PRAISE FOR
The Labyrinth of the Spirits

"A colossal achievement. . . . a genre-crossing delight. . . . Publishers dream of novels that appeal to habitual readers and to those seeking one big book to last a holiday, and that is what Zafón's quartet has delivered. His trick is to have linked multiple genres—fantasy, historical, romance, metafictional, police-procedural, and political—through prose of atmospheric specificity."

—*The Guardian*

"Carlos Ruiz Zafón is a gifted storyteller who knows how to capture his readers' attention. Packed with suspense, *The Labyrinth of the Spirits* is a gripping edge-of-your-seat thriller. As you read this chilling thriller, you feel as if your pounding heart is missing a beat."　　　　　　　　　　　　—*Washington Book Review*

"A compelling, multifaceted, and haunting work of art told by a master storyteller. To say that the writing is brilliant is an understatement. Carlos Ruiz Zafón respects every word, taking his time to develop and do justice to the major, minor, and irrelevant characters, places, things, or situations in order to recreate a dark time in Spain's history and ensure that the reader not only bears witness to it but is immersed in it and feels it. . . . An epic novel that is also an ode to writing and to the undying thirst for knowledge through reading."　　　　　　　　　　　　—*Historical Novel Society*

"Intricate and sublime."

—*O: The Oprah Magazine*, 15 Favorite Books of 2018

"Zafón's vision is one of the complexities of human experience, reveling in language."　　　　　　　—*The Sydney Morning Herald*

"A mystery, a love letter to books, and a magical adventure all wrapped up in one, this book is a masterful work of literature that will invigorate your love of reading."　　　　　　—*Bustle*

"A gripping and moving thriller set in Franco's Spain that's fully accessible to newcomers. . . . Twenty-nine-year-old Alicia Gris, a capable, insightful operative working for the Spanish secret police . . . will remind readers of Lisbeth Salander. . . . Fans of complex and literate mysteries featuring detectives with integrity working under oppressive and corrupt regimes will be well satisfied."

—*Publishers Weekly* (starred review)

"Ruiz Zafón clearly has had a great deal of fun in pulling this vast story together. . . . His ability to keep track of a thousand threads while, in the end, celebrating the power of storytelling is admirable. . . . A satisfying conclusion to a grand epic that, of course, will only leave its fans wanting more."

—*Kirkus Reviews* (starred review)

"Gothic, operatic, and in many ways old-fashioned, this is a story about storytelling and survival, with the horrors of Francoist Spain present on every page. Compelling. . . . This is for readers who savor each word and scene, soaking in the ambience of Barcelona, Zafón's greatest character (after, perhaps, the irrepressible Fermín Romero de Torres)."

—*Booklist*

"*The Labyrinth of the Spirits* is the sublime culmination to a truly outstanding series. Set in Barcelona from 1938 through the 1970s, these books deftly combine the world of bookselling, the long shadow of the Spanish Civil War, gothic literary interplay, wonderfully salty characters, sublime dialogue and verbal sparring, along with elaborate and satisfying exposition. Taken together or individually they represent a reading experience not to be missed. . . . Reading *Labyrinth* first would have given a sublime insight into any of the other books . . . as long as you actually open a door to the labyrinth and enter it, all is well. As to not reading the *Cemetery of Forgotten* books at all, that is obviously a grave error."

—*PW ShelfTalker*

"A literary feast!"   —Barnes & Noble "September Pick"

"Zafón is a master storyteller, combining the postmodern and the traditional in an enchanting hymn to literature. . . . Magnificent. . . . A dizzying tale of drama, intrigue, and passion."

—*The Mail on Sunday* (UK)

THE CEMETERY
OF FORGOTTEN BOOKS

THIS BOOK IS part of a cycle of novels set in the literary universe of the Cemetery of Forgotten Books. Although each work within the cycle presents an independent, self-contained tale, they are all connected through characters and storylines, creating thematic and narrative links.

Each individual installment in the Cemetery of Forgotten Books series can be read in any order, or separately, enabling the reader to explore the labyrinth of stories along different paths that, when woven together, lead into the heart of the narrative.

THE
LABYRINTH
OF THE SPIRITS

A NOVEL

CARLOS RUIZ
ZAFÓN

TRANSLATED BY LUCIA GRAVES

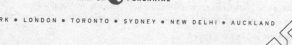

HARPER PERENNIAL

NEW YORK • LONDON • TORONTO • SYDNEY • NEW DELHI • AUCKLAND

HARPER ● PERENNIAL

Permission for use of photographs:

Dies Irae: Aerial view of Barcelona, 17 March 1938. Archivio Storico dell'Aeronautica Militare Italiana.
Kyrie: Sunlight and shadows on the pavements of Madrid's Gran Vía, 1953. Copyright © Fons Fotogràfic F. Català-Roca—Arxiu Històric del Col·legi d'Arquitectes de Catalunya.
City of Mirrors: "Book Day, 1932," Barcelona. Copyright © Gabriel Casas i Galobardes. Fons Gabriel Casas de l'Arxiu Nacional de Catalunya.
The Forgotten: Line 12 tram (at the junction of Avda. Diagonal and Avda. Sarrià), 1932–1934, Barcelona. Copyright © Gabriel Casas i Galobardes. Fons Gabriel Casas de l'Arxiu Nacional de Catalunya © Núria Casas—ANC.
Agnus Dei: Atocha Station against the sunlight, Madrid, 1953. Copyright © Fons Fotogràfic F. Català-Roca—Arxiu Històric del Col·legi d'Arquitectes de Catalunya.
Libera Me: Elegance on Madrid's Gran Vía, 1953. Copyright © Fons Fotogràfic F. Català-Roca—Arxiu Històric del Col·legi d'Arquitectes de Catalunya.
Barcelona: Calle del Bisbe, Barcelona, 1973. Copyright © Fons Fotogràfic F. Català-Roca—Arxiu Històric del Col·legi d'Arquitectes de Catalunya.
Colophon: Sagrada Familia staircase, Barcelona. Copyright © Fons Fotogràfic F. Català-Roca—Arxiu Històric del Col·legi d'Arquitectes de Catalunya.

Francesc Català-Roca (Valls, Spain, 1922–Barcelona, 1998) was one of the great photographers of the twentieth century; the atmosphere he captures has a strong affinity with the literary universe of Carlos Ruiz Zafón.
Gabriel Casas (Barcelona, 1892–1973), an outstanding photojournalist of the period between the wars, was known for his innovative techniques. Although he was a victim of postwar repression, his work has recently been rediscovered.

Originally published as *El Laberinto de los Espíritus* in Spanish in 2016 by Planeta.

Designed by Fritz Metsch

FIRST HARPER PERENNIAL PAPERBACK EDITION PUBLISHED 2019.

Library of Congress Cataloging-in-Publication Data has been applied for.
Library and Archives Canada Cataloguing in Publication information is available upon request.

ISBN 978-0-06-266870-7 (pbk.)
ISBN 978-1-4434-5400-1 (Canada)

19 20 21 22 23 LSC 10 9 8 7 6 5 4 3 2 1

DANIEL'S
BOOK

I

THAT NIGHT I dreamed that I was going back to the Cemetery of Forgotten Books. I was ten years old again, and again I woke up in my old bedroom feeling that the memory of my mother's face had deserted me. And the way one knows things in a dream, I knew it was my fault and my fault only, for I didn't deserve to remember her face because I hadn't been capable of doing her justice.

Before long my father came in, alerted by my anguished cries. My father, who in my dream was still a young man and held all the answers in the world, wrapped me in his arms to comfort me. Later, when the first glimmer of dawn sketched a hazy Barcelona, we went down to the street. For some arcane reason he would only come with me as far as the front door. Once there, he let go of my hand, and I understood then that this was a journey I had to undertake on my own.

I set off, but as I walked I remember that my clothes, my shoes, and even my skin felt heavy. Every step I took required more effort than the previous one. When I reached the Ramblas, I noticed that the city had become frozen in a never-ending instant. Passersby had stopped in their tracks and appeared motionless, like figures in an old photograph. A pigeon taking flight left only the hint of a blurred outline as it flapped its wings. Motes of sparkling dust floated in the air like powdered light. The water of the Canaletas fountain glistened in the void, suspended like a necklace of glass tears.

Slowly, as if I were trying to advance underwater, I managed to press on across the spell of a Barcelona trapped in time, until I came to the threshold of the Cemetery of Forgotten Books. There I paused, exhausted. I couldn't understand what invisible weight I was pulling behind me that barely allowed me to move. I grabbed the knocker and beat the door with it, but nobody came. I banged the large wooden door with my fists, again and again, but the keeper ignored my pleas. At last I fell on my knees, utterly spent. Then, as I gazed at the curse I had dragged behind me, it suddenly became clear to me that the city and my destiny would be forever caught in that haunting, and that I would never be able to remember my mother's face.

*

It was only when I'd abandoned all hope that I discovered it. The piece of metal was hidden in the inside pocket of that school jacket with my initials embroidered in blue. A key. I wondered how long it had been there, unbeknown to me. It was rusty and felt as heavy as my conscience. Even with both hands, I could hardly lift it up into the keyhole. I struggled to turn it with my last bit of breath. But just as I thought I would never manage it, the lock yielded and slowly the large door slid open inward.

A curved gallery led into the old palace, studded with a trail of flickering candles that lit the way. I plunged into the dark and heard the door closing behind me. Then I recognized the corridor flanked by frescoes of angels and fabulous creatures: they peered at me from the shadows and seemed to move as I went past. I proceeded down the corridor until I reached an archway that opened out into a large hall with a vaulted ceiling. I stopped at the entrance. The labyrinth fanned out before me in an endless mirage. A spiral of staircases, tunnels, bridges, and arches woven together formed an eternal city made up of all the books in the world, swirling toward a grand glass dome high above.

My mother waited for me at the foot of the structure. She was lying in an open coffin, her hands crossed over her chest, her skin as pale as the white dress that covered her. Her lips were sealed, her eyes closed. She lay inert in the absent rest of lost souls. I moved my hand toward her to stroke her face. Her skin was as cold as marble. Then she opened her eyes and fixed them on me. When her darkened lips parted and she spoke, the sound of her voice was so thunderous it hit

4

me like a cargo train, lifting me off the floor, throwing me into the air, and leaving me suspended in an endless fall while the echo of her words melted the world.

You must tell the truth, Daniel.

*

I woke up suddenly in the darkness of the bedroom, drenched in cold sweat, to find Bea's body lying next to me. She hugged me and stroked my face.

"Again?" she murmured.

I nodded and took a deep breath.

"You were talking. In your dream."

"What did I say?"

"I couldn't make it out," Bea lied.

I looked at her and she smiled at me with pity, I thought, or maybe it was just patience.

"Sleep a little longer. The alarm clock won't go off for another hour and a half, and today is Tuesday."

Tuesday meant that it was my turn to take Julián to school. I closed my eyes, pretending to fall asleep. When I opened them again a couple of minutes later, I found my wife's face observing me.

"What?" I asked.

Bea leaned over and kissed me gently on my lips. She tasted of cinnamon. "I'm not sleepy either," she hinted.

I started to undress her unhurriedly. I was about to pull off the sheets and throw them on the floor when I heard the patter of footsteps behind the bedroom door.

Bea held back the advance of my left hand between her thighs and propped herself up on her elbows.

"What's the matter, sweetheart?"

Standing in the doorway, little Julián looked at us with a touch of shyness and unease. "There's someone in my room," he whispered.

Bea let out a sigh and reached out toward Julián. He ran over to take shelter in his mother's embrace, and I abandoned all sinful expectations.

"The Scarlet Prince?" asked Bea.

Julián nodded shyly.

"Daddy will go to your room right now and give him such a kicking he'll never come back again."

Our son threw me a desperate look. What use is a father if not for heroic missions of this caliber?

I smiled at him and winked. "A major kicking," I repeated, looking as furious as I could.

Julián allowed himself just a flicker of a smile. I jumped out of bed and walked along the corridor to his bedroom. The room reminded me so much of the one I had at his age, a few floors farther down, that for a moment I wondered if I wasn't still trapped in my dream. I sat on one side of his bed and switched on the bedside table lamp. Julián lived surrounded by toys, some of which he'd inherited from me, but especially by books. It didn't take me long to find the culprit, hidden under the mattress. I took that little book with black covers and opened to its first page.

THE LABYRINTH OF THE SPIRITS VII
Ariadna and the Scarlet Prince

TEXT AND ILLUSTRATIONS BY VÍCTOR MATAIX

I no longer knew where to hide those books. However much I sharpened my wits to find new hiding places, my son managed to sniff them out. Leafing quickly through the pages, I was assailed by memories.

When I returned to our bedroom, having banished the book once more to the top of the kitchen cupboard—where I knew my son would discover it sooner rather than later—I found Julián in his mother's arms. They had both fallen asleep. I paused in the half-light to watch them from the open door. As I listened to their deep breathing, I asked myself what the most fortunate man in the world had done to deserve his luck. I gazed at them as they slept in each other's arms, oblivious to the world, and couldn't help remembering the fear I'd felt the first time I saw them clasped in an embrace.

2

I'VE NEVER TOLD anyone, but the night my son Julián was born and I saw him in his mother's arms for the first time, enjoying the blessed calm of those who are not yet aware what kind of place they've arrived at, I felt like running away and not stopping until there was no more world left to run from. At the time I was just a kid and life was still a few sizes too big for me, but however many flimsy excuses I try to conjure up, I still carry the bitter taste of shame at the cowardice that possessed me then—a cowardice that, even after all those years, I have not found the courage to admit to the person who most deserved to know.

*

The memories we bury under mountains of silence are the ones that never stop haunting us. Mine take me back to a room with an infinitely high ceiling from which a lamp spread its faint ocher-colored light over a bed. There lay a girl, still in her teens, holding a baby in her arms. When Bea, vaguely conscious, looked up and smiled at me, my eyes filled with tears. I knelt by the bed and buried my head in her lap. I felt her holding my hand and pressing it with what little strength she had left.

"Don't be afraid," she whispered.

But I was. And for a moment whose shame has pursued me ever since, I wanted to be anywhere except in that room and in my own skin. Fermín had witnessed the scene from the door and, as usual, had read my thoughts even before I was able to articulate them. Without granting me a second to open my big mouth, he pulled my arm and, leaving Bea and the baby in the safe company of his fiancée, Bernarda, led me out to the hallway, a long angular corridor that melted into the shadows.

"Still alive in there, Daniel?" he asked.

I nodded vaguely as I tried to catch the breath I seemed to have dropped along the way. When I turned to go back into the room, Fermín restrained me.

"Listen, next time you show your face in there, you could use a bit more composure. Luckily Señora Bea is still half knocked out and almost certainly missed much of the dress rehearsal. If I may make a constructive suggestion, I think a blast of fresh air would do wonders. It would help us get over the shock and allow us to attempt a second landing with a bit more flair."

Without waiting for an answer, Fermín grabbed my arm and escorted me down the long passageway. We soon reached a staircase that led to a balustrade suspended somewhere between Barcelona and the heavens. A cold, biting breeze caressed my face.

"Close your eyes and take three deep breaths," Fermín advised. "Slowly, as if your lungs reached down to your shoes. It's a trick I learned from a Tibetan monk I met during a brief but educational stint as receptionist-slash-accountant in a little port-side brothel. The rascal knew his business . . ."

As instructed, I inhaled three times as deeply as I could, and another three for good measure, taking in the benefits of the pure air promised by Fermín and his Tibetan guru. My head felt a bit giddy, but Fermín steadied me.

"Mind you don't go catatonic on me, now," he said. "Just smarten up a bit. The situation calls for temperance, not petrifaction."

I opened my eyes to the sight of deserted streets and the city asleep at my feet. It was around three in the morning, and the Hospital de San Pablo was sunk in a shadowy slumber, its citadel of domes, towers, and arches weaving arabesques through the mist that glided down from the top of Mount Carmelo. I gazed silently at that indifferent Barcelona that can only be seen from hospitals, a city oblivious to the fears and hopes of the beholder, and I let the cold seep in until it cleared my mind.

"You must think me a coward," I said.

Fermín held my gaze and shrugged."Don't overplay it. What I think is that you're a bit low on blood pressure and a bit high on stage panic—which excuses you from responsibility and mockery. Luckily, a solution is at hand."

He unbuttoned his raincoat, a vast emporium of wonders that doubled as a mobile herbalist's shop, museum of odds and ends, and carrier bag of curiosities and relics picked up from a thousand flea markets and third-rate auctions.

"I don't know how you can carry all those trinkets around with you, Fermín."

"Advanced physics. Since my slender yet toned physique consists mostly of muscular fibers and lean cartilage, this cargo reinforces my gravitational field and provides firm anchoring against forces of nature. And don't imagine you're going to distract me that easily with comments that piddle outside the bucket. We haven't come up here to swap stickers or to whisper sweet nothings."

After that bit of advice, Fermín pulled out a tin flask from one of his countless pockets and began unscrewing the top. He sniffed the contents as if he were taking in the perfumes of paradise and smiled approvingly. Then he handed me the bottle and, looking solemnly into my eyes, gave me a nod. "Drink now or repent in the afterlife."

I accepted the flask reluctantly. "What's this? It smells like dynamite."

"Nonsense. It's just a cocktail designed to bring the dead back to life—as well as young boys who feel intimidated by life's responsibilities. A secret master formula of my own invention, made with firewater and aniseed shaken together with a feisty brandy I buy from the one-eyed gypsy who peddles vaguely legal spirits. The mixture is rounded off with a few drops of Ratafia and Aromas de Montserrat liqueurs for that unmistakable Catalan bouquet."

"God almighty."

"Come on, this is where you tell the men from the boys. Down the hatch in one gulp, like a legionnaire who crashes a wedding banquet."

I obeyed and swallowed the concoction. It tasted like gasoline spiked with sugar. The liquor set my insides on fire, and before I could recover Fermín indicated that I should repeat the operation. Objections and intestinal earthquake aside, I downed the second dose, grateful for the drowsy calm the foul drink had conferred on me.

9

"How's that?" Fermín asked. "Better now? Truly the elixir of champions, eh?"

I nodded with conviction, gasping and loosening my neck buttons.

Fermín took the opportunity to take a gulp of his gunge, then put the flask back into his raincoat pocket. "Nothing like recreational chemistry to master the emotions. But don't get too fond of the trick. Liquor is like rat poison or generosity—the more you make use of it, the less effective it becomes."

"Don't worry."

Fermín pointed to a pair of Cuban cigars that peeped out of another of his raincoat pockets, but he shook his head and winked at me. "I had kept aside these two Cohibas, stolen on impulse from the humidifier of my future honorary father-in-law, Don Gustavo Barceló, but we'd better keep them for another day. You're not in the best of shape, and it would be most unwise to leave the little babe fatherless on his opening day."

Fermín gave me a friendly slap on the back and let a few seconds go by, allowing time for the fumes of his cocktail to spread through my veins and a mist of drunken sobriety mask the silent panic that had seized me. As soon as he noticed the glazed look in my eyes and the dilated pupils that announced the general stupefaction of my senses, he threw himself into the speech he'd probably been dreaming up all night long.

"Daniel, my friend. God, or whoever fills in during his absence, has seen fit to make it easier to become a father than to pass one's driving test. Such an unhappy circumstance means that a disproportionate legion of cretins, dimwits, and bona fide imbeciles flaunt paternity medals and consider themselves fully qualified to keep procreating and ruining forever the lives of the unfortunate children they spawn like mice. That is why, speaking with the authority bestowed on me by the fact that I too find myself ready to embark on the enterprise of getting my beloved Bernarda knocked up as soon as possible, once my gonads and the holy matrimony certification she is demanding sine qua non allow me—so that I may follow you in this journey of great responsibility that is fatherhood—I must declare, and I do declare that you, Daniel Sempere Gispert, tender youngster on the verge of maturity, despite the thin faith you feel at this moment in yourself and in your feasibility as a paterfamilias, are and will be an exemplary father, even if, generally speaking, sometimes you seem born the day before yesterday and wetter behind the ears than a babe in the woods."

By the middle of his oration my mind had already drawn a blank, either as a result of the explosive concoction or thanks to the verbal fireworks set off by my good friend. "Fermín," I said, "I'm not sure I grasp your meaning."

Fermín sighed. "What I meant, Daniel, was that I'm aware that right now you feel you're about to soil your undies and that all this is overwhelming, but as your saintly wife has informed you, you must not be afraid. Children, at least yours, Daniel, bring joy and a plan with them when they're born, and so long as one has a drop of decency in one's soul, and some brains in one's head, one can find a way to avoid ruining their lives and be a parent they will never have to be ashamed of."

I looked out of the corner of my eye at that little man who would have given his life for me and who always had a word, or ten thousand, with which to solve my every problem and my occasional lapses into a state of spiritual indecision. "Let's hope it's as easy as you describe it, Fermín."

"In life, nothing worthwhile is easy, Daniel. When I was young I thought that in order to sail through the world you only needed to do three things well. First, tie your shoelaces properly. Second: undress a woman conscientiously. And third: read a few pages for pleasure every day, pages written with inspiration and skill. I thought that a man who has a steady step, knows how to caress, and learns how to listen to the music of words will live longer and, above all, better. But time has shown me that this isn't enough, and that sometimes life offers us an opportunity to aspire to be more than a hairy bipedal creature that eats, excretes, and occupies a temporary space in the planet. And so it is today that destiny, with its boundless lack of concern, has decided to offer you that opportunity."

I nodded, unconvinced. "What if I don't make the grade?"

"If there's one thing we have in common, Daniel, it's that we've both been blessed with the good fortune of finding women we don't deserve. It is clear as day that in this journey they are the ones who will decide what baggage we'll need and what heights we'll attain, and all we have to do is try not to fail them. What do you say?"

"That I'd love to believe you wholeheartedly, but I find it hard."

Fermín shook his head, as if to make light of the matter. "Don't worry. The mixture of spirits I've poured down you is clouding what little aptitude you have for my refined rhetoric. But you know that in these matters I have a lot more miles on the clock than you, and I'm normally as right as a truckload of saints."

"I won't argue that point."

"And you'll do well not to, because you'd be knocked out in the first round. Do you trust me?"

"Of course I do, Fermín. I'd go with you to the end of the world, you know that."

"Then take my word for it and trust yourself as well. The way I do."

I looked straight into his eyes and nodded slowly.

"Recovered your common sense?" he asked.

"I think so."

"In that case wipe away that doleful expression, make sure your testicular mass is safely stored in the proper location, and go back to the room to give Señora Bea and the baby a hug, like the man they've just made you. Make no mistake about it: the boy I had the honor of meeting some years ago, one night beneath the arches of Plaza Real, the boy who since then has given me so many frights, must remain in the prelude of this adventure. We still have a lot of history to live through, Daniel, and what awaits us is no longer child's play. Are you with me? To that end of the world, which, for all we know, might only be around the corner?"

I could think of nothing else to do but embrace him. "What would I do without you, Fermín?"

"You'd make a lot of mistakes, for one thing. And while we're on the subject of caution, bear in mind that one of the most common side effects derived from the intake of the concoction you have just imbibed is a temporary softening of restraint and a certain overexuberance on the sentimental front. So now, when Señora Bea sees you step into that room again, look straight into her eyes so that she realizes that you really love her."

"She knows that already."

Fermín shook his head patiently. "Do as I say," he insisted. "You don't have to tell her in so many words, if you feel embarrassed, because that's what we men are like and testosterone doesn't encourage eloquence. But make sure she feels it. These things should be proven rather than just said. And not once in a blue moon, but every single day."

"I'll try."

"Do a bit more than try, Daniel."

And so, stripped, thanks to Fermín's words and deeds, of the eternal and fragile shelter of my adolescence, I made my way back to the room where destiny awaited.

*

Many years later, the memory of that night would return when, seeking a late-night refuge in the back room of the old bookshop on Calle Santa Ana, I tried once more to confront a blank page, without even knowing how to begin to tell myself the real story of my family. It was a task to which I had devoted months or even years, and to which I had been incapable of contributing a single line worth saving.

Making the most of a bout of insomnia, which he attributed to having eaten half a kilo of deep-fried pork rinds, Fermín had decided to pay me a visit in the wee hours. When he caught me agonizing in front of a blank page, armed with a fountain pen that leaked like an old car, he sat down beside me and checked the tide of crumpled folios spread at my feet. "Don't be offended, Daniel, but have you the slightest idea of what you're doing?"

"No," I admitted. "Perhaps if I tried using a typewriter, everything would change. The advertisements say that Underwood is the professional's choice."

Fermín considered the publicity promise, but shook his head vigorously. "Typing and writing are different things, light-years apart."

"Thanks for the encouragement. What about you? What are you doing here at this time of night?"

13

Fermín tapped his belly. "The consumption of an entire fried-up pig has left my stomach in turmoil."

"Would you like some bicarbonate of soda?"

"No, I'd better not. It always gives me a monumental hard-on, if you'll forgive me, and then I really can't sleep a wink."

I abandoned my pen and my umpteenth attempt at producing a single usable sentence, and searched my friend's eyes.

"Everything all right here, Daniel? Apart from your unsuccessful storming of the literary castle, I mean . . ."

I shrugged hesitantly. As usual, Fermín had arrived at the providential moment, living up to his natural role of a roguish deus ex machina.

"I'm not sure how to ask you something I've been turning over in my mind for quite a while," I ventured.

He covered his mouth with his hand and let go a short but effective burp. "If it's related to some bedroom technicality, don't be shy, just fire away. May I remind you that on such issues I'm as good as a qualified doctor."

"No, it's not a bedroom matter."

"Pity, because I have fresh information on a couple of new tricks that—"

"Fermín," I interrupted. "Do you think I've lived the life I was supposed to live, that I've not fallen short of expectations?"

My friend seemed lost for words. He looked down, sighing.

"Don't tell me that's what's behind this bogged-down-Balzac phase of yours. Spiritual quest and all that . . ."

"Isn't that why people write—to gain a better understanding of themselves and of the world?"

"No, not if they know what they're doing, and you—"

"You're a lousy confessor, Fermín. Give me a little help."

"I thought you were trying to become a novelist, not a holy man."

"Tell me the truth, Fermín. You've known me since I was a child. Have I disappointed you? Have I been the Daniel you hoped for? The one my mother would have wished me to be? Tell me the truth."

Fermín rolled his eyes. "Truth is the rubbish people come up with when they think they know something, Daniel. I know as much about truth as I know about the bra size of that fantastic female with the pointy name and pointier bosom we saw in the Capitol Cinema the other day."

"Kim Novak," I specified.

"Whom may God and the laws of gravity hold forever in their glory. And no, you have not disappointed me, Daniel. Ever. You're a good man and a good friend. And if you want my opinion, yes, your late mother, Isabella, would have been proud of you and would have thought you were a good son."

"But not a good novelist." I smiled.

"Look, Daniel, you're as much a novelist as I'm a Dominican monk. And you know that. No pen or Underwood under the sun can change that."

I sighed and fell into a deep silence. Fermín observed me thoughtfully.

"You know something, Daniel? What I really think is that after everything you and I have been through, I'm still that same poor devil you found lying in the street, the one you took home out of kindness, and you're still that helpless, lost kid who wandered about stumbling on endless mysteries, believing that if you solved them, perhaps, by some miracle, you would recover your mother's face and the memory of the truth that the world had stolen from you."

I mulled over his words; they'd touched a nerve. "And if that were true, would it be so terrible?"

"It could be worse. You could be a novelist, like your friend Carax."

"Perhaps what I should do is find him and persuade *him* to write the story," I said. "Our story."

"That's what your son Julián says, sometimes."

I looked at Fermín askance. "Julián says *what*? What does Julián know about Carax? Have you talked to my son about Carax?"

Fermín adopted his official sacrificial lamb expression. "Me?"

"What have you told him?"

Fermín puffed, as if making light of the matter. "Just bits and pieces. At the very most a few, utterly harmless footnotes. The trouble is that the child is inquisitive by nature, and he's always got his headlights on, so of course he catches everything and ties up loose ends. It's not my fault if the boy is smart. He obviously doesn't take after you."

"Dear God . . . and does Bea know you've been talking to the boy about Carax?"

"I don't interfere in your marital life. But I doubt there's much Señora Bea doesn't know or guess."

"I strictly forbid you to talk to my son about Carax, Fermín."

He put his hand on his chest and nodded solemnly. "My lips are sealed. May the foulest ignominy fall upon me if in a moment of tribulation I should ever break this vow of silence."

"And while we're at it, don't mention Kim Novak, either. I know you only too well."

"On that matter I'm as innocent as the Lamb of God, which taketh away the sin of the world: it's the boy who brings up that subject, he's not stupid by half."

"You're impossible."

"I humbly accept your unfair remarks, because I know they're provoked by the frustration of your own emaciated ingenuity. Does Your Excellency have any other names to add to the blacklist of unmentionables, apart from Carax? Bakunin? Mae West?"

"Why don't you go off to bed and leave me in peace, Fermín?"

"And leave you on your own to face the danger? No way. There must at least be one sane and responsible adult among the audience."

Fermín examined the fountain pen and the pile of blank pages waiting on the table, assessing them with fascination, as if he were looking at a set of surgical instruments. "Have you figured out how to get this enterprise up and running?"

"No. I was doing just that when you came in and started making obtuse remarks."

"Nonsense. Without me you can't even write a shopping list."

Convinced at last, and rolling up his sleeves to face the titanic task before us, he sat himself down on a chair beside me, looking at me with the fixed intensity of someone who scarcely needs words to communicate.

"Speaking of lists: look, I know as much about this novel-writing business as I do about the manufacture and use of a hair shirt, but it occurs to me that before beginning to narrate anything, we should make a list of what we want to tell. An inventory, let's say."

"A road map?" I suggested.

"A road map is what people rough out when they're not sure where they're going, to convince themselves and some other simpleton that they're going somewhere."

"It's not such a bad idea. Self-deceit is the key to all impossible ventures."

"You see? Together we make an invincible duo. You take notes, and I think."

"Then start thinking aloud."

"Is there enough ink in that piece of junk for a round trip to hell and back?"

"Enough to start walking."

"Now all we need to decide is where we begin the list."

"What if we begin with the story of how you met her?" I asked.

"Met who?"

"Who do you think? Our Alice in the Wonderland of Barcelona."

A shadow crossed his face. "I don't think I've ever told anyone that story, Daniel. Not even you."

"In that case, what better entrance could there be to the labyrinth?"

"A man should be allowed to take some secrets to his grave," Fermín objected.

"Too many secrets may take that man to his grave before his time."

Fermín raised his eyebrows in surprise. "Who said that? Socrates? Myself?"

"No. For once it was Daniel Sempere Gispert, the simpleton, only a few seconds ago."

Fermín smiled with satisfaction, peeled a lemon Sugus, and put it in his mouth. "It's taken you years, but you're starting to learn from the master, you rascal. Would you like a Sugus?"

I accepted the piece of candy because I knew it was the most treasured possession in my friend Fermín's estate, and he was honoring me by sharing it.

"Have you ever heard that much-abused saying that all's fair in love and war, Daniel?"

"Sometimes. Usually by those who favor war rather than love."

"That's right, because when all's said and done, it's a rotten lie."

"So, is this a story of love or war?"

Fermín shrugged. "What's the difference?"

And so, under cover of midnight, a couple of Sugus, and the spell of memories that were threatening to disappear in the mist of time, Fermín began to connect the threads that would weave the end and the beginning of our story . . .

Excerpt from
The Labyrinth of the Spirits
(*The Cemetery of Forgotten Books*, volume IV),
by Julián Carax.
Edited by Émile de Rosiers Castellaine.
Paris: Éditions de la Lumière, 1992.

DIES IRAE

~❦~

BARCELONA
MARCH 1938

HE WAS WOKEN by the roll of the sea. When he opened his eyes, the stowaway perceived a darkness that seemed to stretch into infinity. The swaying of the ship, the stench of salt residue, and the sound of water scratching at the hull reminded him that he was not on dry land. He set aside the sacks that had served him as a bed and stood up slowly, scanning the long line of columns and arches that made up the ship's hold.

The sight was dreamlike, he thought, a submerged cathedral peopled by what looked like booty taken from a hundred museums and palaces. He noticed the outline of a fleet of luxury cars, covered with semitransparent cloths, amid a set of sculptures and paintings. Next to a large grandfather clock he spotted a cage containing a splendid parrot. The bird observed him severely, questioning his stowaway status.

A bit farther on he caught sight of a copy of Michelangelo's David, which some individual on an impulse had crowned with the three-cornered hat of the Civil Guard. Behind it, an army of ghostly dummies, all wearing period dresses, seemed caught in a never-ending Viennese waltz. On one side, leaning against the bodywork of a luxurious hearse with glass sides—coffin included—was a pile of old posters in frames. One of them announced a bullfight at the Arenas ring dating from before the war.

The name of a certain Fermín Romero de Torres appeared among the list of horseback bullfighters. As his eyes stroked the letters, the secret passenger, at the time still known by a name he would soon have to leave behind in the ashes of that war, silently mouthed those words.

FERMÍN
ROMERO DE TORRES

A good name, he told himself. Musical. Operatic. On a par with the epic and harrowing existence of a lifelong stowaway. Fermín Romero de Torres, or the thin little man stuck to a very large nose who was soon to adopt that name, had remained hidden in the bowels of a merchant ship that had left Valencia two nights earlier. Miraculously, he'd managed to slip aboard, hiding in a large trunk full of old rifles that was camouflaged among all kinds of merchandise. Some of the guns were wrapped up in sealed bags with a knot that protected them from the damp, but the rest were uncovered, piled up one on top of the other, and looked more likely to explode in the face of some unfortunate militiaman—or in his own face, if he leaned where he shouldn't—than to bring down the enemy.

Every half hour, to stretch his legs and alleviate the numbness caused by the cold and the damp oozing from the walls of the hull, Fermín would venture through the web of containers and supplies in search of something edible, or, failing that, something that would help him kill time. In one of his expeditions he'd befriended a small mouse with long experience of these circumstances. After an initial period of distrust, the mouse began to approach him timidly and, nestling snugly in the warmth of his lap, shared the bits of hard cheese that Fermín had found in one of the food crates. The cheese, or whatever that greasy, leathery substance was, tasted like soap, and as far as Fermín's gastronomic knowledge went, there was no indication that any cow or other ruminant had had a hand or a hoof in the matter of its production. But a wise man admits there is no accounting for taste, and if there was, the abject poverty of those days clearly altered the saying, so that they both enjoyed the feast with the enthusiasm that comes only from months of accumulated hunger.

"Dear rodent friend, one of the advantages of this war business is that from one day to the next, pigswill can be considered a dish fit for the gods, and even a cleverly skewered piece of shit on a stick begins to give off an exquisite bouquet of Parisian boulangerie. This semimilitary diet of soups made with dirty water and bread crumbs mixed with sawdust hardens the spirit and heightens the sensibility of the palate to such a degree that eventually even a piece of cork can taste of serrano ham if there's nothing better to eat."

The mouse listened patiently to Fermín while they devoured the food stolen by the stowaway. Sometimes, feeling satisfied, the rodent would fall asleep at his feet. Fermín gazed at the little creature, guessing that they had made good friends because deep down they resembled one another.

"You and I are two of a kind, mate, enduring the scourge of the erect ape with philosophy, and finding what we can find to survive it. Let's hope to God that in the not too distant future all primates will be extinguished in one fell swoop and sent to push up daisies with the diplodocus, the mammoth, and the dodo, so that you, hardworking, peaceful creatures who are content to eat, fornicate, and sleep, can inherit the earth, or at least share it with the cockroach and some other coleopteran."

If the little mouse disagreed, he showed no signs of it. Theirs was a friendly coexistence, neither of them searching for a dominant role: a gentlemanly agreement. During the day they heard the sound of the sailors' footsteps and voices reverberating in the bilge. On the rare occasions when a member of the crew ventured down there, normally to steal something, Fermín would hide again in the rifle crate he'd just vacated and, lulled by the sea and the aroma of gunpowder, surrender to a little nap. On his second day on board, while exploring the bazaar of wonders hidden in the stomach of that leviathan, Fermín, a modern Jonah and a free-thinking scholar of the Holy Scriptures during his spare time, discovered a box full of beautifully bound Bibles. The discovery struck him as daring and colorful, to put it mildly, but since there was no other literary menu to choose from, he borrowed a copy and, with the help of a candle also on loan from the cargo, read aloud to himself and his traveling companion, highlighting hand-picked fragments, especially from the juicier Old Testament, which he had always considered far more entertaining and gruesome than the New.

"Pay attention, sir, for now cometh an ineffable parable of deep symbolism, spiced up with enough cases of incest and mutilation to scare the feces out of the Brothers Grimm themselves."

The two whiled away the hours and the days sheltered by the sea until, at dawn on March 17, 1938, Fermín opened his eyes and discovered that his friend the rodent was gone. Perhaps listening to a few episodes of the Revelation of Saint John on the previous night had frightened the little mouse, or maybe he could sense that the journey was coming to an end and it was advisable to make oneself scarce. Feeling stiff after another night encased in the icy cold that drilled into his bones, Fermín staggered over to the viewpoint provided by one of the portholes, through which poured the breath of a scarlet dawn. The circular window was only about a foot and a half above the waterline, and Fermín could see the sun rising over a wine-colored sea. He walked across the hold, dodging crates of munitions and a pile of rusty bicycles tied together with ropes, until he reached the opposite side and had a look. The hazy beam of the harbor's lighthouse swept across the ship's hull, projecting momentary flashes of light through all the portholes in the hold. Farther on lay the city of Barcelona, enveloped in a halo of mist that crept between watchtowers, domes, and spires. Fermín smiled to himself, briefly forgetting the cold, as well as the bruises covering his body, a consequence of brawls and misfortunes experienced in his previous port of call.

"Lucía . . . ," he murmured, recalling the face whose memory had kept him alive during the worst predicaments.

He pulled out the envelope he'd carried in the inside pocket of his jacket since he left Valencia and sighed. The daydreaming vanished almost instantly. The ship was much closer to the port than he'd imagined. Any self-respecting stowaway knows that the hardest part isn't smuggling oneself on board: what is difficult is getting out of the situation safe and sound and abandoning the boat without being seen. If he held any hopes of treading land with his own two feet and with all his bones in the right place, he'd better start formulating an escape strategy. While he listened to the footsteps and the increasing activity of the crew on deck, Fermín could feel the ship beginning to veer and the engines reduce speed as they entered the mouth of the harbor. He put the letter back in his pocket and quickly removed all signs of his presence, hiding the remains of the used candles, the sacks that had served as bedding, the Bible of his contemplative readings, and the leftover bits of cheese substitute and rancid biscuits. He then did his best to close the boxes he'd opened in search of sustenance, hammering back the nails with the heels of his worn-out boots. As he looked at his meager footwear, Fermín told himself that as soon as he'd reached dry land and kept his promise, his next objective would be to get hold of a pair of shoes that didn't look as if they'd been filched from a morgue. While he busied himself in the hold, the stowaway peered through the portholes and saw the vessel moving ever closer to the port of Barcelona. He pressed his nose against the glass one last time, feeling a shiver when he noticed the silhouette of Montjuïc Castle with its military prison on the top of the hill, presiding over the city like a bird of prey.

"If you're not careful, you'll end up there," he whispered.

In the distance, he could see the needle-like profile of the monument to Christopher Columbus, who, as usual, was pointing the wrong way, mistaking the Balearic archipelago for the American continent. Behind the confused discoverer was the entrance to the Ramblas that rose toward the heart of the old town, where Lucía awaited. For a moment he imagined her scented presence between the sheets. A feeling of guilt and shame removed that image from his thoughts. He had betrayed his promise.

"You wretch," he muttered.

Thirteen months and seven days had passed since he'd last seen her, thirteen months that weighed on him like thirteen years. The last image he was able to steal before returning to his hiding place was the outline of Our Lady of Mercy, the city's patron saint, standing on the dome of her basilica opposite the port, looking as if she was about to fly off over the rooftops of Barcelona. He commended his soul and his miserable body to her, for although he hadn't set foot in a church since he was nine, when he'd mistaken the chapel of his native village for the public library, Fermín swore to whoever could and wished to listen to him that if the Virgin Mary—or any representative with leverage in heavenly matters—interceded on his behalf and led him to safe harbor without suffering any serious mishaps or fatal injuries, he would redirect his life toward spiritual contemplation and become a regular customer of the prayer book industry. Having concluded his promise, he crossed himself twice and rushed

27

back to hide again in the rifle crate, lying on the bed of arms like a corpse in a coffin. Just before closing the lid, Fermín caught sight of his companion, the little mouse, observing him from the top of a pile of boxes that rose to the ceiling of the hold.

"Bonne chance, mon ami," he whispered.

A second later he plunged into the darkness that smelled of gunpowder, the cold metal of the rifles touching his skin, the die already cast.

2

AFTER A WHILE, Fermín noticed that the rumbling of the engines had stopped and the ship was swaying, lying at rest in the calm waters of the harbor. It was too early for them to have reached the docks, by his reckoning. After two or three ports of call on the journey, his ears had learned to read the protocol and the cacophony that issued from a docking maneuver, from the casting off of the mooring rope and the hammering sound of the anchor chains to the groaning of the ship's frame under the strain of the hull as it was being dragged against the dock. Aside from an unusual stir of footsteps and voices on deck, Fermín recognized none of those signs. For some reason the captain had decided to stop the boat earlier, and Fermín, who after almost two years of war had learned that the unexpected often goes hand in hand with the unwelcome, gritted his teeth and made the sign of the cross once again.

"My little Virgin, I renounce my irreverent agnosticism and all the malicious suggestions of modern science," he murmured, confined in the makeshift coffin he shared with thirdhand rifles.

His prayer did not take long to be answered. Fermín heard what sounded like another vessel, a smaller one, approaching and scraping the hull of the ship. Moments later, almost martial footsteps landed on the deck amid the bustle of the crew. Fermín swallowed hard. They had been boarded.

3

THIRTY YEARS AT SEA, Captain Arráez thought, and the worst always comes when you reach land. He stood on the bridge, watching the group of men who had just climbed up the steps on the port side. They brandished their guns threateningly and pushed the crew aside, clearing the way for the man he supposed was their leader.

Arráez was one of those seamen whose skin and hair had a coppery glaze from the sun and the sea air, and whose watery eyes always seemed veiled with tears. As a young man he believed that you went to sea in search of adventure, but time had taught him that adventure was always waiting in the port, and with nefarious motives. There was nothing to fear at sea. On dry land, however, and more so in those days, he was often overcome by nausea.

"Bermejo," he said, "grab the radio and let the port know that we've been detained momentarily and will be arriving with some delay."

Next to him, Bermejo, his first mate, went pale and was hit by one of those trembling fits he'd been prone to during the recent months of bombings and skirmishes. Formerly a boatswain in pleasure cruises along the Guadalquivir, poor Bermejo didn't have the stomach for the job. "Who do I say has detained us, Captain?"

Arráez's eyes rested on the silhouette that had just stepped onto his deck. Wrapped in a black raincoat and sporting gloves and a fedora, he was the only one who didn't seem armed. Arráez observed him as he walked slowly across the deck. His gait indicated a perfectly calculated calm and disinterest. His eyes, hidden behind dark lenses, skimmed across the faces of the crew, while his face was totally expressionless. At last he stopped in the middle of the deck, looked up toward the bridge, and uncovered his head to convey a greeting with his hat while he offered a reptilian smile.

"Fumero," murmured the captain.

Bermejo, who was white as chalk and seemed to have shrunk at least ten centimeters since that individual had meandered across the deck, looked at the captain.

"Who?" he managed to articulate.

"Political police. Go down and tell the men they're not to fool around. And then, as I said, radio the port."

Bermejo nodded, but made no sign of moving. Arráez fixed his eyes on his. "Bermejo, I said go down. And make sure you don't piss yourself, for God's sake."

"Yes, Captain."

Arráez remained alone on the bridge for a few moments. It was a clear day, with crystal skies and clouds like fleeting brushstrokes that would have delighted a watercolorist. For a second he considered fetching the revolver he kept under lock and key in his cabin, but that naive idea brought a bitter smile to his lips. He took a deep breath and, buttoning up his frayed jacket, left the bridge and walked down the steps to the deck where his old acquaintance was waiting for him, holding a cigarette playfully between his fingers.

4

"CAPTAIN ARRÁEZ, WELCOME to Barcelona."

"Thank you, Lieutenant."

Fumero smiled. "Major, now."

Arráez assented, holding the gaze of those two dark lenses behind which it was hard to guess where Fumero's sharp eyes were looking. "Congratulations."

Fumero offered him one of his cigarettes. "No, thank you," said Arráez.

"Quality merchandise," Fumero insisted. "American."

Arráez accepted the cigarette and put it in his pocket. "Do you wish to inspect the papers and licenses, Major? Everything is up to date, with the permits and stamps of the Generalitat government."

Fumero shrugged, coldly exhaling a puff of smoke and gazing at his cigarette ember with a hint of a smile. "I'm sure your papers are all in order. Tell me, what cargo are you carrying?"

"Supplies. Medicines, arms, and ammunition. And a few lots of confiscated property for auction. The inventory, with the government stamp from the Valencia delegation, is at your disposal."

"I didn't expect anything less from you, Captain. But that's between you and the port and customs officers. I'm a simple servant of the people."

Arráez nodded his head calmly, reminding himself not to take his eyes off those dark, impenetrable lenses for one second. "If you would be kind enough to tell me what you're looking for, Major, it will be my pleasure . . ."

Fumero gestured for him to join him, and they both wandered down the length of the deck while the crew watched expectantly. After a few minutes, Fumero stopped, took one last drag, and threw his cigarette overboard. Leaning on the rail, he gazed at Barcelona as if he'd never seen the city before. "Can you smell it, Captain?"

Arráez waited a moment before replying. "I'm not quite sure what you're referring to, Major."

Fumero tapped his arm affectionately. "Take a deep breath. Slowly. You'll see how you notice it."

Arráez exchanged a glance with Bermejo. The members of the crew looked at one another in confusion. Fumero turned around and with a gesture encouraged them to breathe in too.

"No? Nobody?"

The captain tried to force a smile that didn't reach his lips.

"Well, I can certainly smell it," said Fumero. "Don't tell me you haven't noticed it."

Arráez nodded vaguely.

"Of course," Fumero insisted. "Of course you can smell it. Like me, and like everyone here. It's the smell of a rat. That disgusting rat you're hiding on board."

Arráez frowned in bewilderment. "I can assure you—"

Fumero raised a hand to silence him. "When a rat sneaks in, there's no way of getting rid of it. You give it poison, and it eats it. You set up a rat trap, and it shits on it. A rat is the most difficult thing in the world to get rid of. Because rats are cowards. Because they hide. Because they think they're cleverer than you." Fumero took a few seconds to savor his words. "And do you know what is the only way of destroying a rat, Captain? How to really exterminate a rat, once and for all?"

Arráez shook his head. "I don't know, Major."

Fumero smiled, baring his teeth. "Of course not. Because you're a seaman, and there's no reason why you should know. That's my job. That's the reason why the Revolution has brought me into the world. Observe, Captain. Observe and learn."

Before Arráez could respond, Fumero walked off toward the prow and his men followed him. The captain then realized that he'd been wrong. Fumero was armed. He wielded a shiny revolver in his hand, a collector's piece. Traversing the deck, he roughly pushed aside any crew members standing in his way and ignored the entrance to the cabins. He knew where he was going. At a signal his men surrounded the hatch that sealed off the hold and waited for the order. Fumero leaned over the metal sheet and gently knocked on it with his knuckles, as if he were knocking on the door of an old friend.

"Surprise!" he chimed.

When the men had practically ripped off the hatch and the bowels of the ship were exposed to daylight, Arráez went back to the bridge to hide. He'd already witnessed enough in two years of war. The last thing he saw was Fumero licking his lips like a cat a second before disappearing, revolver in hand, into the hold of the ship.

5

AFTER DAYS OF being confined to the hold, breathing the same stuffy air, Fermín noticed the aroma of a fresh breeze coming in through the hatch and filtering through the cracks in the crate of weapons. He tilted his head to one side and through the narrow chink between the lid and the edge of the box managed to see an array of dusty light beams sweeping the hold. Flashlights.

The white, hazy light caressed the shapes of the cargo, revealing transparencies in the cloths covering the cars and works of art. The sound of footsteps and the metallic echo resounding in the bilge slowly drew closer. Fermín gritted his teeth and mentally went over all the steps he'd taken before he returned to his hiding place. The sacks, the candles, the bits of food or footprints he might have left throughout the cargo area. He didn't think he'd forgotten anything. They'd never find him there, he told himself. Never.

It was then that Fermín heard that harsh, familiar voice saying his name in a soft singsong tone, and his knees turned to jelly.

Fumero.

The voice, and the footsteps, sounded very close. Fermín shut his eyes like a child terrorized by a strange sound in the darkness of his room. Not because he thinks this is going to protect him, but because he doesn't dare acknowledge the silhouette towering by his bedside, bending over him. At that very moment Fermín heard the slow footsteps only centimeters away. Gloved fingers caressed the lid of the box like a snake slithering over the surface. Fumero was whistling a tune. Fermín held his breath and kept his eyes closed. Drops of cold sweat slid down his forehead, and he had to clench his fists to stop the trembling in his hands. He dared not move a single muscle, fearing that the mere touch of his body against the bags of rifles might produce an infinitesimal sound.

Perhaps he'd been mistaken. Perhaps they would find him. Perhaps there was no corner in the world where he could hide and live one more day to tell the tale. Perhaps, after all, that day was as good as any other to leave the show. Come to think of it, nothing stopped him kicking open that box and confronting Fumero, brandishing one of those rifles on which he was lying. Better to die riddled with bullets in two seconds flat than at the hands of Fumero and his toys, after two weeks hanging from the ceiling of a dungeon in Montjuïc Castle.

He felt the outline of one of the guns, searching for the trigger, and clutched it firmly. Until then it hadn't occurred to him that in all probability it wasn't loaded. What did it matter? With his marksmanship, he was as likely to shoot himself in the foot as to hit Columbus's eye on his monument. He smiled at the thought and held the rifle with both hands over his chest, looking for the hammer. He'd never before fired a gun, but he told himself that good luck is always on the side of beginners. It was at least worth a try. He tightened the hammer and prepared to blow off Francisco Javier Fumero's head on his way to heaven or hell.

*

A second later, however, the footsteps faded away, depriving him of his chance of glory and reminding him that great lovers—whether practicing or aspiring—were not born to be eleventh-hour heroes. He allowed himself a deep breath and rested his hands on his chest. His clothes stuck to him like a second skin. Fumero and his henchmen were walking away. Fermín imagined their figures engulfed by the shadows of the hold and smiled with relief. Perhaps there hadn't been a tip-off. Maybe this was nothing but a routine control.

Just then the footsteps stopped. A deathly silence followed, and for a few moments all Fermín could hear was the sound of his own heartbeat. Then, like an almost imperceptible sigh, came the minuscule tapping of something tiny and light walking over the lid of the box, just above his face. He recognized the faint odor, somewhere between sweet and sour. His traveling companion, the little mouse, was sniffing at the chinks in the boards, probably detecting the smell of his friend. Fermín was about to hiss lightly and chase it away when a deafening roar filled the hold.

The high-caliber bullet blew the rodent to bits instantly and bored a clean entry hole on the lid of the box about five centimeters from Fermín's face. Blood dripped through the cracks and fell on his lips. Fermín then felt a tickling sensation on his right leg. As he lowered his eyes to look, he realized that the missile's path had almost brushed his leg, burning a tear in his trousers before drilling a second exit hole in the wood. A line of hazy light cut through the darkness of his hideaway, following the bullet's trajectory. He heard the footsteps approaching again and stopping next to the rifle box. Fumero knelt down beside it. Fermín caught the gleam of his eyes in the thin gap between the lid and the box.

"As usual, making friends among the plebs, eh? You should have heard the screams of your friend Amancio when he told us where we'd find you. A couple of wires on the balls, and you heroes sing like goldfinches."

Facing that look and everything he knew about it, Fermín felt that if he hadn't sweated out what little courage he had left, trapped in that coffin full of guns, he would have wet himself with panic.

"You smell worse than your friend the rat," whispered Fumero. "I think you need a bath."

He could hear the erratic footsteps and the turmoil of the men as they moved boxes and knocked down objects in the hold. While this was taking place, Fumero did not move from where he was. His eyes sounded the darkness inside the box like a serpent at the entrance to a nest, patiently. Before long, Fermín felt a powerful hammering on the box. At first he thought they were trying to break it up. But when he saw the tips of nails appearing under the lid, he understood that what they were doing was sealing down the rim. In a second the millimeter-wide opening that had previously been visible all around the lid vanished. He'd been buried in his own hiding place.

Fermín then realized that the box was moving, that it was being pushed and shoved across the floor, and that, following Fumero's orders, a few members of the crew were coming down to the hold. He could imagine the rest. He felt about a dozen men lifting the box with levers and heard the canvas straps encircle the wood. He also heard the rattling of chains and felt the sudden upward pull of the crane.

6

ARRÁEZ AND HIS crew watched the trunk swaying in the breeze six meters above deck. Fumero emerged from the hold and put his dark glasses on again, smiling with satisfaction as he looked up toward the bridge, raising a hand to his head in a mock military salute.

"With your permission, Captain, we will now proceed to exterminate the rat you carried on board in the only way that is fully effective."

Fumero signaled to the man operating the crane to lower the

container a few meters until it was level with his face. "Your dying wish, or a few words of contrition?"

The crew gazed at the box in utter silence. The only sound that seemed to emerge from inside was a whimper, like the cry of a terrified small animal.

"Come on, don't cry, it's not that bad," said Fumero. "Besides, you won't be alone. You'll be meeting up with a whole lot of friends who can't wait to see you . . ."

The trunk rose in the air again, and the crane began to rotate toward the gunwale. When it was hanging about ten meters above sea level, Fumero turned toward the bridge again. Arráez was observing him with glazed eyes, muttering under his breath.

"Son of a bitch," Fumero managed to lip-read.

Then he gave a nod, and the container, carrying two hundred kilos of rifles and just over fifty kilos of Fermín Romero de Torres, plunged into the icy dark waters of Barcelona's port.

7

THE FALL INTO the void barely gave Fermín time to hold on to the walls of the trunk. When it hit the water, the pile of rifles shifted upward and crashed against the top of the box. For a few seconds the container floated, rocking gently like a buoy. He struggled to remove the dozens of rifles under which he'd been buried. A strong smell of salt residue and diesel reached his nostrils. Then he heard the sound of water gushing in through the hole left by Fumero's bullet. A second later he felt its rising coldness as it flooded the floor. Panic-stricken, he tried to crouch down to reach the bottom of the trunk. As he did so, the weight of the rifles moved to one side and the container listed. Fermín fell headlong on the guns. In complete darkness he groped through the pile of weapons beneath his hands and began to shove them aside, searching for the hole through which the water was entering. No sooner had he managed to place a dozen or so rifles behind his back than these would tumble over him again and push him toward the bottom of the box, which was still listing. Water covered his feet and ran through his fingers. It had reached his knees by the time he managed to find the hole and cover it as best he could by pressing with both hands. He then heard gunshots on the ship's deck and the impact of bullets hitting the wood. Three new holes opened up behind him, and a greenish light filtered through, allowing Fermín to make out how fiercely the water was pouring in. In a few moments it was up to his waist. He screamed in terror and anger, trying to reach one of the holes with one hand, but a sudden jolt pushed him backward. The sound engulfing the trunk made him shudder, as if a beast were swallowing him. Water rose to his chest, and the cold took his breath away. It became dark again, and Fermín realized that the box was sinking irretrievably. His right hand yielded to the water's pressure. In the dark, the freezing sea swept his tears away as he tried to catch one last mouthful of air.

The current sucked in the wooden carcass and dragged it relentlessly to the bottom. A small chamber of air, just about a hand span in height, had been trapped in the top part of the box. Making a huge effort, Fermín managed to lift himself and catch another gulp of oxygen. Moments later, the box hit the seabed and, after leaning to one side, became beached in the mud. Fermín banged and kicked the lid, but the wood was securely nailed on and wouldn't budge. The last remaining centimeters of air seeped out through the cracks. Cold and utter darkness invited him to succumb, but with no air his lungs were burning and he felt as if his head was about to explode under the pressure. Faced with the certainty that he only had a few seconds left to live, he fell into a blind panic and, grabbing one of the rifles, started banging the lid with the butt. At the fourth blow the weapon fell apart in his hands. He groped around in the dark, and his fingers brushed against one of the bags protecting a rifle that floated about in a trapped air bubble. Fermín grabbed the bag with both hands and started banging again with what little strength he had left, praying for an impossible miracle.

The bullet produced a dull vibration as it exploded inside the bag. The shot, almost at point-blank, made a hole in the wood the size of a fist. A streak of light lit up the interior. Fermín's hands now reacted before his brain. He aimed the weapon at the same point and pulled the trigger again and again. But water had already filled the bag, and none of the bullets exploded. He grabbed another rifle and fired through the bag. The first two shots didn't work, but at the third shot Fermín felt his arms jerk back and saw the hole in the wood getting larger. He emptied the rifle of ammunition until his lean, battered body managed to push through the gap. The edges of the splintered wood bit into his skin, yet the promise of that ghostly light and the sheet of brightness he could glimpse on the surface would have helped him cross a field of knives.

The murky water of the port burned his eyes, but Fermín kept them open. An underwater forest of lights and shadows rocked to and fro in the greenish gloom. Below him lay a scene of debris, skeletons of sunken boats, and centuries of mud. He looked up toward the columns of hazy light falling from above. The merchant ship's hull was silhouetted against the surface, forming a large shadow. He reckoned that that part of the port was at least fifteen meters deep, perhaps more. If he managed to reach the surface on the other side of the ship's hull, maybe nobody would notice his presence and he'd be able to survive. Giving himself a push by pressing his feet against the remains of the box, he began to swim up. Only then, as he slowly rose to the surface, were his eyes able to catch a fleeting glimpse of the ghostly vision hiding in the depths. He realized that what he had taken to be seaweed and discarded nets were actually bodies swaying in the dark. Dozens of handcuffed corpses, their legs bound together and chained to stones or blocks of cement, formed an underwater cemetery. The flesh on their faces had been peeled away by the eels that slithered through their limbs, and their hair fluttered in the current. Fermín recognized the shapes of men, women, and children. At their feet lay suitcases and bundles half buried in mud. Some of the bodies were already so decomposed that all that was left of them were bones peeping through tattered bits of clothes. The corpses formed an endless gallery that disappeared into the darkness. Fermín closed his eyes and a second later emerged into life, discovering that the simple act of breathing was the most marvelous experience of his entire existence.

8

FOR A FEW moments Fermín remained stuck like a limpet to the ship's hull as he recovered his breath. A marker buoy floated about twenty meters away. It resembled a small lighthouse: a cylinder crowned by a lantern, set on a circular base with a cabin. It was painted white with red stripes and swayed gently, like a metal island running adrift. If he managed to reach it, Fermín worked out, he could hide inside the buoy's cabin and wait for the right moment to risk gaining dry land unseen. Nobody seemed to have noticed him, but he didn't want to push his luck. He inhaled as much air as his battered lungs could take and dived underwater again, making his way toward the buoy with uneven strokes. As he did so he avoided looking down, preferring to think he'd suffered a hallucination and the ghoulish garden of corpses swaying in the current below him was nothing more than a pile of fishing nets trapped in rubble. He emerged a few meters from the buoy and swam hurriedly around it to hide. After checking the deck of the ship, he assured himself that for the moment he was safe and that everyone on board, including Fumero, presumed him dead. But as he scrambled onto the platform, he noticed a motionless figure observing him from the bridge. For a moment Fermín held his gaze. He couldn't identify the man, but judging from his clothes, he assumed it was the ship's captain. He rushed into the tiny cabin and collapsed in a heap, shivering with cold and imagining that in a few seconds he would hear them coming to get him. It would have been preferable to drown inside that box. Now Fumero would lock him in one of his cells and take his sweet time with him.

He'd been waiting for what seemed like an infinity, resigned to the fact that his adventure had finally come to an end, when he heard the ship's engines start up, and the blare of the foghorn. Peeping fearfully through the cabin window, he saw the ship move away toward the docks. He lay down, exhausted, in the lukewarm embrace of the sun that seeped through the window. Perhaps, after all, Our Lady of the Unbelievers had taken pity on him.

FERMÍN REMAINED ON his tiny island until evening tinted the sky and the streetlamps in the harbor cast a sparkling net over the water. After scanning the docks, he decided that his best bet was to swim up to the swarm of boats clustered in front of the fish market and use a mooring rope or a trawling pulley attached to the prow of one of the anchored vessels to climb up to dry land.

Just then he noticed a shape outlined in the mist that swept across the inner harbor. A rowboat was approaching, with two men on board. One of them rowed, and the other sat in the stern, scouring the shadows with a lantern that tinged the fog with an amber light. Fermín swallowed hard. He could have jumped into the water and prayed that the mantle of twilight would conceal him so he could escape yet again, but he'd reached the end of his prayers and didn't have a breath of resistance left in his body. He came out of his hiding spot with his hands up and faced the advancing boat.

"Lower your hands," said the man carrying the lantern.

Fermín screwed up his eyes. It was the same person he'd seen watching him from the bridge a few hours earlier. Fermín looked him in the eye and nodded as he accepted his hand and jumped onto the boat. The man at the oars handed him a blanket, and the exhausted castaway wrapped himself up in it.

"I'm Captain Arráez," the man with the lantern said, "and this is my first mate, Bermejo."

Fermín tried to stammer something, but Arráez stopped him. "Don't tell us your name. It's none of our business."

The captain reached out for a Thermos flask and poured Fermín a cupful of warm wine. He clutched the tin cup with both hands and drank until he'd drained the last drop. Three more times Arráez filled the cup, and Fermín felt the warmth return to his body.

"Are you feeling better?" asked the captain.

Fermín nodded.

"I'm not going to ask you what you were doing on my ship, or what's between you and that skunk Fumero, but you'd better be careful."

"I do try, believe me. But fate doesn't seem inclined to collaborate."

Arráez handed him a bag. Fermín had a quick look inside. It contained a handful of dry clothes, at least six sizes too large for him, and some money.

"Why are you doing this, Captain?" he asked. "I'm just a stowaway who's got you into big trouble."

"I'm doing this because I damn well want to," replied Arráez, to which Bermejo mumbled his agreement.

"I don't know how to thank you for—"

"Just don't sneak onto my ship as a stowaway again. Go on, change your clothes."

Arráez and Bermejo watched him take off those sodden rags and helped him put on his new outfit, an old sailor's uniform. Before abandoning his threadbare jacket forever, Fermín searched the pockets and pulled out the letter he'd been guarding for weeks. The sea water had rubbed out the ink and the envelope was just a piece of wet paper that fell apart in his hands. Fermín closed his eyes and burst into tears.

Arráez and Bermejo looked at one another anxiously. The captain put his hand on Fermín's shoulder. "Don't be upset, man, the worst is over."

Fermín shook his head. "It's not that   it's not that."

He got dressed slowly and kept what was left of the letter in the pocket of his new short coat. When he noticed the dismay on the faces of his two benefactors, he dried his tears and smiled at them. "I'm sorry."

"You're all skin and bones," remarked Bermejo.

"It's this transient war interval," said Fermín apologetically, trying to adopt a livelier, more optimistic tone. "But now that my luck is changing, I foresee a cornucopia of fine foods in my future and a life of contemplation during which I'll fatten up with sausages while I reread the Bard's best sonnets. A couple of days of vigorously ingesting black pudding and cinnamon biscuits, and I'll look as round as a beach ball. Believe it or not, left to my own devices I put on weight faster than a Wagnerian soprano."

"If you say so," said Arráez. "Do you have somewhere to go?"

Fermín, now poised like an admiral minus the ship in his new outfit, his stomach throbbing with the warm wine, nodded enthusiastically.

"Is a woman waiting for you?" asked the seaman.

Fermín smiled sadly. "She's waiting, but not for me."

"I see. Was that letter for her?"

Fermín nodded again.

"And that's why you've risked your life and returned to Barcelona? To deliver a letter?"

"She's worth it." Fermín shrugged. "And I promised a good friend that I'd do this."

"He's dead?"

Fermín lowered his eyes.

"Some bits of news are best not given," ventured Arráez.

"A promise is a promise."

"When was the last time you saw her?"

"Just over a year ago."

The captain gazed at Fermín for a while. "A year is a long time these days," he said. "People are quick to forget. It's like a virus, but it helps one survive."

"I hope I catch it, then," said Fermín, "because it's just what I need."

10

IT WAS GETTING dark when the rowboat left Fermín at the foot of the steps to the Atarazanas dock. He merged into the mist shrouding the port, one more figure among the stevedores and sailors making their way up to the streets of the Raval, known in those days as the Chinese quarter. As he mixed with them, he was able to make out bits of their half-whispered conversations: the Fascist air force had paid them a visit the day before, one of many that year, and they were expecting more air raids that night. One could sense the fear in those men's voices and in their eyes, but having survived the day, Fermín told himself that whatever the night had in store for him couldn't be any worse. As luck would have it, a candy peddler, who was already beating a retreat with a cartful of confectionary, crossed his path. Fermín stopped him and inspected his wares meticulously.

"I have caramel-coated almonds like the ones from before the war," offered the merchant. "Would the gentleman like some?"

"My kingdom for a Sugus sweet."

"Got one little bag left. Strawberry flavor."

Fermín's eyes opened wide. The very mention of the succulent treat made his mouth water. With some of the funds provided by Captain Arráez he was able to acquire the entire bag, which he proceeded to open with the eagerness of a condemned man.

The misty light of the Ramblas streetlamps—like the first taste of a Sugus sweet—had always seemed to Fermín one of those things for which it was worth living another day. That evening, however, as he walked up the boulevard, Fermín noticed a squad of night watchmen moving from lamp to lamp, ladder in hand, turning off the lights that still shone on the paving. He approached one of them and stood by, observing his hurried movements. When the watchman stepped off the ladder and noticed Fermín's presence, he paused and looked at him out of the corner of his eye.

"Good evening, boss," Fermín said cordially. "You won't be offended if I ask you why you're leaving the city in the dark?"

The watchman simply pointed his finger to the sky and, picking up his ladder, moved on to the next lamp. For a moment Fermín remained where he was, staring at the strange sight of the Ramblas as they sank into shadow. All around him, cafés and shops were beginning to close their doors, and the facades were lit up by the faint glow of moonlight. He set off again, rather apprehensively, and soon caught sight of what looked like a nocturnal procession: a large group of people carrying bundles and blankets were heading for the entrance to the metro station. Some carried lit candles and oil lamps, others walked in the dark. When he passed the steps leading down to the metro, Fermín glanced at a boy who couldn't have been more than five years old. He was clutching his mother's hand, or maybe it was his grandmother's, because in that feeble light all those poor souls looked as if they'd aged prematurely. Fermín was about to give him a friendly wink, but the boy had his eyes riveted on the sky. He was staring at the web of dark clouds coming together on the horizon as if he could see something hidden inside it. Fermín followed the boy's eyes and felt the brush of a cold wind that was beginning to sweep through the city, smelling of phosphorus and charred wood. Just before his mother dragged him down the stairs toward the tunnels of the metro, the boy gave Fermín a look that froze his blood. Those five-year-old eyes reflected the blind terror and despair of an old man. Fermín looked away and set off again, passing a local policeman who was guarding the entrance to the station.

The policeman pointed at him. "If you leave now, you won't find any room later. And the shelters are full."

Fermín nodded but hurried on, moving further into a Barcelona that seemed ghostly to him, a never-ending gloom where outlines could barely be made out in the dim, flickering light of candles and oil lamps placed on balconies and inside entrance halls. When at last he reached Rambla de Santa Mónica, he spied a narrow, somber front door in the distance. Sighing despondently, he set off toward his meeting with Lucía.

II

SLOWLY FERMÍN WALKED up the narrow staircase, and with each step he could feel his determination and courage evaporating. He had to confront Lucía and tell her that the man she loved, the father of her daughter and the face she had been hoping to see for over a year, had died in a prison cell in Seville. On the third-floor landing he waited by the door, not daring to knock. He sat on the steps and buried his head in his hands. He remembered Lucía's precise words spoken thirteen months earlier. She had held his hands and, looking into his eyes, had said, "If you love me, don't let anything happen to him. Bring him back to me."

Fermín pulled the envelope out of his pocket and stared at the pieces in the dark. He crumpled them between his fingers and threw them into the shadows. He had got up and was about to flee down the stairs when he heard the door open behind him. Then he paused.

*

A girl of about seven or eight was watching him from the doorway. She was carrying a book in her hands and had one finger between the pages as a bookmark. Fermín smiled at her and raised a hand in greeting.

"Hello, Alicia," he said. "Do you remember me?"

The girl looked at him a little distrustfully, doubting.

"What are you reading?"

"*Alice in Wonderland.*"

"You don't say! Can I see?"

She showed him the book but didn't let him touch it. "It's one of my favorites," she said, still a little suspicious.

"One of mine too," replied Fermín. "Anything to do with falling down a hole and bumping into madmen and mathematical problems is something I consider highly autobiographical."

The girl bit her lips to hold back the laughter provoked by the peculiar visitor's words. "Yes, but this one was written for me," she said mischievously.

"Of course it was. Tell me, Alicia, is your mother at home?"

She didn't answer, but opened the door a bit farther, turned, and walked into the flat without saying a word.

Fermín paused in the doorway. The flat was dark inside, except for what looked like the glimmer of an oil lamp at the end of a narrow corridor.

"Lucía?" he called, his voice trailing off in the shadows. He rapped on the door with his knuckles and waited. "Lucía? It's me."

He waited another few seconds, and when no reply came, he stepped into the flat and advanced along the corridor. All the doors were closed. When he reached the end of the passage, he found himself in a living room that doubled as a dining room. The oil lamp rested on the table, projecting a soft, yellowish halo. He could see the outline of an old woman facing the window. She sat on a chair, her back turned to him.

Fermín stopped. Only then did he recognize her. "Doña Leonor . . ."

The woman who had seemed so old couldn't have been more than forty-five. Her face was lined with bitterness and her eyes looked glazed, tired of hating and weeping in solitude. Leonor was looking at him without saying a word. Fermín took a chair and sat down next to her. He held her hand and smiled almost imperceptibly.

"She should have married you," she murmured. "You're ugly, but at least you've got a head on your shoulders."

"Where's Lucía, Doña Leonor?"

The woman looked away. "They took her. About two months ago."

"Where to?"

Leonor didn't reply.

"Who were they?"

"That man . . ."

"Fumero?"

"They didn't ask for Juan Antonio. They were looking for her."

Fermín hugged her, but Leonor didn't move.

"I'll find her, Doña Leonor. I'll find her and bring her home."

The woman shook her head. "He's dead, isn't he? My son?"

Fermín remained silent for a few moments.

"I don't know, Doña Leonor."

She looked at him angrily and slapped his face. "Liar."

"Doña Leonor . . ."

"Go," she moaned.

Fermín stood up and moved away a few steps. Little Alicia watched him from the corridor. He smiled at her, and the girl walked slowly over to him. Then she took his hand and held it tight. He knelt down in front of her. He was about to tell her that he'd been a friend of her mother's, hoping to come up with some story with which to placate the look of abandonment that had taken hold of her, but at that very instant, while Leonor drowned her tears in her hands, Fermín heard a faraway rumble raining down from the sky. When he looked up toward the window, he noticed that the glass was beginning to tremble.

FERMÍN WALKED OVER to the window and drew back the net curtain. He gazed up at the narrow slice of sky trapped between the cornices that framed the narrow street. The rumble was more intense now and sounded much closer. His first thought was that a storm was approaching from the sea, and he imagined black clouds stealing over the docks and tearing down sails and masts as it advanced. But he'd never seen a storm that sounded like metal and fire. The mist broke up into shreds, and when the sky cleared, he saw them. They emerged from the dark like large steel insects, flying in formation. He gulped and turned to look first at Leonor, then at Alicia, who was shaking; the child still held her book in her hands.

"I think we should get out of here," said Fermín.

Leonor shook her head. "They'll fly past," she said almost in a whisper. "Like last night."

Fermín scanned the skies again and happened to see a group of six or seven planes leaving the formation. He opened the window, and when he put his head out he thought the roar of the engines was coming up the Ramblas. Then there was a high-pitched whistling sound, like a drill piercing its way down from the skies. Alicia stopped her ears with her hands and ran to hide under the table. Leonor stretched out her arms to hold her, but something stopped her. Seconds before the shell hit the building, the screech became so intense that it seemed to come out of the very walls. Fermín thought the noise was going to rupture his eardrums.

And then, silence.

A sudden impact shook the building, as if a train had just dropped from the clouds and was slicing through the roof and every flat as it would through cigarette paper. He saw words being formed by Leonor's lips, but couldn't hear them. In just a fraction of a second, dazed by a block of solid noise that froze time, Fermín saw the wall behind Leonor crumble into a white cloud, while a sheet of fire surrounded the chair she was sitting on and swallowed her. The suction from the explosion tore half the pieces of furniture right off the floor, leaving them suspended in the air before they went up in flames. He was hit by a wave of burning air, like flaming gasoline, that hurled him against the window with such force he went straight through the glass and crashed against the metal bars of the balcony. The coat given to him by Captain Arráez smoldered and burned his skin. When he tried to stand up and remove it, he felt the floor shudder under his feet. Seconds later, the central structure of the building collapsed before his eyes in a downpour of debris and embers.

Fermín stood up and tore off his smoldering jacket. He peered into the sitting room. A shroud of smoke, dark and acid, licked the walls that were still standing. The explosion had pulverized the heart of the building, leaving only the facade and a first line of rooms around a crater. What remained of the staircase now climbed over the crater's edge. Beyond what had been the corridor through which he had come in, there was nothing,

"Motherfuckers," he spat out. He couldn't hear his own voice through the screeching sound that burned his eardrums, but his skin felt the wave of a new explosion not far from there. An acid wind, reeking of sulfur, electricity, and burned flesh, swept up the street, and Fermín saw the glow of the flames splattering the skies of Barcelona.

13

A SEARING PAIN mauled Fermín's muscles as he staggered into the room. The explosion had flung Alicia against the wall, and the child's body had become wedged between a collapsed armchair and one of the corners of the room. She was covered in dust and ashes. He knelt down and grabbed her under the shoulders. When she felt his touch, Alicia opened her eyes. They were bloodshot, and her pupils were dilated. Fermín saw his own battered figure reflected in them.

"Where's Grandma?" murmured Alicia.

"Grandma has had to go. You should come with me. You and me. We're going to get out of here."

Alicia nodded. Fermín took her in his arms and felt her clothes, checking her for wounds or fractures. "Is anything hurting?"

The girl put a hand to her head.

"It will pass," said Fermín. "Ready?"

"My book . . ."

Fermín looked for the book among the rubble. He found it, a bit singed but still in one piece, and handed it to her. Alicia grabbed it as if it were an amulet.

"Don't lose it, eh? You must tell me how it ends."

Fermín got to his feet with the girl in his arms. Either Alicia weighed more than he expected, or he had even less strength than he thought to get out of that place. "Hold tight." ·

Fermín turned around and, skirting the vast hole left by the explosion, moved slowly along the bit of tiled corridor that remained standing—now reduced to a mere ledge—until he reached the staircase. From there he discovered that the shell had penetrated as far down as the basement of the building, and a pool of fire had flooded the first two floors. Peering through the stairwell, he noticed that the flames were rising slowly, step by step. He clutched Alicia firmly and rushed up the stairs. If they managed to reach the terraced roof, he told himself, he'd be able to jump from there to the adjoining building. Perhaps he'd live to tell the tale.

14

THE DOOR TO the terraced roof was a solid oak panel, but the blast had blown it off its hinges and Fermín was able to kick it open. Once he was on the rooftop, he set Alicia down and collapsed against the edge of the facade to catch his breath. He inhaled deeply. The air smelled of burned phosphorus. For a few seconds Fermín and Alicia remained silent, unable to believe the sight unfolding before their eyes.

Barcelona was a mantle of darkness riddled with columns of fire and plumes of black smoke that swayed like tentacles in the sky. A couple of blocks from there, the Ramblas formed a river of huge flames and clouds of smoke, snaking toward the town center.

Fermín seized the girl's hand and pulled her. "Come on, we can't stop."

They had only taken a few steps when a new roar filled the sky and shook the structure beneath them. Fermín looked behind him and noticed a powerful brightness rising near Plaza de Cataluña. A bolt of red lightning swept over the city's rooftops in a matter of seconds. Then the firestorm died away, turning into a downpour of ashes through which the roar of engines could be heard again. The squadron flew very low through the thick, swirling smoke that spread over Barcelona: Fermín could see the reflection of the city's flames shining on the bellies of the aircraft. He followed the planes' flight with his eyes and saw clusters of bombs raining over the rooftops of the Raval quarter. Some fifty meters from their terraced roof, a row of buildings exploded one after the other, as if they'd been attached to a load of dynamite. The shock wave smashed hundreds of windows into a rain of glass and uprooted everything it found on the neighboring terraces. A dovecote on the adjacent building collapsed onto the cornice, then fell onto the opposite side of the street, knocking down a water tank that plunged into the void and burst with an enormous bang when it hit the pavement. Fermín could hear cries of panic in the street.

Fermín and Alicia were paralyzed. Unable to take another step, they remained immobile for a few seconds, their eyes glued to the swarm of airplanes that kept battering the city. Fermín sighted the docks of the harbor, sown with half-sunken ships. Huge panels of blazing diesel spread over the water's surface, swallowing those who had jumped into the sea and were trying desperately to swim away. The sheds and hangars on the quayside raged with flames. A chain-reaction explosion of fuel tanks demolished a row of enormous cargo cranes. One by one, the huge metal structures crashed down on the freighters and fishing boats moored to the quayside, burying them underwater. In the distance, through the sulfur and diesel mist, Fermín could see the airplanes turning around over the sea, preparing for another pass.

He closed his eyes and let the dirty, hot wind drive the sweat off his body. "Here I am, you sons of bitches. Why don't you damn well hit me, once and for all."

15

WHEN HE THOUGHT all he could hear was the sound of the airplanes approaching again, Fermín registered the voice of the girl by his side. He opened his eyes and saw Alicia. The child was tugging at him as hard as she could, yelling in panic. Fermín turned around. What remained of the building was crumbling away like a sand castle in the tide. They dashed off to the edge of the terraced roof and managed to jump over the wall that separated it from the adjacent building. Fermín tumbled over as he fell, then felt a sudden sharp pain in his left leg. Alicia was pulling him again and helped him back on his feet. He felt his thigh and noticed blood seeping through his fingers. The glow from the flames lit up the wall over which they'd just vaulted, revealing a crest made of bits of sharp, bloodstained glass. Nausea clouded Fermín's eyes, but he took a deep breath and kept moving. Alicia was still pulling him. Dragging his leg, which left a dark, shiny trail on the tiles, Fermín followed the girl across the terraced roof until they reached the wall separating it from the building that looked down on Calle Arco del Teatro. He managed to clamber up a pile of wooden crates stacked against the partition wall and look over into the neighboring roof terrace. An ominous-looking structure rose before him, an old palace with sealed windows and a majestic facade that looked as if it had been submerged for decades in the depths of a swamp. The building was crowned by a large frosted-glass dome, its top shaped like a lantern tower, above which a lightning conductor held the quivering silhouette of a dragon.

The wound on Fermín's leg was throbbing, and he had to hold on to the cornice of the partition wall to avoid collapsing. He could feel the warm blood inside his shoe and again felt nauseous. He knew he was about to lose consciousness. Alicia looked at him, terrified. Fermín did his best to smile.

"It's nothing," he said. "Just a scratch."

In the distance, the airplane squadron had already circled over the sea and flown over the breakwater in the port on its way back to the city.

Fermín held his hand out for Alicia. "Hold tight."

The girl shook her head slowly.

"We're not safe here," he said. "We need to cross over to the next terrace and find the way down to the street, and from there to the metro," he added with little conviction.

"No," mumbled the child.

"Give me your hand, Alicia."

The girl hesitated, but in the end she gave him her hand. Fermín pulled her up firmly, setting her on top of the wooden crates. Once she was there, he lifted her to the edge of the cornice. "Jump."

Alicia held her book against her chest and shook her head. Fermín heard the rattle of the machine guns riddling the rooftops behind them and pushed the girl over. When Alicia landed on the other side of the wall, she turned to stretch a hand up to Fermín, but her friend wasn't there. He was still holding on to the cornice on the other side of the wall. He was pale, and his eyelids were beginning to droop, as if he could barely remain conscious.

"Run," he snapped with his last breath. "Run."

Fermín's knees gave way, and he fell backward. He heard the rattle of the airplanes flying right above them, and before he closed his eyes, he saw a cluster of bombs falling from the sky.

16

ALICIA RAN DESPERATELY across the roof terrace toward the large glass dome. She never knew where the shell burst, whether it grazed the façade of one of the buildings or exploded in midair. All she could perceive was a wall of compressed air hitting her brutally from behind, a deafening gale that flung her up in the air and propelled her forward. A gust skimmed past her, carrying bits of burning metal. It was then she felt an object the size of a fist stab her sharply in the hip. The impact made her spin in the air and then thrust her against the glass dome. She fell through a curtain of splintered glass into the void, the book slipping from her hands.

For what seemed an eternity Alicia plummeted through the dark. Finally an extended sheet of canvas broke her fall. The material buckled under her weight, leaving her lying faceup on what looked like a wooden platform. Fifteen meters above, she could see the hole her body had left in the dome's glass. She tried to lean over on her side, but discovered that she couldn't feel her right leg and could barely move her body from the waist down. She looked around and noticed that the book she thought she'd lost was lying on the edge of the platform.

Using her arms, she dragged herself to the book and touched its spine with her fingertips. A new explosion shook the building, and the vibration hurled the book into the void. Alicia peeped over the edge and saw it plunge, its pages fluttering, into the abyss. The glow from the flames flashing over the clouds spilled a beam of light through the darkness. Alicia blinked a few times in disbelief, doubting her eyes. She had landed on top of a towering spiral that sprawled into an endless labyrinth of corridors, passageways, arches, and galleries, resembling an enormous cathedral. But unlike the cathedrals she knew, this one was not made of stone.

It was made of books.

The shafts of light pouring from the dome revealed a knot of staircases and bridges branching in and out of that structure, each one bordered by thousands and thousands of volumes. At the foot of the chasm she glimpsed a bubble of light, moving slowly. The light paused. A man with white hair was holding a lamp far below her, gazing upward. A deep pain stabbed Alicia's hip, and she felt her sight clouding over. Soon she closed her eyes and lost all sense of time.

*

Alicia woke to find herself being lifted gently into someone's arms. Through half-open eyes, she saw that she was moving down an endless corridor that split into dozens of galleries opening up in every direction, galleries made with walls and more walls crammed with books. She was being carried by the man with the white hair she had seen at the foot of the labyrinth, and noticed his vulturine features. When they reached the bottom of the structure the keeper of that place took her through the large hall under the vaulted ceiling, to a corner where he settled her on a makeshift bed. "What's your name?" he asked.

"Alicia," she murmured.

"I'm Isaac."

With a look of concern, the man examined the wound throbbing in the little girl's hip. He covered her with a blanket and, holding up her head, brought a glass of fresh water to her lips. Alicia sipped avidly. The keeper's hands settled her head on a pillow. Isaac smiled at her, but his eyes betrayed deep anguish. Behind him, forming what she thought was a basilica erected out of all the libraries in the world, rose the labyrinth she had seen from the summit.

Isaac sat on a chair next to her and held her hand. "Now you must rest."

He extinguished the lantern, and a bluish darkness engulfed them, sprinkled with small flashes of fire that trickled down from above. The seemingly impossible geometry of the book-labyrinth faded into the vastness, and Alicia thought she was dreaming all this, that the bomb had exploded in her grandmother's sitting room, that she and her friend had never escaped from that blazing building.

Isaac watched her with sadness. Through the walls came the sound of the bombs, of the sirens and the fire spreading death through Barcelona. A nearby explosion shook the walls and the floor beneath them, bringing up clouds of dust. In her bed, Alicia shuddered. The keeper lit a candle and left it resting on a low table next to her. The candlelight outlined the prodigious structure rising in the center of the hall, a vision that lit up Alicia's eyes moments before she lost consciousness.

Isaac sighed.

"Alicia," he said at last. "Welcome to the Cemetery of Forgotten Books."

17

FERMÍN OPENED HIS eyes to an immensity of celestial white. A uniformed angel was bandaging his thigh. Beyond, a corridor full of stretchers disappeared into infinity.

"Is this purgatory?" he asked.

The nurse raised her eyes and looked at him askance. She did not appear to be a day older than eighteen, and Fermín thought that for an angel on the divine payroll, she was much better looking than the pictures given out at first communions and christenings suggested. The presence of impure thoughts could only mean one of two things: improvement on the physical front or imminent eternal condemnation.

"It goes without saying that I renounce my villainous unbelief and subscribe word for word to both Testaments, the New and the Old, in whatever order Your Angelical Grace esteems best."

When she noticed that the patient was regaining consciousness and could speak, the nurse made a sign, and a doctor who looked as if he hadn't slept for a week walked over to the stretcher. Lifting Fermín's eyelids with his fingers, the doctor examined his eyes.

"Am I dead?" asked Fermín.

"Don't exaggerate. You're a little beat-up, but in general quite alive."

"So this isn't purgatory?"

"Wishful thinking. You're in the Hospital Clínico. In other words, in hell."

While the doctor was examining his wound, Fermín considered the turn of events and tried to remember how he'd gotten there.

"How are you feeling?" asked the doctor.

"A bit confused, to tell you the truth. I dreamed that Jesus Christ paid me a visit, and we held a long and profound conversation."

55

"What about?"

"Soccer, mostly."

"That's because of the sedatives we gave you."

Fermín nodded with relief. "That's what I thought when the Lord confessed himself a Real Madrid fan."

The doctor smiled briefly and mumbled instructions to the nurse.

"How long have I been here?"

"About eight hours."

"Where's the child?"

"Baby Jesus?"

"No. The girl who was with me."

The nurse and the doctor exchanged glances.

"I'm sorry," the doctor said, "but there was no girl with you. As far as I know, it was a miracle someone found you, on a roof terrace in the Raval quarter, bleeding to death."

"And they didn't bring a girl in with me?"

The doctor lowered his eyes. "Alive? No."

Fermín tried to sit up. The nurse and the doctor held him down on the stretcher.

"I need to get out of here, Doctor. There's a defenseless child out there who needs my help."

The doctor gave the nurse a nod, and she quickly took a bottle from the medicine trolley and began preparing an injection. Fermín shook his head, but the doctor held him firmly. "I'm afraid I can't let you go yet. I'm going to ask you to be a bit patient. We don't want things to get worse."

"Don't worry, I have more lives than a cat."

"And less shame than a politician, which is why I'm also going to ask you to stop pinching the nurses' behinds when they change your bandages. Are we clear?"

Fermín felt the prick of the needle in his right shoulder and the cold spreading through his veins.

"Can you ask again, Doctor, please? Her name is Alicia."

The doctor loosened his grip and let his prey rest on the stretcher. Fermín's muscles melted into jelly and his pupils dilated, turning the world into a dissolving watercolor. The faraway voice of the doctor was lost in the echo of his descent. He felt he was falling through cotton-wool clouds, fading into the liquid balm with its promise of a chemical paradise, as the whiteness of the corridor fragmented into a powdery light.

18

FERMÍN WAS DISCHARGED halfway through the afternoon; the hospital could no longer cope with the numbers of wounded, and whoever wasn't dying was deemed fit to leave. Armed with a wooden crutch and some new clothes lent to him by a dead man, he managed to climb onto a tram outside the Hospital Clínico and travel back to the streets of the Raval. There he began to walk into cafés, grocers, and any other shops that were still open, asking in a loud voice whether anyone had seen a girl called Alicia. People looked at the wiry, gaunt little man and shook their heads silently, thinking that, like so many others, this poor soul was searching in vain for his dead daughter: one more body among the nine hundred—a hundred of them children—that would be picked up in the streets of Barcelona on that eighteenth day of March in 1938.

When evening fell, Fermín walked all the way down the Ramblas. Trams derailed by the bombs were still lying there, smoldering, with their dead passengers on board. Cafés that just hours earlier had been packed with customers were now ghostly galleries full of bodies. Pavements were awash in blood. None of the people trying to take the wounded away, cover up the dead, or simply flee anywhere or nowhere could remember having seen the girl he was describing.

Even so, Fermín didn't lose hope, not even when he came across a row of corpses lying on the pavement in front of the opera house, the Gran Teatro del Liceo. None of them looked older than eight or nine.

Fermín knelt down. Next to him, a woman stroked the feet of a boy with a black hole the size of a fist in his chest. "He's dead," she said, although Fermín hadn't asked. "They're all dead."

All night long, while the city removed the rubble and the ruins of dozens of buildings went on burning, Fermín walked from door to door through the whole of the Raval quarter, asking for Alicia.

Finally, at dawn, he couldn't take another step. He collapsed on the stairs outside the Church of Belén, and after a while a local policeman in a bloodstained uniform, his face smudged with cinders, sat down next to him. When the policeman asked him why he was crying, Fermín threw his arms around him. He wanted to die, he told him. Fate had placed the life of a little girl in his care, and he'd betrayed her and hadn't known how to protect her. If either God or the devil had even a hint of decency left in them, he went on, this fucking world would come to an end tomorrow or the next day, because it didn't deserve to go on existing.

The policeman, who had been tirelessly pulling out bodies from the rubble for hours, including those of his wife and six-year-old son, listened to him calmly.

"My friend," he said at last. "Don't lose hope. If there's anything I've learned from this lousy world, it's that destiny is always just around the corner. It might look like a thief, a hooker, or a lottery vendor, its three most usual personifications. And if you ever decide to go and find it—remember, destiny doesn't make house calls—you'll see that it will grant you a second chance."

MASKED BALL

❦

MADRID

1959

His Excellency

Don Mauricio Valls y Echevarría

and

Doña Elena Sarmiento de Fontalva

cordially invite you to the

Masked Ball

that will take place in the

Palacete Villa Mercedes

of Somosaguas, Madrid

on November 24, 1959

from 7:00 p.m.

R.S.V.P. to the Protocol Service

of the Ministry of National Education

before November 1.

I

THE ROOM EXISTED in perpetual darkness. For years the drapes had been drawn, sewn together to prevent any hint of brightness from filtering through. The only source of light grazing the shadows was a copper wall lamp. Its dull ocher-colored halo revealed the outline of a bed crowned by a canopy from which hung a diaphanous veil, behind which Mauricio Valls could perceive his wife Elena's static figure. It looks like a hearse, Mauricio Valls thought as he peered at her silhouette.

She lay there motionless in the bed that had been her prison for the last decade, once it had become impossible to sit her in the wheelchair. As the years went by, the disease that was wasting her bones away had twisted Doña Elena's skeleton, reducing it to an unrecognizable tangle of limbs in constant agony. A mahogany crucifix stared down at her from above the headboard, yet heaven, in its infinite cruelty, refused to grant her the blessing of death.

It's my fault, Valls thought. He does it to punish me.

He could hear Elena's tortured breathing through the echoes of the orchestra's strains and the voices of the guests—over a thousand of them—who were downstairs, in the garden. The nurse on night shift rose from the chair next to the bed and walked quietly over to Valls. He couldn't remember her name. The nurses watching over his wife never lasted more than two or three months in their job, however high their salary. He didn't blame them.

"Is she asleep?" he asked.

The nurse shook her head. "No, Minister, but the doctor has already given her the evening injection. She's been restless all afternoon. She's better now."

"Leave us."

The nurse nodded and left the room, closing the door behind her. Valls moved closer. He drew back the gauze curtain and sat on the

63

edge of the bed. Closing his eyes for a moment, he listened to Elena's rasping breath while he absorbed the bitter stench emanating from her body. He heard the sound of her nails scratching the sheet. When he turned, with a false smile on his lips and the serene expression of calm and endearment frozen on his face, Valls discovered that his wife was looking at him with blazing eyes. The illness for which the most expensive doctors in Europe had been unable to provide a cure, or even a name, had deformed her hands and turned them into knots of rough skin that reminded him of the claws of a reptile. Valls took what had once been his wife's right hand and confronted her glare, which flashed with anger and pain. Perhaps with hatred, Valls hoped. The very thought that the poor creature could still hold the slightest bit of affection for him or for the world seemed too cruel.

"Good night, my love."

For almost two years now, Elena had all but lost the use of her vocal cords, and to form a word required a huge effort. Even so, she responded to his greeting with a guttural moan that seemed to stem from the very depths of the deformed body one could just about visualize under the sheets.

"I hear you've had a bad day," he went on. "The medication will soon take effect, and you'll be able to sleep."

Valls didn't wipe off his smile, nor did he let go of the hand that aroused both revulsion and fear in him. The scene would take place as it did every day. He would speak to her in a low voice for a few minutes while he held her hand, and she would observe him with those blazing eyes until the morphine calmed the pain and the fury, whereupon Valls could leave that room at the end of the first-floor corridor, and not return until the following day.

"Everybody is here. Mercedes wore her new long dress, and I'm told she danced with the son of the British ambassador. They're all asking after you and send you their love."

While he reeled off his ritual of banalities, his eyes rested on the small tray lying on the metal table next to her bed, holding medical instruments and syringes. The table was covered with a piece of red velvet, and in the dim light the morphine phials shone like precious stones. His voice became suspended, his empty words lost in the air.

Elena's eyes had followed his and were now fixed on him imploringly, her face covered in tears. Valls gazed at his wife and sighed. He leaned over to kiss her forehead.

"I love you," he whispered.

When she heard those words, Elena turned her head and closed her eyes. Valls stroked her cheek and stood up. He drew the veil and walked across the room, buttoning up his dinner jacket and cleaning his lips with a handkerchief, which he dropped onto the floor before leaving.

2

A FEW DAYS earlier, Mauricio Valls had asked his daughter, Mercedes, to come up to his office at the top of the tower, so that he could find out what she wanted for a birthday present. The days of beautiful porcelain dolls and storybooks had passed. Mercedes, whose only remaining childlike traits were her laughter and the devotion she felt toward her father, declared that her greatest and only wish was to be able to attend the masked ball that was going to take place in the mansion that bore her name.

"I'll have to talk to your mother," Valls lied.

Mercedes hugged and kissed him, sealing the unspoken promise she knew she'd secured. Before speaking to her father, she had already chosen the dress she was going to wear: a dazzling wine-colored gown made in a Parisian haute-couture workshop for her mother, which Doña Elena herself had not worn even once. The dress, like hundreds of other fine garments and jewels from the stolen life her mother had never lived, had been confined for fifteen years to one of the wardrobes of the luxurious and solitary dressing room, next to the unused marital bedroom on the second floor. For years, when everyone thought she was asleep in her bedroom, Mercedes would sneak into her mother's room and borrow the key hidden in the fourth drawer of a chest of drawers next to the door. The only night nurse who had dared mention her presence was fired unceremoniously and without compensation when Mercedes accused her of stealing a bracelet from her mother's dressing table—a bracelet she herself had buried in the garden behind the fountain with the angels. The others never dared open their mouths, pretending not to notice her in the permanent half-light that shrouded the room.

In the middle of the night, key in hand, Mercedes would slip into the dressing room in the west wing, an isolated, spacious room smelling of dust, mothballs, and neglect. Holding a candle in one hand, she would walk down the aisles bordered by glass cabinets packed with shoes, jewelry, dresses, and wigs. Cobwebs dangled over the corners of that mausoleum of garments and memories, and little Mercedes, who had grown up in the wealthy solitude of a privileged princess, imagined that all those marvelous outfits and precious stones belonged to a broken, ill-fated doll confined to a cell at the end of the first-floor corridor, who would never be able to show them off.

Sometimes Mercedes would leave the candle on the floor, put on one of those dresses, and dance to the sound of an old wind-up music box that tinkled out the melody of *Scheherazade*. A sudden feeling of pleasure would seize her as she imagined her father's hands on her waist, swirling her around the large dance hall while everyone looked on with envy and admiration. When the first lights of dawn began to filter through the chinks in the curtain, Mercedes would return the key to the chest of drawers and hurry back to her bed, where she pretended to sleep until a maid roused her just before seven.

The night of the masked ball, nobody imagined that the dress hugging her figure so impeccably could have been made for anyone but her. As she slid around the dance floor to the strains of the orchestra in the arms of one or another partner, Mercedes felt the eyes of hundreds of guests upon her, caressing her with lust and longing. She knew her name was on everyone's lips, and she smiled to herself as she picked up snatches of conversation in which she was the protagonist.

It was almost nine o'clock of that long-anticipated evening when Mercedes, much against her will, abandoned the dance floor and headed toward the staircase of the main house. She had hoped to be able to dance at least one number with her father, but he hadn't turned up, and nobody had seen him yet. Don Mauricio had made her promise—it was his condition for allowing her to go to the dance—

that she would return to her room at nine o'clock, and Mercedes was not going to upset him. "Next year."

*

On the way she heard a couple of her father's government colleagues talking, two senior gentlemen who hadn't stopped staring at her with their glazed eyes all night. They were muttering that Don Mauricio had been able to buy everything in life with the fortune of his poor wife, including a strangely springlike evening in the middle of Madrid's autumn, in which to show off his little tart of a daughter before the cream of society. Intoxicated by champagne and the twirls of the waltz, Mercedes turned to answer back, but a figure came out to meet her and gently held her arm.

Irene, the governess who had been her shadow and her solace for the past ten years, smiled warmly at her and pecked her on the cheek. "Pay no attention to them," she said, taking her arm.

Mercedes smiled and shrugged.

"You're looking gorgeous. Let me have a good look."

The girl lowered her eyes.

"This dress is stunning and fits you like a glove."

"It was my mother's."

"After tonight it will always be yours and nobody else's."

Mercedes gave a little nod, blushing at the compliment, though it came tinged with the bitter taste of guilt. "Have you seen my father, Doña Irene?"

The woman shook her head.

"It's just that everyone is asking after him . . ."

"They'll have to wait."

"I promised him I'd only stay until nine. Three hours less than Cinderella."

"In that case we'd better hurry before I turn into a pumpkin," the governess joked halfheartedly.

They followed the path across the garden under a festoon of lamps that lit up the faces of strangers; strangers who smiled when she went by as if they knew her, their champagne flutes shining like poisoned daggers.

67

"Is my father going to come down to the dance, Doña Irene?" asked Mercedes.

The governess waited until she was far enough away from indiscreet ears and prying eyes before replying. "I don't know. I haven't seen him all day."

Mercedes was about to answer when they heard some sort of commotion behind them. They turned to discover that the band had stopped playing and that one of the two gentlemen who had muttered maliciously when Mercedes walked by was about to address the guests. Before Mercedes could ask who the man was, the governess whispered in her ear: "That's Don José María Altea, minister of the interior."

A young official handed a microphone to the politician, and the murmuring of the guests dropped to a respectful silence. The musicians adopted a solemn expression and looked up at the minister, who smiled as he gazed at the compliant and expectant audience. Altea surveyed the hundreds of faces observing him, nodding to himself. Finally, in a slow, deliberate manner, and with the calm and authoritarian composure of a preacher who knows the meekness of his flock, he drew the microphone to his lips and began his homily.

3

"DEAR FRIENDS, IT is for me a great pleasure and honor to be able to say a few words before such a distinguished audience—an audience gathered here today to pay a heartfelt and well-deserved tribute to one of the great men of this new Spain, reborn from the ashes of war. And it is all the more gratifying for me to make this address in a year that marks the twentieth anniversary of the glorious triumph of the national crusade of liberation, a triumph that has placed our country at the very acme of world nations. A Spain led by the Generalissimo with God's help, and wrought with the valor of men like the one who welcomes us to his home and to whom we owe so much. A key man in the development of this great nation—which today fills us with pride and is the envy of the West—and a key man in its immortal culture. A man that I am proud and grateful to count as one of my best friends: Don Mauricio Valls y Echevarría."

A flood of applause ran through the crowd from one end of the garden to the other. Even the servants, the bodyguards, and the musicians joined in. Altea weathered the ovations and bravos with a benevolent smile, nodding his head paternally and calming the enthusiasm of those gathered around him rather like a cardinal blessing the congregation.

"What can one say about Don Mauricio Valls that has not been said already? His irreproachable and exemplary career goes back to the very origins of our movement and is carved into our history in gold letters. But it has perhaps been in this field, that of arts and letters, if I may be so bold, where our admired and beloved Don Mauricio has distinguished himself in an outstanding manner, bestowing on us achievements that have taken this country's culture to new heights. Not content with having contributed to building the solid foundations of a regime that has brought with it peace, justice, and prosperity to the Spanish people, Don Mauricio has also been aware that man cannot live on bread alone and has established himself as the shining star in our cultural Olympus. Illustrious author of immortal titles; founder of the Instituto Lope de Vega, which has taken our literature and our language to all corners of the world, and which this year alone has opened offices in twenty-two world capitals; tireless and superb publisher; discoverer and champion of great literature and of the most sublime culture of our time; architect of a new way of understanding and realizing arts and ideas . . . Words cannot describe our host's enormous contribution to the formation and education of today's and tomorrow's Spaniards. His work at the head of the Ministry of National Education has promoted the fundamental structures of our knowledge and creativity. It is therefore only fair to declare that without Don Mauricio Valls, Spanish culture would not have been what it is. His hallmarks and his brilliant vision will accompany us for generations, and his everlasting works will remain standing on the highest point of the Spanish Parnassus for all time."

An emotional pause gave rise to a new round of applause, during which quite a number of people were beginning to look around for the honored absentee, the man of the moment whom nobody had seen all evening.

"I could go on, but don't wish to extend myself, as I know many of you will wish to express your thanks and admiration to Don Mauricio personally, and I add myself to that number. I would only like to share with you the message of personal affection, gratitude, and heartfelt homage to my cabinet colleague and dearest friend Don Mauricio Valls that was sent to me only a few minutes ago by the head of state, Generalissimo Franco, from El Pardo Palace, where urgent matters of state have kept him from attending."

A sigh of disappointment, glances exchanged between those present, and a solemn silence served as introduction to the reading of the note Altea pulled out of his pocket.

"My dear friend Mauricio, universal Spaniard and indispensable collaborator, who has done so much for our country and our culture: Doña Carmen and I send you our warmest wishes and would like to express our gratitude in the name of all Spaniards for twenty years of exemplary service . . ."

Altea raised his eyes and his voice to round off his performance with a "Viva Franco!" and "Arriba España!" chorused enthusiastically by the audience and generating a forest of arms raised in salute and not a few tearful eyes. Altea himself joined in the thunderous applause inundating the garden. Before leaving the stage, the minister made a sign to the bandleader, who, ensuring the ovation did not die down into murmurings, took it into a waltz that promised to maintain the elation in the air for the rest of the evening. Yet by the time it became clear that the Generalissimo was not coming, many of the guests dropped their masks on the floor and began to make their way to the exit.

4

VALLS HEARD THE distant ripples of the applause that had closed Altea's speech as it merged into the orchestra's next number. Altea, "his great friend and esteemed colleague," who for years had been trying to stab him in the back: that message from the Generalissimo excusing his absence must have been music to his ears. Valls cursed Altea and his bunch of hyenas, that pack of new centurions already called "the poisoned flowers" by more than one: they had sprouted in the regime's shadows and were beginning to fill key positions in the administration. Most of them were prowling about the garden right now, drinking his champagne and nibbling his canapés. Sniffing his blood. Valls put the cigarette he was holding to his lips, but there was just a hint of ash left on it. Vicente, his chief personal bodyguard, was observing him from the other end of the corridor and walked over to offer him one of his own.

"Thanks, Vicente."

"Congratulations, Don Mauricio," his loyal guard dog intoned.

Valls nodded, smiling bitterly to himself. Vicente, ever faithful and respectful, returned to his place at the end of the passage, where, if one didn't look carefully, he seemed to melt into the wallpaper.

Valls took a first drag and observed the wide corridor that opened before him through the curtain of his cigarette smoke. Mercedes called it "the portrait gallery." The corridor circled the entire third floor and was filled with paintings and sculptures that lent it an air of a grand museum bereft of viewers. Lerma, the curator of the Prado Museum, who took care of Valls's collection, was always reminding him that he shouldn't smoke there and that sunlight could damage the paintings. Valls took a second drag on his cigarette to Lerma's health. He realized that what Lerma was trying to say, though he didn't have the nerve, was that those pieces deserved better than to be confined in a private home, however splendid the setting, or however powerful its owner; their natural place was a museum where they could be admired and enjoyed by the public, those insignificant souls who clapped in ceremonies and queued up in funerals.

Valls sometimes enjoyed sitting on one of the plush armchairs dotted around the portrait gallery to admire his treasures. Many of the works had been lent to him, or simply seized from the private collections of citizens who had ended up on the wrong side of the conflict. Others came from museums and palaces under his ministry's jurisdiction, by way of a permanent loan. He liked to recall those summer afternoons when little Mercedes—who wasn't even ten at the time—sat on his knees and listened to the stories hidden behind each one of those marvels. Valls took refuge in those memories, in his daughter's look of fascination when she heard him talk about Sorolla and Zurbarán, about Goya and Velázquez.

*

More than once Valls had wanted to believe that while he could sit there, ensconced in the light and dreamlike quality of the paintings, those days shared with Mercedes, days of glory and fulfillment, would never slip away. For some time now Mercedes hadn't come to spend the afternoon with him and listen to his masterly accounts of the golden age of Spanish painting, but the very act of seeking refuge in that gallery still comforted him: it made him forget that Mercedes was now a woman he had not recognized in her formal dress, dancing under the gaze of greed and desire, suspicion and malice. Soon, very soon, he would no longer be able to protect her from that world of shadows that didn't deserve her, a world that lurked, baring its teeth, beyond the walls of the house.

He quietly finished his cigarette and stood up. The hum of the band and of the voices in the garden could just be made out behind the drawn curtains. Without turning his head, he walked over to the staircase leading to the tower. Vicente, emerging from the dark, followed him, his footsteps barely audible behind Valls's back.

5

AS SOON AS he inserted the key in the office keyhole, Valls knew the door was open. He paused, his fingers still holding the key, and turned around. Vicente, who was waiting at the foot of the stairs, read his eyes and crept up, pulling out a revolver from inside his jacket. Valls moved aside a few steps, and Vicente signaled to him to lean against the wall. Once Valls was safe, Vicente cocked the revolver's hammer and very slowly turned the doorknob. Pushed by its own weight, the panel of carved oak moved gently toward the dim interior.

Keeping the revolver pointed, Vicente scanned the shadows. A bluish halo filtered through the windows, outlining Valls's office. His eyes scanned the large desk, the admiral's armchair, the oval library, and the leather sofa on the Persian carpet covering the floor. Nothing moved in the shadows. Vicente felt the wall, searching for the switch, and turned on the light. There was no one there. He lowered his weapon, putting it back inside his jacket as he took a few more steps into the room. Behind him, Valls watched from the entrance. Vicente turned and shook his head.

"Perhaps I forgot to lock up when I left this afternoon," said Valls, without much conviction.

Vicente stood in the middle of the office and looked around him carefully as Valls stepped into the room and walked over to his desk. Vicente was checking the locks on the windows when the minister noticed it. The bodyguard heard him stop dead. He turned to look over his shoulder.

The minister's eyes were glued to the desk. A cream-colored folio-sized envelope rested on the leather sheet covering the central part of the table. Valls felt the hairs on his hands stand on end, as if a blast of ice-cold air were assailing his body.

"Everything all right, Don Mauricio?" asked Vicente.

"Leave me alone."

Valls was still staring at the envelope. For a few seconds the bodyguard hesitated. "I'll be outside if you need me," he said at last.

Valls nodded. Vicente walked reluctantly toward the door. When he closed it behind him, the minister stood motionless in front of his desk, looking at that piece of parchment as if it were a viper about to leap at his neck.

He walked around the desk and sat in his chair, crossing his fists under his chin. Almost a minute went by before he placed his hand on the parcel. He felt the contents and then, his pulse racing, inserted his finger under the gummed flap and opened it. The strip was still moist, so it came unstuck easily. He picked the envelope up by one of its bottom corners and raised it. The contents slipped onto the desk. Valls closed his eyes and sighed.

The book was bound in black leather and had no title on the cover, only a design that suggested the image of a descending spiral staircase viewed from above.

Valls's hand shook: he closed it into a fist, pressing hard. A note peeped out of the pages of the book, and he pulled it out. It was a yellowish piece of paper, torn out of a ledger, with two columns of red horizontal lines. In each column there was a list of numbers. At the bottom of the page, these words were written in red ink:

Your time is coming to an end.
You have one last chance.
At the entrance to the labyrinth.

Valls felt he needed air. Before he realized what he was doing, his hands were rummaging around in the main drawer of the desk, grabbing the revolver he kept there. He put the barrel into his mouth, his finger tensed on the trigger. The gun tasted of oil and gunpowder. A wave of nausea swept over him, but he held the revolver with both hands and kept his eyes closed to hold back the tears falling down his face. Then he heard her footsteps and her voice on the stairs. Mercedes was talking to Vicente by the office door. Valls put the revolver back in the drawer and dried his tears on the sleeve of his dinner jacket. Vicente tapped at the door with his knuckles. Valls took a deep breath and waited a moment. The bodyguard knocked again. "Don Mauricio?" he called. "It's your daughter."

"Let her in," said Valls in a faltering voice.

The door opened and Mercedes came in, wearing her wine-colored dress and an enthralled smile that was wiped off her face the moment she saw her father. Vicente watched anxiously from the doorway. Valls gave him a nod and signaled for him to leave them alone.

"Are you all right, Daddy?"

Valls smiled broadly and stood up to embrace her. "Of course I'm all right. And all the better for seeing you."

Mercedes felt her father's arms holding her tight as he buried his face in her hair and smelled her, just as he used to do when she was a child, as if he thought that inhaling the aroma of her skin could protect him against all the evils in the world.

When at last he let go of her, Mercedes looked into his eyes and noticed how red they were. "What's the matter, Daddy?"

"Nothing."

"You know you can't fool me. You can fool others, but not me."

Valls smiled. He looked at the clock on his desk: it was five past nine. "As you can see, I keep my promises," she said, reading his thoughts.

"I've never doubted that."

Mercedes stood on her toes and glanced at the desk. "What are you reading?"

"Nothing. Just rubbish."

"Can I read it too?"

"It's not the sort of thing for a young girl to read."

"I'm not a young girl anymore," replied Mercedes, giving him a mischievous smile and twirling around to show off her dress and her demeanor.

"I can see. You're a grown woman."

Mercedes put her hand on her father's cheek. "And is that what makes you sad?"

Valls kissed his daughter's hand and shook his head. "Of course not."

"Not even a little?"

"Well, yes, a little."

Mercedes laughed. Valls imitated her, the taste of gunpowder still in his mouth.

"They were all asking after you at the party . . ."

"My evening got rather complicated. You know how these things are."

Mercedes nodded cunningly. "Yes. I know . . ."

She wandered around her father's office, a secret world full of books and closed cupboards, running her fingertips gently over the tomes on the bookshelves. She noticed her father looking at her with misty eyes and stopped. "You're not going to tell me what's wrong, are you?"

"Mercedes, you know I love you more than anything in the whole world, and I'm very proud of you, don't you?"

She looked unsure. Her father's voice seemed to be hanging from a thread, his self-possession and arrogance torn from him.

"Of course, Daddy . . . and I love you too."

"That's all that matters. Come what may."

Her father was smiling at her, but Mercedes could see he was crying. She'd never seen him cry and felt frightened, as if her world might suddenly fall apart. Her father dried his tears and turned away from her. "Tell Vicente to come in."

Mercedes walked over to the door, but stopped before opening it. Her father still had his back to her, looking at the garden through the window.

"Daddy, what's going to happen?"

"Nothing, my love. Nothing's going to happen."

Then she opened the door. Vicente was already waiting on the other side, with that impenetrable, harsh expression that always gave her a chill.

"Good night, Daddy," she murmured.

"Good night, Mercedes."

Vicente nodded at her respectfully and stepped into the office. Mercedes turned around to look, but the bodyguard gently closed the door in her face. The girl put her ear to the door and listened.

"He's been here," she heard her father say.

"That's not possible," said Vicente. "All the entrances were secured. Only the house staff had access to the top floors. I have men posted on all the staircases."

"I'm telling you he's been here. And he has a list. I don't know how he got hold of it, but he has a list . . . Oh God."

Mercedes swallowed hard.

"There must be a mistake, sir."

"Have a look for yourself . . ."

A long silence followed. Mercedes held her breath.

"The numbers seem correct, sir. I don't understand . . ."

"The time has come, Vicente. I can't hide any longer. It's now or never. Can I count on you?"

"Of course, sir. When?"

"At dawn."

They fell silent, and shortly afterward Mercedes heard footsteps approaching the door. She ran down the stairs and didn't stop until she reached her room. Once she got there, she leaned against the door and collapsed onto the floor. A curse was spreading through the air, she thought. That night would be the last of the turbid fairy tale they'd been acting out for too many years.

6

SHE WOULD ALWAYS remember that dawn for its cold grayness, as if winter had decided to tumble down without warning and sink Villa Mercedes in a lake of mist that emerged from the edge of the forest. She woke up when just a hint of metallic brightness grazed her bedroom windows. She had fallen asleep on her bed with her dress on, and when she opened the window, the cold, damp morning air licked her face. A carpet of thick fog was sliding over the garden, slithering through the remains of the previous night's party. The black clouds covering the sky traveled slowly, heavy with an impending storm.

Mercedes stepped out into the passage, barefoot. The house was buried in deep silence. She walked along the shadowy corridor, circling the whole west wing until she reached her father's bedroom. Neither Vicente nor any of his men were posted by the door, as had been routine for the past few years, since her father had begun to live in hiding, always protected by his trustworthy gunmen. It was as if he feared that something was going to jump out of the walls and plunge a dagger into his back. She had never dared ask him why he had adopted that habit. It was enough for her to catch him sometimes with an absent expression, his eyes poisoned with bitterness.

She opened the door to her father's bedroom without knocking. The bed hadn't been slept in. The cup of chamomile tea that the maid left on Don Mauricio's bedside table every night hadn't been touched.

Mercedes sometimes wondered whether her father ever slept, or whether he spent most nights awake in his office at the top of the tower. The flutter of a flock of birds flying off from the garden alerted her. She went over to the window and saw two figures walking toward the garage. Mercedes pressed her face against the glass. One of the figures stopped and turned to look up in her direction, as if he'd felt her gaze on him. Mercedes smiled at her father, who stared back at her blankly, his face pale, looking older than she could ever remember.

At last Mauricio Valls looked down and stepped into the garage with Vicente, who carried a small suitcase. Mercedes panicked. She had dreamed about this moment a thousand times without understanding what it meant. She rushed down the stairs, stumbling over bits of furniture and carpets in the steely gloom of daybreak. When she reached the garden, the cold, cutting breeze spat in her face. She hurried down the marble staircase and ran toward the garage through a wasteland of discarded masks, fallen chairs, and garlands of lanterns still blinking and swaying in the mist. She heard the car's engine start and the wheels steal across the gravel drive. By the time Mercedes reached the drive, which led to the front gates of the estate, the car was already speeding away. She ran after it, ignoring the sharp gravel cutting her feet. Just before the mist swallowed the car forever, her father turned his head one last time, throwing her a despairing look through the rear window. She went on running until the sound of the engine was lost in the distance, and the spiked gates at the entrance to the estate rose before her.

An hour later Rosaura, the maid who came every morning to wake her up and dress her, found her sitting at the edge of the swimming pool. Her feet were dangling in the water, which was tinted with threads of her blood. Dozens of masks drifted over its surface like paper boats.

"Señorita Mercedes, for heaven's sake . . ."

The girl was trembling when Rosaura wrapped her in a blanket and took her back to the house. By the time they reached the marble staircase, it was starting to sleet. A hostile wind stirred through the trees, knocking down garlands, tables, and chairs. Mercedes, who had also dreamed about this moment, knew that the house had begun to die.

KYRIE

~✦~

MADRID

DECEMBER

1959

I

SOON AFTER TEN in the morning, a black Packard drove up Gran Vía under the downpour and stopped opposite the entrance to the old Hotel Hispania. Her bedroom window was shrouded by the rain trickling down the pane, but Alicia could see the two emissaries, as gray and cold as the day, getting out of the car in their regulation raincoats and hats. Alicia looked at her watch. Good old Leandro hadn't even waited fifteen minutes before setting the dogs on her. Thirty seconds later the phone rang. She picked it up at the first loud ring. She knew perfectly well who would be at the other end.

"Señorita Gris, good morning and all that," Maura's hoarse voice intoned from reception. "A couple of lizards who reek of political police have just asked for you very rudely and stepped into the elevator. I've sent them up to the fourteenth floor to give you a couple of minutes in case you might want to evaporate."

"That's very kind of you, Joaquín. What are you into today? Anything good?"

Shortly after the fall of Madrid, Joaquin Maura had ended up in Carabanchel Prison. When he came out, sixteen years later, he discovered that he was an old man, his lungs were ruined and his wife, six months pregnant when he was arrested, had managed to get an annulment and was now married to a bemedaled lieutenant-colonel who had furnished her with three children and a modest house on the outskirts of town. From that first short-lived marriage there remained a daughter, Raquel, who grew up convinced that he had died before her mother gave birth to her. The day Maura went to see her surreptitiously on her way out of a shop on Calle Goya, where she worked selling fabrics, Raquel thought he was a beggar and gave him a few coins. Since then Maura had scraped by, living in a dingy room next to the boilers in the basement of the Hispania, doing the night shift and all the shifts he was allowed to do, rereading cheap detective novels, and chain-smoking short Celtas in his lodge while he waited for death to put things in their place and take him back to 1939, from where he should never have emerged.

"I'm in the middle of a romance that makes no sense at all. It's called *The Crimson Tunic*, by someone called Martín. It's part of an old series, *The City of the Damned*. It was lent to me by that little fat guy Tudela in room 426, who always finds odd things in the Rastro flea market. The story is about your part of the world, Barcelona. You might feel like reading it."

"I won't say no."

"Very good. And keep your eye on that pair. I know you can fend for yourself, but those two don't leave a pretty shadow."

Alicia hung up and calmly sat down to wait for Leandro's jackals to sniff her out. At most, two or three minutes before they stuck their noses around, she reckoned. She lit a cigarette and waited in the armchair facing the door, which she'd left open. The long dark corridor leading to the elevators opened up before her. An odor of dust, old wood, and the threadbare carpet covering the floor of the passageway flooded the room.

The Hispania was an exquisite ruin in a perpetual state of decadence. Built in the early 1920s, the hotel had seen its years of glory among Madrid's large luxury buildings but fell into disuse after the civil war. After two decades of decline, it had become a graveyard where the dispossessed, the doomed, lost souls with nothing and no one in their lives, languished in drab rooms that they rented by the week. The hotel had hundreds of rooms, but half of them were empty and had been for years. A number of floors were closed off, and eerie tales spread among the guests, recounting what sometimes took place in those long bleak passages: an elevator would stop and open its doors when nobody had pressed the button, and for a few seconds a yellowish beam of light would shine out from the car, revealing what looked like the innards of a sunken liner. Maura had told her that the switchboard often rang in the early hours with calls from rooms nobody had occupied since the war. When he answered, there was never anyone on the line, except the time he heard a woman weeping; when he asked what he could do for her, another voice, dark and deep, said to him: "Come with us."

"From then on, I'm damned if I take calls from any room after midnight," Maura admitted to her once. "Sometimes I think this place is like a metaphor, you know? Of the whole country, I mean. I feel it's cursed because of all the blood that was spilled and is still on our hands, however much we insist on pointing the finger at others."

"You're a poet, Maura. Not even all those detective novels manage to dampen your lyric vein. What Spain needs is thinkers like you to bring back the great national art of conversation."

"Laugh at me all you want. It's easy when you're on the regime's payroll, Señorita Gris. Although I'm sure that with what you must make, an important person like you could afford to move somewhere better and not rot in this dungeon. This is no place for a refined, classy mademoiselle like you. People don't come here to live, they come here to die."

"As I said. A poet."

"Get lost."

Maura wasn't all that mistaken in his philosophical remarks, and as time went by the Hispania began to be known, among select circles, as Suicide Central. Decades later, when the hotel had already been closed for some time and finally the demolition engineers went through the building, floor by floor, placing the explosive charges that would tear it down forever, rumor had it that in a number of rooms they'd found corpses that had lain mummified on beds or in bathtubs for years, its old night manager among them.

2

SHE SAW THEM emerge from the shadows of the corridor for what they were, two puppets made up to frighten people who still took life at face value. She'd seen them before, but she'd never bothered to remember their names. All those dummies from the secret police looked the same to her. They stopped in the doorway and gave the room a studied look of contempt before resting their eyes on Alicia and showing her the wolfish smile Leandro must have taught them on their first day at school.

"I don't see how you can live here."

Alicia shrugged and finished her cigarette, waving a hand toward the window. "I like the views."

One of Leandro's men laughed halfheartedly, and the other muttered disapprovingly under his breath. They came into the room, had a peek at the bathroom, and examined the place from top to bottom as if they hoped to find something. The younger one, who still oozed inexperience and tried to make up for it with attitude, pretended to take an interest in the collection of books piled up against the wall, practically filling half the room. He slid his forefinger along the spines. "You're going to have to lend me one of your lovely romantic novels," he sneered.

"I didn't know you could read."

The novice turned around, scowled, and took a step forward, but his colleague, and presumably his boss, stopped him, sighing wearily. "Go on," he said to Alicia, "powder your nose. They're expecting you at ten."

Alicia showed no signs of leaving her chair. "I'm on mandatory sick leave. Leandro's orders."

The novice, who apparently had felt his manliness tarnished, plonked his ninety-plus kilos of muscle and bile close to Alicia and offered her a smile that was clearly well practiced in prison cells and midnight raids. "Don't fuck with me—I'm not in the mood today, sunshine. Don't make me have to drag you out of that chair."

Alicia turned her eyes on him. "It's not about whether you're in the mood, it's about whether you've got the balls."

Leandro's thug glared at her for a few seconds, but when his partner grabbed his arm and pulled him away, he decided to break into a more gentle smile and put his hands up as a sign of truce. To be continued, thought Alicia.

The leader of the twosome checked his watch and shook his head. "Come on, Señorita Gris, it's not our fault. You know how these things work."

I know, Alicia thought. I know only too well. She pressed both hands against the sides of the armchair and stood up. The two henchmen watched her stagger over to a chair. On it lay what looked like a harness made up of fine lengths of string and a set of leather straps.

"May I help you?" asked the novice, his voice malicious.

Alicia ignored them both. She picked up the contraption and went into the bathroom with it, leaving the door ajar. The older man looked away, but the novice couldn't help finding an angle from which to dwell on Alicia's reflection in the mirror. He saw her remove her skirt and, grabbing the harness, place it over her hips and her right leg as if she were putting on some exotic sort of corset. When she adjusted the fasteners, the harness hugged her figure like a second skin, giving her the appearance of a mechanical doll. It was then that Alicia looked up and the thug met her eyes in the mirror: cold eyes, devoid of all expression. He smiled with delight and, after a long pause, turned back into the room, not without catching a fleeting glimpse of that black stain on Alicia's side, a tangle of scars that seemed to sink into her flesh as if a red-hot drill had rebuilt her hip. The officer noticed his superior looking at him severely.

"You cretin," he heard him mutter.

Moments later Alicia emerged from the bathroom.

"Don't you have another dress?" asked the older policeman.

"What's wrong with this one?"

"I don't know. Something a little more discreet, maybe?"

"Why? Who else is at this meeting?"

His only response was to hand her a walking stick that was leaning against the wall and point to the door.

"I haven't put my makeup on."

"You look fine. But if you like, you can do that in the car. We're already late."

Alicia refused the stick and walked out to the corridor without waiting for them, limping slightly.

A few minutes later they were traveling silently through the streets of Madrid in the rain. Sitting on the back seat of the black Packard, Alicia looked up at the profiles of domes and statues along the cornices of Gran Vía. Angel-driven chariots and stone sentinels kept watch from above. It looked to her as if the lead-gray skies had disgorged a snaking reef of colossal, somber buildings, all piled up against each other: petrified creatures that had swallowed entire cities. At her feet, the canopies of grand theaters and the fronts of cafés and fancy shops gleamed beneath the rain. Closer to the ground, people were just tiny sketches with vapor coming out of their mouths, walking past under a swarm of umbrellas. On days such as this, Alicia thought, one began to agree with good old Maura and believe that the dark shadows of the Hispania stretched right across the country, from one end to the other, without letting in a single chink of light.

3

"TELL ME ABOUT this new operative you're proposing. Gris, did you say?"

"Alicia Gris."

"Alicia? A woman?"

"Is that a problem?"

"I don't know. I've heard about her more than once, but always as Gris. I'd no idea she was a woman. Some may question the choice."

"Your superiors?"

"Our superiors, Leandro. We can't allow another mistake like the Lomana one. They're getting nervous in El Pardo."

"With all due respect, the only mistake was that they didn't explain clearly from the start why they needed someone from my unit. Had I known what it was about, I would have chosen another candidate. That was not a task for Ricardo Lomana."

"I don't set the rules, nor do I control the information. It all comes from above."

"I realize that."

"Tell me about Gris."

"Señorita Gris is twenty-nine and has been working for me for twelve years. She's a war orphan. She lost her parents when she was eight. She was brought up in the Patronato Ribas, a Barcelona orphanage, until she was thrown out when she was fifteen for disciplinary reasons. For a couple of years she took to living on the streets, working for a black marketeer and second-rate criminal called Baltasar Ruano, who ran a gang of teenage thieves, until the Civil Guard got their hands on him and he was executed, like so many others, in Campo de la Bota."

"I hear that she's—"

"That's not a problem. She can manage on her own, and I can assure you she knows how to defend herself. It's a wound she sustained in the war, during the Barcelona bombings. It's never been an obstacle when it comes to performing her duty. Alicia Gris is the best agent I've recruited in my twenty years of service."

"Then why hasn't she turned up when she was expected?"

"I understand your frustration and apologize once again. Alicia can be somewhat unruly at times, but so are almost all exceptional agents in this line of work. A month ago we had a routine disagreement about a case she was working on. I suspended her temporarily without pay. Not to turn up at her appointment today is her way of saying she's still annoyed with me."

"Your relationship sounds more personal than professional, if you'll allow my opinion."

"In my field one can't exist without the other."

"I worry about this contempt for discipline. We can't afford any more mistakes in this matter."

"There won't be any more."

"That had better be true. We're putting our necks on the line. Yours and mine."

"Leave it in my hands."

"Tell me more about Gris. What makes her so special?"

"Alicia Gris sees what the rest don't see. Her mind works differently from the rest. Where everyone else sees a locked door, she sees a key. Where others lose track, she picks up the trail. It's a gift, one could say. And the best thing is that no one sees her coming."

"Is that how she resolved what they called the case of the Barcelona Dolls?"

"The wax brides. That was the first case Alicia worked on for me."

"I've always wondered whether that story about the civil governor was true . . ."

"All that happened years ago."

"But we have time, no? While we wait for the damsel."

"Of course. It happened in 1947. At the time I'd been posted to Barcelona. We were informed that during the past three years the police had discovered at least seven bodies of young women in different corners of the city. They turned up sitting on a park bench, at a tram stop, in a café on the Paralelo . . . They even found one kneeling in a confessional in the parish church of El Pino. They were all perfectly made up and dressed in white. There wasn't a drop of blood in their bodies, and they smelled of camphor. They looked like wax dolls. Hence the name."

"Did they know who they were?"

"Nobody had ever reported their disappearance, so the police thought they might be prostitutes. This was confirmed later on. Months went by without any more bodies appearing, and the Barcelona police closed the case."

"And then another one turned up."

"Correct. Margarita Mallofré. They found her sitting in an armchair in the lobby of the Hotel Oriente."

"And this Margarita was the darling of . . . ?"

"Margarita Mallofré worked in a rather exclusive brothel on Calle Elisabets, which catered to, let's say, unusual tastes provided at high prices. It emerged that the civil governor at the time was a regular customer, and the deceased was his favorite."

"For what reason?"

"It seems that Margarita Mallofré was the one who managed to remain conscious longest, despite the governor's special attentions. Hence the gentleman's preference."

"So much for His Excellency."

"The fact is that thanks to that connection, the case was reopened, and because of the delicate nature of the matter, I was put in charge. Alicia had just started working for me, and I assigned it to her."

"Wasn't it too lurid a matter for a young girl?"

"Alicia was a very unusual young girl, and not easily shocked."

"And how did the matter end?"

"It ended quickly. Alicia spent a few nights sleeping rough, keeping an eye on the entrances and exits of the main bordellos in the Raval quarter. She discovered that whenever there was a routine police raid, the clients would sneak out through some concealed door, and that sometimes the young girls or boys working there did the same thing. Alicia decided to follow them. They hid from the police in doorways, in cafés, and even in the sewers. Most of them were caught and made to spend a night in prison, or worse still, but that's neither here nor there. Others managed to dodge the police. And the ones who did always ended up in the same place: the junction of Calle Joaquín Costa and Calle Peu de la Creu."

"What did she find there?"

"At first glance, nothing special. A couple of grain warehouses. A grocer's. A garage. And a textile mill whose owner, someone called Rufat, had had a few brushes with the police because of his tendency to go overboard when he applied corporal punishment to some of his female workers, one of whom had lost an eye. Rufat was a frequent client of the establishment where Margarita Mallofré worked until her disappearance."

"The kid works fast."

"That's why the first thing she did was eliminate Rufat. He was a brute, but he had no link to the case beyond the coincidence that he was a regular visitor to the establishment. Which was only a few streets away from his own business."

"And then? Back to square one?"

"Alicia always says that things follow not their apparent logic, but instead an inner logic."

"And what logic could there be in this case, according to her?"

"What Alicia calls the simulation logic."

"You've really lost me now, Leandro."

"The short version is that Alicia believes that everything that happens in society and in public life is a staging, a mere simulation of what we are trying to pass off as reality, but in fact isn't."

"Sounds Marxist."

"Don't worry. Alicia is the most skeptical person I know. According to her, all ideologies and creeds, without distinction, are brain inflammations induced by low intellect. In a word, simulations."

"Even worse. I don't know why you're smiling, Leandro. I don't find this funny. I'm feeling an increasing dislike for this young lady. She's good-looking, at least?"

"I don't run a hostess agency."

"Don't get angry, Leandro, I was only joking. How does that story end?"

"Once Rufat was no longer a suspect, Alicia began to peel off what she calls the onion skins."

"Another one of her theories?"

"Alicia says that every crime is like an onion: you have to cut through lots of layers to find out what's hidden inside, and on the way you must shed a few tears."

"Leandro, sometimes I marvel at the fauna you recruit."

"My work consists in finding the right tool for each task. And keeping it sharpened."

"Be careful you don't cut yourself one of these days. But go back to the onion story. I was enjoying that."

"By peeling off the layers of each of the businesses and establishments located at the road junction where the vanished girls had last been seen, Alicia discovered that the garage belonged to the old charity almshouse known as the Casa de la Caridad."

"Another dead end."

"In this case, *dead* is the key word."

"I'm lost again."

"That garage was used to house part of the fleet of hearses belonging to the city council, and there was also a storeroom for coffins and funeral sculptures. In those days, the municipal funeral services were still managed by the almshouse, and most of its menial employees, from gravediggers to young helpers, were godforsaken people: convicts, beggars, and so on. In other words, miserable souls who had ended up there because they had no one else in the world. Applying her skills, which are plenty, Alicia managed to get employed as a typist in the administrative department of the Casa de la Caridad. Soon she discovered that on the nights when there were police raids, the girls from the neighboring brothels ran to hide in the garage of the funeral services. It was always easy for them to persuade any of the poor souls who worked there to let them hide in one of the carriages in exchange for their favors. Once the danger was over, and the benefactors' desires had been satisfied, the girls went back to their posts before daybreak."

"But . . ."

"But they didn't all go back. Some were never seen again. Alicia discovered that among the people working there, there was one character unlike the rest. Like her, he was a war orphan. They called him Quimet, because he had a boyish face and such a pleasant manner that all the widows wanted to adopt him and take him home with them. The fact is that this so-called Quimet was an outstanding student and already very skilled in funeral arts. What caught her attention was that he was a collector and had a photograph album of porcelain dolls that he kept in his desk. He said he wanted to get married and form a family, and that was why he was looking for the right woman, pure and clean, both in spirit and in flesh."

"The simulation?"

"Decoy would be a better word here. Alicia started to watch him every night, and it didn't take her long to discover that her suspicions had been well founded. It turned out that when one of those women who'd gone astray went to Quimet for help, if the girl satisfied all his requirements of height, complexion, looks, and build, far from demanding a sexual payment, he would pray with her and assure her that with his help and that of the Holy Virgin Mary, nobody would ever find her. The best hiding place, he argued, was a coffin. Nobody, not even the police, would dare to open a coffin to see what's inside. The girls, captivated by Quimet's childlike face and gentle manners, would lie down in the coffin and smile at him when he closed the lid and sealed them inside. There he would let them suffocate. Then he would undress them, shave their pubes, wash them from head to foot, bleed them, and inject an embalming liquid into their hearts, which he then pumped through their bodies. Once they had been reborn as wax dolls, he would apply makeup and dress them in white.

Alicia also discovered that all the clothes that had been found on the bodies came from the same bridal shop on Ronda San Pedro, just two hundred meters away. One of the employees remembered having served Quimet more than once."

"What a gem."

"Quimet would spend a couple of nights with the dead bodies, emulating, so to speak, some sort of marital life, until the bodies began to smell of dead flowers. At that point, always before daybreak, when the streets were still deserted, he would take them to their new eternal life in one of the hearses and then stage their discovery."

"Holy Mother of God . . . Stuff like that only happens in Barcelona."

"Alicia was able to discover all this and more, just in time to rescue what would have been Quimet's eighth victim from one of the coffins."

"And was it established why he did it?"

"Alicia found out that when he was a boy, Quimet had spent a whole week locked up with his mother's corpse in a flat on Calle de la Cadena, until the smell alerted the neighbors. It seems that his mother had committed suicide by swallowing poison when she found out that her husband had left her. Unfortunately, none of this could be verified because Quimet took his own life during his first night in the Campo de la Bota prison, after leaving his dying wishes written on the wall of his cell. He wanted to have his body shaved, washed, and embalmed, and then, dressed in white, be exhibited in perpetuity in a glass coffin next to one of his wax brides, in the shop window of the El Siglo department store. Apparently his mother had worked there as a shop assistant. But, speaking of the devil, Señorita Gris must be about to arrive. A little brandy to remove the bad taste from the anecdote?"

"One last thing, Leandro. I want one of my men to work with your agent. I don't want another unreported disappearance like Lomana's."

"I think that's a mistake. We have our own methods."

"The condition isn't negotiable. And Altea agrees with me."

"With all due respect . . ."

"Leandro, Altea had already wanted to put Hendaya on the case."

"Another mistake."

"I agree. That's why I've convinced him to let me do things my way, for the moment. But the condition is that one of my men must supervise your operative. It's that, or Hendaya."

"I see. Who were you thinking of?"

"Vargas."

"I thought he had retired."

"Only technically."

"Is this a punishment?"

"For your agent?"

"For Vargas."

"More like a second chance."

4

THE PACKARD CIRCLED Plaza de Neptuno under the deluge, then turned up Carrera de San Jerónimo toward the white, French-style silhouette of the Gran Hotel Palace. They stopped in front of the main entrance, and when the doorman came over to open the passenger door, holding a large umbrella, the two secret-police officers turned their heads and gave Alicia a look that was somewhere between a threat and a plea.

"Can we leave you here without you making a scene, or must we drag you in so you don't give us the slip again?"

"Don't worry; I won't show you up."

"Do we have your word?"

Alicia nodded. Getting in and out of a car on a bad day was never easy, but she didn't want that pair to see her looking even more crushed than she actually was: as she stood up, she concealed the piercing pain in her hip with a smile. The doorman walked with her to the entrance, protecting her against the rain with the umbrella; a battalion of concierges and valets seemed to be waiting for her, ready to escort her through the hall to her appointment. When she noticed the two flights of stairs rising from the lobby to the grand dining hall, she knew she should have taken the walking stick. She pulled out a pillbox from her handbag and swallowed a pill. Before beginning the ascent, she breathed in deeply.

A couple of minutes and dozens of steps later, she stopped to catch her breath outside the doors to the dining hall. The concierge who had accompanied her noticed the film of perspiration on her forehead. Alicia smiled reluctantly. "From here on, I think I can manage all by myself, if you don't mind."

"Of course. As you please, miss."

The concierge left discreetly, but Alicia didn't need to look back to know that he was still watching her and would not take his eyes off her until she'd entered the dining hall. She dried her forehead with a handkerchief and studied the scene.

Barely a whisper of voices and the tinkling of a teaspoon slowly turning in a china cup. The Palace dining hall opened up before her, possessed, it seemed, by dancing flashes that dripped down from the large dome beneath the hammering rain. She had always thought the structure resembled a huge glass willow tree that hung like a canopy of rose windows taken from a hundred cathedrals and put together in remembrance of the Belle Époque. Nobody could accuse Leandro of having bad taste.

Under that bubble of multicolored glass, only one table was taken among a large number of empty ones. Two figures were being watched diligently by half a dozen waiters, who maintained the exact distance from the table that was too far to overhear their conversation but close enough to read their gestures. After all, the Palace, unlike her temporary address, the Hispania, was a first-class establishment. A creature of bourgeois habits, Leandro lived and worked there. Literally. He had occupied suite 814 for years and liked to carry out his business in that dining hall, which, as Alicia suspected, allowed him to believe that he lived in Proust's Paris and not in Franco's Spain.

She trained her eyes on the two diners. Leandro Montalvo, sitting, as usual, facing the entrance. He was a man of average height, with the soft and rounded build of a well-to-do accountant. Hiding behind oversize horn-rimmed glasses that helped him conceal his sharp eyes. Affecting the relaxed and affable air of a provincial lawyer, the sort who enjoys operettas, or a successful bank clerk who likes visiting museums after work. *Good old Leandro.*

Next to him, sporting a British-style suit that didn't match his rugged looks, sat an individual with smoothed-down hair and mustache, nursing a glass of brandy. His face looked familiar. One of those usual personalities in the newspapers, a veteran of posed photographs that always included the inevitable eaglet on the flag and some predictable painting of an equestrian scene. Gil de something, she told herself. Secretary General of Fried Bread, or whatever.

Leandro looked up and smiled at her from afar. He motioned her to come closer, the way one calls a child or a puppy. Suppressing her limp at the expense of a shooting pain on her side, she crossed the dining hall slowly. As she did so, she noticed two men from the ministry at the far end, in the shadows. Armed. Stock-still, like waiting reptiles.

"Alicia, I'm so glad you were able to find a gap in your schedule to have a coffee with us. Tell me, have you had breakfast?"

Before she could reply, Leandro raised his eyebrows, and two of the waiters standing by the wall proceeded to set a place for her at the table. While they poured her a glass of freshly squeezed orange juice, Alicia felt the bigwig's gaze slowly boring into her. It wasn't hard to see herself through his eyes. Most men, including professional observers, confused seeing with looking and almost always stopped at obvious details that deterred any reading beyond those irrelevancies. Leandro used to say that to disappear into the eyes of one's opponent was a skill that could take one a whole lifetime to learn.

Hers was an ageless face, sharp-featured yet malleable, with only a few lines of shadow and color. Alicia changed her appearance every day according to the role she had to play in whatever fable Leandro had selected to stage his maneuvers and intrigues. She could be shade or light, landscape or figure, depending on the libretto. In days of truce she would vanish within herself and retreat into what Leandro called the transparency of her darkness. Her hair was black and her complexion pale, made for midwinter suns and indoor lounges. Her greenish eyes shone in the half-light, and she would fix them sharply on onlookers to distract them from her figure, which was fragile but not easy to avoid. When necessary she would conceal it under loose-fitting clothes so as not to draw furtive glances in the street. But close up her presence came into focus and she exuded a somber mood, which Leandro found vaguely disturbing. Her mentor had instructed her to try to keep it under wraps. "You're a night creature, Alicia, but here we all hide in daylight."

"Alicia, allow me to introduce you to the Right Honorable Señor Manuel Gil de Partera, director of the General Police Corps."

"It's an honor, Your Excellency," declared Alicia, offering him her hand. The director didn't take it, as if he were afraid she might bite him.

Gil de Partera observed her as if he hadn't yet decided whether she was a schoolgirl with more than a touch of wantonness that was unnerving him, or a species he didn't even know how to begin to classify. "The director has been good enough to ask for our help in solving a rather delicate matter that requires an extraordinary amount of discretion and diligence."

"Of course," said Alicia, in such a meek and angelic voice that it earned her a gentle kick from Leandro under the table. "We're at your disposal to assist you in all we can."

Gil de Partera went on observing her with that poisoned mixture of suspicion and desire that her presence usually elicited in gentlemen of a certain age. What Leandro always referred to as the perfume of her presence, or the side effects of her looks, was, in her mentor's opinion, a double-edged sword she hadn't yet learned to wield with absolute precision. In this case, and judging by the clear discomfort Gil de Partera seemed to feel in her proximity, Alicia was convinced that the blade would turn against her. Here comes the offensive, she thought.

"Do you know anything about hunting, Señorita Gris?" he asked.

She hesitated for an instant as she searched for her mentor's eyes.

"Alicia is essentially an urban creature," Leandro intervened.

"One learns a lot from hunting," lectured the director. "I've had the privilege of sharing a few hunts with the Generalissimo, and it was he who showed me the fundamental rule all hunters must adopt."

Alicia nodded repeatedly, as if she found it all fascinating. Leandro, meanwhile, had smeared jam over a piece of toast and handed it to her. Alicia accepted it almost without noticing.

The director was still caught up in his lecture. "A hunter has to understand," he said, "that at a critical moment in the hunt, the role of the prey and that of the hunter become confused. The hunt, the real hunt, is a duel between equals. You don't know who you really are until you shed blood."

There was a pause, and after a few seconds of theatrical silence demanding deep reflection on what had just been revealed to her, Alicia put on a respectful expression. "Is that also a maxim of the Generalissimo?"

Leandro gave her a warning stamp on the foot under the table.

"I'll be frank, young lady," the director said. "I don't like you. I don't like what I've heard about you, and neither do I like your tone or the fact that you think you can keep me waiting for half the morning, as if your crappy time were more valuable than mine. I don't like the way you look at people, and even less the sarcastic tone with which you address your superiors. Because if there's one thing that pisses me off in this life, it's people who don't know their place in the world. And what pisses me off even more is having to remind them."

Alicia looked down submissively. The temperature in the dining hall seemed to have plunged ten degrees at a stroke.

"I beg you to forgive me, sir, if I—"

"Don't interrupt me. If I'm here talking to you, it's because of the trust I have in your superior, who for some reason that escapes me thinks you're the right person for the job I need to entrust him with. But don't make any mistakes with me: from this very moment you're answerable to me. And I don't have the patience or the generous disposition of Señor Montalvo here."

Gil de Partera fixed his eyes on her. They were black, and the spider's web of small red capillaries covering his cornea seemed about to burst. Alicia imagined him all dressed up with a feathered hat and marshal's boots, kissing the royal buttocks of the head of state during one of those hunts, when the elders of the nation would burst open the prey placed within firing range by a squadron of servants—after which they'd smear their genitals with them, the aroma of gunpowder and chicken blood making them feel like virile conquerors, for the glory of God and the Fatherland.

"I'm sure Alicia didn't mean to offend you, dear friend," said Leandro, who was probably relishing the scene.

Alicia corroborated her superior's words with a serious and contrite nod of her head.

"Needless to say, the content of what I'm about to tell you is strictly confidential, and for all intents and purposes this conversation has never taken place. Any doubt on this point or any other, Gris?"

"Absolutely none, sir."

"Good. Then for God's sake, eat your piece of toast, so we can get down to business."

5

"WHAT DO YOU know about Don Mauricio Valls?"

"The minister?" asked Alicia.

The young woman stopped for a moment to consider the avalanche of images of the long and widely publicized career of Don Mauricio Valls that came to her mind. A spruce, arrogant profile, always standing in the most prominent position in every photograph and among the finest company, receiving honors and dispensing undisputed wisdom to the applause and admiration of the court clique. Canonized in his lifetime, raised to the altar by his own efforts, with the help of the country's self-proclaimed intelligentsia, Mauricio Valls was the embodiment among mortals of the quintessential Spanish Man of Letters, Gentleman of Arts and Thought. Awarded endless prizes and homage. Described, without irony, as the emblematic figure of the country's cultural and political elite. Minister Valls was always preceded by his press clippings and all the regime pomp. His lectures in major Madrid venues always drew the cream of society. His lauded articles on current affairs became articles of faith. The pack of reporters who ate from the palm of his hand bent over backward to flatter him. His occasional recitals of poetry and monologues taken from his celebrated plays—which he performed as a two-hander with leading figures of the stage—were always sold out. His literary works were considered the epitome of achievement, and his name was already inscribed in the roll call of the great masters. Mauricio Valls, radiance and intellect of Iberia, lighting up the world.

"We know what we see in the press," Leandro interjected. "Which, to be honest, for some time now, has been pretty thin compared to what it used to be."

"Nonexistent, in fact," Gil de Partera confirmed. "I'm sure, young woman, you haven't failed to notice that since November 1956, over three years ago, Mauricio Valls, Minister for National Education (or for Culture, as he himself likes to say) and, if I may say so, the apple of the eye of the Spanish press, has practically disappeared from view and has hardly been seen at any official function."

"Now that you mention it, sir . . . ," Alicia agreed.

Leandro turned toward her and, exchanging a conspiratorial look with Gil de Partera, put her in the picture. "The fact is, Alicia, that it's not by chance or out of personal choice that the minister has been unable to offer us his fine intellect and flawless talents."

"I see you've had occasion to deal with him, Leandro," Gil de Partera cut in.

"I had that pleasure long ago, just briefly, during my years in Barcelona. A great man, and someone who has best exemplified the values and deep significance of our intellectual class."

"I'm sure the minister would agree with you wholeheartedly."

Leandro smiled politely, fixing his gaze on Alicia again before he began to speak.

"Sadly, the business that brings us here today is not the indisputable merits of our dear minister, or the enviable health of his self-esteem. If Your Honor, Señor Gil de Partera, will allow, I don't think I would be speaking out of turn if I say that the prolonged absence of Don Mauricio Valls from public life in the last few years has been due to the suspicion that there is, and has been for years, a plot to carry out an attempt on his life."

Alicia raised her eyebrows and swapped glances with Leandro.

"In order to support the investigation opened by the General Police Corps, and following a request from our friends in the Ministry of the Interior, our unit assigned an agent to assist with the investigation, although we weren't officially involved in it and in fact, were not aware of its details," Leandro explained.

Alicia bit her lip. Her superior's eyes made it clear that question time had not started yet.

"For reasons we haven't yet been able to clarify," Leandro continued, "that agent has broken off contact, and we've been unable to track him down for a couple of weeks. This puts into context the mission for which His Excellency has kindly asked for our collaboration."

Leandro looked at the veteran policeman and gestured to him to take over. Gil de Partera cleared his throat and adopted a somber expression. "What I am going to tell you is strictly confidential and cannot leave this table."

Alicia and Leandro both nodded.

"As your superior has already explained, on the second of November 1956, during an event organized in his honor in Madrid's Círculo de Bellas Artes, Minister Valls was the object of a failed attempt on his life, apparently not for the first time. The news was kept under wraps, a decision agreed upon as the best option by both the cabinet and the minister himself, who didn't wish to alarm his family or his collaborators. An investigation was opened and is still ongoing, but despite all the efforts of the General Police Corps and a special unit of the Civil Guard, we still haven't been able to establish the circumstances surrounding this crime and other similar ones that may have taken place before the police were alerted. Naturally, from that very moment, the minister's police escort and all security measures were reinforced, and his public appearances were canceled until further notice."

"What has the investigation yielded so far?" Alicia cut in.

"The investigation concentrated on a series of anonymous letters that Don Mauricio had been receiving for some years and to which he hadn't attached much importance. Shortly after the failed attack, the minister informed the police of the existence of these threatening letters. The initial investigation revealed that in all likelihood they'd been sent by someone called Sebastián Salgado, a thief and murderer who was serving a sentence in the prison of Montjuïc Castle, in Barcelona, until about two years ago. As you are probably aware, Don Mauricio Valls had been the governor of that prison at the start of his career in the service of the regime, to be precise between 1939 and 1944."

"Why didn't he warn the police about the anonymous letters sooner?" asked Alicia.

"As I said, he explained that at first he hadn't attached much importance to them, although he admitted that perhaps he should have done so. At the time he told us that the tone of the messages was so cryptic that he couldn't work out their meaning."

"And what is the tone of these supposed threats?"

"Mostly vague. In the letters the author says that 'the truth' cannot be concealed, that 'the time of justice' has come for 'the children of death' and that 'he,' presumably the author, awaits him 'at the entrance to the labyrinth.'"

"Labyrinth?"

"As I said, the messages are cryptic. They may refer to something that only Valls and whoever wrote them knew about. Although apparently the minister wasn't able to interpret them either. Maybe they're the work of a lunatic. We can't eliminate that possibility."

"Was Sebastián Salgado already a prisoner in the castle when Valls was appointed governor?"

"Yes. We've checked Salgado's records. In fact, he was sent to the prison in 1939, right after Mauricio Valls was the governor. The minister explained that he remembered him vaguely as being a quarrelsome individual, and this gave credibility to our theory that he was very likely the person who sent the letters."

"When exactly was he released?"

"Just under two years ago, in fact. Clearly, the dates don't coincide with the murder attempt in the Círculo de Bellas Artes, or with the earlier ones. Either Salgado worked with someone outside the prison, or he was only being used as a decoy to confuse the trail. This last possibility is becoming more feasible as the investigation advances. As you'll see in the dossier I'm going to leave with you, the letters were all sent from the post office in Pueblo Seco, Barcelona, where the mail from the inmates of Montjuïc Castle is taken."

"How do you know which letters stamped in that post office come from the prison and which don't?"

"All the ones originating from the castle have an identifying stamp affixed to them by the prison office before going into the mail sack."

"Aren't the prisoners' letters checked?"

"Yes, in theory. In practice, as has been confirmed by the very people responsible, only on certain occasions. In any case, nobody was aware that threatening messages to the minister had been detected. It's also possible that because of the obscure nature of the language used, the prison censors didn't notice anything relevant."

"If Salgado had an accomplice or various accomplices outside the prison, could they have handed him the letters so that they were sent from the prison?"

"Yes, possibly," said Gil de Partera. "Salgado had the right to one personal visit per month. In any case, it wouldn't make any sense if it had happened that way. It would have been much easier to send the letters by regular post and not be exposed to detection by the prison censors."

"Unless they specifically wanted to prove that the letter had been sent from the prison," Alicia pointed out.

Gil de Partera nodded.

"There's one thing I don't understand," Alicia continued. "If Salgado had been in Montjuïc all that time, and wasn't released until a couple of years ago, I imagine that means he'd received the maximum thirty-year sentence. So what's he doing out in the street?"

"You don't understand it, nor does anyone else. Indeed, Sebastián Salgado was supposed to serve at least another ten years when he was unexpectedly granted a special pardon by the head of state. And there's more. The pardon was processed at the request of the minister Don Mauricio Valls, and under his good auspices."

Alicia let out a laugh of astonishment. Gil de Partera threw her a severe look.

"Why would Valls do something like that?" asked Leandro, quickly coming to her rescue.

"Against our advice, and alleging that the investigation was not producing the expected results, the minister deemed that the release of Salgado might help uncover the identity and location of the party, or parties, involved in sending him those threats and the alleged attempts on his life."

"Sir," said Alicia, "you refer to these facts as 'alleged'—"

"Nothing is clear in this matter," Gil de Partera interrupted. "That doesn't mean that I doubt, or that we should doubt, the word of the minister in question."

"Of course. Going back to Salgado's release. Did it produce the results the minister was expecting?"

"No. We had him watched twenty-four hours a day from the moment he left the prison. The first thing he did was rent a room in a cheap hotel in the red-light district, where he paid for a month in advance. Apart from that, all he did was go to the Estación del Norte every day and spend hours gazing at the checked-luggage lockers in the station's entrance hall, or perhaps keeping them under surveillance. Occasionally, he also visited an old secondhand bookshop on Calle Santa Ana."

"Sempere & Sons," murmured Alicia.

"That's right. Do you know it?"

Alicia nodded.

"Our friend Salgado doesn't seem to fit the profile of a regular reader," Leandro suggested. "Do we know what he hoped to find in one of the station's baggage lockers?"

"We suspect he had some sort of booty hidden there, the fruit of crimes he committed before he was arrested in 1939."

"Was the suspicion confirmed?"

"In the second week of his release, Salgado visited the Sempere & Sons bookshop one last time and then made his way to the railway station, as he did every day. That day, however, instead of sitting down in the entrance hall to stare at the lockers, he walked over to one of them and put a key in. He pulled a suitcase out of the locker and opened it."

"What was inside it?" asked Alicia.

"Air," pronounced Gil de Partera. "Nothing. His booty, or what-ever it was he'd hidden there, had disappeared. The Barcelona police were about to arrest him on his way out of the station when Salgado collapsed in the rain. The officers had noticed that when he left the bookshop, two of its employees followed him to the station. Once Salgado lay stretched out on the ground, one of those two employees knelt down beside him for a few seconds and then left. When the policemen reached Salgado, he was already dead. It could be a case of divine justice, the robbed robber and all that, but the autopsy revealed needle marks on his back and on his clothes, and traces of strychnine in his blood."

"Could it have been the two bookshop employees? The accom-plices get rid of their bait once he's no longer any use to them, or once they realize their safety has been jeopardized because they're being watched by the police."

"That was one of the theories, but it was ruled out. In fact, any-one who'd been at the station could have murdered him without Sal-gado even noticing. The policemen were keeping a close eye on the two bookshop employees and did not see any direct contact between them and Salgado until Salgado collapsed, presumably dead."

"Could they have administered the poison in the bookshop, before Salgado set off toward the station?" asked Leandro.

This time it was Alicia who replied. "No. Strychnine acts very fast, even more so in an older man, and one whose physical condition had presumably been affected by spending almost twenty years in a dungeon. No more than two minutes would have elapsed between the prick and his death."

Gil de Partera looked at her, holding back an expression of approval. "That's right. The most likely explanation is that somebody else was in the station that day, someone who went unnoticed by the police officers and had decided the moment had come to get rid of Salgado."

"What do we know about these two bookshop employees?"

"One of them is Daniel Sempere, the son of the owner. The other answers to Fermín Romero de Torres, whose trail in the records is confused and shows signs of documentary impersonation. Perhaps to establish a false identity."

"What was their connection to the case, and what were they doing there?"

"That wasn't established."

"And weren't they questioned?"

Gil de Partera shook his head. "Once again, by express instructions from Minister Valls. Against our own judgment."

"What about the trail leading to Salgado's accomplice or accomplices?

"At a standstill."

"Perhaps the minister will change his mind now and allow you to . . ."

Gil de Partera unearthed his wolfish veteran policeman's smile.

"That's what I was coming to. Exactly nine days ago, at daybreak, the day after the masquerade ball organized in his Somosaguas residence, Don Mauricio Valls abandoned his home in a car, accompanied by his chief bodyguard, Vicente Carmona."

"Abandoned?" asked Alicia.

"Nobody has seen him or had any news from him since. He's vanished from the face of the earth without a trace."

A long silence fell over the dining hall. Alicia searched Leandro's eyes.

"My men are working tirelessly," he continued, "but for the moment we've got nothing. It's as if Mauricio Valls had evaporated the moment he stepped into that car."

"Did the minister leave a note, or some indication of where he was going before he departed?"

"No. The theory we're considering is that the minister, for some reason we can't quite follow, had at last discovered who was sending him those threats and decided to confront that person himself with the help of his trusted bodyguard."

"And that way perhaps fall into a trap," Leandro concluded. "'The entrance to the labyrinth.'"

Gil de Partera nodded repeatedly.

"How can we be certain that the minister didn't know from the start who was sending him those notes and why?" Alicia now queried.

Both Leandro and Gil de Partera threw her a disapproving look.

"The minister is the victim, not the suspect," the latter put in quickly. "Don't confuse the facts."

"How can we help you, my friend?" asked Leandro.

Gil de Partera took a deep breath and waited a few moments before replying.

"My department has limited procedures. We were kept in the dark on this subject until it was too late. I admit we may have made some mistakes, but we're doing everything in our power to resolve the matter before it gets into the news. Some of my superiors believe that, given the nature of the case, your unit could come up with some additional angle that would help us resolve this question as soon as possible."

"Is that also what you believe?"

"To be honest, Leandro, I no longer know who or what to believe. But what I'm quite sure of is that if we don't find Valls safe and sound very soon, Altea will unleash a storm and put his old friend Hendaya on the case. And neither of us wants that to happen."

Alicia looked inquiringly at Leandro, who shook his head almost imperceptibly. Gil de Partera chuckled bitterly under his breath. His eyes were bloodshot. He looked as if he hadn't slept more than two hours a night for a week.

"I'm telling you as much as I know, but what I don't know is whether I've been told the whole truth. I can't be any clearer. We've spent the last nine days groping around in the dark, and every hour that goes by is another hour lost."

"Do you think the minister is still alive?" asked Alicia.

Gil de Partera looked down and said nothing for a long time. "It's my duty to think that he is," he said finally, "and that we'll find him safe and sound before any of this can leak out, or the case is taken out of our hands."

"And we'll be behind you on this matter," Leandro agreed. "Be in no doubt that we'll do all we can to help you with your investigation."

Gil de Partera nodded, looking at Alicia with ambivalence. "You'll work with Vargas, one of my men."

For a moment Alicia hesitated. She searched Leandro's eyes, but her superior decided to stare into his coffee cup.

"With all due respect, sir," she said, "I always work alone."

"You'll work with Vargas. There's no room for discussion on this point."

"Of course," agreed Leandro, oblivious to Alicia's blazing eyes. "When can we start?"

"Yesterday."

At a sign from the director, one of his officials came over and handed him a bulky envelope. Gil de Partera set it on the table and stood up, not trying to conceal his haste to be anywhere else but that dining hall. "All the details are in the dossier. Keep me informed." He shook Leandro's hand and, with barely a glance at Alicia, stood up to leave.

They watched him recede through the large dining hall with his men in tow, and then sat down again. For a few minutes neither of them said a word, Alicia gazing into space and Leandro meticulously slicing a croissant, spreading butter and strawberry jam on it and then eating it slowly, his eyes shut.

"Thanks for the support," said Alicia.

"Come on. I hear Vargas is a talented man. You'll like him. And you might learn something."

"Lucky me. Who is he?"

"A veteran in the Force. He used to be a heavyweight. He's been moved to the reserve for a while, apparently due to a difference of opinion with the head office. Something happened, they say."

"A pariah? Am I so worthless that I don't even deserve a top-class chaperone?"

"He has class, no doubt about that. The trouble is that his loyalty and faith in the regime have been questioned more than once."

"Surely they're not expecting me to convert him."

"All they expect is that we don't make any noise, and we make them look good."

"Fabulous."

"It could be worse," said Leandro, putting an end to it.

"Does 'worse' mean this business of inviting his 'old friend,' that Hendaya guy?"

"Among other things."

"Who is Hendaya?"

Leandro looked away. "Best if you don't have to find out."

A long silence ensued, during which Leandro took the opportunity to pour himself another cup of coffee. He had the irritating habit of holding the saucer with one hand under his chin and taking small sips. On days like this, almost all his habits, which Alicia knew so well, seemed irritating to her.

Noticing her expression, he gave her a benevolent, paternal smile. "If looks could kill."

"Why didn't you tell the director that I resigned two weeks ago, and I'm no longer in the service?"

Leandro set the cup down on the table and wiped his lips with his napkin. "I didn't want to embarrass you, Alicia. May I remind you that we're not a chess club. One can't just join or leave the service by filling in a form. We've had this conversation a few times already, and to be honest, I'm hurt by your attitude. Because I know you better than you know yourself, and because I think so highly of you, I allowed you two weeks' holiday so you could rest and think about your future. I understand that you're tired. So am I. I understand that you sometimes don't like what we do. Neither do I. But it's our job and our duty. You knew that when you joined."

"I was seventeen when I joined. And it wasn't out of choice."

Leandro smiled like a proud teacher confronting his most brilliant student. "Your soul is an old soul, Alicia. You've never been seventeen."

"We decided that I was leaving. That was the deal. Two weeks don't change anything."

Leandro's smile was getting cold, like his coffee. "Grant me this last favor, and then you'll be free to do whatever you want."

"No."

"I need you in this, Alicia. Don't make me beg. Or force you."

"Hand it to Lomana. I'm sure he's dying to collect some points."

"I was wondering when you'd bring up the subject. I've never quite understood what the problem was between you and Ricardo."

"Incompatible personalities," suggested Alicia.

"In fact, Ricardo Lomana is the agent I loaned to the police a few weeks ago, and he hasn't been returned. Now they tell me he's disappeared."

"Fat chance. Where the hell is he?"

"Part of the disappearing act consists in not revealing that detail."

"Lomana isn't the sort to disappear. There must be a reason why he's not giving any signs of life. He's found something."

"That's what I think, too, but insofar as we don't have any news from him, we can only speculate. And that's not what they pay us to do."

"What do they pay us to do?"

"To solve their problems. And this is a very serious problem."

"And couldn't I also disappear?"

Leandro shook his head. He looked at her for a long time, a pained expression on his face.

"Why do you hate me, Alicia? Haven't I been like a father to you? A good friend?"

Alicia stared at her mentor. She had a knot in her stomach, and words didn't come to her mouth. She'd spent two weeks trying to get Leandro out of her mind, and now that she was facing him again, she realized that sitting there, beneath the grand dome of the Hotel Palace, she was once again that miserable teenager who would probably never have reached her twentieth birthday, had Leandro not gotten her out of that hole.

"I don't hate you," she said at last.

Leandro smiled again, that warm smile that forgave everything, that understood everything. "Perhaps you hate yourself, what you do, who you serve, all that crap that surrounds us and rots us inside a little bit more each day. I understand you. I've also been through that." He rested his hand on Alicia's and squeezed it hard. "Help me solve this last matter, and I promise you'll be able to leave afterward. Disappear forever."

"That simple?"

"That simple. You have my word."

"Where's the catch?"

"There's no catch."

"There's always a catch."

"Not this time. I can't keep you beside me forever if you don't want that. However much it may hurt." Leandro held out his hand. "Friends?"

Alicia hesitated, but finally she held hers out too. He took it to his lips and kissed it. "I'm going to miss you when all this is over. And you'll miss me too, even if you don't see it that way now. You and I make a good team."

"Birds of a feather flock together."

"Have you thought about what you're going to do later?"

"When?"

"When you're free. When you disappear, as you say."

Alicia shrugged. "I haven't thought about it."

"I thought I'd taught you to be a better liar, Alicia."

"Perhaps I'm no use for anything else."

"You've always wanted to write," Leandro suggested. "A new Laforet?"

Alicia looked at him with indifference.

He smiled. "Will you write about us?"

"No. Of course not."

Leandro nodded. "It wouldn't be a good idea, you know that. We operate in the shadows. Unseen. It's part of the service we offer."

"Of course I know. You don't have to remind me."

"A shame, because there would be so many stories to tell, wouldn't there?"

"See the world," murmured Alicia.

"Excuse me?"

"What I'd like to do is travel and see the world. Find my place. If it exists."

"On your own?"

"Do I need anyone else?"

"I suppose you don't. For creatures like us, solitude can be the best company."

"It suits me fine."

"One of these days you'll fall in love."

"What a pretty title for a ballad."

"You'd better get going. Unless I'm completely wrong, Vargas must be waiting for you outside."

"It's a mistake."

"This interference annoys me more than it annoys you, Alicia. It's obvious that they don't trust either of us. Be diplomatic and don't scare him. Do it for me."

"I always am. And I don't scare anyone."

"You know what I mean. Besides, we won't be competing with the police. We're not even going to try. They have their investigation, their methods and procedures."

"What do I do, then? Smile and hand out sugared almonds?"

"I want you to do what you do best. Notice what the police are not going to notice. Follow your instinct, not the procedure. I want you to do all the things the police won't do because it's the police and because they're not my Alicia Gris."

"Is that a compliment?"

"Yes, and an order."

Alicia took the envelope containing the dossier that was lying on the table and stood up. As she did so, Leandro noticed how she put her hand on her hip and pressed her lips to hide the pain.

"How much are you taking?" he asked.

"Nothing in these last two weeks. A couple of pills every now and then."

Leandro sighed. "We've talked about this a number of times, Alicia. You know you can't do that."

"I am doing it."

Her mentor shook his head, muttering under his breath. "I'll make sure they send you four hundred grams this afternoon to your hotel."

"No."

"Alicia . . ."

She turned and walked away from the table without limping, biting her tongue, swallowing her pain and her angry tears.

6

WHEN ALICIA LEFT the Gran Hotel Palace, the driving rain had stopped and a veil of vapor rose from the pavement. Thick beams of light stabbed the center of Madrid from the dome of passing clouds, like spotlights combing through a prison courtyard. One of them swept through Plaza de las Cortes and revealed a Ford parked a few yards from the hotel entrance. Leaning against the hood stood a silver-haired man in a black coat, calmly smoking a cigarette and watching people walk by. She guessed he must be in his mid-fifties, but he looked well muscled and in good shape for his age. He had the solid appearance of someone who has made the most of his stint in the armed forces and spends little time at his desk.

As if he'd sniffed her in the air, he turned toward Alicia and smiled like a matinee idol. "Can I help you at all, miss?"

"I hope so. My name is Gris."

"Gris? You're Gris?"

"Alicia Gris. Of Leandro Montalvo's unit. Gris. You must be Vargas." The man nodded vaguely. "They didn't tell me—"

"Last-minute surprises," she said quickly. "Do you need a few moments to recover?"

The policeman took a final drag of his cigarette and looked at her intently through the curtain of smoke he exhaled. "No."

"Wonderful. Where do you want to begin?"

"They're expecting us in the Somosaguas villa. If that's all right with you."

Alicia nodded. Vargas threw the cigarette stub onto the street and walked around the car while she installed herself in the passenger seat. He sat at the wheel, his eyes staring straight ahead, the car keys on his lap. "I've heard a lot about you. I didn't think you were so . . . young."

Alicia gave him an icy look.

"This is not going to be a problem, is it?" asked the policeman.

"A problem?"

"You and me."

"I see no reason why it should be."

He looked at her with more curiosity than suspicion. Alicia gave him one of those sweet, catlike smiles that irritated Leandro so much. Vargas chuckled and started the car, mumbling under his breath.

"Nice car," Alicia remarked after a while.

"Courtesy of police headquarters. Consider it a sign that they're taking this matter seriously. Do you drive?"

"I can barely open a bank account in this country without permission from a husband or father."

"I see."

"Allow me to doubt that."

They drove on in silence for the next few minutes. Vargas kept looking at Alicia out of the corner of his eye. She pretended not to notice as through this methodical and intermittent observation the policeman x-rayed her by installments, making the most of red lights and pedestrian crossings. When they came to a halt in the middle of a traffic jam on Gran Via, Vargas pulled out an elegant silver cigarette case, opened it, and handed it to her. Virginia tobacco, imported. She declined. He put a cigarette to his lips and lit it with a gold-plated lighter, which Alicia could have sworn had the Dupont logo on it. Vargas liked beautiful, expensive things. While he lit his cigarette, Alicia noticed him glancing at her hands, clasped over her lap, perhaps searching for a wedding ring. Vargas himself sported a rather large one.

"Family?" asked the policeman.

Alicia shook her head. "You?"

"Married to Spain."

"Very exemplary. And the ring?"

"Other times."

"Aren't you going to ask me what someone like me is doing working for Leandro?"

"Is it any business of mine?"

"No."

"Well, then."

As they left the city's traffic behind them and headed toward Casa de Campo Park, the awkward silence returned. Vargas's eyes continued to scrutinize her bit by bit. He had a cold, metallic gaze, his gray irises shining like freshly cut diamonds. Alicia wondered whether, before falling out of favor, her enforced partner had been an acolyte or merely a mercenary. The first of these infested every layer of the regime and multiplied like infected warts, safeguarded by flags and proclamations; the second remained silent and merely kept the machinery working. She wondered how many people he'd rubbed out throughout his career in the Force, whether he lived with the guilt or whether he'd already lost count. Perhaps, with his gray hair, his conscience had also grown, and this had ruined his ambitions.

"What are you thinking?" asked Vargas.

"I was wondering whether you like your job."

Vargas chuckled again.

"Aren't you going to ask me whether I like mine?"

"Is that any business of mine?"

"I suppose it isn't."

"Well, then."

Realizing that the conversation had no future, Alicia pulled out the dossier supplied by Gil de Partera and started looking through it. At first glance there wasn't much there. Notes from the police officers. The statement of the minister's personal secretary. A couple of pages devoted to the supposed frustrated attack against Valls; procedural guidelines from the two inspectors who opened the case; and excerpts from records relating to Vicente Carmona, Valls's bodyguard. Either Gil de Partera trusted them even less than Leandro had suggested, or the top men in his department had been twiddling their thumbs for the past week.

"Were you expecting more?" asked Vargas, reading her thoughts.

Alicia fixed her attention on the trees of Casa de Campo Park.

"I didn't expect anything less," she mumbled. "Who are we going to see?"

"Mariana Sedó, Valls's personal secretary for the last twenty years. She's the person who reported the minister's disappearance."

"That's a lot of years for a secretary."

"According to gossip she's much more than that."

"Lover?"

Vargas shook his head. "I think Doña Mariana's tastes lie more on the other shore. What people say is that she's the one who steers the ship, and that nothing was done or decided in Valls's office without her consent."

"Behind every bad man there's always a worse woman. People also say that."

Vargas smiled. "Well, I'd never heard that. I'd been warned that you were somewhat irreverent."

"What else have you been warned about?"

Vargas turned toward her and winked.

"Who is Hendaya?" asked Alicia.

"Excuse me?"

"Hendaya. Who is he?"

"Rodrigo Hendaya?"

"I suppose."

"Why do you want to know?"

"One can never know too much."

"Has Montalvo mentioned Hendaya in connection with this matter?"

"The name came up in the conversation. Who is he?"

Vargas sighed. "Hendaya is a butcher. The less you know about him, the better."

"Do you know him?"

Vargas ignored her question. They made the rest of the journey without exchanging a single word.

7

THEY'D BEEN DRIVING for almost fifteen minutes through avenues speckled with armies of uniformed gardeners when a boulevard of cypress trees opened up before them, leading to the spiked gates of Villa Mercedes. The sky had acquired a leaden color; fine drops of rain spattered on the windshield. A porter, waiting by the entrance to the estate, opened the door to let them in. On one side stood a sentry box, where a guard holding a rifle responded with a nod to Vargas's greeting.

"Have you been here before?" asked Alicia.

"A couple of times since last Monday. You're going to love it."

The car glided along the fine-gravel path, winding around groves and ponds. Alicia gazed at the parade of statues, pools, and fountains, and the faded rose gardens, disintegrating in the autumn wind. A narrow railway track could be glimpsed here and there among bushes and dead flowers, while farther away, on the far edge of the property, Alicia noticed the outline of what looked like a miniature station. A steam locomotive bearing two cars waited by the platform under the drizzle.

"A toy for the girl," Vargas explained.

Soon the profile of the main residence rose before them, an over-large mansion that seemed to have been conceived to dwarf and frighten visitors. Two large houses, one on either side of it, stood at a distance of about a hundred meters from the mansion. Vargas stopped the car opposite the wide staircase leading to the main entrance. A butler in uniform, waiting with an umbrella at the foot of the stairs, instructed them to drive over to a nearby building. As Vargas drove down the path to the garage, Alicia was able to take in the whole outline of the mansion.

"Who pays for all this?" she asked.

Vargas shrugged.

"You and I, I suppose. And perhaps Valls's wife, who inherited a fortune from her father, Enrique Sarmiento."

"The banker?"

"One of the bankers of the Crusade, as the papers called it," Vargas specified.

Alicia remembered having heard Leandro mention Sarmiento. How he and a group of bankers had financed the Nacionales during the civil war, lending them in large measure funds looted from the defeated side, in a mutually beneficial agreement. "I've heard that the minister's wife is ill," she said.

"That's one way of putting it."

The garage attendant opened one of the doors and signaled for them to park the car inside. Vargas lowered the window, and the guard recognized him. "Leave it wherever you like, boss. And the keys in the ignition, please . . ."

Vargas gave him a nod and drove into the garage, a structure consisting of a succession of vaults supported by wrought-iron columns stretching away into an impenetrable darkness. A string of luxury cars was lined up along the walls, the shine of their chromium plating vanishing into the distance. Vargas found a gap between a Hispano-Suiza and a Mercedes-Benz.

The garage attendant had followed them and gave him the thumbs-up. "Nice one you're driving today, chief," he remarked as they got out of the car.

"As the young lady was coming today, the bosses let me take the Ford," said Vargas.

The attendant looked like a cross between a homunculus and a mouse. He appeared to be held upright inside his blue overalls thanks to a jumble of dirty rags hanging from his belt and a film of grease that preserved him from the elements. After staring at Alicia from head to toe, the attendant bowed ostentatiously and, when he thought she didn't notice, gave Vargas a conspiratorial wink.

"Great guy, Luis," Vargas said to Alicia. "I think he lives here, in the garage itself, in a shed behind the repair shop."

They walked toward the exit, passing Valls's museum pieces on wheels, while Luis, behind them, busied himself polishing the Ford energetically with rag and spit while enjoying Alicia's gentle swaying and the shape of her ankles.

Vargas covered Alicia with the umbrella they'd been offered as the butler came over to meet them.

"I hope you've had a good journey from Madrid," said the butler solemnly. "Doña Mariana is expecting you." He bore that cold and vaguely condescending smile of career servants who, as the years go by, start to believe that their masters' lineage has tinged their own blood blue and granted them the privilege of looking down on others. As they walked the distance separating them from the main house, Alicia noticed that he kept glancing at her surreptitiously, trying to make out from her gestures and clothes what her role was in the show.

"Is the young lady your secretary?" he asked, fixing his eyes on Alicia.

"The young lady is my boss," replied Vargas.

The servant dropped his arrogant manner, which was replaced with a stiff expression worthy of being framed. His lips remained sealed and his eyes glued to his shoes the rest of the way.

The main door led to a large entrance hall with a marble floor, from which staircases, corridors, and galleries branched out. They followed the butler to the reading room, where a middle-aged woman was waiting with her back to the door, facing the view of the garden under the rain.

The woman turned as soon as she heard them come in, giving them an icy smile. "I'm Mariana Sedó," she said as the butler closed the door behind him and retired to enjoy his momentary bewilderment. "Don Mauricio's personal secretary."

"Vargas, from Central Police Headquarters, and this is my partner, Señorita Gris."

The secretary took her time conducting the inevitable inspection. She began with Alicia's face, registering the color of her lips, then the cut of her dress, and finally the style of her shoes with a grimace of intolerance and contempt, quickly buried in the serene and sorrowful expression the circumstances demanded. Motioning them to sit down on a leather sofa, Mariana chose a chair, which she placed near a small table bearing a tray with a steaming teapot and three cups. As the secretary proceeded to fill the cups, Alicia assessed the feigned smile behind which Doña Mariana took cover and concluded that Valls's eternal guardian exuded a malicious aura, midway between that of a fairy godmother and a voracious praying mantis.

"How may I help you?" asked Doña Mariana. "I've spoken to so many of your colleagues these last few days that I'm not sure there's anything left to say."

"We're grateful for your patience, Doña Mariana," said Alicia. "We're well aware that these are difficult moments for the family and for you."

The secretary nodded with an air of patience, exhibiting the studied demeanor of the faithful servant to perfection. Her eyes, however, betrayed irritation at having to deal with second-rate subordinates. The way in which she focused on Vargas and avoided acknowledging Alicia added another layer of contempt. Alicia could see that Vargas hadn't missed the slightest detail: she decided let him take the lead while she listened.

"Doña Mariana," he began, "from the official report and your statement to the police, we're assuming that you were the first person to notify the authorities of the absence of Don Mauricio Valls."

The secretary nodded. "The day of the masked ball," she explained, "Don Mauricio had given a number of permanent staff the day off. I took advantage of this to go to visit my goddaughter in Madrid. The following day, although Don Mauricio hadn't told me he would need me, I returned in the early morning, at about eight o'clock, and began to go through his mail and his datebook as I always do. I went up to the office and saw that the minister wasn't there. A few minutes later, one of the maids informed me that his daughter Mercedes had said her father left by car very early with Vicente Carmona, his chief bodyguard. I found it odd, because when I went through his datebook I noticed that Don Mauricio had added, in his own handwriting, an informal meeting that morning at ten here, in Villa Mercedes, with Pablo Cascos, the sales director of Ariadna."

"Ariadna?" asked Vargas

"It's the name of a publishing company owned by Don Mauricio," the secretary explained.

"That detail doesn't appear in your statement to the police," said Alicia.

"Excuse me?"

"The meeting Don Mauricio had himself set up for that morning. You didn't mention this to the police. May I ask why?"

Doña Mariana smiled somewhat condescendingly, as if she thought the question were trivial. "Since the meeting never took place, I didn't think it was relevant. Should I have?"

"You have now, and that's what matters," said Vargas amicably. "It's impossible to remember every detail—that's why we're taking advantage of your kindness and insisting so much. Please continue, Doña Mariana."

Valls's secretary accepted the apology and went on, although she ignored Alicia, looking only at Vargas.

"As I said, I found it odd that the minister should have left without alerting me beforehand. I asked the servants, and they informed me that apparently the minister hadn't slept in his room. He'd been in his office all night."

"Do you spend your nights here, in the main building?" Alicia interrupted.

Doña Mariana looked offended. She shook her head, pressing her lips together. "Of course not."

"I'm sorry. Do go on, if you'd be so kind."

Valls's secretary huffed impatiently. "Shortly afterward, at about nine o'clock, Señor Revuelta, the head of security at the house, told me he wasn't aware that Vicente Carmona and the minister had planned to be anywhere that morning, and that, furthermore, the fact that they left together without any other escort was highly irregular. At my request, Señor Revuelta consulted first with the staff at Don Mauricio's ministry and then spoke to the Ministry of the Interior. No one had any news of him, but we were told they'd call us as soon as they could locate him. It was then that Mercedes, Don Mauricio's daughter, came to see me. She was crying, and when I asked her what the matter was, she told me that her father had left and would never return."

"Did Mercedes say why she thought that?" asked Vargas.

Doña Mariana only shrugged.

"What did you do then?"

"I called the secretariat at the Ministry of the Interior and spoke first with José Moreno and later with the head of police, Señor Gil de Partera. The rest you already know."

"That was the point at which you mentioned the anonymous letters the minister had been receiving."

Doña Mariana gave herself a moment to reply. "That's right. The subject arose during the conversation with Señor Gil de Partera and his subordinate, someone called García—"

"García Novales," Vargas completed.

The secretary nodded.

"The police, of course, were already aware of the existence of those letters. They'd been supplied with copies for months. It so happens that that morning, when I was going through the minister's date-book in his office, I found the folder in which he kept them."

"Did you know he kept them?" asked Alicia.

Doña Mariana shook her head,

"I thought he'd destroyed them after showing them to the police at the time of the investigation, after the incident in the Círculo de Bellas Artes, but I realized I'd been mistaken, and Don Mauricio had been looking at them. I mentioned this to your superiors."

"Why do you think Don Mauricio took so long to inform the police, or the security staff, of the existence of those letters?" Alicia asked again.

Doña Mariana turned away from Vargas for a moment, her predatory eyes settling on Alicia.

"Young lady, you must understand that the volume of letters received by a man as important as Don Mauricio is vast. A large number of people and associations decide to write to the minister, and quite often there are eccentric or simply crazy letters, which I throw away, so Don Mauricio doesn't even see them."

"And yet you didn't throw those letters away."

"No."

"Did you know the person identified by the police as the most likely to have sent them? Sebastián Salgado?"

"No, of course not," the secretary snapped.

"But you knew of his existence?" Alicia insisted.

"Yes. I remembered him from the time the minister had been processing his pardon, and later from the time the police reported on the result of their investigation into the letters."

"Of course, but before that, do you remember ever having heard Don Mauricio mention Salgado's name? Perhaps years ago?"

Doña Mariana remained silent for a while. "I might have," she said finally. "I'm not sure."

"Could he have mentioned him?"

"I don't know. Perhaps he did. I think he did."

"And this would have been in . . ."

"March 1948."

Alicia frowned with surprise. "You remember the date clearly, yet you're not sure he mentioned the name Salgado?"

Doña Mariana blushed. "In March 1948, Don Mauricio asked me to organize an informal meeting with the successor in his post as governor of the prison in Montjuïc Castle, Luis Bolea."

"For what purpose?"

"I gathered it was an informal get-together, a courtesy meeting."

"And were you present during that courtesy meeting, as you call it?"

"Only every now and then. It was a private conversation."

"But perhaps you were able to catch the occasional fragment. Accidentally. As you went in and out of the room . . . taking in the coffee . . . Perhaps from your desk at the entrance to Don Mauricio's office . . ."

"I don't like what you're insinuating, young woman."

"Anything you can tell us will help us find the minister, Doña Mariana," Vargas put in. "Please."

The secretary hesitated. "Don Mauricio asked Señor Bolea about some of the prisoners who had been under his charge. He wanted to find out details, such as whether they were still in the prison or had been released, moved to another prison, or died. He didn't say why."

"Do you remember any of the names that were mentioned?"

"There were lots of names. And that was many years ago."

"Was Salgado one of them?"

"Yes, I think it was."

"Any other name?"

"The only name I remember well is Martín. David Martín."

Alicia and Vargas looked at one another. He wrote the name down in his notebook.

"Any more?"

"Perhaps a surname that sounded more like French, or foreign. I can't remember. As I said, it was years ago. How can that be important now?"

"We don't know, Doña Mariana. Our duty is to explore all the possibilities. Going back to the letters . . . When he showed you the first one, can you remember his reaction? Did the minister say anything that struck you as unusual?"

The secretary shook her head. "He didn't say anything in particular. He didn't seem to think it was important. He put it in a drawer and told me that if any more letters like that one arrived, I should hand them to him personally."

"Unopened?"

Doña Mariana nodded.

"Did Don Mauricio ask you not to mention the existence of those letters to anyone?"

"There was no need. I'm not in the habit of talking about Don Mauricio's business to those whom it doesn't concern."

"Does the minister usually ask you to keep secrets, Doña Mariana?" asked Alicia.

Valls's secretary pressed her lips together but didn't reply. Instead she turned impatiently to Vargas. "Do you have any more questions, Captain?"

Disregarding Doña Mariana's attempt to avoid her, Alicia leaned forward to place herself directly in the secretary's line of vision. "Did you know that Don Mauricio was planning to ask the head of state for Sebastián Salgado's pardon?"

The secretary looked Alicia up and down, no longer making any effort to hide her disdain and hostility. Then she looked at Vargas for support, but he had his eyes fixed on his notebook. "Of course I knew," she said.

"Didn't it surprise you?"

"Why should it have surprised me?"

"Did he say why he'd decided to do that?"

"For humanitarian reasons. He'd heard that Sebastián Salgado was very ill and did not have long to live. He didn't want him to die in prison. He wanted him to be able to see his loved ones and die with his family around him."

"According to the police report," Alicia objected, "after almost twenty years in prison Sebastián Salgado no longer had any living relatives or close friends."

"Don Mauricio is an ardent defender of national reconciliation, of healing the wounds of the past. Perhaps you find that hard to understand, but there are some people who are blessed with Christian charity and generosity of spirit."

"That being so, do you know whether Don Mauricio has requested other similar pardons during the years you've worked for him? Perhaps for some of the hundreds or thousands of political prisoners who passed through the prison when he was in charge?"

Doña Mariana wielded a frosty smile, sharp as a poisoned knife. "No."

Alicia and Vargas glanced briefly at one another. *Give up*, Vargas's look said. It was clear they weren't getting anywhere pursuing that line of inquiry.

Alicia leaned forward once more and again caught Doña Mariana's uncooperative gaze. "We're almost done, Doña Mariana. Thank you for your patience. The minister's appointment you mentioned earlier, with the sales representative of Editorial Ariadna—"

"Señor Cascos."

"Señor Cascos, thank you. Do you know what was going to be discussed?"

Doña Mariana stared at her as if making an effort to ignore how absurd the question seemed to her. "Matters concerning the publishing house, of course."

"Of course. Does the minister usually meet up with members of staff from his private businesses, here, in his home?"

"I don't know what you mean."

"Do you remember the last time it happened?"

"Quite frankly, no."

"What about the meeting with Señor Cascos. Did you arrange it?"

Doña Mariana shook her head. "As I said, he himself put it down in his datebook, in his own handwriting."

"Is it usual for Don Mauricio to fix appointments or meetings without telling you, 'in his own handwriting'?"

The secretary glared at Alicia.

"No."

"And yet in your statement to the police you didn't mention this fact."

"I've already said that at first it seemed irrelevant to me. Señor Cascos is one of Don Mauricio's employees. I didn't think there was anything unusual about the fact that they'd agreed to meet. It wasn't the first time."

"Oh, wasn't it?"

"No. They'd met before a number of times."

"In this house?"

"Not that I know of."

"Did you arrange those meetings, or did Don Mauricio arrange them himself?"

"I can't remember. I'd have to go through my notes. Why does it matter either way?"

"Forgive my insistence, but when Señor Cascos turned up for the meeting that morning, did he tell you that the minister wanted to talk to him?"

Dona Mariana thought about it for a few seconds. "No. At that moment our main concern was to establish the whereabouts of Don Mauricio, and it didn't occur to me that whatever he had to discuss with a mid-level employee could be a priority."

"Is Señor Cascos a mid-level employee?" asked Alicia.

"Yes."

"Just to clarify, and for reference only, what would your level be, Doña Mariana?"

Vargas gave Alicia a discreet kick. The secretary stood up, her face assuming a severe expression to indicate that the meeting had concluded. "If you'll excuse me, and there's nothing else I can help you with . . ." She pointed to the door, a polite but firm invitation to depart. "Even in his absence, Don Mauricio's affairs require my attention."

Vargas nodded and stood up, ready to follow Doña Mariana toward the exit. He'd already begun leaving when he noticed that Alicia was still seated on the sofa, sipping the cup of tea that she hadn't even noticed during the conversation. Vargas and the secretary turned toward her.

"In fact, yes, there is one more thing you can do to help us, Doña Mariana," she said.

*

127

They followed Doña Mariana through a maze of corridors until they reached the staircase leading up to the tower. Valls's secretary showed them the way mutely, without looking back, an almost tangible shadow of hostility trailing her. The sheets of rain licking the facade cast a somber atmosphere through curtains and windowpanes, creating the impression that Villa Mercedes was submerged under the waters of a lake. On their way they passed an entire army of servants and other staff members of Valls's small empire, who bowed their heads when they saw Doña Mariana, more than one stopping and moving to one side to bend over in obeisance. Observing this ritual of hierarchies, Vargas and Alicia exchanged an occasional bewildered glance.

At the foot of the spiral staircase leading up to the office in the tower, Doña Mariana took an oil lamp hanging on the wall and adjusted the intensity of the flame. They ascended, enveloped in a bubble of amber light that dragged their shadows along the walls. When they reached the office door, the secretary turned, for once ignoring Vargas as she fixed Alicia with her poisonous stare. Smiling calmly, Alicia stretched out an open palm.

Doña Mariana handed her the key, her lips tightly pressed together. "Don't touch anything. Leave everything just as you found it. And when you've finished, return the key to the butler before you leave."

"Thank you so much, Doña—" said Vargas.

Doña Mariana turned and set off down the stairs without replying, taking the lamp with her and leaving them in the semidarkness of the landing.

"It couldn't have gone better," Vargas said dryly. "Let's see how long it takes Doña Mariana to get on the phone to García Novales and tear us to pieces. Especially you."

"Under a minute," Alicia agreed.

"Something tells me that working with you is going to be a treat."

"Light?"

Vargas pulled out his lighter and brought the flame to the keyhole so that Alicia could insert the key. The doorknob let out a metallic groan as it turned.

"It sounds like a rat trap," Vargas said.

Alicia gave him a cunning smile in the light of the flame, which Vargas would have preferred not to see.

Vargas blew out the flame and pushed the door inward. "Abandon all hope ye who enter here."

8

ALICIA AND VARGAS stepped into what felt like the main cabin in a luxury yacht. An aura of gray light hovered in the air. Leaden skies and tears of rain sealed the windows.

The office was oval in shape. A large desk of fine wood stood at its center. Around it, most of the wall space was lined with spiraling bookshelves that seemed to form a bow as they rose toward the glass lantern at the top of the tower. Only one section was clear of books: it resembled a mural but was made up of dozens of small framed photographs packed together on the wall directly across from the desk. Alicia and Vargas walked over to examine it. All the images were of the same face and traced a photographic biography. A pale-faced girl with fair hair grew up before the eyes of the observer, from childhood to adolescence and first youth—the trail of a life in a hundred snapshots.

"It looks like the minister loves someone even more than he loves himself," said Alicia.

Vargas stayed on another moment or two, gazing at the portrait gallery, while Alicia went over to Valls's desk. She pulled out the admiral's chair and sat down on it, then placed her hands on the sheet of leather covering the table and glanced around the room.

"How does the world look from there?" asked Vargas.

"Small."

Alicia turned on the desk lamp. A warm, powdery light filled the room. She opened the first drawer in the desk and found a carved wooden box.

Vargas walked over and sat on a corner of the table. "If it's a humidor, I want the first Montecristo," he said.

Alicia opened the box. The inside was lined with blue velvet and seemed shaped to hold a revolver, but now it was empty. Vargas leaned over and stroked the edge of the box. He smelled his fingers, then nodded.

She pulled open the next drawer. It contained a collection of cases, all neatly lined up as if they were part of an exhibition. "They seem like little coffins," she said.

"Show me the corpse," said Vargas.

Alicia opened one of the cases. It contained a black-lacquered fountain pen with a white star on the tip of its cap. She pulled it out and smiled as she felt its weight, then pulled off the cap and slowly twisted one of the ends. A gold and platinum nib that seemed wrought by a cabal of wise men and goldsmiths shone in her hands.

"Is that the magic fountain pen of Fantômas?" asked Vargas.

"Almost. This is the first fountain pen produced by Montblanc. It dates back to 1905. A very expensive piece."

"And how do you know that?"

"Leandro has one exactly like it."

"It's more your sort of thing."

Alicia put the pen back in the case and closed the drawer. "I know. Leandro promised he'd give it to me the day I retired."

"And that will be?"

"Soon."

She tugged at the third and last drawer, but it was locked. She glanced at Vargas.

He shook his head. "If you want the key, go down and ask your friend Doña Mariana."

"I wouldn't like to bother her when she's so busy with 'Don Mauricio's affairs.'"

"So?"

"I thought at headquarters you were given courses on breaking and entering."

Vargas sighed. "Move out of the way."

The policeman knelt down in front of the set of drawers and

pulled out of his jacket an ivory handle, from which he then unfolded a double-edged serrated blade. "Don't think you're the only one who knows about collectors' pieces. Pass me that paper knife."

Alicia handed it to him, and he began to force the lock with the blade, at the same time using the paper knife to push at the gap between the drawer and the desk.

"Something tells me this isn't the first time you've done this," Alicia observed.

"Some people go to soccer games, and others force locks. You've got to have some hobby."

The operation took a little over two minutes. With a metallic snap, the lock gave way and the paper knife sank into the drawer. Vargas pulled out the blade. There wasn't a single scratch or dent on it.

"Tempered steel?" asked Alicia.

Vargas folded the knife neatly by pressing the tip of the blade on the floor, and put it back in the inside pocket of his jacket.

"One day you must let me play with that contraption," said Alicia.

"If you behave yourself," said Vargas as he opened the drawer.

They both looked expectantly inside. It was empty.

"Don't tell me I've forced open a minister's desk for nothing."

Alicia didn't reply. She knelt down next to Vargas and felt the inside of the drawer, rapping on the base and sides with her knuckles.

"Solid oak," said the policeman. "They don't make furniture like this anymore."

Alicia frowned, puzzled.

Vargas got to his feet. "We're not going to find anything here. We'd do better going to headquarters to inspect Salgado's letters."

Alicia, who was still feeling the inside of the drawer and the base of the one above it, ignored him. There was a space of about three centimeters between the bottom of the second drawer and the end of the side panels of the one below.

"Help me get it out," she said.

"Not content with breaking the lock, you now want to pull the whole desk to pieces," Vargas muttered, signaling her to move out of the way and pulling out the drawer. "You see? Nothing."

Alicia grabbed the drawer and turned it over. Stuck to the back panel of the base with a cross formed of two pieces of insulating tape was what looked like a book. Carefully pulling off the tape, she lifted out the volume.

Vargas felt the adhesive side of the tape. "It's recent."

Alicia set the book on the desk, sat down again, and pulled it toward the lamp. Vargas knelt beside her and looked at her with interest.

The volume contained roughly two hundred pages and was bound in black leather. There was no title on the cover or the spine. The only distinctive mark was a golden spiral embossed on the cover, creating a sort of optical illusion: when you held the book, you felt as if you were looking down a spiral staircase descending into the deep.

Alicia opened the book. The first three pages each bore an ink drawing of a chess piece with vaguely human features: a bishop, a pawn, and a queen with black eyes and vertical pupils, like those of a reptile. On the next page was the title of the book:

THE LABYRINTH OF THE SPIRITS VII
Ariadna and the Scarlet Prince

TEXT AND ILLUSTRATIONS BY VÍCTOR MATAIX

Beneath the title, and spilling over the page to its left, was an illustration in black ink, the image of an eerie city with buildings that had faces. Clouds slid through the rooftops like snakes. Bonfires and pyres of smoke rose from the streets, and a large blazing cross presided over the city from a mountaintop. Alicia could make out the landmarks of Barcelona—but it was a different Barcelona, a city that seemed to sketch out a nightmare seen through the eyes of a child. She turned over a few more pages, pausing at an illustration of what was undoubtedly the Temple of the Sagrada Familia. In the drawing the structure seemed to have come to life; the unfinished cathedral crept like a dragon, the four towers of the Nativity door rippling against sulfur-colored skies, ending in heads that spewed out fire.

"Have you ever seen anything like this?" asked Vargas.

Alicia shook her head slowly. For about two minutes she immersed herself in the strange universe projected by those pages. Images of a traveling circus populated by creatures who shunned the light; of an endless cemetery standing with its swarm of mausoleums and souls rising up to heaven, passing through clouds; of a ship stranded on a beach strewn with wreckage and a huge tide of corpses trapped beneath the water's surface. And ruling over that ghostly Barcelona from the top of the cathedral's lantern tower, gazing at the streets that swirled below, a silhouette clad in a tunic that fluttered in the wind, an angel's face with wolfish eyes: the Scarlet Prince.

Alicia closed the book, intoxicated by the strange and perverse power it exuded. Only then did she realize that what she was holding in her hands was only a children's storybook.

9

AS THEY WALKED down the tower staircase, Vargas took Alicia's arm gently and stopped her. "We'll have to tell Doña Mariana that we found this book and we're taking it with us."

She fixed her eyes on his hand, and he removed it apologetically. "I thought I heard her say she would rather not be bothered again."

"Well, at least it will have to be included in the report . . ."

Alicia gave him an impenetrable look. In the half-light, Vargas thought, those green eyes shone like coins sinking into a pond, lending their mistress a somewhat spectral air.

"I mean as evidence," the policeman specified.

"Of what?" Alicia's tone was cold, cutting.

"What the police find during an investigation . . ."

"Technically the police didn't find it. I found it. All you've done is act as locksmith."

"Listen . . ."

Alicia sailed down the stairs before he could reply.

Vargas groped his way down behind her. "Alicia . . ."

When they reached the garden, they were greeted by a drizzle that clung to their clothes like powdered glass. One of the maids had lent them an umbrella, but before Vargas was able to open it, Alicia headed for the garage without waiting for him.

The policeman hurried after her and managed to cover her with the umbrella. "You're welcome," he said.

Alicia limped slightly, he noticed, and was pressing her lips together.

"What the matter?"

"Nothing. It's an old wound. The damp doesn't help. It's not important."

"If you like, you can wait here, and I'll go and get the car."

Once again, Alicia didn't seem to hear him. Her eyes were lost in the distance as she stared at a vision between the trees: a structure veiled by the rain.

"What?" asked Vargas.

She walked off, leaving him holding the umbrella.

"For God's sake," mumbled the policeman, following her again.

When he caught up with her, Alicia only pointed toward what looked like a conservatory buried in the depths of the garden. "There was someone there," she said. "Watching us."

"Who could it be?"

Alicia stopped for a moment and hesitated. "You go ahead to the garage. I'll come in a minute."

"Are you sure?"

"Take the umbrella, at least . . ."

Vargas watched her walk away in the rain, limping slightly, until she faded into the mist, one more shadow in the garden.

SHE FOUND HERSELF walking along a path of pale stone. Lines of moss nestled in the cracks between carved slabs that looked, Alicia thought, like tombstones stolen from a graveyard. The path wound through the willows, their branches oozing raindrops and grazing her skin as she passed, like arms trying to hold her back. Beyond the trees she glimpsed the structure of what at first she had mistaken for a conservatory but, closer up, looked more like a neoclassical pavilion. The miniature railway tracks that followed the perimeter of the estate ran along the front of the pavilion, with a platform, like a little station, by its main entrance. Alicia stepped over the rails and walked up the steps to the front door, which was ajar. Her hip throbbed, a sharp stabbing pain that made her think of barbed wire wrapped around her bones. She paused for a moment to catch her breath, then pushed the door inward. It gave way with a faint groan.

Her first thought was that she was in a ballroom that had been abandoned for years. A trail of footprints marked the dust covering the diamond-patterned wooden floor. From the ceiling hung two lamps with crystal droplets, like frost flowers.

"Hello?" she called.

The echo of her voice traveled through the room, but there was no reply. The footprints trailed off into the gloom. A little farther away she made out a dark wooden display cabinet covering an entire wall, divided into small pigeonholes like funeral niches. Alicia took a few steps forward, following the trail on the floor, but stopped when she realized that she was being watched. Glass eyes emerged from the shadows, framed by an ivory face that smiled with an expression of malice and defiance. The doll had red hair and wore a black silk outfit.

Alicia walked on a couple of meters and then noticed that the doll wasn't alone. Each of those compartments housed a small being dressed in finery—over a hundred figures, all of them smiling, all of them looking without blinking. They were the size of tiny children, and even in the gloom she could appreciate their meticulous, exquisite finish, from the shining nails to the small white teeth peeping behind glossy lips to the pupils within each iris.

"Who are you?" The voice came from the back of the room, where a figure was seated on a chair in the corner.

"I'm Alicia. Alicia Gris. I didn't mean to scare you."

The figure stood up and approached her very slowly. It emerged from the shadows into the dim light filtering in through the entrance, and Alicia recognized the face of the girl in the set of photographs she'd seen in Valls's office. "You've got a lovely collection of dolls," she said.

"Hardly anyone likes them. My father says they look like vampires. Most people are frightened by them."

"That's why I like them," said Alicia.

*

Mercedes observed that curious presence intently. For a second she thought the stranger had something in common with the pieces in her collection, as if one of them had not become frozen in an ivory childhood and had grown up to become a woman of flesh, blood, and shadow.

The woman called Alicia smiled and held out her hand. "Mercedes, right?"

Mercedes nodded and shook her hand. Something in those cold, penetrating eyes calmed her and gave her confidence. She reckoned the woman was not quite thirty, but like the dolls in the display cabinet, the closer Mercedes looked at her, the more difficult it was to determine her age. She had a slender figure and dressed the way Mercedes herself would secretly like to dress, had she not been certain that both her father and Doña Irene would never have allowed it. This woman exuded that indefinable air that Valls's daughter knew could captivate men and make them behave like children, or lick their lips like old men when she went by. She'd seen her arrive with that policeman and go into the house. The very idea that somebody high up could have thought of that creature as the ideal person to find her father seemed to her both incomprehensible and hopeful.

"You've come about my father, haven't you, miss?"

Alicia nodded. "There's no need to be all formal and call me 'miss.' I'm not much older than you."

Mercedes shrugged. "I was brought up to address everyone politely."

"I was brought up to behave as if I came from a good home, and look at me now."

Mercedes gave a little laugh, slightly embarrassed. She wasn't used to laughing, Alicia thought: she laughed the same way as she observed the world, like a child hiding in the body of a woman. Or a woman who had lived almost all her life in a children's storybook, peopled by servants and dolls with glass hearts.

"Are you a policewoman?" Mercedes asked.

"Something like that."

"You don't look like one."

"Nobody is what they seem."

Mercedes considered those words. "I suppose you're right."

"Can we sit down?"

"Of course." Mercedes rushed over to a corner to grab a couple of chairs and placed them within the pool of light coming through the door. Alicia sat down with care and when the girl noticed the agony in her face, she helped her. Alicia smiled weakly, cold sweat covering her forehead. Mercedes hesitated for a moment but then dried Alicia's forehead with a handkerchief she carried in her pocket. Alicia's skin was so fine and soft that she wanted to stroke it with her fingers. She banished the idea from her thoughts and felt herself blushing without really knowing why. "Are you better?"

Alicia nodded.

"What is it?"

"It's an old wound. From when I was a little girl. Sometimes, if it's raining or there's a lot of humidity, it hurts."

"An accident?"

"Something like that."

"I'm sorry."

"These things happen. Do you mind if I ask you a few questions?"

The girl's eyes filled with anxiety. "About my father?"

Alicia nodded again.

"Are you going to find him?"

"I'm going to try."

Mercedes looked at her longingly. "The police won't be able to find him. You'll have to do it."

"What makes you say that?"

Valls's daughter lowered her eyes. "Because I think he doesn't want to be found."

"Why would that be?"

Mercedes continued looking crestfallen. "I don't know."

"Doña Mariana says that the morning your father left, you told her you thought he'd left forever, that he wasn't going to return."

"It's true."

"Did your father say something that evening that would make you think such a thing?"

"I don't know."

"Did you speak to him on the night of the ball?"

"I went up to his office to see him. He didn't come down to the party at any point. He was with Vicente."

"Vicente Carmona, the bodyguard?"

"Yes. He was sad. He was odd."

"Did he tell you why?"

"No. My father only tells me what I want to hear."

Alicia laughed. "All fathers do that."

"Does yours too?"

Alicia replied with a smile, and Mercedes didn't insist. "I remember he was looking at a book when I went into his office," she said instead.

"Do you remember whether it was a book with a black cover?"

Mercedes looked surprised. "I think so. I asked him what it was, and he said it wasn't a book for young ladies. I felt as if he didn't want me to see it. Perhaps it was a banned book. "

"Does your father have banned books?"

Mercedes nodded, again looking slightly embarrassed.

"They're in a locked cupboard, in his ministry office. He doesn't know that I know."

"He won't find out from me. Tell me, does your father often take you to his office in the ministry?"

Mercedes shook her head. "I've only been there twice."

"And in town?"

"In Madrid?"

"Yes, in Madrid."

"I've got everything I need here," she said, rather unconvinced.

"Perhaps we could go into town together sometime. For a stroll. Or to the cinema. Do you like going to the cinema?"

Mercedes bit her lip. "I've never been. But I'd like to. Go with you, I mean."

Alicia patted her hands and gave her a winning smile. "We'll go and see a Cary Grant film."

"I don't know who that is."

"He's the perfect man."

"Why?"

"Because he doesn't exist."

Mercedes laughed again with that sad laughter that seemed imprisoned inside her.

"What else did your father say that night? Do you remember?"

"Not much. He said he loved me. And that he'd always love me, come what may."

"Anything else?"

"He was nervous. He wished me good night and then stayed there, talking to Vicente."

"Were you able to hear what they were saying?"

"It's not right to listen behind closed doors . . .".

"I've always thought that's how you get to hear the best conversations," Alicia suggested.

Mercedes smiled mischievously. "My father thought that someone had been there. During the party. In his office."

"Did he say who?"

"No."

"What else? Anything that struck you as unusual?"

"Something about a list. He said someone had a list. I don't know who."

"Do you know what kind of list he meant?"

"No, I don't. A list of numbers, I think. I'm sorry. I'd like to be able to help you more, but that's all I managed to hear . . ."

"You've helped me a lot, Mercedes."

"Really?"

Alicia nodded and stroked Mercedes's cheek. Nobody had caressed her like that since ten years earlier, when her mother had been confined to her bed and the bones in her hands had ended up like hooks.

"What do you think your father meant when he said 'come what may'?"

"I don't know."

"Had you ever heard him say that before?"

Mercedes fell silent and stared straight at Alicia.

"Mercedes?"

"I don't like talking about that."

"About what?"

"My father told me never to talk about it to anyone."

"But I'm not anyone. You can talk to me."

"If my father found out that I'd told you—"

"He won't find out."

"Do you swear?"

"I swear. Cross my heart and hope to die."

"Don't say that."

"Tell me, Mercedes. What you tell me will remain between you and me. You have my word."

Mercedes looked at her, her eyes brimming with tears. Alicia pressed her hand.

"I must have been seven or eight, I don't know. It was in Madrid, at the Sisters of the Holy Infant Jesus School. Every afternoon my father's bodyguards would come and fetch me from school. We girls all waited in the cypress-tree patio for our parents or maids to come and pick us up at five thirty. The lady often came. She always stood on the other side of the gates, looking at me. Sometimes she smiled at me. I didn't know who she was. But she was there almost every day. She would signal to me to come closer, although she scared me a bit. One afternoon, the security guards were late. Something had happened in Madrid, in the center of town. I remember that all the other cars came and took the other girls away, and I was left alone, waiting. I'm not quite sure how it happened, but when one of the cars was leaving, the lady slipped in through the gates. She came up to me and knelt down before me. Then she hugged me and began to cry. She was kissing me. I got frightened and started shouting. The nuns came out. The security guards arrived, and I remember that two of the men grabbed her by her arms and dragged her away. The lady shouted and cried. I remember that one of my father's men punched her in the face. Then she pulled out something she'd been hiding in her handbag. It was a gun. The bodyguards moved out of the way, and she ran toward me. Her face was covered in blood. She hugged me and told me she loved me and I should never forget her."

"What happened next?"

Mercedes swallowed hard. "Then Vicente came closer and shot her in the head. The lady collapsed at my feet in a pool of blood. I remember because one of the nuns picked me up and took off my shoes, which were stained with the lady's blood. She handed me over to one of the bodyguards, who took me along to the car with Vicente. Vicente started up the engine and we drove off very fast, but through the rear window I could see two of the security men dragging the lady's body away . . ."

Mercedes searched Alicia's eyes, and Alicia hugged her.

"That night my father told me that that lady was mad. He said the police had arrested her a few times for trying to kidnap children from Madrid schools. He told me that nobody would ever hurt me, and that now I had nothing to worry about. And he told me never to tell anyone what had happened that day. Come what may. I never returned to the school. Doña Irene became my tutor, and I was schooled at home from then on . . ."

Alicia let Mercedes cry in her arms, stroking her hair. A desperate calm was falling over the girl when Alicia heard the horn of Vargas's car in the distance and stood up. "I have to go now, Mercedes. But I'll come back. And we'll go to Madrid and I'll take you to the cinema. But you must promise me you'll be all right until then."

Mercedes took her hands and nodded. "Will you find my father?"

"I promise."

Alicia kissed her on the forehead and walked away, limping. Mercedes sat on the floor, hugging her knees in the shadows of her dolls' world, now broken forever.

II

THE DRIVE BACK to Madrid was marked by rain and silence. Alicia sat with her eyes closed and her head leaning on the misted-up window, her mind a thousand miles away. Vargas watched her out of the corner of his eye, throwing the occasional bait here and there to see if he could draw her into conversation and fill the void that had persisted since they'd left Villa Mercedes.

"You were hard over there with Valls's secretary," he ventured. "To put it mildly."

"She's a harpy," retorted Alicia in an unfriendly murmur.

"If you'd rather, we can talk about the weather."

"It's raining," said Alicia. "What else do you want to talk about?"

"You could tell me what happened in there, in the garden cottage."

"Nothing happened."

"You were there for half an hour. I hope you weren't tightening the screws on anyone else. It would be good if we didn't get everyone against us on the first day. Just saying."

Alicia didn't reply.

"Listen, this only works if we work together. Sharing information. Because I'm not your chauffeur."

"Then perhaps it won't work. I can take taxis if you prefer. It's what I usually do."

Vargas sighed.

"Pay no attention to me, OK?" Alicia replied. "I'm not feeling very well."

Vargas observed her carefully. She kept her eyes closed and clutched her hip in agony.

"Shall we go to a pharmacy or something?"

"What for?"

"I don't know. You don't look too good."

"Thanks."

"Can I get you something for the pain?"

Alicia shook her head. Her breathing sounded labored.

"Shall we stop for a moment?" Vargas said at last. He spotted a roadside restaurant a few hundred meters farther on, next to a service station, where about a dozen trucks had congregated. He left the main road and stopped opposite the entrance. Then he walked around the car and opened the door, offering Alicia his hand.

"I can manage alone."

After two attempts, Vargas held her below her shoulders and pulled her out of the car. He picked up the handbag she'd left on the seat and hung it over her arm. "Can you walk?"

Alicia nodded, and they made their way to the restaurant door. Vargas held her gently by the arm, and she, for once, did nothing to rebuff his help. When they entered the bar, the policeman made a brief inspection of the place, as was his habit, locating entrances and exits and checking those present. A group of truck drivers were talking at a table covered with a paper tablecloth, house wine, and soda-water siphons. Some of them turned to have a look at Alicia and Vargas, but as soon as they met his eyes, they buried their faces and thoughts in their plates of stew without a murmur. The waiter, looking the part of the innkeeper in an operetta, was walking past with a trayful of cups of coffee. He pointed them toward what must have been the restaurant's best table, separated from the plebs and with a view of the road.

"I'll be with you in a second," he said.

Vargas led Alicia to the table and settled her in a chair with her back to the other customers. He sat down opposite and looked at her expectantly. "You're beginning to frighten me."

"Don't get too carried away."

The waiter returned swiftly, all smiles and attentiveness in welcoming such distinguished and unexpected visitors. "Good afternoon, will madam and the gentleman wish to have lunch? We have a delicious stew today, made by my wife, but we can also prepare whatever you like. A little fillet steak . . ."

"Some water, please," said Alicia.

"Right away."

The waiter hurried off to fetch a bottle of mineral water and returned armed with a couple of menus handwritten on thick cardboard. He poured two glasses of water and, guessing that his presence would be best appreciated for its brevity, withdrew with a bow, saying, "I'll leave the menu with you in case you want to have a look at it."

Vargas mumbled a thank-you, while Alicia drank her glass of water as if she'd just crossed the desert.

"Are you hungry?"

She took her bag and stood up. "I'm just going to the bathroom. You order for me." As she walked past Vargas, she put a hand on his shoulder and smiled weakly. "Don't worry. I'll be fine." She hobbled off toward the ladies' room and disappeared behind the door.

The waiter watched her from the bar, probably wondering what the relationship was between that man and such an unusual young woman.

*

Alicia closed the bathroom door and bolted it. The room stank of disinfectant and was hemmed in by discolored tiles covered in obscene drawings and infelicitous witticisms. A narrow window framed a ventilator through whose blades slanted sharp beams of dusty light. Alicia went over to the sink and leaned on it, opening the tap to let the water run. It reeked of rust. She opened her bag and with shaking hands pulled out a metal case from which she took a syringe and a phial with a rubber top. She plunged the needle into the phial and half filled the cylinder, then rapped it with her fingers and pushed the piston down until a thick, shiny drop formed on the tip of the needle. Alicia then walked over to the toilet, closed the lid, sat down, and, propping herself up against the wall with her left hand, pulled her dress up to her hip. She felt the inside of her thigh, breathed deeply, and plunged the needle a couple of centimeters above the top of her stocking, emptying the contents.

Seconds later she felt the rush. The needle fell from her hands, and her mind clouded over while a cold sensation spread through her veins. She leaned against the wall and let a couple of minutes go by without thinking of anything except that ice-cold snake creeping through her body. For a moment she felt she was losing consciousness. She opened her eyes to find herself in a foul-smelling broom-cupboard of a room that she didn't recognize. A distant sound, of someone knocking on the door, roused her.

"Alicia, are you all right?"

It was Vargas's voice.

"Yes," she forced herself to say. "I'll be right out."

The policeman's footsteps took a while to move away. Alicia cleaned the blood trickling down her thigh and smoothed down her dress. She washed her face in the sink and dried it with a piece of thick paper hanging from a nail on the wall. Before leaving, she looked at her face in the mirror. It reminded her of one of Mercedes's dolls. She put on some lipstick and tidied up her clothes. Taking a deep breath, she prepared herself for her return to the world of the living.

When she got back to the table, she sat down opposite Vargas and gave him her sweetest smile. He was holding a glass of beer, which he didn't seem to have tasted, and looked at her with undisguised concern.

"I ordered a fillet steak for you," he said at last. "Rare. Protein."

Alicia nodded to indicate that she thought his choice was perfect.

"I didn't know what to ask for, but you strike me as a carnivore."

"Bleeding meat is all I eat," Alicia remarked. "If possible from innocent creatures."

He didn't laugh at her joke. Alicia caught her own image in his eyes. "You can say it."

"Say what?"

"What you're thinking."

"What am I thinking?"

"That I look like Dracula's girlfriend."

Vargas frowned.

"That's what Leandro always says," said Alicia in a friendly tone. "It doesn't bother me. I'm used to it."

"That isn't what I was thinking."

"I'm sorry about earlier."

"There's nothing to be sorry about."

The waiter came over carrying two dishes and an obliging grin.

"Fillet steak for the young lady . . . and the house stew for the gentleman. Anything else? A bit more bread? A glass of wine from the local winery?"

Vargas shook his head. Alicia glanced at the steak on her plate, flanked by French fries, and sighed.

"If you like, I can cook it a bit longer," the waiter offered.

"It's fine, thanks."

They began to eat in silence, exchanging the occasional conciliatory look and smile. Alicia wasn't hungry, but she made an effort and pretended to enjoy her steak.

"It's good. How's your stew? Makes you want to marry the cook?"

Vargas put down his spoon and leaned back in the chair. Alicia knew he was observing her dilated pupils and drowsy face.

"How much did you inject?"

"It's none of your business."

"What sort of a wound is it?"

"The sort a well-brought-up young lady doesn't talk about."

"If we're going to be working together, I need to know what to expect."

"We're not engaged. This will last a couple of days. You don't need to introduce me to your mother."

Vargas didn't show the slightest hint of a smile.

"It's from when I was a child. During the bombings, in the war. The doctor who rebuilt my hip hadn't slept for twenty hours, and he did his best. I think I still carry a couple of souvenirs in there from Mussolini's air force."

"In Barcelona?"

Alicia nodded.

"I had a colleague in the Force who came from there. He lived for twenty years with a piece of shrapnel the size of a stuffed olive stuck to his aorta."

"Did he die in the end?"

"Run over by a newspaper delivery van as he stood outside a railway station."

"One can never trust the press. At the slightest chance, they'll do you in. What about you? Where did you spend the war?"

"Here and there. Mostly in Toledo."

"In or out of the siege?"

"What difference does it make?"

"Mementoes?"

Vargas unbuttoned his shirtfront and showed her a circular scar on the right-hand side of his chest.

"May I?" asked Alicia.

Vargas nodded. Alicia leaned forward and felt the scar with her fingers. Behind the bar, the waiter dropped the glass he was drying.

"It looks like the real thing," said Alicia. "Does it hurt?"

Vargas buttoned up his shirt again. "Only when I laugh. Honestly."

"With this work, you can probably barely afford all the aspirin you need."

Vargas smiled at last. Alicia raised her glass of water.

"A toast to our sorrows."

The policeman held up his glass, and they toasted. They ate in silence, Vargas mopping up the stew with bread and Alicia picking at her meat here and there. Once she'd pushed her plate to one side, he started stealing her remaining fries, which was almost the whole serving.

"So what's the plan for this afternoon?" he asked.

"I thought you could stop by headquarters to get a copy of Salgado's letters and see whether there is anything new on that front. And if there's enough time, pay a visit to that Cascos guy at the publishing house, Ariadna. There's something there that doesn't quite add up."

"Don't you want us to go and see him together?"

"I have other plans. I thought I'd pay a visit to an old friend who might be able to lend us a hand. It's better if I see him on my own. He's a peculiar character."

"If he's a friend of yours, that goes without saying. Is the inquiry about the book?"

"Yes."

Vargas signaled to the waiter to bring the bill. "Don't you want a coffee, a dessert, or something else?"

"In the car you can treat me to one of your imported cigarettes."

"This isn't a ruse to get rid of me at the first opportunity, is it?"

Alicia shook her head. "We'll meet at seven in the Café Gijón and 'share information.'"

Vargas looked at her severely. She raised a hand solemnly. "Promise."

"You'd better. Where should I drop you?"

"Recoletos. It's on your way."

12

THE YEAR ALICIA GRIS arrived in Madrid, her mentor and puppet master Leandro Montalvo taught her that to keep your sanity, you must have a place in the world where you can lose yourself if necessary. That place, that last refuge, is a small annex of the soul, and when the world reverts to its absurd comedy, you can always run there, lock yourself in, and throw away the key. One of Leandro's most irritating habits was that he was always right. In time, Alicia ended up bowing to the evidence, deciding that perhaps she did need to find her own protected space. The absurdities of the world no longer seemed the stuff of comedy: they had become mere routine. And for once, destiny chose to deal her a good hand of cards. Like all great discoveries, it happened when she least expected it.

One faraway day during her first autumn in Madrid, when a downpour caught her strolling down Paseo de Recoletos, Alicia noticed a classical-style palace through the trees. Thinking it must be a museum, she decided to shelter there until the storm was over. Soaked to the skin, she walked up the grand staircase bordered by regal-looking statues, not noticing the name written on the lintel. A man with a listless gait and the piercing look of an owl had peeped out of the main door to watch the spectacle offered by the storm when he saw her arrive. Those bird eyes settled on Alicia as if she were a small rodent.

"Hello there," Alicia improvised. "What do you exhibit in here?"

Clearly unimpressed by her opening, the man inspected her through enlarged pupils. "We exhibit patience, young lady, and sometimes astonishment at the audacity of ignorance. This is the National Library."

Be it out of compassion or boredom, the gentleman with the owlish look informed her that she'd just set foot in one of the greatest libraries in the world, that over twenty-five million volumes awaited her inside. But if she'd come with the idea of using the bathrooms or reading fashion magazines, she had better turn around and catch pneumonia in the outdoor world.

"May I ask Your Lordship who you are?" asked Alicia.

"I haven't seen any lordships for years, but if you're referring to this humble person, let it be known that I'm the director of this house, and that one of my favorite pastimes is chucking out bumpkins and intruders."

"I understand, but I wish to become a member."

"And I wish I'd written *David Copperfield*, yet here I am, getting old and with no decent body of work to show for it. What's your name, dear?"

"Alicia Gris, at your service, and Spain's, sir."

"Not having given birth to any contemporary classic doesn't stop me from appreciating irony or impertinence. I can't answer for Spain, there being too many voices pretending to speak for her out there already, but I can't see how you could serve me, except to remind me that the years are advancing. However, I don't consider myself an ogre, and if your wish to become a member is sincere, I won't be the one to keep you in total illiteracy. My name is Bermeo Pumares."

"It's an honor, sir. I place myself in your expert hands to receive the guidance that will rescue me from ignorance and allow me, under your command, to cross the threshold of this Arcadia."

Bermeo Pumares raised his eyebrows and reconsidered his opponent.

"I'm beginning to get the vague impression that you can rescue yourself very well on your own, and that your ignorance is less sizable than your boldness, Señorita Gris. I'm also well aware that encyclopedic gluttony has ended up warping my speech, making it veer toward the baroque, but there's no need to make fun of an old teacher, either."

"It would never occur to me to do such a thing."

"I see. By their words ye shall know them. I like you, Alicia, even though I may not give that impression. Come inside and go over to the counter. Tell Puri that Pumares said to issue a card for you."

"How can I thank you?"

"By dropping by and reading good books, whichever you feel like reading, not what I or anyone else says you've got to read. I may be a touch dogmatic, but I'm not a pedant."

"You can be quite sure I will."

That afternoon Alicia got her reader's card and passed the first of many afternoons in the main reading room, getting acquainted with some of the treasures that centuries of human ingenuity had managed to conjure up. More than once she looked up from her page and found the owlish gaze of Don Bermeo Pumares, who liked ambling around the room to see what everyone was reading. He would gruffly eject those who had nodded off or were whispering, because, as he said, for slumbering minds and inane conversations the big outdoor world offered plenty of opportunity.

One day, after Alicia had proved her interest and voracious reading throughout an entire year, Bermeo Pumares invited her to follow him to the back room of the palatial building, into a section closed to the general public. There, he explained, lay the library's most precious volumes. The only readers allowed in were certain academics and scholars distinguished enough to obtain a special reader's card for their research work.

"You've never told me what you do in your more worldly activities, but I have a sneaking suspicion you may be a researcher yourself, and I'm not talking about inventing new penicillin treatments, or even unearthing incunabula among the ruins of Cistercian monasteries."

"You're on the right track."

"I've never been on the wrong track in my life. The problem with this dear country of ours is with the tracks themselves, not with those of us walking along them. The mysterious ways of our Lord, as they say."

"In my case, the mysterious ways are not those of the Lord, but what Your Eminence would call the machinery of state security."

Bermeo Pumares nodded slowly. "You're full of surprises, Alicia. A box of surprises one doesn't dare open, just in case."

"Wise decision."

Pumares handed her a card with her name on it. "In any case, I wanted to make sure, before leaving, that you had a researcher's card, so you can come along here whenever you feel in the mood."

"Before leaving?"

Pumares's expression turned serious. "Don Mauricio Valls's secretary has seen fit to inform me that I've been retroactively removed from my post, and that my last day at the head of this institution was yesterday, Wednesday. It seems that the minister's decision is the result of various factors, notable among which are, on the one hand, the minimal enthusiasm exhibited by my person toward the revered principles of the regime, whatever those may be, and on the other, the interest shown by the brother-in-law of one of our country's most prominent men in taking over the reins of this fine institution. Some cretin must believe that the title of chief librarian is as impressive in certain circles as an invitation to the presidential box at Real Madrid Stadium."

"I'm very sorry, Don Bermeo. I really am."

"Don't be sorry. Rarely in our country's history has a qualified person—or at least someone not completely incompetent—found himself heading a cultural institution. Strict controls and numerous specialized staff are in place to prevent this from happening. Meritocracy and the Mediterranean climate are by necessity incompatible. I suppose it's the price we pay for having the best olive oil in the world. The fact that an experienced librarian has actually run the National Library, even if only for fourteen months, was an unforeseen accident that the illustrious minds guiding our destinies have remedied, all the more so when there's no end of cronies and relatives to fill the post. All I can say is that I'll miss you. Alicia. You, your mysteries, and your jibes."

"Same here."

"I return to my beautiful Toledo, or what they've left of it, hoping I can rent a room in some peaceful country house on a hill with a decent view of the city. A place where I can spend the rest of my wasted existence peeing on the banks of the Tajo and rereading Cervantes and all his bitter rivals—most of which didn't live far from Toledo and failed to alter the course of this ship in the slightest, despite all the gold and all the verse of their century."

"And couldn't I help you? My trade isn't poetry, but you'd be surprised at my range of stylistic resources with which to stir up what should be left alone."

Pumares looked at her at length. "You wouldn't surprise me; you'd scare me, and I'm only bold enough with idiots. Besides, even if you're not aware of this, you've already helped me enough. Good luck, Alicia."

"Good luck, master."

Bermeo Pumares smiled, a wide and open smile. It was the first and last time Alicia saw him do that. He shook her hand firmly, lowering his voice. "Tell me something, Alicia. Out of curiosity, apart from your devotion to Mount Parnassus, knowledge, and all those exemplary things, what is it that really brings you to this place?"

She shrugged. "A memory."

The librarian raised his eyebrows.

"A childhood memory. Something I once dreamed when I was on the point of dying. That was a long time ago. A cathedral made of books . . ."

"And where was that?"

"In Barcelona. During the war."

The librarian nodded slowly, smiling to himself. "And you say you dreamed it? Are you sure?"

"Almost sure."

"Certainty is reassuring, but one can only learn by doubting. One more thing. The day will come when you'll have to rummage around where you shouldn't, and disturb the bottom of some murky pond. I know because you're not the first or the last person passing through this place with the same shadow as the one I see in your eyes. And when that day comes, and it will come, be assured that this house conceals far more than it appears to do, and that people like me come and go, but there's someone here who might one day be of use to you." Pumares pointed to a black door at the end of a vast arched gallery filled with books. "Behind that door there's a staircase that leads to the library's basements. Floors and floors of endless corridors with millions of books, many of which are incunabula. During the civil war alone half a million volumes were added to the collection to save them from being burned. But that's not the only thing down there. I suppose you've never come across the legend of the Recoletos palace vampire?"

"No."

"But you must admit that the idea intrigues you, at least for its melodramatic tone."

"I can't say it doesn't. But are you being serious?"

Pumares winked at her. "I already told you once that, despite appearances, I know how to appreciate irony. I leave you with that thought. Mull it over. And I hope you'll never stop coming to this place, or to another similar one."

"I'll do so, as a toast to your health."

"Better to the health of the world, which is in the doldrums. Take good care of yourself, Alicia. I hope you find the path that I missed."

And that was how, without saying another word, Don Bermeo Pumares crossed the researchers' gallery one last time and then the large reading room of the National Library and continued through its doors without once turning his head to look back until he'd stepped out through the entrance on Paseo de Recoletos and set off, walking toward oblivion, one more drop amid the unending flood of lives shipwrecked in gray ancestral Spain.

And that was also how, months later, the day came when her curiosity was greater than her prudence, and Alicia decided to go through that black door and dive into the shadows of the basement floors hidden beneath the library, to unravel its secrets.

A LEGEND IS a lie that has been whipped up to explain a universal truth. Places where lies and fantasy pepper the earth are particularly apt for the development of these tales. The first time Alicia Gris lost her way in the dark corridors of the library basements in search of the supposed vampire and its legend, all she found was a subterranean city peopled by hundreds of thousands of books, waiting silently among cobwebs and echoes.

Few are the occasions when life allows us to stroll through our dreams, caressing a lost memory with our hands. More than once, while she explored that place, Alicia stopped in the dark, expecting to hear once again the explosion of the bombs and the metallic roar of the airplanes. After two hours spent wandering about, floor after floor, she didn't meet a soul: only a couple of gourmet bookworms making their way up the spine of a collection of Schiller verse in search of a snack. On her second incursion, this time armed with a flashlight she'd bought at an ironmonger's in Plaza de Callao, she didn't even meet her friends the worms, but as she was leaving, after an exploratory hour and a half, she discovered a note pinned on the door that said:

Pretty flashlight.
But don't you ever change your colors?
In this country that is almost an eccentricity.

Yours sincerely,
Virgilio

The following day, Alicia stopped at the ironmonger's again to buy another flashlight, just like hers, and a packet of batteries. Sporting the same blue coat, she walked into the farthest part of the bottom floor and sat down next to a collection of novels by the Brontë sisters, her favorite books since her years at the orphanage. There she pulled out the marinated porkloin sandwich and the beer she'd bought at the Café Gijón and tucked into her lunch. Afterward, with a full stomach, she nodded off.

The sound of footsteps in the shadows roused her. Soft steps, like feathers being dragged along the dust. She opened her eyes and saw needles of amber light filtering through the books on the other side of the corridor. The bubble of light moved along slowly, like a jellyfish. Alicia sat up and brushed the bread crumbs off her lapels. Seconds later, a dark profile turned the corner of the corridor and kept moving forward in her direction, the steps faster now. The first thing Alicia noticed was the eyes, blue and reared in a world of darkness. The skin was as pale as the pages of an unread book, the hair straight and combed back.

"I've brought you a flashlight," said Alicia. "And batteries."

"What a kind gesture."

The voice was hoarse and oddly high-pitched.

"My name is Alicia Gris. You must be Virgilio."

"Touché."

"This is just a formality, but I need to ask you whether you're a vampire."

Virgilio smiled questioningly. Alicia thought he looked like a moray eel when he did that.

"If I were, I'd be dead by now, given the garlicky stench emanating from the sandwich you've just polished off."

"So you don't drink human blood."

"I prefer orange Fanta. Are you making up these questions as you go, or did you write them down in advance?"

"I'm afraid I've been the object of a practical joke."

"And who isn't? That's the essence of life. Tell me, how can I help you?"

"Señor Bermeo Pumares told me about you."

"That's what I imagined. Scholastic humor."

"He mentioned that you might be able to help me if I ever needed help."

"And do you?"

"I'm not sure."

"Then that means you don't. May I see the flashlight?"

"It's yours."

Virgilio accepted the gift and inspected it.

"How many years have you been working here?"

"About thirty-five. I started with my father."

"Did your father also live down in these depths?"

"I think you're mistaking us for a family of crustaceans."

"Is that how the legend of the vampire-librarian began?"

Virgilio's laughter sounded like sandpaper. "There's never been such a legend," he assured her.

"So Señor Pumares invented it to pull my leg?"

"Technically speaking, he didn't invent it. He got it out of a novel by Julián Carax."

"I've never heard of him."

"Most people haven't. It's very entertaining. It's about a diabolical murderer who lives in hiding in the basement of the Bibliothèque Nationale in Paris and uses his victims' blood to write a demonic book with which he hopes to ward off Satan himself. A delight. If I manage to find it, I'll lend it to you. Tell me, are you a policewoman or something like that?"

"Something like that."

*

During that year, in between the shady tasks and other dirty jobs Leandro pressed on her, Alicia visited Virgilio in his underground domain whenever she had the chance. Eventually, the librarian became her only real friend in town. Virgilio always had books ready to lend her, and his choices were always perfect.

"Listen, Alicia, don't misunderstand me, but one of these evenings, would you like to come to the cinema with me?"

"So long as it's not to see a film about saints or exemplary lives."

"May the immortal spirit of Don Miguel de Cervantes strike me down right now, should it ever occur to me to suggest we see an epic film on the triumph of the human spirit."

"Amen," said Alicia.

Sometimes, when Alicia had no assignment, they'd stroll over to one of the cinemas on Gran Vía to catch the last show. Virgilio loved Technicolor, biblical stories, and films about Romans, which allowed him to see the sun and enjoy the muscular torsos of the gladiators without restraint. One night, when he was walking her back to the Hotel Hispania after they'd watched *Quo Vadis*, Alicia stopped in front of a bookshop window on Gran Vía. He stood there, looking at her.

"Alicia, if you were a young boy I'd ask for your hand, to indulge in illicit cohabitation."

She held out her hand to him, and he kissed it.

"What lovely things you say, Virgilio."

The man smiled, with all the sadness of the world in his eyes.

"That's what comes from being well read. One already knows all the verses and all the tricks of fate."

Some Saturday afternoons, Alicia would buy a few bottles of orange Fanta and go over to the library to listen to Virgilio's stories about obscure authors nobody had ever heard of, authors whose ill-fated biographies were sealed in the book-lined crypt of the lowest basement floor.

"Alicia, I know it's none of my business, but this thing with your hip . . . What happened?"

"The war."

"Tell me."

"I don't like to talk about it."

"I can imagine. But that's precisely why. Tell me. It will do you good."

Alicia had never told anybody the story of how a stranger had saved her life the night Mussolini's air force, recruited to support the Nacionales, had bombed Barcelona without pity. She surprised herself as she listened to her tale and realized that she'd forgotten nothing. She could still perceive the smell of sulfur and burned flesh in the air.

"And you never found out who that man was?"

"A friend of my parents. Someone who really loved them."

She didn't realize until Virgilio handed her a handkerchief that she'd been crying, and that, however embarrassed and angry she felt, she couldn't stop herself.

"I've never seen you cry."

"Nor has anyone else. And you'd better hope it doesn't happen again."

*

That afternoon, after visiting Villa Mercedes and sending Vargas off to sniff around police headquarters, Alicia walked over to the National Library. As they knew her well, she didn't even have to show her card. She crossed the reading room and headed for the wing reserved for researchers. A large number of academics were daydreaming at their desks when Alicia passed discreetly by on her way to the black door at the far end. Over the years she'd learned to decipher Virgilio's habits. It was early afternoon, so he would probably be putting away the incunabula used by the scholars that morning on the third floor. There he was, armed with the flashlight she had given him, whistling to a melody on the radio and absentmindedly swaying his pale skeleton in time to the music. The uniqueness of the scene made such an impression on her she felt it worthy of its own legend.

"Your tropical rhythm is fascinating, Virgilio."

"The *clave* tempo does get under your skin. Have they let you out early today, or have I got the day wrong?"

"I'm on a semiofficial visit."

"Don't tell me I'm being arrested."

"No, but your knowledge is being sequestered temporarily to be put at the service of the national interest."

"If that's the case, tell me how I can help."

"I'd like you to have a quick look at something."

Alicia pulled out the book she'd found hidden in Valls's desk and handed it to him. Virgilio took it and switched on the flashlight. As soon as he saw the design of the coiled staircase on the cover, he looked Alicia straight in the eyes. "But have you even the remotest idea of what this is?"

"I was hoping you'd be able to enlighten me."

Virgilio looked over his shoulder, as if he feared there might be someone else in the passageway, and motioned with his head toward a door. "We'd better go to my office."

Virgilio's office was a cubicle squeezed into the end of a corridor on the lowest floor. One got the feeling that the room had grown out of the walls as a result of the pressure of those millions of volumes stacked floor upon floor, a sort of cabin formed of books, lever-arch files, and all sorts of peculiar objects, from glasses full of paintbrushes and sewing needles to spectacles, magnifying glasses, and tubes of pigments. Alicia guessed that this was where Virgilio undertook the occasional emergency surgery on damaged volumes. The cubicle's pièce de resistance was a small fridge, full of orange Fanta. Virgilio pulled a couple bottles out and served them. Then, armed with his special magnifying glasses, he placed the book on a piece of red velvet and slipped on a pair of silk gloves.

"From all this ceremonial, I deduce the volume is a rare one—"

"Shhh," said Virgilio. For the next few minutes he examined the Víctor Mataix book with fascination, licking his lips at every page, stroking each illustration, and savoring every engraving as if it were some fiendishly choice dish.

"Virgilio, you're making me nervous. Say something, for God's sake!"

The man turned around, his ice-blue eyes amplified by the magnifier of those watchmaker's lenses. "I suppose you can't tell me where you found it," he began.

"That's right."

"This is a collector's piece. If you like, I can tell you who you could sell it to for a very good price, although you'd have to be careful because this is a censored book, not only by the government but also by the Holy Mother Church."

"This one and hundreds of others. What can you tell me about it that I can't imagine?"

Virgilio removed his magnifier glasses and drank half a Fanta in one gulp. "I'm sorry, I got all emotional," he confessed. "I haven't seen one of these treats for at least twenty years . . ."

He leaned back in his moth-eaten armchair, his eyes shining. Alicia knew that the day prophesied by Bermeo Pumares had arrived.

14

"AS FAR AS I know," Virgilio explained, "eight books of the series *The Labyrinth of the Spirits* were published in Barcelona between 1931 and 1938. I can't tell you much about the author, Víctor Mataix. I know he worked occasionally as an illustrator of children's books and that he published a few novels under a pseudonym in a third-rate publishing house called Barrido & Escobillas. It was rumored that he was the illegitimate son of an industrialist from Barcelona who had made his fortune in South America and disowned both Víctor and his mother—a relatively popular actress at the time in the theaters of the Paralelo district. Mataix also worked as a set designer and produced catalogs for a toy manufacturer in Igualada. In 1931 he published the first installment of *The Labyrinth of the Spirits*, under the title *Ariadna and the Underwater Cathedral*. Published by Orbe, if I'm not mistaken."

"Does the expression 'the entrance to the labyrinth' mean anything to you?"

Virgilio tilted his head. "Well, in this case, the labyrinth is the city."

"Barcelona."

"The other Barcelona. The Barcelona of the books."

"A kind of hell."

"Whatever."

"And where is the entrance?"

Virgilio shrugged, looking pensive. "A city has a lot of entrances. I don't know. Can I think about it?"

Alicia nodded. "What about Ariadna? Who is she?"

"Read the book. It's worth it."

"Give me a preview."

"Ariadna is a girl, the protagonist of all the novels in the series. Ariadna was the name of Mataix's eldest daughter, for whom he presumably wrote the books. The character is a reflection of his daughter. Mataix was also partially inspired by the *Alice in Wonderland* books, which were his daughter's favorites. Don't you find that fascinating?"

"Can't you see how I'm trembling with emotion?"

"When you behave like this, you're insufferable."

"But you do suffer me. That's why I love you so much. Go on, tell me more."

"Oh, what a cross I have to bear. Celibate and with even fewer prospects than Le Fanu's Carmilla . . ."

"The book, Virgilio, back to the book . . ."

"Well, the thing is that Ariadna was Mataix's Alice, and instead of a Wonderland, he invented a Barcelona of horrors, an infernal town, a nightmare. With every book the backdrop—which is as much a protagonist as Ariadna and the extravagant characters she comes across during her adventures, or perhaps more so—becomes increasingly sinister. The last known book of the series, *Ariadna and the Machines of the Averno*, published in the middle of the civil war, is about a besieged city that in the end is invaded by the enemy. The resulting carnage makes the fall of Constantinople look like a Laurel and Hardy film."

"Did you say the last known book?"

"There are those who think that when he disappeared after the war, Mataix was concluding his ninth and last book of the series. In fact, years ago large sums were being offered among book collectors to anyone who could get hold of that manuscript, but as far as I know, it was never found."

"And how did Mataix disappear?"

Virgilio shrugged. "Barcelona after the war? What better place to disappear?"

"And would it be possible to find more books of this series?"

Virgilio finished his Fanta while he shook his head slowly. "That would be very difficult. About ten or twelve years ago I heard that two or three copies of *The Labyrinth* were discovered at the bottom of a box in the Cervantes Bookshop in Seville, and they fetched a lot of money. Right now, I'd say the only possibility of finding anything would be in the bookshop of Costa, the antiquarian in Vic, or else in Barcelona. Gustavo Barceló, perhaps, or maybe, if you're very lucky, at Sempere's, but I wouldn't get too excited."

"Sempere & Sons?"

Virgilio looked at her in surprise. "You know it?"

"I've heard of it."

"I'd try Barceló first. He's the one who deals in special items and is in touch with top collectors. And if Costa has it, Barceló will know."

"Would Barceló be willing to talk to me?"

"I gather he's semiretired, but he always finds time for a good-looking young lady. You know what I mean."

"I'll doll myself up."

"Pity I won't be there to see it. You're not going to tell me what all this is about, are you?"

"I still don't know, Virgilio."

"Can I ask you a favor?"

"Of course."

"When this business you're dealing with is over, if it does indeed end and you're still in one piece and still have this book, bring it to me. I'd love to spend a few hours with it alone."

"And why shouldn't I come out of it in one piece?"

"Who knows? If there's one thing all Mataix's *Labyrinth* books have in common, it's that anyone who touches them has a bad ending."

"Another one of your legends?"

"No. This one is true."

*

At the end of the nineteenth century, an island in the shape of a literary café came unstuck from the mainland of reality. From then on it has floated about, frozen in time, at the mercy of history's currents, through the grand avenues of an imagined Madrid, where it can usually be found beached a few steps away from the National Library and flying the flag of the Café Gijón. There it awaits, a drifting hourglass ready to save any castaway who arrives with a parched spirit or a dry palate, offering them, just for the price of a coffee, the chance to look at themselves in the mirror of memory and for a moment believe they'll live forever.

Evening was falling when Alicia crossed the avenue toward the doors of the Café Gijón. Vargas was waiting at a table by the window, savoring one of his imported cigarettes and watching the passersby with his policeman's eye. When he saw her come in, he looked up and signaled to her. Alicia sat down and managed to catch a waiter's attention as he passed by. She asked for a coffee to shake off the cold that had clung to her in the basement of the library.

"Have you been waiting long?" Alicia asked.

"All my life," replied Vargas. "Fruitful afternoon?"

"Depends. How about you?"

"I can't complain. After dropping you off I went by Valls's publishing house to pay a visit to Pablo Cascos Buendía. You were right. There's something there that doesn't quite add up."

"And?"

"Cascos himself turns out to be little more than an oaf. Full of himself, but still an oaf."

"The simpler they are, the more dashing they think they are."

"First of all, our friend Cascos offered me a luxury tour of the offices and then proceeded to rhapsodize about the extraordinary person and exemplary life of Don Mauricio, as if his own life depended on it."

"You're probably not far wrong. People like Valls usually drag behind them an endless court of sycophants and enablers."

"I must say, there was no shortage of either of those. Still, Cascos did seem a bit nervous. He could smell something and didn't stop asking questions."

"Did he say why Valls had asked him to come to his home?"

"I had to tighten the screws quite a bit. At first he wouldn't say a word."

"And then you criticize me."

"When it comes to creeps and social climbers, I can work wonders, I must admit."

"Go on."

"Let me check my notebook, because there's a long story there. . . . Here it is. Listen. It turns out that when he was younger, Don Pablito was engaged to a damsel named Beatriz Aguilar. This Beatriz ditched the poor guy when he was doing his military service and ended up marrying, on the way to the maternity ward, as it were, someone called Daniel Sempere, the son of the owner of a secondhand bookshop in Barcelona called Sempere & Sons. This was Sebastián Salgado's favorite bookshop, which he visited a number of times as soon as he was out of prison, probably to catch up with the literary hits of the past twenty years. If you recall the report that comes with the file, two employees of the said bookshop, one of them Daniel Sempere, followed Salgado to the railway station the day he died."

Alicia's eyes flashed electricity. "Go on, please."

"Getting back to our man, Cascos. The fact is that our resentful hero, Cascos Buendía, the cuckolded second lieutenant, lost contact with his paramour, the lovely Beatriz, who, so Pablito swears, was and is a beauty that in a fair world would have ended up with him and not with a nobody like Daniel Sempere."

"Don't cast your pearls before swine," Alicia suggested.

"Without knowing her, and after spending half an hour with Cascos, I was glad for Doña Beatriz. That's the background. Now we take a leap forward in time to the middle of 1957, when after parading his CV and letters of recommendation from family members through most companies in Spain, Pablo Cascos receives an unexpected call from Editorial Ariadna, founded in 1947 by Don Mauricio Valls, who is still today its main shareholder and president. Cascos is summoned to an interview, and there he is offered a job in the sales department as representative for Aragon, Catalonia, and the Balearics. At good pay and with the possibility of promotion. Pablo Cascos is delighted to accept and starts working. Some months go by, and one day, out of the blue, Don Mauricio Valls turns up in his office and tells him he wants to take him to Horcher for lunch."

"Wow. How grand."

"Cascos did find it strange that the president of the publishing house and the most celebrated figure of Spanish culture should invite a mid-level employee, as Doña Mariana would say, whom he'd never met personally, to the flagship restaurant of the glorious Fascists, in whose basement they probably keep the Fuhrer's ashes in a cookie jar. Between appetizers, Valls gives him an account of all the good things he's heard about Cascos and his work in the sales department."

"And Cascos buys that?"

"Not quite. He's an idiot, but not that stupid. He senses there's something odd and begins to wonder whether the job he accepted is what he'd imagined. Valls continues with the pantomime until coffee is served. Then, when they've both become great friends and the minister has promised him a golden future in the company and told him he's thinking of him as senior management material for the publishing house, he lets the cat out of the bag."

"A small favor."

"Exactly. Valls comes out with his love for old bookshops, mainstay and sanctuary of the miracle of literature, in particular his love for the Sempere bookshop, for which he has a special fondness."

"Does Valls say where this fondness comes from?"

"He doesn't specify. He's a bit more precise when it comes to his interest in the Sempere family, in particular in an old friend of the owner's deceased wife, Isabella, Daniel's mother."

"Had Valls met this Isabella Sempere?"

"From what Cascos figured out, he'd met not only Isabella but also a good friend of hers. Guess who? Someone called David Martín."

"Bingo."

"Curious, isn't it? The mysterious name remembered, in extremis, by Doña Mariana during that distant conversation between the minister and his successor as the head of the Montjuïc Castle prison."

"Go on."

"Basically, Valls then spelled out his request. The minister would be eternally grateful if Cascos could, deploying his charm, ingenuity, and past devotion for Beatriz, contact her again and, let's say, repair the burned bridges."

"Seduce her?"

"To put it one way."

"What for?"

"To find out whether that man, David Martín, was still alive and had got in touch with the family at any point during all those years."

"Why didn't Valls himself ask the Semperes?"

"Again, Cascos asked him the same question."

"And the minister replied . . ."

"That it was a delicate subject, of a personal nature, and for unrelated reasons he would rather just sound things out and find out whether there was any basis in his suspicion that Martín was somewhere behind the scenes."

"What happened?"

"Well, Cascos, bold as brass, began to write flowery letters to his old lover."

"Did he get any answers?"

"Ah, you mischievous pixie, I can see you appreciate a good bedroom intrigue . . ."

"Focus, Vargas."

"Sorry. As I was saying, not at first. Beatriz, recent mother and wife, ignores the advances of this would-be Don Juan. But Cascos doesn't give up and begins to realize he's got a golden opportunity to recover what was taken away from him."

"Storm clouds in the marriage of Beatriz and Daniel?"

"Who knows? Too young a couple, married in a rush and with a child on the way before tying the knot . . . a perfect picture of fragility. The fact is that weeks go by and Bea doesn't reply to his letters. And Valls keeps insisting. Cascos begins to fret. Valls implies an ultimatum. Cascos sends a final letter to Beatriz, summoning her to a tryst in a suite at the Ritz."

"And Beatriz turns up?"

"No. But Daniel does."

"The husband?"

"Exactly."

"Had Beatriz told him about the letters?"

"Or he'd found them. . . . It doesn't matter either way. The thing is that Daniel Sempere turns up at the Ritz, and when Cascos opens the door in Casanova attire—perfumed bathrobe, slippers, and a glass of champagne in hand—good old Daniel beats the crap out of him until Cascos's face looks like the Rock of Gibraltar."

"I like the sound of Daniel."

"Hang on a minute. According to Cascos, whose face is still bruised, Daniel very nearly finished him off, and would have succeeded if the thrashing hadn't been interrupted by a plainclothes policeman who happened to be passing by."

"What?"

"This last bit doesn't seem to add up. My impression is that the policeman was no such thing, but a friend of Daniel's."

"And then?"

"Then Cascos returned to Madrid looking like a piece of toast, his tail between his legs and fear in his bones, thinking of what he was going to tell Valls."

"What did Valls say?"

"He listened to him without saying a word and made him swear he wouldn't tell anyone what had happened or what he'd asked him to do."

"And that's it?"

"That's what it looked like until, a few days before he disappeared, Valls phoned him again and asked him to come around to his home to talk about something. Although he didn't specify what that was, it might have been related to the Semperes, Isabella, and the mysterious David Martín."

"A meeting to which Valls never turned up."

"And that's as far as the story goes," Vargas concluded.

"What do we know about this David Martín? Were you able to gather any information about him?"

"Very little. But what I've found is promising. A forgotten author and, get this, a prisoner in Montjuïc Castle between 1939 and 1941."

"Coinciding with Valls and Salgado," remarked Alicia.

"Classmates, one could say."

"And once he leaves the prison, what happens to David Martín after 1941?"

"There is no after. The police records have him as 'disappeared and deceased during an attempted escape.'"

"And translated, that would mean . . . ?"

"In all likelihood a summary execution and burial in a ditch or a common grave."

"On Valls's orders?"

"Most probably. At that time Valls would have been the only person with the authority and power to do it."

Alicia weighed all that up for a few moments. "Why would Valls look for a dead man he himself had ordered executed?"

"Sometimes dead men aren't completely dead. Take El Cid, for example."

"Then let's suppose that Valls thinks Martín is still alive . . ."

"That would make sense."

"Alive and seeking vengeance. Perhaps pulling Salgado's strings in the shadows, waiting for the moment when he can get his revenge."

"Old friends made in prison are not easily forgotten," Vargas agreed.

"What isn't clear is what relationship there can be between Martín and the Semperes."

"There must be something, all the more so if Valls himself stopped the police from following that thread and preferred to use Cascos to investigate."

"Perhaps that something is the key to all this."

"Do we or don't we make a good team?"

Alicia noticed a feline smile lifting the corners of Vargas's mouth. "What else?"

"Wasn't that enough?"

"Out with it."

Vargas lit a cigarette and took a deep puff, studying the spirals of smoke creeping through his fingers. "Later, as you were still visiting your friend, after I'd practically solved the case single-handedly, only for you to get the medals for it, I went by headquarters to pick up the letters from Sebastián Salgado, the prisoner, and took the liberty of consulting my friend Ciges, the police graphologist. Don't worry, I didn't tell him what it was about, nor did he ask. I showed him four sheets of paper at random, and after having a good look at them, he told me there were quite a number of signs on the accents and in at least fourteen different letters and ligatures that ruled out a right-handed person. The angle of the ink strokes on the paper and the pressure—or something like that."

"And where does that take us?"

"To the fact that the person who wrote those threatening letters to Valls is left-handed."

"So?"

"So if you took some time to read the Barcelona Police report of Sebastián Salgado's surveillance after his surprising release in January 1958, it specifies that the comrade lost his left hand during his prison years and wore a prosthetic porcelain hand. It seems that during one of the interrogations someone overplayed his hand, if you'll excuse the pun."

Alicia seemed about to say something, but she suddenly fell silent, her gaze miles away. In less than a minute she'd started to grow pale, and Vargas noticed a film of perspiration on her forehead.

"Anyway," he said, "our quick-witted one-handed Salgado could not have written those letters. Alicia, are you listening? Are you all right?"

The young woman suddenly stood up and put on her coat.

"Alicia?"

Alicia picked up the folder that lay on the table with Salgado's supposed letters and glanced absently at Vargas.

"Alicia?"

She made her way to the door, with Vargas's baffled eyes fixed on her back.

15

THE PAIN WORSENED the moment she stepped out. She didn't want Vargas to see her like that. She didn't want anyone to see her like that. The looming episode was going to be a bad one. That damned Madrid cold. The midday dose had only bought her a bit of time. She tried to manage the first stabs in the hip by breathing slowly and went on walking, taking each step carefully. She hadn't even reached Plaza de Cibeles when she had to stop and hold on to a lamppost while a spasm clenched her, like an electric current eating away at her bones. She could feel people walking by, staring surreptitiously.

"Are you all right, miss?"

She nodded without even looking up. When she recovered her breath, she stopped a taxi and asked to be taken to the Hispania. The driver looked at her rather nervously, but didn't say anything. It was getting dark, and the lights on Gran Vía were already sweeping up all and sundry in the gray tide of those who were leaving their cavernous offices to go home and those who had nowhere to go. Alicia pressed her face against the window and closed her eyes.

When she reached the Hispania, she asked the taxi driver to help her out. She gave him a good tip and made her way to the entrance hall, holding on to the walls. As soon as he saw her come in, Maura, the receptionist, jumped up and ran to her side, looking worried. He put his arm around her waist and helped her reach the elevators.

"Again?" he asked.

"It will soon pass. It's this weather . . ."

"You don't look at all well. Shall I call the doctor?"

"There's no need. Upstairs I've got the medicine I need."

Maura nodded rather hesitantly.

Alicia patted his arm. "You're a good friend, Maura. I'll miss you."

"Are you going somewhere?"

Alicia smiled and stepped into the elevator as she waved goodnight.

"By the way, I think you have company," Maura said as the doors were closing.

She limped down the long dark corridor to her room, clinging to the wall, passing dozens of closed doors that sealed off empty rooms. On nights like this, Alicia suspected she must be the only living occupant left on that floor, although she always felt that somebody was watching her. Sometimes, if she stopped in the dark, she could almost feel the breath of the permanent residents on the back of her neck, or the touch of fingers on her face. When she reached her room at the end of the passage, she paused for a moment, panting.

She opened the door, not bothering to turn on the light. The neon billboards of Gran Vía's theaters projected a flickering beam that spread a dim Technicolor radiance over the room. The figure in the armchair had its back to the door, and a lighted cigarette in one hand, from which a spiral of smoke wove arabesques in the air.

"I thought you'd come to see me at the end of the afternoon," said Leandro.

Alicia staggered over to the bed and collapsed on it, exhausted. Her mentor turned and sighed, shaking his head. "Shall I prepare it for you?"

"I don't want anything."

"Is this some form of atonement for your sins, or do you enjoy suffering unnecessarily?" Leandro stood up and approached the bed. "Let me have a look."

He leaned over her and felt her hip with a clinical coldness. "When did you have your last jab?"

"At lunchtime. Ten milligrams."

"That not enough, for starters. You know that."

"Perhaps it was twenty."

Leandro muttered to himself. He walked over to the bathroom and went straight to the cabinet. There he found a metal case and returned to Alicia's side. He sat on the edge of the bed, opened the case, and started to prepare the injection. "I don't like it when you do that, Alicia. You know it."

"It's my life."

"When you punish yourself this way, it's also my life. Turn over."

Alicia closed her eyes and turned on her side. Leandro lifted her dress up to her waist. He unfastened her harness and took it off. Alicia was moaning with pain, squeezing her eyes shut and breathing with difficulty.

"This hurts me more than it hurts you," said Leandro. He grabbed her thigh and held her down on the bed. Alicia was shaking when he plunged the needle in the wound on her hip. She let out a muffled cry, and her whole body tensed up like a steel cable for a few seconds. Leandro pulled the needle out slowly and left the syringe on the bed. Slowly, he lessened the pressure on her leg and turned her body around until she was lying faceup. He pulled down her dress and gently placed her head on the pillow. Alicia's forehead was bathed in sweat. He pulled out a handkerchief and dried it for her.

She looked at him, glassy-eyed. "What time is it?" she murmured.

Leandro stroked her cheek.

"It's early. Rest now."

16

ALICIA WOKE UP in the dark room to discover Leandro outlined against the armchair next to her bed. He held the Víctor Mataix book in his hands and was reading it. While she was asleep, he must have gone through her pockets, her handbag, and probably all the drawers in the room.

"Better?" he asked, without looking up from the book.

"Yes," said Alicia.

Waking up was always accompanied by a strange lucidity and the feeling of frozen jelly sliding through her veins. Leandro had covered her with a blanket. She felt her body and realized she was still wearing her day clothes. She pulled herself up and leaned against the headboard. The pain was now just a weak, muffled throb buried in the cold. Leandro bent forward and handed her a glass.

She took a couple of sips. It didn't taste of water. "What's this?"

"Drink it."

Alicia drank the liquid. Leandro closed the book and left it on the table.

"I've never really understood your literary tastes, Alicia."

"I found it hidden inside the desk of Valls's office."

"And you think it might have some connection with our business?"

"For the moment I'm not ruling anything out."

"You're beginning to sound like Gil de Partera. How's your new partner?"

"Vargas? He seems efficient."

"Trustworthy?"

Alicia shrugged.

"Coming from someone who doesn't trust her own shadow, I'm not sure whether to take your uncertainty as a sign that you're converting to the faith in the regime."

"Take it as you please."

"Are we still at war?"

Alicia sighed and shook her head.

"This wasn't a courtesy call, Alicia. I have things to do, and there are people at the Hotel Palace who've been waiting to have dinner with me for quite a while. What can you tell me?"

The young woman gave Leandro a brief summary of the day's events and let him digest it in silence, as was his habit. He stood and walked over to the window. Alicia watched his still outline against the lights of Gran Vía. His fragile arms and legs, attached to a disproportionate torso, lent him the air of a spider hanging in its web. She didn't interrupt his meditation. She'd learned that Leandro liked to take his time to scheme and conjecture, savoring every piece of information and working out how to extract the greatest possible damage from it.

"I suppose you didn't tell Valls's secretary that you'd found that book and were going to take it with you," he pointed out at last.

"No. Only Vargas knows that I have it."

"It would be best if things stopped there. Do you think you can convince him not to tell his superiors?"

"Yes. At least for a few days."

Leandro sighed, slightly annoyed. He turned away from the window and returned unhurriedly to the armchair. He settled down, crossed his legs, and devoted a few moments to examining Alicia with forensic eyes. "I'd like Dr. Vallejo to see you."

"We've already discussed this."

"He's the best specialist in the country."

"No."

"Let me make an appointment for you. Just a visit. You don't need to commit to anything."

"No."

"If you're going to continue speaking in monosyllables, then at least introduce a little variation."

"OK."

Leandro took the book from the table again and leafed through it, smiling to himself.

"You find it amusing?"

Leandro shook his head slowly. "No. In fact it makes my hair stand on end. I was just thinking that it seems to be tailor-made for you."

He ran his eyes over the pages, pausing here and there with a skeptical expression. Finally he returned the book to Alicia and gazed at her. He had a Jesuitical look, the sort that sniffs out sins before they are even formed in one's mind and administers penitence with a mere blink.

"Your important dinner at the Palace must be getting cold," said Alicia.

Leandro gave her his ecumenical assent. "Don't get up. Rest. I've left ten one-hundred phials for you in the bathroom cabinet."

Alicia pressed her lips angrily but kept silent. Leandro nodded and made his way to the door. Before leaving the room, he stopped and pointed his finger at her. "Don't do anything stupid."

Alicia joined her hands as if in prayer and smiled.

17

ONCE FREE FROM Leandro's presence, Alicia bolted the door, got under the shower, and abandoned herself to the steam and the needles of hot water for almost forty minutes. She didn't bother to turn on the light, but stood in the faint glow that filtered through the bathroom window, letting the water rub the day off her. The Hispania boilers were probably buried in some part of hell, and the metallic rattle of water pipes behind the walls created a hypnotic music. When she thought her skin was about to peel off in shreds, she turned off the taps and stayed there a couple more minutes, listening to the drip of the shower and the murmur of the traffic on Gran Vía.

Later, wrapped in a towel and with a full glass of white wine for company, she lay on the bed with the dossier Gil de Partera had given them that morning and the folder of letters allegedly penned by Sebastián Salgado, or by the possibly deceased David Martín, addressed to Minister Valls.

She began with the dossier, comparing her findings so far with the official version from police headquarters. Like so many police reports, what mattered wasn't what it included: the interesting part was what was left out. The report on the supposed attack against the minister in the Círculo de Bellas Artes formed a masterpiece in the genre of inconsistent and overblown conjecture. All it contained was an unverified refutation of Valls's words, who argued that he'd seen somebody among the audience who intended to make an attempt on his life. The only colorful note was a reference to one of the alleged witnesses of the alleged plot in connection with a presumed individual who had allegedly been seen behind the scenes wearing a sort of mask, or something that covered part of his face.

Alicia let out a sigh of boredom. "All we needed now was El Zorro," she muttered to herself.

After a while, tired of flicking through documents that seemed whipped up to provide the dossier with a swift coat of varnish, she abandoned it and began to look through the letters.

She counted about a dozen messages, all written on sheets of yellowing paper peppered with erratic handwriting, the longest barely two short paragraphs. They had been written with a worn nib that made the ink flow irregularly, so that some lines were saturated and others hardly seemed to have scratched the page. The author's writing rarely seemed to link one character with the next, giving the impression that the text was written out letter by letter. The subject matter was repetitive, insisting on the same points in every message: the phrases "the truth," "the children of death," and "the entrance to the labyrinth" appeared again and again.

Valls had been receiving the messages for years, but only in the end had something pushed him into taking action. "What?" whispered Alicia.

The answer was almost always in the past. That had been one of Leandro's first lessons. Once, when they were leaving the funeral of one of the senior officers of the secret police in Barcelona, which Leandro had obliged Alicia to attend (as part of her education, he had stated), her mentor had pronounced those words. Leandro's thesis was that after a particular point in a man's life, his future is invariably in his past.

"Isn't that obvious?" Alicia had said.

"You'd be surprised at how often one looks in the present or in the future for answers that are always in the past."

Leandro had a penchant for didactic aphorisms. On that occasion Alicia thought he was talking about the deceased, or perhaps even about himself and the wave of darkness that seemed to have pulled him like a tide toward power, like so many celebrated individuals who had climbed up the gloomy architecture of the regime. The chosen, she'd ended up calling them. Those who always stayed afloat in the murky waters, like scum. A distinguished group of champions reborn in a cloak of decay, creeping through the streets of that barren land like a river of blood surging up from the sewers. Alicia realized she had borrowed that image from the book she'd found in Valls's office: blood that surged up through the drains and was slowly flooding the streets. *The labyrinth.*

She dropped the letters on the floor and closed her eyes. The cold in her veins from that poison always opened a door to the dark back room of her mind. It was the price she paid for muting the pain. Leandro knew that. He knew that beneath the frozen mantle, where there was no pain or consciousness, her eyes were able to see through the dark, hear and feel what others couldn't even imagine, hunt down the secrets others thought they'd buried in their wake. Leandro knew that every time Alicia sank into those black waters and returned with a trophy in her hands, she left behind part of her being and of her soul. And that she hated him for it. She hated him with the anger that can only be felt by one who knows her maker all too well.

She suddenly sat up and went to the bathroom. She opened the small cabinet behind the mirror and found the phials Leandro had left for her, perfectly lined up. Her prize. She grabbed them with both hands and threw them forcefully into the sink. The clear liquid drained through the broken glass and disappeared.

"Fucking bastard," she murmured.

Shortly afterward the phone rang in the bedroom. For a few seconds, Alicia stared at her reflection in the mirror and let the phone ring. She was expecting the call. She went back to the room and picked up the receiver. She listened without saying anything.

"They've found Valls's car," said Leandro at the other end.

She kept silent. "In Barcelona," she said at last.

"Yes," Leandro confirmed.

"And not a sign of Valls."

"Or of his bodyguard."

Alicia sat on the bed, her eyes lost in the lights that bled on the window.

"Alicia? Are you there?"

"I'll take the first train tomorrow morning. I believe it leaves Ato- cha at seven."

She heard Leandro sigh and imagined him lying on his bed in the suite of the Gran Hotel Palace.

"I don't know whether that's a good idea, Alicia."

"Would you rather leave it in the hands of the police?"

"You know that I worry about you being alone in Barcelona. It's not good for you."

"Nothing's going to happen."

"Where will you stay?"

"Where do you think?"

"The apartment on Calle Aviñón . . ." Leandro sighed. "Why not in a good hotel?"

"Because that's my home."

"Your home is here."

Alicia looked around the room, her prison for the last few years. Only Leandro could think this coffin could be a home. "Does Vargas know?"

"The news came from headquarters. If he doesn't know, he'll know early tomorrow morning."

"Anything else?"

She heard Leandro breathing deeply.

"I want you to call me every day without fail."

"All right."

"Without fail."

"I said I would. Good night."

She was about to put the phone down when Leandro's voice reached her through the receiver. She put it back to her ear.

"Alicia?"

"Yes."

"Be careful."

18

SHE HAD ALWAYS known that one day she would return to Barcelona. The fact that she was going to do this during her last job for Leandro added a layer of irony that could not have escaped her mentor. She imagined him pacing around his suite, pensive, his eyes on the telephone, tempted to pick up the receiver and call her again, order her to stay in Madrid. Leandro didn't like it when his puppets tried to cut their strings. More than one of them had attempted it, only to discover that this was not a profession for lovers of happy endings. But Alicia had been different. She was his favorite. She was his masterpiece.

She poured herself another glass of white wine and lay down to wait for the call. The temptation to disconnect the phone crossed her mind. The last time she'd done that, two of his stooges had turned up at her doorstep to escort her as far as the hallway, where Leandro was waiting for her—a Leandro she had never seen before, devoid of his calm expression, consumed by anxiety. On that occasion he had looked at her with a mixture of suspicion and eagerness, as if he couldn't quite decide whether to hug her or order his men to beat her to a pulp with their rifle butts then and there. "Don't ever do anything like that to me again," he'd said. It was two years since that night.

She waited for Leandro's call until late that evening, but it never came. His need to find Valls and please the upper echelons of the regime must be great, she thought, if he was letting her out of her cage. Convinced that neither of them would get any sleep that night, Alicia decided to take refuge in the only place where she knew Leandro had never been able to reach her—the pages of a book. She picked up the black volume she'd found hidden in Valls's office and opened it, ready to enter the mind of Víctor Mataix.

Before she reached the end of the first paragraph, she'd already forgotten that what she was holding in her hands was a piece of evidence in the investigation. She let herself be lulled by the perfume of the words and was soon lost among them, succumbing to the torrent of images and rhythms that oozed from the story of Ariadna's adventures and her descent into the depths of that enchanted Barcelona. Every paragraph, every sentence, seemed written in a musical key. The narrative drew her eyes through a cadence of timbres and colors that sketched a theater of shadows in her mind. She read without pause for two hours, relishing every sentence and dreading the moment she would reach the end. When, upon turning the last page, she came across the illustration of a curtain crashing down on a stage and making the text evaporate into shadowy dust, Alicia closed the book over her chest and lay down in the dark, her gaze still lost in the adventures of Ariadna in her labyrinth.

Bewitched by the magic of that story, she closed her eyes and tried to sleep. She imagined Valls in his office, hiding the book behind a drawer and turning the key in its lock. Of all the things he could have hidden, he'd chosen that book before disappearing. Slowly, exhaustion began to drip over her body. Throwing off the towel, she slipped naked under the sheets. She lay on one side, curled up into a ball, her hands linked between her thighs. It occurred to her that this was probably the last night she would ever sleep in that room, the room that had been her cell for years. She lay there, waiting, listening to the murmurings and groans of the building that was already sensing her absence.

She got up shortly before dawn, with barely enough time to pack a few essentials and leave the rest behind as a donation for the invisible hotel guests. She stared at her little city of books piled up against the walls and smiled sadly. Maura would know what to do with her friends.

Day was just breaking when she walked across the lobby, with no intention of bidding farewell to the lost souls of the Hispania. She had almost reached the door when she heard Maura's voice behind her.

"So it was true," said the concierge. "You're leaving."

Alicia stopped and turned around. Maura was observing her, leaning on a mop that sported as much mileage as he did. He smiled so as not to cry, his eyes betraying immense sadness.

"I'm going home, Maura."

The concierge nodded repeatedly. "You're doing the right thing."

"I've left my books upstairs. They're for you."

"I'll look after them."

"And the clothes. Do what you think best. Someone in the building might want them."

"I'll take them to the Red Cross. There are lots of creeps around here, and I wouldn't like to find that smart aleck Valenzuela sniffing around where he has no business."

Alicia went over to the little man and embraced him. "Thanks for everything, Maura," she whispered in his ear. "I'm going to miss you."

Maura dropped the mop handle and put his trembling arms around her. "Forget all about us as soon as you get home," he said in a broken voice.

She was going to kiss him good-bye, but Maura, knight of the doleful countenance and old school, held out his hand. Alicia shook it.

"Someone called Vargas might call and ask for me."

"Don't worry. I'll get him off your back. Go on, off you go."

She got into a taxi that was waiting by the hotel entrance and asked the driver to take her to Atocha. A leaden blanket covered the city, and frost shrouded the car windows. The taxi driver looked as if he'd spent the night, or the entire week, at the wheel, barely clinging to the world with the cigarette butt hanging from his lips. He watched her through the rearview mirror. "Are you going or returning?" he asked.

"I don't know," replied Alicia.

When she arrived at the station, she saw that Leandro had gotten there ahead of her. He was waiting at a table in one of the cafés next to the ticket offices, reading a newspaper and playing with his coffee spoon. Two of his heavies were posted against columns, a few meters away. When he saw her, Leandro folded the newspaper and smiled paternally.

"Getting up early won't make the sun rise any sooner," said Alicia.

"Reciting proverbs doesn't suit you, Alicia. Sit down. Have you had breakfast?"

She shook her head and sat down at the table. The last thing she wanted was to annoy Leandro just when she was about to put six hundred kilometers between them.

"There are some common habits among normal people, like eating breakfast or having friends. They would do you good, Alicia."

"Do you have many friends, Leandro?"

Alicia noticed the steely glimmer in her boss's eyes, a hint of warning, and she looked down. She dutifully accepted the cup of coffee and the pastry served by the waiter at Leandro's request and took a few sips under his watchful eye.

He pulled an envelope out of his coat and handed it to her. "I've reserved a first-class compartment just for you. I hope you don't mind. There's also some money there. Today I'll put the rest into the Hispano account. If you need any more, let me know."

"Thank you."

Alicia nibbled the pastry. It was dry and rough, and she found it hard to swallow. Leandro didn't take his eyes off her. She sneaked a look at the clock hanging high up on the wall.

"You still have ten minutes," said her mentor. "Relax."

Groups of passengers were beginning to walk past on their way to the platform. Alicia curled her hands around the cup just for something to do with them. The silence between them was painful.

"Thanks for coming to say good-bye," she ventured.

"Is that what we're doing? Saying good-bye?"

Alicia shook her head. They continued sitting there, mutely, for a couple of minutes. At last, when Alicia was beginning to think the cup would shatter into a thousand pieces under the pressure of her grip, Leandro stood up, buttoned up his coat, and calmly tied his scarf. He put on his leather gloves and, smiling benevolently, leaned over to kiss Alicia on the cheek. His lips were cold, and his breath smelled of mint. Alicia sat there, motionless, barely daring to breathe.

"I want you to call me every day. Without fail. Starting tonight, as soon as you arrive, so I know that all is well."

She didn't say anything.

"Alicia?"

"Every day, without fail," she recited.

"No need for the singsong."

"Sorry."

"How are you managing the pain?"

"Well. Better. Much better."

Leandro pulled a pill bottle out of his coat pocket and handed it to her. "I know you don't like to take anything, but you'll be grateful for this. It's not as strong as the injectable sort. One pill, no more. Don't take it on an empty stomach, and especially not with alcohol."

Alicia accepted the bottle and put it into her handbag. She wasn't going to start an argument now. "Thanks."

Leandro nodded and made his way toward the exit, escorted by his men.

The train was waiting beneath the station's vaulted ceiling. On the platform, a very young-looking porter asked to see her ticket. He led her to the first-class carriage, which was standing empty at the head of the train. Noticing that she was limping slightly, he helped her up the steps and accompanied her to her compartment, where he lifted the suitcase into the luggage rack and raised the window curtain. The glass was misted up, and he wiped it with his jacket sleeve. A troupe of passengers glided along the platform, which shone like a mirror in the humid early-morning air. Alicia offered the porter a tip: he bowed before leaving and closed the compartment door.

She collapsed into her seat and looked absently at the station lights. Soon the train began to crawl, and Alicia abandoned herself to the gentle swaying of the carriage while she imagined the sun rising over Madrid, anchored in mist. And then she saw him. Vargas was racing down the platform, trying in vain to catch the train. He very nearly touched the carriage with his fingers, and even met Alicia's impenetrable eyes as she observed him impassively through the window. At last Vargas gave up, his hands on his knees and a bitter, breathless laugh on his lips.

As the city receded into the distance, the train entered a plain with no visible horizon, stretching endlessly. Behind that wall of darkness, Alicia felt, Barcelona had already scented her trail in the wind. She imagined the city opening like a black rose and for a moment was filled with the calm of inevitability that comforts the accursed—or perhaps, she told herself, it was just tiredness. Little did it matter now. She closed her eyes and surrendered to sleep while the train, clearing the shadows, slowly hastened toward the labyrinth of the spirits.

CITY OF MIRRORS

❧

BARCELONA

DECEMBER

1959

I

COLD. A COLD that bites the skin, cuts the flesh, and slices through the bones. A damp cold that clamps one's muscles and burns one's insides. Cold. For that first moment of consciousness it's the only thing he can think of.

It is almost pitch-dark. Only a thin sliver of light filters through from above, a breath of deathly light that clings to the shadows and hints at the limits of the space in which he is confined. His pupils dilate, and he's able to make out an area the size of a small room. The walls are made of bare stone. Moisture oozes from them and glistens in the gloom, as if dark tears were sliding down them. The floor is made of rock and sodden with something that doesn't look like water. There is a powerful stench in the air. He notices a row of thick, rusty bars, and beyond them some steps leading up in the dark.

He's in a cell.

Valls tries to stand up, but his legs won't support him. After barely a step his knees buckle, and he falls to one side, hitting his face against the floor, cursing. He tries to recover his breath. He remains there for a few minutes, dejected, his face glued to the slimy film that covers the floor, giving off a metallic, slightly sweet smell. His mouth is dry, as if he'd swallowed earth, and his lips are chapped. He tries to touch them with his right hand, but realizes he can't feel his hand, as if there was nothing there below the elbow.

He manages to prop himself up with his left arm. Raising his right hand in front of his face, he looks at it against the light, a yellowish gleam that tints the air. The hand is shaking. He can see it shake, but he can't feel it. He tries to open and close his fist, but his muscles don't respond. Only then does he notice that he is missing his index and middle fingers. In their place are two dark stains: shreds of skin and flesh dangle from them. Valls wants to scream, but his voice is broken and he only manages to produce an empty cry. He lets himself slump backward and closes his eyes. He starts breathing through his mouth to avoid the strong smell that poisons the air. As he does so, he is reminded of something from his childhood: a faraway summer in the country house his parents had outside Segovia, and an old dog that went down to the cellar to die. Valls remembers the nauseating smell that took hold of the house, how it was similar to the smell that now burns his throat. But this is much worse; this hardly allows him to think. After a while, minutes or perhaps hours, he is overcome by exhaustion and falls into a troubled drowsiness, somewhere between sleeplessness and sleep.

He dreams he is traveling in a train where he is the only passenger. The locomotive is galloping furiously over clouds of black steam toward a maze of factories shaped like cathedrals, pointed towers and a mass of bridges and roofs conjured up into a tangle of incomprehensible angles beneath a bloodstained sky. Shortly before entering a tunnel that seems to have no end, Valls looks out of the window and sees that the entrance is guarded by two large statues of angels with open wings, sharp teeth visible between their lips. A battered sign hanging from the lintel reads:

BARCELONA

The train hurtles into the tunnel with a hellish roar. When it emerges at the other end, the silhouette of Montjuïc rises before him, with the castle outlined on the hilltop, enveloped in an aura of crimson light. Valls feels his guts tighten. A ticket inspector, bent over like an old, storm-battered tree, is approaching along the corridor and stops in front of Valls's compartment. He wears a badge on his uniform that reads SALGADO.

"Your stop, Governor . . ."

The train climbs up the winding road he remembers so well and enters the prison premises. It stops in a dark corridor, and he alights. The train sets off again and disappears into darkness. Valls turns around and realizes that he's become trapped in one of the prison cells. A dark figure is watching him from the other side of the bars.

When Valls tries to explain to him that there's been a mistake, that he's on the wrong side, that he's the prison governor, his voice won't reach his lips.

The pain comes later, pulling him out of his dream like an electric current.

*

The smell of carrion, the darkness, and the cold are still there, but now he barely notices them. The only thing he can think of is the pain. A pain as he's never known before. As he's never been able to imagine. His right hand is burning. It feels as if he's plunged it into a bonfire and can't pull it out. He grabs his right arm with his left hand. Even in the shadows he can see that the two dark stains where his fingers should be are suppurating, oozing what looks like a thick and bloody liquid. He screams in silence.

The pain helps him remember.

The images of what has happened begin to form in his mind. He revisits the moment when Barcelona emerges in the distance, silhouetted against the early-evening sky. Through the windshield, he watches the town rise like the great backdrop for a funfair performance and remembers how much he hates that place. His loyal bodyguard, Vicente, drives silently, concentrating on the traffic. If he's scared, he doesn't show it. They drive along avenues and streets where he sees people wrapped up, hurrying through a curtain of snow that drifts in the air like glass mist. They head straight up a boulevard to the higher part of town, and soon they're on a road that zigzags up toward the ridge of Vallvidrera. Valls recognizes that strange citadel of facades suspended from heaven. The city's lower zones are left behind, a carpet of darkness below, melting into the sea. The funicular climbs the hillside like a serpent of golden light, outlining the grand modernist villas that shore up the mountain. There, sunk among the trees, he glimpses the outline of the old rambling house. Valls swallows hard. Vicente glances at him, and Valls gives him a nod. It will all be over very soon. Valls pulls back the hammer of the revolver in his hand. It is already dark when they reach the entrance to the villa. The gates are open. The car drives into the weed-infested garden, around the fountain—dry and covered in ivy. Vicente stops the car opposite the stairs that lead to the front door. He turns off the engine and pulls out his revolver. Vicente never uses a gun, only a revolver. A revolver, he says, never gets jammed.

"What time is it?" Valls asks in a tiny voice.

Vicente doesn't have time to reply. It all happens very fast. The bodyguard has just pulled the key out of the ignition when Valls notices a figure on the other side of the car window. He hasn't seen it approach. Without a word, Vicente pushes Valls aside and shoots. The window shatters a few centimeters from Valls's head. He feels a shower of glass shards lashing at his face. The roar of the shot deafens him, a piercing whistle stabbing his ears. Before the cloud of gunpowder floating inside the car has time to settle, the door on the driver's side suddenly opens. Vicente turns, revolver in hand, but with no time to fire another shot because something has slit his throat. He clutches his neck with both hands. Dark blood runs through his fingers. For a brief moment their eyes meet, Vicente's haunted by disbelief. A second later the bodyguard slumps over the steering wheel and sets off the horn. Valls tries to hold him, but Vicente leans to one side, and half his body is left hanging out of the car. Valls holds the revolver in both hands and points toward the blackness beyond the driver's open door. Then he senses someone's breath behind him, and when he turns to shoot, all he notices is a sharp, ice-cold blow on his hand. He feels the metal on the bone, and nausea clouds his vision. The revolver falls on his lap, and he sees blood flowing along his arm. The figure looms, holding the bloodstained knife in one hand, the blade dripping. Then the figure tries to open the car door, but the door is stuck. Two hands grab Valls by the neck and tug at him angrily. Valls feels himself being pulled out of the car through the gap in the window and being dragged up the gravel path to the broken marble steps. He hears soft footsteps approaching. The moon lights up what in his delirium he takes for an angel and then for an apparition of death. Valls faces those eyes and realizes his mistake.

"What are you laughing at, you son of a bitch?" the voice asks.

Valls smiles. "You look so much like her," he murmurs.

Valls closes his eyes and waits for the coup de grâce. It doesn't come. He feels his angel spitting on his face. The angel's footsteps move away. God, or the devil, takes pity on him, and at some point he loses consciousness.

He can't remember whether all that happened hours, days, or weeks ago. Time has ceased to exist in this cell. All is cold now, and pain and darkness. He feels a sudden spasm of rage. Dragging himself to the bars, he bangs on the cold metal until his skin smarts. He is still holding on to them when a band of light opens above, revealing a staircase that leads down to the cell. Valls hears footsteps and looks up hopefully. He stretches his hand beyond the bars, imploringly. His jailer gazes at him from the shadows, motionless. Something covers his face, reminding Valls of the frozen expression on a mannequin in one of Gran Vía's shop windows.

"Martín? Is that you?" asks Valls.

He gets no reply. The jailer just stares at him without saying a word. At last Valls nods, as if wishing to imply that he understands the rules of the game.

"Water, please," he groans.

For a long time the jailer remains impassive. Then, when Valls thinks he's imagined it all and the man's presence is only an image from the delirium caused by pain and by the infection that is eating him alive, the jailer walks down a few steps.

Valls smiles submissively. "Water," he begs.

The spurt of urine splashes his face, burning the cuts that cover it. Valls howls and jerks back. He drags himself backward until he hits the wall, and there he cringes and curls up into a ball. The jailer disappears up the stairs, and the light goes out again behind the echo of a heavy door closing.

This is when he realizes he's not alone in the cell. Vicente, his loyal bodyguard, is sitting in the corner, leaning against the wall. He doesn't move. Only the shape of his legs is visible. And the hands. The palms and fingers are swollen and have a purple hue.

"Vicente?"

Valls drags himself over there but stops when he notices how close the stench is. He takes shelter in the opposite corner and doubles himself up, hugging his knees and burying his face between his legs to get away from the smell. He tries to conjure up the image of his daughter, Mercedes. He imagines her playing in the garden, in her dollhouse, traveling in her private train. He imagines her as a child, with those eyes of hers fixed on his, those all-forgiving eyes that shed light where there had always been darkness.

After a while he surrenders to the cold, the pain and exhaustion, and feels he's again losing consciousness. Perhaps it is death, he thinks, hopeful.

2

FERMÍN ROMERO DE Torres woke with a start, his heart throbbing like a machine gun. He felt as if the world was sitting on his chest. The hands of the alarm clock confirmed his worst suspicions. It wasn't even midnight. He'd only half slept for an hour before his insomnia had charged at him again like a runaway tram. Next to him, Bernarda snored like a little calf, blissfully asleep in the arms of Morpheus.

Fermín, I think you're going to be a father.

Pregnancy had made her more enticing than ever, her blossoming beauty and her entire self a feast of curves into which he would gladly have dug his teeth at that very moment. He was considering finishing off the job with his characteristic "midnight express service," but he didn't dare wake her and break that heavenly peace radiating from her face. He knew that if he did, there would be two alternative outcomes: either the H-bomb of hormones that oozed from her pores would explode, and Bernarda would transform into a wild tigress who would slice him up, or else the spark of lust would turn out to be a damp squib, rendering his saintly wife a prey to fears, including the thought that any attempt at docking anywhere near her nether regions might put the baby at risk. Fermín didn't blame her. Bernarda had lost the first child they'd conceived just before their marriage. Such was the sadness that had come over her that Fermín feared he was going to lose her forever. In time, just as the doctor had promised them, Bernarda was once again in the family way, and had returned to life. But now she lived with the constant panic that she might lose the baby, and sometimes she even seemed to be afraid to breathe.

But, dearest love, the doctor said it would be fine.

That doctor is a scoundrel. Like you.

A wise man is one who doesn't stir up volcanoes, revolutions, or pregnant females. Fermín left the marital bed and tiptoed to the dining room of the modest flat in Calle Joaquín Costa where they had settled after their honeymoon. He'd thought of drowning his sorrows and his lust in a Sugus, but a quick glance at the larder revealed that he was down to zero supplies. Fermín felt his soul drop to his slippers. This was serious. Then he remembered that in the foyer of the Estación de Francia there was always a peddler selling confectionary and cigarettes who kept his stand there until midnight. He was known as Blind Diego, and he was normally very well stocked with sweets and indecent jokes. Fermín's mouth watered in anticipation at the very thought of a lemon Sugus. He didn't lose a second getting out of his pajamas and slipping into one of his Siberian wintry outfits. Thus attired, he set off down the street to satisfy his basic instincts and walk off his insomnia.

The Raval quarter is the land of insomniacs, for although it never sleeps, it invites you to forget. However many sorrows you drag along with you, you'll only have walked a few steps before bumping into someone who will remind you that there's always another person with a far worse set of cards than yours in the game of life. On that night of crossed destinies, a yellowish miasma made up of urine, gas lamps, and sepia-toned echoes drifted through the tangle of narrow streets like a spell, or a warning, depending on the beholder.

Fermín navigated the choir of shouts and waves of effluvia courtesy of the riffraff that livened up alleyways as dark and twisted as the fantasies of a bishop. He emerged at last at the foot of the statue of Columbus. A gaggle of seagulls had conspired to dye it guano-white in a murky homage to the Mediterranean diet. Fermín headed straight along the boulevard toward the railway station, without daring to look back lest he glimpse the sinister silhouette of Montjuïc Castle looming on the top of the hill.

Packs of American sailors roamed the area surrounding the port, looking for fun and the chance of cultural exchanges with ladies of easy virtue who'd be willing to teach them the basic vocabulary and three or four novel tricks of the trade. He remembered Rociíto, solace of so many dark nights of his youth, a good soul with a generous bosom who more than once had rescued him from loneliness. He imagined her with her fiancé, the prosperous tradesman from Reus who had removed her from active service a year ago, traveling around the world like the lady she had always been and perhaps feeling, for once, that life was smiling on her.

*

Thinking about Rociíto and people with hearts of gold—that rare species constantly threatened with extinction—Fermín soon arrived at the station. He spotted Blind Diego, who was about to close for the night, and hurried toward him.

"Hey, Fermín. At this time of night I imagined you'd be pestering the wife," said Diego. "Short on Sugus?"

"Run out."

"I've got lemon, pineapple, and strawberry."

"Make it lemon. Five packets."

"And one on the house."

Fermín paid, adding a tip. Without counting them, Diego put the coins in a leather pouch that hung from his belt, like a tram conductor. Fermín had never understood how Blind Diego knew whether he was being cheated or not, but he knew. Diego had been born sightless, but he could see them coming. He lived alone in a windowless room in a *pensión* on Calle Princesa, where his best friend was a transistor radio on which he listened to soccer matches and the news bulletins that amused him so much.

"You've come to see the trains, eh?"

"Old habits," said Fermín.

He watched Diego set off toward the room where not even bedbugs were waiting for him, and he thought of Bernarda, asleep in their bed and smelling of rose water. He was about to go back home but decided to step into the great nave of the station, that cathedral of steam and iron through which he'd returned to Barcelona one distant night in 1941. Fermín had always thought that destiny, though keen to ambush innocent people from behind and if possible with their pants down, also enjoyed nesting in railway stations whenever it took a refreshment break. This is where tragedies and romances began and ended, as did escapes and returns, betrayals and absences. Life, some said, is a railway station where one almost always enters, or gets put into, the wrong carriage.

Those thoughts, no deeper than a cup of coffee, usually came to Fermín in the small hours of the night, when his body was tired of tossing and turning but his head kept on spinning like a top. Determined to swap his cheap philosophy for the austere comfort of a wooden bench, he walked under the station's curved vault. A design, he thought, with a clear message from its shrewd architect to the fresh arrivals: that the future is born crooked in Barcelona.

Fermín settled on the bench, unwrapped a Sugus, and popped it in his mouth. Absorbed in his sweet nirvana, he became mesmerized by the railway lines, which seemed to draw together as they vanished into the night. After a while he felt the ground shaking under his feet and saw the headlights of a locomotive breaking the shroud of midnight. A couple of minutes later the train entered the station, riding on a cloud of steam.

A blanket of sea mist swept in over the platforms, eerily enveloping the passengers as they alighted after their long journey. Happy faces were in short supply. Fermín watched them as they passed, taking in their weary expressions and smart clothes, fantasizing on prior incidents and circumstances that had brought them to the city. He was starting to relish his new role as an instant biographer of anonymous citizens when he saw her.

She stepped out of the carriage wrapped in a veil of white steam, just the way Fermín had learned to expect his beloved Marlene Dietrich to emerge in a station—be it in Berlin, Paris, or any other place that had never existed, in that glorious black-and-white twentieth century of the Capitol Cinema matinees. The woman—for although she couldn't even be thirty, he would never have thought of describing her as a young girl, a chick, or any other of the terms currently in vogue—walked with a slight limp, lending her a somewhat intriguing and vulnerable air.

Her sharp features and presence exuded light and shade at the same time. If he'd had to describe her to his friend Daniel, he would have said she looked like one of the ghostly midnight angels that sometimes peeped out of the novels by his old cell-block pal in the prison of Montjuïc, David Martín. In particular she reminded him of the ineffable Chloé, the protagonist of many stories of doubtful decorum in the *City of the Damned* series, which had robbed him of so much sleep in his long sessions of feverish reading. From those novels he'd acquired an encyclopedic knowledge on the art of poisoning, the turbulent passions of criminal minds, and the techniques and variety in the making and wearing of women's undergarments. Perhaps it was time to return to those wild Gothic romances, he told himself, before his spirit and his gonads dried up inexorably.

Fermín watched the woman as she drew near, and they exchanged glances. It was just a fleeting moment, an accidental gesture from which he quickly fled, lowering his head and allowing her to walk by. Fermín buried his eyes in his coat and faced the other way. The passengers were disappearing toward the exit, the woman with them. He stayed there, glued to his seat, almost trembling, until the station master went up to him.

"Listen, there are no more trains arriving tonight and you can't sleep here . . ."

Fermín nodded and left, dragging his feet. When he reached the entrance hall, he looked around, but there was no sign of her. He hurried out to the street, where a cold breeze brought him back to the reality of winter.

"Alicia?" he asked the wind. "Is that you?" Sighing, he set off into the shadows of the streets, telling himself that it was not possible, that those eyes he'd met were not the same eyes he'd abandoned that faraway night of fire during the war, and that the girl he'd tried to save, Alicia, must have perished that night along with so many others. Not even his nemesis, destiny, could have such a perverse sense of humor.

Perhaps it was a ghost who had returned from the dead to remind him that someone who lets a child die doesn't deserve to bring descendants into this world, he speculated. The promptings of the Almighty were unknowable, said the priests. This had to have a scientific explanation, he told himself. Like an early-morning hard-on.

Clinging to that empirical principle and sinking his teeth into a Sugus or two, Fermín started walking back to the warm bed where Bernarda waited for him, convinced that nothing happened by chance and that sooner or later he would uncover that mystery or else that mystery would uncover him, once and for all.

3

WHILE PROCEEDING TOWARD the exit, Alicia noticed the figure sitting on a bench by the platform entrance, looking at her out of the corner of his eye—a small, scrawny man whose face orbited around a prominent nose, his features vaguely reminiscent of a Goya painting. He wore a coat that was far too big for him, making him look like a snail carrying his shell. Alicia could have sworn he wore newspaper pages folded under his clothes to keep himself warm, or for goodness knows what other reason, a practice she had not seen since the first postwar years.

The simplest thing would have been to forget him and tell herself he was only another nameless face, caught in the flood of the dispossessed, still floating around the dark areas of large cities almost twenty years after the end of the war—hoping perhaps that history would remember Spain and rescue the country from oblivion. The simplest thing would have been to think that Barcelona would give her at least a few hours' respite before making her confront her fate. She walked past him without looking back and went straight to the exit, praying to the devil that he hadn't recognized her. Twenty years had passed since that night, and she'd only been a child at the time.

Outside the station she climbed into a taxi and asked the driver to take her to number 12, Calle Aviñón. Her voice shook as she pronounced those words. The car drove straight up Paseo Isabel II toward

Vía Layetana, dodging a pas de deux of intersecting trams that lit up the mist with blue electric sparks crackling on the overhead cables. Alicia scanned Barcelona's somber outlines through the window: the arches and towers, the narrow streets penetrating the old town, the lights of Montjuïc Castle far up in the distance. Home, dark home, she told herself.

At that time of night there was hardly any traffic. Ten minutes later, they'd reached their destination. The taxi driver left her by the front door of 12 Calle Aviñón, and after thanking her for the tip, which doubled the fare on the meter, he set off down the road, heading for the port. Alicia abandoned herself to the cold breeze that carried with it that neighborhood smell of an old Barcelona not even the rain could dispel. She caught herself smiling. In time, even bad memories dress up for the occasion.

*

Her home was just a few steps away from the intersection with Calle Fernando, opposite the old Gran Café. Alicia was fumbling for her keys in her coat pocket when she heard the front door opening. She looked up to meet the smiling face of Jesusa, the caretaker.

"Jesus, Mary and Joseph," Jesusa intoned, visibly excited.

Before Alicia could reply, Jesusa caught her in one of her boa-constrictor embraces and riddled her face with kisses that smelled of aniseed. "Let's have a good look at you," said the caretaker as she freed her.

Alicia smiled. "Don't tell me I'm too thin."

"Men might say that, and for once they'd be right."

"You can't imagine how I've missed you, Jesusa."

"You shameless flatterer. Let me give you another kiss that you don't deserve. All that time goodness knows where, without coming, or calling, or writing, or anything at all . . ."

Jesusa Labordeta was one of those war widows with enough spirit and determination for nine lives she had never been able to live—and never would. For fifteen years she'd been working as a caretaker in the building. She occupied a tiny apartment with two rooms at the far end of the entrance hall, which she shared with a radio tuned to a station featuring romantic soaps, and a half-dead dog she'd rescued from the street. She'd christened the mutt Napoleon, even though he could barely capture the street corner in time to perform his early-morning urinary duties, and often ended up dropping his load under the row of mailboxes in the hall. She complemented her miserable wages by mending and sewing up old clothes for half the neighborhood. Loose tongues—and most tongues were loose in those days—liked to say that Jesusa was as fond of anise liqueur as of tight-trousered sailors, and that sometimes, when she went overboard with the bottle, she could be heard weeping in her minute home while poor Napoleon howled with fear.

"Come on in, it's fiendishly cold out here."

Alicia followed her indoors.

"Señor Leandro called this morning to let me know you were coming."

"Always so thoughtful, Señor Leandro."

"He's a gentleman," declared Jesusa, who had always put him on a pedestal. "He speaks so well and lovely . . ."

The building had no elevator, and the stairs seemed to have been put in by the architect as a deterrent. Jesusa walked ahead, and Alicia followed her as best she could, dragging her case step by step.

"I've aired the apartment and tidied the place up a bit, 'cause it really needed it. Fernandito helped me—I hope you don't mind. As soon as he heard you were coming, he didn't stop pestering me until I allowed him to make himself useful . . ."

Fernandito was Señora Jesusa's nephew. A blameless soul of whom even a saint could take advantage, he was dangerously prone to the classic attacks of adolescent infatuation. To spice it all up, Mother Nature had enjoyed herself endowing him with the looks of a bumpkin. He lived with his mother in the next building and worked for a grocer's as a delivery boy, although the bulk of his toils and talents was devoted to the composition of elaborate amorous verse dedicated to Alicia, in whom he saw an irresistible mixture of the Lady of the Camellias and the wicked queen in *Snow White*, only racier. Shortly before Alicia left Barcelona, three years earlier, Fernandito had declared his eternal love to her, his readiness to provide her with at least five offspring, God willing, and the promise that his body, soul, and other earthly belongings would always be hers, in exchange for a farewell kiss.

"Fernandito, I'm at least ten years older than you," Alicia had told him at the time, drying his tears. "You shouldn't think such things, it's not right."

"Why don't you love me, Señorita Alicia? Am I not man enough for you?"

"Fernandito, you're man enough to sink the Spanish Armada, but what you must do is find yourself a girlfriend who is your age. In a couple of years you'll realize that I was right. All I can offer you is my friendship."

Fernandito's pride was like an earnest young boxer with more willingness than talent: it didn't matter how many blows it took, it always came back for more. "Nobody will ever love you more than I do, Alicia," he said. "Nobody."

The day she was due to take the train to Madrid, Fernandito, who by dint of listening to boleros on the radio carried melodrama in his bloodstream, was waiting for her at the station dressed in his Sunday best, polished shoes, and the implausible air of an aspiring matinee idol, though somewhat on the short side. He carried a bunch of red roses that had probably cost him a month's salary and insisted on handing her a passionate love letter that would have made Lady Chatterley blush but only made Alicia cry, and not in the way poor Fernandito longed for. Before Alicia could step onto the train and get safely away from the would-be Casanova, Fernandito summoned up all the courage and nerve he'd been bottling up since puberty and gave her an almighty kiss, the sort of kiss only a fifteen-year-old can give, making her feel, if only for a while, that there was still hope for the world.

"You're breaking my heart and sending me to an early grave, Señorita Alicia," he sobbed. "I'll die from weeping. I've heard that this is a medical certainty. The tear ducts dry up and end up bursting the aorta. They were talking about it on the radio the other day. You'll see, they'll send you the funeral notice, and then you'll be sorry."

"Fernandito, there's more life in one of your tears than I could live if I made it to a hundred."

"That sounds like something you've got out of a book."

"No book can do you justice, Fernandito, unless it's a treatise on biology."

"Leave, go off with your deceit and your heart of stone. One day, when you feel you're all alone with no one to turn to, you'll miss me."

Alicia kissed him on his forehead. She would have kissed him on the lips, but that would have killed him. "I'm missing you already. Take care, Fernandito. And try to forget me."

*

At last they reached the top floor. When Alicia realized she was standing in front of the door to her old home, she emerged from her trance.

Jesusa opened the door and switched on the light. "Don't worry," she said, as if she'd read her thoughts. "The boy has a lovely girlfriend now and has wised up no end. Come along in."

Alicia left her suitcase on the floor and walked into the flat. Jesusa stood waiting in the doorway. There were fresh flowers in a vase in the entrance hall, and the place had a pleasant smell of cleanliness. She went through the rooms and walked along the corridors slowly, as if she were visiting the apartment for the first time.

Hearing Jesusa behind her, setting the keys on the table, she came back into the dining room. The caretaker was looking at her with a half smile.

"As if three years hadn't gone by, right?"

"As if thirty had gone by," replied Alicia.

"How long are you staying?"

"I still don't know."

Jesusa nodded.

"Well, you must be tired. You'll find something for your dinner in the kitchen. Fernandito filled your larder. If you need anything, you know where to find me."

"Thank you so much, Jesusa."

The caretaker looked away. "I'm glad you're home again."

"Me too."

Jesusa closed the door, and Alicia heard her footsteps fading down the stairs. She drew back the curtains and opened the windows to take a look at the street. Below spread the ocean of terraced rooftops covering Barcelona's old town, and in the distance rose the towers of the cathedral and the basilica of Santa María del Mar. She scanned the outline of Calle Aviñón and caught sight of a figure withdrawing into the dark doorway of La Manual Alpargatera, the espadrille shop on the other side of the street. Whoever it was, the person was smoking, and the smoke ascended in silvery spirals up the building's facade. Alicia kept her eyes fixed on that point for an instant but then gave up. It was too soon to start imagining threatening shadows. There would be enough time for that.

She closed the windows and, although she wasn't hungry, sat at the kitchen table and ate a little bit of bread and cheese and some dried fruit and nuts. Then she opened a bottle of white wine she'd found on the table, tied with a red ribbon. The gesture had all the hallmarks of Fernandito, who still remembered her weaknesses. She poured herself a glass and sipped the wine with her eyes closed.

"Let's hope it's not poisoned," she said. "To your health, Fernandito."

The wine was excellent. Alicia poured herself a second glass and huddled up in the sitting-room armchair. She discovered that her radio still worked. Slowly she sipped the wine, a good vintage Penedès, and after a while, tired of the news bulletins that reminded the listeners, in case they'd forgotten, that Spain was the envy and the light of all nations in the world, she turned off the radio and decided to unpack the suitcase she'd brought. After dragging it into the middle of the dining room, she opened it on the floor. Looking at the contents, she wondered why she'd bothered to burden herself with clothes that seemed like remnants from another life, with possessions that, in fact, she had no intention of ever using again. She was tempted to close the suitcase and ask Jesusa, in the morning, to donate it to the Sisters of Charity. The only thing she pulled out was a revolver and two packets of bullets. The firearm had been a gift from Leandro in her second year of service, and Alicia suspected it had a past history her mentor had preferred not to mention.

What's this? The Great Captain's gun?

If you'd rather, I can find you a gun for young ladies, with an ivory grip and two golden barrels.

And what do I do with this, aside from using it to practice shooting poodles?

Make sure nobody practices on you.

In the end Alicia had accepted that heavy piece as she'd done with so many of Leandro's offerings, in a tacit agreement of submission and pretense, where the unmentionable was sealed with a cold smile of politeness and a veil of silence, allowing her to look in the mirror and carry on deceiving herself on the purpose of her life. She held the weapon in her hands and felt its weight, then opened the cylinder. Seeing that it was unloaded, she emptied one of the bullet boxes on the floor and inserted all six bullets, taking her time. She stood up and walked over to the packed bookcase covering one of the walls. Jesusa and her army of feather dusters had left not a speck of dust or a trace of her three-year absence anywhere. She pulled a leather-bound copy of the Bible out from its place next to a French translation of *Doctor Faustus* and opened it. The pages had been hollowed out with a knife, making a perfect case for her private artillery. After hiding the gun in the Bible, she slipped it back on the bookshelf. "Amen," she intoned.

She closed her suitcase and went to the bedroom. Freshly ironed and perfumed sheets welcomed her; tiredness from the train journey and the warmth of the wine in her bloodstream did the rest. She closed her eyes and listened to the murmur of the city whispering in her ear.

That night Alicia again dreamed that it was raining fire. She was jumping over the rooftops of the Raval quarter, fleeing from the roar of the bombs while buildings collapsed all around her in columns of fire and black smoke. Swarms of aircraft overflew at a low altitude, machine-gunning those running through the narrow streets as they tried to reach the shelters. When she peeped over a cornice of Calle Arco del Teatro, she saw a woman and four children fleeing in panic toward the Ramblas. A torrent of missiles swept the street, and their bodies burst into pools of blood and entrails as they ran. Alicia closed her eyes, and that is when the explosion happened. She felt it before hearing it, as if a train had charged against her in the dark. A stabbing pain shot through her side, and the flames lifted her up in the air and flung her against a skylight through which she fell, wrapped in blades of red-hot glass. She plunged into the void.

A few seconds later, something broke her fall. She'd landed on a wooden balcony suspended at the top of a huge structure. She crawled over to the edge and, looking down into the darkness, thought she saw the outline of a spiral framework in the faint reddish glow reflected by the clouds.

Alicia rubbed her eyes and looked down again into the shadowy space. Below her lay a fantastically designed citadel made entirely of books. After a while she heard footsteps approaching up one of the staircases of the labyrinth. A man with thinning hair knelt down beside her and examined the wounds covering her body. Holding her in his arms, he took her through tunnels, down stairs, and under bridges until they reached the base of the structure. There he laid her on a bed and saw to her wounds. Holding her tight, he kept her from death's door while the bombs went on falling furiously. A fiery light filtered through the dome, allowing the child Alicia to gaze at the flickering images of that place, the most marvelous she had ever seen: a basilica made of books hidden in a palace that had never existed, a place she could only return to in dreams. Somewhere like that could only belong to the other side, to the place where her mother, Lucía, waited for her, and where her own soul had remained imprisoned.

At dawn the man with the sparse hair picked her up in his arms again, and together they walked through the streets of Barcelona, streets filled with blood and flames. At last they came to an orphanage. There a doctor covered in ashes looked at them and shook his head, muttering under his breath.

"This doll is broken," he said, turning his back on them.

And then, as she had so often dreamed, Alicia looked at her own body and recognized it as a scorched wooden puppet, still smoking, its strings cut off and dangling. Nurses with no eyes came off the walls, snatched the doll from the hands of the good Samaritan, and dragged it to a vast hangar. There stood a colossal mountain, made up of bits and pieces of hundreds, even thousands, of dolls like her. The nurses threw her onto the pile and went away, laughing.

ALICIA WAS WOKEN by the wintry sun rising above the rooftops. This would be her first and last day of freedom in Barcelona, she thought as she opened her eyes. Vargas would probably show his face there that very evening.

She decided that her first stop of the day would be Gustavo Barceló's bookshop, which was nearby, on Calle Fernando. Remembering Virgilio's advice about the bookseller and his soft spot for young women of a suggestive appearance, she decided to dress up for the occasion. When she opened her old wardrobe she found that, in preparation for her arrival, Jesusa had washed and ironed all her clothes and left them smelling of lavender. Alicia brushed her old fighting colors with her fingertips, feeling the texture of the dresses that seemed smart enough for her mission. Then, to celebrate the fact that during her absence a new boiler had been installed in the building, she took a shower that flooded the apartment with steam.

Wrapped up in a towel, she stepped into the dining room, tuning the radio to a station that always played Count Basie music. Any civilization capable of producing that sound surely had a future. Back in her bedroom she threw off the towel and pulled on a pair of seamed stockings she had bought in one of her self-rewarding expeditions to La Perla Gris. She chose a pair of low-heeled shoes that would have earned Leandro's disapproval and slipped into a black wool dress she had never worn, which showed off her figure perfectly. She made herself up without rushing, caressing her lips with blood-red lipstick. The icing on the cake was her red coat. Then, just as she had done every morning when she lived in Barcelona, she went down to breakfast in the Gran Café.

Miquel, the veteran waiter, famous in the neighborhood because he never forgot a face, a name, or an outstanding bill, recognized her as soon as she came through the door, waving from behind the bar as if three years hadn't passed since her last visit. Alicia sat down at one of the tables by the large window and looked around the old coffee shop, deserted at that time of the morning. There was no need for her to order anything. Miquel came over with a tray and served her usual breakfast: a cup of coffee and two pieces of toast with butter and strawberry jam, next to a copy of the morning paper, hot off the press.

"I see you haven't forgotten, Miquel."

"We haven't seen you around here for a while, but it hasn't been that long, Doña Alicia. Welcome home."

Alicia ate her breakfast unhurriedly while she leafed through the newspaper. She'd forgotten how much she enjoyed starting the day like this, taking in the endless pantomime of Barcelona's public life as reflected in the pages of *La Vanguardia*, licking the strawberry jam off her lips, and letting half an hour go by as if she had all the time in the world.

Once the ritual was over, she went up to the bar, where Miquel was polishing wineglasses in the muted light of morning. "What do I owe you, Miquel?"

"I'll put it on your bill. See you tomorrow at the same time?"

"God willing."

"You're looking very elegant. A formal meeting?"

"Even better. A book meeting."

5

IT WAS ONE of those steely winter Barcelona mornings, when a sprinkle of powdery sunshine invites you to take a stroll. Gustavo Barceló's bookshop was opposite the arches of Plaza Real, just a couple of minutes' walk from the Gran Café. Alicia set off, escorted by a brigade of street sweepers armed with brooms and hoses. The pavements on Calle Fernando were flanked by emporiums that looked more like sanctuaries than ordinary retailers: sweet shops that made one think of a silversmith's workshop, tailor's shops straight out of an opera scene, and Barceló's bookshop, a museum in which one felt tempted to live, rather than just browse around. Before crossing the threshold, Alicia paused to enjoy the sight of the beautifully displayed glass cabinets and bookshelves beyond the shop window. Inside, a young shop assistant in blue overalls was standing on a stepladder, dusting the top shelves. She pretended not to have seen him and walked straight into the shop.

"Good morning!" hailed the shop assistant.

Alicia turned and offered him a smile that could have opened a safe.

The young man scurried down the ladder and planted himself behind the counter, hanging the rag over his shoulder. "What can I do for you, madam?"

"Miss," Alicia corrected him as she calmly pulled off her gloves.

The young man nodded, spellbound. The simplicity of these situations never ceased to surprise her. Blessed be the silliness of men of goodwill on this earth.

"Could I speak to Don Gustavo Barceló, please?"

"Señor Barceló is not here at present . . ."

"Would you know when I might find him?"

"Let me see. . . . The truth is that Don Gustavo no longer comes by the shop unless he has a meeting with a client. Don Felipe, the manager, has gone to Pedralbes to value a collection, but he'll be back at noon."

"What's your name?"

"Benito, at your service."

"Look, Benito, I can see you're smart. I'm sure you'll be able to help me."

"Certainly."

"You see, it's a rather delicate subject. I need to speak to Señor Barceló as a matter of urgency. As it so happens, a close relative of mine, a great collector, has recently acquired a unique piece that he would be very interested in selling, and he'd like Don Gustavo to act as middleman and adviser in the transaction in order to maintain his anonymity."

"I see," said the young man, his voice faltering.

"The piece in question is a copy in perfect condition of one of the books of *The Labyrinth of the Spirits*, by someone called Víctor Mataix."

The young man looked at her with eyes like saucers. "Mataix, you said?"

Alicia nodded. "Does that ring a bell?"

"If you would be so kind as to wait a minute, miss, I'll try to contact Don Gustavo right away."

Alicia smiled meekly. The shop assistant disappeared behind a curtain into the back room, and a few seconds later Alicia heard him dialing a number, then speaking hurriedly in a hushed voice.

"Don Gustavo, excuse me if I . . . Yes, I know this is not the time . . . No, I haven't gone . . . Yes, sir, yes sir, I beg you . . . Of course I like my job . . . No, please . . . One second, just one second . . . Thank you." The young man paused to recover his breath. "There's a young lady here who says she has a Víctor Mataix in perfect condition for sale."

A long silence.

"No, I'm not making this up. What? No. I don't know who she is. No, I'd never seen her before. I don't know. Young, very elegant . . . Well yes, I'd say so . . . No, they don't all seem to me . . . Yes, sir, right away, sir . . ."

The young man appeared in the doorway to the back room, all smiles. "Don Gustavo wants to know when would be a good time for you to meet him."

"First thing this afternoon?"

The young man nodded and disappeared again. "She says this afternoon. Yes. I don't know. I'll ask her . . . Then I won't ask her . . . Whatever you say, Don Gustavo. Yes, sir. Right away. Rest assured. Yes, sir. You too."

When the assistant reappeared, he looked relieved.

"Everything all right, Benito?" Alicia inquired.

"Never better. Excuse the manners. Don Gustavo is a saint, but he has his quirks."

"I understand."

"He said he'd be delighted to meet you this afternoon at the Equestrian Club, if that would suit you. He's having lunch there today and will be there all afternoon. Do you know where it is? Casa Pérez Samanillo, Balmes, on the corner of Avenida Diagonal?"

"I know it. I'll tell Don Gustavo you've been a great help."

"Most grateful."

Alicia was about to leave when the young man, perhaps wishing to prolong her visit a few more moments, walked around the counter and offered to accompany her to the exit.

"Funny, isn't it?" he improvised, sounding rather nervous. "It's been years since anyone has seen a single book of the *Labyrinth* series, and this month, so far, you're the second person who has come to the bookshop to talk about Mataix."

Alicia stopped. "You don't say. And who was the other person, if I may ask?"

Benito assumed a serious expression, as if he'd talked too much.

Alicia put her hand on his arm and pressed it affectionately. "Don't worry, it will remain between us. I'm just curious."

The assistant looked doubtful. Alicia leaned slightly toward him.

"He was a man from Madrid who looked like a policeman. He showed me some sort of badge," he said.

"Did he tell you his name, perhaps?"

Benito shrugged. "Right now I don't remember . . . I remember him because he had a cut on his face."

Alicia's smile made Benito feel even more agitated.

"On the right cheek? The scar?"

The boy turned pale.

"Was the name Lomana, perhaps?" asked Alicia. "Ricardo Lomana?"

"It might be . . . I'm not sure, but—"

"Thanks, Benito. You're a star."

Alicia was already walking down the street when the shop assistant stuck his head out of the door and called out, "Miss? You haven't told me your name . . ."

Alicia turned around and threw Benito a smile that left its mark on him all day and part of the night.

6

AFTER HER VISIT to Barceló's bookshop, Alicia allowed herself to be tempted by the old haunts as she meandered through the rambling Gothic quarter, bound for the second stop of her day. She walked slowly, her thoughts focused on Ricardo Lomana and his strange disappearance. Deep down, it didn't surprise her that she'd already run across his trail. Time had taught her that quite often she and Lomana were hot on each other's heels when following the same track. Nine times out of ten she was the one who got there first. The only remarkable thing on this occasion was that only a few weeks ago Lomana—who, as Gil de Partera had explained when he entrusted them with the mission, had started investigating the case of Valls's anonymous letters—should have been asking questions about the Víctor Mataix books. Lomana might be a lot of things, but he wasn't stupid. The good news in all that was that if Lomana had arrived at the *Labyrinth* books on his own, Alicia could take that as evidence that her instinct was not failing her. The bad news was that, sooner or later, she was going to bump into him. And their encounters rarely ended well.

According to rumors in the unit, Ricardo Lomana had been an old disciple of the ill-fated Inspector Fumero in Barcelona's political branch, and the most sinister of all the creatures Leandro recruited over the years—and there were quite a few. During her years in Leandro's pay, Alicia had had more than one brush with Lomana. The most recent had taken place a couple of years back when Lomana, fired up with brandy and resentment because Alicia had solved a case in which he'd been stuck hopelessly for months, had followed her one night to her room in the Hispania and sworn that one day, when Leandro wasn't there to protect her, he'd find the right moment and place to hang her from the ceiling and take his time to work her over, making good use of his toolbox.

You're not the first or the last classy tart Leandro comes up with, darling, and when he tires of you, I'll be waiting. And I promise we're going to have a great time, especially you, with that flesh of yours made for the irons . . .

From that meeting Lomana had obtained a kneeing to his pride that left him on sick leave for two weeks, a double fracture to his arm, and a cut on his cheek that required eighteen stitches. For her part, the encounter cost Alicia a couple of weeks of insomnia, staring at the door of her hotel room in the dark, with the revolver on her bed-side table and an ominous foreboding that the worst still lay ahead in the return match.

She decided to banish Lomana from her thoughts and enjoy that first morning in the streets of Barcelona. As she continued her lei-surely stroll in the sun, she measured each step, pausing to window-shop at the slightest hint of pressure on her hip. Over the years she had learned to read the signs and avoid, or at least postpone, the in-evitable. She and her pain were old rivals, veterans who know one an-other well, exploring one another mutually and sticking to the rules of the game. Even so, that first walk without the harness clinging to her body was well worth the price she knew she would pay later.

It wasn't even ten o'clock when she walked up Puerta del Ángel and, as she turned the corner into Calle Santa Ana, saw the shop window of the old bookshop, Sempere & Sons. Across the street from the bookshop was a small café. Alicia decided to go in and take one of the tables by the window. A rest would do her good.

"What will it be, miss?" asked a waiter who looked as if he hadn't left the premises for at least twenty years.

"An espresso. And a glass of water."

"House tap water, or bottled mineral water?"

"What would you recommend?"

"That depends on how much calcium is already in your blood-stream."

"I'll have bottled water. Room temperature, please."

"On its way."

*

A couple of coffees and half an hour later, she hadn't seen a single person stop by the bookshop, not even to glance at the shop window. Sempere's ledgers must be gathering cobwebs at the speed of light. The temptation to cross the street, enter that enchanted bazaar, and spend a fortune was strong, but it was not the right moment. What she had to do now was observe. Another half hour went by, with nothing much happening. She was beginning to consider whether or not to weigh anchor when she saw him. He looked distracted as he walked, his head in the clouds, a half smile on his lips, with that calm expression of one who is lucky enough not to know how the world works. She had never seen a photograph of him, but she knew who he was before he approached the shop door.

Daniel.

Alicia smiled unconsciously. When Daniel Sempere reached the bookshop, its door opened outward, and a young woman who didn't look a day older than twenty came out to meet him. Hers was one of those fresh beauties, the sort that writers of radio soaps would describe as coming from within, the sort of beauty that makes love-prone saps addicted to stories about golden-hearted angels drool and sigh. She had the touch of innocence, or modesty, of a girl from a good family, and she dressed as if she suspected the type of chassis she carried under her clothes but didn't dare acknowledge it. The famous Beatriz, Alicia told herself, a Snow White, perfumed with innocence, in the land of the dwarves.

Beatriz stood on her toes and kissed her husband's lips. A chaste kiss, a quick brush of joined lips. Alicia couldn't help noticing that Beatriz was the type of woman who closed her eyes when she kissed, even if this was her lawful little husband, letting him put his arm around her waist. Daniel, on the other hand, still kissed like a schoolboy. An early marriage hadn't yet taught him how to hold a woman, where the hands should go, and what to do with his lips. Clearly nobody had taught him. Alicia felt her smile vanish, and a streak of malice invaded her. "Will you bring me a glass of white wine?" she asked the waiter.

On the other side of the street, Daniel Sempere said good-bye to his wife and stepped into the bookshop. Beatriz, in her tasteful but low-budget clothes, set off toward Puerta del Ángel, mingling with the crowd. Alicia studied her waist and the undulations described by her hips. "God, if I could dress you, my princess," she murmured.

"You were saying, miss?"

Alicia turned to find the waiter standing there with the glass of white wine, looking at her with a mixture of enthrallment and appre-hension. "What was your name?" she asked.

"Mine?"

Alicia looked all around the café, confirming that they were alone. "Do you see anyone else?"

"Marcelino."

"Why don't you sit down with me, Marcelino? I don't like to drink alone. Well, that's a lie. But I like it less."

The waiter gulped.

"If you like, I could buy you a drink," offered Alicia. "A beer?"

Marcelino looked at her, stiff as a ramrod.

"Sit down, Marcelino. I don't bite."

The young man sat down opposite her. Alicia smiled at him sweetly. "Do you have a girlfriend, Marcelino?"

The waiter shook his head.

"Some girls don't know what they're missing. Tell me something. Does this place have any other way out, apart from the main door?"

"Excuse me?"

"I was asking, do you have any other way out to an alleyway, or to the entrance hall of the next-door building . . ."

"There's a door to a patio that leads to Bertrellans. Why?"

"I'm asking you because someone is following me."

Marcelino glanced at the street in alarm. "Do you want me to call the police?"

Alicia put her hand on his. The waiter was about to turn into a statue of salt.

"There's no need. It's nothing serious. But I'd rather use a more discreet exit, if that's not a problem for you."

Marcelino shook his head.

"You're a darling. Now, what do I owe you?"

"It's on the house."

"Are you sure?"

Marcelino gave a quick nod.

"It's what I said. There's a whole lot of young girls out there who don't know what's good . . . Tell me, do you have a telephone?"

"Behind the bar."

"Do you mind if I make a call? It's long-distance, but I'll pay for it, all right?"

"Make as many calls as you wish . . ."

Alicia made her way to the bar and found an old telephone attached to the wall. Marcelino, who had remained stuck to the table, was looking at her. She waved at him while she dialed. "Put me through to Vargas, please."

"You're Gris, aren't you?" asked a rather sarcastic voice on the other end of the line. "The captain was expecting your call. I'll put you through."

She heard the receiver being left on a table as the voice summoned her colleague. "Vargas, it's Doña Inés . . . ," she heard one of the police officers say, while another sang the refrain of "Green Eyes."

"Vargas here. How's it going? Have you been dancing *sardanas*?"

"Who is Doña Inés?"

"You. We've been given nicknames here. I'm Don Juan . . ."

"Your pals are so witty."

"You have no idea. There's an abundance of talent here. What news?"

"I just thought you'd be missing me."

"I've been stood up by more promising dates, and I've managed to get over it."

"I'm glad to see you're coping so well. I thought you'd already be on your way here."

"If it was up to me, I'd be happy for you to stay there on your own until you retired."

"And what do your bosses say?"

"They're telling me to get into a car and drive all day and part of the night to be there with you tomorrow."

"Speaking of cars—any news on Valls's?"

"No news. They found it abandoned in . . . let me look at the note . . . Carretera de las Aguas, in Vallvidrera. Is that in Barcelona?"

"Above Barcelona, to be precise."

"Above? As in the sky?"

"Something like that. Any trace of Valls, or of his driver, Vicente?"

"Drops of blood on the passenger seat. Signs of violence. Not a trace of either man."

"What else?"

"That's it. What about you? What do you have to tell me?"

"That I'm the one missing you," said Alicia.

"This business of returning to Barcelona has gone to your head. Where are you now? On a pilgrimage to Our Lady of Montserrat?"

"Almost. Right now I'm staring at the shop window of Sempere & Sons."

"Very productive. Have you spoken to Leandro, by any chance?"

"No. Why?"

"Because he's been pursuing me all morning, asking after you. Please phone him and wish him a Merry Christmas. He's not going to get off my back otherwise."

Alicia sighed. "I will. By the way, I need you to do something for me."

"Apparently that's the new purpose of my life."

"It's a rather delicate subject."

"My specialty."

"I need you to use all your contacts in headquarters to find out in a discreet way what someone called Ricardo Lomana was up to before he vanished into thin air."

"Lomana? The one who disappeared? Bad type."

"You know him?"

"I know of him. Nothing good. I'll see what I can do."

"That's all I'm asking."

On the other end of the phone, Vargas sighed. "I guess I'll be there tomorrow morning. If you like, we can have breakfast together, and I'll let you know what I've found out about your friend Lomana—if I do discover anything, that is. Will you behave yourself and keep out of trouble until I arrive?"

"I promise."

7

MARCELINO WAS STILL watching her from afar, mixing his morbid fascination with quick glances to the street in search of her mysterious follower. Alicia winked at him and made a sign with her forefinger. "Another quick call, and that's it . . ."

She dialed the direct number of the hotel suite. The phone didn't even ring once. He must have been sitting next to the phone, waiting, thought Alicia.

"It's me," she murmured.

"Alicia, Alicia, Alicia," Leandro's voice intoned sweetly. "I don't like you to avoid me. You know that."

"I was going to call you right now. There was no need to send a chaperone after me."

"I'm not following you."

"Somebody is. Haven't you set someone up to shadow me?"

"If I had, it wouldn't have been someone you could detect that easily on your first morning. Who is it?"

"I don't know yet. I was hoping it was one of yours."

"Well, it isn't. Unless it's something to do with our friends at the central police station in Barcelona."

"The local supply must have dried up, for them to have sent me this whiz kid."

"It's not easy to find good people. I should know. Would you like me to make a call and get him off your back?"

Alicia thought about it. "Maybe not. I just had an idea."

"Don't be cruel to him. I don't know who they've assigned to you, but it might have been the most inexperienced guy they've found."

"Am I that easy?"

"On the contrary. What I'm thinking is that nobody would have wanted the job."

"Are you suggesting that I left a bad impression?"

"I've always told you it's important to mind your manners. If you don't, this is what happens. Have you spoken to Vargas?"

"Yes."

"So you're up-to-date about the car? Everything all right in your flat?"

"Yes. Señora Jesusa left everything spotless. She even ironed my first communion dress. Thanks for organizing that."

"I want you to have everything you need."

"Is that why you're sending Vargas?"

"That must have been on his own initiative. Or Gil de Partera's. I told you they didn't trust us."

"I wonder why?"

"What are your plans for today?"

"I've been going around the bookshops, and this afternoon I have an appointment with someone who will be able to clarify a few things about Víctor Mataix."

"So you're still on about that book . . ."

"Even if only to rule it out."

"Do I know him? The person you're meeting?"

"I don't know. He's a bookseller, Gustavo Barceló?"

The pause was almost imperceptible, but Alicia noticed it.

"It doesn't ring a bell. Call me if you find out anything. And if you don't."

Alicia was trying to think of a sharp reply when she heard Leandro hang up. She left a few coins on the bar to cover the drinks and the two phone calls and blew Marcelino a kiss good-bye.

"We keep all this between us, eh, Marcelino?"

The waiter nodded enthusiastically and accompanied Alicia to the back door, which led to an open patio. From there, through a maze of corridors between various buildings in the block, she came to one of those gloomy alleyways, trademark of Barcelona's old town, that are as tight and narrow as the space between a seminarist's buttocks.

The alley went uphill from Calle Canuda to Calle Santa Ana. Alicia walked around the block, and at the corner stopped to take in the scene. A lady was pushing a shopping cart with one hand and with the other trying to drag a child who seemed to have his shoes glued to the ground. A young man wearing a suit and a scarf was standing in front of a shoe-store window, throwing sidelong glances at two pretty young girls with seamed stockings who laughed as they walked past him. A local policeman ambled down the middle of the street, casting suspicious looks here and there. And farther on, stuck to the side of a doorway like a poster, Alicia noticed a short man of such unremarkable appearance that he bordered on invisibility. This specimen was smoking a cigarette and watching the café door nervously while he checked his watch. He wasn't a bad choice, thought Alicia. He looked so insignificant that even boredom wouldn't have noticed him passing by.

She walked up to him and stopped just a few centimeters from the pale nape of his neck. Then she formed an O with her lips and blew.

He jumped and almost lost his balance. When he turned around and saw Alicia, he lost what little color he had left.

"What's your name, sweetheart?" she asked.

If the little man had a voice, he didn't find it. His eyes swiveled around a hundred times before settling on Alicia.

"If you run off, I'll stick a bodkin in your guts. Are we clear?"

"Yes," said the guy.

"That was a joke." Alicia smiled. "I don't do that sort of thing."

The poor wretch was wearing a coat that could have been found in a trash bin, and looked like a cornered rodent. Some spy she'd been assigned. She grabbed him by his lapel and led him quietly to the street corner. "What's your name?"

"Rovira," he muttered.

"Were you the one standing in the doorway of the espadrille shop last night?"

"How do you know?"

"Never smoke against the light of a streetlamp."

Rovira nodded, cursing under his breath.

"Tell me, Rovira, how long have you been in the Force?"

"It would have been two months tomorrow, but if they find out at the police station that you spotted me—"

"There's no need for them to find out."

"No?"

"No. Because you and I, Rovira, are going to help one another. Do you know how?"

"I don't follow, miss."

"Yes, that's the idea, but call me Alicia. We're on the same side, after all."

Alicia searched Rovira's coat pockets and found a packet of cigarettes, the sort they sold in cheap bars and that went well with a *carajillo* coffee. She lit one and put it in the man's mouth. She let him take a couple of puffs and gave him a friendly smile. "A bit calmer now?"

He nodded.

"Tell me, Rovira, why exactly have they chosen you to follow me?"

The man hesitated. "Don't take this the wrong way, miss, but nobody else wanted the job."

"And why's that?"

Rovira shrugged.

"Come on, don't be shy, now that we've been introduced. Spill it out."

"They say you screw people up, and you're bad news."

"I see. Obviously that didn't deter you."

"I tried, but I wasn't given a choice."

"Poor baby. And what does your mission consist of, exactly?"

"I'm to follow you from afar and inform on your whereabouts and what you're doing without you noticing. I told them this wasn't my kind of thing."

"Clearly. So why did you join the police?"

"I wanted to go into the printing business, but my father-in-law is a captain at the central police station."

"I see. And the missus likes uniforms, right?" Alicia placed a maternal hand on Rovira's shoulder. "Rovira, there are times when a man has to have some balls, and if you'll forgive my French, show the world that he was born to pee standing up. And just so you know that you're far more capable than you think, I'm going to give you the chance to prove it: to me, to the police force, to your father-in-law, and to the little wife. Once she sees the stud she has at home, she's going to need to sniff some smelling salts to keep her undies on."

Rovira stared at her, on the verge of a seizure.

"From now on, you'll follow me as you've been ordered to do, but never less than a hundred meters away and trying your best not to let me see you. And when they ask you where I've been and what I've done, you'll tell them what I ask you to tell them."

"But . . . is that legal?"

"Rovira, you're a cop now. Legal is whatever you say is legal."

"I don't know . . ."

"Of course you know. You're a connoisseur of the policing arts. What you're lacking is self-confidence."

Rovira looked dazed. He blinked a few times. "What if I say no?"

"Don't be like that, just when we'd started to become friends. Because if you refuse, I'm going to have to go and see your father-in-law the captain and tell him I saw you climbing up the wall of the Teresian mothers' school and jerking off during the break."

"You wouldn't do that."

Alicia fixed her eyes on his.

"Rovira, you haven't a fucking idea of what I might do."

The man let out a moan. "You're evil."

Alicia pressed her lips together, pretending to sulk. "When I decide to be evil with you, you'll notice it immediately. Tomorrow, first thing, you'll be waiting for me opposite the Gran Café, and I'll tell you what the plan is for the day. Are we clear?"

Rovira seemed to have shrunk a few centimeters during the conversation. He looked at her with pleading eyes. "All this is a joke, isn't it? You're laughing at me because I'm new at the job . . ."

Alicia did her best impression of Leandro's icy look. She shook her head slowly. "It's not a joke, it's an order. Don't fail me. Spain and I are counting on you."

8

AT THE DAWN of the twentieth century, when money still had a whiff of perfume and large fortunes were not only inherited but also put on display, a modernist palace, born from the troubled romance between the dreams of great craftsmen and the vanity of a tycoon, fell from the heavens and was encased forever in the most improbable enclave of Barcelona's Belle Époque.

The so-called Casa Pérez Samanillo had been occupying the corner of Calle Balmes and Avenida Diagonal for half a century in the guise of a mirage, or perhaps a warning. Built originally as a family residence at a time when almost all aristocrats were getting rid of such ostentatious abodes, this paean to abundance seemed like a Parisian coral reef, beaming its coppery light over the streets from its French windows, displaying to mere mortals its grand staircases, halls, and crystal chandeliers with no hint of shame. Alicia had always thought of it as a sort of aquarium where one could observe exotic and undreamed-of forms of life through glass panels.

For years this lavish fossil had ceased to be a family home, and more recently it had become the headquarters of the Equestrian Club of Barcelona, one of those unassailable and elegant institutions left to ferment in all great cities, where people with good names can protect themselves against the smell of sweat given off by those on whose shoulders their illustrious ancestors built their fortunes. Leandro, a fine observer of such situations, said that once the business of food and home has been solved, the next thing humans strive for are reasons to feel superior to others, and resources with which to demonstrate that superiority. The club seemed to have been fashioned for that very end, and Alicia suspected that if Leandro hadn't moved to Madrid years ago, those exquisitely designed halls of fine wood would have provided the perfect stage for her mentor, a residence where he might handle his murky affairs with kid gloves.

Uniformed up to his ears, a footman opened the solemn iron door for her. Inside the foyer stood an illuminated lectern behind which she caught sight of an individual wearing a suit. His face wizened with age, he glanced at her from head to toe a couple of times before granting her a meek smile.

"Good afternoon," said Alicia. "I've arranged to meet Señor Gustavo Barceló here."

The employee looked down at the notebook on the lectern and pretended to study it for a few moments, lending solemnity to the ritual. "And your name is . . . ?"

"Verónica Larraz."

"If you'd be so kind as to follow me—"

The receptionist led her through the sumptuous interior of the palace. As she walked by, the members of the club interrupted their conversations to look at her in surprise. Some almost seemed scandalized. This was clearly not a place that was used to receiving female visitors, and more than one patrician seemed to take her presence as an affront to his ancestral masculinity. Alicia merely returned their attentions with a polite smile. At last she was shown into a reading room facing a large window that looked out onto Avenida Diagonal. There, sitting in a plush armchair, sipping a glass of brandy the size of a fish tank, was a gentleman with majestic features and a no less grand mustache, sporting a three-piece suit, complete with two-toned shoes. The receptionist stopped a couple of meters away and broke into a fainthearted smile.

"Don Gustavo? The visitor you were expecting . . ."

Don Gustavo Barceló, honorary chairman of the Barcelona guild of booksellers and a scholar of everything pertaining to the eternal feminine and its most refined manifestations, stood up to receive Alicia warmly with a deferential bow. "Gustavo Barceló, at your service."

Alicia held out her hand to him, and the bookseller kissed it as he would the hand of a bishop, taking his time and making the most of the moment to look her over properly, probably even noting what size gloves she wore.

"Verónica Larraz," Alicia introduced herself. "It's a pleasure."

"Is Larraz the surname of your collector relative?"

Alicia supposed that Barceló's employee, Benito, had called him as soon as she'd left the bookshop and told him all about the meeting in minute detail.

"No. Larraz is my married name."

"I see. Discretion above all. I quite understand. Please, take a seat."

Alicia sat down in an armchair opposite Barceló and took in the exclusive aristocratic air that emanated from the room's decor.

"Welcome to the illustrious sanctuary of the nouveaux-riches and of those who have fallen on hard times and marry off their children to them, in order to perpetuate the caste," remarked Barceló, following her eyes.

"You're not a full member of the club, then?"

"For years I resisted on grounds of moral hygiene, but in the end circumstances forced me to succumb to the realities of the city and go with the flow."

"It must have its advantages."

"It certainly does. You meet people in need of thinning their excessive inherited disposable income on articles they don't understand or want. It also cures you of any romantic notions you might entertain about the self-appointed elites of this country. And the brandy is superb. Besides, this is a wonderful place for social archaeology. Over a million people live in Barcelona, but when it comes to the crunch, barely four hundred of them hold the keys to every door. This is a city of closed doors where everything depends on who has the key, who the key holder will allow through the door, and on what side of the door one will end up. But I doubt any of this is news to you, Señora Larraz. Is there anything I can offer you, apart from speeches and sermons from an old bookseller?"

Alicia shook her head.

"Of course. No beating around the bush, right?"

"If you wouldn't mind."

"On the contrary. Did you bring the book?"

Alicia opened her bag, pulled out the copy of *Ariadna and the Scarlet Prince*, wrapped in a silk scarf, and handed it to him. Barceló took it with both hands. As soon as his fingers touched the cover, his eyes lit up and a smile of pleasure spread over his lips.

"*The Labyrinth of the Spirits . . .*," he murmured. "I suppose you're not going to tell me how you obtained it."

"The owner would rather that was kept secret."

"I understand. If you'll allow me . . ."

Don Gustavo opened the book and turned the pages slowly, relishing the finding like a gourmet taking pleasure in a unique and unrepeatable dish. Alicia was beginning to suspect that the old bookseller, lost in the pages of the volume, had forgotten her when he suddenly looked up and threw her a questioning glance.

"Pardon my boldness, Señora Larraz, but I have to admit that I can't understand why someone—in this case the collector you are representing—would want to get rid of a piece like this."

"Do you think it would be difficult to find a buyer?"

"Not at all. Give me a phone, and in twenty minutes I'll present you with at least five offers at the high end, minus my ten percent commission. That's not the point."

"And what is the point, Don Gustavo, if you don't mind my asking?"

Barceló downed his glass of brandy. "The point is whether you really want to sell this piece, Señora *Larraz*." Barceló stressed the fictitious surname ironically.

Alicia just smiled timidly. Barceló gave a nod. "There's no need to reply, nor do you need to give me your real name."

"My name is Alicia."

"Did you know that Ariadna, the main character in the series of *The Labyrinth of the Spirits*, is a homage to another Alice, the Lewis Carroll one with her Wonderland, which in this case is Barcelona?"

Alicia feigned surprise, shaking her head slowly.

"In the first book of the series, Ariadna finds a book of magic spells in the attic of a large old house in Vallvidrera where she lives with her parents until they disappear mysteriously one stormy night. Believing that if she could exorcize a spirit from the shadows, she might be able to find them, Ariadna, without realizing it, opens a door between the real Barcelona and its reverse, the accursed reflection of the city. The City of Mirrors . . . The floor cracks beneath her feet, and Ariadna falls down an interminable spiral staircase into the dark until she reaches that other Barcelona, the labyrinth of the spirits, where she is condemned to wander through the circles of hell built by the Scarlet Prince. There she meets ill-fated souls and tries to save them while she searches for her lost parents."

"Does Ariadna manage to find her parents and save some of those souls?"

"No, unfortunately she doesn't. But she tries hard. In her own way she's a heroine, although her flirtations with the Scarlet Prince also turn her slowly into a dark and perverse reflection of herself—a fallen angel, one might say."

"It sounds like an uplifting story."

"It is. Tell me, *Alicia*, is this what you devote your time to? Descending into hell in search of problems?"

"Why would I want to search for problems?"

"Because, as I imagine you've already been told by that dimwit Benito in my employ, not long ago an individual who looked like a butcher from the political police came to the bookshop asking questions similar to the ones you've asked, and I have a feeling that you two are acquainted with one another."

"The individual you're referring to is called Ricardo Lomana, and you're on the right path."

"I'm usually on the right path, miss, however thorny it may turn out to be."

"What exactly did Lomana ask you?"

"He wanted to know whether anyone had recently bought one of Víctor Mataix's books, either at auction, as a private purchase, or on the international market."

"Didn't he ask you any questions about Víctor Mataix?"

"Señor Lomana didn't strike me as a great reader, but I got the impression that he knew everything he needed to know about Mataix."

"And what did you say to him?"

"I gave him the address of a collector who for the last seven years has been buying all the copies of *The Labyrinth of the Spirits* that were not destroyed in 1939."

"All the Mataix books in the market have been bought by the same person?"

Barceló nodded. "All but yours."

"And who is this collector?"

"I don't know."

"You've just told me you gave Lomana his address."

"I gave him the address of the lawyer who represents him and carries out all the transactions in his name. His name is Brians—Fernando Brians."

"Have you spoken to this lawyer Brians, Don Gustavo?"

"I must have spoken to him once or twice, at the most. On the phone. A serious man."

"About matters connected to Víctor Mataix, Don Gustavo?"

Barceló nodded.

"What can you tell me about Víctor Mataix, Don Gustavo?"

"Very little. I know he often worked as an illustrator, that he'd published various novels with those scoundrels Barrido and Escobillas before he started to work on the *Labyrinth* books, and that he lived as a recluse in a house on Carretera de las Aguas, between Vallvidrera and the Fabra observatory, because his wife suffered from some strange disease and he couldn't, or wouldn't, leave her alone. Not much else. That and the fact that he disappeared in 1939, after the Nacionales entered Barcelona."

"Where could I find out more about him?"

"It's difficult. The only person I can think of who could help you is Vilajuana. Sergio Vilajuana, a journalist and writer who knew Mataix. He's a regular customer at the bookshop and the person who knows most about the subject. I remember hearing someone say that Vilajuana was working on a book about Mataix and the whole doomed generation of Barcelona writers who vanished after the war—"

"You mean there are more?"

"Doomed writers? It's a local specialty, like *allioli*."

"And where can I find Señor Vilajuana?"

"Try the newsroom of *La Vanguardia*. But if you'll allow me a bit of advice, you'd better come up with a better story than your secret collector. Vilajuana wasn't born yesterday."

"What would you suggest?"

"Tempt him."

Alicia smiled mischievously.

"With the book. If he's still interested in Mataix, I don't think he'll be able to resist having a look at this copy. These days it's almost as difficult to find a Mataix as it is to find a decent person in an important post."

"Thank you, Don Gustavo. You've been a great help. May I ask you to keep this conversation between us?"

"Of course. Keeping secrets is what keeps me young. That and expensive brandy."

Alicia wrapped the book in the silk scarf again and put it back in her bag. While she was at it, she pulled out her lipstick and shaped her smile as if she were alone, a spectacle that Barceló watched with fascination and delight.

"How does that look?"

"Very distinguished."

She stood up and put on her coat.

"Who are you, Alicia?"

"A fallen angel," she replied, holding out her hand and winking.

"Then you've come to the right place."

Don Gustavo Barceló shook her hand and watched her walk away. He settled back in his large armchair, holding his almost empty brandy glass, lost in thought. Minutes later he saw her walking past the large window. The evening had spread a blanket of crimson clouds over Barcelona, and the setting sun traced the figures of passersby on the pavements of Avenida Diagonal and made the cars shine like red-hot metal tears. Barceló fixed his gaze on that receding red coat until Alicia seemed to evaporate into the shadows of the city.

9

THAT AFTERNOON, AFTER leaving Barceló in the company of fine brandy and finer suspicions, Alicia walked straight down Rambla de Cataluña on her way home, revisiting the parade of elegant shops that were already lighting up their windows. She remembered the days when she had learned to look at those emporiums and their respectable, stylish clientele with envy and mistrust.

She remembered the times she had gone in to steal, and what she had taken, and the shouts of the manager and customers behind her, the fire in her veins when she realized she was being pursued and the sweet taste of revenge and justice after seizing something from people who thought it belonged to them by divine right. She remembered the day her pillaging career ended in a dark, damp room in the basement of Central Police Headquarters on Vía Layetana. The room had no windows, just a metal table nailed to the floor and two chairs. There was a drain in the middle of the room, and the floor was still wet. It smelled of shit, blood, and bleach. The two policemen who had arrested her had shackled her hands and feet to the chair and left her there for hours, giving her plenty of time to imagine all the things they were going to do to her.

"Fumero is going to be so happy when he sees he's got such a young tart waiting for him. He'll give you a real makeover."

Alicia had heard about Fumero. There were loads of stories about him in the streets, and about what happened to the poor devils who ended up in a dungeon like the one in the basement of police headquarters. She didn't know whether she was trembling from cold or from fear, and when hours later the metal door opened and she heard voices and footsteps, she closed her eyes and felt urine running between her thighs and sliding down her legs.

"Open your eyes," said a voice.

A man of medium height with the look of a small-town lawyer was smiling warmly at her through her tears. There was nobody else in the room. The guy, in an immaculate suit and smelling of lemony eau de cologne, gazed at her for a while and then walked around the table and stood behind her. Alicia pressed her lips tight to drown the cry of terror that burned her throat when she felt those hands on her shoulders and his mouth brushing her left ear.

"Don't be afraid, Alicia."

She began to shake violently, swaying on the chair to which she was fastened. She felt the man's hands making their way down her back, and when the pressure gripping her wrists was relieved, it took her a few seconds to realize that her captor had removed her handcuffs. Her circulation slowly returned to her limbs, and with it the pain. The man took her arms and placed them delicately on the table. He sat down next to her and started to massage her wrists. "My name is Leandro," he said. "Better?"

Alicia nodded.

Leandro smiled and let go of her hands. "I'm now going to take the shackles off your ankles. But first I need to make sure that you're not going to do anything silly."

She shook her head.

"Nobody's going to hurt you," said Leandro as he removed the shackles.

When she was free, Alicia stood up and ran for shelter to a corner of the room.

The man's gaze fixed on the puddle of urine under the chair. "I apologize, Alicia."

"What do you want?"

"I want us to have a chat. That's all."

"What about?"

"About the man you've been working for these last two years. Baltasar Ruano."

"I don't owe him anything."

"I know. I want you to know that Ruano has been arrested, together with most of your gang."

Alicia looked at him suspiciously.

"What are they going to do to him?"

Leandro shrugged. "Ruano's finished. He confessed after a long interrogation. He'll be garroted. It's a matter of days. That's good news for you."

Alicia swallowed hard. "What about the others?"

"They're just kids. Reformatory or prison. For the lucky ones, that is. The ones who go back to the streets have their days numbered."

"And me?"

"That depends."

"On what?"

"On you."

"I don't understand."

"I'd like you to work for me."

Alicia observed Leandro without a word as he settled in the chair and gazed at her, smiling.

"I've been watching you for some time, Alicia. I think you have the gift."

"What for?"

"For learning."

"Learning what?"

"To survive. And also to use your skills for something more than filling the pockets of a small-time crook like Ruano."

"And who are you?"

"I'm Leandro."

"Are you with the police?"

"Something like that. Think of me as a friend."

"I don't have any friends."

"We all have friends. It's a matter of knowing how to find them. What I'm proposing to you is that you work for me for the next twelve months. You'll have decent lodgings and a salary. You'll be free to leave whenever you wish."

"What if I decide to leave now?"

Leandro pointed to the door. "If that's what you want, you can go. You can go back to the streets."

Alicia fixed her eyes on the door. Leandro stood up and opened it. Then he went back to the chair, leaving the path open for her. "Nobody is going to stop you if you decide to walk through that door, Alicia. But the opportunity I'm offering you stays here."

She took a few steps toward the door. Leandro made no attempt to stop her.

"And if I stay with you?" she said.

"If you decide to trust me, the first thing will be to find you a hot bath, clean clothes, and dinner at the Siete Puertas restaurant. Have you ever been there?"

"No."

"They serve a delicious seafood rice."

Alicia's stomach rumbled with hunger. "And then?"

"Then you'll go to your new home, where you'll have a room and a bathroom to yourself, and there you'll rest and sleep in your own bed with clean new sheets. And tomorrow, without rushing, I'll come and fetch you and we'll go to my office so I can begin to tell you what I do."

"Why don't you tell me now?"

"Let's say that I devote my time to solving problems and to putting criminals like Baltasar Ruano and others far worse out of circulation, so that they can no longer hurt anybody. But the most important thing I do is find exceptional people like you, who don't know they're exceptional, and teach them to develop their talents so that they can do good."

"Do good," Alicia repeated coldly.

"The world isn't the amoral place you've known until now, Alicia. The world is simply the reflection of those of us who make it up. In fact, the world is only what we make of it between us all. That's why people like you or like me, who are born with a gift, have a responsibility to use it for the good of others. Mine is to know how to recognize talent in others and guide them, so that when the time comes they can make the right decision."

"I have no talent. No gift—"

"Of course you do. Trust me. And above all, trust yourself, Alicia. Because if you so wish, today could be the first day of the life that was stolen from you. If you let me, I'll give it back to you."

Leandro smiled warmly, and Alicia felt an anxious and painful need to hug him. He held out his hand. Step by step, she crossed the room toward him. She placed her hand on that stranger's hand and gazed deep into his eyes.

"Thank you, Alicia. I swear you won't be sorry."

*

The echo of those words, so distant now, slowly died away. Pain was starting to bare its claws, and Alicia decided to walk slowly. She knew that since she left Barceló's club someone had been following her. She could feel someone's eyes caressing her figure from a distance, waiting. When she reached the traffic lights on Calle Rosellón, she stopped and turned around slightly, combing the street behind her with a casual look, scanning the dozens of passersby who had come out to stroll down the Rambla, to show off their uniforms, to see and be seen in the right places. She hoped it would be poor old Rovira, but she couldn't help asking herself whether Lomana might be hiding among all those people, cleverly concealed some thirty meters away in a doorway, or behind a group of pedestrians who could cover him up: observing her, hot on her heels, his hand in his coat pocket, eagerly stroking the knife he had been keeping for her for so long. A block farther down, she sighted the glass front of the Mauri Patisserie, bursting with delicious confectionery, all masterfully presented to sweeten the autumn blues of wellborn ladies. After checking behind her again, she decided to take refuge there for a few moments.

A young woman—her expression solemn and virginal—led her to a table by the window. The Mauri Patisserie had always seemed to Alicia a lavish sugar den where ladies of a certain age and position retired to scheme, sheltering behind exquisite chamomile teas and almost sinful cakes. That afternoon the congregated clientele only confirmed her diagnosis. Tempted to feel like one more among the chosen few, she ordered a cappuccino and a cream Massini cake she had noticed on her way in, which had her name written all over it. While she waited, she smiled back absently at the bejeweled matrons who glanced at her from the other tables, in their armor-plated outfits from Modas Santa Eulalia. It was easy to lip-read their sotto voce comments. If they could pull my skin off in shreds and make themselves a mask with it, she thought, they would.

*

Alicia swallowed half of her cake greedily as soon as it was served. Within a few seconds she felt the sugar rush. She put her hand in her bag, pulled out the bottle Leandro had given her in the station, and opened it, placing one of the pills on the palm of her hand. Before putting it in her mouth she examined it for a few seconds, but a sharp new pang in her hip made up her mind for her. She swallowed the pill with a long gulp of coffee and ate the rest of the cake, just to pad her stomach. For the next half hour she sat there, watching people go by and waiting for the drug to kick in. As soon as she felt the pain drowning in the murky veil of drowsiness that spread through her body, she stood up and paid at the till.

Outside the patisserie she hailed a taxi and gave her address. The taxi driver was in a chatty mood and offered her a long monologue, to which Alicia vaguely agreed. As the narcotic began to freeze her blood, the city lights seemed to fade into a watery mantle, like watercolor stains sliding down a canvas. The traffic sounds seemed to reach her from afar.

"Are you feeling all right?" asked the driver, stopping in front of her flat on Calle Aviñón.

She nodded and paid her fare without waiting for the change. The taxi driver, not altogether convinced, didn't leave until he'd made sure she could fit the key in the lock.

Not wanting to bump into Jesusa or some neighbor eager for long-time-no-see conversations on landings, Alicia started up the stairs at a brisk pace. After what felt like an interminable ascent, marked by moments of darkness and vertigo, she managed to reach the door to her flat. Miraculously, she found her key and let herself in.

Once inside, she took the bottle out of her bag again. She pulled out two more pills with trembling fingers, let the bag fall to the ground by her feet, and walked over to the dining-room table. The bottle of white wine Fernandito had given her was still there. She filled a glass to the rim. Clutching the table with one hand to steady herself, she swallowed the pills in one gulp, raising the empty glass to Leandro's health. *And especially not with alcohol.*

*

Alicia staggered down the corridor to her bedroom, dropping her clothes on the way. Without bothering to switch on the light, she slumped down on the bed and, with great difficulty, tugged the bed-spread over herself. Exhausted, she closed her eyes. The cathedral bells rang in the distance.

10

IN THE DREAM, the stranger had no face. His black silhouette looked as if it had become detached from the liquid shadows that dripped from the ceiling. At first Alicia thought she had seen him watching her from the foot of her bed, but then she realized that he was sitting on the edge, pulling off the sheets that covered her. She felt cold. The stranger was slowly removing his black gloves. She felt his freezing fingers touch her bare belly, searching for the scar that spread over her right hip. The hands of the stranger explored the folds in the wound, and his lips settled on her body.

The warm contact of the tongue caressing the ridge of the scar made her feel nauseous. Only when she heard footsteps walking away along the corridor did she realize she wasn't alone in the apartment.

Fumbling about in the dark for the switch, she turned on her bedside lamp. The light blinded her, and she covered her eyes. She heard steps in the dining room, then the sound of a door closing. When she opened her eyes again, she saw that she was lying naked on her bed, the sheets piled up on the floor. She sat up slowly, holding her head, overwhelmed by vertigo. For a moment she thought she would pass out.

"Jesusa?" she called out nervously.

She picked a sheet off the floor and wrapped herself in it, then managed to walk down the corridor, searching the walls with her hands, groping in the dark. The trail of clothes she'd left hours before had vanished. The dining room was buried in a steely darkness. A bluish gleam filtered through the window, barely outlining the shapes of furniture and bookshelves. She found the switch and turned on the ceiling lamp, her eyes slowly adjusting to the light. As soon as she understood what she was seeing, fear cleared her mind. The scene before her suddenly jumped into sharp relief, as if until that moment she had been looking through a lens that was out of focus.

Her clothes had been gathered on the dining-room table, except for her red coat, which lay on one of the chairs. Her dress was folded with professional expertise, her stockings delicately stretched out with the seams to one side, her underwear smoothed out as if on display in a lingerie shop. Again, she felt a surge of nausea. She walked over to the bookshelves and pulled out the Bible. Opening it, she removed the gun hidden there, letting the empty book slip from her hands. She made no attempt to pick it up. Cocking the hammer, she grasped the revolver in both hands.

Only then did she notice her bag, hanging on the back of one of the chairs. She remembered having dropped it when she came in. She walked over to look at it. It was closed. A shiver ran through her body when she opened it. She let it fall, cursing herself. The Mataix book was no longer there.

Alicia spent the rest of the night in the dark, curled up in a corner of the sofa, her gun in her hands, her eyes fixed on the door, listening to the unending moans of the old building. Daybreak caught her as her heavy eyelids were beginning to close. She sat up and looked at her reflection in the windowpane. Farther away, a blanket of purple spread over the sky, sketching a parade of shadows between the rooftops and towers of the city. Alicia looked out of the window and saw that the lights of the Gran Café were already speckling the pavement. Barcelona had only given her one day's respite.

"Welcome back," she told herself.

II

VARGAS WAS WAITING for Alicia in the dining room of the Gran Café, nursing a steaming cup and rehearsing his smile as a truce offering. She spotted him as soon as she walked out of her front door, his profile outlining a double image on the café window. He was sitting at the same table she had occupied the day before, surrounded by the remains of what must have been a sumptuous breakfast, and by a couple of newspapers. Alicia crossed the street and took a deep breath before opening the café door. When he saw her come in, Vargas stood up and waved nervously. She returned his greeting and approached the table, signaling to Miquel to bring her the usual breakfast. The waiter nodded.

"How was your journey?" asked Alicia.

"Long."

Vargas waited for her to sit down before doing so himself. They eyed one another in silence. His brow was furrowed, and he looked confused.

"What?" asked Alicia.

"I was expecting to be greeted with a curse, or something more in your style."

Alicia shrugged.

"If I were a bit more stupid, I'd almost say you were pleased to see me," he added.

She gave just the hint of a smile. "Don't push it."

"You scare me, Alicia. Has something happened?"

Miquel approached the table with care, carrying Alicia's toast and her cup of coffee. She gave him a nod, and he quickly left, disappearing discreetly behind the bar. Alicia took one of the pieces of toast and gave it a tentative bite.

Vargas shot her a slightly worried look. "So?" he finally asked, impatiently.

Alicia began to summarize the previous day's adventures, and those of the night. Vargas's face grew somber. As she finished telling him how she had spent those hours until dawn, holding her revolver, waiting for the door of the flat to open again, he swore under his breath.

"There's something I don't understand," he said. "You say a man came in while you were asleep and took the book."

"What don't you understand?"

"How do you know it was a man?"

"Because I know."

"So you weren't asleep."

"I was under the effects of the medication. I've already told you."

"What part haven't you told me?"

"The one that's none of your business."

"Did he do anything to you?"

"No."

Vargas looked at her in disbelief. "While I was waiting for you, your friend Miquel here offered me an attic they have upstairs, with a partial view of your home. I'm going to ask him to take my suitcase up, and I'll pay him a couple of weeks in advance."

"You don't need to stay here, Vargas. Go to a good hotel. It's on Leandro."

"It's either this, or I take up residence on your sofa. You choose."

Alicia sighed. She was not in the mood to start a new battle.

"You hadn't told me you had a gun," said Vargas.

"You hadn't asked me."

"And you know how to use it?"

Alicia fixed her eyes on his.

"There I was, thinking you were more the knitting kind," said the policeman. "Will you please always carry it with you? Inside and outside your home."

"Yes, sir. Were you able to discover anything about Lomana?"

"No one in the ministry is saying a word. The impression I got was that they didn't know anything. You must have already heard the police force's version. He was transferred from his unit about a year ago to assist on the case of the anonymous letters to Valls. He did some investigating on his own. He was supposed to report to Gil de Partera. At some point he stopped doing so. Vanished into thin air. What is your history with him?"

"None."

Vargas frowned. "You're not thinking he's the person who came into your apartment last night to steal the book and do whatever it is he did that you won't tell me about?"

"That's you talking, not me."

Vargas was observing her with a quizzical look. "This medication, is it for that wound of yours?"

"No, I take it for fun. How old are you, Vargas?"

He raised his eyebrows in surprise. "Probably twice as old as you, although I'd rather not think about it. Why?"

"You're not starting to see yourself as my father, or anything of the sort, are you?"

"Don't get your hopes up."

"What a shame," said Alicia.

"And don't get all soppy now. It doesn't suit you."

"That's what Leandro says."

"Probably with good reason. If our sentimental interlude is over, why don't you tell me what our plans are for the day?"

Alicia finished her coffee and signaled to Miquel to bring her another.

"You do know that aside from caffeine and cigarettes the body also needs carbohydrates, protein, and all that stuff, don't you?"

"I promise we'll go and have lunch at Casa Leopoldo later today. You're paying."

"What a relief. And before that?"

"Before that we're going to meet my private spy, good old Rovira."

"Rovira?"

Alicia gave him a brief account of her meeting with Rovira the day before. "He must be wandering around out there, frozen stiff."

"Let him freeze his balls off," said Vargas. "And after giving your apprentice his assignment for the day, what's next?"

"I thought we could pay a visit to a lawyer. Fernando Brians."

Vargas nodded unenthusiastically. "Who is he?"

"Brians represents a collector who for years has been buying up all the copies of Mataix novels."

"You're still on about that book. Don't be offended, but wouldn't the sensible thing be to see what they have to tell us at police headquarters about the car Valls was in when he left Madrid? I'm just giving an example of something truly connected with the case in hand."

"That's not a priority."

"Says who? Excuse me, Alicia, but are we still trying to find Minister Valls while it's possible that he may still be alive?"

"The car is a waste of time."

"Yours or mine?"

"Valls's. But if it makes you feel better, OK. You win. Let's follow up on your suggestion."

"Thanks."

12

TRUE TO HIS promise, Rovira was waiting in the street, trembling with cold and looking as if he cursed the day he'd been born and all the days that followed. The spook apprentice seemed to have shrunk noticeably overnight. His anxious grimace suggested the start of an ulcer.

Vargas spotted him before Alicia had pointed him out. "Is that the ace of spies?"

"That's him."

Rovira looked up when he heard approaching footsteps. He gulped when he saw Vargas and searched for his cigarettes with a shaking hand. Alicia and Vargas hemmed him in, one on either side.

"I thought you would come alone," he mumbled, gazing at Alicia.

"You're such a romantic, Rovira."

He breathed out a sort of nervous laugh. Alicia pulled the cigarette from his mouth and threw it far away.

"Hey . . . ," Rovira protested.

Vargas bent over him slightly, making him shrink, if that were possible, a bit more. "You only speak to the young lady when she asks you something. Is that clear?"

Rovira nodded.

"Rovira, this will be your lucky day," said Alicia. "No more standing around in the cold. You're off to the cinema. The Capitol matinees begin at ten, and they're showing a cycle of films with Cheetah the monkey, which you'll love."

"Oscar winning," Vargas corroborated.

"I'm sorry, Doña Alicia, but before your colleague breaks my neck, I'd like to ask you, if it's not too much bother and thanking you in advance for your generosity, whether you could help me a little. I'm not asking for much. Don't tell me to go to the cinema. I'd love to, but if they find out at headquarters, I'll be in big trouble. Let me follow you. At a great distance. If you like, you could let me know where you're going, and that way I'll be out of your hair. I promise you won't even see me. But at the end of the day I have to write a report about where I've been and what I've done, or they'll boil me alive. You've no idea what these people are like. Your colleague can tell you . . ."

Vargas looked at the poor devil with some sympathy. There seemed to be a wimp like him in every police station, the doormat on which everyone cleaned the mud off their shoes.

"You tell me what places I can report on and what places I can't. That way it's a win-win situation for both. I beg you on my knees . . ."

Before Alicia could say a word, Vargas pointed at Rovira and took the floor. "Look here, son, you remind me of Charlie Chaplin, and you seem like a nice guy. This is what I propose: you follow us from afar, and I mean from very afar. Something like from the Pyrenees to the Rock of Gibraltar. If I as much as see you, smell you, or even imagine you at less than two hundred meters, you and I will have a face-to-face, and I don't suppose they'll think much of you showing up at headquarters after I've beaten the shit out of you and they have to pull your head out of your ass."

Rovira seemed unable to breathe for a few seconds.

"Is that understood, or would you like a free sample?" Vargas said.

"Two hundred meters. Done. Let's call it two hundred and fifty, and the extra is on the house. Thank you so much for your generosity and understanding. You won't be sorry. No one will be able to say that Rovira doesn't keep his word—"

"Clear off. Just seeing you gets me going," Vargas grunted in his most unpleasant voice.

Rovira gave him a quick bow and rushed off. Vargas smiled as he watched him slip away among the crowd.

"You're such a softie," murmured Alicia.

"And you're a little angel. Let me call Linares to find out whether they'll let us go and see the car this morning."

"Who is Linares?"

"One of the real ones. We started out together, and he's still a good friend. How many people can you say that about after twenty years in the Force?"

They went back into the café, and Miquel let them use the phone. Vargas called police headquarters on Vía Layetana and launched into a conversational two-step of male camaraderie, foul-mouthed jokes, and studied tough-guy bonding with his pal Linares, eventually getting the go-ahead for checking out the car that was allegedly used by Valls and his driver, gunman, and stooge to travel from Madrid to Barcelona. Alicia followed the conversation as if she was listening to a drawing-room play, enjoying Vargas's knack of flattering his colleagues and coming up with grand statements that said nothing at all.

"All solved," he concluded as he hung up.

"Are you sure? Haven't you thought that perhaps this Linares would have liked to know that you're with me?"

"Of course. That's why I didn't mention it."

"And what will you say when they see me?"

"I'll say we're going out together. I don't know, I'll think of something."

They took a taxi opposite the city hall, setting off just as the traffic on Vía Layetana was beginning to thicken in the tortuous early-morning rush hour. Vargas gazed thoughtfully at the parade of monumental buildings emerging like ships in the morning mist. The taxi driver cast occasional furtive glances in the mirror, probably speculating on the odd couple they made. But soon he was distracted by a sports program on the radio, in which it was furiously debated whether the soccer league was already lost or, on the contrary, there were still reasons to go on living.

13

THEY CALLED IT the Museum of Tears.

The huge pavilion stood in a no-man's-land between the zoo and the beach. A citadel of factories and hangars spread all around it, their backs to the sea, watched over by a great water tower like a circular castle perched at heaven's door. The museum was a relic, a ruin spared from the demolition that had swept away almost all the structures built for the 1888 Universal Exhibition. After years of abandonment, the city had given the pavilion to Central Police Headquarters, which had transformed it into a depot and modern-day catacombs. Stuff had been piling up there, forming an endless forensic warehouse: decades of legal reports, evidence material, plunder, confiscated goods, weapons, and all manner of contraptions, notebooks, and other treasures resulting from over seventy years of dust, crime, and punishment in the city of Barcelona.

The building had a vaulted ceiling not unlike that of the neighboring Estación de Francia. Blades of light fell from its laminated roof, cutting through the darkness and spreading over a tangle of corridors that were hundreds of meters long and even taller than many of the buildings in the central district. A complex system of staircases and footbridges that seemed to dangle from the heights like ghostly stage machinery led to the upper areas, where a nest of documents and objects told the secret history of Barcelona from the closing years of the nineteenth century. During the seven decades of its existence, all kinds of artifacts had become trapped in that limbo, from ancient carriages and motorcars used in crimes to an encyclopedic arsenal of weapons and poisons. The building held enough works of art linked to an inventory of unsolved cases to open several museums. Particularly famous among experts was a collection of stuffed bodies that had been discovered in the basement of a mansion in the San Gervasio neighborhood. The mansion had belonged to a wealthy colonial baron who, in his years of prosperity and glory in Cuba, had developed a predilection for hunting slaves like game. On his return to Europe, he'd left a trail of disappearances among the underclass who frequented the salons and cafés of the Paralelo district, which had never been resolved.

An entire gallery was devoted to glass bottles in which a varied fauna of permanent tenants floated in yellowish embalming fluid. The palace also boasted an impressive armory of daggers, chisels, and other cutting devices that would alarm the most experienced butcher. One of the most famous sections, a securely closed-off pavilion that could only be accessed with permission from the highest authorities, housed materials and documents requisitioned from criminal investigations involving religious and occult matters—an archive said to contain enticing dossiers on members of Barcelona high society in connection with the case of the so-called Lady Vampire of Calle Poniente, as well as correspondence and fees related to the exorcisms performed by the infamous late priest Cinto Verdaguer in an apartment close to Calle Princesa that had never seen the light of day and never would.

The perpetual residence for such a vast exhibition of misdeeds naturally exudes an aura of malevolence that makes visitors want to get out of there as fast as possible, lest they be trapped inside and end up part of the permanent collection. The Museum of Tears was no exception, and although police records referred to it by its official name, Section Thirteen, its reputation and the ever-expanding accumulation of grisly tales stockpiled inside it had earned it its well-known nickname.

A fellow who seemed to be the gatekeeper was already waiting at the Section Thirteen entrance when they arrived. A bunch of keys hung from his belt, and his face would have won top prize in a grave-digger competition.

"That must be Florencio," said Vargas in a low voice before opening the taxi door. "Let me do the talking."

"He's all yours," said Alicia.

They got out of the taxi, and Vargas held out his hand to the guard. "Good morning. Juan Manuel Vargas, from Central Police Headquarters. I spoke to Linares a few minutes ago. He said he was going to call you and let you know I was coming over."

Florencio nodded. "Captain Linares didn't say you were bringing company."

"The young lady is my niece Margarita. She's been kind enough to act as my guide and secretary while I'm in Barcelona for a few days. Didn't they mention it?"

Florencio shook his head and looked at Alicia.

"Margarita, say hello to Florencio. It's Florencio, right? He's *the* authority in Section Thirteen."

Alicia stepped forward and timidly held out a hand. Florencio frowned but led them to the main door and invited them in.

"Have you been here long, Florencio?" asked Vargas.

"A couple of years. Before that I was in the house for ten years." Vargas looked at him, confused.

"The dead house—the morgue," the guard explained. "If you'll please follow me, what you're looking for is in pavilion nine. I've left it ready for you."

What from the outside looked like an old abandoned railway station, inside revealed a gigantic cathedral-like space stretching into infinity. Electrical cables hung in wreaths of lightbulbs that exhaled a golden hue. Florencio guided them through countless galleries peopled with all kinds of gadgets, boxes, and trunks. Alicia sighted an entire collection of stuffed animals and a battalion of mannequins. There were pieces of furniture, bicycles, weapons, paintings, religious statues, and even an eerie enclosure populated exclusively by what looked like automatons from a funfair.

Florencio must have noticed Alicia's look of wonder. He drew closer to her and pointed toward what looked like a circus big top. "You wouldn't believe the things that end up here. There are times when even I don't believe it."

As they penetrated deeper into the mesh of passageways, they noticed a strange litany resembling animal sounds floating in the air. For a moment, Alicia thought she was venturing into a jungle full of tropical birds and prowling wild cats.

Enjoying the bewilderment on their faces, Florencio let out a childish guffaw. "No, you haven't both gone mad, even if this is the perfect place for making you go off your rocker. The noise comes from the zoo, which is just behind. You can hear all sorts of creatures from here. Elephants, lions, and cockatoos. At night the panthers start howling—they make your hair stand on end. But the monkeys are the worst. Like people, only without all the fuss. This way, please. We're almost there . . ."

The car's shape was visible under the thin tarpaulin that covered it. Florencio flicked the cover off expertly, then folded it. He'd already set up a couple of spotlights on tripods placed on either side of the vehicle, and now he connected them to an extension hanging from the electrical cables. Two intense yellow beams transformed the car into a shining metal sculpture. Pleased with his set design, Florencio opened all four doors of the car and moved back a few steps with a bow. "There it is."

"Do you have the technical report at hand?" asked Vargas.

Florencio nodded. "It's in my office. I'll go and fetch it right now." He hurried off, seeming to levitate a few centimeters above the floor.

"You stay on the side of the passenger seat," Vargas told Alicia.

"Yes, dear uncle."

The first thing Alicia noticed was the smell. She looked up at Vargas, who nodded.

"Gunpowder."

The policeman pointed at the dark stains of dry blood splattered over the passenger seat.

"It's not much blood for a bullet wound," Alicia said, considering. "Perhaps a scratch . . ."

Vargas shook his head slowly. "A shot inside the car would have produced an exit wound, and the bullet would be embedded in the bodywork, in the seats. Such a small amount of blood probably comes from another wound, perhaps a blade of some sort. Or from a blow."

Vargas touched the halo of small marks piercing the back of the seat. "Burned," he murmured. "The shot was from the inside to the outside."

Alicia moved away from the seat and looked for the window handle. When she turned it, a thin line of glass shards showed over the edge. On the floor beneath the window were fragments of pulverized glass.

"You see?"

For a few minutes they examined the car from top to bottom, without saying a word. The local police had combed it thoroughly and hadn't left anything of interest for them, except a wad of old road maps in the glove compartment and a spiral notebook with no covers. Alicia leafed through the pages.

"Anything there?" asked Vargas.

"It's blank."

Florencio, who had returned quietly with the technical report, watched them from the shadows. "As clean as a whistle, eh?"

"Was there anything in the car when they brought it here?"

Florencio handed them the report. "It was like this when they brought it in."

Vargas took the report and began going through the inventory of items.

"Is this normal?" asked Alicia.

"Excuse me?" Florencio inquired politely.

"I was asking whether it was normal that the car was not examined here."

"That depends. Usually there is a first inspection at the scene and then a more in-depth one here."

"And was there one?"

"No, not that I know."

"Here in the report it says that the car was found on Carretera de las Aguas. Is that road used a lot?" Vargas wanted to know.

"No. It's more like a dirt track, a few kilometers long, and it winds around the hillside," said Florencio. "There's no real road and no water either, in fact."

The explanation was meant for Vargas, but Florencio winked at Alicia as he spoke. She smiled at the joke.

"The investigators believe the car was abandoned there after the event, but the incident took place somewhere else," Florencio added.

"Any idea why?"

"They found bits of fine gravel in the grooves of the tire treads. Limestone. Not the same sort that covers Carretera de las Aguas."

"What might that mean?"

"If you ask the investigators, they'll tell you there are dozens of places where that sort of gravel is found."

"What if we asked you, Florencio?" said Alicia.

"A landscaped enclosure. Perhaps a park. It could be the entrance patio to a private house."

Vargas pointed at the report. "I can see you two have solved the case already," he interrupted. "But if it's not too much to ask, could we have a copy?"

"That is a copy. You can keep it. Is there anything else I can do for you?"

"If you would be kind enough to call us a taxi . . ."

14

IN THE CAB, Vargas didn't open his mouth. He kept his eyes fixed on the window, his bad mood spreading like poison in the air.

Alicia tapped his knee gently. "Cheer up, man. We're off to Casa Leopoldo."

"They're wasting our time," he mumbled.

"That surprises you?"

He looked at her, fuming.

She smiled calmly. "Welcome to Barcelona."

"I don't see what you find so funny."

Alicia opened her bag and pulled out the notebook she'd found in Valls's car.

Vargas sighed. "Tell me this isn't what I think it is."

"Does it whet your appetite?"

"Leaving aside the fact that removing official evidence is a serious misdemeanor, all I can see is a notebook with blank pages."

Alicia pushed her nail between the rings of the spiral and pulled out a couple of shreds of paper that had gotten trapped inside.

"So?"

"Pulled-out pages."

"Of great use, I'm sure."

Alicia spread the first page of the notebook on the taxi's windowpane. The sunlight brought out the indentation of lines marked on the paper.

Vargas leaned over and screwed up his eyes. "Numbers?"

Alicia nodded. "There are two columns. The first is made up of a sequence of numbers and letters. The second only has numbers. Sequences between five and seven digits. Have a good look."

"I can see. And?"

"The numbers are consecutive. They start with forty thousand three hundred and something and end in forty thousand four hundred and seven or eight."

Vargas's eyes lit up, although a shadow still hovered over his face. "It could be anything," he said.

"Mercedes, Valls's daughter, remembered that her father had said something about a list to his bodyguard the night before he disappeared. A list with numbers . . ."

"I don't know, Alicia. Most likely it's nothing."

"Perhaps," she agreed. "Feeling hungrier now?"

Vargas gave in at last and smiled. "I'm always hungry."

The visit to the Museum of Tears and the possibility—as slim as it was—that the unlikely clue found in the indentations of a blank page might lead somewhere had lifted Alicia's spirits. To sniff a new trail was always a secret pleasure: the perfume of the future, as Leandro liked to call it. Mistaking her good mood for an appetite, Alicia confronted the Casa Leopoldo menu like a Cossack and ordered for both, and for two more as well. Vargas let her do so without complaining, and when the parade of rich food began to flow incessantly and Alicia could barely tackle it, the veteran policeman just muttered under his breath while he made short work of his own servings and a few more.

"When it comes to table-sharing we also make a great team," he remarked, finishing off an oxtail stew with a superb aroma. "You order and I devour."

Alicia nibbled at her food like a bird and smiled.

"I don't want to be a spoilsport, but don't get too excited," said Vargas. "Those numbers might only be references to spare parts jotted down by the driver, or who knows what else."

"That's a lot of spare parts. How's the oxtail?"

"First class. Like one I ate in Córdoba in the spring of 1949, which I still dream about."

"In good company?"

"Better than the present one. Are you investigating me, Alicia?"

"Simple curiosity. Do you have a family?"

"Everyone has a family."

"I don't," she snapped.

"I'm sorry, I didn't—"

"There's nothing to be sorry about. What did Leandro tell you about me?"

Vargas seemed surprised by the question.

"He must have said something," she insisted. "Or you must have asked him something."

"I didn't ask. And he didn't say much."

Alicia smiled coldly. "Between you and me. Go on. What did he tell you about me?"

"Look, Alicia, whatever game goes on between you two has nothing to do with me."

"I see. That means he told you more than you admit."

Vargas faced her. He looked irritated. "He told me you were an orphan. He said you lost your parents during the war."

"What else?"

"He said you have a wound that gives you constant pain. And that this affects your character."

"My character."

"Forget it."

"What else?"

"That you're a solitary person, and you have a problem establishing emotional ties."

Alicia laughed halfheartedly. "Did he say that? Did he use those words?"

"I can't remember exactly. Can we change the subject?"

"Right. Let's talk about my emotional ties."

Vargas rolled his eyes.

"Do you think I have problems establishing emotional ties?"

"I don't know, and it's none of my business."

"Leandro would never pronounce those words—they're a string of clichés. They sound straight out of an advice column in a fashion magazine."

"It must have been me, then, because I'm subscribed to quite a few."

"What did he say exactly?"

"Why do you do this to yourself, Alicia?"

"Do what?"

"Torment yourself."

"Is that how you see me? Like a martyr?"

Vargas looked at her in silence, and finally shook his head.

"What did Leandro say? I promise that if you tell me the truth, I'll never ask you again."

Vargas weighed up the alternatives. "He said you don't think that anyone can love you because you don't love yourself, and that you think nobody has ever loved you. And that you can't forgive the world for it."

Alicia looked down and gave a false laugh. Vargas noticed that her eyes were shining and cleared his throat. "I thought you wanted me to tell you about my family."

Alicia shrugged.

"My parents were from a small village in . . ."

"I meant, did you have a wife and children?" she cut in.

Vargas looked at her, his eyes empty of all expression. "No," he said after a pause.

"I didn't want to annoy you. I'm sorry."

Vargas smiled reluctantly. "You don't annoy me. And you?"

"Do I have a wife and children?"

"Or whatever."

"I'm afraid not."

Vargas raised his glass of wine. "To solitary souls."

Alicia took her glass and touched his, avoiding his eyes.

"Leandro is an idiot," the policeman remarked after a while.

Alicia shook her head slowly. "No. He's simply cruel."

The rest of the meal took place in silence.

15

VALLS WAKES UP in the dark. Vicente's body is gone. Martín must have removed it while he slept. Only that son of a bitch could have thought of locking him up with a corpse. A slimy stain on the floor marks the space where the body had lain. Instead there is a pile of clothes, old but dry, and a small bucket full of water. The water smells dirty, with a whiff of metal, but as soon as Valls moistens his lips and manages to take a gulp, it seems to him the most delicious thing he has ever tasted. He drinks until he quenches a thirst he thought could never be quenched, until his stomach and his throat hurt. Then he removes his filthy bloodstained rags and slips on some of the clothes he finds on the pile. They smell of dust and disinfectant. His right hand has gone numb, and in the place of pain he feels only a dull throbbing. At first he doesn't dare look at the hand, and when he does, he notices that the black stain has spread and now reaches his wrist, as if he had dipped it in a bucket full of tar. He can smell the infection, feel his body rotting away alive.

"It's the gangrene," says a voice in the dark.

His heart misses a beat, and he turns to discover his jailer sitting at the bottom of the stairs, watching him.

"How long have you been there?" Valls asks.

"You're going to lose that hand. Or your life. It's up to you."

"Help me, please. I'll give you whatever you want."

The jailer stares at him impassively.

"How long have I been here?"

"Not long."

"Do you work for Martín? Where is he? Why doesn't he come to see me?"

The jailer stands up. The meager light that filters down from the top of the stairs touches his face. Valls can now see the mask clearly, a piece of flesh-colored porcelain covering half the man's face. The eye behind it doesn't blink.

The jailer approaches the metal bars so Valls can look at him closely. "You don't remember, do you?"

Valls shakes his head slowly.

"You'll remember. There's time enough."

He turns and is about to start up the stairs again when Valls stretches out his left hand through the bars beseechingly. The jailer stops.

"Please," Valls implores. "I need a doctor."

The jailer pulls a packet wrapped in brown paper out of his coat pocket and throws it into the cell.

"You decide whether you want to live or whether you want to rot away slowly, the way you've allowed so many innocents to do."

Before he leaves, he lights a candle and leaves it in a small niche dug into the wall.

"Please, don't go . . ."

Valls hears the footsteps fade and the door close. Then he kneels down to pick up the parcel. He opens it with his left hand. At first he can't make out what he is seeing. Only when he takes the object and looks at it in the light of the candle does he realize.

A carpenter's saw.

16

IN THE DARKEST corner of her heart, Barcelona, mother of labyrinths, holds a mesh of narrow streets knotted together to form a reef of present and future ruins. Intrepid travelers and all manner of lost souls lie forever trapped in this district named the Raval, once the outskirts of the medieval city. When Alicia and Vargas stepped out of Casa Leopoldo, a network of alleyways greeted the couple in all its sinister splendor, populated by dives, brothels, and a whole arsenal of bazaars peddling wares and services away from the eye of the law.

The lavish meal had left Vargas suffering from a light hiccup, which he tried to get rid of by taking deep breaths and tapping his chest with his knuckles.

"This happens because you're a glutton," Alicia decreed.

"You've got some nerve. First you stuff me, then you make fun of me."

A young streetwalker displaying rotund charms observed them with strictly commercial interest. She was standing in a doorway behind which a transistor radio was blaring out a Catalan rumba in all its crossbred glory. "How about a little twosome siesta with your skinny-ribs and a real woman, my love?" the lady of the evening invited.

Vargas shook his head, vaguely embarrassed, and hurried on. Alicia smiled and followed him, exchanging glances with the strapping woman in the doorway, who, seeing her prey walk away, shrugged and gave her the once-over, as if wondering whether this was the latest look preferred by well-shod gentlemen.

"This area is a social calamity," said Vargas.

"Would you like me to leave you alone for a while to see if you can solve it?" asked Alicia. "I think you've just made a friend who'll get rid of your hiccup in a flash."

"Don't prick me. I'm about to burst."

"Would you like some dessert?"

"A magnifying glass. If possible, a huge one."

"I thought you had no faith in those numbers."

"You believe what it's possible to believe, not what you want to believe. Unless you're an idiot, in which case it's the other way around."

"I didn't know indigestion brought out the philosopher in you."

"There are lots of things you don't know, Alicia."

"That's why I learn something new every day."

Alicia put her arm through his.

"Don't get your hopes up," Vargas warned.

"You've already told me that."

"It's the best bit of advice one can give anyone in this life."

"What a sad thought, Vargas."

The policeman looked at Alicia, and in his eyes she saw that he was speaking seriously. Her smile left her lips, and without thinking, she stood on tiptoe and gave him a kiss on the cheek. It was a chaste kiss, full of affection and friendship, a kiss that didn't expect anything and asked for even less.

"Don't do that," said Vargas, setting off again.

The doorway hooker was still watching, Alicia noticed. They looked at each other briefly. The old hand mumbled under her breath, smiling bitterly.

17

CLOUDS HUNG LOW in the afternoon sky. A greenish aura filtered through them, making the Raval quarter look like a small village sunk beneath the waters of a swamp. They walked up Calle Hospital until they reached the Ramblas and from there Alicia guided Vargas through the crowds toward Plaza Real.

"Where are we going?" he asked.

"In search of the magnifying glass you mentioned."

They crossed the square, heading for the passageway under the arches that surrounded it. Alicia stopped in front of a shop window through which one could glimpse a small jungle of wild animals, frozen in a moment of fury and staring at eternity with glass eyes.

Vargas looked up to see the notice over the entrance and, a little further down, to the letters printed on the glazed door:

MUSEUM

WIDOW OF L. SOLER PUJOL

TELEPHONE 404451

"What's this?"

"People call it the Beast Museum, but in fact it's a taxidermist's establishment."

As soon as they stepped into the shop, Vargas was struck by its rich collection of stuffed animals. Tigers, birds, wolves, apes, and a whole troop of exotic species inhabited this improvised museum of natural sciences, which would have delighted, or terrified, more than one expert on exotic fauna from any of the continents. He strolled among the glass cabinets, admiring the skill shown in those pieces of taxidermy.

"Now you've really stopped hiccupping," said Alicia.

Hearing footsteps behind them, they turned to discover a young woman, thin as a rake, observing them with her hands joined over her chest. Her eyes and her general demeanor reminded Vargas of a praying mantis.

"Good afternoon. How may I help?"

"Good afternoon," said Alicia. "I'd like to speak to Matías, if at all possible."

The look of suspicion that colored the eyes of the praying mantis deepened. "And that will be about . . . ?"

"A technical inquiry."

"And may I ask who wishes to see him?"

"Alicia Gris."

The praying mantis gave them a thorough going-over, screwing up her nose with disapproval, before she walked off unhurriedly to the back room.

"I'm discovering a most welcoming Barcelona," whispered Vargas. "I'm thinking of moving here."

"Don't you have enough stuffed glories in the capital?"

"I wish we did. I'm afraid they're all alive and kicking. Who is this Matías? An ex-boyfriend?"

"More like an ex-candidate."

"Heavyweight?"

"Featherweight, I'd say. Matías is a technician here. This place has the best magnifying glasses in town, and Matías has the best eye."

"What about the lamia?"

"I think her name is Serafina. Years ago she was his fiancée. She must be the wife now."

"Maybe one of these days he'll stuff her and put her on one of the shelves, next to the lions, as a finishing touch for the museum of horrors."

"Alicia!" came Matías's euphoric voice, as he welcomed her with a warm smile.

Matías was a small man with nervous gestures. He sported a white lab coat and round spectacles that enlarged his eyes and gave him a rather comical appearance. "It's been a long time," he cried, visibly excited. "I thought you'd left Barcelona. When did you come back?"

Serafina watched, half hidden behind the back room curtain, with eyes as black as tar and an unfriendly expression.

"Matías, this is my colleague, Don Juan Manuel Vargas."

Matías studied him as he shook his hand.

"You have an impressive collection here, Don Matías," Vargas said.

"Oh, most of the pieces are the work of Señor Soler, the founder of the establishment. My teacher."

"Matías is very modest," Alicia interrupted. "Tell him about the bull."

Matías shook his head humbly.

"Don't tell me you also stuff fighting bulls?" asked Vargas.

"No task is impossible for him," said Alicia. "A few years ago a famous matador came here and asked Matías to stuff a beast weighing over five hundred kilos. He'd fought it that afternoon at the Monumental bullring and wanted to present it to a film star with whom he was madly in love . . . Wasn't it Ava Gardner, Matías?"

"The things we do for women, eh?" added Matías, who obviously preferred not to broach the subject.

Serafina coughed threateningly from her sentry post; Matías stood at attention and his smile disappeared.

"So, what can I do for you? Do you have a pet you wish to immortalize? Some memorable piece of game?"

"The truth is that we have a rather unusual request," Alicia began.

"Unusual is usual here. A few months ago, Salvador Dalí himself came through this door to ask whether we could stuff two hundred thousand ants for him. It's not a joke. When I told him I thought it wasn't feasible, he offered to paint my Serafina in an altarpiece of insects and cardinals. Quirks of genius. As you can see, we're never bored here . . ."

Alicia pulled the notebook out of her handbag and opened it. "What we wanted to ask you is whether you could help us decipher the text that appears in relief on this page, using your lenses."

Matías took the paper carefully and examined it against the light. "Alicia always with her mysteries, eh? Come into the workshop. Let's see what can be done."

The taxidermist's workshop and laboratory was a small cave of alchemy and wonders. A complex device with lenses and spotlights hung from the ceiling on metal cables. The walls were crammed with glass cabinets, filled with countless bottles and chemical solutions. Large ocher-colored anatomical atlases flanked the room, presenting the visitor with images of the internal organs, skeletons, and muscles of all types of creatures. Two wide slabs of marble dominated the workshop's center, making the room look like an operating theater conceived for otherworldly specimens. Next to the slabs, small metal tables covered with crimson cloths displayed a collection of the most extravagant surgical instruments Vargas had ever seen.

"Don't mind the smell," the taxidermist warned. "After a few minutes you won't even notice it."

Doubting this, but not wishing to contradict Matías, Alicia accepted the chair she was being offered next to one of the tables and smiled affectionately at him, aware of the longing in the eyes of her old suitor.

"Serafina never comes in here," he said. "She says it smells of dead bodies. But I find it relaxing. Here one sees things the way they are, with no illusions or deceits." He took the piece of paper and extended it over a glass plate. Using a dimmer close to the marble table, he lowered the main light until it was barely visible, then turned on a couple of spotlights hanging from the ceiling. Next, he tugged at a bar held up by pulleys, bringing down a set of lenses articulated on metal arms.

"You never said good-bye," he said without looking up from his work. "I had to find out through the caretaker, Jesusa."

"It was all a bit of a rush, from one day to the next."

"I understand." Matías placed the glass plate between one of the spotlights and a magnifying glass. The beam of light outlined the marks on the page. "Numbers," he remarked.

Adjusting the angle of the magnifying glass, he studied the page with great care. "I could apply a contrast to the paper, but that would probably damage it and we might lose some of the digits . . ."

Vargas went up to a desk in a corner of the room, picking up a couple of blank pieces of paper and a pencil.

"May I?" he asked.

"Of course. Feel free."

The policeman came over to the table and, his eyes fixed on the magnifying lens, began to copy the numbers.

"They look like numbers in a series," suggested Matías.

"Why do you say that?" Alicia asked.

"They're correlated," Matías replied. "If you observe the first three digits of the column on the left, they seem to be part of a series. The rest is also in a sequence. The last two digits only change every three or four numbers."

Matías paused to look at them both with a note of irony. "I suppose it's not worth my asking you what your job is?"

"I'm just an errand boy," Vargas replied, still copying down the numbers.

Matías nodded and gazed at Alicia. "I wanted to send you a wedding invitation, but I didn't know where to send it."

"I'm sorry, Matías."

"It doesn't matter. Time is a great healer, isn't it?"

"That's what they say."

"What about you? Happy?"

"Over the moon."

Matías laughed. "Same old Alicia . . ."

"Unfortunately. I hope Serafina doesn't mind that I've come here."

Matías sighed. "Well, I imagine she has some idea of who you are. There'll be a bit of trouble at dinnertime, but that's all. Serafina seems a bit surly when you don't know her well, but she has a good heart."

"I'm glad you've found someone who deserves you."

Matías looked into her eyes but said nothing. Then he turned around and patted Vargas on the back. "Have you got it all?"

"I'm working on it," said Vargas. He'd been trying to keep out of that hushed conversation, playing the role of the uninvited guest as he copied down the numbers on a piece of paper, barely daring to speak.

"Perhaps we could clip the paper onto a cellophane sheet and place it on the projector."

"I think I've got it all," said Vargas.

Alicia had risen and was wandering around the room as if she were in a museum. Matías watched her, his head lowered. "You've known each other for a while?" he asked Vargas.

"Just a few days. We're working together on an administrative job, that's all."

"Quite a character, right?"

"Excuse me?"

"Alicia."

"Yes, she does have her ways."

"Does she still use the harness?"

"Harness?"

"I made it for her, you know. Made to measure. A masterpiece, though I shouldn't say so myself. I used whalebone and tungsten tapes. It's what we call an exoskeleton. So fine, so lightweight and articulated it's almost like a second skin. She's not wearing it today. I know because of the way she moves. Remind her that she must use it. It's for her own good."

Vargas nodded, as if he understood what the taxidermist was

talking about, and finished taking down the last numbers. "Thank you, Matías," he said. "You've been a great help."

"My pleasure."

The policeman stood and cleared his throat. Alicia turned, and they exchanged glances. Vargas nodded. She approached Matías and gave him a smile that Vargas thought must have hurt him like a stab.

"Well," said Matías tensely. "I hope we won't have to wait another few years to meet again."

"I hope not." Alicia hugged him and whispered something in his ear. Matías nodded, although he left his arms hanging, not putting them around Alicia's waist. After a bit she walked off toward the front door without saying another word.

Matías waited to hear her leave the workshop. Only then did he turn around. Vargas held out his hand, and the taxidermist shook it.

"Take good care of her, Vargas, because she's not going to take care of herself."

"I'll do my best."

Matías smiled weakly and nodded. He was a man who seemed young, Vargas thought, until you looked into his eyes and saw a soul aged by sadness and remorse.

As Vargas walked across the exhibition hall, past the animals posing in the dark, Serafina came out to meet him. "Don't bring her here again," she warned. Her eyes burned with anger, and her lips trembled.

Outside, Alicia was leaning on the edge of the fountain in the square, rubbing her right hip and grimacing with pain. Vargas walked over and sat beside her.

"Why don't you go home and rest?" he said. "Tomorrow's another day."

One look at Alicia was all he needed to offer her a cigarette, and they sat smoking in silence.

"Do you think I'm a bad person?" she asked at last.

Vargas stood and held out his arm. "Come on, lean on me."

In that way, limping and stopping every ten or fifteen meters to ease the pain, they managed to reach her front door. When she tried to pull the keys out of her bag, they fell on the ground. Vargas picked them up, opened the door, and helped her in. Alicia leaned on the wall, moaning. The policeman checked the staircase and, without saying a word, picked her up in his arms and headed up the stairs.

By the time they reached the top floor, Alicia's face was covered in tears of pain and anger. Vargas carried her into the bedroom and laid her gently on the bed. He removed her shoes and put a blanket over her. The bottle with the pills was on the bedside table.

"One or two?" he asked.

"Two."

"Are you sure?"

He gave her two pills and poured a glass of water from the jug on the chest of drawers. Alicia swallowed the pills, breathing with difficulty. Vargas held her hand and waited for her to calm down.

She looked at him, her eyes reddened and her face streaked with tears. "Don't leave me alone, please."

"I'm not going anywhere."

Alicia tried to smile. He turned off the light.

"Get some rest."

He kept her hand in his, listening to her in the dusky room as she held back her tears and shook with pain. Half an hour later he felt her grip loosen as she slipped into a state midway between delirium and sleep, murmuring words that made no sense to him. At last she slowly fell asleep, or lost consciousness. The faint light of evening filtered through the window, outlining her face on the pillow. For a moment Vargas thought she looked dead, and he checked her pulse. Were those tears caused by the wound on her side, or did the pain come from somewhere deeper?

After a while he too began to feel worn out. He retired to the dining room to lie on the sofa, closing his eyes and breathing in Alicia's scent, which lingered in the air.

"No, I don't think you're a bad person," he murmured under his breath, surprising himself. "But sometimes you scare me."

18

IT WAS AFTER midnight when Vargas opened his eyes and found Alicia sitting in a chair next to him, wrapped in a blanket, staring at him in the darkened room.

"You look like a vampire," he managed to say. "How long have you been there?"

"A while."

"I should have warned you that I snore."

"I don't mind. With those pills I wouldn't hear an earthquake."

Vargas sat up and rubbed his face. "If you don't mind my saying so, this sofa is dreadful."

"I don't have much of an eye for furniture. I'll buy some new cushions. Any color preference?"

"As it's for you, black with a pattern of spiders, or skulls and crossbones."

"Did you have any dinner?"

"I ate enough food for a whole week. How are you feeling?"

Alicia shrugged. "Embarrassed."

"I can't see why. How's the pain?"

"Better. Much better."

"Why don't you go back to bed and sleep a bit longer?"

"I've got to call Leandro."

"At this time of night?"

"Leandro doesn't sleep."

"Speaking of vampires . . ."

"If I don't call him, it will be worse."

"Do you want me to go out to the corridor?"

"No," said Alicia, but she'd paused a shade too long.

Vargas nodded. "Look, I'll go down to my luxurious rooms on the other side of the street to have a shower and change my clothes, and then I'll come back."

"There's no need, Vargas. You've done enough for me tonight. Go and get some rest—we're going to have a long day tomorrow. I'll see you in the morning for breakfast."

He looked at her, somewhat unconvinced.

Alicia smiled at him. "I'll be all right. I promise."

"Do you have the revolver at hand?"

"I'll sleep with it as if it were my new teddy bear."

"You've never had a teddy bear. A little devil, perhaps . . ."

Alicia gave him one of those smiles of hers, the kind that opened doors and melted willpower. Vargas lowered his eyes.

"All right, then. Call the prince of darkness and tell him your little secrets," he said on his way out. "And lock the door tight."

"Vargas?"

The policeman stopped in the doorway.

"Thanks."

"Stop thanking me for nothing."

*

She waited while the policeman's footsteps trailed away down the stairs and then picked up the telephone. Before dialing, she took a deep breath and closed her eyes. The direct line to the suite didn't answer. Alicia knew that Leandro kept other rooms at the Gran Hotel Palace, although she had never wanted to ask what he used them for. She called reception.

The night operator was familiar with Alicia's voice, and didn't even have to ask whom she was calling. "One moment, Señorita Gris." Even at that time of night, she hadn't lost her musical singsong. "I'll put you through to Señor Montalvo."

The phone rang only once before the receiver was lifted at the other end. Alicia imagined Leandro sitting in the dark somewhere in the hotel, gazing down at Plaza de Neptuno or looking at the Madrid sky awash with black clouds, awaiting daybreak.

"Alicia," he said slowly, no tone whatsoever in his voice. "I thought you weren't going to call."

"I apologize. I had an episode."

"I'm sorry to hear that. Are you better?"

"I'm fine."

"Is Vargas with you?"

"I'm alone."

"Everything all right with him?"

"Yes. There's no problem."

"If you want me to get rid of him, I could . . ."

"There's no need. I almost prefer to have him handy, just in case."

A pause. In Leandro's pauses there was no breathing, no sound whatsoever. "You're unrecognizable, if you don't mind the observation. Anyhow, I'm glad you two get along. I thought that perhaps you wouldn't quite mesh, given his personal history . . ."

"What history?"

"Nothing. It's not important."

"When you say that, that's when I really get worried."

"Didn't he tell you about his family?"

"We don't speak about personal matters."

"In that case, I don't want to be the one who—"

"What's the matter with his family?"

There was another of Leandro's pauses. Alicia could almost imagine him smiling and licking his lips.

"Vargas lost his wife and his daughter in a traffic accident about three years ago. He was drunk at the wheel. His daughter was your age. He's been through rough times. He was almost thrown out of the Force."

Alicia didn't reply. She could hear Leandro's breathing.

"Didn't he tell you?"

"No."

"I suppose he prefers not to stir up the past. At any rate, I hope there won't be a problem."

"What problem could there be?"

"Alicia, you know I never meddle in your personal life, although by God I sometimes find it hard to understand your tastes and particular preferences."

"I don't know what you mean."

"You know exactly what I mean."

She bit her lip and swallowed the words burning in her mouth. "There won't be any problem," she said at last.

"Excellent. Now tell me, what have you got for me?"

Alicia took a deep breath and clenched her fist so firmly she sank her nails into her skin. When she began her account, her voice had returned to the docile and melodic tone she had learned to cultivate in her dealings with Leandro.

*

During the next few minutes she summed up the events that had taken place since their last conversation. Her narrative had no color and no detail; she just listed all the steps she had taken, without offering the reasons or hunches that had led her to take them. When it came to omissions, most noteworthy was the bit about the theft of the Víctor Mataix book from her home the night before. As he usually did, Leandro listened patiently, without interrupting.

Once she'd finished, Alicia fell silent, taking in Leandro's long pause as he digested her report.

"Why do I get the feeling that you're not telling me everything?"

"I don't know. I don't think I've left out anything relevant."

"To conclude, the search of the car that was allegedly used for—let's call it the getaway—provides no final evidence beyond a few signs of nonfatal violence and a supposed list of numbers that we can't link to anything and that possibly has no connection with the case. On the other hand, we continue with your insistence on the matter of the book by this man called Mataix, a line of inquiry that I worry will lead only to a series of fascinating bibliographical mysteries of zero use in finding Mauricio Valls."

"Any news about the official police investigation?" asked Alicia, hoping to shift the course of the conversation.

"There's no relevant news, and there isn't expected to be any. Suffice it to say that some don't look kindly on the fact that we've been invited to the party, even if it was through the back door."

"Is that why I'm being watched?"

"For that reason, and because they probably can't believe that we will, of course, be pleased to see our friends in the police take all the glory and medals the day we find the minister safe and sound, and hand him over to them, tied up with a red bow."

"If we find him, that is."

"Is your lack of faith a simple affectation, or have you kept something from me?"

"I only meant that it's difficult to find someone who might not want to be found."

"Let's give ourselves the benefit of the doubt and set aside the possible wishes of the minister. Or those of our colleagues at police headquarters. That's why I recommend a certain amount of prudence when it comes to Vargas. Loyalty is a habit that doesn't change in one day."

"We can trust Vargas."

"Said the woman who doesn't even trust herself. I'm not saying anything that you don't already know."

"Don't worry. I'll be careful. Anything else?"

"Call me."

Alicia was about to wish Leandro a good night when she realized that, once again, he had already hung up.

19

THE CANDLELIGHT FADES into a tiny pale-blue flame, floating on a pool of wax. Valls draws the hand he no longer feels into the aura of brightness. His skin has a purplish color, almost black. His fingers are swollen, and his nails, beneath which flows a gelatinous liquid with an indescribable stench, are beginning to fall off. Valls tries to move the fingers, but his hand doesn't respond. It's just a piece of dead flesh stuck to his body, beginning to send black lines up his arm. He can feel the rotten blood in his veins clouding his thoughts, dragging him into a dark, feverish sleep. He knows that if he waits a few more hours, he will lose consciousness. He will die in the narcotic sleep of gangrene, his body just a tangle of carrion that will never see the sunlight again.

The saw his jailer left in the cell is still there. He has considered it various times. He has tried pressing it down on the fingers that no longer belong to him. At first he felt some pain. Now he feels nothing, only nausea. His throat is dry from shouting, moaning, begging for mercy. He knows that sometimes someone comes to see him. When he is asleep. When he's delirious. It is usually the man with the mask, his jailer. Other times it's the angel he remembers seeing by the car door, before a knife cut through his hand and he lost consciousness.

Something has gone wrong. There has been a mistake somewhere in his calculations and suppositions. Martín isn't here, or hasn't wanted to show his face. Valls knows, needs to believe, that all this is the work of David Martín. Only his sick mind could think of doing this to someone.

"Tell Martín I'm sorry, tell him I beg his forgiveness . . . ," he has pleaded a thousand times in the jailer's presence.

He never gets a reply. Martín will let him die there, let him rot a centimeter at a time, not deigning to come down to his cell, even once, to spit in his face.

At some point he loses consciousness again.

*

Valls wakes up soaked in his own urine, convinced this is 1942, and he's back in Montjuïc Castle. His poisoned blood has snatched what little reason he had left. He laughs. I was inspecting the cells, and I've fallen asleep in one of them, he thinks. That's when he notices a hand that isn't his, attached to his arm. Panic takes hold of him. He has seen lots of corpses, during the war and in his years as prison governor, and he knows without needing to be told that the hand he is looking at is a dead man's hand. He creeps along the floor, thinking the hand will drop off, but it follows him. He hits the hand against the wall, and it doesn't come off. He doesn't realize he's screaming when he grabs hold of the saw and starts cutting just above the wrist. The flesh yields like wet clay, but when he hits the top of the bone, a deep nausea invades him. He doesn't stop. He musters all his strength. His howls drown the sound the bone makes when it breaks under the metal. A pool of black blood spreads at his feet. The only thing linking his hand to his body is a shred of skin.

The pain comes later, like a huge wave. It reminds him of a time when he was a child and he touched the naked cable from which a lightbulb hung—in the basement of his parents' home. He collapses backward and feels something rising to his throat. He cannot breathe. He is drowning in his own vomit. It will just take a minute, he tells himself. He thinks of Mercedes and puts all the strength of his being into fixing the image of her face in his mind.

*

Valls barely notices when the cell door opens and the jailer kneels down beside him. He carries a bucket of scalding tar. He grabs Valls's arm and dips it in the bucket. Valls feels the fire.

The jailer is looking into his eyes. "Do you remember now?"

Valls nods.

The jailer sinks a needle into his arm. The liquid flooding into his veins is ice cold and makes Valls think of a clean blue sea. The second injection is the one that brings peace, a sleep with no end and no consciousness.

20

ALICIA WAS AWOKEN by the wind whistling through the cracks in the windows, making the windowpanes vibrate. She looked at the clock on her bedside table: it was a couple of minutes to five in the morning. She let out a sigh. Only then did she notice. The darkness.

She remembered having left the light on in the dining room and the corridor before snatching a few hours' sleep after her conversation with Leandro, but now the flat was plunged in a bluish gloom. She groped for the switch of the bedside table lamp and pressed it. The light didn't go on. Then she thought she could hear footsteps in the dining room, and the sound of a door moving slowly. A piercing cold took hold of her. She grabbed the revolver that had spent the night with her under the sheets and released the safety.

"Vargas?" she called out weakly. "Is that you?"

The echo of her voice drifted through the flat, but there was no answer. Alicia pulled the sheets aside, got up, and stepped into the corridor. The floor was icy under her bare feet. The passageway formed a dark frame around a halo of pale light at the entrance to the dining room. She walked slowly down the corridor, holding up the weapon. Her hand shook. When she reached the dining room, she felt the wall for the light switch and pressed it. Nothing. There was no power. She scanned the shadows, the outline of the furniture, and the dark corners around the room. There was a sour smell in the air. Tobacco, she thought. Or perhaps it came from the flowers Jesusa had left in the vase on the table; they were starting to shed dry petals. She didn't notice any movement, so she walked over to the dining-room sideboard and searched in the first drawer. She found a packet of candles and a box of matches that must have been there since before Leandro had posted her to Madrid. After lighting one of the candles, she held it up, then walked through the flat slowly, the candle in one hand and the revolver in the other. She checked the front door to make sure it was locked, trying to banish the image of Lomana from her mind, smiling and motionless as a wax figure, holding a butcher's knife, waiting for her inside a cupboard or behind a door.

Once she had covered every nook and cranny in the flat and made quite sure there was nobody there, Alicia took one of the dining-room chairs and jammed it against the lock of the front door. Leaving the candle on the table, she crossed to the large window that looked out onto the street. The whole neighborhood was plunged in darkness, the serrated outline of roofs and dovecotes sketched against the dark blue that announced the oncoming dawn. Her face touching the windowpane, she scanned the shadows at street level. A glimmer of light could be seen beneath the arches of the espadrille shop. The embers of a lit cigarette. It was surely just that poor wretch Rovira, Alicia told herself, already doing his early shift at that ungodly hour. She withdrew into the dining room and took two more candles from the sideboard drawer. It was still much too early to go down to the Gran Café to meet Vargas for breakfast, and she knew she wouldn't get back to sleep.

She went over to the bookshelf where she kept some of her best-loved books, most of which she'd read and reread a few times. Four years had gone by since Alicia had revisited her favorite among them all, *Jane Eyre*. She took it down and ran her fingertips over the front cover. When she opened the book, she smiled. There was the stamp: a small devil sitting on a pile of books, an old bookplate given to her by her colleagues in the unit during her first year in Leandro's service, when they still saw her as a mysterious but harmless young girl—a whim of the boss, someone who had not yet awoken jealousy, envy, and resentment among the older members of the team.

Those had been days of poisoned wine and roses, when Ricardo Lomana had decided of his own accord that she would be his personal apprentice. Every Friday he'd given her flowers before inviting her to the cinema or to a dance hall, invitations that Alicia always found some excuse to refuse. Days when Lomana looked at her out of the corner of his eye, thinking she didn't notice, dropping hints or flirtatious remarks that made even the older people in the room blush. A bad beginning makes a bad end, she had thought at the time. She hadn't known the half of it.

Trying to banish Lomana's face from her mind, she carried the book to the bathroom. There she tied up her hair and ran hot water into the bath. After lighting her candles and placing them at the head of the bathtub, she sank into the steaming hot water, letting it dispel the cold that had nestled in her bones, and closed her eyes. After a while she thought she heard footsteps on the stairs. She wondered whether it could be Vargas, coming up to make sure she was still alive, or whether she was imagining things again. The dark stupor induced by the painkillers always left a trail of half-formed pictures when she woke up, as if the dreams she had not been able to dream were trying to push their way through the cracks in her consciousness. She opened her eyes and sat up, resting her chin on the edge of the bath. A couple of voices floated in the air. Neither was Vargas's voice. She stretched out an arm until she touched the revolver resting on the stool next to the bathtub, and listened to the echo of water dripping from the closed tap. She waited a few seconds. The voices had gone silent. Or perhaps they had never been there. Moments later, the footsteps faded away down the stairs. Probably a neighbor leaving home to go to work, she thought.

Alicia left the revolver on the stool again and lit a cigarette. She watched the smoke coil between her fingers, then lay down in the bathtub again and gazed through the window at the bluish blanket of clouds over the city. She picked up the book and went back to the first paragraph. As she turned the pages, the anxiety that had gripped her slowly dissolved. After a while Alicia lost all track of time. Even Leandro couldn't pursue her into the forest of words *Jane Eyre* always conjured up before her eyes. She smiled and returned to the novel, feeling that she was returning home. She could have stayed there all day. Or all her life.

When she got out of the bath, she faced the mirror, staring at the threads of steam rising from her body. The black mark from the old wound on her right hip sketched a poisoned flower spreading its roots beneath her skin. She touched it and felt a slight stab of pain, a warning. After untying her hair, she applied a rose-scented cream over her arms, legs, and belly—a cream Fernandito had once given her in a fit of adolescent devotion, with the distinctive name of Péché Originel. She was on her way back to her bedroom when the power suddenly returned, and all the lights she had been testing went on at once. Startled, she pressed her hands to her chest. Her heart was beating fast. She turned the lights off, one by one, cursing.

Then, standing naked in front of her wardrobe, she took her time to decide. Barcelona forgave many things, but never bad taste. As she slipped on the underwear Señora Jesusa had washed and perfumed, she smiled, imagining the caretaker folding those garments and crossing herself, wondering whether that was what modern young city girls wore nowadays. Next, she put on a pair of sheer stockings. Alicia had made Leandro buy them for her to wear when she had to play the part in the fancy corners of Madrid, or for when she was assigned to one of her boss's intrigues in the dining halls and lounges of the Ritz.

"Can't you make do with a normal brand?" Leandro had protested when he'd seen the price.

"If you want normal, send someone else to do the job."

Making Leandro spend a fortune on finery and books was one of the very few pleasures she got out of the job. Not willing to tempt fate, Alicia decided to wear the harness that day. She fixed the fastener one notch tighter than normal and turned around to check in the mirror that the girdle was well adjusted. It gave her the air of a wicked doll, she thought, a marionette of dark beauty. She'd never been able to get accustomed to the sight. It seemed to insinuate that, deep down, Leandro was right and the mirror told the truth.

"All you lack are the strings," she told herself.

For the day's uniform she chose a formal-looking purple dress and a pair of Italian shoes that at the time had cost the equivalent of a month's wages in an elegant shoe shop on Rambla de Cataluña, where the shop assistant had called her "honey." She put on her makeup carefully, sketching the character. A dark, shiny burgundy lipstick made a finishing touch that she was positive would have earned Leandro's disapproval. She didn't want Vargas to find the slightest hint of weakness in her face when he saw her arrive. Experience had taught her that modesty always invited scrutiny. Before leaving the apartment, she checked herself one last time in the hallway mirror, approving of what she saw. You'd break your own heart, she thought, if you had one.

It was just getting light when Alicia crossed the street to the doors of the Gran Café. Before going in she caught sight of Rovira, already positioned at the corner, wearing a scarf that covered his face up to his nose and rubbing his hands. She thought of going over to him and spoiling his day, but let him be. Rovira waved at her from afar and ran to hide.

When she stepped into the café, she saw that Vargas had already settled down in what seemed to have become his official table. The policeman was devouring a monumental meat sandwich and washing it down with a large cup of coffee while he went through the list of numbers they had managed to scrape together with the help of the taxidermist. When he heard her come in, he raised his head and looked her up and down. She sat at the table without saying a word.

"You smell very nice," Vargas said. "Like a cream cake." With that he went straight back to the pleasures of his breakfast and to the list.

"How can you eat that at this time of morning?" asked Alicia.

The policeman shrugged and offered her a bite of the enormous sandwich. Alicia turned her face away, and Vargas renewed his attack with another huge bite.

"Did you know that in Catalan the word for sandwich means 'between breads'?" Vargas remarked. "Isn't that amusing?"

"Enough to fall over backward."

"And—wait for it—the Catalan word for 'bottle' sounds like ampoule, as for an injection!"

"A couple of days in Barcelona, and you've become a polyglot."

Vargas smiled like a shark. "I'm glad you've lost last night's sweetness. That means you're feeling better. Have you seen Jiminy Cricket, shitting himself with cold out there?"

"His name is Rovira."

"I forgot you hold him in such high esteem."

Miquel had walked over timidly, carrying a tray with slices of toast and a pot of steaming coffee. It was half past seven, and there was nobody else in the café. Miquel, a master of discretion, had withdrawn as always to the farthest point of the bar to pretend he was busy doing something. Alicia poured herself some coffee, and Vargas returned once more to his numbers, going over them one by one, as if he hoped that their meaning would be revealed by spontaneous generation. The minutes dragged by in a thick silence.

"You're looking very elegant," said Vargas at last. "Are we going somewhere smart?"

Alicia swallowed hard and cleared her throat. He looked up.

"About last night . . . ," she began.

"Yes?"

"I wanted to apologize. And thank you."

"There's nothing to apologize about, and even less to thank me for." A shadow of shyness veiled his severe expression.

Alicia smiled weakly at him. "You're a good person."

Vargas looked down. "Don't say that."

She nibbled at her piece of toast with no appetite. Vargas was watching her.

"What?"

"Nothing. I like to see you eat."

Alicia flashed her teeth, gave the piece of toast a big bite, and smiled.

"What's the plan?" he said.

"Yesterday we concentrated on the car. Let's pay a visit to the lawyer, Brians, today."

"As you wish. How do you want to do this?"

"I was thinking that I could be the young, naive heiress who has discovered she owns a copy of a Víctor Mataix book and wants to sell it. Don Gustavo Barceló told me that Brians represents a collector who is interested in buying all the Mataix books on the market, etcetera."

"You as the naive young lady. Promising. What about me. Who am I supposed to be? The squire?"

"I thought you could be my loyal, mature, and loving husband."

"Fabulous. The cat woman and the old captain, couple of the year. I don't think he'll buy it, even if he got the lowest grades in law school."

"I don't expect him to. The idea is rather to arouse his suspicions so that he makes a false move."

"I see. So what do we do then? Do we follow him?"

"You're quite the mind reader, Vargas."

*

When they set off down the road, a dazzling sun had managed to break through and was combing the rooftops. Vargas gazed at the facades and hidden corners bordering Calle Aviñón with the placid expression of a provincial seminarist on a weekend trip. Soon he noticed that Alicia kept turning her head to look back over her shoulder every few meters. He was about to ask whether something was wrong when he followed her eyes. Rovira was trying unsuccessfully to hide discreetly in a doorway, about fifty meters away.

"I'm going to spell it out to that little piece of shit," murmured Vargas.

Alicia held on to his arm. "No, it's best if you leave him."

She waved at Rovira and smiled. The man looked both right and left, hesitated for a moment, and, realizing he'd been discovered, returned the greeting timidly.

"Useless idiot," spat Vargas.

"Better him than someone else. At least this one is on our side, if he knows what's good for him."

"If you say so."

Vargas signaled to Rovira to move further back and stick to the agreed distance. The man nodded and raised two thumbs.

"Look at him," said Vargas. "He must have seen that at the movies."

"Isn't that where people learn how to live nowadays, in the cinema?"

"That's what the world's come to."

They left Rovira behind and continued walking.

"I don't like having this cretin tailing us," Vargas insisted. "I don't know why you trust him. God knows what he's telling them at headquarters."

"The fact is, I feel rather sorry for him."

"I think a couple of knuckle sandwiches wouldn't be amiss. You don't have to witness it if you don't want to. I'll catch him on my own at some point and leave him to soak."

"You eat too much protein, Vargas. It affects your disposition."

21

IF CLOTHES MAKETH the man, an office and a good address make, or unmake, the lawyer. In a city well provided with lawyers to be found in sumptuous offices inside the regal, stately buildings of Paseo de Gracia and other elegant streets, Don Fernando Brians had gone for a far more modest address.

From a distance Alicia and Vargas sighted the building, which was roughly a hundred years old and listing vaguely to one side, at the intersection of Calle Mercé and Calle Aviñón. The ground floor was occupied by a tapas bar that looked more like a refuge for forgotten bullfighters and fishermen on payday. The bartender, a tiny man shaped like a spinning top and sporting a plump mustache, had come outdoors armed with a mop and a steaming bucket that stank of bleach. He was whistling a popular tune and performing juggling tricks with a toothpick between his lips while he washed the pavement clean of urine, drunken vomit, and other miscellaneous souvenirs from the early hours, characteristic of the narrow streets leading to the port.

Piles of boxes and dusty bits of furniture flanked the front door of the building. A trio of young men, sweating profusely, had paused to recover their breath and polish off some baguette sandwiches with strips of mortadella peering over the sides.

"Is this the office of Señor Brians, the lawyer?" Vargas asked the bartender, who had interrupted his mopping to have a good look at them.

"Top floor," the man said, pointing upward with his index finger. "But they're in the middle of moving." He smiled as Alicia walked past, revealing his yellowed teeth. "A little coffee and a madeleine, miss? It's on the house."

"Some other day. Once you've shaved off that bush," Alicia replied without stopping.

The three young men applauded the jibe, which the bartender took sportingly. Vargas followed her into the building to the stairs, a sort of spiral that looked more like an intestinal tract than an architectural design.

"Is there an elevator?" Vargas asked one of the boys.

"If there is, we haven't seen it."

They ascended the building's five floors until they came to a landing teeming with boxes, filing cabinets, clothes hangers, chairs, and paintings of pastoral scenes that looked like they'd been rescued from a flea market at a few céntimos apiece. Alicia peeked her head around the office door, an apartment in full battle cry where nothing seemed to be in the right place and almost everything was stuffed in overfull boxes or on the move. Vargas tried the doorbell, which didn't work, then knocked on the door.

"Hello!"

A peroxide blonde with hair amassed into a rigid perm appeared in the corridor. The young lady sporting the prodigious helmet was wearing a flower-print dress and matching rouge.

"Good morning," said Alicia. "Is this Señor Brians's office?"

The young lady took a few steps toward them and gazed at them in surprise. "It is. Or was. We're moving. Can I help you?"

"We'd like to speak to the lawyer."

"Do you have an appointment?"

"I'm afraid not. Is Señor Brians in?"

"He usually gets in a bit later. Likes to take his time, you know, make an entrance . . . Perhaps you'd like to wait in the bar downstairs."

"If you don't mind, we'd rather wait here. There are lots of floors to climb."

The secretary sighed and nodded. "As you wish. As you can see we're in a real mess here."

"We're aware of the situation," Vargas said quickly. "We'll try not to bother you."

Alicia's sweet smile and in particular Vargas's looks seemed to have softened the secretary's distrust. "Follow me, please," she said, and guided them down the long corridor that cut through the offices. On either side there were rooms packed with full boxes, ready for the move. The bustle had stirred up shining particles that tickled their nostrils, and they continued their voyage through the remains of the shipwreck until they came to a large corner room at the end. It looked like the last standing bastion in the workplace.

"If you'd be so kind . . . ," said the secretary, showing them in.

The room was, in fact, all that remained of Brians's office. It presented a mass of shelves and files stacked in precarious heaps against the walls. The main exhibit was a desk of fine wood that looked as if it had survived a fire, and behind it a glass cabinet containing the entire collection of Aranzadi law books, randomly piled together.

Alicia and Vargas sat down on a couple of improvised stools by the French window, which opened onto a balcony with a view of the statue of Our Lady of Mercy perched on the dome of the basilica, on the other side of the street.

"You could ask the Virgin Mary to have pity on us. She pays no attention to me," the secretary remarked. "Who shall I announce?"

"Jaime Valcárcel and wife," said Alicia before Vargas could even blink.

The woman nodded diligently, although her eyes brushed mischievously past Vargas, as if she wanted to remark on the age difference and let him know that she had no problem forgiving this peccadillo in a handsome fellow like him.

"I'm Puri, at your service. I don't think Señor Brians will be long. Can I offer you anything while you wait? Mariano from the bar brings up a few madeleines and a Thermos flask with coffee every morning, in case you'd like some . . ."

"I wouldn't say no . . . ," Vargas allowed.

Puri smiled happily.

"I'll bring it along right away."

They saw her march off with a suggestive swing of the hips that did not escape Vargas.

"Enough of Mariano and his madeleines," muttered Alicia under her breath.

"We all make do as best we can."

"How can you possibly still be hungry after eating a whole pig?"

"Some of us still have blood in our veins."

"Maybe it's Señorita Puri who has awoken your wilder side."

Before Vargas could reply, the abovementioned returned, carrying a plateful of madeleines and a large cup of steaming coffee, which the policeman readily accepted.

"Forgive me for serving it like this, but everything is in boxes . . ."

"Don't worry. Thanks so much."

"And why is it you're moving?" asked Alicia.

"The landlord, he wants to hike up the rent. . . . He's a greedy oaf. I hope the entire building gets vacant, and the rats move in."

"Amen," Vargas agreed. "And where will you go now?"

"I wish I knew. We had a verbal agreement for an office nearby, behind the post office, but the work they were doing to modify the space for us has been delayed, and we'll have to wait at least another month. For the moment all this is going into a storage warehouse owned by the lawyer's family."

"And where are you going to be meanwhile?"

Puri sighed. "An aunt of the lawyer's, who died not long ago, had an apartment on Calle Mallofré, in Sarriá, and it looks like we're moving there for the moment. As you can see, we live from one day to the next . . ."

Alicia and Vargas looked over Brians's decommissioned office again, taking in the air of bankruptcy it exuded. Alicia's eyes paused on a frame containing what looked like the parody of a graduation photograph. It was a portrait of Brians as a young man, or so she imagined, surrounded by people in rags and starving prisoners shackled up to their necks. Beneath the image were these words:

FERNANDO BRIANS
DEFENDER OF LOST CAUSES

Alicia stood up and walked over to have a look at the tableau. Puri joined her, shaking her head. "There he is, the saint of Barcelona's magistrates' courts. . . . That's a joke his classmates played on him years ago, when he was young. And he hasn't changed. He even thinks the whole thing is funny enough to display it where the clients can see it."

"Doesn't the lawyer have clients who are more . . ."

"Prosperous?"

"Solvent."

"There are one or two, but all it takes is for Don Fernando to meet some poor, godforsaken devil in the street, and he'll bring him up to the office and sign him pro bono. . . . He's a bleeding heart, is what he is. And this is the result."

"Don't worry. We're the paying sort," Vargas put in.

"God bless you. How are the madeleines?"

"Memorable."

While Vargas was giving a practical demonstration of his hearty appetite, much to Puri's delight, they heard a crash that sounded like someone bumping into something, followed by a prolonged stumble that ended in a loud curse.

Puri rolled her eyes. "The lawyer will see you right away."

Fernando Brians looked like a public-school teacher. He wore a secondhand suit and a faded tie that had probably not been knotted afresh in weeks. The soles of his shoes shone like river stones. He cut a slender, nervous figure and despite his age still sported a good head of gray hair and penetrating eyes behind black horn-rimmed glasses—the sort that had been fashionable before the war. He looked as much like a Barcelona lawyer as his secretary Puri looked like a nun. Yet Alicia thought that despite the modest context framing his professional life, Fernando Brians retained the irreverent demeanor of those who have never been told that time has passed and they should adopt a more respectable and settled manner.

"What can I do for you?" Brians asked, sitting down on a corner of the desk and looking at them with a mixture of curiosity and skepticism. Perhaps he had a soft spot for lost causes, but he seemed to be nobody's fool.

Vargas spoke first, pointing to Alicia. "If you don't mind, sir, I'll let my wife explain our case to you. She's the one in charge."

"As you wish."

"Shall I take notes, Don Fernando?" asked Puri, who was watching the scene from the doorway.

"There won't be any need. You'd better go and keep an eye on the movers. They're blocking the street with boxes, and the van won't be able to get through."

Puri nodded, disappointed, and went off on her mission.

"You were saying?" said Brians, picking up where they'd left off. "Or your wife was, who is the one in charge . . ."

His slightly steely tone made Alicia wonder whether Gustavo Barceló, the bookseller she'd spoken to in the Equestrian Club, had warned the lawyer about her possible visit. "Señor Brians," she began, "an aunt of my husband Jaime has recently died and left us a collection of works of art, as well as a library of extremely valuable books."

"My condolences. Do you perhaps need help with executing the will, or—"

"The reason why we've come to see you is that among the books in this collection, there is one by an author named Víctor Mataix. It's part of a series of novels published in Barcelona in the thirties—"

"*The Labyrinth of the Spirits*," said Brians, finishing the sentence.

"Precisely. We've been told that you represent a collector who is very interested in acquiring all extant copies by this author, and that's why we thought it would be a good idea—"

"I see," said Brians, abandoning the corner of his desk and taking shelter in the armchair.

"Perhaps you would be so kind as to put us in touch with your client, or, if you prefer, give us his details so that we can—"

Brians was nodding, more to himself than to Alicia's suggestions. "Unfortunately, I can't do that."

"Excuse me?"

"I can't give you that information, or put you in touch with my client."

Alicia gave him a conciliatory smile. "And may I ask why?"

"Because I don't know him."

"I'm sorry, I don't understand."

Brians sat back in his armchair and linked his hands over his chest, rubbing his thumbs together. "My relationship with this client has been conducted strictly by correspondence through a secretary. I've never seen him in person, nor do I know his name. As usually happens with some collectors, he prefers to remain anonymous."

"Even with his own lawyer?"

Brians smiled stiffly and shrugged.

"So long as he pays the bill, right?" Vargas ventured.

"Well, if you're in touch by letter with his secretary, you will at least have an address where you can write to him," Alicia suggested.

"It's a PO box whose number, needless to say, I cannot give you for reasons of confidentiality. Just as I can't give you the name of his secretary, since I'm not authorized to divulge any information about my clients that they do not wish to make public. It's a simple formality, but you must understand that I have to observe it."

"We do understand. Even so, how can you get hold of books for your client's collection if afterward there's no way of contacting him directly to let him know there's an opportunity?"

"Believe me, Señora—Valcárcel?—if my client is interested in buying a book that is in your possession, he will be the one to notify me. I'm simply an intermediary."

Alicia and Vargas looked at one another.

"Goodness," the policeman improvised. "We've obviously been mistaken, my dear."

Brians stood up and walked around the desk, holding out his hand with a smile that had all the signs of a farewell. "I'm very sorry not to be able to help you in this matter, and I must apologize for the appearance and state of my office. We're in the middle of a move, and I wasn't expecting any clients today."

They shook hands and let Brians guide them to the front door as he hopped about, avoiding obstacles and clearing the path for them.

"If you'll allow me a bit of impartial advice," he said, "in your place I'd talk to a good secondhand bookseller and get him to spread the word. If you have a genuine Mataix, there will be no lack of buyers."

"Any suggestions?"

"Barceló, next to Plaza Real, or Sempere & Sons, on Calle Santa Ana. Or Costa in Vic. Those are your three best options."

"We'll do that. Thank you so much."

"You're most welcome."

Alicia didn't open her mouth during their descent to the entrance hall of the building. Vargas followed her at a prudent distance. Before stepping through the front door, she stopped to look at one of the piles of boxes left there by the removal crew.

"What now?" Vargas said.

"Now we wait."

"What for?"

"For Brians to make a move."

Alicia knelt down by one of the closed boxes. She glanced briefly at the door and, seeing nobody around, pulled a label off the cardboard and put it in her pocket.

"Can you tell me what you're doing?"

Alicia walked out into the street without replying. To his surprise, the moment Vargas stepped out, she went into the bar on the corner. Mariano, the bartender and champion of the morning madeleines, was still mopping the pavement, and seemed even more surprised than Vargas to see her entering his establishment. He quickly leaned the mop against the wall and followed her, drying his hands on the cloth hanging from his belt.

Vargas sighed and went in behind them.

"A little coffee and madeleines for the young lady?" Mariano proposed.

"A glass of white wine."

"At this hour?"

"When do you start serving white wine?"

"For you, twenty-four hours a day. A smooth Penedès?"

Alicia nodded. Vargas sat on the stool next to her. "Do you really think your plan is going to work?" he asked.

"There's no harm in trying."

Mariano returned with the glass of wine and a plateful of olives on the house. "A little beer for the gentleman?"

Vargas shook his head. He watched Alicia relishing her wine. There was something about the geometry of her lips caressing the glass, about the shape of her pale neck throbbing as the liquid went through it, that lit up the day.

She noticed his look and raised an eyebrow. "What?"

"Nothing."

Alicia raised the glass. "Do you disapprove?"

"God forbid."

Alicia was downing the last drop of wine when the figure of the lawyer sped past the bar's front window. Swapping a quick glance, Alicia and Vargas dropped a few coins on the bar and left the place without a word.

22

IT WAS WELL known to everyone in the Force that when it came to the art of following or even chasing citizens—whether or not they were suspects—Vargas was unequaled. When asked what his secret was he would say that what mattered, more than discretion, was knowing how to make good use of the lay of the land. What was essential, he argued, was not what the pursuer could see or guess, but what was within range of the pursued person's vision. That and good legs. As soon as they began to follow the lawyer, Vargas realized that Alicia had not only mastered the discipline to perfection but even raised it to a fine art. Her exhaustive knowledge of the old town's mesh of narrow streets and alleyways allowed her to follow Brians unnoticed.

Alicia walked more confidently than the day before. Vargas supposed she must be wearing the girdle the taxidermist had told him about. The way she moved her hips was different, and she seemed more upright. She led him through that maze, indicating pauses, taking shelter in blind spots, and following Brians's route without the lawyer realizing what she was doing. For almost twenty minutes they trailed the lawyer through the dense grid of passageways that rose from the port to the town center. More than once they caught a glimpse of him stopping at an intersection, looking back to make sure nobody was following him. His only mistake was to look the wrong way. Finally they saw him turn into Calle Canuda and head for the Ramblas, mixing with the crowd that already filled the central boulevard. Only then did Alicia stop for a few seconds.

"He's going to the metro," she murmured, holding Vargas back with her arm.

Mingling with the surge of people along the Ramblas, keeping about ten meters back, Alicia and Vargas followed Brians to the metro entrance next to the Canaletas fountain. The lawyer rushed down the stairs and into the web of tunnels that led to the so-called Avenida de la Luz.

More like a boulevard of darkness and sorrow than an avenue of light, this extravagant and ghostly mall had been designed by some enlightened soul who hoped to create an underground Barcelona by gaslight. The project, however, had never come close to fulfilling that vision. A budding graveyard through which gusts of air coughed up the scent of charcoal and electricity from the metro tunnels, Avenida de la Luz had become a refuge for those who shunned the surface and the sun.

Vargas scanned the long, gloomy line of mock-marble columns that bordered the shoddy bazaars and dimly lit cafés, then turned to Alicia. "The city of vampires?"

"Something like that."

Alicia and Vargas followed Brians down the underground avenue, the lines of columns on either side shielding them from view. The lawyer walked on almost to the end, not showing any interest in the shops bordering the avenue.

"Perhaps he's allergic to sunlight," suggested Vargas.

Brians walked straight past the Catalan Railways' ticket office and continued down the vast gallery. Only then did it become obvious where he was heading.

The Avenida de la Luz Cinema loomed ahead, a somber fantasy marooned in that strange subterranean Barcelona. Its amusement-park lights and old posters for rereleases had been tempting the tunnel creatures—sacked office clerks, truant schoolchildren, and sleazy pimps—to its matinees since shortly after the civil war. Brians walked up to the ticket office and bought a ticket.

"Don't tell me our lawyer goes to the cinema halfway through the morning," said Vargas.

At the entrance, the usher opened the door for Brians, and he disappeared under the canopy announcing that week's program: a double bill with *The Third Man* and *The Stranger*. A somewhat evil-looking Orson Welles bearing an enigmatic smile looked down from a poster, framed by flickering lightbulbs.

"At least he has good taste," Alicia said.

As Vargas and Alicia went through the velvet curtains sealing the entrance, they were hit by an aroma of old cinema and unspeakable sadness. The projector's beam cut through a thick cloud that seemed to have been trapped for decades over the stalls. There were only three or four people in the entire cinema. Rows of empty seats sloped down to the screen, where a treacherous Harry Lime ran through the phantasmagoria of Vienna's sewer tunnels, in a series of spectral images that seemed, to Alicia, straight out of Víctor Mataix's book.

"Where is he?" whispered Vargas in her ear.

She pointed toward the bottom of the stalls. Brians had taken a seat in the fourth row. They moved down the side passage, where a row of seats was backed up against the wall, as on an underground train. Halfway down, Alicia slipped into one of the rows, sitting in the middle.

Vargas sat down beside her. "Have you seen this film?"

Alicia nodded. She'd seen it at least six times and knew the dialogue by heart.

"What's it about?"

"Penicillin. Keep quiet."

The wait turned out to be shorter than they thought. The film was still running when Alicia, glancing over her shoulder, saw a figure advancing down the side aisle. She nudged Vargas, who was by now utterly engrossed in the film.

The stranger wore a dark coat and carried a hat in his hand. Alicia clenched her fists. The visitor stopped by the row where the lawyer was sitting, and stood staring calmly at the screen. A moment later he stepped into the row just behind Brians, sitting in a seat diagonally behind the lawyer.

"Knight's move," whispered Vargas.

For the next couple of minutes the lawyer showed no sign of having noticed the presence of the stranger, nor did the stranger seem to communicate with him in any way. Vargas looked at Alicia skeptically. Even she began to think that perhaps it was a simple coincidence— two strangers in a cinema with no more connection than a nearsightedness that made them prefer to sit in the front rows. It was only when the sound of gunshots filled the hall, ending the thousand lives of the evil Harry Lime, that the stranger leaned toward the seat in front of him, and Brians turned slightly. The sound track took away his words, and all Alicia was able to establish was that the lawyer had spoken a couple of sentences and given the stranger a piece of paper. Afterward, ignoring one another, they settled back in their seats and continued watching the film.

"In my day I would have arrested them on grounds of being fairies," said Vargas.

"Pity we're no longer living in the golden days of your Stone Age Spain," replied Alicia.

When the projector flooded the screen with the grandiose final shot, the stranger stood up. He withdrew slowly toward the side aisle, and while the disillusioned heroine walked along the deserted avenue of the old Vienna cemetery, he put on his hat before slinking off to the exit. Alicia and Vargas didn't turn their heads or otherwise suggest that they had noticed his presence, but their eyes were fixed on the figure sprinkled by the vaporous flicker of the projector. The brim of the hat cast a shadow over his face, but not enough to hide a bizarrely smooth, shiny ivory surface, like the face of a dummy. Alicia shivered.

Vargas waited for the stranger to disappear behind the entrance curtain before leaning over. "Is it me, or was that guy wearing a mask?"

"Something like that. Come on, let's get out before he slips away."

At that moment, before they had time to stand up, the lights went on and the end credits disappeared from the screen. Brians had stood up and was making his way toward the side aisle. In just a few seconds he would walk past and see them sitting there.

"What now?" whispered Vargas, lowering his head.

Alicia grabbed the back of the policeman's neck and pulled his face toward hers.

"Embrace me," she whispered.

Vargas put his arms around her with the zeal of a practicing schoolboy. Alicia pulled him toward her. Their lips almost touching, they became entwined in what looked like one of those furtive kisses that in those days were only seen in the back rows of local cinemas and in dark doorways at midnight. Vargas closed his eyes.

As soon as Brians had left the cinema hall, Alicia pushed Vargas away and stood up. "Let's go."

Outside the cinema, Brians was walking down the central lane of the underground avenue in the same direction as he had come. There was no trace of the stranger with the mannequin face. Some twenty meters farther along, Alicia spotted the stairs that led to the crossing of Calle Balmes and Calle Pelayo, and they hurried toward them. A stabbing pain ran up Alicia's right leg, and she held her breath. Vargas grabbed her arm.

"I can't go any faster," she announced. "You go on ahead. Quick."

Vargas leaped up the stairs while she leaned against the wall, recovering her breath. Emerging into the daylight, the policeman found himself staring at the entire length of Calle Balmes. He looked around in confusion. He didn't know the city well and had lost his bearings. By then the traffic was very thick. The center of Barcelona was flooded with cars, buses, and trams. Curtains of pedestrians moved across the pavements beneath a dusty sunlight bearing down from on high. Vargas put a hand on his forehead to protect himself from the light and swept the intersection with his eyes, ignoring the shoving of passersby. A thousand black coats and hats were parading every which way. He'd never find the stranger, he thought.

The peculiar texture of the stranger's face gave him away. He was already on the other side of the street, walking toward a car parked on the corner of Calle Vergara. Vargas tried to cross, but the mass of vehicles pushed him back to the pavement amid a bellow of horns. On the other side the stranger was getting into the car—a Mercedes-Benz, at least fifteen or twenty years old.

By the time the traffic lights changed, the car was already driving away. Vargas ran after it and managed to get a good look before it was swallowed by the river of traffic. On his way back toward the mouth of the metro station, he walked past a local policeman, who gave him a disapproving look; he must have seen Vargas try to cross the street against a red light and dive in among the cars. Vargas nodded meekly and raised a hand in apology.

Alicia was waiting expectantly on the pavement.

"How are you feeling?" Vargas asked.

She ignored his question and shook her head impatiently.

"I managed to see him get into a car. A black Mercedes," said Vargas.

"Plate number?"

He nodded.

23

THEY TOOK SHELTER in Café Nuria at the top of the Ramblas, sitting by the window. Alicia asked for a glass of white wine, the second one that day. She lit a cigarette and let her eyes roam through the mass of people flowing down the Ramblas, as if she was gazing at the largest aquarium in the world. Vargas watched her raise her glass with trembling fingers and draw it to her lips.

"No lecture?" she asked, not looking away from the window.

"To your health."

"You didn't say anything about the guy with the mask. Are you thinking the same thing as me?"

He shrugged doubtfully.

"The report concerning the alleged attack on Valls in the Círculo de Bellas Artes mentioned a man with a covered face," she said.

"It could be," Vargas conceded. "I'm going to make a few calls."

Once alone, Alicia let out a sigh of pain and pressed her hand against her hip. She thought about taking half a tablet but decided against it. Making the most of the fact that Vargas was using the phone at the far end of the coffee shop, she signaled to the waiter to bring her another glass and take away the first, which she polished off in one gulp.

Vargas returned a quarter of an hour later, his little notebook in his hand. The glow in his eyes foretold news. "We're in luck. The car is under the name of Metrobarna S.L. It's a property investment company, or at least that's how it's registered. The main office is here, in Barcelona. Paseo de Gracia, number six."

"That's just around the corner. Give me a couple of minutes to recover, and we'll go there."

"Why don't you leave this one to me, Alicia, and go home to rest for a while? I'll come by later and tell you what I've found out."

"Are you sure?"

"Positive. Go on."

Outside, in the Ramblas, the sky seemed to have cleared at last. It shone with that electric blue that sometimes bewitches Barcelona winters, persuading the gullible that nothing can go wrong.

"Straight home, OK? No technical stops," Vargas warned. "I'm getting to know you."

"Yes, sir. Don't solve the case without me."

"Don't worry."

She watched him head off toward Plaza de Cataluña and waited a couple of minutes. Years ago she'd discovered that when a woman exaggerated symptoms of pain, adopting the helpless expression of a frail maiden in distress, she could manipulate any man who needed to feel that she required his protection and guidance—and that applied to almost the entire male contingent on the census, excepting Leandro Montalvo, who had taught her most of the tricks in her armory and could also invariably sense the ones she had picked up herself. As soon as Alicia was sure that she'd got rid of Vargas, she changed her route. Going home could wait. She needed time to think and observe from the shadows. And above all, there was something she wanted to do—on her own, and in her own way.

*

The Metrobarna offices were located on the top floor of a celebrated modernist block. The massive structure, its facade covered in ocher stone and its roof crowned with pinnacles and domed turrets, was known as Casa Rocamora. It oozed the fastidious craftsmanship and grand melodrama pervading certain examples of architecture only found on the streets of Barcelona. Vargas paused on the corner to look at the spectacle of balconies, galleries, and Byzantine geometry. A street watercolorist had set up his easel on the corner, and was giving the finishing touches to an impressionist take on the building. When he noticed Vargas's presence, he smiled politely.

"Beautiful image," Vargas congratulated him.

"We do our best. Policeman?"

"That obvious?"

The artist gave him a bitter smile.

Vargas pointed at the picture. "Is it for sale?"

"It will be in just under half an hour. Interested in the building?"

"Increasingly. Does one have to pay to go in?"

"Don't give them any ideas."

A lift straight out of Jules Verne's dreams took Vargas up to an office door, on which a weighty golden sign bore these words:

METROBARNA LTD

PROPERTY INVESTMENT & MANAGEMENT

He pressed the bell. A sound like the chime of a grandfather clock echoed from within, and a few seconds later the door opened, revealing the delicate figure of a receptionist in oversmart clothes, framed by a sumptuous hallway. In some firms, opulence was communicated with intentional malice.

"Good morning," Vargas stated in an official tone, showing his badge. "Vargas, Central Police Headquarters. I'd like to speak to the manager, please."

The receptionist looked at him in surprise. Presumably the type of visitor she was used to receiving in that office was somewhat classier.

"Do you mean Señor Sanchís?"

Vargas replied with a nod and stepped into an entrance hall, its walls lined with blue velvet and dotted with delicate watercolors of Barcelona's emblematic facades and buildings. Vargas suppressed a smile when he recognized the style of the corner painter.

"May I ask what this is about, Officer?" asked the receptionist behind his back.

"Captain," Vargas corrected her without turning around.

The receptionist cleared her throat and, realizing she was not getting an answer, sighed. "Señor Sanchís is at a meeting right now. If you wish . . ."

Vargas turned around and looked at her coldly.

"I'll let him know right away, Captain."

Vargas nodded unenthusiastically. The receptionist rushed off in search of reinforcements. This was followed by a quick succession of hushed voices, sounds of doors opening and closing, and hurried steps along corridors. A minute later she was back, this time with a docile smile as she invited him to follow her. "If you'll be so kind, the director will see you in the boardroom."

He walked down a long passageway flanked by pompous office rooms where spruced-up lawyers in three-piece suits dealt with the day's business with the seriousness of skilled traders. Statues, paintings, and top-quality carpets outlined the route leading him to a large room with a glazed balcony that afforded an angel's-eye view of the entire Paseo de Gracia. An impressive board-meeting table presided over a series of armchairs, glass cabinets, and fine wood moldings.

"Señor Sanchís will be with you in a moment. Can I offer you anything while you wait? A coffee?"

Vargas shook his head. The receptionist vanished as soon as she could, leaving him on his own.

The policeman studied the scenery. The Metrobarna offices reeked of money. The carpet at his feet alone probably cost quite a bit more than he received from several years' salary. Vargas walked around the board table, caressing the lacquered oak wood with his fingers and taking in the perfume of excess. The stage set, with its shapes and designs, distilled that oppressive and exclusive air of institutions devoted to the alchemy of money, reminding the visitor that even if he thought he was inside, he would, in fact, always be outside the proverbial bank counter.

The room was decorated with numerous portraits of different sizes. Most of them were photographs, but there were also some oil paintings and a few charcoal sketches signed by an assortment of official and prestigious portrait artists of the last decades. Vargas studied these. The same person appeared in all the images, a gentleman with silvery hair and a patrician expression glancing at the lens, or the easel, with a calm smile and ice-cold eyes. The protagonist of those pictures clearly knew how to pose and choose his company. Vargas leaned over to take a closer look at one of the photographs, in which the gentleman with the cold eyes appeared with a group of important-looking men in hunting gear, smiling like lifelong friends as they stood on either side of a younger-looking General Franco. Vargas went through the cast of figures taking part in the hunting scene and was drawn to one particular participant. He stood in the second row and smiled enthusiastically, as if he were trying hard to stand out.

"Valls," Vargas murmured.

The door of the room opened behind him, and he turned around to encounter a lean, almost fragile-looking middle-aged man, with scant fair hair as fine as a baby's. The man wore an impeccably tailored alpaca suit that matched his gray eyes, steady and penetrating.

"Good morning. My name is Ignacio Sanchís, director general of this company. I gather, from what Lorena tells me, that you wish to speak to me. I'm sorry I've kept you waiting. We're preparing the annual shareholders' meeting, and we're rather snowed under. How can I help you, Captain?"

Sanchís exuded a cultivated air of friendliness and utmost professionalism. His eyes transmitted both warmth and authority while he cataloged Vargas meticulously. Vargas was certain that before ending his introductory sentence, Sanchís already knew the brand of the shoes he was wearing and how old his second-rate suit was.

"This face looks familiar," said the policeman, pointing at one of the oil paintings hanging in the room.

"That's Don Miguel Ubach," Sanchís said, smiling benevolently at the ignorance or ingenuousness of the man speaking to him. "Our founder."

"Of the Banca Ubach?" asked Vargas. "The Gunpowder Banker?"

Sanchís offered him a light, diplomatic smile, but his look grew colder. "Don Miguel Ángel never liked that nickname, which, if you don't mind my saying so, does not do the person justice."

"I heard that it was the Generalissimo himself who gave it to him, for his services," Vargas ventured.

"I'm afraid that's not the case. The nickname was conferred on Don Miguel by the red press during the war. The Banca Ubach, together with other institutions, helped finance the campaign of national liberation. A great man to whom Spain is hugely indebted."

"For which no doubt he has been generously rewarded . . . ," mumbled Vargas.

Sanchís ignored his words without losing any of his cordiality.

"And what is the relationship between Don Miguel Ángel and this company?" Vargas inquired.

Sanchís cleared his throat. "When Don Miguel Ángel died in 1948, the Banca Ubach was divided into three companies," he said patiently. "One of these was the Banco Hipotecario e Industrial de Cataluña, which was absorbed by the Banca Hispanoamericana de Crédito eight years ago. Metrobarna was created at that time to manage the property investment portfolio that was on the bank's balance sheet."

Sanchís pronounced those words as if he had recited them often, with the expert and absent air of a museum guide instructing a group of tourists while eyeing his watch. "But I'm sure that the company's history doesn't interest you that much," he concluded. "How can I help you, Captain?"

"It's a small matter, probably unimportant, Señor Sanchís, but you know the routine with these things. One has to check everything."

"Of course. I'm listening."

Vargas pulled out his notebook and pretended to be reading through a few lines. "Could you confirm whether a car with the license plate B-74325 belongs to Metrobarna?"

Sanchís looked at him in bewilderment.

"I really don't know. . . . I'd have to ask . . ."

"I imagine the company has a fleet of cars. Am I wrong?"

"No, you're right. We have four or five cars, if—"

"Is one of them a Mercedes-Benz? Black? A fifteen- or twenty-year-old model?"

A shadow of anxiety crossed Sanchís's face. "Yes . . . It's the car Valentín drives. Has something happened?"

"Valentín, you say?"

"Valentín Morgado, a driver who works for this firm."

"Your own private driver?"

"Yes. For years now. . . . May I ask what—"

"Is Señor Morgado in the office now?"

"I don't think so. He had to take Victoria to the doctor first thing this morning."

"Victoria?"

"Victoria is my wife."

"And your wife's family name is . . . ?"

"Ubach. Victoria Ubach."

Vargas raised his eyebrows in surprise. Sanchís nodded, vaguely irritated. "Daughter of Don Miguel Ángel, yes."

The policeman winked at him, as if he wished to imply that he admired the golden marriage that had taken him to the top of the company.

"Captain, please explain what this matter is about . . ."

Vargas smiled in a friendly, relaxed manner. "As I was saying, it's nothing important. We're investigating an accident that took place this morning on Calle Balmes. Someone was run over, and the suspect's car sped off. Don't worry, it's not yours. But two witnesses have declared that they saw a black car parked right there, on the corner, and the car fits the description and license plate of the black Mercedes driven by . . ."

"Valentín."

"Exactly. In fact, both witnesses have declared that when the accident took place, the driver of the Mercedes was inside the car. That is why we're interested in locating him, in case he was able to see anything that could help us identify the driver who fled the scene."

Sanchís looked concerned as he listened to the story, although he also seemed visibly relieved that his car and his driver were not involved in the accident. "That's terrible. Any fatalities?"

"Yes, unfortunately there is one. An elderly lady who was taken to the Hospital Clínico, where she was pronounced dead on arrival."

"I'm terribly sorry. Of course, whatever we can do to help to—"

"All I need is to be able to speak to your employee, Valentín."

"Yes, of course."

"Do you know whether Señor Morgado took your wife anywhere else this morning, after the visit to the doctor?"

"I'm not sure. I don't think so. Yesterday Victoria mentioned that she had visitors coming to the house around lunchtime today. . . . Maybe Valentín had gone out to do some errands. Some mornings, if my wife or I don't need him, he delivers documents or letters from the office."

Vargas pulled out a card and handed it to him.

"Would you be so kind as to ask Señor Morgado to get in touch with me as soon as possible?"

"Don't worry. I'll make sure he's located and gets the message. I'll do that right away."

"He probably won't be able to help us, but we have to go through the formalities."

"Of course."

"One last thing. Does Señor Morgado, by any chance, have any distinctive feature?"

Sanchís nodded. "Yes. Valentín was wounded during the war. Part of his face is disfigured because of a mortar explosion."

"How many years has he been working for you?"

"At least ten. Valentín was already working for my wife's family, and he's a trusted person in this house. I can confirm that."

"One of the witnesses mentioned something about a mask covering part of his face. Could that be so? I just want to make sure this is the right person."

"That's right. Valentín wears a prosthesis covering his lower jaw and left eye."

"I don't want to take up any more of your time, Señor Sanchís. Thank you so much for your help. I'm sorry I interrupted your meeting."

"Don't worry at all. My pleasure. It's a duty and an honor for a Spaniard to collaborate with the State Security Forces."

As Sanchís was leading Vargas to the exit, they passed a large carved door behind which lay a monumental library with a view of Paseo de Gracia. Vargas stopped a moment and peeped inside. The library stretched out like a Versailles gallery that seemed to occupy the entire side of the building. Floor and ceiling were lined with polished wood, so shiny they were like two mirrors facing each another, in which columns of books multiplied to infinity.

"Impressive," said Vargas. "Are you a collector?"

"A modest one," replied Sanchís. "Most of these books come from the collection of the Ubach Foundation, although I must admit that books are my weakness and my escape from the world of finance."

"I understand you. In my own humble way, I do the same," said

Vargas. "My hobby is serving arrest warrants on rare and unique books. My wife says it's the policeman in me."

Sanchís gave a nod, keeping his polite and patient expression, although his eyes were betraying mounting fatigue and a desire to rid himself of the policeman as soon as possible.

"Are you interested in rare books, Señor Sanchís?"

"Most books in this collection are eighteenth- and nineteenth-century Spanish, French, and Italian texts, although we also have an excellent selection of German literature and philosophy, as well as English poetry," the director explained. "I suppose that among some circles this would already be considered rare enough." Sanchís took Vargas's arm gently but firmly and led him back to the corridor and toward the front door.

"I envy you, Señor Sanchís. If only . . . I have limited means and must make do with more modest items."

"There are no modest books, only arrogant ignorance."

"Of course. That's exactly what I told a secondhand bookseller whom I've asked to find a series of novels by a forgotten author. The name might ring a bell. Mataix. Víctor Mataix."

Sanchís held his gaze impassively, then shook his head slowly. "I'm sorry, I've never heard of him."

"That's what everyone tells me. A man can devote his whole life to writing, and then nobody remembers his words . . ."

"Literature is a cruel lover that easily forgets its suitors," said Sanchís, opening the door to the landing.

"Much like justice. Luckily there is always someone who, like you and me, is ready to give them both a nudge."

"That's life: it forgets us all too soon. Now, if there's nothing else I can do for you . . ."

"No, thank you again for your help, Señor Sanchís."

24

AS HE LEFT the building, Vargas noticed the watercolorist, who was putting away his tools and lighting an old sailor's pipe. Vargas smiled at him from a distance and walked over.

"Hey, it's Chief Inspector Maigret," cried the artist.

"The name is Vargas."

"Dalmau," the painter introduced himself.

"How is it going, Master Dalmau? Have you finished your painting?"

"A painting is never finished. The trick is to know at what point to leave it unfinished. Are you still interested?" The artist lifted the rag covering the canvas and showed him the watercolor.

"It looks like something out of a dream," said Vargas.

"The dream is yours for ten duros plus whatever you think fit."

The policeman pulled out his wallet. The artist's eyes shone like the embers in his pipe. Vargas handed him a one-hundred-peseta note.

"That's too much."

Vargas shook his head. "Consider me the day's patron."

The painter wrapped up the watercolor with brown paper and string.

"Can one make a living doing this?" asked Vargas.

"The picture-postcard industry has hit us hard, but there are still people with good taste."

"Like Señor Sanchís?"

The artist raised an eyebrow and looked at him suspiciously. "I thought there was something fishy going on here. I hope you're not going to get me in trouble now."

"Has Sanchís been a customer for long?"

"A few years."

"Have you sold him lots of pictures?"

"Quite a few."

"Does he like your style that much?"

"He buys them out of pity, I think. He's a very generous man, at least considering he's a banker."

"Perhaps he has a bad conscience."

"He wouldn't be the only one. There's loads of those in this country."

"Are you referring to me?"

Dalmau muttered a curse under his breath and folded his easel.

"Are you leaving? I thought you'd be able to tell me something about Señor Sanchís."

"Look, if you like I'll give you back your money. And you can keep the picture. Hang it in one of the dungeons in the police station."

"The money is yours. You've earned it."

The artist hesitated. "What do you want with Sanchís?"

"Nothing. I'm just curious."

"That's the same thing the other policeman said. You're all alike."

"The other policeman?"

"Sure. Pretend you know nothing about it."

"Could you describe my colleague to me? There might be another note if you lend me a hand."

"There's little to describe. Another thug like you. Although this one had a scar on his face."

"Did he give you his name?"

"We didn't get that close."

"When was that?"

"Some two or three weeks ago."

"Here?"

"Yes, here. In my office. Can I go now?"

"You don't need to be afraid of me, boss."

"I'm not afraid of you. I've seen it all before with your type. But I'd rather have a change of scene, if you don't mind."

"Have you been locked up?"

The artist chuckled disdainfully.

"La Modelo?"

"Montjuïc. From 1939 to 1943. There's nothing you can do to me that you haven't done already."

Vargas took out his wallet, ready to make a second payment, but the painter refused it. He pulled out the money Vargas had given him and let it fall to the ground. Then he took his easel and paint box and walked away with a limp. Vargas watched him disappear up Paseo de Gracia. He knelt down to pick up the note and headed off in the opposite direction, carrying the picture under his arm.

*

Ignacio Sanchís walked over to the boardroom window and observed the policeman talking to the watercolorist on the corner. A couple of minutes later he saw the policeman strolling off toward Plaza de Cataluña, carrying what looked like a picture he had bought from the artist. Sanchís waited until he'd lost sight of Vargas among the crowd. Then he stepped into the corridor and made his way to reception.

"I'll be out a few minutes, Lorena. If Lorca calls, from the Madrid office, pass him over to Juanjo."

"Yes, Señor Sanchís."

Sanchís didn't wait for the elevator, but walked down the stairs. When he stepped out into the street, he felt a slight breeze grazing his forehead and realized it was covered in sweat. He made his way to the café next to Radio Barcelona on Calle Caspe, and asked for a *cortado*. While his coffee was being prepared, he walked over to the public telephone at the far end and dialed a number he knew by heart.

"Brians," replied a voice on the other end of the line.

"A policeman called Vargas has just paid me a visit."

A long silence.

"Are you calling from the office phone?" asked Brians.

"Of course not," said Sanchís.

"They've also been here this morning. The policeman and a girl. They said they had a Mataix for sale."

"Do you know who they are?"

"He's obviously a policeman. I didn't like her one bit. As soon as they left, I did what you said. I phoned the number you gave me and hung up immediately to signal Morgado to meet at our usual place. I saw him barely an hour ago. I thought he'd already warned you."

"Something unexpected turned up. Morgado had to go back to the house."

"What did the policeman ask you?"

"He wanted to know about Morgado. Some nonsense about an accident. They must have followed you. For all I know, they tricked you."

The lawyer sighed. "Do you think they've got the list?"

"I don't know. But we can't run any risks."

"What do you want me to do?" asked Brians.

"No meetings with Morgado and no calls until further notice," Sanchís ordered. "I'll contact you if necessary. Go back to the office and act as if nothing had happened. If I were you, I'd leave the city for a while."

The banker put down the phone. He walked past the bar, pale-faced.

"Your *cortado*, boss," said the waiter.

Sanchís looked at him as if he didn't know what he was doing there, and left the café.

25

MAURICIO VALLS HAS seen too many people die to believe there is anything beyond death. Coming back to life from the purgatory of antibiotics, narcotics, and hopeless nightmares, he opens his eyes to the wretchedness of his cell. The clothes he was wearing have disappeared. He's naked and wrapped in a blanket. He lifts the hand he does not have to his face and discovers the stump, cauterized with tar. He stares at it for a long time, as if trying to find out who is the owner of the body in which he has awakened. Bit by bit, his memory returns, dripping images and sounds. After a while he remembers everything except the pain. Perhaps there is a merciful God after all, he tells himself.

"What are you laughing at?" asks a voice. The woman who, in his delirium, he had taken to be an angel, is staring at him from behind the iron bars. There is no compassion or emotion in her eyes.

"Why didn't you let me die?"

"Death is too good for you."

Valls nods. He's not sure who he is speaking to, although something about this woman seems extremely familiar.

"Where is Martín? Why hasn't he come?"

The woman looks at him with a suggestion of scorn and sadness. "David Martín is waiting for you."

"Where?"

"In hell."

"I don't believe in hell."

"Have patience. You'll believe." The woman withdraws into the shadows and begins to climb the stairs.

"Wait. Don't leave. Please."

She stops.

"Don't go. Don't leave me here alone again."

"There are some clean clothes there. Get dressed," she says before disappearing up the stairs.

Valls hears a metal door closing. He finds the clothes in a bag, in a corner of the cell. They're old clothes that are too large for him, but they're moderately clean, even though they smell of dust. He throws off the blanket and eyes his naked body in the half-light. He can make out bones and tendons under the skin where once there was a thick layer of fat. He gets dressed. It's not easy to dress with only one hand, or do up trousers or a shirt with only five fingers. What he is most grateful for is a pair of socks and shoes with which he can hide his feet from the cold. At the bottom of the bag there's something else. A book. He instantly recognizes the black leather binding and the outline of a scarlet spiral staircase engraved on the cover. He rests the book on his lap and opens it.

THE LABYRINTH OF THE SPIRITS III
Ariadna and the Theatre of Shadows

TEXT AND ILLUSTRATIONS BY VÍCTOR MATAIX

Valls keeps turning the pages and stops at the first illustration. It shows the carcass of an old theater in ruins, on whose stage stands a girl dressed in white, a fragile look in her eyes. Even in the candle-light he recognizes her.

"Ariadna . . . ," he whispers.

He closes his eyes and holds on to the bars of the cell with one hand.

Perhaps hell does exist.

26

A VELVET SUN was painting the streets with innocence. Alicia strolled through the crowds milling around the center of town as she mulled over a scene she had read in the last pages of *Ariadna and the Scarlet Prince*. In this scene, Ariadna met with a street vendor who sold masks and dead flowers by the entrance to the city of the dead, the great southern necropolis. She had arrived there in a ghostly tram with no driver or passengers. The tram had a notice on the front that read:

DESTINY

The vendor was blind, but he could hear Ariadna approaching and asked her whether she wanted to buy a mask. The masks he sold in his cart, he explained, were made with the remains of doomed souls who inhabited the cemetery. By wearing them, one could outwit the fates and perhaps survive one more day. Ariadna admitted that she didn't know what her destiny was, and that she thought she had lost it when she fell into the haunted Barcelona ruled by the Scarlet Prince. The vendor smiled and replied with these words:

Most of us mortals never get to know our real destiny; we're just trampled by it. By the time we raise our heads and see it moving off down the road, it's already too late, and we have to walk the rest of the way along the straight and narrow ditch that dreamers call maturity. Hope is no more than the belief that that moment hasn't yet come, that we might still manage to see our real destiny when it draws near and jump on board before the chance of being ourselves disappears forever, condemning us to live in emptiness, missing what should have been and never was.

Alicia remembered those words as if she had them engraved on her skin. Nothing is more surprising or frightening than what one already knows. That midday, as she placed her hand on the doorknob of the old Sempere & Sons bookshop, she felt the presence of that life still to be lived and wondered whether it wasn't already too late.

She was greeted by the tinkle of the entrance bell, the perfume emanating from thousands of pages waiting to be read, and a faint luminosity that wove the scene into the texture of dreams. It was all just as she remembered it, from the endless pale wooden shelves to the last speck of dust caught in the beams of light filtering through the shop window. Everything except herself.

She stepped into that room as if she were going back into a forgotten memory. For a moment she told herself that this place could have been her destiny if the war hadn't snatched from her everything she possessed, if it hadn't maimed her and abandoned her on the streets of an accursed land. If it hadn't turned her into one more puppet in a show from which she knew she could never escape. She realized that the vision she could divine inside the four walls of the Sempere & Sons bookshop was the life that had been stolen from her.

The gaze of a small boy pulled her out of her daydreaming. He couldn't have been more than two or three years old and was installed inside a white wooden playpen next to the counter. Crowned by a mass of fine fair hair that shone like gold, he had risen to his feet, holding on to the edge of the playpen and looking straight at Alicia, studying her as if she were some exotic specimen. Alicia melted into one of those honest smiles she could summon up on cue. The little boy seemed to be sizing up her smile while he played with a rubber crocodile. Then, in a notable feat of air acrobatics, he proceeded to fire off the toy in a parabolic flight that left it at her feet. Alicia knelt down to pick up the crocodile, and then she heard the voice.

"For heaven's sake, Julián! What are you up to . . . "

Alicia heard footsteps approaching around the counter, and when she stood up she saw her. Beatriz. Close up, she seemed as beautiful as she was described by fools and busybodies who, as expected, felt inclined to say little else about her. She was graced with the unassuming and youthful femininity of a woman who has experienced motherhood before reaching twenty, but the look in her eyes was that of a woman twice her age, penetrating and inquisitive. In that brief instant in which their hands touched, when Alicia handed her little Julián's toy and their eyes met, they both felt they were confronting a looking glass through time.

Alicia gazed at the child and told herself that, in another life, she could well have been that young woman with her serene angelic appearance, a woman who surely must give rise to longings and sighs in the neighborhood, the very image of the perfect wife in fashion ads. Beatriz, virtue incarnate, also gazed at the stranger, a dark reflection of her own self, a Bea she could never or would never dare be.

"I'm sorry about the boy," said Bea. "He's quite determined that everyone should like crocodiles as much as he does. You'd think he could like puppies or teddy bears like other children, but no . . ."

"A sign of good taste," said Alicia. "All those other children are silly, aren't they?"

The child nodded a few times, as if at last he'd found a sane person in the universe. Bea frowned. The way that woman looked reminded her of the stylized, exquisitely evil witches in the storybooks Julián loved so much. Her son must have thought likewise, because he had stretched his arms out as if he wanted her to pick him up.

"It looks like you've made a friend," said Bea. "And don't imagine Julián will go off with just anyone . . ."

Alicia looked at the boy. Having never held a baby or child, she had no idea how to do it.

Bea must have sensed her bewilderment, because she took Julián in her arms. "Don't you have children?"

The visitor shook her head.

She probably eats them, thought Bea, lapsing into spite. Julián was still looking at Alicia, entranced.

"Julián, is that his name?"

"Yes."

Alicia stepped closer to the child and leaned forward so that their eyes were level. Julián smiled, delighted.

*

Surprised at her son's reaction, Bea let him stretch out his hand to the woman's face. Julián touched her cheek and her lips. When he stroked her, Bea thought the customer's eyes were filling with tears, or perhaps it was just the reflection of the midday sun. The woman moved away swiftly and turned around.

She was wearing gorgeous clothes, and as far as Bea could see, very expensive. The sort of clothes she would sometimes stop to look at in the most exclusive shop windows in Barcelona, only to walk away daydreaming about them. She was pencil-slim, and her expression was vaguely theatrical. And she wore a glossy red lipstick that Bea would never have dared show off in public. Only occasionally had she painted her lips that color for Daniel in private, when he got her a bit tipsy with muscatel and asked her to do what he called "a fashion parade."

"I love your shoes," said Bea.

The woman turned around again and smiled, her teeth flashing. Julián was trying to clap, a clear indication that he liked everything about her, from the shoes whose price could not even be asked to the velvety eyes that seemed to hypnotize like the eyes of a snake.

"Were you looking for anything in particular?"

"Well, I'm not sure. I had to leave almost all my books behind when I moved, and now that I've returned to Barcelona, I feel as if I've been shipwrecked."

"Are you local?"

"Yes, but I've been away a few years."

"In Paris?"

"Paris? No."

"I said that because of your clothes. And your look. You have a Parisian look."

Alicia swapped glances with little Julián. Still besotted with her, he nodded as if that business of her Parisian origins had been his idea, not his mother's.

"Do you know Paris?" asked Alicia.

"No. Well, only from books. But next year we'll go and celebrate our anniversary there."

"That's what I call a good husband."

"Oh, he doesn't know yet." Bea laughed nervously. Something in that woman's gaze made her speak too much.

Alicia gave her a conspiratorial wink. "Even better. Some things are far too important to be left in men's hands."

"Is this your first time in the bookshop?" asked Bea, wanting to change the subject.

"No. In fact, when I was a child, I used to come here with my parents. This is where my father bought me my first book. . . . Although that was many years ago. Before the war. But I have very good memories, and I told myself it was the best place to begin rebuilding my lost library."

Bea felt butterflies in her stomach at the thought of imminent business. For a long time now sales had been poor, and those words sounded like celestial music.

"Well, we're here to assist you in anything you need. What we don't have in the shop we can find for you in a matter of days or even hours."

"That's good to know. Are you the owner?"

"I'm Bea. This is my father-in-law's bookshop, but we all work here, all the family . . ."

"Your husband also works with you? How lucky."

"I'm not sure if I agree with you," joked Bea. "Are you married?"

"No."

Bea swallowed hard. Once more she'd said too much. That was the second personal question she had asked that promising customer for no reason.

Alicia read her thoughts and smiled. "Don't worry, Bea. My name is Alicia."

She held out her hand, and Bea shook it. Julián, who didn't miss a thing, also lifted his hand, trying his luck. Alicia shook it too.

Bea laughed. "You have such a knack with them, you should have kids yourself."

As soon as she'd said those words she bit her tongue. *Bea, please shut up.*

The woman called Alicia didn't seem to have heard her. She was gazing absently at the full bookshelves, lifting her hand and almost caressing the books without touching them. Bea took advantage of the fact that she had her back turned to have another good look at her.

"You might like to know that we offer special prices for collections . . ."

"May I stay and live here?" asked Alicia.

Bea laughed again, this time without much conviction. She looked at her son, who would clearly have handed over the shop keys to the stranger.

"Steinbeck . . . ," she heard her murmur.

"We have an entire new series that includes a number of his novels. It has just arrived . . ."

Alicia picked up one of the volumes, opened it, and read a few lines at random. "It's like reading a musical score."

Bea thought she was talking to herself, lost among the books, and had forgotten about her and the child. She left her alone and let her wander through the bookshop undisturbed. Alicia would pick up a book here and there and leave it on the counter. A quarter of an hour later she had piled up a respectable tower of books.

"We also do deliveries . . ."

"Don't worry, Bea. I'll send someone around to collect them this afternoon. But I'll take this one with me. This card has convinced me. It says: 'Recommended by Fermín: *The Grapes of Wrath*, by the roguish Johnny Steinbeck, is a symphony of words suitable for alleviating cases of stubborn stupidity and favoring the prophylaxis of the meninx in cases of cerebral constipation provoked by an excess of adherence to the norms of official idiocy.'"

Bea rolled her eyes and pulled the card off the cover. "Forgive me, this business of recommendation cards is one of Fermín's latest ideas. I try to find them all and pull them off before the customers discover them, but he keeps on hiding them all over the place . . ."

Alicia laughed. Her laughter was cold, like crystal. "Is this Fermín one of your employees?"

Bea nodded. "Something like that. He describes himself as literary adviser and bibliographic detective for Sempere & Sons."

"He sounds like quite a character."

"You have no idea. Isn't it true, Julián, that Uncle Fermín is quite something?"

The child clapped.

"One is as bad as the other," Bea explained. "I don't know who is the more childish of the two . . ."

Bea started to look at the prices of the different volumes, noting them down in the sales ledger. Alicia observed her: she showed a confidence that left no doubt as to who was in charge of the accounts in that household.

"With our discount, that will come to . . ."

"No discounts, please. Spending money on books is a pleasure that I don't want you to lessen."

"Are you sure?"

"Positive."

Alicia paid for the purchase, which Bea started to wrap up for its collection that afternoon.

"You're taking quite a few treasures," said Bea.

"I hope they'll be the first of a long list."

"Well, here we are, at your service."

Alicia held out her hand. Bea shook it.

"It's been a pleasure. I'll be back soon."

Bea nodded contentedly, though she thought that Alicia's remark sounded vaguely threatening.

"Any time. We'll be here for anything you may need . . ."

Alicia blew a kiss to Julián, who looked as if he was in a trance. They both watched her put on her gloves with catlike movements and make her way to the door, drumming out a rhythm with those high heels. Just as Alicia was leaving, Daniel arrived. Bea watched her husband, openmouthed, holding the door for Alicia and melting into a smile that deserved at least a slap in the face. Bea rolled her eyes and sighed. Julián, next to her, made the noises he usually made when he was delighted with something, whether it was one of Uncle Fermín's stories or a hot bath.

"You're all the same," Bea murmured.

Daniel stepped into the bookshop, to be met by Bea's icy look.

"That woman, who was she?" he asked.

27

ALICIA DIDN'T PAUSE until she reached the corner of Puerta del Ángel. Only then, hiding among the crowds, did she stop by one of the Casa Jorba department store window displays and dry the tears falling down her face. This is my life, she thought. She faced her image in the glass and let the anger burn her inside.

"You idiot," she said out loud.

On her way back she abandoned herself to what, years ago, had been her favorite walk, covering twenty centuries in twenty minutes. She walked down from Puerta del Ángel to the cathedral, and from there she slipped around the curve of Calle de la Paja, bordering the remains of the Roman walls, and descended toward Calle Aviñón through the Call, the old Jewish Quarter. She had always preferred the streets she didn't have to share with trams and cars. There, in the heart of old Barcelona, where neither machines nor their disciples could penetrate, Alicia wanted to believe that time flowed in circles and that if she didn't venture beyond those narrow streets through which the sun only dared to tiptoe, perhaps she would never grow old and would be able to return to a hidden time, rediscover the path she should never have left. Perhaps her moment hadn't yet passed. Perhaps there was still a reason for her to go on living.

Before the war, when she was a child, Alicia had often taken that route, holding on to her parents' hands. She remembered walking past the shop window of Sempere & Sons with her mother and stopping for a moment to meet the gaze of a sad-faced boy observing her from behind the glass pane. Daniel, perhaps? She remembered the day her mother bought her her first book, an anthology of poems and legends by Gustavo Adolfo Bécquer. She remembered all those nights she was unable to sleep, believing that Maese Pérez, the ghostly organist, would be hovering by her door at midnight. She recalled how she longed to return to the enchanted book bazaar where a thousand and one stories awaited her. Perhaps in that other lost life Alicia would now have been on the other side of that counter, putting books in other people's hands, making a note of the title and its price in the accounts book, and dreaming about that journey to Paris with Daniel.

*

As she approached her home, she began to feel a dark resentment rising in her again: a bitterness that dragged her down to that shadowy room of her soul, with no mirrors or windows, in which she lived. For a moment she imagined herself turning around and returning to the bookshop to meet that woman straight out of a story, Beatriz the Pure, and her smiley cherub. She saw herself holding Beatriz by the neck against the wall, digging her nails into that velvety skin, putting her own face so close to that white soul that Bea could peep into the chasm hiding in Alicia's eyes. And then she saw herself licking Bea's lips to taste the honeyed happiness blessing the lives of people among whom Leandro had always said Alicia could never count herself: normal people.

She stopped at the intersection of Calle Aviñón and Calle Fernando, just a few meters from her home, and hung her head, filled with shame. She could almost hear Leandro laughing at her in some corner of her mind. *My dear Alicia, creature of the shadows, don't hurt yourself by dreaming you can be that little house princess waiting for her champion to come home, filled with joy as she takes care of her adorable children. You and I are what we are, and the less we look at ourselves in the mirror, the better.*

"Are you feeling all right, Señorita Alicia?"

She opened her eyes to discover a familiar face, a fragment from the past. "Fernandito?"

A warm smile spread over the lips of her loyal old admirer. Time had taken with it a poor boy with a feverish mind and a fast-beating heart, and returned a good-looking young man. And yet, despite all the years gone by, his gaze was still as entranced as on the day he had come to bid her farewell in the Estación de Francia.

"It's such a joy to see you again, Señorita Alicia. You look just the same. What am I saying? Even better."

"It's only because you see me with favorable eyes, Fernandito. You're the one who has changed."

"That's what people tell me," the boy agreed, seemingly happy with the improvement.

"You've put on a load of muscle," said Alicia. "I'm not sure I can go on calling you Fernandito. Now you look like Don Fernando."

Fernandito blushed and looked down. "You can call me whatever you like, Señorita Alicia."

She leaned over and kissed him on the cheek, which was beginning to show a stubble. Fernandito froze in astonishment and then, in a fit of rapture, threw his arms around her. "I'm glad you've come back home. We've all missed you a lot."

"Can I treat you to a . . . ?" Alicia said quickly. "Do you still like cinnamon milk shakes so much?"

"I've moved on to rum *carajillo*."

"What testosterone can't achieve . . ."

Fernandito laughed. Despite his newly developed muscles, the hint of a beard, and his new deep voice, he still laughed like a child. Alicia took his arm and dragged him to the Gran Café, where she asked for a *carajillo* coffee with the best Cuban rum in the house, and a glass of Alella white wine. They toasted for the years of absence, and Fernandito, intoxicated by the rum and Alicia's presence, told her he had a part-time job doing deliveries for a grocer's shop in the neighborhood, and a girlfriend called Candela he'd met at the parish Sunday school.

"Promising," Alicia remarked. "When are you getting married?"

"Married? Those are Aunt Jesusa's fancies. I've barely managed to get Candela to kiss me. She thinks that if there isn't a priest present, it's a sin."

"If there's a priest present, it spoils the fun."

"That's what I say. Besides, with the small amount I earn at the grocer's, I can't save a duro for the wedding. Imagine, I signed forty-eight installment payments for the Vespa . . ."

"You've got a Vespa?"

"A beauty. It's thirdhand, but I've had it painted and it looks amazing. One of these days I must take you for a ride. It cost me an arm and a leg, and it will go on costing me. We're a bit tight—the whole family is—since my father got ill and had to leave his job at the rayon factory. All those fumes from the acid. Poor man, they've eaten his lungs away."

"I'm so sorry, Fernandito."

"That's life. But for the moment my salary is all that comes into our home, and I'm going to have to find something better."

"What would you like to do?"

He smiled enigmatically. "Do you know what I've always wanted to do? Work with you."

"But you don't even know what I do, Fernandito."

"I'm not as stupid as I look, Señorita Alicia."

"I never thought you were stupid."

"A bit of a dreamer, and a bit naive, sure—what can I say that you haven't experienced yourself? But I have enough brains to know that you're in the business of mysteries and intrigues."

She smiled. "I suppose that's one way of putting it."

"And don't think I go around talking out of school, eh? Mum's the word."

Alicia looked into his eyes. Fernandito gulped. Peering into those depths always set his pulse racing.

"Would you really like to work with me?" she asked at last.

Fernandito's eyes were popping out of his head. "Nothing in the world would make me happier."

"Not even marrying Candelita?"

"Don't be mean. Sometimes you're very mean, Señorita Alicia . . ."

Alicia nodded, agreeing with the accusation.

"Look," he said, "I don't want you to think I'm getting my hopes up. I know I'll never love anyone the way I've loved you, but that's my problem. I've known for a long time that you'll never love me."

"Fernandito . . ."

"Let me finish. Now that at last I feel bold enough to speak to you frankly, I wouldn't like to leave anything unsaid. I don't think I'll ever again pluck up enough courage to tell you what I feel."

She gave an approving nod.

"What I'm trying to say, and I know it's none of my business, and don't get angry with me if I'm telling you this, is that it's OK if you don't love me because I'm a poor idiot, but one day you'll have to love somebody. Life's a bitch and too short to live like this . . . alone."

Alicia looked down. "We don't choose who we love, Fernandito. Perhaps it's just that I don't know how to love anyone, and I don't know how to let anyone love me."

"I don't believe that. Is that your boyfriend, that hunk of a policeman who goes around with you?"

"Vargas? No. He's just a work colleague. And a good friend, I think."

"Maybe I can be too."

"A friend, or a work colleague?"

"Both things. If you'll let me."

For a long time Alicia kept silent. Fernandito waited without saying a word, watching her with religious devotion.

"What if it was dangerous?" she asked finally.

"More dangerous than carrying boxes full of bottles up the staircases in this neighborhood?"

She nodded.

"From the moment I met you, I knew you were the dangerous sort, Señorita Alicia. I'm only asking you to give me an opportunity. If you see I'm no good, fire me. No questions asked. What do you say?" Fernandito held out his hand.

Instead of shaking it, Alicia took it and kissed it as if he were a damsel, then placed it against her cheek. The boy went the color of a ripe peach.

"Fine. A week's trial. If after a few days you see that this isn't for you, we terminate the agreement."

"Really?"

Alicia nodded.

"Thank you so much. I won't fail you. I swear."

"I know, Fernandito. I haven't the slightest doubt."

"Will I need to be armed? I say that because my father still has his militiaman's rifle—"

"So long as you're armed with prudence, that should be enough."

"And what does the mission consist of?"

"In being my eyes."

"Whatever you say."

"What do they pay you per month at the grocer's?"

"A pittance."

"Multiply that by four, and you'll get your basic salary per week. Plus incentives and bonuses. And I'll cover your monthly payments for the Vespa. That's for starters. Does it seem fair?"

Fernandito nodded, hypnotized. "You know that for you I would work for nothing. I'd pay, even."

Alicia shook her head. "No more doing things for nothing, Fernandito. Welcome to capitalism."

"Don't they say that's really bad?"

"Worse. And you're going to love it."

"When do I begin?"

"Right away."

28

VARGAS CLUTCHED HIS stomach as if he'd suddenly developed an ulcer. "You said what to that kid?"

"His name is Fernandito. And he's not much of a kid. He's almost as big as you. And besides, he has a Vespa."

"Holy Mother of God. Not happy with complicating my life, now you want to drag innocent souls into your machinations?"

"That's what it's about. What we need in this enterprise is some innocent person."

"I thought that idiot Rovira filled that gap. By the way, he's been following me all morning. Hadn't they told him to follow you?"

"Maybe he's not as stupid as he seems."

"And this Fernandito, what is he? A fresh victim for your Countess Báthory bath?"

"You're becoming better-read by the day, Vargas. But no. Fernandito is not going to shed a drop of blood. Sweat, if anything."

"And tears. Don't think I haven't noticed the way he looks at you with those mournful eyes."

"When have you seen that?"

"When you were hypnotizing him down there, in the café. You two looked like a queen cobra and a baby rabbit."

"I thought only Rovira was spying on me."

"I saw you when I walked by, on my way back from Metrobarna."

Alicia muttered something under her breath, as if to play down the matter, while she poured some white wine into one of her fine glasses. She took a first sip and leaned on the table. "Tell me how you got on, and forget about Fernandito for the moment."

Vargas huffed and collapsed on the sofa. "Where do I begin?"

"Try the beginning."

Vargas summed up his visit to Metrobarna and his resulting impressions. Alicia listened to him quietly, walking up and down the apartment, wineglass in hand, nodding every now and then.

When he'd finished, she went over to the window and downed her glass of wine. Then she turned to the policeman with an expression that filled him with anxiety. "I've been thinking, Vargas."

"God help us."

"With all this stuff you've discovered today about Señor Sanchís and his profitable marriage connections, his driver, the trail of the Mataix books, Brians and the Semperes—"

"Don't forget the invisible man, your ex-colleague Lomana."

"I'm not forgetting. The fact is that you and I alone won't be able to follow up all these leads. And the knot is tightening."

"Around our necks?"

"You know what I mean. All these leads are connected in some way. The more we pull at them, the closer we'll be to finding the way in."

"When you get metaphorical, I'm lost."

"We're waiting for someone to make a false move, that's all."

"Is that how you solve your cases? Through false moves?"

"It's more efficient to let others make mistakes than to trust we'll guess correctly first time around."

"What if we're the ones who make a false move?"

"If you have a better system, I'm all ears."

Vargas raised his hands to signal a truce. "And what about this Fernandito. What's he going to do?"

"He'll be our eyes wherever we can't be present. Nobody knows who he is, and nobody is expecting him."

"You're turning into Leandro."

"I'll pretend I didn't hear you say that, Vargas."

"Pretend whatever you like. How are you planning to sacrifice the little partridge?"

"Fernandito will begin by following Sanchís. Division of labor increases productivity."

"That smells like a trap. What about me—what do I do?"

"I'm thinking it through."

"What you're trying to do is get rid of me again."

"Don't be stupid. When have I done anything like that?"

Vargas groaned. "And while you're thinking it through, what else are you planning to do?" he asked.

"Devote time and attention to the Sempere family."

At that moment they heard a noise behind the door of the apartment, like the sound of something heavy falling, and a moment later the doorbell rang.

"Are you expecting anyone?" asked the policeman.

"Will you answer the door?"

Vargas stood up reluctantly and went to the door.

A flushed Fernandito stood in the doorway, panting. "Good afternoon," he said. "I'm bringing Señorita Alicia's books." Fernandito held out a conciliatory hand.

Vargas ignored the gesture. "Alicia, the errand boy is here for you."

"Don't be grumpy. Let him in." Alicia stood up and walked over to the door. "Come in, Fernandito—pay no attention to him."

When he saw her, the boy's face lit up. He lifted the box with the books and walked into the flat. "May I? Where shall I leave them?"

"Right here, by the bookshelves."

Fernandito did as instructed and took a deep breath, wiping the sweat from his brow.

"You brought them like that, carrying all that weight?"

The boy shrugged. "Well, on the motorbike. But of course, since the building doesn't have an elevator . . ."

"What dedication, *Fernandito*," said Vargas. "A shame I don't happen to have a medal for bravery at hand."

Ignoring Vargas's sarcasm, Fernandito concentrated his attention on Alicia. "It wasn't that bad, Señorita Alicia. I'm used to delivering groceries."

"That's what's made you so strong. Go on, Vargas, pay him."

"What?"

"An advance for his services. And give him something extra for gas."

"And how am I supposed to pay this?"

"Out of the expenses account. You're the treasurer. Don't make that face."

"What face?"

"As if you had a urinary infection. Go on, pull out your wallet."

Fernandito shifted uneasily, seeing Vargas's ominous look. "Listen, if there's a problem, I'll—"

"There isn't a problem," Alicia cut in. "Captain?"

Vargas grunted and pulled out his wallet. He counted a couple of notes and handed them to Fernandito.

"More," whispered Alicia.

"What?"

"Give him at least double that amount."

Vargas pulled out two more notes. Fernandito, who had probably never seen so much money together in his entire life, accepted it in amazement.

"Don't spend it all on candy," mumbled Vargas.

"You won't regret it, Señorita Alicia. Thank you so much."

"Hey, kid, I'm the one who's paying," said the policeman.

"Can I ask you a favor, Fernandito?" asked Alicia.

"Just say the word."

"Go down and get me a pack of cigarettes."

"American?"

"You're a darling."

Fernandito ran off down the stairs—skipping, from the sound of it.

"So much for the altar boy," Vargas observed.

"You're jealous," said Alicia.

"Oh, of course."

"What's the picture?" asked Alicia, noticing the canvas Vargas had brought with him.

"I thought it would look wonderful above your sofa."

"Is it by your new friend, Señor Sanchís's favorite painter?"

The policeman nodded.

"Do you think Sanchís is our book collector?"

Vargas shrugged.

"And the chauffeur . . . ?"

"Morgado. I've already called headquarters to ask for information on him. I'll get news tomorrow."

"What are you thinking, Vargas?"

"I'm thinking that perhaps you're right, whether I like it or not. The knot, or whatever it is, is getting tighter."

"You don't seem altogether convinced."

"I'm not. There's something that doesn't add up."

"What?"

"I'll know when I see it. But I get the feeling that we're looking from the wrong angle. Don't ask me why. I can feel it in my bones."

"I think so too," Alicia agreed.

"Are you going to tell Leandro?"

"I'm going to have to tell him something."

"If you'll allow a suggestion, leave Fernandito out of the newsreel."

"I wasn't planning to include him."

A few moments later they heard the boy rushing up the stairs.

"Go on. Open the door. And be a bit nicer to him. He needs solid male role models if he's going to be a useful member of society."

Vargas shook his head and opened the door. Fernandito stood there anxiously, the pack of cigarettes in his hand.

"Come in, kid. Cleopatra awaits."

Fernandito hurried in with the cigarettes. Alicia opened the packet with a smile and put one in her mouth. The boy quickly pulled out a lighter for her.

"I didn't know you'd started smoking, Fernandito."

"No, no . . . I just use it as a flashlight. Half the staircases in this neighborhood are pitch-dark."

"You see, Vargas? Don't you think Fernandito has the makings of a detective?"

"A veritable junior Marlowe."

"Pay no attention to him, Fernandito. When they get older, they become embittered. It's all that quinine in the white hair."

"Keratin," snapped Vargas.

Alicia waved her hand as if to brush away Vargas's comment. "May I ask you another favor, Fernandito?"

"That's what I'm here for."

"This one is trickier. Your first mission."

"I'm all ears."

"You need to go over to Paseo de Gracia, number six."

Vargas looked at her, suddenly alarmed. Alicia put a finger to her lips.

"The offices of a company called Metrobarna are in that building."

"I know it."

"You do?"

"They own half the buildings in this area. They buy them, throw out the old people who live there, giving them practically nothing, and sell them again at ten times the price."

"Smart, eh? Well, it turns out that the director general is someone called Ignacio Sanchís. I want you to follow him from the moment he leaves his office. Become his shadow—tell me where he goes, what he does, who he talks to . . . everything. Will you manage with the Vespa?"

"She's the queen of the road. Even Nuvolari couldn't escape me when I'm on the Vespa."

"This time tomorrow, come here and tell me what you've found out. Any questions?"

Vargas lifted a hand.

"I'm referring to Fernandito."

"Everything is crystal clear, Señorita Alicia."

"Off you go, then. And welcome to the world of intrigue."

"I won't fail you. Nor you, Captain." Fernandito rushed off into a promising career in the world of intrigue and detection.

Vargas stood openmouthed, staring at Alicia's catlike eyes as she enjoyed her cigarette.

"Have you gone mad?"

She ignored his question, gazing out the window at the blanket of clouds creeping in from the sea. The setting sun had tinted it red, but a web of black ribbons was swirling about, thick and dark. An electric spark pulsated through the clouds, as if a large flare had lit up among them.

"There's a storm coming," Vargas murmured.

"I'm famished," declared Alicia, turning around.

He was astounded.

"I never thought I'd hear you say that."

"There's a first time for everything. Will you buy me dinner?"

"I don't know what with. I gave your admirer almost everything I had. Tomorrow I'll have to go to the bank and withdraw some more money."

"Tapas would do."

"Tell me where."

"Do you know La Barceloneta?"

"I think I've already had more than enough with the normal Barcelona."

"Could you go for a good bomb?"

"Excuse me?"

"A spicy one, not one made of gunpowder."

"Why am I guessing that this is another of your tricks?"

29

UNDER A LIGHTNING-MESHED sky, they walked down to the port. A forest of masts fought a wind blowing in from the sea, carrying the scent of electricity.

"There's a big one coming," Vargas announced.

They skirted the lines of warehouses opposite the docks, large cavernous buildings that looked like grand old markets.

"My father used to work here, in the sheds," Alicia said, pointing.

Vargas kept silent, waiting for her to say more. "I thought you were an orphan," he said at last.

"I wasn't born one."

"At what age did you lose them? Your parents."

Alicia buttoned up the collar of her coat and quickened her pace. "We'd better hurry or we'll get wet."

When they reached La Barceloneta, the first drops were falling. Thick, isolated drops, like bullets of water that burst on the cobbles and machine-gunned the trams sliding down the avenue along the docks. A jumble of narrow streets stretched out before them, covering a neck of land in a grid that reminded Vargas of a large cemetery. "It looks like an island," he remarked.

"You're not far off. Now it's the fishermen's quarter."

"And before?"

"Do you want a history lesson?"

"As an appetizer for your bombs . . ."

"Centuries ago, all you could see here was sea," Alicia explained. "Eventually the beginning of the breakwater was built, and slowly the sediment dragged in by the sea against the dike formed an island."

"How do you know all these things?"

"Because I read. Try it sometime. During the War of Succession, Philip V's troops demolished a substantial part of the Ribera quarter to build the Ciudadela fortress. After the war, many of the people who had lost their homes moved here."

"Is that why you Barcelonians are such monarchists?"

"For that reason, and just to be contrarian. It improves one's circulation."

The first downpour chased them furiously until they reached an alleyway. Before them rose a facade that at first glance looked like a cross between a portside tavern and a roadside bar. It would not have won any design competition, but the aroma coming from it made Vargas's stomach rumble. The sign above the door read LA BOMBETA.

A group of locals who were battling over a card game raised their eyebrows slightly when they saw Vargas and Alicia come in. Vargas realized that they had identified him as a cop the moment he set foot in the place. A rough-mannered waiter glared at them from behind the bar and pointed to a table in a corner, far from the local clientele.

"It doesn't look like one of your places, Alicia."

"One comes here not for the sights but for the bombs."

"And, I suspect, for something else."

"Well, it's not far."

"Far from where?"

Alicia pulled a piece of paper out of her pocket and set it on the table. Vargas recognized the tag Alicia had pulled off one of the movers' boxes outside the lawyer's office that morning.

"From the warehouse where Brians has temporarily stored all his papers and files," she said.

Vargas rolled his eyes.

"Don't play hard to get, Vargas. You're not expecting to have everything handed to us on a silver platter, are you?"

"I was hoping I wouldn't have to break the law."

The rude waiter planted himself in front of them with a questioning look.

"Bring us four bombs and two beers," Alicia instructed, without taking her eyes off Vargas.

"Estrella or draft beer?"

"Estrella."

"Bread with oil and tomato?"

"A couple of slices. Toasted."

The waiter nodded and walked off without more ado.

"I've always wondered why you Catalans rub tomato on the bread," said Vargas.

"And I've always wondered why nobody else does."

"What other surprises do you have in store for me, aside from housebreaking?"

"Technically speaking, it's a warehouse. I don't think it's a home for anything but rats and spiders."

"How could I refuse, then? What else are you turning over in that devilish head of yours?"

"I was thinking about that cretin you went to see, Cascos—Valls's employee in Editorial Ariadna."

"The spurned lover."

"Pablo Cascos Buendía," Alicia recited. "Beatriz Aguilar's ex-fiancé. I can't get him out of my head. Don't you find it odd?"

"What isn't odd in this whole affair?"

"The almighty minister secretly poking around in the family history of some humble Barcelona booksellers . . ."

"We'd decided that he suspected they might know something about David Martín, whom he also suspected of being behind the threats and attacks against him."

"Yes, but what does David Martín have to do with the Semperes? And what have they got to do with this whole story?" Alicia remained pensive for a while before going on. "There's something there. In that place. In that family."

"Is that why you've decided to make home visits to Sempere & Sons without warning me?"

"I needed something new to read."

"You should have bought yourself a comic book. To approach the Semperes too soon could be dangerous."

"Are you afraid of a family of booksellers?"

"I'm afraid of letting the cat out of the bag before we know what we're treading on."

"I think it's worth the risk."

"Something you've decided unilaterally."

"Beatriz Aguilar and I got along very well," said Alicia. "She's such a delightful girl. You'd fall in love with her at first sight."

"Alicia . . ."

She smiled mischievously.

The beers and the plate of *bombas* arrived just in time to interrupt the conversation. Vargas eyed that curious invention, a sort of large ball of breaded potato filled with spicy meat. "So how does one eat this?"

Alicia skewered a *bomba* with her fork and sank her teeth in it.

Outside, the storm pounded the street savagely, and the waiter had gone over to the door to watch the downpour.

Vargas observed Alicia as she devoured the feast. There was something about her that he hadn't noticed before. "When dusk falls," he said, "you seem to revive . . ."

She took a sip of beer and looked him in the eyes. "I'm a night creature."

"No need to convince me."

30

THE STORM HAD left a mist in its wake that swept through the streets of La Barceloneta and glistened in the glow of the streetlamps. Just a few isolated drops were falling when they stepped outside, as the echoes of the tempest disappeared in the distance.

The address Alicia had extracted that morning from Fernando Brians's storage boxes—a warehouse where the lawyer was to stow his furniture, filing cabinets, and all the surplus junk accumulated over decades—was on the grounds of Vapor Barcino, an old locomotive and boiler factory abandoned during the civil war. After barely two minutes' walk through deserted, icy-cold alleyways, they came to the entrance of the old factory. An ancient railway track, partly buried under their feet, made its way into the factory grounds. A large stone portal bearing the words VAPOR BARCINO presided over the entrance. Beyond it was a wasteland of run-down warehouses and workshops, a graveyard for the wonders of the age of steam.

"Are you sure it's here?" asked Vargas.

Alicia nodded and went in ahead of him. They walked past a locomotive stranded in a large puddle, among wheelbarrows, water pipes, and the shell of a discarded boiler, where a flock of seagulls had made their nest. The birds stood there stock-still, watching them go by with eyes that flashed in the twilight. A row of posts supported a tangle of electrical cables from which a few dangling lamps cast a faint light. The factory bays had been numbered and marked with wooden signs.

"Ours is number three," said Alicia.

Vargas looked around him. A couple of starving cats meowed from the shadows. The air smelled of charcoal and sulfur. They walked by a deserted guard's cabin.

"Shouldn't there be a guard around here?"

"I think Brians is a lawyer with a preference for low-cost solutions," Alicia suggested.

"The defender of lost causes," Vargas recalled. "He stays in character . . ."

She approached the entrance to the bay marked with a 3. Recent tracks from the moving van's tires were still visible on the mud in front of a large wooden door bolted with metal bars. A smaller door cut into the main panel was locked with a chain and a rusty padlock the size of a fist.

"How are we for brute force?" asked Alicia.

"You're not expecting me to bite it open, are you?"

"I don't know. Do something manly."

The policeman pulled out his revolver and inserted the barrel point-blank into the padlock's hole. "Move away," he ordered.

Alicia put her hands over her ears. The echo of the shot rippled through the enclosure. Vargas pulled the gun out of the padlock, which fell to his feet, dragging the chain with it. Then he kicked the door open.

A web of shadows spread through the bay, out of which peered the ruins of a thousand and one palaces. From the vaulted ceiling hung a network of cables dotted with bare bulbs. Vargas followed the circuit along the walls until he found an electrical box sticking out of the wall and pressed the main switch. The bulbs lit up in slow succession, just strands of yellowish, flickering lights, as in a ghostly funfair. The current produced a low humming sound, like a cloud of insects fluttering in the dark.

They walked down the corridor that ran through the bay, with enclosures on either side protected by wire fencing. A notice hung at the entrance to each enclosure, bearing the number of the lot, the month and year of the storage expiration, and the owner's surname or company name. Each of those subdivisions housed a world in itself. In the first enclosure they saw hundreds of old typewriters, adding machines, and cash registers, stacked up like a fortress. The next one contained a huge selection of crucifixes, figures of saints, confessionals, and pulpits.

"One could start a convent with all that," said Alicia.

"Maybe you're still in time . . ."

Farther on they came across a dismantled merry-go-round behind which, barely visible, lay the broken remains of a traveling fair. On the other side of the corridor was a collection of coffins and funeral paraphernalia—all in the ornate nineteenth-century style—including a glass baldachin, containing a silk bed on which one could still see the imprint left by some worthy deceased soul.

"Jesus Christ . . . ," murmured Vargas. "Where does all this come from?"

"Mostly from fortunes that went downhill, families that had already fallen into disgrace before the war, and companies that have vanished into the black hole of time."

"Are you sure someone still remembers that all this is here?"

"Someone is still paying the rent."

"Makes your hair stand on end."

"Barcelona is a haunted house, Vargas. What happens is that you tourists never think of looking behind the curtain. Look, here it is."

Alicia stopped in front of one of the compartments and pointed to the notice:

BRIANS-LLORAC

FAMILY

NO: 28887-BC-56. 9-62

"Are you sure you want to do this?"

"I didn't think you'd be so squeamish, Vargas. I'll take the blame."

"Whatever you say. What exactly are we looking for?"

"I don't know. Something that connects Valls, Salgado, David Martín, the Semperes, Brians, your list with the undecipherable numbers, the Mataix books, and now Sanchís and his faceless driver. If we find that piece, we'll find Valls."

"And you think it's here?"

"We won't know until we find it."

The enclosure was sealed with a simple padlock, the sort you can buy at any hardware store. It yielded at the fifth blow of the revolver's butt. Not wasting a second, Alicia slipped inside.

"It smells as if a corpse was dumped here," Vargas griped.

"It's the sea breeze. All those years in Madrid have made you lose your sense of smell."

Vargas cursed and followed her in. A pile of wooden boxes covered with tarpaulins formed a passageway leading to a sort of yard, where the relics of various generations of the Brians dynasty seemed to have been scattered by the force of a tornado.

"The lawyer must be the black sheep of the family," Vargas said. "I'm not an antiquarian, but there's at least a fortune or two here."

"Then I hope your sense of legal rectitude will stop you filching one of Grandma Brians's silver ashtrays."

Vargas pointed to the hodgepodge of dinner sets, mirrors, chairs, books, sculptures, chests, wardrobes, console tables, chests of drawers, bicycles, toys, skis, shoes, suitcases, paintings, vases, and thousands of other belongings piled up to form a haphazard mosaic that looked more like catacombs than anything else. "What century would you like to start with?"

"Brians's files. We're looking for medium-sized cardboard boxes. It shouldn't be too difficult. The moving men must have chosen the closest free space to the entrance to drop off the lawyer's stuff. Anything that isn't covered with a thick coat of dust is a possible candidate. Would you rather start left or right? Or is that a stupid question?"

After a few minutes' wandering around through a jungle of junk that had probably been there since before either of them had been born, they discovered a pyramid of boxes still sporting a tag identical to the one Alicia had pulled off. Vargas stepped forward and began to place them in a row, while she opened them and went through their contents.

"Is this what you were looking for?" asked Vargas.

"I don't know yet."

"A perfect plan," muttered the policeman.

It took them over half an hour to separate the boxes containing documents from the ones full of books and office supplies. They were unable to examine the documents properly in the anemic glow of the bulbs hanging high above them, so Vargas went off in search of something that would provide a better light. He came back after a while with an old copper candlestick and a handful of thick candles that looked as if they had never been used.

"Are you sure those aren't dynamite cartridges?" asked Alicia.

Vargas flicked on the lighter, holding the flame a centimeter from the first candle, which he handed to her. "Will you do the honors?"

The candles spread a bubble of brightness, and Alicia began to check, one by one, the spines of the folders that could be seen when they opened the boxes.

Vargas watched her anxiously. "What shall I do?"

"It's arranged by dates. Beginning in January 1934. I'll search by date, and you search by name. Start with the most recent files, and we'll meet in the middle."

"Search for what?"

"Sanchís, Metrobarna . . . Anything that might allow us to link Brians with—"

"Fine," Vargas interjected.

For almost twenty minutes they checked through the boxes without saying a word, exchanging occasional glances or a shake of the head.

"There's nothing here about Sanchís or Metrobarna," said the policeman. "I've already looked through five years, and there's nothing."

"Keep looking. Maybe it's under Banco Hipotecario."

"There's nothing about banks. All these clients are nobodies, to use the technical legal term—"

"Keep looking."

Vargas nodded and submerged himself again in the ocean of papers and dossiers as the candles dripped, leaving a cluster of wax tears running down the candlestick. After a while he noticed that Alicia was silent and had stopped her search. He looked up at her.

She was immobile, her eyes riveted on a pile of folders she had pulled out of one of the boxes.

"What?" asked Vargas.

Alicia showed him a thick folder. "Isabella Gispert . . ."

"Of the Sempere & . . ."

She nodded. She showed him another folder labeled MONTJUÏC 39-45. Drawing closer, Vargas knelt down by the box and began to go through the folders.

He pulled out a few. "Valentín Morgado . . ."

"Sanchís's chauffeur."

"Sempere/Martín . . ."

"Let me see." Alicia opened the folder. "Is this our David Martín?"

"That's what it looks like . . ." Vargas stopped. "Alicia?"

She looked up from David Martín's dossier.

"Look at this," said Vargas.

The folder he handed her was at least three centimeters thick. When she read the name of the file, she felt a shiver.

"Víctor Mataix . . . ," she said, unable to suppress a smile.

"I'd say we have enough with this."

Alicia was about to close the box when she noticed a yellowed envelope at the bottom. She picked it up and inspected it in the candlelight. It was a foolscap envelope, sealed with wax. She blew on the layer of dust covering it and read a word written in ink, the only word on the envelope.

Isabella

"We're going to take all of this," she said. "Close the boxes and try to leave them more or less as we found them. It might be days, if not weeks, before Brians has a new office and notices some of the dossiers are missing."

Vargas nodded, but before he'd lifted the first box off the floor, he stopped dead and turned around.

Alicia had also heard it. Footsteps. The sound of footsteps on the layer of dust covering the enclosure. She blew out the candles, while Vargas pulled out his revolver.

A silhouette was outlined in the doorway: a man wearing a ragged uniform, watching them. He carried a lantern and a cudgel that shook so much it gave the poor man away: he was obviously more frightened than a warehouse mouse.

"What are you doing here?" the guard stammered. "You're not allowed in after seven."

Alicia straightened up slowly and smiled at him. Something in her expression must have made his blood freeze, because he took a step back and brandished his cudgel with a threatening gesture.

Vargas placed the barrel of the revolver against his temple. "Unless you'd like to use it as a suppository, please drop the stick."

The guard dropped it and stood there, petrified. "Who are you?"

"Friends of the family," said Alicia. "We'd forgotten some things. Is there anyone else here with you?"

"I cover all the bays. You're not going to kill me, are you? I have a wife and children. Look, I've got a picture of them in my wallet . . ."

Vargas pulled the wallet out of the guard's pocket. He removed the money, which he dropped on the floor, and put the wallet in his coat.

"What's your name?" asked Alicia.

"Bartolomé."

"I like your name. It's very masculine."

The guard was trembling.

"Look, Bartolomé, this is what we're going to do. We're going home, and you're going to do the same thing. Tomorrow morning, before coming here, you're going to buy a couple of new padlocks and substitute the one at the entrance and the one on this enclosure. And you're going to forget that you saw us. What do you think of the deal?"

Vargas cocked the revolver.

Bartolomé gulped. "I think it's good."

"And just in case you suddenly feel bad about it, or someone questions you about it, remember—the salary they pay you wouldn't be worth it, and your family needs you."

Bartolomé nodded. Vargas took his finger off the trigger and withdrew the weapon.

Alicia smiled at the guard as if they were old friends. "Go on, go home and get yourself a glass of nice warm brandy. And pick up your money . . ."

"Yes, ma'am." Bartolomé knelt down and picked up what little cash he carried in his wallet.

"Don't forget your stick."

The man picked it up and tied it to his belt. "Can I go now?"

"There's nobody stopping you."

Bartolomé hesitated a few moments but then began to retreat toward the exit. Before his silhouette was lost in the shadows, Alicia called him. "Bartolomé?"

The guard's footsteps stopped.

"Remember, we have your wallet, and we know where you live. Don't make us have to pay you a visit. My colleague here has a very bad temper. Good night."

They heard him scampering off as fast as he could.

31

MIQUEL CAME UP to the apartment carrying a couple of Thermos flasks with hot coffee and a whole tray of pastries fresh from the oven of his friend's bakery on the corner. The pastries smelled divine. Once they'd divided up the folders, they sat on the floor facing each other. Alicia polished off three pastries in a row and filled a large cup with coffee, which she began to sip while engrossed in the first of the files stolen from Brians's boxes. After a bit she raised her head and noticed that Vargas was gazing at her, looking rather embarrassed.

"What?"

He pointed to her skirt, which Alicia had pulled up so she could lean against the sofa.

"Don't be childish. Can't be anything you haven't seen before, I hope. Concentrate on what you're supposed to be doing."

Vargas didn't reply, but he changed position to avoid seeing those fine seams in her stockings, which disturbed his focus on the gripping legalistic prose of the defender of lost causes' dossiers and summary proceedings.

As they journeyed silently into dawn on the wings of caffeine and sugar, a landscape with figures slowly emerged out of the documentation. On a large sketch pad, Alicia drew what looked like a map, with notes, dates, names, arrows, and circles. Every now and then Vargas would find something relevant and hand it to her. There was no need to say anything; she just glanced at it and nodded. She seemed to have a prodigious skill for establishing links and connections, as if her brain spun a hundred times faster than the brains of other mortals. Vargas began to sense the process governing his colleague's mind and, far from questioning it or trying to work out its internal logic, he simply acted as a filter, providing the data with which she was constructing her map, piece by piece.

Two and a half hours passed before Vargas paused. "I don't know about you, but I'm wiped out." He had gone through all the files allotted to him when they divided up the tasks. The caffeine he'd substituted for his blood was already losing strength, and his eyes could no longer focus.

"Go to sleep," suggested Alicia. "It's late."

"What about you?"

"I'm not sleepy."

"How is that possible?"

"The night and I, you know."

"Do you mind if I lie down on your sofa for a while?"

"It's all yours, although I can't promise I won't make any noise."

"Not even a brass band would wake me."

*

The cathedral bells did wake him. He opened his eyes to see a thick mist floating in the air, smelling of coffee and American tobacco. The sky above the rooftops was the color of young wine. Alicia was still sitting on the floor, a cigarette between her lips. She had taken off her skirt and her blouse, and was wearing only a black negligée that induced anything but calm. Vargas managed to creep over to the bathroom. There, he stuck his head under the tap and looked at himself in the mirror.

He found a blue silk robe hanging on the bathroom door and threw it at Alicia. "Cover up."

She caught it in mid-flight, stood up, stretched, and put it on.

"I'm going to open the window before the fire brigade comes to get us out of here," Vargas warned her.

A breath of fresh air penetrated the living room, and the swirl of smoke slipped out like a ghost trapped in a dark spell. Vargas stared at the remains of the two coffee Thermos flasks, the tray of pastries reduced to sugar dust, and the two ashtrays overflowing with cigarette stubs smoked to the very end. "Tell me all of this has been worth it," he pleaded.

Apart from the remains of the battle, Alicia had left a tangled pile of about a dozen sheets from the sketching pad. She picked them up and began to stick them on the wall with tape until they formed a circle. Vargas went over to look. She licked her lips like a satisfied cat.

The policeman shook the Thermos flasks to see whether there was anything left in them and managed to fill half a cup. He placed a chair in front of Alicia's diagram and nodded. "Impress me."

She tied up her silk dressing gown and pulled her hair back into a knot. "Do you want the long version or the short one?"

"Begin at the beginning, and we'll see how it goes."

Alicia stood in front of her mural like a schoolteacher, though she looked more like a Victorian geisha with suspicious night habits.

"Montjuïc Castle, between 1939 and 1944," she began. "Mauricio Valls is the prison governor, having just married Elena Sarmiento, daughter and heiress of a wealthy industrialist close to the regime who belongs to a sort of cabal of bankers, business owners, and members of the nobility, known as Franco's Crusaders because, to a large extent, they're financing the coffers of the Nacionales. Among them are Don Miguel Ángel Ubach, founder and main shareholder of the Banco Hipotecario, from whose head office emerges the investment firm Metrobarna you visited yesterday."

"All that is there?"

"In Brians's file notes, yes."

"Go on."

"During the years when Valls was governor of Montjuïc Prison, the following individuals coincide at some point as prisoners and as clients represented by Fernando Brians: first, Sebastián Salgado, alleged author of the threats sent by post to Valls for years and re-splendent beneficiary of a pardon arranged by the minister, which gets him out of prison. He survives in the outside world for about six weeks. Second, Valentín Morgado, ex-sergeant of the Republican army, included in an amnesty of 1945 thanks to a heroic act he per-formed in prison: according to Brians's notes, he saved a captain of the castle's regiment from dying in an accident during the rebuild-ing of one of the castle walls. When he leaves the prison, having signed up for a parole and rehabilitation program backed by a group of wealthy patricians with a bad conscience, Morgado is hired as a hand in the Ubach family garages, where in time he is promoted to chauffeur. When Ubach, the banker, dies, Morgado enters the service of his daughter Victoria, who marries your friend Sanchís, director general of Metrobarna."

"Is there more?"

"I'm only just beginning. Third, David Martín. An ill-fated writer, accused of a series of bizarre crimes committed before the war. Martín had managed to escape from the police in 1930, and eventu-ally ends up in France. For reasons that are unclear he tries to return incognito to Barcelona, but is arrested in Puigcerdá, a town in the Pyrenees, soon after crossing the border into Spain in 1939."

"What connection does David Martín have with all this, apart from having been in prison during those years?"

"That's where it starts to get interesting. Martín is the only one of these prisoners who is not directly a client of Brians. The lawyer is hired to represent Martín at the request of Isabella Gispert."

"Of Sempere & Sons?"

"The mother of Daniel Sempere, yes. Gispert was her maiden name. She allegedly died of cholera, shortly after the end of the war in 1939."

"Allegedly?"

"According to Brians's personal notes, there are elements pointing to the possibility that Isabella Sempere was murdered. Poisoned, to be precise."

"Don't tell me . . ."

"Exactly, by Mauricio Valls. The result of an unhealthy obsession and an unrequited desire, or so supposes Brians, who obviously can't prove anything, or doesn't dare."

"And Martín?"

"David Martín is the object of another of Valls's unhealthy obsessions, according to Brians's notes."

"Does the minister have any other sort of obsessions?"

"It seems that while Martín was in prison, Valls was trying to force him to write books that the future minister intended to publish later under his own name, to satisfy his vanity and his yearning for literary renown, or whatever. Unfortunately, according to Brians, David Martín is a sick person who has been slowly losing his mind. He hears voices and thinks he's in touch with a character of his own invention, someone called Corelli. While in prison, Martín's ravings, plus the fact that during the last year of his life Valls decides to put him in solitary confinement at the very top of one of the castle towers, earn him the nickname among the inmates of the Prisoner of Heaven."

"This is starting to have a very Alicia feel about it."

"In 1941, seeing that his plan for manipulating the writer wasn't working, Valls apparently orders two of his lackeys to take David Martín to an old mansion next to Güell Park and murder him. Something unexpected happens there, and Martín manages to escape alive."

"So David Martín is alive?"

"We don't know. Or Brians doesn't know."

"But he suspects it."

"And probably Valls does too—"

"—who thinks he's the one who has been sending him the threats and has been trying to murder him. To avenge himself."

"That's my hypothesis," Alicia agreed. "But it's only a conjecture."

"There's more still?"

She smiled. "I've left the best for the end."

"Fire away."

"Four: Víctor Mataix, author of the series *The Labyrinth of the*

Spirits, of which you and I found a volume hidden in Valls's desk, and which, according to what his daughter Mercedes remembers about the night he disappeared, was the last document the minister consulted before evaporating from the face of the earth."

"What's the connection between Mataix and the other three?"

"Mataix appears to have been a friend and old colleague of David Martín, back in the thirties, when they were both hired to write novels by installments under pseudonyms for a publishing house called Barrido & Escobillas. Brians's notes hint that Mataix may have been the victim of a similar plan to the one Valls had tried on Martín. Who knows, perhaps Valls was trying to recruit ghost writers so he could build a body of work that would give him a name and a reputation in the literary world. It's obvious that Valls hated seeing himself relegated to the role of regime jailer, a position obtained through his marriage of convenience, and he aimed much higher."

"There must be something else. What happened to Mataix?"

"Mataix is sent to Montjuïc in 1941, moved there from La Modelo. A year later, if you want to believe the official report, he committed suicide in his cell. He was probably shot and his body thrown into a common grave, with no record remaining."

"And the unhealthy obsession in this case is . . ."

Alicia shrugged. "In this case Brians does not jot down any suppositions, but I'd like to draw your attention to the fact that when Mauricio Valls starts his own publishing company in 1947, he christens it Ariadna, the name of the protagonist in the books of *The Labyrinth of the Spirits* series."

Vargas sighed and rubbed his eyes, trying to process everything Alicia had just told him. "Too many coincidences," he said at last.

"I agree," said Alicia.

"Let's see if I understand this. If all these connections exist, and we, or rather you, have been able to establish them within three days, how is it possible that the police and the higher echelons of the state, after an investigation that went on for a number of weeks, are still at a loss?"

Alicia bit her lower lip. "That's what worries me."

"Do you think they don't want to find Valls?"

She thought about it. "I don't think they can afford that option. Valls isn't somebody who can just disappear and be forgotten."

"So?"

"Perhaps they just want to know where he is. And perhaps they don't want the real motives for his disappearance to come out into the open."

Vargas shook his head and rubbed his eyes again. "Do you really think that Morgado, Salgado, and Martín, three ex-prisoners under Valls's yoke, could have devised a plan to take their revenge on Valls and at the same time avenge their fallen colleague, Víctor Mataix? Is that what you're thinking?"

Alicia shrugged. "Perhaps it's not Morgado, the driver. Perhaps it's Sanchís, his boss, who is involved."

"Why would Sanchís do something like that? He is a regime man, married to the heiress of one of the great fortunes of the country . . . a budding Valls. Why would someone like him want to get himself implicated in this kind of mess?"

"I don't know."

"What about the list of numbers we found in Valls's car?"

"It could be anything. Or have nothing to do with this. A coincidence. You yourself said that, remember?"

"Another coincidence? In my twenty years in the police force I've come across fewer real coincidences than people who told the truth."

"I don't know, Vargas. I don't know what those numbers mean."

"Do you know what really doesn't add up for me in all this?"

Alicia nodded again, as if she could read his thoughts. "Valls."

"Valls," Vargas agreed. "Without going into the sordid scheming of his years in Montjuïc, and whatever it was he did—poison Isabella Gispert and murder or try to murder David Martín, Mataix, and God knows who else—basically, we're talking about a low-class butcher, a jailer linked to the middle rungs of the regime. There are thousands like him. You pass them in the street every single day. Connected, with friends and acquaintances in the big jobs, sure, but ass-kissers when all's said and done. Lackeys and aspiring hopefuls. How does a guy like that manage to climb, in just a few years, from the sewers of the regime to the highest point?"

"A good question, isn't it?" said Alicia.

"Get that special little head of yours to give it an answer, and you'll find the piece we're missing so that all this rigmarole falls into place."

"You're not going to help me?"

"I'm beginning to doubt whether I should. Something tells me that discovering the key to this puzzle could be far more dangerous than not finding it, and I was hoping to retire with a full pension in a few years' time and devote myself to reading Lope de Vega's plays, from the first to the last."

Alicia collapsed onto the sofa, her enthusiasm flagging. Vargas finished his cold coffee and sighed. He walked over to the window and took a deep breath. In the distance, the cathedral bells tolled again, and the policeman watched the sun beginning to cast threads of light between dovecotes and bell towers.

"Do me a favor," he said. "For the moment, not a word about all this to Leandro or to anyone else."

"I'm not mad," Alicia cut in.

Vargas closed the window and went over to her. She was beginning to show signs of exhaustion.

"Isn't it time you started getting into your coffin?" asked Vargas. "Come on."

He took her hand and led her to the bedroom, then pulled back the blanket and signaled to her to get inside. Alicia let her dressing gown fall to the ground and got in between the sheets. He covered her up to her chin and looked at her with a smile.

"Aren't you going to read me a bedtime story?"

"Get lost." Vargas bent down to pick up the dressing gown and walked over to the door.

"Do you think they're leading us into a trap?" asked Alicia.

He weighed her words. "Why do you say that?"

"I don't know."

"One sets one's own traps. And all I know is that you need to rest."

Vargas began to close the door.

"Will you be out there?"

He nodded. "Good morning, Alicia," he said, closing the bedroom door.

32

VALLS HAS LOST all track of time. He doesn't know whether he's been in this cell for days or for weeks. He hasn't seen the sunlight since one far-away afternoon when he was traveling up the road to Vallvidrera in the car, sitting beside Vicente. His hand hurts, and when he tries to scratch it, he can't find it. He feels spasms in fingers that no longer exist and a stabbing pain in the knuckles, as if someone were nailing iron spikes into his bones. For some hours, or days, his side has been hurting. He can't see the color of the urine that falls into the brass pail, but he thinks it's darker than usual, tinged with blood. The woman hasn't returned, and Martín still hasn't appeared. He can't understand. Isn't this what Martín wanted? To see him rotting away in a cell?

The faceless and nameless jailer checks on him once a day, or so Valls believes. He has started to measure the days by the man's visits. He brings Valls water and food. The food is always the same: bread, rancid milk, and sometimes a sort of dry meat like salted tuna that he finds hard to chew because most of his teeth are getting loose. Two have already fallen out. Sometimes he runs his tongue over his gums and tastes his own blood, feeling his teeth giving way to the pressure.

"I need a doctor," he says when the jailer arrives with the food.

The jailer hardly ever speaks. He barely looks at him.

"How long have I been here?" Valls asks.

The jailer ignores his questions.

"Tell her I want to speak to her. To tell her the truth."

On one occasion he wakes up and discovers there's someone else in the cell. It's the jailer. He is holding something shiny in his hand. Perhaps it's a knife. Valls makes no attempt to protect himself. He feels the prick in his buttock and the cold. It's just another injection.

"How long are you going to keep me alive?"

The jailer straightens up and walks over to the cell door. Valls grabs his leg. A kick in the stomach winds him. He spends hours curled up into a ball, moaning with pain.

That night he dreams about his daughter Mercedes again, when she was just a little girl. They're in their estate in Somosaguas, in the garden. Valls has been held up speaking to one of his servants, and loses sight of her. When he looks for her, he finds her footprints on the path leading to the dolls' house. Valls steps into the dark building and calls his daughter. He finds her clothes and a trail of blood.

The dolls are licking their lips with feline glee. They have devoured her.

33

WHEN VARGAS OPENED his eyes again, the midday light was pouring through the windows. The hands of the grandfather clock, a nineteenth-century contraption Alicia must have picked up at some antiques bazaar, were nearing twelve o'clock.

He heard high heels tapping around the living room and rubbed his eyelids. "Why didn't you wake me up earlier?"

"I like to hear you snore. It's like having a bear cub in the house."

Vargas sat up and remained seated on the edge of the sofa. He put his hands on his lower back and rubbed it. He felt as if his backbone had been pushed through a candy-making machine. "If you want a bit of advice," he said, "don't grow old. It offers no advantages."

"I thought so," said Alicia.

The policeman got up, battling with cramp and creaking joints. Alicia stood in front of the sideboard mirror, carefully applying her lipstick. She was wearing a black wool coat with a belt around the waist, black seamed stockings, and vertigo-inducing high heels.

"Going somewhere?"

She turned around full circle, as if parading on the catwalk, and grinned at him. "Do I look good?"

"Who are you planning to kill?"

"I have an appointment with Sergio Vilajuana, the journalist from *La Vanguardia*. The one Barceló, the bookseller, told me about."

"The expert on Víctor Mataix?"

"And on other things, I hope."

"And may I ask how you got him involved?"

"I told him I had a Mataix book and wanted to show it to him."

"*Had* is the correct tense. I might remind you, your book has been stolen, and you don't have anything."

"Technicalities. I haven't lost the knack. And besides, I have myself."

"God help us . . ."

Topping off Alicia's attire was a hat with a net veil that covered half her face. She took a last glance in the mirror.

"Can you tell me what that outfit is supposed to be?"

"It's a Balenciaga."

"That's not what I meant."

"I know," she said on her way to the door. "I'll be back soon."

"May I use your bathroom?"

"As long as you don't leave any hairs in the bath."

*

Arranging the meeting with Vilajuana hadn't been as easy as Alicia had implied. In fact, she'd first had to contend with a cagey secretary in the newsroom, who was eager to send her packing. A few maneuvers later, she managed to get Vilajuana on the line. Having listened to her initial pitch, he sounded less convinced than a mathematician at a bishops' tea party.

"You say you have a Mataix book? Of the *Labyrinth* series?"

"*Ariadna and the Scarlet Prince.*"

"I thought there were only three copies left."

"Mine must be the fourth."

"And you say Gustavo Barceló sends you?"

"Yes. He told me he was a great friend of yours."

Vilajuana laughed. Alicia could hear the hustle and bustle in the newsroom at the other end of the line.

"I'll be in the library of the Real Academia de Buenas Letras de Barcelona, after twelve o'clock," he said at last. "Do you know it?"

"I've heard of it."

"Ask for me in the secretary's office. And bring the book."

34

LOST IN A square hidden beneath the shadow of the cathedral stands a stone portico. An inscription on its arch reads:

Real Academia de Buenas Letras
de Barcelona

Alicia had occasionally heard about the place, but like most of her fellow citizens, she knew almost nothing about that institution housed behind the walls of an old palace, a relic of medieval Barcelona. She knew, or guessed, that the academy was made up of an illustrious company of wise men, scribes, and serious addicts to literature and the arts, sworn to protect learning and the written word, who had been gathering there since the end of the eighteenth century, determined to ignore the outside world's enthusiastic efforts to oppose and disdain such eccentricities.

A perfume of stones and the mandatory aura of mystery followed her as she stepped through the doorway into the inner patio, where a wide stairway led up to the reception room. There she was intercepted by an individual with a leathery face who looked as if he'd been there since the dawn of the last century. He regarded her with suspicion and asked her whether she was Señorita Gris.

"That's me."

"I thought so. Señor Vilajuana is in the library," he said, pointing inside. "We ask visitors to be silent."

"Don't worry, I took my vows this very morning."

The guard dog showed no intention of smiling at her joke. She decided to thank him and set off in search of the library, as if she knew where to find it. That was always the most efficient way of slipping into any place with restricted access: behave as if you know where you're going and require no clearance or directions. The strategy of gaining entry is not unlike seduction: if you ask for permission, you've lost before you've begun.

Alicia wandered at ease, nosing around halls filled with statues and strolling down palatial corridors until she stumbled across a kindly bookworm who identified himself as Polonio and offered to guide her to the library.

"I've never seen you around here," he remarked. His experience with the feminine gender did not seem to have ventured beyond Petrarch's verses.

"It's your lucky day."

She found Sergio Vilajuana in the company of the muses and the almost fifty thousand volumes that made up the academy's library. The journalist had settled down at one of the tables and was facing a small citadel of sheets of paper covered in marginal notes and crossed-out words. Vilajuana had the pensive poise of a British scholar relocated to the fairer climes of the Mediterranean. He wore a gray wool suit, a tie with a pattern of golden nibs, and a saffron-colored scarf over his shoulders. Nibbling the top of a fountain pen, he murmured under his breath as he tried to trap a sentence that refused to land on the page.

Alicia let the echo of her footsteps announce her presence as she walked into the room. Vilajuana emerged from his daydream and looked up. Replacing the top of the pen, he rose courteously. "Señorita Gris, I presume."

"Call me Alicia, please." Alicia held out her hand, which Vilajuana shook with a polite but cautious smile. His small, keen eyes observed her as he asked her to sit down, wavering between suspicion and curiosity.

Alicia pointed to the pages dotted around the table, some still damp with ink. "Have I interrupted you?"

"I'd say you've rescued me."

"Bibliographic research?"

"My inaugural speech for being received into this institution."

"Congratulations."

"Thank you. I wouldn't like to sound brusque, Señorita Gris, Alicia, but I've been waiting to see you for a few days, and I think we can dispense with the small talk."

"I gather, then, that Don Gustavo Barceló has spoken to you about me?"

"In some detail, if I may be so bold. Let's say you made a deep impression on him."

"It's one of my specialties."

"I can see that. In fact, some of your old colleagues at police headquarters also send you their regards. Don't be surprised. We journalists are like that too. We ask questions. It's a bad habit we acquire over the years." Abandoning all attempts at diplomacy, he looked her straight in the eye. "Who are you?"

Alicia considered lying, just a little, or even lying her head off, but something in that look told her it would be a grave tactical mistake. "Someone who wants to find out the truth about Víctor Mataix."

"A club that recently seems to be gaining more and more followers. May I ask why?"

"I'm afraid I can't answer your question."

"Without lying, you mean."

Alicia nodded. "Something I won't do, out of respect."

Vilajuana's smile returned, this time overflowing with irony. "And you think that flattering me will prove more profitable than lying?"

She fluttered her eyelashes and adopted her sweetest expression. "You can't reproach me for trying."

"I see Barceló wasn't exaggerating. If you can't tell me the truth, tell at least why you can't."

"Because if I did, I would put you in danger."

"In other words, you're protecting me."

"In a way, yes."

"So I should be grateful and help you. Is that the idea?"

"I'm glad to see you're beginning to see things my way."

"I'm afraid I'm going to need some more motivation. And not just cosmetic. The flesh is weak, but after one reaches middle age, common sense tends to prevail again."

"So they say. How about an alliance of mutual convenience? Barceló told me you're working on a book on Mataix and the lost generation of those years."

"The word *generation* might be rather exaggerated, and *lost* is poetic license, for want of a better term."

"I'm speaking about Mataix, David Martín, and others . . ."

Vilajuana raised his eyebrows. "What do you know about David Martín?"

"Things that I'm sure would interest you."

"As, for example?"

"As, for example, the details of the indictments against Martín, Mataix, and other prisoners who supposedly disappeared in the prison of Montjuïc Castle between 1940 and 1945."

Vilajuana's gaze remained fixed on her. His eyes were shining. "Have you spoken to Brians, the lawyer?"

Alicia just nodded.

"I know for a fact that he keeps his mouth shut."

"There are other ways of finding out the truth," Alicia insinuated.

"At police headquarters they say that is another of your skills."

"Sour grapes," replied Alicia.

"It's our national pastime," Vilajuana agreed. Despite himself, he seemed to be enjoying the sparring.

"Even so, I don't think calling the police station and asking about me is a very good idea, especially now. I say this for your own good."

"I'm not that simple, young lady. I didn't make the call, and my name hasn't been mentioned. As you can see, I also do my best to protect myself."

"I'm glad to hear it. These days you can never be too cautious."

"What everyone seems to agree upon is that you're not to be trusted."

"In some places and at certain moments, that's the best compliment one can get."

"I won't deny that. Tell me, Alicia, won't all this, by chance, have something to do with our ineffable minister Don Mauricio Valls and his neatly forgotten past as a jailer?"

"What makes you say that?"

"The face you made when I mentioned him."

Alicia hesitated for a moment. Vilajuana nodded to himself, as if she'd confirmed his own suspicions.

"And if that were the case?" asked Alicia.

"Let's say it would contribute toward getting me slightly interested. What sort of exchange did you have in mind?"

"Strictly literary. You tell me what you know about Mataix, and I promise you access to all the information I have at my disposal once I've solved the matter I'm dealing with now."

"And until then?"

"My eternal gratitude and the satisfaction of knowing you've done the right thing by helping a poor damsel in distress."

"I see. I must admit that at least you're more convincing than your—I'm presuming—colleague."

"Excuse me?"

"I'm referring to the one who came to visit me a couple of weeks ago, and whom, by the way, I haven't seen again," said the journalist. "Don't you people exchange information during break? Or are we talking about a competitor?"

"Do you remember his name? Lomana?"

"It could be. I've forgotten. Aging, as I said."

"What did he look like?"

"Far less tempting than you."

"Did he have a scar on his face?"

Vilajuana nodded, and his eyes sharpened. "Did you give it to him, perhaps?"

"He cut himself shaving. He's always been the hairy sort. What did you tell Lomana?"

"Nothing he didn't already know."

"Did he mention Valls?"

"Not explicitly, but I could tell he was interested in the years Mataix spent in Montjuïc Castle and his friendship with David Martín. You don't have to be a genius to put two and two together."

"And you haven't seen him or spoken to him since?"

Vilajuana shook his head.

"Lomana can be quite persistent," said Alicia. "How did you get rid of him?"

"I told him what he wanted to hear. Or what I thought he wanted to hear."

"Which was . . ."

"He seemed very interested in the house where Víctor Mataix and his family lived until his arrest in 1941, on Carretera de las Aguas, on the hillside of Vallvidrera."

"Why the house?"

"He asked me what the phrase 'the entrance to the labyrinth' meant. He wanted to know whether it referred to a particular place."

"And . . ."

"I told him that in the novels from the *Labyrinth* series, the 'entrance,' the place through which Ariadna 'falls' into the subterranean world of that other Barcelona, is the house where she lives with her parents, which is none other than the house where the Mataix family lived. I supplied him with the address and directions. It's not anything he couldn't have found himself by spending an hour in the land registry. Perhaps he thought he'd find a treasure there, or something better. Am I right?"

"Did Lomana say who he was working for?"

"He showed me a badge. Like they do in films. I'm no expert, but it looked genuine. Do you also have one of those badges?"

Alicia shook her head.

"A pity. A femme fatale working for the regime is something I thought could only happen in a Julián Carax novel."

"Are you a Carax reader?"

"Of course! The patron saint of all Barcelona's ill-fated novelists. You two should meet. You look like you just walked out of one of his books."

Alicia sighed. "This is important, Señor Vilajuana. The lives of various people are at stake."

"Mention just one. With a name and surnames, if possible. That way I may be able to take all this a bit more seriously."

"I can't do that."

"Of course. For my own security, I suppose."

She nodded. "Even if you don't believe me."

The journalist clasped his hands over his lap and sat back in his chair, pensive. Alicia sensed that she was losing him. It was time to throw out some more bait. "How long is it since you've seen Valls make a public appearance?" she let out.

Vilajuana unclasped his hands, his interest stirred again. "Go on."

"Not so fast. The deal is that you tell me what you know about Mataix and Martín, and I tell you what I can as soon as I can. And it's a lot. You have my word."

Vilajuana chuckled but nodded slowly. "Including Valls?"

"Including Valls," Alicia lied.

"I suppose there's no point in me asking you to show me the book."

Alicia donned the sweetest smile ever.

"You've also lied to me about that?"

"Only partly. I had the book until two days ago, but I've lost it."

"I'm supposing that wasn't because you left it behind in a tram."

She shook her head.

"The deal, if you'll allow the amendment, is as follows," said Vilajuana. "You tell me where you found the book, and I'll tell you what you want to know."

Alicia was about to say something when the journalist raised a warning forefinger. "One more mention of my personal security, and I'll have to wish you good-bye and good luck. Taking for granted that what you say to me stays between us . . ."

She thought it over for quite a while. "Do I have your word?"

Vilajuana put his hand on top of the pile of papers he was working on.

"I swear on my inaugural speech to the Real Academia de Buenas Letras de Barcelona."

Alicia acquiesced. She looked around her, making sure they were alone in the library. The journalist watched her expectantly.

"I found it a week ago, in Mauricio Valls's home, hidden in the personal desk of his office."

"And may I know what you were doing there?"

Alicia leaned forward. "Investigating his disappearance."

Vilajuana's eyes lit up like a flare. "Swear to me that you'll be giving me the exclusive on this story and whatever derives from it."

"I swear to it on your inaugural speech."

Vilajuana's eyes were glued to hers. Alicia didn't even blink. The journalist gathered a few blank sheets of paper from the table and handed them to her, together with his fountain pen.

"Here," he said. "I think you might want to take a few notes . . ."

35

"I MET VÍCTOR Mataix about thirty years ago, in the autumn of 1928, to be precise. I was starting off on my career, working in the newsroom of *The Voice of Industry*, doing a bit of everything and just about getting by. At the time, Víctor Mataix was writing serialized novels under different pseudonyms for a publishing house owned by a couple of scoundrels, Barrido and Escobillas: they were notorious for swindling everyone, from their authors to their suppliers of ink and paper. They also published David Martín, Ladislao Bayona, Enrique Marqués, and the entire starving young generation of prewar Barcelona authors. When the monthly advances from Barrido & Escobillas weren't enough to make ends meet, which was often, Mataix wrote pieces commissioned by a number of newspapers, including *The Voice of Industry*, from short stories to some magnificent travel columns about places he'd never visited. I remember one titled 'The Mysteries of Byzantium' that at the time I considered a masterpiece, and which Mataix invented from beginning to end with no more documentation than a set of old postcards of Istanbul."

Alicia sighed. "And there am I, believing everything I read in the papers."

"Sure, you look just the type. But those were other times, when the pens that told lies in newspapers did so with a certain flair. The fact is that on more than one occasion I had to cut down Mataix's texts just as we were going to press to make room for some last-minute publicity or an ill-timed column from one of the publisher's friends or relatives. One day, when Mataix had come to the office to get paid for his contributions, he came up to me. I thought he was going to tell me off, but instead he shook my hand, introduced himself as if I didn't know who he was, and thanked me for being the one who handled the scissors on his pieces, when there was no other option. 'You have a good eye, Vilajuana,' he said. 'I hope you don't lose your touch here.'

"Mataix had the gift of elegance. I'm not referring to his clothes, although he always dressed impeccably, with his three-piece suit and his round wire-rimmed glasses, which lent him a Proustian air, but without the madeleines. No, I mean in his manners, in the way he addressed people and the way he spoke. He was what old-school editors in chief call a rare bird. Besides, he was a generous man, who did favors without being asked and without expecting anything in return. In fact it was he who, shortly afterward, recommended me for a job at *La Vanguardia*: thanks to him I was able to escape from *The Voice of Industry*. By then Mataix hardly wrote for the papers anymore. He'd never liked it in the first place, and only did it to bump up his income in times of need. One of the series of novels he wrote for Barrido & Escobillas, *The City of Mirrors*, was quite popular at the time. I think that between them, he and David Martín kept the whole Barrido & Escobillas team afloat, and they worked incessantly. Martín, in particular, lost what little health and sanity he had left after frying his brains at the typewriter. Mataix, for family reasons, enjoyed a more comfortable situation."

"He came from a well-to-do family?"

"Not exactly, but he had a stroke of luck—or maybe he didn't, depending on how you look at it. He inherited the property of an uncle of his, Ernesto, a somewhat eccentric character known as the Sugar Cube Emperor. Mataix was Ernesto's favorite nephew, or at least the only member of the family he didn't detest. So, shortly after he got married, Víctor Mataix was able to move into an imposing old house next to the Carretera de las Aguas, on the slopes of Vallvidrera, which his uncle Ernesto had left him, together with some shares in a company of imported goods he'd established when he returned from Cuba."

"So Uncle Ernesto was a rich colonial?"

"More like the poster boy for them all. He'd left Barcelona aged seventeen without two sticks to rub together, his hand in other people's pockets. The Civil Guard were on the lookout for him, aiming to break his legs, but he miraculously managed to stow away in a merchant ship en route to Havana."

"And how did the Americas treat him?"

"Much better than he treated them. When Uncle Ernesto returned to Barcelona on his own ship, dressed in white linen and with a Scandinavian wife thirty years his junior, just acquired by mail order, more than four decades had gone by. In that time, the Sugar Cube Emperor had won and lost fortunes, his own and other people's, both in the sugar business and in the arms trade. Thanks to a well-stocked battalion of lovers and mistresses, he'd engendered enough bastard children to populate all the Caribbean islands and committed atrocities that, had there been a God on duty and a little justice, would have guaranteed him bed and breakfast in hell for ten thousand years."

"Had there been," said Alicia.

"Still, one could say that although there was no justice, there was at least a spot of irony. Such is heaven. They say that shortly after returning from Cuba, the Sugar Cube Emperor began to lose his mind thanks to a poison supplied during his last tropical dinner by a resentful mulatto cook, pregnant with malice and goodness knows what else. The loaded colonial ended up blowing his brains out in the attic of the house he'd only just moved into, convinced that there was something living in the house, something that crept along the walls and the ceiling and smelled like a serpent's nest. . . . Something that slid nightly into his bedroom and nestled up beside him in his bed, to suck away his soul."

"Impressive," said Alicia. "Are the theatrical touches yours?"

"I borrowed them from Mataix, who included the anecdote, with some operatic embellishments, in one of the *Labyrinth* novels."

"What a shame."

"Reality never beats fiction, at least not quality fiction."

"And reality in this case was . . ."

"In all probability something more mundane. The most reliable theory was already put forward on the day of Ernesto the nabob's funeral, a huge event that took place in the cathedral in the presence of the bishop, the mayor, and all the menagerie of the city council. Not to mention all those to whom Uncle Ernesto had lent money, there to make quite sure he was dead so they wouldn't have to give it back to him. But, as I was saying, the gossip of the day was that the only thing that slid between the sugar tycoon's sheets was the housekeeper's daughter, a seventeen-year-old girl not to be messed around with, who later in life acquired fame and fortune as a cabaret artist in the Paralelo theaters, calling herself Doris Laplace, and that what she sucked every night was not precisely his soul."

"So, the suicide . . ."

"Assisted, it would appear. Everything seems to suggest that the magnate's long-suffering new wife—and they say Nordic women are cold!—after putting up with years of marriage and serial infidelity, finally flipped her lid. One midsummer's night she shot him in the face, the rumor goes, with the hunting gun he always kept next to his bed in case the Anarchists arrived."

"An exemplary tale."

"The lives of saints and sinners, a classic Barcelona genre. Whatever the true version of events, the fact is that the mansion was abandoned for years. Its reputation for spells and curses linked to it since the wealthy colonial baron placed the first stone never went away, not even when the newlyweds Mataix and his wife, Susana, settled there. Admittedly, the house was quite something. Once Mataix offered me a deluxe tour that sent shivers up my spine—though I have to admit I'm someone who prefers musical comedies and light romance. There were stairs that led nowhere, a corridor with mirrors placed to make you think someone was following you, and a cellar where a mosaic on the bottom of a swimming pool depicted the face of the mogul's first Cuban wife, Leonor, who at nineteen, convinced that she was pregnant by a snake, had committed suicide by sticking a hairpin into her heart."

"How sweet. And is that where you sent Lomana?"

Vilajuana smiled cunningly.

"Did you tell him all this stuff about evil spirits from the great beyond and the haunted house on the hill? Lomana can be very superstitious and apprehensive about these things . . ."

"I shouldn't say this, but that's the impression I got. I didn't take much of a liking to the guy, so I preferred not to ruin his surprise by offering him any unrequested information."

"Do you believe in these things? Spells and curses?"

"I believe in literature. And sometimes in the art of gastronomy, especially when it involves a good paella. The rest are just fibs or half measures, depending on how you look at it. I have a feeling that we're quite similar in this respect. About literature, not gastronomy."

"So what happened then?" asked Alicia, eager to return to the story about Mataix.

"To tell you the truth, I never heard Mataix complain about interference from the hereafter or anything like that. I'd say he believed in all this baloney even less than in the political harangues that in those days had already turned this country into a cackling henhouse. He'd just married Susana, with whom he was madly in love, and worked relentlessly in an office looking down on the whole of Barcelona. Susana was a frail, delicate creature. Her skin was almost transparent, and when you embraced her, you felt she might break. She tired very easily and sometimes spent the whole day in bed, too weak to get up. Mataix was always worrying about her, but he loved her to bits, and I think she loved him too. I visited them there a couple of times, and although I must admit that, as I said, the house was a bit sinister for my taste, they did seem happy, despite everything. At least at first.

"When Mataix went down to the city, as he used to say, he often came into the offices of *La Vanguardia,* and we'd go out to lunch together, or for a coffee. He always talked to me about the novel he was writing and would hand me a couple of pages to get my opinion, even if afterward he'd pay little attention to my comments. He used me as a guinea pig, so to speak. In those days Mataix was still a mercenary. He wrote under goodness knows how many pseudonyms at a fixed price per word. Susana's health required constant medical attention and pricey medication, and Mataix would only allow the best specialists to see her. If this meant he had to work flat out at the expense of his own health, little did he care. Susana dreamed of getting pregnant. The doctors had already told her it would be complicated. And costly."

"But the miracle occurred."

"Yes. After several miscarriages and years of hardship, Susana became pregnant in 1931. Mataix lived in constant fear that she would lose the baby again, and perhaps her life. But for once everything went well. Susana had always wanted a daughter, so she could name her after a sister she had lost when she was a child."

"Ariadna."

"During the years when they were trying to conceive a child, Susana asked Mataix to begin a new book, different from all the others he'd written until then. A book that would only be for the girl she was dreaming of. Literally. Susanna said she'd seen her in dreams and had spoken to her."

"Is that the origin of the *Labyrinth* books?"

"Yes. Mataix started writing the first installment of the series with the adventures of Ariadna in a magical Barcelona. I think he also wrote them for himself, not just for Ariadna. I always thought that the *Labyrinth* books were, in a way, a warning."

"About what?"

"About what was coming. You must have been very young then, just a child, but in the years before the war, things already looked very bad. You could smell it. It was in the air . . ."

"There's a good title for your book."

Vilajuana smiled.

"Do you think Mataix foresaw what was going to happen?"

"He did, and so did many others. You had to be blind not to see it. He often spoke about it. Once or twice I heard him say that he was thinking of leaving the country, but Susana didn't want to leave Barcelona. She thought that if they left, she would never get pregnant. And then it was too late."

"Tell me about David Martín. Did you know him?"

Vilajuana rolled his eyes. "Martín? A little. I came across him on two or three occasions. Mataix introduced me to him one day when we'd arranged to meet in Bar Canaletas. They'd been good friends since they were very young, before Martín got a few screws loose, but Mataix was still very fond of him. To be honest, I thought he was the strangest person I'd met in my entire life."

"In what sense?"

Vilajuana hesitated a few moments. "David Martín was a brilliant man, probably too brilliant for his own good. But in my modest opinion he was completely unhinged."

"Unhinged?"

"He was mad. Mad as a hatter."

"What makes you say that?"

"Call it intuition. Martín heard voices . . . and I don't mean the voices of the muses."

"Do you mean he was schizophrenic?"

"Who knows? What I do know is that Mataix was worried about him. Very worried. Mataix was like that—he worried about everyone except himself. It seems that Martín had got himself into God knows what sort of trouble, and after that they hardly saw each other anymore. Martín avoided people."

"Didn't he have family who could help him?"

"He didn't have anyone. And if he did, he always ended up pushing them away. His only connection with the real world was a young girl he'd taken on as an apprentice, someone called Isabella. Mataix thought Isabella was the only person who kept Martín alive, doing her best to protect him from himself. Mataix used to say that the only real demon was Martín's brain, which was eating him alive."

"The only demon? Were there more?"

Vilajuana shrugged. "I wouldn't know how to explain it to you without making you laugh."

"Try me."

"Well, the thing is this: Mataix once told me that David Martín thought he'd signed a contract with a mysterious publisher to write some sort of sacred text, a kind of bible for a new religion. Don't look at me like that. According to Mataix, he used to meet up every so often with this character, someone called Andreas Corelli, to receive instructions from beyond the grave, or something like that."

"And Mataix naturally doubted Corelli's existence."

"'Doubted' is putting it mildly. He had him well placed on his list of improbable figures, somewhere between Spring-Heeled Jack and the Tooth Fairy. Mataix asked me to make inquiries in publishing circles to see if we could find the alleged publisher. I did make inquiries. I left no stone unturned."

"And?"

"The only Corelli I found was a Baroque composer called Arcangelo Corelli. You could call him the Vivaldi's Vivaldi."

"So who was the Corelli that Martín was working for, or imagined he was working for?"

"Martín thought he was some other sort of *arcangelo*, a fallen one."

The journalist placed two fingers on his forehead like horns and smiled mockingly.

"The devil?"

"With tail and hoofs. A Mephistopheles with a Savile Row tailor who had arrived from hell and drawn Martín into a Faustian pact to create an accursed book, the foundation of a new religion that would set fire to the world. As I was saying, mad as a hatter. And that's how he ended."

"You mean in Montjuïc Prison?"

"That was a bit later. At the start of the thirties David Martín, as a result of his delusions and that strange alliance with his tormentor, had to get the hell out of Barcelona when the police accused him of a series of crimes that were never solved. Apparently he managed to escape by the skin of his teeth. But imagine how mad he must have been that he could think of nothing better to do but return to Spain during the war. They arrested him in Puigcerdá, shortly after he'd crossed the Pyrenees, and he ended up in Montjuïc Castle. Like so many others. And like Mataix himself a bit later. That's where they met up again after not having seen each other for years . . . a sad end if ever there was one."

"Do you know why he returned? Even if Martín wasn't altogether sane, he must have realized that if he went back to Barcelona, he'd be arrested sooner or later . . ."

Vilajuana shrugged. "Why do we make such stupid mistakes in life?"

"For love, for money, out of spite . . ."

"Deep down you're a romantic, I knew it."

"For love, then?"

"Who knows. I don't know what else he was hoping to find in a place where half the country was murdering the other half in the name of some colored rags."

"The so-called Isabella?"

"I don't know. . . . I haven't found that part of the jigsaw yet."

"Was Isabella the same person who a bit later married the bookseller Sempere?"

Vilajuana looked at her, somewhat surprised. "How do you know that?"

"Let's say I have my sources."

"Which it would be nice if you shared with me."

"As soon as I can. You have my word. So was Isabella that same person?"

"Yes. She was. Isabella Gispert, the daughter of the owners of the Gispert grocers, which is still behind Santa María del Mar. She was the person destined to become Isabella de Sempere."

"Do you think Isabella was in love with David Martín?"

"May I remind you that she married the bookseller Sempere, not Martín."

"That doesn't prove anything," replied Alicia.

"I suppose it doesn't."

"Did you know her? Did you know Isabella?"

Vilajuana nodded. "I was at her wedding."

"Did she seem happy?"

"All brides are happy on their wedding day."

This time it was Alicia's turn to smile maliciously. "What was she like?"

The man lowered his eyes. "I only spoke to her once or twice."

"But she must have made an impression."

"Yes. Isabella made an impression."

"And?"

"And she seemed to me one of those very rare people who make this dog's world a place worth visiting."

"Did you go to the funeral?"

Vilajuana nodded slowly.

"Is it true she died of cholera?"

A shadow crossed the journalist's face. "That's what they said."

"But you don't believe it."

The journalist shook his head.

"So, why don't you tell me the rest of the story?"

"In all honesty, it's a very sad story that I'd rather forget."

"Is that why you've spent so many years writing a book about it? A book I'm sure you know you'll never be able to publish. At least not in this country . . ."

Vilajuana smiled sadly. "Do you know what David Martín said to me, the last time I saw him? It was on a night when the three of us, Mataix, Martín, and me, had drunk a glass too many in El Xampanyet to celebrate Víctor finishing his first *Labyrinth* book."

Alicia shook her head.

"I don't know why, but the conversation drifted toward the old subject of writers and alcohol. Martín, who could drink a bathful of liquor and still remain lucid, told me something that night that I have never forgotten. 'One drinks to remember, and one writes to forget.'"

"Maybe he wasn't as mad as he seemed."

Vilajuana nodded silently, his face overwhelmed with memories.

"Then tell me what you've been trying to forget for so many years."

"Don't say I didn't warn you," Vilajuana said.

THE FORGOTTEN:

Víctor Mataix and the End of Barcelona's
Lost Generation

by Sergio Vilajuana

(Ediciones Destino, Barcelona, 1989)

One does not need to be Goethe to know that sooner or later any
writer worth his salt will come across his Mephistopheles. Kind-
hearted writers, if they exist, will offer him their soul. The rest will
sell him the soul of any of the gullible people who stand in their way.

The above is the opening paragraph of *Ink and Sulfur,* a lighthearted piece bursting with irony, written by Víctor Mataix in 1933
and presumably inspired by the misfortunes of his friend and colleague David Martín.

Víctor Mataix, who was worth his salt and that of a few others,
came across his own Mephistopheles one day in the autumn of 1937.

If living off literature had already been a tightrope act until then,
the outbreak of the war swept away what was left of the precarious
publishing business that had provided Mataix with his purpose and
upkeep. People still wrote and published, but the genre that now
prevailed was propaganda, pamphlets, and eulogies at the service of
grandiose causes soaked in noise and blood. In a matter of months
Mataix found himself, like so many others, with no other way of
making a living but from other people's charity and through chance,
and the odds were usually short in those days.

His last publishers, to whom he had entrusted the series of novels called *The Labyrinth of the Spirits,* were two shrewd gentlemen
named Revells and Badens. Badens, a noted gourmand and connoisseur of fine foods and products of the land, had retired temporarily to his farmhouse in the Ampurdán to grow tomatoes and study
the secrets of truffles, while awaiting for the madness of the times
to abate. He was a born optimist: squabbles made him sick, and he
wanted to believe that the conflict would last no longer than two or

three months, after which Spain would return to its natural state of chaos and absurdity, where there was always room for literature, good food, and business. Revells, a fine scholar of power games and political theater, had chosen to stay in Barcelona and keep his offices open, even if barely idling. The literature section had been relegated to an uncertain limbo, and the bulk of the business now concentrated on printing speeches, leaflets, and exemplary stories that exalted the heroes of the moment, who varied from week to week thanks to inside struggles and the intimations of a hidden civil war within the declared civil war that affected the Republican side. Less optimistic than his partner, who continued to send him crates of splendid tomatoes and garden vegetables, Revells suspected that the situation was going to drag on for some time yet and end worse than badly.

Revells and Badens, however, still paid Mataix a small salary out of their savings, as an advance on future works. Despite his reservations, Mataix accepted it reluctantly. Revells ignored his objections and insisted. When the discussion inevitably drifted into scruples, or what the publisher called "a load of bullshit from someone who hasn't really gone hungry yet," he smiled ironically. "Víctor," he reassured him, "don't weep on our account: you'll make it up to us one day, I'll make sure you do."

Thanks to his publishers, Mataix managed to provide his family with some food, a situation that was beginning to be quite privileged. Most of his colleagues were in far more precarious and dramatic situations. Some had joined the militia in a fit of passion and romanticism. "We'll exterminate the Fascist rat in its putrid den," they sang. More than one of them reproached him for not joining them. It was a time when large numbers of people turned the propaganda posters covering the city into their creed and conscience. "If you're not prepared to fight for your freedom you don't deserve it," they told him. Mataix, who suspected they were right, was filled with remorse. Should he abandon Susana and his daughter Ariadna in the large house on the hill and set off to meet the massed ranks of the so-called Nacionales? "I don't know what nation they're talking about, but it's not mine," a friend told Mataix, who had gone to see him off at the station. "And it's not yours either, even if you don't have the courage to come out and defend it." Mataix went home feeling ashamed of himself. When he got there, Susana threw her arms around him and burst into tears. She was shaking. "Don't leave us," she begged. "Ariadna and I are your country."

As the war advanced, Mataix discovered that he couldn't write. He would sit for hours in front of his typewriter, staring at the horizon beyond the large windows. In time, he began to go down to the city almost every day, to look for opportunities, he said, or to escape from himself. Most of his acquaintances were by then begging favors in the shady black market of servitude that spread in the shadow of the war. Rumor had it among starving men of letters that Mataix received a nonrefundable salary from Revells and Badens. "Envy is the gangrene of writers," his old friend Martín had already warned him. "It rots us while we're alive until oblivion hacks us down unceremoniously." In a matter of months his acquaintances were no longer acquainted with him. When they saw him approaching in the distance, they would cross over to the opposite pavement, murmuring among themselves, laughing scornfully. Others passed him by, averting their eyes.

The initial months of the war had left Barcelona plunged in a strange somnolence of fear and internal skirmishes. The Fascist rebellion had failed in Barcelona in the first few days after the coup, and there were those who wanted to believe that the war was now a distant event, that in the end it would be seen as just one more piece of bravado from generals with little stature and even less shame. In a matter of weeks, they said, everything would return to the feverish abnormality that characterized the country's public life.

*

Mataix no longer believed that. And he was scared. He knew that a civil war is never just one fight, but a tangle of large or small fights bound to one another. Its official memory is always established by chroniclers entrenched on the winning or the losing side, but it is never the story of those who are trapped between the two, those who seldom set the bonfire alight. Martín used to say that in Spain an opponent may be scorned, but anyone who does things his own way and refuses to swallow what he doesn't agree with is hated. At the time, Mataix hadn't believed him. But he was beginning to think that the only sin never forgiven in Spain was that of refusing to take sides, to join one flock or another. And where there are flocks of sheep, the hungry wolves always make an appearance. Sadly for him, Mataix had learned all this and was beginning to smell blood in the air. There would be time enough later on to hide the dead and invent stories. Now was the moment to pull out the knives and pay homage to cruelty. Wars soil everything, but they clean the memory.

That fateful day of 1937 when his destiny was about to change, Mataix had gone down to the city center to meet up with Revells. Whenever they met, the publisher invited him to lunch at the Bar Velódromo, close to the offices of Ediciones Orbe, on Avenida Diagonal, and slipped him an envelope under the table with enough money to keep his family for a couple more weeks. That day, for the first time, Mataix refused to accept it. This is how he describes the scene in his *Memory of Darkness*, a sort of fictionalized chronicle of the war and the years that took him to prison, which was never published, and in which he is one more character, seen by an omniscient narrator who might or might not be the Grim Reaper:

*

The glazed front of the large Bar Velódromo stood at the point where Calle Muntaner loses its elegant slope, just a few steps from Avenida Diagonal. Its aquarium light and its cathedral ceilings offered asylum and a lounge where coffee substitutes were served to those who still tried to believe that life went on, and that tomorrow, or perhaps the day after tomorrow, would be just another day. Revells always chose a corner table from which he could observe the whole room and see who came in and out.

"No, Señor Revells. I can no longer accept your charity."

"It's not charity, it's an investment. Believe me, Badens and I are convinced that in ten or twenty years you'll be one of the best-selling authors in the whole of Europe. And if I'm wrong, I'll become a priest and Badens will eat mortadella instead of truffles. I swear on this dish of snails *a la llauna.*"

"You and your silly remarks."

"Take the money."

"No."

"All those millions of Spaniards, and I've come across the only one who won't take money from under a table."

"What does your crystal ball say about that?"

"Look, Víctor, I'd be happy to accept a book in exchange for an advance, but at the moment we can't publish it. You know that."

"Then I'll have to wait."

"Years might go by. There are people in this country who are not going to stop until they've all massacred one another. Here, when people lose their mind, which is quite often, they're capable of shooting themselves in the foot if they think that by doing so they'll make their neighbor lame. This is going to go on for a long time. Trust me."

"In that case it's better to die of hunger than to live to see it."

"Very heroic. Forgive me if I'm not sobbing with emotion. Is this what you want for your wife and daughter?"

Mataix closed his eyes and sank into his own misery. "Don't say that."

"Well, then, don't you talk such nonsense. Just take the money, for God's sake."

"I'll give it all back to you. To the last céntimo."

"I've never doubted that. Go on, eat a bit. You haven't tasted a thing. And take some of this bread home. And by the way, come by the office: there's a crateful of wonderful garden vegetables from the Ampurdán sent to you by Badens. Please, you must take something, the office is starting to look like a greengrocer's."

"Are you leaving?"

"I have things to do. Take care, Víctor. And keep writing. We'll be publishing again one day, you'll see, and I'm counting on you to make us rich."

The publisher headed off and left Mataix sitting alone at the table. He knew that Revells had only come to give him the money, that once he'd accomplished his mission he'd preferred to leave and save him the embarrassment and humiliation of feeling he was unable to provide for his family without charity.

He was finishing his food and starting to put the leftover pieces of bread in his pockets when a shadow fell on his table. He looked up and saw a young man wearing the remains of a ragged suit, holding a folder of the kind that piled up in the courts and registry offices. He looked too frail and destitute to be some political commissar out to get Mataix.

"Do you mind if I sit down?"

Mataix shook his head.

"My name is Brians. Fernando Brians. I'm a lawyer, though I might not look like one."

"Víctor Mataix, writer, though I might not look like one either."

"What times these are, don't you think? Anyone who is anyone is a nobody, and anyone who just a couple of days ago was a nobody is now someone."

"A lawyer and a philosopher, it would appear."

"And all at a very attractive price," Brians agreed.

"I'd love to be able to hire you to defend my pride, but I'm afraid I'm short of funds."

"Don't worry. I already have the client."

"So what's my role in this story?" asked Mataix.

"The lucky artist who has been selected for a very lucrative job."

"You don't say. And who is your client, if I may ask?"

"A man who values his privacy."

"And who doesn't?"

"Those who have none."

"Forget the philosopher for a moment, and call in the lawyer," said Mataix, cutting him short. "How can I help you, or your client?"

"My client is someone of great importance and even greater wealth. One of those men who have it all, as they say."

"Those are the ones who always want more."

"In this case 'more' includes your services," Brians said.

"What services can a novelist offer in wartime? My readers don't want to read, they want to kill one another."

"Have you ever thought of writing a biography?"

"No. I write fiction."

"Some would argue that no genre is more fictitious than a biography."

"With the possible exception of an autobiography," Mataix granted.

"Precisely. As a novelist you have to accept that when it comes to the crunch, a story is a story."

"As a novelist, I only accept advances. Cash preferred."

"We'll be coming to that. But, just speaking theoretically, wouldn't you say that a chronicle is made up of words, of language?"

Mataix sighed. "Everything is made up of words and language," he replied. "Even a lawyer's sophistry."

"And what is a writer but a worker of the language?"

"Someone with no professional prospects when people stop using their brain and start thinking with their ass, for want of a better expression."

"You see? Even when it comes to sarcasm, you have a touch of elegance."

"Why don't you stop beating around the bush, Señor Brians."

"My client couldn't have put it better."

"While we're in the mood for sarcasm, if your client is so important and powerful, aren't you a somewhat low-profile lawyer to represent him? No offense."

"None taken. In fact, you're absolutely right. I'm representing someone through a third party."

"Please explain," said Mataix.

"My services have been requested by a prestigious firm that acts for the client."

"Lucky you. And why doesn't some member of this top-notch firm make an appearance around here?"

"Because they're in the Nacionales' zone. Technically speaking, of course. The client himself is in Switzerland, I believe."

"Excuse me?"

"My client and his lawyers are under the auspices and protection of General Franco," Brians explained.

Mataix checked the surrounding tables apprehensively. Nobody seemed to be paying any attention, but those were times when even walls had sharp ears. "This must be a joke," he said, lowering his voice.

"I can assure you it isn't."

"Please get up and get the hell out of here. I'll pretend I haven't seen you or listened to you."

"Believe me, Señor Mataix, I understand you perfectly. But I can't do that."

"Why not?"

"Because if I go out through that door without having secured your services, I don't think I'll be alive tomorrow. Nor will you and your family, either."

There was a long silence. Mataix grabbed Brians by his lapels. The lawyer looked at him with infinite sadness.

"You're telling the truth . . . ," Mataix murmured, more to himself than to the lawyer.

Brians nodded.

Mataix let go of him. "Why me?"

"The client's wife reads all your books. She says she likes the way you write. Especially your love stories. The others, not so much."

The writer covered his face with his hands.

"If it's any consolation, the salary is unbeatable."

Mataix looked at Brians through his fingers. "And what do they pay you?"

"They let me go on breathing and they take care of my debts, which are not small. But only if you agree."

"And if I don't?"

Brians shrugged. "I'm told that hired assassins are very affordable in Barcelona these days."

"How do I know . . . how do *you* know that these threats are believable?"

Brians looked down. "When I asked that question, they sent me a parcel containing the left ear of my office partner, Jusid. They tell me that every day that goes by without a reply, they'll send me another parcel. As I said, hired guns come cheap in Barcelona."

"What's your client's name?" inquired Mataix.

"I don't know."

"Then what, in fact, do you know?"

"That the people who work for him don't mess around."

"What about him?"

"I know he's a banker. Important. I know, or sense, that he's one of the two or three bankers financing General Franco's army. I know, or it has been implied to me, that he's a vain man, very sensitive to the way history might judge him, and that his wife—as I said, a devoted reader of your work—has convinced her husband that he needs a biography that reflects his achievements, his magnificence, and his prodigious contribution to the good of Spain and the world."

"Every son of a bitch needs a biography," declared Mataix. "It's the most dishonest genre in the entire catalog."

"I'm not going to contradict you, Señor Mataix. Do you want to hear the good news?"

"Do you mean the bit about staying alive?"

"One hundred thousand pesetas deposited in an account in your name in the National Swiss Bank of Geneva on acceptance of the job, and a hundred thousand more on publication."

Mataix stared at him in astonishment.

"While you take in the figure, please let me explain the procedure. Once you've accepted and signed the contract, you'll begin to receive a biweekly emolument through my office, which will continue during the development of the work, without affecting the global total of your fees. Furthermore, you'll receive, again through me, a document that apparently already exists, containing a first version of my client's biography."

"So I'm not the first?"

Brians shrugged again.

"What happened to my predecessor?" asked Mataix. "Have they also sent him to you in little pieces?"

"I don't know. I believe the client's wife thought his work had no style, class, or savoir faire."

"I don't know how you can joke about this sort of thing."

"It's better than jumping in front of a train. In any case, this document, which from what I've been told is in a very rudimentary state, will serve as a source of information and something to work from. Your task is to write an exemplary biography of this person based on the pages you've been sent. You have a year to do this. After going through the notes sent by the client, you'll have another six months to incorporate the required changes, polish up the text, and prepare the manuscript for publication. And if you'll allow the comment, the best thing is that there's no need for you to sign the book. Nobody need ever know that you wrote it. In fact, your silence and mine are essential requirements for the transaction."

"Why's that?"

"Perhaps I should have said from the start that the book is in fact an autobiography. You will ghostwrite it in the first person, and my client will sign it."

"I imagine it already has a title."

"The working title is *I, XXXXXX: Memoirs of a Spanish Financier*. I believe they'll admit alternative suggestions."

Then Mataix did something that neither he nor Brians expected. He burst out laughing. He laughed until he cried, and the other people in the café turned to look at him askance, wondering how anyone would want to guffaw like that when things were going from bad to worse. When he recovered his composure, Mataix took a deep breath and looked at Brians.

"Am I to understand that that was a yes?"

"Is there any alternative?"

"That you and I get a bullet in the head tomorrow morning, or the day after, as we walk down the street, and that they do the same to your family and to mine, sooner rather than later."

"Where do I sign?"

A few days later, after a succession of sleepless nights, remorse, and speculations, Mataix could bear it no longer. He went to see his publisher in Ediciones Orbe. Revells hadn't lied: the offices exuded a delicate perfume straight from the gardens of the Ampurdán. Whole crates from Badens's vegetable sanctuary were lined up along the corridors, among piles of books and heaps of unpaid bills. Revells listened carefully to Mataix's account while he sniffed a splendid tomato that he shifted playfully from hand to hand.

"What do you think?" asked Mataix when he finished his story.

"Divine. Just smelling it makes me feel hungry."

"I'm referring to my dilemma," Mataix insisted.

Revells set the tomato on the table. "That you had no choice but to accept."

"You're saying this because you know it's what I want to hear."

"I'm saying this because I like to see you alive, and because we've advanced you a lot of money that we hope to recoup someday. Have you received the stack of papers yet?"

"Part of it."

"And . . . ?"

"They make you want to throw up."

"Were you expecting Shakespeare's sonnets?"

"I don't know what I was expecting."

"At least you must have started guessing. You must have figured out who the person is."

"I have an idea," said Mataix.

Revells's eyes shone in anticipation. "Tell me . . ."

"From what I've read, I suspect it's Ubach."

"Miguel Ángel Ubach? Holy shit. The Gunpowder Banker?"

"I don't think he likes being called by that name."

"Too fucking bad. If he doesn't like it, he should have financed a welfare fund and not a war."

"What do you know about him—you who know everything about everyone?" asked Mataix.

"Only about those who matter."

"I know the world of nobodies and good-for-nothings has no romance for you."

Revells ignored the jibe, fascinated as he was by this high-flying thriller. He leaned his head outside his office door and called one of his trusted staff, Laura Franconi.

"Laura, come here a sec, if you can . . ."

While they waited, Revells walked restlessly around the office. After a few moments, dodging a couple of crates full of onions and leeks, Laura Franconi came through the door. Seeing Mataix, she smiled and went over to give him a kiss. Petite and vivacious, Laura was one of those active minds that makes an establishment work as smooth as silk.

"What do you think of our fruit and vegetable stall?" she asked. "How about some zucchini?"

"Our friend Mataix here has just made a deal with the war gods," said the publisher.

Mataix sighed. "Why don't you look out of the window and blare it out through a megaphone?"

Laura Franconi closed the office door and looked at him anxiously.

"Tell her," said Revells.

Mataix gave her a summary of the facts, but Laura didn't need any help to fill in the bits between the lines. When he'd finished, she just put her hand on his shoulder, looking concerned.

"By the way," asked Revells, "has that son of a bitch Ubach got a publisher who will bring out that horror?"

Laura threw him a caustic look.

"I'm only suggesting a business opportunity," Revells said. "I don't know why you have to be so squeamish in times like these."

"I'd appreciate your help and advice," Mataix reminded him.

Laura took his hand and looked him in the eye. "Accept the money. Write whatever that bighead wants you to write, and then get the hell out of this country forever. I recommend Argentina. Plenty of space, and the steaks are out of this world. Plus there's a handy ocean in between."

Mataix observed Revells.

"Amen," said the publisher. "I couldn't have put it better."

"Any suggestion that doesn't involve crossing the world and exiling my family?"

"Look, Mataix. Whatever you do, you're on thin ice. If Ubach's side wins—and he's got plenty of cards in his favor—I have a hunch that once you've offered him your services, your existence will become uncomfortable, and more than one person will want you out of the way. And if the Republic wins, and someone finds out that you collaborated with one of Franco's money men, I can picture you in a secret police dungeon, all expenses paid."

"Fabulous."

"We can help you flee. Badens has contacts with a merchant fleet company, and we could get you and your family to Marseilles in a matter of days. From there, it would be up to you. I'd listen to Laura and head for the Americas. North or South, it doesn't matter. It's a case of putting plenty of distance between here and wherever you go."

"We'll come and visit you," Laura promised. "Unless of course you end up having us all as guests, the way things are going in this country . . ."

"And we'll bring you tomatoes and delicious vegetables for all those barbecues you're going to enjoy with your two-hundred-thousand-peseta booty," declared Revells.

Mataix sighed. "My wife doesn't want to leave Barcelona."

"I'm guessing that you haven't told her anything," said Revells.

Mataix shook his head. Revells and Laura exchanged glances.

"And I don't want to go anywhere, either," said the writer. "This is my home, for better or worse. It's in my blood."

"The same thing happens with malaria," remarked Revells, "and it's not always healthy."

"Do you have a vaccination against Barcelona?"

"Deep down, I understand you. I'd feel the same way. Although I wouldn't say no to seeing the world with a well-lined pocket. And you don't have to decide right away. You have a year and a half to think about it. As long as you don't hand in the book and the war continues, everything will be on hold. Do what you do with us, never keeping to deadlines and leaving us in the dark."

Laura gave Mataix a sympathetic tap on his back. Revells took the wonderful sample of wild flora from the Ampurdán and handed it to him.

"Would you like a tomato?"

*

Only part of the manuscript of *Memory of Darkness* has survived, but everything seems to point to the fact that Mataix decided to give in. There are no signs of him handing in a first version of Miguel Ángel Ubach's autobiography until well into 1939. Indeed, when the war came to an end and Franco's troops made their victorious entry into Barcelona, he was still working on revisions and changes he'd been asked to make—most of which presumably came from Federica, Ubach's wife, whose devotion to Fascism was linked to a great sensitivity for literature and the arts. Once he'd handed in the final manuscript, in 1940, Mataix might have considered his publishers' advice to try to leave the country with his family and his fees, but in the end he ignored the warning and decided to stay. The most likely reason for that decision, which he kept postponing, was that his wife was pregnant again, this time with their second daughter.

By then Ubach had already returned triumphant to Spain, enjoying the highest levels of acclaim and gratitude among the top echelons of the regime, thanks to his work as banker for the national crusade. Those were days of revenge, but also of rewards. All circles of Spanish life were being restructured, and while many people were cast into oblivion, internal exile, and poverty, just as many acolytes rose to fill posts of power and prestige. There wasn't a single corner of public life where that purge was not undertaken with relentless zeal. Becoming a turncoat, a deeply rooted Spanish tradition, grew into an art form. The war had left hundreds of thousands of dead, but even more forgotten and damned. Many of the old acquaintances and colleagues who had looked down on Mataix with such scorn reappeared, desperate, begging for his help, his recommendation and compassion. Most of them would soon end up in prison, where they would linger for years until what was left of them was snuffed out forever. A few were summarily executed. Others took their own lives, or died from illness or sadness.

Some, predictably the most pretentious and untalented, switched sides. As protégés and courtiers of the regime, they made all the progress they had been unable to achieve by their own merits. Politics can sometimes be a shelter for mediocre and failed artists. There they can prosper, gain power with which to lend themselves airs, and above all, get back at all those who, through their own work and talent, have achieved what they've never come even close to achieving, while they declare, with a look of holiness and sacrifice, that everything they do is for the country.

In the summer of 1941, two weeks after the birth of Sonia, the second daughter of Susana and Víctor Mataix, something unexpected happened. The family was enjoying a sunny, peaceful Sunday in their home near Carretera de la Aguas when they heard a stream of cars approaching. Out of the first car came four armed men in suits. Mataix feared the worst, but then he noticed the second car, a Mercedes almost identical to the one used by Generalissimo Franco, out of which emerged a gentleman with faultless manners, together with a blond lady covered in jewels and dressed as if she was going to a royal coronation. They were Miguel Ángel Ubach and his wife, Federica.

Mataix, who had never told his wife the truth about the book in which he'd buried over a year and a half of his life—the book that had saved her life—felt the floor sink under his feet. Susana, looking confused, asked him who those illustrious visitors crossing the garden were. It was Doña Federica who would speak for him throughout that long afternoon. While Don Miguel Ángel retired to Mataix's office to discuss matters that concern men only, between snifters of brandy and the Cuban cigars he had brought with him as a gift, Doña Federica became the best friend of that poor commoner who, still weak after the birth of her second daughter, could barely stand. Even so, Doña Federica allowed her to get up and go to the kitchen to prepare a cup of tea which she didn't deign to touch and some dry biscuits she wouldn't even have given to her dogs, and watched her limp around while she sat in the company of those two girls, Ariadna and little Sonia, who, quite inexplicably, were the most beautiful things she'd seen in her life. How could those two sweet creatures, so full of light and life, have been born from that couple of starving nobodies? Sure, perhaps Mataix had some talent, but basically he was like all other artists, a servant, and besides, the only really good book he'd written was *The House of the Cypress Trees*. All the rest were nothing special, disappointing her with their unintelligible and macabre plots. "The only really good one was the first," she had told Mataix right away when they shook hands, disappointed too by how distant he seemed, as if he were not happy to see her. That Mataix had married that uncouth woman who didn't even know how to dress or speak confirmed her suspicions. He had been useful to pass the time, but he would never have a place among the greats.

Despite all that, it was with the best of smiles that Doña Federica endured the company of that poor wretch, who was doing everything she could to please her. Susana kept asking questions about her life, as if she could hope to understand it. Doña Federica barely listened. She only had eyes for those two children. Ariadna looked at her suspiciously, the way all children did, and when Doña Federica asked her, "Tell me, darling, who do you think is prettiest, your mommy or me?" she ran to hide behind her mother.

It was getting dark when Ubach and Mataix emerged from the study and Don Miguel Ángel decided to put an end to the impromptu visit. He embraced Mataix and kissed Susana's hand. "You're a charming couple," he declared. The Mataixes accompanied the illustrious spouses to their Mercedes-Benz and watched them leave, escorted by the other two cars, beneath a starry sky that promised a horizon of peace and, perhaps, of hope.

A week later, shortly before dawn, two more cars returned to the Mataixes' house. This time they were black cars with no license plates. Out of the first car came a man in a dark raincoat, who identified himself as Lieutenant Javier Fumero, from the political police division. With him was a meticulously dressed man, with spectacles and a haircut that suggested a middling bureaucrat, who observed the scene from the passenger seat, never leaving the car.

Mataix had come out to meet them. Using his revolver, Fumero struck Mataix so hard on the face that he broke his jaw and knocked him down. His men picked him up and dragged him, screaming, to one of the cars. Fumero wiped his bloody hands on his raincoat and went into the house to search for Susana and the girls. He found them hiding inside a wardrobe, trembling. When Susana refused to hand over her daughters, Fumero kicked her hard in the stomach. He took little Sonia in his arms and grabbed Ariadna by the hand as she wept in terror. He was about to leave the room when Susana threw herself on his back and dug her nails into his face. Without batting an eyelid, he handed the girls to one of his men, who was watching from the doorway, and turned around. He grabbed Susana by her neck and flung her on the floor. Then he knelt down on top of her, crushing her chest, and looked into her eyes. Unable to breathe, Susana gazed at that stranger who was staring at her with a smile. She saw him pull a cutthroat razor from his pocket and unfold it. "I'm going to open up your guts and string them around your neck like a necklace, you fucking whore," he said calmly.

Fumero had pulled her clothes off and was starting to play around with the blade when the man who had remained in the car, the icy bureaucrat, put a hand on his shoulder and stopped him.

"There's no time," he warned.

The men walked away, leaving her there. Susana dragged herself, bleeding, down the stairs. She listened to the drone of the departing cars through the trees until she lost consciousness.

THE

FORGOTTEN

I

WHEN VILAJUANA ENDED his story, his eyes looked glazed and his voice was dry. Alicia dropped her head, remaining silent. After a while, the journalist cleared his throat, and she smiled weakly at him.

"Susana never saw her husband or her children again. She spent two months visiting police stations, hospitals, and charity homes, asking after them. Nobody knew anything. One day, in despair, she decided to phone Federica Ubach. A servant answered the phone and passed the line on to a secretary. Susana explained what had happened and told the man that Señora Ubach was the only person who could help her. 'She's a friend of mine,' she said."

"Poor woman," murmured Alicia.

"Two days later she was picked up in the street and taken to the women's mental hospital. She remained there a few years. They say she escaped some time later. Who knows. Susana was lost forever."

A long silence ensued.

"What happened to Víctor Mataix?" asked Alicia.

"Brians, the lawyer, who some time earlier had been hired by Isabella Gispert to try to help David Martín, found out through Martín that Mataix had also ended up in Montjuïc Castle. He was held in solitary confinement by an express order of the prison governor, Don Mauricio Valls, not allowed to go out to the yard with other inmates, receive visits, or have any form of communication with anyone. Martín, who had himself been sent to one of the isolation cells more than once, was the only person who had been able to speak to Mataix, exchanging words across the passage. That's how Brians knew what had happened. I imagine that by then the lawyer must have felt very remorseful and partly to blame, so he decided to help all those poor devils trapped in the prison. Martín, Mataix . . ."

"The defender of lost causes . . . ," said Alicia.

379

"He was never able to save them, of course. Martín was murdered by order of Valls, or so they said. Mataix was never heard of again. His death is still a mystery. And as for Isabella, with whom poor Brians had fallen in love, as did everyone who met her, she had preceded them, also in extremely suspicious circumstances. Brians never got back on his feet again after all that. He's a good man, but he's frightened, and anyhow, there's nothing he can do, either."

"Do you think Mataix is still there?"

"In the castle? I hope God isn't that cruel."

Alicia nodded, trying to take it all in.

"And you?" asked Vilajuana. "What do you plan to do?"

"What do you mean?"

"Are you just going to sit there and do nothing, after hearing all this?"

"My hands are as tied as those of Brians. Or perhaps even more."

"How convenient."

"With all due respect, you don't know anything about me."

"Then tell me. Help me complete the story. Tell me what I can do."

"Do you have a family, Vilajuana?"

"A wife and four children."

"And you love them?"

"More than anything in the world. Why are you asking me?"

"Do you want me to tell you what you must do? Really?"

Vilajuana nodded.

"Finish writing your speech. Forget about Mataix. About Martín. About Valls and everything you've told me. And forget about me. I was never here."

"That wasn't the deal," Vilajuana protested. "You've tricked me."

"Welcome to the club," said Alicia, walking out.

2

NOT LONG AFTER leaving the Real Academia and stepping out of Palacio Recasens, Alicia was turning the corner into a narrow street when she had to stop to throw up. She held on to the cold stone wall and closed her eyes, tasting the bile on her lips. She tried to take a deep breath and restrain herself, but nausea hit again and she almost fell to her knees.

If she didn't fall, it was because someone held her up. When she turned around, she was confronted with the obliging face of Rovira, the apprentice spy, who looked at her with deep concern.

"Are you all right, Señorita Gris?"

She tried to recover her breath. "What on earth are you doing here, Rovira?"

"Well . . . I saw you wobbling from afar and . . . I'm sorry."

"I'm fine. Go away."

"You're crying, miss."

"Clear off, you idiot," she lashed out, raising her voice and pushing him away with both hands.

Rovira shrugged and hurried off, looking wounded. Alicia leaned against the wall. She dried her tears with her hands and, pressing her lips together angrily, set off again.

On her way home she found a street vendor and bought some eucalyptus sweets from him to drive the acid taste from her mouth. Then she started slowly up the stairs. When she reached the door to her apartment, she heard voices inside. Perhaps Fernandito had come by for new instructions, she thought, or to report on his mission. Perhaps he'd patched things up with Vargas.

She opened the door and saw Vargas standing by the window. Sitting on the sofa with a cup of tea in his hand, smiling calmly, was Leandro Montalvo. In the doorway, Alicia felt her cheeks paling.

Leandro stood up. "And there was I, thinking you'd be glad to see me, Alicia."

Alicia took a few steps forward, removing her coat as she glanced at Vargas. "I . . . I didn't know you were coming. If I'd known . . ."

"It's been a bit of a last-minute thing. I arrived last night, but in fact I couldn't have chosen a better moment."

"May I offer you anything?" Alicia improvised.

Leandro held out his cup. "Captain Vargas here has been very kind and made me a splendid cup of tea."

"Señor Montalvo and I have been discussing the details of the case," said Vargas.

"Oh, good . . ."

"Come on, give me a kiss, Alicia, I haven't seen you for days."

She went up to Leandro and brushed his cheek with her lips.

A glint in his eyes informed her that he'd noticed the bile on her breath. "Everything all right?"

"Yes. A bit of an upset stomach. It's nothing."

"You must take better care of yourself. If I'm not around to keep an eye on you, you don't bother."

Alicia nodded and smiled meekly.

"Go on, sit down. Tell me. The captain says you've had a busy morning. You went to see a journalist, I believe."

"In the end he stood me up. He probably didn't have anything to tell me."

"You can't rely on anyone in this country."

"That's what Vargas says."

"Luckily there are still some people who work, and who work well. Like you two, who've practically resolved the case."

"Have we?" Alicia glanced at Vargas, who lowered his eyes.

"Well, all this stuff about Metrobarna, the chauffeur, and that Sanchís guy . . . I'd say we've almost got this in the bag, as they say. The trail is very solid."

"It's only circumstantial. Nothing more."

Leandro laughed politely. "See what I was saying, Vargas? Alicia is never satisfied with herself. She's a perfectionist."

"I wonder where she gets it from," Vargas said drily.

Alicia was about to ask him what he was doing in Barcelona when the door of the apartment suddenly opened and Fernandito walked into the sitting room, panting after his race up the stairs.

"Fresh news, Señorita Alicia! You'll never guess what I discovered!"

"I hope you're going to tell me that you've found my order at last," she snapped, her eyes fixed on his. "I suppose you left it in the building across the street by mistake."

"Goodness," said Leandro. "Who is this obliging young man? Aren't you going to introduce us?"

"It's Fernandito. The boy from the grocery."

Fernandito gulped and nodded.

"So? You haven't brought it?" Alicia asked, scowling.

Fernandito stared at her mutely.

"I said eggs, milk, bread, and two bottles of white Perelada. And also olive oil. Which is the bit you haven't understood, you simpleton?"

Fernandito read the urgency in Alicia's eyes and nodded again, looking contrite. "I'm sorry, Señorita Alicia. It's all been a mistake. Manolo says it's ready now, and please to forgive him. It won't happen again."

Alicia snapped her fingers a few times. "Go on, then. What are you waiting for?"

Fernandito nodded once again and made himself scarce.

"They can't get anything right," Alicia spat.

"That's why I live in a luxury hotel," said Leandro. "Everything is resolved with a simple phone call."

Alicia assumed a calm smile and went back to Leandro's side. "And to what do we owe the honor of your having left the comfort of the Palace for my humble abode?"

"I'd like to say that I missed your sarcasm, but the truth is that I bring good and bad news."

Alicia shot a quick glance at Vargas, who simply nodded.

"Sit down, please. You're not going to like this, Alicia, but I want you to know it wasn't my idea, and I haven't been able to do anything to avoid it."

She noticed Vargas withdrawing into himself.

"Avoid what?" she asked.

Leandro left the cup on the table and paused, as if he were gathering courage to give her the news. "Three days ago the police investigation revealed that last month Don Mauricio Valls had been in touch by phone on three different occasions with Señor Ignacio

Sanchís, director general of Metrobarna. That same morning, in the early hours, during a search of the company's Madrid offices, the police found documents showing that a number of share purchase operations of the Banco Hipotecario, Metrobarna's parent company, had taken place between its manager, Don Ignacio Sanchís, and Don Mauricio Valls. According to the police technical division, these operations were the subject of important procedural irregularities, and there was no record of the transactions having been duly reported to the Banco de España. When one of the clerks of the head office was questioned, he denied having any knowledge or record of such operations."

"Why were we not kept informed?" asked Alicia. "I thought we were part of the investigation."

"Don't blame Gil de Partera, or the police. It was my decision. At the time I didn't know that your investigation was going to lead you to Sanchís by another route. Don't look at me like that. When Gil de Partera told me about this business, I thought it best to wait for the police to confirm whether we were facing something relevant to the case or just a simple trading irregularity that would have been beyond the scope of our investigation. If at any given moment the lines had crossed over, of course I would have told you. But you two got ahead of me."

"I can't quite get to the bottom of this matter," said Alicia. "Shares?"

Leandro gestured for her to be patient. "The police continued investigating and found more signs of questionable transactions between Sanchís and Mauricio Valls. Most of them included the purchase of shares and promissory notes from the Banco Hipotecario, purchases that had taken place for almost fifteen years behind the back of the company's board and management. We're talking about significant amounts. Millions. At Gil de Partera's request, or rather, following his orders, I set off for Barcelona last night, where the police were ready to arrest and interrogate Sanchís sometime today or tomorrow, as soon as they had confirmation that Valls had used funds obtained through the fraudulent sale of Banco Hipotecario debt securities to pay off a mortgage he'd taken out against the lands and building works of Villa Mercedes, his private residence in Somosaguas. The technical report from the police suggests that Valls had been blackmailing Sanchís for years to obtain illicit funds stolen from the balance sheet of the bank and its companies—funds that Sanchís had disguised with fictitious transactions between shell companies to hide the identities of the real receivers."

"You're saying that Valls must have blackmailed Sanchís. What with?"

"That's what we're trying to establish right now."

"Are you telling me that all of this is about money?"

"Isn't it almost always?" replied Leandro. "Of course, everything came to a head this morning, when Captain Vargas told me about the result of your investigations."

Alicia threw Vargas another look.

"I've just spoken to Gil de Partera, and we've compared your discoveries with those of the police. Appropriate action has been taken immediately. I'm sorry this happened while you were absent, but it couldn't wait."

Alicia kept looking furiously first at Leandro, then at Vargas.

"Vargas did what he had to do, Alicia," said Leandro. "As a matter of fact, it upsets me to see that you didn't keep me up to date with your investigation as we'd arranged. But I know you, and I know you didn't do it in bad faith—I know you don't like to let the cat out of the bag until you're sure. I don't either. That's why I didn't mention any of this to you until I was quite sure it was connected to our investigation. Quite frankly, I was just as surprised as you to hear about all this. I didn't know you were trailing Sanchís. Like you, I was expecting something else. Had things worked out differently, I would have preferred a few more days to get to the bottom of it before taking action. Unfortunately, this is a case in which we can't afford to take all the time we'd like."

"What have they done with Sanchís?"

"Sanchís is being questioned at the police station as we speak. He's been there for a couple of hours, cooperating with the police."

Alicia put her hands on her temples and closed her eyes, pale as a tombstone. Vargas stood up, poured white wine into a glass, and offered it to her.

"Gil de Partera and all his team have expressed their gratitude and have asked me specifically to congratulate you both for the excellent job and service you have rendered the country," Leandro remarked.

"But . . ."

"Alicia, I beg you. No."

She downed her glass of wine and leaned her head against the wall. "You said that you also had some good news," she said at last.

"That was the good news," Leandro explained. "The bad news is that you and Vargas have been taken off the case. The investigation will now be exclusively in the hands of a new appointment made by the Ministry of the Interior."

"Who?"

Leandro pressed his lips together.

Vargas, who had been silent until now, poured a glass of wine, this time for himself, and looked sadly at Alicia. "Hendaya," he said.

Alicia looked at both men in bewilderment.

"Who the hell is Hendaya?"

3

THE CELL STANK of urine and electricity. Sanchís had never noticed that electricity had a smell—sweetish, metallic, like the odor of spilled blood. The air in the cell was stuffy, saturated with that aroma that made his stomach turn. In a corner the generator buzzed, making the light-bulb vibrate. The bulb dangled from the ceiling, projecting a milky light over damp walls that seemed to be covered in scratches.

Sanchís made an effort to keep his eyes open. By now he could barely feel his arms or his legs, which were tied with wire to the metal chair, so tightly that it cut his skin. "What have you done with my wife?"

"Your wife is safely at home. In perfect health. Who do you think we are?"

"I don't know who you are."

The voice acquired a face, and for the first time Sanchís confronted those crystal-clear, steely eyes, so blue they looked liquid. The face was angular, but with soft features. The man speaking to him looked like a matinee idol, one of those handsome men who well-to-do ladies steal a glance at and feel a rush between their legs. He dressed with extraordinary elegance. Gold cuff links engraved with the eagle of the national shield gleamed on the cuffs of his dry-cleaned shirt.

"We are the law," said the speaker, smiling as if they were good friends.

"In that case, let me go. I've done nothing wrong."

The man, who had drawn up a chair and was sitting opposite Sanchís, nodded sympathetically. Sanchís noticed that there were at least two more people in the cell, leaning against the wall in the shadows.

"My name is Hendaya. I'm sorry we've had to meet in these circumstances, but I like to think that you and I are going to be good friends. Friends respect one another, and don't keep secrets to themselves."

Hendaya gave a nod, and two of his men came over to the chair and began to cut Sanchís's clothes into shreds with a pair of scissors.

"I learned practically everything I know from a great man—Inspector Francisco Javier Fumero, who has a plaque in his name in this building. Fumero was one of those men who are sometimes not fully appreciated. I think this is something that you, Sanchís, my friend, can understand better than most, because the same thing happened to you. Isn't that right?"

Sanchís, who had started to tremble when he saw how his clothes were being snipped off him, stammered out, "I don't . . . know what you—"

Hendaya raised a hand, cutting him off. "We're among friends, Sanchís. Just as I said. We don't need to keep secrets from one another. The good Spaniard has no secrets. And you're a good Spaniard. The trouble is that sometimes people can be spiteful. We must admit it. We're the best country in the world, nobody can doubt that, but occasionally envy gets the better of us. And you know that. All those comments about how you married the boss's daughter, how you married for money, how you didn't deserve being made director general, how this, how that . . . As I say, I understand you. And I understand that when a man's honor and his self-respect are put in doubt, he gets angry. Because when a man's got balls, he gets angry. And you've got them. A good pair of balls."

Sanchís's voice drowned in a howl when the man operating the generator clamped the pincers on his testicles. "Please, don't hurt me, no . . ."

"Don't cry, man, we haven't done anything to you yet. Come on, look at me. Look me in the eye."

Crying like a baby, Sanchís looked up.

Hendaya was smiling at him. "Let's see, Sanchís. I'm your friend. This is just between you and me. No secrets. You help me, and I'll take you home to be with your wife, which is where you should be. Don't cry, man. I don't like to see a Spaniard cry, for fuck's sake. The only people who cry here are those who are holding something back. But we have nothing to hide here, have we? There are no secrets here. Because we're among friends. I know you've got Mauricio Valls. And I understand. Valls is a bastard. Yes, yes. I can say that: I don't have any qualms about saying that. I've seen the documents. I know Valls was forcing you to break the law. Making you sell shares that didn't exist. I don't know much about these things. Can't get my head around all this finance stuff. But even someone as ignorant as me can see that Valls was forcing you to steal for him. I'll tell you clearly: this individual may be a minister, but he's a shit. And believe me, this is something I *do* understand, something I have to see every day. But you know what this country is like. You're valued according to what friends you have. It's like that, I'm afraid. And Valls has lots of friends. The sort of friends who are in charge. But everything has a limit. There comes a point when one has to say: Enough. And you've wanted to take the law into your own hands. Look, I understand. But that's a mistake. That's what we're here for. It's our job. Right now all we want is to find that rogue Valls, so that everything is cleared up. So you can go home to your wife. So that we can put Valls into jail once and for all, and he can answer for what he's done. And so I can go off on holiday—it's high time I did, I tell you. And then we forget about it all. You do understand, don't you?"

Sanchís tried to say something, but his teeth chattered so much the words were incomprehensible.

"What are you saying, Sanchís? If you don't stop shaking, I can't hear what you're saying."

"What shares?" he managed to articulate.

Hendaya sighed. "You disappoint me, Sanchís. I thought we were friends. And one mustn't insult one's friends. This is not going well. I'm making it easy for you because deep down I understand what you've done. Perhaps others wouldn't understand, but I do. Because I know what it's like to have to put up with this sort of rabble who think they're above everything. So I'm going to give you a second chance. Because I like you. But just a bit of advice from a friend: sometimes one has to know when it's not a good idea to get all cocky."

"I don't know what . . . shares you're talking about," stammered Sanchís.

"Stop sniveling, for fuck's sake. Can't you see what an uncomfortable position you're putting me in? I must leave this room with results. It's that simple. You understand that. Basically, it's very straightforward. When life gives it to you up the ass, it's best to pretend you're a faggot. And life is about to fuck you in the backside big-time, my friend. Don't make things difficult for yourself. Men a hundred times tougher than you have sat in this chair and only lasted a quarter of an hour. You're a bit high and mighty. Don't force me to do what I don't want to do. For the last time: tell me where you've got him, and all will be forgotten. You'll be back with your wife tonight, unhurt."

"Please," Sanchís begged, "don't do anything to her. . . . She's not well."

Hendaya sighed and slowly drew closer to Sanchís, until his face was just a few centimeters away. "Look here, you bastard," he said, his tone infinitely colder. "If you don't tell me where Valls is, I'm going to fry your balls until you crap on your mother's memory, and then I'm going to get that little wife of yours and peel the flesh off her bones with a pair of hot pliers, slowly, so she knows that the crybaby she married is to blame for what's happening to her."

Sanchís closed his eyes and whimpered.

Hendaya shrugged and walked over to the generator. "It's your party."

The banker smelled that metallic odor again and felt the vibration on the floor under the soles of his feet. The lightbulb flickered a couple of times. Afterward, all was fire.

4

LEANDRO WAS HOLDING the receiver and nodding. He'd been on the phone for forty-five minutes. Vargas and Alicia were watching him. Between them they'd polished off the bottle of wine. When Alicia got up to look for a new one, Vargas held her back, muttering "No" under his breath. She threw herself into chain-smoking, her eyes glued on Leandro, who listened and nodded slowly.

"I understand. No, of course not. I realize. Yes, sir. I'll tell them. You too."

Leandro put down the phone and gave them a languid look, exuding relief and concern in equal measure.

"That was Gil de Partera," he said at last. "Sanchís has confessed."

"Confessed? To what?" asked Alicia.

"All the pieces are beginning to fall into place. It's been confirmed that the story goes back a long way. It seems that Valls and Miguel Ángel Ubach, the financier, met shortly after the war. At the time Valls was a rising star in the regime, having proved his loyalty and reliability while running Montjuïc Prison, not exactly a pleasant job. Apparently, through a consortium set up to reward individuals who had made an outstanding contribution to the national cause, Ubach handed Valls a package of shares from the reconstituted Banco Hipotecario, which grouped together various financial institutions that had been dissolved after the war."

"You're talking about the looting and dividing up of the booty," Alicia cut in.

Leandro gave a patient sigh. "Be careful, Alicia. Not everyone is as broad-minded and tolerant as me."

Alicia bit her tongue. Leandro waited to catch her submissive look before he continued. "In January 1949 Valls was due to receive another package of shares. That had been the arrangement, made verbally. But because Ubach had died unexpectedly in an accident the year before—"

"What accident?" interrupted Alicia.

"A fire in his home, in which he and his wife died while they slept. Don't interrupt me, Alicia, please. As I said, when Ubach died, certain discrepancies arose concerning his will, which apparently didn't mention those arrangements. The matter became complicated because the executor named by Ubach was a young lawyer who worked in the practice that represented him."

"Ignacio Sanchís," said Alicia.

Leandro threw her a warning look. "Yes, Ignacio Sanchís. As his executor, Sanchís also became the legal guardian of Victoria Ubach, the couple's daughter, until she came of age. And yes, before you interrupt me yet again, when Victoria was nineteen he married her, which provoked much gossip and a bit of a scandal. Rumor had it that Victoria and her future husband already had an illicit relationship when she was in her teens. People also said that Ignacio Sanchís was just an ambitious upstart, since the will left most of the Ubachs' estate to Victoria, and there was a considerable age gap between them. Besides, Victoria Ubach had a history of emotional instability. They say that when she was still very young, she ran away from home and disappeared for six months. But that's just gossip. What really matters in all this is that when Sanchís took over the running of the Banca Ubach on behalf of the shareholders, he refused to give Valls what he claimed was owed to him, promised by the deceased. At that moment Valls had to sheathe his sword, as they say, and keep his mouth shut. It wasn't until years later, when he'd been made a minister and acquired a considerable amount of power, that he decided to force Sanchís to hand over what he considered his, and more. He threatened to accuse Sanchís of having been involved in Victoria's 'disappearance' in 1948 to hide the pregnancy of a minor, and of having kept her hidden in a private clinic on the Costa Brava—near San Feliu de Guíxols, I believe—where the Civil Guard found her about four months later, wandering along the beach, confused and showing signs of malnutrition. Everything seems to point to the fact that Sanchís gave in. Through a number of illegal operations, Sanchís gave Valls a very large sum in shares and negotiable notes from the Banco Hipotecario. A large amount of Valls's estate came from there, and not from his father-in-law, as had sometimes been suggested. But Valls wanted more. He kept putting pressure on Sanchís, who never forgave him for having involved his wife Victoria, making use of her reputation and her adolescent escapade to get what he wanted. Sanchís tried to protest and approached different bodies, but everyone closed the door on him, saying Valls was too powerful, too close to the top of the regime to touch. Besides, to do so would have implied stirring up the matter of the rewards distributed at the end of the war, something nobody wished to do. Sanchís was warned very seriously to forget all about it."

"Which he didn't do."

"Evidently not. Not only did he not forget, but he decided to take revenge. And that's where he made a real mistake. He hired investigators to poke around into Valls's past. That's how they came across Sebastián Salgado, a rogue who was still rotting away in Montjuïc Prison, and also discovered a series of shady incidents and abuses Valls committed against a number of inmates and their families during his years as prison governor. There turned out to be a long list of possible candidates to take the lead in a supposed revenge against Valls. The only thing missing was a convincing narrative. So Sanchís devised a plot to avenge himself on the minister, by manufacturing what would look like a political or personal vendetta stemming from the minister's dark past. He began to send threatening letters through Salgado, whom he had offered a sum of money for acting, so to speak, as bait—money he would receive after obtaining the pardon that was being processed for him. Sanchís knew the letters would be tracked, and that the tracking would lead to Salgado. He also hired a former Montjuïc prisoner, someone called Valentín Morgado, who had more than enough reasons not to feel the slightest affection for Valls. Morgado had been released in 1945, but he blamed Valls for his wife's death from an illness while he'd been imprisoned. Morgado was hired as a chauffeur for the family. It was Morgado—with the help of an old prison guard, a guy called Bebo, who received a considerable amount of money from Sanchís, as well as a low-rent flat in Pueblo Seco, owned by Metrobarna—who supplied his benefactor with information concerning the prisoners most severely punished by Valls during his years in Montjuïc. One of them, David Martín, a writer with serious mental problems known to the other inmates as the Prisoner of Heaven, turned out to be the ideal candidate for Sanchís's plot. It seems that Martín had disappeared under strange circumstances after Valls ordered two of his men to take him to a large house near Güell Park and murder him. Martín, who had lost his mind completely while in solitary confinement in one of the towers of the castle, managed to escape, and Valls always feared that one day he would return to take his revenge, because he blamed Valls for the murder of a woman called Isabella Gispert. Are you following me?"

Alicia nodded.

"Sanchís planned to convince Valls of the existence of a conspiracy to make public his abuses and crimes against prisoners under his governorship. The hidden hand behind it all would be Martín's, and that of other former prisoners. They wanted to make him nervous, force him to come out of the cocoon of protection his position afforded and confront them in person. The only way he could silence them would be to destroy them before they destroyed him."

"But it was all just a trap," Alicia pointed out.

"A perfect trap, because when the police investigated, they would discover the components of personal revenge and financial chicanery that Valls himself had taken care to cover up. And Salgado was the perfect bait. He could be easily linked to other prisoners, and in particular to David Martín, the supposed hidden hand in the shadows. Even so, Valls kept his sangfroid for years. But after the alleged 1956 attempt perpetrated by Morgado in the Círculo de Bellas Artes in Madrid, Valls began to lose his cool. He arranged for Salgado to be released so he could follow him, hoping he'd lead him to Martín; but Salgado was eliminated—the ex-prisoner died just when he thought he was about to recover some old booty he'd left hidden in one of the lockers of the Estación del Norte, shortly before being arrested in 1939. Salgado was no longer useful, and silencing him would leave a dead trail.

"Valls also committed a number of important slips that created false trails. He forced Pablo Cascos, an employee in one of his companies, Editorial Ariadna, to contact a member of the Sempere family with whom Cascos had had a relationship, namely Beatriz Aguilar. The Semperes are the owners of a secondhand bookshop that Valls thought Martín may have been using as a shelter. They may even have been Martín's accomplices, since Martín had had some sort of relationship with Isabella Gispert, the late wife of the bookshop's owner and mother of Daniel Sempere, the present manager and Beatriz's husband. And yes, now you can interrupt me again, before you have a fit."

"What about Mataix's books? How do you explain the presence of the book I found hidden in Valls's desk—which, as his daughter Mercedes said, was the last thing he consulted before disappearing?"

"As part of the same strategy. Mataix had been a friend and colleague of Martín's, and a prisoner in Montjuïc. Bit by bit the pressure, the threats, and his imaginings of a conspiracy in the shadows got the better of Valls. He decided to go in person to Barcelona, together with his trusted man Vicente, to confront the man he believed to be his nemesis, David Martín. The police suppose—and I agree with them—that Valls thought he was going to a clandestine meeting with Martín, where he could get rid of him once and for all."

"But Martín had been dead for years, like Mataix."

"Exactly. The people waiting for him were, in fact, Sanchís and Morgado."

"Wouldn't it have been easier for Valls to let the police take charge of David Martín, if he thought Martín was alive?"

"Yes, but Martín might reveal information on the death of Isabella Gispert, among other things, destroying Valls's reputation."

"That makes sense, I suppose. And then?"

"Once they'd caught him, Sanchís and Morgado moved Valls to the old Castells factory in Pueblo Nuevo, which has been closed for years but belongs to the property consortium of Metrobarna. Sanchís has confessed that they tortured him for hours and then got rid of his body in one of the factory ovens. While I was talking to Gil de Partera, he received confirmation that the police had found remains of bones that they think could belong to Valls. They've requested Valls's dental X-rays, to check whether the remains are in fact those of the minister. I imagine we'll know either tonight or tomorrow morning."

"So the case is closed?"

Leandro nodded. "The part that concerns us, at least. It still remains to be seen whether there were other accomplices, and how far-reaching the implications of Ignacio Sanchís's plot were."

"And will this be reported to the press?"

Leandro smiled. "Of course not. At this very moment there's a meeting in the Ministry of the Interior to determine what will be announced and how. I don't know any more details."

A long silence ensued, barely interrupted by the sound of Leandro as he sipped his tea, his eyes fixed on Alicia's.

"All this is a mistake," she murmured at last.

Leandro shrugged. "Perhaps. But it's no longer in our hands. The task that was required of us—to track down Valls's whereabouts—has been accomplished. And it has produced results."

"That's not true," protested Alicia.

"That's how it is perceived by voices with more authority than mine and, needless to say, than yours, Alicia. We have to know when to let go of things. All we need do now is remain discreet and let matters take their natural course."

"Señor Montalvo is right, Alicia," said Vargas. "There's nothing more we can do."

"It seems like we've done enough already," said Alicia coldly.

Leandro shook his head disapprovingly. "Captain, would you mind giving us a couple of minutes?"

Vargas stood up. "Of course. In fact, I'm going to go over to my rooms on the other side of the street to call police headquarters and get my orders."

"I think that's an excellent idea."

Vargas avoided Alicia's eyes as he walked past her. He held out his hand to Leandro, who shook it amiably.

"Thanks so much for your help, Captain. And for taking such good care of my Alicia. I am greatly indebted to you. Don't hesitate to knock on my door if you ever need my help with anything."

Vargas nodded and left discreetly. Once they were alone, Leandro beckoned Alicia to come and sit next to him on the sofa. She obeyed reluctantly.

"A great man, Vargas," he said.

"And with an even greater mouth."

"Don't be unfair. He's proved he's a good policeman. I like him."

"I think he's single."

"Alicia, Alicia . . ." Leandro put a fatherly arm around her shoulders, with a hint of an embrace. "Go on, let it out before you explode. Get it out of your system."

"All this is a pile of shit."

Affectionately, Leandro drew her toward him. "I agree. It's a botched job. It's not the way you and I do things, but in the ministry they were getting very nervous. And El Pardo sent the message that enough is enough. It's better this way. I wouldn't have liked it if they'd started to think or say that we were the ones who weren't getting results."

"What about Lomana? Has he reappeared?"

"Not for the moment, no."

"It's odd."

"It is. But it's one of the loose ends that is sure to be resolved in the next few days."

"There are lots of loose ends," Alicia pointed out.

"Not that many. The Sanchís bit is pretty solid. A well-documented matter involving a lot of money and a personal betrayal. We have a confession and proof to support it. It all adds up."

"Apparently."

"Gil de Partera, the minister of the interior, and El Pardo all think the case has been resolved."

Alicia opened her mouth to say something, but closed it again.

"This is what you wanted, Alicia. Don't you see?"

"What I wanted?"

Leandro looked at her sadly. "Your freedom. To get rid of me, of the wicked Leandro, forever. To disappear."

"Do you mean it?"

"I gave you my word. That was the deal. One last case. And then your freedom. Why do you think I've come to Barcelona? All this could have been settled over the phone without leaving the Gran Hotel Palace. You know how much I dislike traveling."

"Then why did you come?"

"To tell you face-to-face. And to say that I'm your friend, and always will be." Leandro took her hand and smiled. "You're free, Alicia. Free forever."

Her eyes filled with tears. Despite herself, she hugged Leandro.

"Whatever happens," said her mentor, "whatever you do, I want you to know that I'll always be there. For whatever you may need. No obligations or commitments. The ministry has authorized me to transfer one hundred and fifty thousand pesetas, which will be in your account by the end of this week. I know you're not going to need me or miss me, but if it's not too much to ask, call me every now and then, even if it's only at Christmas. Will you do that?"

Alicia nodded. Leandro kissed her on the forehead and stood up.

"My train leaves in an hour. I'd better make a start for the station. Don't come to see me off. I won't hear of it. I don't like scenes, as you know."

She walked with him to the door. Just as he was leaving, Leandro turned. For the first time in her life, she thought he suddenly looked shy and embarrassed.

"I've never told you what I'm about to say, because I didn't know whether I had a right to do so, but I think I can now. I have loved you and I love you like a daughter, Alicia. Perhaps I haven't known how to be the best of fathers, but you've been the greatest happiness in my life. I want you to be happy. And that, truly, is my last order."

5

SHE WANTED TO believe him. She wanted to believe him with the yearning that comes with the suspicion that truth hurts, and that cowards live longer and better, even if they do so in the prison of their own lies.

She looked out the window to watch Leandro walk over to the car waiting for him on the corner. A driver with dark glasses held the door open for him. It was one of those huge black cars, tanks with tinted windows and a cryptic license plate that were sometimes seen plowing though the traffic like hearses; the sort everyone moved out of the way to avoid because they knew, without having to ask, that they didn't carry normal people, and the best thing was to step aside. Before he got into the car, Leandro turned around for a second, looked up toward her window, and waved. When Alicia tried to swallow, she found that her mouth was dry. She wanted to believe him.

She spent an hour chain-smoking, walking up and down the apartment like a caged animal. More than once, more than ten times, she went over to the window to scan the other side of the street, hoping to see Vargas in his rooms above the Gran Café. There was no sign of him. He'd had plenty of time to call Madrid and receive his orders. He had probably gone out for a stroll, to clear his head, walking through that Barcelona to which he would soon say good-bye. The last thing he must have wanted right then was to be in Alicia's company and run the risk of having his eyes pulled out for having told Leandro everything.

He had no option.

She would have liked to believe that too.

As soon as Leandro left, she'd started to feel a stabbing pain in her hip. At first she'd ignored it, but now she could feel a dull ache throbbing with her pulse. It felt as if someone was trying to nail a picture hook into her by gently hitting it with a hammer. She could imagine the tip of the metal scratching the bone's surface and slowly digging in. She swallowed half a pill with another glass of wine and lay down on the sofa to wait for the drug to take effect. She knew she was drinking too much. She didn't need Vargas or Leandro to look at her and remind her. She could feel it in her blood and in her breath. But it was the only thing that calmed her anxiety.

*

Alicia closed her eyes and began to go over Leandro's account. He himself had taught her, when she was barely a child, to always listen and read with the headlights on. "The eloquence of an explanation," he had told her, "is directly proportional to the intelligence of the person expressing it, in the same way as its credibility is proportional to the stupidity of the person listening to it."

Sanchís's confession, in the version recounted by Gil de Partera to Leandro, was perfect at first sight, especially as it didn't seem perfect. It explained almost everything that had taken place yet left a few loose ends, as usually occurs with the most credible explanations. Truth is never perfect, never squares with all expectations. Truth always poses doubts and questions. Only lies are one hundred percent believable, because they don't need to justify reality, they simply have to tell us what we want to hear.

Fifteen minutes later the pill began to act. Slowly the pain lessened, until all Alicia felt was a sharp prickling she was used to ignoring. She stretched an arm under the sofa and pulled out the storage box containing the files they'd stolen from Brians's furniture warehouse. She couldn't help smiling at the thought that Leandro had spent the morning resting his illustrious bum on that information, without realizing. She had a quick look through the folders inside the box. Much of it, or the bit that mattered, had already been incorporated into the official narrative of the case. As she rummaged around the bottom of the box, however, she recovered the envelope with just the word ISABELLA on it in longhand. She opened it and pulled out a notebook. A piece of fine cardboard slid off the first page.

It was an old photograph, beginning to fade around the edges. The image showed a young girl with fair hair and lively eyes who smiled at the camera, her whole life ahead of her. Something about that face reminded Alicia of the young man she'd passed on her way out of the Sempere & Sons bookshop. She turned it over and immediately recognized Brians's handwriting:

Isabella

Even the strokes in each letter and the way Brians had avoided adding the surname spoke of a strong feeling. It was not only guilt that was eating away at the defender of lost causes, but also desire. She left the photograph on the table and flicked through the notebook. All the pages were written in a clean, distinct writing that was obviously feminine. Only women write this clearly, without hiding behind absurd flourishes—at least when they're writing for themselves and for nobody else. Alicia turned back to the first page and began to read:

My name is Isabella Gispert, and I was born in Barcelona in 1917. I'm twenty-two years old and I know I will never reach my twenty-third birthday. I write these words knowing for certain that I only have a few days left to live, and that I will soon have to leave behind those to whom I am most indebted in this world: my son Daniel and my husband Juan Sempere, the kindest man I have ever known. I will die without having merited all the trust, love, and devotion he has given me. I'm writing for myself, taking with me secrets that don't belong to me and knowing that nobody will ever read these pages. I'm writing to reminisce and to cling to life. My only wish is to be able to remember and understand who I was and why I did what I did while I am still able to do so, and before the consciousness that I already feel weakening abandons me forever. I'm writing even if it hurts, because loss and pain are the only things that keep me alive, and I'm afraid of dying. I'm writing to tell these pages what I can't tell those I love, for fear of hurting them and putting their lives in danger. I'm writing because as long as I'm able to remember, I will be with them one more minute . . .

For a whole hour Alicia lost herself in the pages of that notebook, oblivious to the world, the pain, or the uncertainty in which Leandro's visit had left her. For an hour, all that existed was the story told by those words, a story that, even before she reached the last page, she knew she would never forget. When she came to the end and closed Isabella's confession over her chest, her eyes were veiled with tears, and all she could do was take a hand to her lips and suppress a scream.

*

This is how Fernandito found her, a little later. After knocking a few times on the door and getting no reply, he stepped in and saw her curled up into a ball, crying like he'd never seen anyone cry before. He didn't know what to do except kneel down and put his arms around her, while Alicia moaned with pain as if someone had set fire to her heart.

6

SOME FOLKS JUST can't win, Fernandito told himself. He'd spent years dreaming about holding Alicia in his arms, and when at long last it happened, the resulting scene proved to be the saddest he could ever have imagined. He propped her up and stroked her head gently, trying to calm her down, not able to think what else to do or say. He had never seen her like that. In fact, he'd never imagined her like that. In all the fantasies Fernandito had placed over the years on the private altar of his adolescent yearnings, Alicia Gris was always indestructible, hard as a diamond that cut through everything.

When at last she stopped sobbing and looked up, Fernandito encountered a broken Alicia, her eyes reddened and her smile so fragile it looked as if she was going to splinter into a thousand pieces of glass.

"Are you feeling better?" he murmured,

Alicia looked into his eyes and, without warning, kissed him on the lips.

Fernandito, who felt a fire lighting up entire provinces of his body and soul he didn't know existed, stopped her. "Señorita Alicia, I don't think this is what you want to do now. You're confused."

She lowered her face and licked her lips. Fernandito knew he would carry that image etched on his brain to the grave and possibly beyond.

"I'm sorry, Fernandito," she said, getting up.

He also got to his feet and then offered her a chair, which Alicia accepted.

"This will stay between us, all right?"

"Of course," he said, thinking that even if he'd tried, he wouldn't have known what or whom to tell.

Alicia looked around her, and her eyes paused on a box filled with bottles and food, standing in the middle of the dining room.

"It's your order," Fernandito explained. "I thought it would be best if I showed up with the shopping, in case the gentleman who was here before was still around."

Alicia smiled and nodded. "What do I owe you?"

"It's on the house. They didn't have Perelada, but I brought you a Priorato, which according to Manolo is fabulous. I don't know much about wine. Although, if I may volunteer a suggestion—"

"I shouldn't drink so much. I know. Thank you, Fernandito."

"May I ask what happened?"

Alicia shrugged. "I'm not sure."

"But you're better, aren't you? Say you're feeling better."

"Much better, thanks to you."

Fernandito, who wasn't sure whether to believe her, simply nodded. "Actually, I'd come to tell you what I've found out," he said.

Alicia looked at him questioningly.

"About the guy you asked me to follow," he explained. "Sanchís?"

"I'd forgotten about that. I think we might be too late, I'm afraid."

"Are you saying that because of the arrest?"

"Did you see him being arrested?"

Fernandito nodded. "Early this morning, I planted myself opposite his offices on Paseo de Gracia, just as you said. There was a nice old-timer there, a street painter, and when he saw me watching the front door, he told me to give Captain Vargas his regards. Does he also work for you?"

"He's an independent operator—an artist. And what happened?"

"I recognized Sanchís because he came out wearing a very fine suit, and the painter told me that yes, he was the individual in question. He got into a taxi, and I followed him on the Vespa to the Bonanova district. He lives in a house on Calle Iradier, one of those that sweep you off your feet. He must have a good eye for business, because that area is pricey as hell, and the house—"

"He has a good eye for marriages," said Alicia.

"Right. Lucky him. Well, the thing is that soon after he arrived, a car and a police van turned up, and a whole lot of cops filed out. There were at least seven or eight of them. They looked like very bad news. First they surrounded the house, and then one of them, dressed rather fancy for a cop, rang the doorbell."

"And while all that was going on, where were you?"

"Under cover. On the other side of the street there's a large house where they're doing some construction, and it's easy to hide. You see, I take precautions."

"And then?"

"A few minutes later they took Sanchís out, handcuffed and in his shirtsleeves. He was protesting, but one of the cops hit him behind his knees with a billy club, and they dragged him to the van. I was going to follow them, but I got the impression that the fancy-dressed cop was giving the large old house the evil eye, like he could smell me. The van sped off really fast, but the car stayed behind. They moved it farther up the street, so it couldn't be seen from the house. Just in case, I decided to stay put and out of sight."

"You did the right thing. In that sort of situation, never push it. If you lose the trail, you lose it. Better that than losing your head."

"That's what I thought. My father always says that once you lose your ass, the rest follows starting with your head."

"Wise words."

"The thing is, I was beginning to get rather nervous. I was wondering whether I should leave when a second car drove up to the front door of the house. A very flashy Mercedes. An odd-looking fellow got out."

"Odd-looking?"

"Plain weird. He wore some kind of mask, as if he was missing half his face, or something like that."

"Morgado."

"You know him?"

"That's Sanchís's chauffeur."

Fernandito nodded, all enthusiastic again, sharing the mysteries of his adored Alicia. "I thought he might be. He was dressed for the part. So, he got out of the car and went into the house. A bit later he came out again, this time accompanied by a lady."

"What was she like?"

"Young. Like you."

"Do I look young to you?"

Fernandito gulped. "Don't tease me now. As I said, she was young. Not more than thirty, but she dressed as if she were older. Like a rich lady. Since I didn't know who she was, I gave her a technical nickname: Myrna Loy, you know, like the one in the movies?"

"Is that your type?"

"Stop it."

"You weren't far off, anyway. Her name is Victoria Ubach, or Sanchís. She's the wife of the banker they arrested."

"I knew it. These crooks always marry someone much younger and much richer."

"You know what you must do, then."

"I'd be useless at that sort of thing. But going back to the events: they both got into the Mercedes. She sat in the front, next to the driver, and I found that odd. As soon as they drove off, the other police car started to follow them."

"And you behind them."

"Of course."

"How far did you follow them?"

"Not far from there. The Mercedes went into a whole lot of narrow, elegant streets—the sort that smell of eucalyptus trees, where you only see maids and gardeners passing by—until we got to Cuatro Caminos, and from there to Avenida del Tibidabo. I was almost ironed flat by the blue tram."

"You should wear a helmet."

"I've got a US army regulation helmet that I bought at the Encantes flea market. It looks great on me. I've written 'Private Fernandito' on it, with a thick felt-tip pen—"

"Get to the point, Fernandito."

"Sorry. I followed them up Avenida del Tibidabo, up to where the tram line ends."

"They were going to the funicular stop?"

"No. The chauffeur and Myrna—Señora . . . Ubach—continued along the street that goes around it, and then the car drove into the house that's on that hill, just above the avenue, the one that looks like a fairy-tale castle and you can see from all over the place. It's got to be the prettiest house in all of Barcelona."

"It is. It's called El Pinar," said Alicia, who remembered having seen it a thousand times as a child when she was allowed out of the orphanage on Sundays, and liked to imagine herself living there in the company of a huge library and a night view of the city at her feet, spreading like a magic carpet sown with stars. "What about the police?"

"In the police car there were two dog-faced thugs. One of them posted himself by the front door of the house while the other went into La Venta restaurant to make a phone call. I waited there for almost an hour, but there were no movements whatsoever. In the end, when one of the officers gave me a look I didn't like, I came back to tell you what had happened and await your orders."

"You've done a stellar job, Fernandito. You clearly have what it takes for this business."

"Do you think so?"

"I'm going to promote you with immediate effect from Private Fernandito to what in English is called a corporal."

"And what is that?"

"Pull out a dictionary, Fernandito. People who don't learn languages have their brains turned into cauliflower mush."

"The things you know. . . . What are your orders, then?"

Alicia thought for a few seconds. "I want you to change your clothes, into something dark, and put on a cap. Then you go back there and keep watch. But leave the Vespa parked farther away, just in case the policeman who looked at you recognizes it."

"I'll leave it next to the Hotel La Rotonda and then take the blue tram up."

"Good idea. Then try to see what's going on inside the house, but don't take any risks. None whatsoever. At the slightest hint that someone may have noticed you, leg it. Understood?"

"Yessir."

"Come back in two or three hours and give me an update."

Fernandito rose to his feet, ready to resume his duties. "And meanwhile, what are you going to do?"

Alicia made a gesture that seemed to imply she was going to do a pile of things, or none at all.

"You won't go and do something silly, will you?" said Fernandito.

"What makes you say that?"

The boy looked at her rather anxiously from the door. "I don't know."

This time Fernandito went down the stairs slowly, every step feeling like a reproach. Alone again, Alicia returned Isabella's notebook to the box under the sofa. She stepped into the bathroom and splashed her face with cold water, then took off the clothes she was wearing and opened the wardrobe.

She chose a tight black dress that, in Fernandito's estimation, would have made Myrna Loy green with envy. On her twenty-second birthday—Isabella's age at the time of her death—Leandro had told Alicia he would give her whatever she wanted. She had asked for that dress, which she'd been admiring for two months in a boutique on Calle Rosellón, and a matching pair of black suede French shoes. Leandro had spent a fortune without complaining. The saleswoman, who didn't dare inquire whether Alicia was his daughter or his lover, told him that few women could carry off a dress like that one. After leaving the boutique, Leandro took Alicia to dinner at La Puñalada. Almost all the tables were taken by what one could charitably call businessmen, who drooled like hounds when they saw her walk by and then gazed enviously at Leandro. "They're looking at you like that because they think you're an expensive hooker," said Leandro before toasting to her health.

She hadn't worn that dress again until that afternoon. As she made up her character in front of the mirror, outlining her eyes and letting her lipstick accentuate her lips, Alicia smiled maliciously. "After all, that's what you are," she told herself. "A very expensive hooker."

When she stepped out into the street, she told herself she was just going to stroll around aimlessly. But deep down she knew that Fernandito was right. Perhaps she was going to do something really silly.

7

THAT AFTERNOON, IGNORING common sense, Alicia walked down the stairs with an inkling of where her feet would take her. The shops on Calle Fernando were already lit up, shedding strokes of color on the pavement. A scarlet halo faded in the sky, outlining cornices and rooftops high above the street. People came and went on their way to the metro station, their daily shopping, or their ticket to oblivion. Alicia joined the flow of pedestrians toward the City Hall square, where she passed a squadron of nuns flocking in perfect formation. She smiled at them, and one nun crossed herself at the sight of her. She continued navigating the river of walkers along a street bordering the walls of the cathedral.

There she walked under the papier-mâché Gothic bridge, letting herself be enveloped, as the tourists were, by the charm of that medieval-looking citadel, a set design most of which was barely ten years older than her. Past the bridge, a photographer on the hunt for liquid shadows had mounted a fabulous Hasselblad on a tripod and was framing the perfect composition and exposure for the fairy-tale image. He was a severe-looking individual with shrewd eyes hiding behind enormous square glasses, which conferred on him the air of a wise, patient turtle.

The photographer became aware of her presence and gazed at her with curiosity. "Would you like to look through the lens, mademoiselle?"

Alicia nodded timidly. The photographer showed her how to do it. She peeped into the artist's eyes and laughed at the perfect artifice of shadows and perspectives he'd created, reinventing a corner she had passed by hundreds or thousands of times in her life.

"The eye sees; the camera observes," the photographer explained. "Like it?"

"It's astonishing," Alicia admitted.

"This is just the composition and the perspective. The secret is in the light. You must look through the lens, imagining there will be a liquid glow. The shadow will be tinged by a soft, evanescent layer, as if it had been raining light . . ."

The photographer had all the hallmarks of a true professional, and Alicia wondered where that image would end up.

The turtle of the magic light read her thoughts. "It's for my book," he explained. "What's your name?"

"Alicia."

"Don't be alarmed, but I'd like to take a picture of you, Alicia."

"Of me? Why?"

"Because you're a creature of light and shadow, like this city. What do you say?"

"Here? Now?"

"No. Not now. Something on your mind is weighing you down today, and doesn't allow you to be yourself. And the camera would pick that up. At least, mine would. I want to take a picture of you when you've taken that load off your mind and the light can see you as you are, not as you've been made to be."

Alicia blushed for the first and last time in her life. She had never felt so naked as she did, facing the eyes of that peculiar character.

"Think about it," said the photographer. He pulled a card out of his jacket pocket and handed it to her with a smile.

FRANCESC CATALÁ-ROCA
Photographic Studio since 1947

Calle Provenza 366, Ground Floor. Barcelona

Alicia put the card away and hurried off, leaving the master alone with his art and his keen eye. Hiding among the crowds teeming around the cathedral area, she pressed on, walking straight up Puerta del Ángel until she reached Calle Santa Ana and could see the window of the Sempere & Sons bookshop.

You're still in time not to ruin everything. Walk past and keep walking.

She positioned herself on the other side of the street, taking shelter in a doorway from which she could see inside the shop. The somber blue evening of a Barcelona winter was falling over the city, an invitation to defy the cold and wander through the streets.

Leave this place. What do you think you can do?

She caught sight of Bea helping a customer. Next to her stood an older man who Alicia guessed must be her father-in-law, Señor Sempere. Little Julián was sitting on the counter, leaning on the cash register, engrossed in a book that he held over his knees, a book almost bigger than him. Alicia smiled.

Suddenly Daniel emerged from the back room, carrying a pile of books that he left on the counter. Julián raised his head and looked at his father, who ruffled his hair. The boy said something, and Daniel laughed. He leaned over and kissed the boy's forehead.

You have no right to be here. This is not your life, and this isn't your family. Clear off and crawl back to the hole you came out of.

She observed Daniel as he sorted out the books he'd left on the counter. He was separating them into three different piles, almost stroking them as he dusted them and lined them up neatly. She wondered what the touch of those hands and those lips would be like. She forced herself to turn her head and move away a few steps. Was it indeed her duty, or her right, to reveal what she knew to people who surely would live more happily in blissful ignorance? Happiness, or the closest to it any moderately intelligent creature can aspire to, spiritual peace, is what evaporates on the way between belief and knowledge.

One last look. To say good-bye. Good-bye forever.

Before she even realized it, she was standing opposite the shop window again. She was about to leave when she noticed that little Julián was watching her, as if he'd smelled her presence. Alicia stood motionless in the middle of the street, the people walking past dodging her as if she were a statue. With considerable skill, Julián clambered off the counter, using a stool as a step. Without his parents noticing—Daniel was wrapping up the books, and Bea, together with her father-in-law, was still with the customer—Julián walked across the shop to the door and opened it. He stood in the doorway looking at Alicia, grinning from ear to ear. Alicia shook her head. Julián started to walk over to her. By then Daniel had realized what was happening, and his lips formed his son's name. Bea turned around and rushed into the street. Julián had reached Alicia's feet and was hugging her. She took him in her arms, and that is how Bea and Daniel found them.

"Señorita Gris?" asked Bea, midway between surprise and alarm. All the kindness and warmth Alicia had perceived in Bea the day they'd met seemed to have disappeared the moment Bea saw that stranger with her son in her arms.

Alicia handed the boy to Bea and swallowed hard. Bea hugged Julián tightly and took a deep breath. Daniel, who was looking at Alicia with a mixture of fascination and hostility, took a step forward and stood between her and his family.

"Who are you?"

"It's Señorita Alicia Gris," Bea explained behind him. "She's a customer."

Daniel gave a nod, but a shadow of a doubt fell on his face.

"I'm very sorry. I didn't mean to scare you. The boy must have recognized me, and . . ."

Julián was still staring at her, mesmerized, unaware of his parents' concern. To make matters worse, Señor Sempere looked out of the shop door. "Have I missed something?" he said.

"Nothing, Dad, just that Julián almost got away . . ."

"It's my fault," said Alicia.

"And you are . . ."

"Alicia Gris."

"The lady who placed the big order? But please, come in, it's cold outside."

"In fact, I was just leaving . . ."

"I won't hear of it. Besides, I see you've already made friends with my grandson. Don't imagine he'll go off with just anyone. Not at all."

Señor Sempere held the door open and invited Alicia in. She exchanged glances with Daniel, who nodded, looking calmer now.

"Come in, Alicia," Bea agreed.

Julián held a hand out to her.

"As you can see, you have no choice now," said Granddad Sempere.

Alicia smiled and stepped into the shop. The perfume of books enveloped her. Bea had put Julián down on the floor. The child grabbed her hand and led her to the counter.

"He's quite taken with you," remarked the grandfather. "Tell me, have we met before?"

"I used to come here when I was a child, with my father."

Sempere gazed at her. "Gris? Juan Antonio Gris?"

Alicia nodded.

"Good heavens! I can't believe it. . . . It must be years since I last saw him and his wife! They used to come by almost every week. . . . Tell me, how are they?"

Alicia felt her mouth go dry. "They died. During the war."

Grandfather Sempere sighed. "I'm so sorry. I didn't know."

Alicia tried to smile.

"So you have no family left?"

Alicia shook her head. Daniel noticed the young woman's eyes shining with tears. "Dad, don't interrogate her," he said.

Granddad Sempere looked crestfallen. "Your father was a great man. And a good friend."

"Thank you," murmured Alicia, barely able to speak. An overlong silence ensued.

Daniel came to the rescue. "Would you like a drink? It's my father's birthday today, and we're inviting all our customers to a glass of liqueur from Fermín's vintage cellar."

"I don't recommend it," whispered Bea behind Alicia's back.

"By the way, where's Fermín gone?" asked the granddad. "Shouldn't he be back by now?"

"He should be," said Bea. "I sent him to get the champagne for the dinner, but since he refuses to go to Don Dionisio's grocery, he's wandered off to some dive near the Borne. He says that Dionisio mixes rancid church wine with soda and a few drops of cat pee to give it color. And I'm tired of arguing with him."

"Don't be alarmed," said the grandfather, turning to Alicia. "Our Fermín is like that. When he was young, Dionisio was a member of the Falangist Party, and Fermín is always having a go at him. He'd rather die of thirst than buy a bottle of anything from him."

"Happy birthday." Alicia smiled.

"Listen, I'm sure you'll say no, but . . . why don't you stay and have dinner with us? There'll be a big group, but . . . for me it would be an honor to have the daughter of Juan Antonio Gris among us tonight."

Alicia looked at Daniel, who smiled weakly.

"Thank you so much, but—"

Julián gripped her hand.

"As you can see, my grandson insists. Go on, say you'll stay. We'll be among family."

Alicia looked down and shook her head slowly. She felt Bea's hand on her back and heard her whisper, "Stay."

"I don't know what to say . . ."

"Don't say anything. Julián, why don't you show Señorita Alicia your first book? Wait till you see this . . ."

Julián ran off to look for a notebook he had smudged with drawings, scribbles, and incomprehensible inscriptions. He showed it to her enthusiastically.

"His first novel," said Daniel.

Julián looked at her expectantly.

"It looks great . . ."

The child clapped, happy with the critical reception. Grandfather Sempere, who must have been the same age her father would have been had he lived, glanced at Alicia with the sad look that seemed to have followed him through life. "Welcome to the Sempere family, Alicia."

8

THE BLUE TRAM climbed slowly, a small raft of golden light making its way like a ship through the night mist. Fernandito traveled on the back platform. He'd left his Vespa parked next to the Hotel La Rotonda. He saw it fade in the distance and then looked out to face the long avenue of mansions that flanked the route, deserted castles sheltered by small woods, fountains, and gardens of statues, where nobody was ever to be seen. Great fortunes are never at home.

At the top of the avenue loomed the silhouette of El Pinar through slivers of low clouds. Towers, gables, and lines of serrated dormer windows crowned a forbidding vision resting on a hill from which the whole of Barcelona could be seen. On a clear day you could probably make out the island of Mallorca from that hilltop, thought Fernandito. That night, however, a thick blanket of darkness shrouded the house.

Fernandito gulped. The mission Alicia had entrusted him with was beginning to make him apprehensive. According to an uncle of his who had lost an arm and an eye in the war, one can only be a hero when one is genuinely afraid. Someone who faces danger fearlessly is just an idiot. Fernandito wasn't sure whether Alicia was expecting him to be a hero or a simpleton. Perhaps a subtle combination of both, he concluded. The salary was unbeatable, granted, but the image of Alicia weeping inconsolably in his arms would have been enough to make him tiptoe into hell, and even pay for it.

*

The tram dropped him off at the top of the avenue and vanished again in the mist, its lights fading on the downward journey like a hazy mirage. The small square was deserted at that late hour. A solitary streetlamp barely revealed the shape of two black cars parked outside the La Venta restaurant. Police, thought Fernandito. He heard the drone of an approaching vehicle and rushed to find a dark spot near the funicular station. Soon he caught sight of headlights cutting through the night. The car, which he identified as a Ford, stopped only a few meters from where he was hiding.

Out of the car emerged one of the two men he'd seen that very morning arresting Sanchís, the banker. Something made him different from the rest. He exuded a classy air, a dash of high breeding and refined manners. He was dressed like a gentleman at a fine cigar club, in the sort of formal attire one saw in shop windows such as Gales or Gonzalo Comella. It didn't fit in with the more modest, everyday garments worn by the other plainclothes policemen who accompanied him. His cuff links shone in the gloom and his shirt cuffs looked as if they'd been pressed at the dry cleaner's. It was only when the man walked under the streetlamp's halo that Fernandito was able to see that these were dotted with dark stains. Blood.

The policeman stopped and turned toward the car. For a second, Fernandito thought he'd noticed him, and his stomach shrank to the size of a marble. But the policeman only addressed the driver of the Ford, smiling politely.

"Luis, I'll be here a while. If you like you can leave. Remember to clean the back seat. I'll let you know when I need you."

"Very good, Captain Hendaya."

Hendaya pulled out a cigarette and lit it, savoring it unhurriedly as he watched the car driving off down the avenue. He seemed possessed by a strange calm, as if no concern in the world could spoil that moment alone with himself. Buried in the shadows, afraid of even breathing, Fernandito observed him. The man called Hendaya smoked like a movie star, transforming the act into a show of style and poise. He turned his back on Fernandito and walked over to the vantage point, a balcony from which one could view the city. After a while, taking his time, he dropped his stub on the ground, put it out cleanly with the tip of one patent-leather shoe, and made his way toward the entrance of the house.

As soon as Hendaya had rounded the corner of the street that bordered El Pinar and disappeared, Fernandito emerged from his hiding place. His forehead was drenched with cold sweat. Some hero Alicia had got herself. He hurried after Hendaya, who had entered the property through an archway in the wall that fenced off the estate. On the entry lintel, above a pair of metal gates, were inscribed the words EL PINAR. Beyond the gates Fernandito saw what appeared to be a path of stone steps that climbed through the garden up to the house. He peeped in and glimpsed the silhouette of Hendaya, leaving a trail of smoke behind him as he moved gradually up the steps.

Fernandito waited until Hendaya had reached the top of the path. A couple of police officers had come out to meet him, and seemed to be giving him an account of events. After a brief exchange Hendaya went into the villa, followed by one of the men. The other remained posted at the top of the steps, guarding the front door.

Fernandito weighed his options. He couldn't take that path without being seen, and the sight of the blood on Hendaya's cuffs didn't exactly encourage him to pull any heroic stunts. He took a few steps back and studied the wall surrounding the grounds. The street, a narrow road that snaked along the mountainside, was deserted. Fernandito walked along it until he caught sight of what looked like the back of the house. He climbed carefully up the wall and from there managed to grab a branch, lowering himself into the garden. It suddenly occurred to him that if there were dogs, they would detect his scent in a matter of seconds, but after a few moments he established something even more disquieting. There was no sound at all. Not a leaf shook among the trees, no murmur of birds or insects stirred the air. The place was dead.

The house's elevated position on the top of a hill created the illusion that it was closer to the street than it actually was. Fernandito had to clamber up the slope between trees and paths overrun by bushes until he reached the paved lane that circled around from the main entrance. Once on the path, he followed it to the villa's rear facade. All the windows were dark except for a couple of small casements in a corner hidden between the house and the top of the hill, which he guessed must be the kitchen window. Fernandito crept up to it and, keeping his face away from the dim light spreading out through the glass, peered inside.

He recognized her immediately: the woman he'd seen coming out of Sanchís's house with the chauffeur. She lay slumped on a chair, strangely still, her face to one side, as if she were unconscious. Yet her eyes were open.

Only then did he notice that she was bound, hand and foot, to the chair. A shadow fell across her. Hendaya and the other policeman had come in. Hendaya pulled up a chair and sat facing the woman. He spoke to her for a couple of minutes, but Señora Sanchís showed no signs of hearing him. She looked away, as if Hendaya wasn't there. After a while the policeman shrugged and placed his fingers gently on the banker's wife's chin, turning her face toward him. He'd begun speaking to her again when the woman spat in his face. Hendaya instantly slapped her so hard he knocked her onto the floor, where she remained, collapsed, tied to the chair. The officer with Hendaya, and another one Fernandito hadn't noticed before—he must have been leaning against the wall under the window Fernandito was spying through—approached her and pulled the chair upright again.

Hendaya wiped the spit off his face with his hand and then smeared it on Señora Sanchís's blouse.

At a signal from Hendaya, the two police officers left the kitchen. They returned shortly afterward, bringing in the chauffeur Fernandito had seen that morning, picking up the banker's wife. He was handcuffed.

Hendaya nodded, and the two men forced the man to lie down on a wooden table in the middle of the kitchen. Then they tied his hands and feet to the four table legs. Meanwhile, Hendaya removed his jacket and folded it neatly over the chair. He went up to the table, leaned over the driver, and pulled off the mask that covered half his face. Hidden under it was a terrible wound that had disfigured the man's face from his chin to his forehead; part of the jaw and his cheekbone were missing.

Once the chauffeur had been immobilized, the two officers brought the chair on which the banker's wife was sitting close to the table. One of them held the woman's head with his hands, so that she could not look away. Fernandito felt a wave of nausea, and tasted bile in his mouth.

Hendaya knelt down next to the banker's wife and whispered something in her ear. She didn't even open her mouth: her face was frozen in anger. The policeman stood up. He stretched an open hand toward one of the officers, who handed him a gun. Then he inserted a bullet in the chamber and placed the gun's barrel just above the driver's right knee. For a moment he glanced at the woman, expectantly. Finally he shrugged again.

The roar of the gunshot and the driver's screams pierced the windowpanes and stone walls. A fine mist of blood and pulverized bone spattered the woman's face. She began to shout. The driver's body was convulsing as if an electric current was running through him. Hendaya walked around the table, placed another bullet in the chamber, and pressed the barrel against the driver's other kneecap. A pool of blood and urine spread over the table, dripping onto the floor. For a second, Hendaya looked at the woman. Fernandito closed his eyes and braced himself for the second shot. When he heard the yells, the nausea got worse, and he doubled over. Vomit rose up his throat and spilled over his chest.

He was trembling when the third shot rang out. The chauffeur no longer screamed. The woman in the chair was stammering, her face covered with tears and blood. Hendaya knelt down next to her once more, listening to her while he stroked her face and nodded. When he seemed to have heard what he wanted, he got up and, with barely one last look at him, shot the driver in the head. He returned the gun to the officer and walked over to a corner, where he washed his hands in a sink. Then he slipped on his jacket and his coat.

Fernandito suppressed his retching and moved away from the window, sliding down toward the bushes. He tried to find the path back along the hill to the tree he'd used to jump over the wall. He was perspiring like never before, a cold sweat that stung his skin. His hands and legs shook as he climbed up the wall. When he jumped over to the other side, he fell flat on his face and threw up again. At last, feeling there was nothing left inside him, he staggered down the road. As he passed the gate through which he'd seen Hendaya enter, he heard voices drawing nearer. He hurried on and ran to the little square.

*

A tram waited at the stop, an oasis of light in the darkness. There were no passengers on board, only the conductor and the driver, who were chatting and sharing a Thermos flask of coffee to keep away the cold. Fernandito got in, ignoring the conductor's look.

"Young man?"

Fernandito fumbled around in his jacket pocket and handed over some coins.

The conductor gave him his ticket. "You're not going to throw up here, are you?"

The boy shook his head. He sat down in the front, by a window, and closed his eyes, trying to take a deep breath and think about his

Vespa waiting for him at the foot of the avenue. He could hear a voice talking to the conductor, and the tram swayed gently as a second passenger got in. Fernandito heard footsteps approaching. He clenched his teeth. Then he felt the touch. A hand resting on his knee. He opened his eyes.

Hendaya was gazing at him with a friendly smile. "Are you feeling all right?"

Fernandito froze. Trying not to look at the red marks dotted over Hendaya's shirt collar, he nodded.

"Are you sure?"

"I think I've had too much to drink."

Hendaya gave him a sympathetic smile. The tram began its descent. "A bit of bicarbonate of soda with the juice of half a lemon. When I was young, that was my secret. And then to sleep."

"Thanks," said Fernandito. "I'll do that as soon as I get home."

The tram was sliding down at a snail's pace, caressing the hook-shaped curve that crowned the avenue. Hendaya leaned back in his seat opposite Fernandito and smiled at him. "Do you live far?"

The boy shook his head. "No. Twenty minutes on the metro."

Hendaya felt his coat and pulled out what looked like a small paper envelope from an inside pocket. "A eucalyptus sweet?"

"I'm all right, thanks."

"Go on, take one," Hendaya encouraged him. "It will do you good."

Fernandito accepted a sweet and began to peel off the wrapper with trembling fingers.

"What's your name?"

"Alberto. Alberto García." Fernandito popped the sweet in his mouth. His mouth was dry, and it stuck on his tongue. He forced a smile of satisfaction.

"How's that?" asked Hendaya.

"Very good, thank you so much. It's true, it really helps."

"I told you it would. Tell me, Alberto García. Can I see your ID?"

"Excuse me?"

"Your ID card."

Fernandito gulped the saliva he didn't have and started searching his pockets. "I don't know. . . . I think I must have left it at home."

"You know you can't go out without ID, don't you?"

"Yes, sir. My father is always reminding me. I'm a bit of a disaster."

"Don't worry. I understand, but don't let that happen again. I'm telling you for your own good."

"It won't happen again."

The tram was now heading down the last stretch toward the final stop. Fernandito glimpsed the dome of the Hotel La Rotonda and a white point caught by the tram's headlights. The Vespa.

"Tell me, Alberto. What were you doing here at this time of night?"

"I went to see my uncle. The poor man is very ill. The doctors say he won't live long."

"I'm very sorry." Hendaya pulled out one of his cigarettes. "You don't mind, do you?"

Fernandito shook his head, offering his best smile. Hendaya lit the cigarette. The tobacco embers tinted his pupils the color of copper.

The boy felt those eyes digging into his mind like needles. *Say something*

"What about you?" he suddenly asked. "What are you doing around here this time of night?"

Hendaya let the smoke filter through his lips. He had the smile of a jackal.

"Work," he said.

They both fell silent during the last few meters of the journey. When the tram stopped, Fernandito stood up and, after saying a courteous good-bye to Hendaya, made his way to the back. He got off the tram and walked at a leisurely pace toward the Vespa, then knelt down to open the padlock. Standing on the step of the tram, Hendaya watched him coldly.

"I thought you were going to take the metro home," he said.

"Well, I meant it was nearby. A few stops away."

Fernandito put his helmet on, as Alicia had recommended, and fastened the strap. Slowly, he told himself. He lowered the Vespa off the stand with a gentle push, and moved it along a meter or so to the end of the pavement. Hendaya's shadow loomed in front of him, and Fernandito felt the policeman's hand on his shoulder. He turned around.

Hendaya was smiling at him paternally. "Come on. Get off and hand me the keys."

He barely noticed that he was nodding and handing the policeman the motorbike's keys with a tremulous hand.

"I think you'd better come with me to the station, *Alberto*."

9

GRANDFATHER SEMPERE LIVED in a small apartment just above the bookshop on Calle Santa Ana. For as far back as the family could remember, the Semperes had always lived in that building. Daniel had been born there, and grew up in the apartment. When he married Bea, he moved only a few floors up, to the attic flat. Perhaps one day Julián would also settle in the same block. The Semperes traveled through books, not maps.

Old Sempere's apartment was a modest-looking home, haunted by memories. Like so many other homes in the old city, it exuded a vaguely depressing atmosphere, insistent on preserving that nineteenth-century-style furniture to protect the innocents from the dreams of the present.

Gazing at the scene, with Isabella Gispert's words still fresh in her mind, Alicia couldn't help feeling her presence in that room. She saw Isabella stepping on the same tiles, sharing the bed with Señor Sempere in the tiny bedroom she'd noticed as she walked down the corridor. Alicia had stopped for a moment as she passed the half-open door, imagined Isabella giving birth to Daniel in that very bed and dying in it, poisoned, barely four years later.

"Please, go in, Alicia, and I'll introduce you to the rest," Bea urged her as she closed the bedroom door behind her.

Joining two tables together—which filled the dining room from one end to the other and even part of the corridor—Bea had achieved the miracle of seating the eleven guests invited to celebrate the patriarch's birthday. Daniel was still downstairs, closing the bookshop, while his father, Julián, and Bea had accompanied Alicia up the stairs. Bernarda, Fermín's wife, was already waiting there. She had set the table and was giving the last touches to a stew that sent out a heavenly aroma.

"Bernarda, come, let me introduce you to Señorita Alicia Gris."

Bernarda wiped her hands on her apron and folded her arms around her.

"Do you know when Fermín is coming?" Bea asked her.

"Oh, Señora Bea, I'm up to my back teeth with that scoundrel's tale about the bubbly wine he says is full of pee. Forgive me, Señorita Alicia, but my husband is as pigheaded as a fighting bull and doesn't stop talking nonsense. You must pay no attention to him."

"If he takes much longer, I can see us toasting with tap water," said Bea.

"No, you won't," boomed a theatrical voice from the dining-room doorway.

The owner of that resonant instrument turned out to be a family friend called Don Anacleto, who lived in the same block, a secondary school teacher and, according to Bea, a man of verse in his free time. Don Anacleto proceeded to kiss Alicia's hand with a formality that would have looked outdated at Kaiser Wilhelm's wedding. "At your service, beautiful stranger."

"Don Anacleto, don't bother our visitors," Bea interrupted him. "Did you say you'd brought something to drink?"

Don Anacleto showed her two bottles wrapped in brown paper. "Forewarned is forearmed," he said. "Being privy to the controversy arisen between Fermín and that grocer of notorious Fascist sympathies, I decided to come armed with a couple of bottles of sweet moonshine passing for aniseed from the bar across the street, in order to solve any temporary shortage of bubbly spirits."

"It's not Christian to toast with aniseed," said Bernarda. "Much less *moonshine*."

Don Anacleto, who couldn't keep his eyes off Alicia, smiled with a worldly-wise air, to imply that such considerations only worried provincial people.

"So it will be a pagan toast, under Venus's influence," the teacher argued, giving Alicia a wink. "And tell me, would you, damsel of such remarkable presence, do me the honor of sitting next to me?"

Bea pushed the teacher to the other end of the room. "Don Anacleto," she warned him, "move along and don't overwhelm Alicia with your windy talk. You're sitting there at the junior end of the table until you prove you can join the adults."

Don Anacleto shrugged and went over to express his best wishes to the birthday man while two more guests entered the room. One of them was a fine-looking man in a suit, trim and dapper as a model, who introduced himself as Don Federico Flaviá, the neighborhood watchmaker, and displayed exceedingly polished manners.

"I adore your shoes," he told her. "You must tell me where you got them."

"Calzados Summun, on Paseo de Gracia," Alicia replied.

"Of course. They couldn't come from anywhere else. If you'll excuse me, I'm going to wish my friend Sempere a happy birthday."

With Don Federico came a cheery-looking young girl called Merceditas who was clearly and quite naively smitten with the elegant watchmaker. When she was introduced to Alicia, the girl looked her up and down, assessing her with alarm. After praising Alicia's good looks, elegance, and style, she ran off to Don Federico's side, to keep him as far away from her as was humanly possible in that limited space. If the dining room already looked crowded, when Daniel came through the door and had to slip in among the guests, any moving about began to look precarious. The last person to arrive was a young girl who couldn't have been more than twenty and radiated the shining spirit and easy beauty of the very young.

"This is Sofía, Daniel's cousin," Bea explained.

"Piacere, signorina," Sofía said.

"In Spanish, Sofía," Bea corrected her, explaining that the girl came from Naples and was living with her uncle while she studied at Barcelona University.

"Sofía is a niece of Daniel's mother, who died years ago," murmured Bea, who obviously didn't wish to mention Isabella's name.

It was painful for Alicia to see Granddad Sempere's devotion and sadness as he hugged her. It didn't take her long to find a framed photograph in the display cabinet, in which she recognized Isabella in her wedding dress, next to a Señor Sempere looking centuries younger. Sofía was the spitting image of Isabella. Out of the corner of her eye, Alicia saw Sempere gazing at her so adoringly and with such sadness that she had to look away.

Bea, who had noticed Alicia making the connection when she saw the wedding photograph, muttered something under her breath, then said to Alicia, "She doesn't do him any good. She's a lovely girl, but I can't wait for her to go back to Naples."

Alicia just nodded in response.

"Why don't you start sitting down?" ordered Bernarda from the kitchen. "Sofía, darling, come over and give me a hand. I need a bit of young blood here."

"Daniel, what about the cake?" asked Bea.

Daniel huffed and rolled his eyes. "I forgot . . . I'll go down right now."

Looking sideways at Don Anacleto, Alicia noticed that he was trying hard to creep toward her end of the dining room. She instantly hit on a plan. When Daniel walked past her on his way to the door, she followed him.

"I'll come with you. The cake's on me."

"But—"

"I insist."

A moment later Bea was left staring at them, frowning, as they disappeared through the door.

"Everything all right?" asked Bernarda next to her.

"Yes, of course . . ."

"I'm sure she's a saint," whispered Bernarda, "but I don't want her sitting next to my Fermín. And if you don't mind my saying so, neither do I want to see her next to Danielito, bless him."

"Don't be silly, Bernarda. We've got to seat her somewhere."

"Better be safe than sorry, is all I'm saying."

*

They walked in silence down the stairs. Daniel led the way. When he reached the ground floor, he stepped ahead and held the front door open for Alicia.

"The cake shop is right here, near the corner," he said, as if it weren't obvious; the shop's neon sign was clearly visible, just a few steps away.

Inside the shop, the woman in charge raised her hands to the heavens with relief. "Thank goodness. I thought you weren't coming, and we'd have to eat the cake ourselves . . ." Her voice trailed off as she became aware of Alicia. "How can I help you, miss?"

"We're together, thanks," said Alicia.

The shop owner's eyebrows catapulted halfway up her forehead. Her look, brimming with mischief, was mirrored on the faces of her two assistants, who had peeped over the counter for the occasion.

"Look at Danielito," murmured one of them in a flattering tone. "And there we were, thinking he was born yesterday."

"Shut your trap, Gloria, and bring out Señor Sempere's cake," the boss cut in, letting her underlings know that even the use of slander had to observe proper seniority in her establishment.

The other assistant, a catlike creature with a chubby figure—no doubt the result of eating too many leftover sponge fingers and custard tarts—watched Daniel with delight, enjoying his embarrassment.

"Felisa, have you nothing better to do?" the boss asked her.

"No."

By then Daniel's blush had turned the color of a ripe raspberry, and he couldn't wait to get out of there, with or without the cake. The two confectioners didn't stop shooting glances at Alicia and Daniel—sizzling glances that could have fried doughnuts in midair. At last Gloria appeared with the cake, a prize-entry exhibit, which the confectionary trinity proceeded to protect with cardboard arches before carefully placing it in a large pink box.

"Cream, strawberry, and lots of chocolate," said the cake maker. "I've put the candles in the box."

"My father loves chocolate," Daniel told Alicia, as if it needed an explanation.

"Mind the chocolate, Daniel, it can make you blush," said Gloria, still poking fun at him.

"And get you all excited," Felisa finished off.

"How much is that?" Alicia stepped forward and placed a twenty-five-peseta note on the counter.

"And on top of it, she's paying . . . ," murmured Gloria.

The manageress dawdled over the counting of the change, giving it to Alicia a coin at a time. Daniel picked up the box and walked over to the door.

"Say hello to Bea," was Gloria's parting shot.

The cake-makers' giggles followed them as they stepped out into the street, their eyes glued to them like soft fruit on an Easter cake.

"Tomorrow you'll be the talk of the entire neighborhood," Daniel predicted.

"I hope I haven't got you into trouble, Daniel."

"Don't worry. Generally speaking, I'm quite good at getting into trouble on my own. Pay no attention to the Medusa trio. Fermín says the meringue has gone to their heads."

This time Daniel let Alicia walk ahead, waiting until she'd gone up a whole flight of stairs before following her. Clearly he didn't want to be climbing up two stories with his eyes caught on her swaying hips.

The arrival of the cake was greeted with an ovation and shouts reminiscent of a great sporting victory. Daniel raised the box for all to see as if he were displaying an Olympic medal, and then took it to the kitchen. Alicia noticed that Bea had kept a place for her between Sofía and little Julián, who was sitting next to his grandfather. She took her seat, aware that the guests were casting her sidelong glances. When Daniel returned from the kitchen, he sat at the other end of the table, next to Bea.

"Shall I serve the soup, then, or shall we wait for Fermín?" Bernarda asked.

"I'd say he's the one who'll land in the soup if we don't eat soon," proclaimed Don Anacleto.

Bernarda had begun to fill the soup bowls when they heard a crash behind the door and the echo of various glass bottles tumbling down. A few seconds later, a triumphant Fermín materialized, carrying, two in each hand, the bottles of champagne, miraculously saved.

"Fermín, you had us drinking sour muscatel," protested Don Anacleto.

"Throw out that foul drink that is tarnishing your goblets, ladies and gentlemen," announced Fermín, "for the wine vendor hath just arrived from yonder vineyard to delight your palate with a beverage that will make you urinate flowers."

"Fermín!" cried Bernarda. "Your language!"

"But, my little rosebud, don't you know that on this riverbank micturating to leeward is as natural and pleasurable as—"

Fermín's loquacity and rhetoric suddenly froze. Stock-still, he was staring at Alicia as if he'd just seen a ghost. Daniel grabbed his arm and forced him to sit down.

"Come on, let's eat," announced Señor Sempere, who had also noticed Fermín's momentary lapse.

The choreography of glasses, laughter, and jokes began to take over, but Fermín, who held his empty spoon in his hand and couldn't keep his eyes off Alicia, was as silent as a tomb. Alicia pretended to be unaware, but even Bea was beginning to look uncomfortable. Daniel nudged Fermín and whispered something quickly in his ear. Tensely, Fermín sipped a spoonful of soup. Fortunately, although the trademark eloquence of the bibliographic adviser to Sempere & Sons had been silenced by Alicia's presence, Don Anacleto's tongue was living a second youth thanks to the champagne, and soon they were all regaled with his customary analysis of the country's ills.

The teacher, who saw himself as the sentimental heir and bearer of the eternal flame of Don Miguel de Unamuno (with whom he shared a more than remarkable physical resemblance), began, as usual, to present an apocalyptic panorama, announcing the imminent sinking of the Iberian Peninsula into the oceans of the blackest ignominy. Fermín, who normally enjoyed undercutting Don Anacleto's improvised table talk with sly remarks like "The index of punditry in a society is inversely proportional to its intellectual solvency" and "When people choose overheated opinions over cold facts, the social order reverts to a moronocracy," was so unforthcoming that the teacher, having no rivals or opposition, tried to wind him up.

"The fact is," he said, "that our country's leaders have run out of ideas on how to brainwash its people. Don't you agree, Fermín?"

Fermín shrugged. "I don't know why they bother. In most cases a quick rinse does the job."

"There goes the anarchist," Merceditas blurted out.

Don Anacleto smiled happily, seeing that at last he'd kick-started the debate, his favorite hobby.

Fermín puffed up. "Look, Merceditas, only because I know for a fact that your reading of the newspaper begins and ends on the horoscope page, and today we're celebrating the birthday of the elder of this house—"

"Fermín, could you pass the bread, please?" interrupted Bea, trying to keep the party from falling into discord.

Fermín nodded and beat a retreat. Don Federico, the watchmaker, came to the rescue by breaking the tense silence.

"So tell us, Alicia, what is your profession?"

Merceditas, who didn't look favorably upon the deference and attention everyone was paying to the surprise guest, threw herself into the ring. "And why should a woman have a profession? Isn't it enough to take care of a home, a husband and children, just as our parents taught us to do?"

Fermín was about to say something, but Bernarda put her hand on his wrist and he bit his tongue.

"Yes, but Alicia is single. Isn't that right?" Don Federico insisted.

Alicia smiled demurely.

"Not even a boyfriend?" asked Don Anacleto in disbelief.

She smiled modestly, shaking her head.

"This is a scandal! Indelible proof that there are no more worthwhile young men in the country. If I were twenty years younger . . . ," said Don Anacleto.

"Better make that fifty years younger," Fermín interjected.

"Manhood is ageless," replied Don Anacleto.

"Let's not mix heroics with urology."

"Fermín, there are minors at the table," Señor Sempere warned.

"If you mean Merceditas . . ."

"You should wash your mouth and your thoughts with bleach, or you'll end up in hell," Merceditas assured him.

"Well, I'll save on heating."

Don Federico raised his hands to silence the discussion. "Come on . . . with everyone talking at once, we're not letting her speak."

Calm was restored, and they all turned to Alicia.

"So," Don Federico invited her again, "you were going to tell us what you do for a living . . ."

Alicia gazed at the audience, all hanging on her words. "The fact is that today was my last day at work. And I don't know what I'm going to do from now on."

"You must have thought of something," remarked Señor Sempere.

She looked down. "I thought I would like to write. Or at least try to."

"Bravo!" cried the bookseller. "You'll be our new Laforet."

"Rather our Pardo Bazán," intervened Don Anacleto, who shared the widespread national opinion that living writers, unless they were in their death throes and had one leg already in the grave, deserved no esteem whatsoever. "Don't you agree, Fermín?"

"I would agree, dear friend, were it not because I have a feeling that when Pardo Bazán looked herself in the mirror, she noticed a certain air of the gun dog about her, whereas our Señorita Gris here looks more like a heroine from the darkest night, and I don't imagine she can quite see her image in a mirror."

There was a deep silence.

"And what could you possibly mean by that, you know-all?" Merceditas chided him.

Daniel grabbed Fermín's arm and dragged him into the kitchen.

"It means that if men moved their brains a tenth of the times they move their mouths, this world would work much better," said Sofía, who until that moment seemed to have had her head in the clouds, observing proper adolescent etiquette.

Señor Sempere turned his eyes toward that niece life had sent him to bless or torment his golden years. As so often happened, for a moment he thought he was seeing and hearing his Isabella through the ocean of time.

"Is that what they teach these days in the arts faculty?" asked Don Anacleto.

Sofía shrugged and returned to her limbo.

"God almighty, what a world awaits us," the teacher said.

"Don't worry, Don Anacleto. The world is always the same," Señor Sempere reassured him. "The truth is, it doesn't wait for anyone, and races past you at the first hurdle. How about a toast for the past, the future, and those of us who are between the two?"

Little Julián raised his glass of milk enthusiastically, seconding the proposal.

Meanwhile Daniel had cornered Fermín in the kitchen, far from the sight and hearing of the guests. "Can you tell me what the hell's the matter with you, Fermín?"

"That woman isn't what she says she is, Daniel. There's something fishy going on here."

"And what's that, if you don't mind my asking?"

"I don't know, but I'm going to find out what shady ruse she's plotting. I can smell it from here, like that cheap perfume Merceditas has showered herself with, vainly hoping to confuse the watchmaker and get him to leave fairyland."

"And how do you plan to find out?"

"With your help."

"No way. Don't you dare get me mixed up in this."

"You already are. Don't let yourself be dazzled by the insidious femme fatale routine. She's a minx, as sure as my name is Fermín."

"May I remind you that the minx is my dear father's guest of honor?"

"Aaaah . . . And have you asked yourself how this all too convenient coincidence came about?"

"I don't know. And I don't care. Coincidences don't get questioned. That's why they are coincidences."

"Is that your meager intellect speaking, or your post-teenage glands?"

"What is speaking is common sense, which you must have had removed the same day as your shame."

Fermín laughed sarcastically.

"She doesn't do things by halves," he declared. "She's buttered up your father and you at the same time, and all in the presence of your beautiful wife."

"Stop talking nonsense. They're going to hear us."

"Let them hear me," cried Fermín, raising his voice. "Loud and clear."

"Fermín, I beg you. Let's have my father's birthday in peace."

Fermín screwed up his eyebrows and tightened his lips. "On one condition."

"All right. What?"

"That you help me unmask her."

Daniel rolled his eyes and sighed.

"How do you propose to do that? By dint of more verses?"

Fermín lowered his voice.

"I have a plan . . ."

*

True to his promise, Fermín showed exemplary manners for the rest for the dinner. He laughed at Don Anacleto's jokes, treated Merceditas as if she were Marie Curie, and every now and then cast Alicia altar-boy glances. When the moment came for the toast and the cutting of the cake, Fermín delivered a long, impassioned speech that he'd prepared, eulogizing the host. This brought about a round of applause and a heartfelt embrace from the man who was being honored.

"My grandson will help me blow out the candles, won't you, Julián?" the bookseller announced.

Bea turned off the dining-room lamps, and for a few moments, they were all caught in the candles' flickering light.

"Make a wish, my friend," Don Anacleto reminded him. "If possible in the shape of a plump widow in the flower of maturity and vigor."

Bernarda delicately removed the teacher's champagne glass and replaced it with a glass of mineral water, exchanging glances with Bea, who nodded.

Alicia watched that spectacle almost in a trance. She feigned a friendly calm, but her heart was beating fast. She had never been in a gathering like this. All the birthdays she remembered had been spent with Leandro or alone, usually hidden in a cinema, the same one in which she hid almost every New Year's Eve, only to curse that awful habit they had of interrupting the film at midnight and turning on the lights for ten minutes before going back to the film. As if it weren't insulting enough having to spend the night in the empty stalls of a cinema, with six or seven other solitary souls with nobody and nowhere to go back to, they had to rub their noses in it. That feeling of camaraderie, of belonging and affection that went far beyond the jokes and discussions, was something Alicia didn't know how to handle.

Julián had taken her hand under the table, and was pressing it hard, as if, of all those present, only a child could understand how she felt. Had it not been for him, she would have burst into tears.

When all the toasts were over, Bernarda was offering coffee or tea, and Don Anacleto was doling out cigars, Alicia stood up. Everyone looked at her in surprise.

"I wanted to thank you all for your hospitality and your kindness. And very particularly you, Señor Sempere. My father always held you in great esteem, and I know he would have been very happy that I was able to share this special evening with all of you. Thank you very much."

They all looked at her with what seemed like pity, or perhaps she only saw in others what she herself felt inside. She gave little Julián a kiss and headed for the door. Bea got up and followed her, still holding her napkin.

"I'll come with you, Alicia . . ."

"No, please. Stay here with your family."

Before leaving, Alicia walked past the display cabinet and took one last look at Isabella's photograph. She sighed with relief as she disappeared down the stairs. She needed to get out of that place before she started believing that it could be hers one day.

*

Alicia's departure provoked a wave of murmurs among the guests. Grandfather Sempere had put Julián on his knees and was observing the boy. "Have you fallen in love so soon?" he asked.

"I think it's time our little Casanova went off to bed," said Bea.

"And I should follow his example," Don Anacleto added, rising from the table. "You young wild things, stay on at the party. Life is too short . . ."

Daniel was about to heave a sigh of relief when Fermín gripped his arm and stood up. "Oh, Daniel, we'd forgotten to bring up those boxes from the basement."

"What boxes?"

"Those boxes."

The two slipped out toward the door before the sleepy and surprised eyes of the bookseller.

"Every day I understand this family less," he said.

"I thought I was the only one," murmured Sofía.

*

When they stepped out of the front door, Fermín took a quick look at the bluish passageway sketched out by the streetlamps on Calle Santa Ana and signaled to Daniel to follow him.

"What now?"

"Now we hunt the vamp," replied Fermín.

"No way."

"Burying your empty head in the sand will only make it worse. Let's move it before she gives us the slip."

Without waiting for an answer, Fermín set off toward the corner of Puerta del Ángel. There he took shelter under the canopy of the Casa Jorba department store and scanned the dark night, strewn with low clouds that crept over the rooftops. Daniel joined him.

"There she goes, the serpent of paradise."

"For goodness sake, Fermín, don't do this to me."

"Hey, I held up my part of the deal. Are you a man of your word or a wimp?"

Daniel cursed his bad luck, and the two, going back to their golden days as second-rate detectives, set off on the trail of Alicia Gris.

10

THEY FOLLOWED HER, staying close to doorways and canopies, until they reached the end of the avenue. There the street opened out into a vast esplanade stretching toward the cathedral, where the ancient neighborhood used to be before it was flattened by air raids during the war. A liquid moon splattered the pavement, and Alicia's silhouette left the wake of a shadow in the air.

"Have you noticed?" asked Fermín as they watched her starting up Calle de la Paja.

"Noticed what?"

"Someone's following us."

Daniel turned to scan the silvery darkness tinting the streets.

"There. In the entrance to the toy shop. See?"

"I can't see a thing."

"The ember of a cigarette."

"So . . . ?"

"It's been following us since we left."

"Why would anyone want to follow us?"

"Maybe he's not following us. Maybe he's following her."

"This is making less sense by the minute, Fermín."

"On the contrary. It's becoming increasingly clear that something ominous is going on here . . ."

They followed Alicia's trail along Calle Baños Nuevos, a narrow chasm through ancient buildings that seemed to join in a shadowy embrace over the winding route.

"I wonder where she's going?" murmured Daniel.

The answer came soon. Alicia stopped by a front door on Calle Aviñón, opposite the Gran Café. They saw her enter the building. They walked past and took shelter a couple of doors farther down.

"And now what?"

Fermín's answer was to point toward the facade of La Manual Alpargatera, a shop a few doors up the street. Daniel realized that his friend was right. They were being followed, or Alicia was. Hiding under the arches of the espadrille-shop entrance, barely visible, was a small figure wearing a cheap bowler hat.

"At least he seems to be on the small side," Fermín reckoned.

"And what's that got to do with anything?"

"It'll prove a tactical advantage for you, once you get into fisticuffs with him."

"Great. And why does it have to be me?"

"Because you're the younger of us two, and when it comes to dishing out a thrashing, what matters is brute force. I provide the strategic vision."

"I have no intention of dishing out a thrashing to anyone."

"Don't get all squeamish on me now, Daniel. As the Lord is my witness, you already proved your warrior's zeal when you smashed that jerk Cascos Buendía's face in at the Ritz. Don't think I've forgotten."

"It was not my best hour," Daniel admitted.

"No need to make excuses. May I remind you that the swine was sending lovey-dovey letters to your wife to soften her up, following orders from that worm Valls. Yes, yes, the same worm whose slimy path you've been tracking in the Ateneo newspaper library since spring last year. Don't think for a second I hadn't noticed."

Daniel hung his head in defeat. "Any other secret you don't know about me?"

"Haven't you wondered why the hell it is there's been no sign of Valls for so long?"

"Every single day," Daniel admitted.

"Or where Salgado's booty ended up, the one he'd hidden in the baggage locker?"

Daniel nodded.

"Who says this fox isn't another one of Valls's minions? Possibly the worst one . . ."

Daniel closed his eyes. "You win, Fermín. What do we do?"

*

When she reached her apartment, Alicia noticed the strip of light under the door and recognized the smell of Vargas's cigarettes in the air. She went in without saying a word, leaving her bag and coat on the dining-room table. Facing the window, with his back to the door, Vargas was smoking. He too was silent. She poured herself a glass of white wine and collapsed on the sofa. In her absence, Vargas had pulled out the box with the documents stolen from Brians's warehouse from under the sofa. Isabella's notebook lay on the table.

"Where have you been all day?" asked Alicia finally.

"Wandering around," Vargas replied. "Trying to clear my head."

"Any luck?"

He turned and looked at her warily. "Are you going to forgive me for telling Leandro everything?"

Alicia took a sip of wine and shrugged. "If you're looking for a confessor, there's a church just before you get to the Ramblas. I believe they do shifts until midnight."

Vargas lowered his eyes. "If it's any consolation, I got the impression that Leandro already knew most of what I told him. That he only needed confirmation."

"That's what always happens with Leandro," said Alicia. "One never reveals anything to him, just clarifies some detail or other."

Vargas sighed. "I had no choice. He could sense something. If I hadn't told him what we'd found, I would have shown you up."

"You don't owe me an explanation, Vargas. What's done is done."

The silence grew thicker.

"What about Fernandito?" asked Alicia. "Hasn't he come back?"

"I thought he'd be with you."

"What else are you not telling me, Vargas?"

"Sanchís . . ."

"Out with it."

"He's dead. A cardiac arrest while they were taking him from police headquarters to the Hospital Clínico. That's what the report says."

"Motherfuckers . . . ," murmured Alicia.

The policeman slumped down on the sofa next to her. They gazed at one another. She filled her glass of wine again and offered it to him. Vargas downed it in one gulp.

"When must you go back to Madrid?"

"I've been given five days' leave," said Vargas. "And a five-thousand-peseta voucher."

"Congratulations. Perhaps you'd like to burn it all on a pilgrimage with me to see the Virgin of Montserrat. They say she works wonders for the troubled conscience."

Vargas smiled sadly. "I'm going to miss you, Alicia. Even if you don't believe it."

"Of course I believe it. But don't get your hopes up. I won't miss you."

Vargas smiled to himself. "What about you? Where have you been?"

"Visiting the Semperes."

"How did that happen?"

"A birthday party. Long story."

Vargas nodded, as if that made all the sense in the world.

Alicia pointed at Isabella's notebook. "Have you been reading while you waited?"

Again Vargas nodded.

"Isabella Gispert died knowing that bastard Valls had poisoned her," said Alicia.

The cop put his hands on his face and pushed his hair back. He looked as if every year of his life was weighing on his soul. "I'm tired," he said at last. "I'm tired of all this shit."

"Why don't you go back home?" asked Alicia. "Make them happy. Take your pension and retire to your country house in Toledo to read Lope de Vega. Wasn't that the plan?"

"And do like you? Live off literature?"

"Half the country lives off make-believe. I don't think two more will make much of a difference."

"How was it with the Semperes?"

"Good people."

"I see. And you're not used to it. Right?"

"No."

"That used to happen to me, too. You'll get over it. What are you planning to do with Isabella's notebook? Are you going to give it to them?"

"I don't know," Alicia admitted. "What would you do?"

Vargas considered the question. "I would destroy it," he declared. "The truth isn't going to do anyone any good. And it might put them in danger."

Alicia nodded. "Unless . . ."

"Think this through before saying it, Alicia."

"I think I've already thought it through."

"I thought we were going to let it pass, and just be happy."

"You and I are never going to be happy, Vargas."

"Put like that, woman, how can I refuse?"

"You don't need to tag along. It's my problem."

Vargas smiled at her. "You're my problem, Alicia. Or my salvation, even if the thought makes you laugh."

"I've never saved anyone."

"It's never too late to begin."

He stood up, collected her coat, and handed it to her. "What do you say? Shall we screw up our lives forever, or would you rather let the years go by, only to find out that you haven't a shred of talent for writing, and for me to accept that Lope only works when performed onstage?"

Alicia slipped her coat on.

"Where would you like to begin?" asked Vargas.

"By the entrance to the labyrinth . . ."

*

Daniel shivered with cold in his doorway hideout. Fermín, despite being as thin as a rake and sporting a build mainly composed of cartilage, seemed happy as a clam, passing the time by humming a *son montuno* while he lightly swayed his hips in his tropical style.

"I can't understand how you're not cold, Fermín. I'm frozen shitless."

Fermín undid a couple of buttons to reveal the folded newspaper lining he wore under his clothes.

"Applied science," he explained. "This and a few well-chosen memories of the little mulatto girl I had in Havana in my younger days."

"Holy Mary . . ."

Daniel was considering walking over to the Gran Café to ask for a piping-hot coffee with a generous dash of brandy when they heard a creak from the door to Alicia's building and saw her come out, accompanied by a solidly built guy with a military look about him.

"Look at the Tarzan our minx has found herself," remarked Fermín.

"Stop calling her a minx. Her name is Alicia."

"It's time you got over your puberty. You're a family man and a father now. Let's go."

"And what do we do about the other one?"

"The spy? Don't worry. I'm formulating a devastating strategy as we speak."

Alicia and the big fellow, who clearly belonged to the forces of law and order, turned into Calle Fernando toward the Ramblas. Following Fermín's plan, they walked casually past the spy, who had buried himself in the shadows of the street corner without acknowledging their presence. At that time of night the street was more lively than usual, thanks to a contingent of sailors on the hunt for a cultural exchange and the odd rake from the better part of town, come down to the city's bowels to satisfy his illicit bedroom urges. Fermín and Daniel used each gaggle of pedestrians as a curtain until they reached the arches leading to Plaza Real.

"Look, Daniel, this is where we met. Remember? The years go by, but it still smells of piss. It's the eternal Barcelona that never fades away . . ."

"Don't get all mushy, now."

Alicia and the policeman were crossing the square toward the exit that led to the Ramblas.

"They're going to catch a taxi," Fermín deduced. "The show's beginning."

They turned and caught sight of the spy peeping through the arches.

"Can you elaborate?" asked Daniel.

"Go up to him and kick him in the gonads as hard as you can. He's just a weakling, and I'm sure he'll oblige."

"Do you have an alternative plan?"

Fermín sighed, exasperated. He then noticed a local policeman calmly patrolling the square, staring in amazement at the generous cleavage of a couple of tarts posted outside the main door of the Hostal Ambos Mundos.

"Make sure you don't lose sight of your darling angel and the big guy," ordered Fermín.

"What about you? What are you going to do?"

"Look and learn from the master."

Fermín shot off in the direction of the policeman, whom he saluted, military style, and with great ceremony. "Chief," he said. "I find it my painful duty to report a crime against decorum and decency."

"And what crime might that be?"

"Can Your Excellency make out the tadpole over there, hiding lustfully under that cheap and smelly coat and pretending to pass for a model citizen?"

"You mean that kid?"

"That's no kid, boss. It is with a heavy heart that I certify, so help me God, that beneath that stinky coat he's as naked as a newborn baby. What's more, he's been disgracefully swinging his dick at some ladies, and spewing language I wouldn't dare repeat to a crew of sailors."

The policeman grabbed his billy club energetically. "Are you sure?"

"As God is my witness. There he goes, a pig through and through, in search of new opportunities to strike again."

"Well, then, he's in for a rude awakening." The policeman pulled out his whistle and pointed at the suspect with his club. "Hey, you there! Stop!"

Realizing the fix he'd been put into, the spy ran off, the policeman trailing behind him. Fermín, satisfied with his distracting ploy, hurried over to join Daniel, who was waiting by the taxi rank.

"Where are they?"

"They just got into a cab. There they go."

Fermín pushed Daniel into the second taxi. The driver, a master juggler of the toothpick in the mouth, looked at them through his rearview mirror. "I'm not going to Pueblo Nuevo," he warned.

"That's your loss. See the taxi over there?"

"Cipriano's cab?"

"That's the one. Follow it and don't lose him. It's a matter of life and death, and a good tip."

The taxi driver set the meter running and smiled acidly. "I thought these things only happened in American movies."

"Your prayers have been answered. Step on it, and eyes on the prize."

11

THE TWENTY MINUTES it took them to reach the police station felt like twenty years. Fernandito traveled in the back seat, next to Hendaya, who was smoking in silence and every now and then offered him a smile and a "Relax, don't worry" that curdled his blood. Two of Hendaya's men sat in the front. Neither of them spoke a word during the entire journey. It was a cold night, but although the car was freezing inside, Fernandito could feel the sweat trickling down his sides. He watched the city file past behind the car windows as if he were bidding farewell to a place to which he would never return. Pedestrians and cars went by just meters away, unreachable. When they came to the crossing of Calle Balmes and Gran Vía and stopped at a red light, he felt the urge to open the door and break into a run, but his body didn't respond. Seconds later, when the car started off again, he realized that the doors were locked.

Hendaya gave him a friendly pat on the knee. "Relax, Alberto, it will only take a minute."

When the car stopped in front of the police station, a couple of officers in uniform who were guarding the entrance approached the car. After opening the door for Hendaya and nodding to the orders he murmured, they grabbed Fernandito by the arm and led him indoors. The officer sitting in the passenger seat, who didn't get out, watched as they were taking him away. Fernandito saw him say something to his colleague in the driver's seat and smile.

Fernandito had never been inside Central Police Headquarters on Vía Layetana. He was one of the many inhabitants of Barcelona who, if by chance they found themselves in the area and needed to walk past the ominous building, would cross over to the other side of the street and hurry on. He found the interior as dark and cavernous as legend had it. Once the light from the street faded behind him, he noticed a vague smell of ammonia. The two officers held both his arms, and his feet responded with a mixture of slow steps and just letting himself be dragged along. As passages and corridors multiplied, Fernandito felt as if something was nibbling at his guts. An echo of voices and footsteps floated in the air, and a cold, gray semidarkness permeated everything. Furtive looks settled on him for an instant, then turned away with indifference. He was pulled along a flight of stairs, but couldn't tell whether they were going up or down. The lightbulbs hanging from the ceiling flickered every now and then, as if the power were being supplied in dribs and drabs. They went through a door on which the words SOCIAL INVESTIGATION BRIGADE were engraved on frosted glass.

"Where are we going?" he mumbled.

The two officers ignored his words, just as they'd ignored his presence during the entire journey, as if they were transporting a bundle. They led him through a somber hall populated with metal tables, all of them empty except for a reading lamp that shed a yellow bubble of light on each one. At the far end, an office with glass walls awaited. Inside the office was a hardwood desk facing two chairs.

One of the officers opened the door and told him to go in. "Sit down there," he said without looking him in the eye. "And keep still."

Fernandito ventured forward a few steps. The door closed behind him. He sat down meekly and took a deep breath. Looking over his shoulder, he saw that the two officers had sat down at one of the tables in the hall. One of them offered the other a cigarette. They were smiling.

At least you're not in a cell, he told himself.

*

A long hour went by during which Fernandito's greatest display of bravery was, after forty minutes of despair, to move from one chair to the other. Then, incapable of continuing any longer anchored to those seats, which seemed to shrink with every minute he sat in them, he stood up and, arming himself with something that was not quite bravery—something, in fact, much closer to panic—he was about to knock on the glass wall to claim his innocence and demand that the officers guarding him let him go when a door opened behind him, and Hendaya's figure stood out against the light. "I'm sorry about the delay, Alberto. I was held up by a small administrative matter. Have you been offered a cup of coffee?"

Had he been able to, Fernandito would have swallowed ages ago, but his mouth was like sandpaper. He sat down again without waiting to be told.

"Why am I here?" he demanded. "I've done nothing wrong."

Hendaya smiled calmly, as if the boy's state of nerves had touched him. "Nobody is saying you've done anything wrong, Alberto. Are you sure you don't want a coffee? Water?"

"What I want is to go home."

"Of course. Right away."

Hendaya picked up a phone that was on his desk and pushed it toward Fernandito. He took the receiver off the hook and handed it to him.

"Go on, Alberto, call your father. Ask him to bring your ID card and come here to fetch you. I'm sure your family must be worried about you."

12

A RING OF clouds was sliding down the hillside. The taxi's headlights revealed the outlines of grand mansions peeking through the trees along the road up to Vallvidrera.

"I can't go into Carretera de las Aguas," said the taxi driver. "Since last year access has been restricted to residents and municipal vehicles. You just have to stick your nose in, and one of them ticket fairies hidden between those bushes will jump out with his notebook and hand you a prescription. But I can leave you at the entrance . . ."

Vargas showed him a fifty-peseta note. The taxi driver's eyes rested on the vision like flies on honey. "Listen, I don't have change for that . . ."

"If you wait for us, we won't need it. And the city council can go suck themselves."

The taxi driver grumbled but concurred with the monetary logic. "I guess I see your point," he concluded.

When they reached the entrance to the road—just a narrow unpaved ribbon that bordered the amphitheatre of hills guarding Barcelona—the taxi driver drove on with care. "Are you sure it's this way?"

"Just keep going a bit further."

The old house of the Mataixes stood about three hundred meters from the start of the Carretera de las Aguas. Soon the taxi's headlights fell on a half-open spiked gate on one side of the dirt road. Farther in, one could just about make out the jagged outline of dormer windows and towers peering through the ruins of a garden that had been abandoned for far too long.

"It's here," said Alicia.

The taxi driver glanced quickly at the place and then looked at them unenthusiastically in the rearview mirror. "You sure this is the place? Looks abandoned to me . . ."

Alicia ignored his words and got out of the car.

"You wouldn't have a flashlight on you, by any chance?" asked Vargas.

"Extras aren't included in the initial fare. Are we still talking ten duros?"

Vargas pulled out the fifty-peseta note again and showed it to him. "What's your name?"

The hypnotic effect of the dough in all its glory dazzled the taxi driver. "Cipriano Ridruejo Cabezas, at your service."

"Cipriano, this is your lucky night. Could we find a flashlight for the young lady? We wouldn't want her to trip over and twist her ankle."

The man bent down and delved into his glove compartment, emerging with a sizable long flashlight. Vargas grabbed it and got out of the taxi, but first he tore the note in two and handed the driver one half. "The other half when we return."

Cipriano sighed, examining the half note as if he was staring at an expired lottery ticket. "If you return, that is," he mumbled.

Alicia had already slipped through the narrow opening in the gate. Her silhouette could be seen gliding along a moonlit passage through the undergrowth. Vargas, who was double her size, had to struggle with the rusty bars to follow. Beyond the gate a paved path wound its way around the house up to the main entrance, which was on the other side. The cobblestones under his feet were covered in dry leaves.

Vargas followed Alicia up to a balustrade perched on the edge of the hillside, from where the whole of Barcelona could be contemplated. In the distance, the sea glowed beneath the moonlight, forming a pool of red-hot silver.

*

Alicia examined the facade of the large house. The images she had conjured up while she listened to Vilajuana's account now materialized before her eyes. She imagined the house in better days, the sun caressing the ocher stone of the walls and speckling the pond below the fountain that now lay dry and full of cracks. She imagined Mataix's daughters in that garden and the writer and his wife watching them from the French windows in the sitting room. The home of the Mataix family had been reduced to an abandoned mausoleum, its shutters swaying in the breeze.

"A crate of the best white wine if we leave this for tomorrow and return in the daylight," proposed Vargas. "Two, if need be."

Alicia snatched the flashlight from his hands and walked over to the entrance. The door was open, and the remains of a rusty padlock lay on the threshold. Alicia pointed the flashlight at the bits of metal and knelt down to examine them. She picked up a piece that looked as if it had been part of the main lock and examined it. It seemed to have been burst from the inside.

"A shot in the piston," Vargas said, behind her. "High-caliber burglars."

"If they were burglars, that is." Alicia dropped the piece of metal and stood up.

"Can you smell what I'm smelling?" the policeman asked.

Alicia answered with a nod and, walking into the entrance hall, paused at the foot of a staircase of pale marble that climbed up in the gloom. The beam of the flashlight swept across the darkness spreading up the stairs. The skeleton of an old glass lamp dangled from up high.

"I wouldn't trust that staircase," warned Vargas.

They went up slowly, one step at a time. The flashlight dispelled the shadows within a range of four or five meters before blurring into a pale halo that sank into the dark. The stench they had noticed as they came in still hung in the air, but as they walked up the stairs a cold, damp breeze brushed their faces, seeming to come from the floor above.

The first-floor landing formed a hall from which stemmed a wide corridor with a row of skylights that let the moonlight through. Most of the doors had been wrenched off, and the rooms were bare, with no curtains or furniture. Alicia and Vargas walked down the corridor, inspecting those dead spaces. The floor was coated with a film of dust, like a carpet of ashes that creaked under their feet.

Alicia shone the flashlight at a line of footprints that vanished into the shadows. "It's recent," she murmured.

"A beggar, I imagine," said Vargas, "or some lowlife creature who slipped in to see if there was anything left to pillage."

Alicia paid no attention to his words as she followed the trail. The two made their way through the house, following the footprints until they came to the southeast corner. There the trail faded. Alicia stopped in the doorway of what clearly must have been the master bedroom. There was barely any furniture left, and the pillagers had even pulled the paper off the walls. The ceiling had started to collapse, and part of its old paneling hung like an open bellows, creating a false perspective that made the room seem deeper than it really was. The black hole of the cupboard where Mataix's wife had hidden in vain to protect her daughters was visible at the far end. Alicia felt a pang of nausea.

"There's nothing left here," said Vargas.

Alicia walked back to the hall at the top of the stairs from which they'd explored the floor. The stench they'd noticed upon entering was more noticeable there, a putrid aroma that seemed to rise from the very depths of the house. She walked slowly down the stairs, Vargas's footsteps behind her. As she was making her way to the exit, she noticed a movement on her right and stopped. She approached a doorway to a sitting room with large windows. Some of the wooden floorboards had been pulled up, and among the remains of an improvised fire were burned pieces of chairs and charred, blackened book spines.

A wooden panel swayed gently at the far end of the room: behind it lay a well of darkness. Vargas stopped next to Alicia and pulled out his revolver. They moved very slowly toward the opening, keeping a safe distance between them. When they reached the wall, Vargas opened the door, which was encased within the wall paneling, and gave a nod. Alicia pointed the flashlight's beam into the darkness. A long staircase descended into the basement. A draft rose from below, reeking with the smell of carrion. She covered her mouth and nose. Vargas nodded once more, and led the way. They went down slowly, feeling the walls on either side and testing each step in case they missed their footing and fell into the void.

At the bottom of the stairs they found themselves in what at first glance looked like a huge room with a vaulted ceiling, occupying the entire structure of the house. The room was flanked by a row of horizontal windows through which shafts of light shone dimly, caught in a misty miasma rising from the floor. She was about to take a step forward when Vargas stopped her. Only then did she realize that what she had thought was a tiled floor was in fact water. The rich colonial's underground swimming pool had lost its emerald green and was now a black mirror. They moved closer to the edge, and Alicia swept the surface with her beam of light. A web of greenish algae swayed beneath the water. The stench came from there.

Alicia pointed to the bottom of the pool. "There's something down there."

She brought the flashlight closer to the surface. The water took on a ghostly clarity.

"Do you see it?" asked Alicia.

A dark mass swayed at the bottom of the pool, slithering slowly. Vargas looked around and found the pole of what looked like a brush for cleaning the pool. All the fibers had come off it years ago, but the metal head was still stuck to the end. Vargas plunged the pole into the water and tried to reach the dark shape. When he touched it, it turned upon itself and seemed to unfurl bit by bit.

"Careful," warned Vargas.

He felt the metal end touch something firm and tugged at it energetically. The shadow began its ascent from the bottom of the pool. Alicia took a few steps back.

Vargas was the first to realize what was happening. "Move away," he murmured.

Alicia recognized the suit instantly: she'd gone with him to a tailor's on Gran Vía the day he bought it. The face that emerged on the water's surface was as white as chalk, the eyes like two ovals of polished marble, a dark web of capillaries around the irises. The scar on his cheek, which she herself had left on him, had become a purple mark that looked as if it had been seared with a branding iron. The head fell to one side, exposing the deep cut that had sliced his throat.

Alicia closed her eyes and let out a sob. She felt Vargas's hand on her shoulder.

"It's Lomana," she managed to say.

When she opened her eyes again, the body was sinking, until it was finally left suspended underwater, turning upon itself, arms outstretched.

Alicia turned to Vargas, who was looking at her anxiously. "Vilajuana told me he'd sent him here. Someone must have followed him."

"Or perhaps he came across something he wasn't expecting to find."

"We can't leave him in this place. Like this."

Vargas shook his head. "I'll take care of that. For the time being, let's get out of here."

The policeman took her arm and guided her gently toward the stairs. "Alicia, that body has been there for at least two or three weeks. Since before you arrived in Barcelona."

She closed her eyes and nodded in agreement.

"That means," he said, "that whoever went into your apartment and stole the book, it wasn't Lomana."

"I know."

They were about to climb up again when Vargas suddenly stood still and held her back. The sound of footsteps creaking on the floor above reverberated through the vaulted room. They followed the movement of the footsteps with their eyes. The policeman listened, his expression inscrutable.

"There's more than one person," he whispered.

For a moment the footsteps seemed to stop, and then they moved away again. Alicia was going to take a quick look up the stairs when she noticed a noise above them. They heard the stairs creak and the echo of a voice, and glanced at one another. Alicia switched off the flashlight and they positioned themselves one on either side of the doorway at the bottom of the stairs, hiding in the shadows. Vargas pointed his gun at the staircase and cocked the hammer. The footsteps were getting closer. Seconds later a figure emerged. Before the stranger could take another step, Vargas had placed the barrel of his revolver on the newcomer's temple, ready to blow his head to pieces.

13

ALTHOUGH HE'D EXPERIENCED it on countless occasions, the touch of a gun's barrel on his skin—like the consistency of crème brûlée—was something to which Fermín had never grown accustomed.

"It goes without saying that we come in peace," he uttered, closing his eyes and raising his hands to signal unconditional surrender.

"Fermín, is that you?" asked an astonished Alicia.

Before Fermín could reply, Daniel poked his head around the doorframe, freezing when he saw the weapon that Vargas was still pointing at his friend's head.

The policeman breathed out and lowered the revolver. Fermín gave an anxious sigh.

"Can you tell me what the hell you're doing here?"

"You just stole my line," said Fermín.

Alicia faced the accusing looks of Daniel and Fermín and weighed her options.

"Just as I was telling you, Daniel," said Fermín. "Look at her, ever the evil schemer, like the treacherous lamia she is."

"What's a lamia?" asked Vargas.

"Don't be offended, musketeer, but if you traded the firearm for the dictionary, it would work wonders for your vocabulary."

Vargas took one step forward, and Fermín five back. Alicia raised a hand to signal a truce.

"I think you owe us an explanation, Alicia," said Daniel.

She looked him straight in the eye and nodded, producing a smile that was enough to dispel all suspicion from the world.

Fermín nudged Daniel. "Daniel, keep your blood flow above the belt and don't let yourself be taken in."

"No one wants to take anyone in here, Fermín," said Alicia.

"Perhaps that's what you should tell the bathing beauty," murmured Fermín, pointing at the murky pool water. "An acquaintance of yours?"

"There's an explanation for this," Alicia began.

"Alicia . . . ," Vargas warned.

She made an appeasing gesture and moved closer to Fermín and Daniel. "Unfortunately, it's not a simple one."

"Try us. We're far less stupid than we look. I speak for myself, because my friend here, Daniel, may be still struggling with some growing pains."

"Let her speak, Fermín," Daniel snapped.

"I've seen less poisonous tongues in the cobras they keep in the zoo."

"Why don't we get out of here first," Alicia proposed, "and go somewhere where we can talk calmly?"

Vargas muttered under his breath, clearly disapproving.

"How do we know it's not a trap?" asked Fermín.

"Because I'll let you choose the place," said Alicia.

Daniel and Fermín swapped glances.

*

They walked across the garden and returned to the taxi to find Cipriano at the mercy of a dark cloud of tobacco and a momentous radio chat show pounding on about questions of vital concern to the public: the soccer league and the potential impact of Kubala's left-foot bunion in the run-up to the Madrid-Barcelona match the next Sunday. Size dictated that Vargas should sit in the passenger seat and the other three squeeze together, as best they could, in the back seat.

"Weren't there just two of you?" asked the driver, wondering, perhaps, whether he hadn't smoked one too many Celtas.

Vargas replied with a grunt. Alicia was engrossed in her mysteries, perhaps plotting the formidable lie she was surely going to try to shove down their throats, Fermín suspected. His friend Daniel seemed too dazzled by the contact between the crafty vamp's thigh and his right leg to articulate a single word or thought.

Realizing that he was the only adult in full command of his senses, Fermín decided to call the shots. "Look, boss," he said, "kindly drive us to the Raval quarter and leave us by the door of Can Lluís." The very mention of his favorite restaurant in the known universe, a spiritual refuge of sorts in trying times, restored his vitality. A brush with law-enforcement officers likely to blow his brains out always kindled his appetite.

Cipriano reversed the car as far as the Vallvidrera road and initiated the descent back to Barcelona. As they slid down the hillside, Fermín discreetly studied the character sitting in the passenger seat, scooped up by Alicia from God knows where to play the forbidding strongman. His entire persona smelled of police—the heavyweight variety. Vargas must have sensed Fermín's eyes boring into the back of his neck, because he turned around and gave him one of his searing looks, the sort that would stir up the guts of any miscreant and leave him in a state of severe constipation. The little man Alicia called Fermín seemed to him like a creature escaped from the pages of a picaresque epic.

"Don't get overconfident on account of my wimpish appearance," Fermín said, eying him defiantly. "All you see here is ironclad muscle and killing instinct. Think of me as a plainclothes ninja."

You think you've seen everything in this line of work, Vargas thought, and then the Good Lord sees fit to send you a golden nugget as a farewell present.

"Fermín, isn't it?"

"Who's asking?"

"Call me Vargas."

"Lieutenant?"

"Captain."

"I hope Your Excellency holds no conscientious objection to fine dining and gourmet Catalan cuisine."

"None whatsoever. To tell you the truth, I'm starving. Is this Can Lluís good?"

"Sublime," replied Fermín. "Like one of Rita Hayworth's thighs in net stockings."

Vargas smiled.

"Those two have already made friends," said Alicia. "What brings men together are the urges of their stomachs and their loins."

"Pay no attention to her, Fermín," said Vargas. "Alicia never eats, at least not solids. She feeds herself by sucking from the souls of the innocent."

Fermín and Vargas reluctantly exchanged a conspiratorial smile.

"Did you hear that, Daniel?" said Fermín. "Confirmed by a captain of the police department, no less."

Alicia turned to Daniel, who was looking at her out of the corner of his eye. "Foolish words fall on deaf ears."

"Don't worry," said Fermín. "I don't think he's registered anything after the word *sucking*."

"Why don't you all shut up so we can ride in peace?" Daniel suggested.

"It's the hormones," said Fermín. "The boy is still growing."

And so, each in their own silence, accompanied by the drone of the radio's grandiose account of the soccer league, they arrived at the doors of Can Lluís.

14

FERMÍN DISEMBARKED FROM the taxi like a famished castaway making land after weeks clinging to a plank of wood. The owner of Can Lluís, an old friend of Fermín's, received him with an embrace and greeted Daniel warmly. He eyed Vargas and Alicia uncertainly, but after Fermín whispered something in his ear, he nodded, inviting them in. "Only today we were talking about you with Professor Alburquerque, who had lunch here, and wondering what adventures you might be caught up in."

"Nothing of note," said Fermín, "just small domestic intrigues. I'm not the sleuth I used to be."

"If you like, you can have the table at the far end. It will be more peaceful there . . ."

They settled in a corner of the dining room, Vargas instinctively taking a seat facing the entrance.

"What would you like?" asked the manager.

"Surprise us, my friend," said Fermín. "I've already had a preliminary dinner, but with all this excitement I wouldn't say no to a late-night snack, and our captain here could eat a bull and requires a crash course on the local cuisine. Kindly bring the young ones a couple of lemonades and let them sip that, to see if they come out of their apathy."

"A glass of white wine for me, please," said Alicia.

"I have a very good Penedès."

She nodded.

"So, why don't I bring you a few tapas to start with and we take it from there?"

"Motion approved unanimously," Fermín declared.

The manager set off to the kitchen with the order, leaving them with no more company than a heavy silence.

"You were saying, Alicia?" Fermín asked encouragingly.

"What I'm going to tell you must remain between us," she warned. Daniel and Fermín looked straight at her.

"You're going to have to give me your word," Alicia insisted.

"One gives one's word to someone who has one," said Fermín. "And for the moment you, with all due respect, have not shown us any proof at all that this may be the case."

"Well, you're going to have to trust me."

Fermín exchanged glances with Vargas. The policeman shrugged. "Don't look at me. That's what she told me a few days ago, and look where I am now."

Soon a waiter appeared with a tray and placed a few small dishes and a bit of bread on the table. Fermín and Vargas instantly attacked the offering, while Alicia slowly savored her glass of white wine, holding a cigarette between her fingers. Daniel stared at the table.

"What do you think of the fare?" asked Fermín.

"Tremendous," Vargas agreed. "Enough to awaken the dead."

"Try this portion of *fricandó*, Captain—prime Catalan beef stew that will make you want to dance the *sardana* in your long johns."

Daniel observed this odd couple, who couldn't have been more different from each other, frantically wolfing down everything that had been put in front of them. "How many dinners are you capable of eating, Fermín?" he asked.

"As many as pop up within shooting distance. The youth of today who did not live through the war cannot understand it, my friend."

Vargas nodded, licking his fingers. Alicia, who was watching the show with the detached calm of someone waiting for the rain to die down, signaled to the waiter to bring her a second glass of white wine.

"Doesn't that go to your head if you don't throw in something solid?" asked Fermín, mopping up the plate with a piece of bread.

"It doesn't worry me if it does," replied Alicia. "So long as it stays up there."

Once the coffees were on the table, together with a succession of fine liqueurs, Fermín and Vargas leaned back in their chairs with a satisfied expression, and Alicia stubbed out her cigarette in the ashtray.

"I don't know about the rest of you, but I'm all ears," said Fermín.

Alicia leaned forward and lowered her voice. "I'm assuming you both know who the minister Mauricio Valls is."

"My friend Daniel has heard of him." Fermín smiled craftily. "I've had my brushes with him as well."

"You will have noticed, then, if you've been paying attention, that for some time he's barely been seen in public."

"Now you mention it . . . Although the expert here on Valls is Daniel. Whenever he has a spare moment, he goes down to the newspaper library at the Ateneo to investigate the life and miracles of the great man, an old family acquaintance."

Alicia glanced at Daniel.

"About three weeks ago, Mauricio Valls disappeared from his residence in Somosaguas without leaving a trace. He left at dawn together with his main bodyguard in a car that was found abandoned in Barcelona a few days later. No one has seen him since."

Alicia studied the turbulent torrent of emotions lighting up Daniel's eyes.

"The police investigation suggests that Valls may have been the victim of a conspiracy, seeking to avenge some supposed fraudulent deals in connection with a number of bank shares."

Daniel was looking at her in bewilderment and growing indignation.

"When you say 'the investigation,'" Fermín intervened, "who are you referring to?"

"The police department, and other law-enforcement agencies."

"I can see Captain Vargas in that role, but you, quite frankly . . ."

"I work, or rather worked, for one of the services that have given their support to the police in this investigation."

"And does such service have a name?" asked Fermín skeptically. "Because you don't look like a member of the Civil Guard's women's section."

"No."

"I see. And the deceased we've just had the pleasure of seeing floating tonight?"

"An old colleague of mine."

"So I suppose what's put you off your food is grief—"

"All this is just a load of lies," Daniel cut in.

"Daniel . . . ," said Alicia, placing a conciliatory hand on his.

He pulled his hand away and faced her. "What's all this about you being an old friend of the family, then? Visiting the bookshop, my wife, my son, sneaking into my family?"

"Daniel, this is complicated. Let me—"

"Is Alicia even your real name? Or did you borrow it from one of my father's old memories as well?"

It was now Fermín who had his eyes fixed on her, as if he were facing a ghost from the past.

"Yes. My name is Alicia Gris. And I haven't lied about who I am."

"Only about everything else," Daniel shot back.

Vargas kept silent, letting Alicia lead the conversation. She sighed, showing heartfelt embarrassment and guilt that he didn't think for a second were genuine.

"During the investigation we came across evidence that Mauricio Valls had been acquainted with your mother, Doña Isabella, and with an old inmate of Montjuïc Prison called David Martín. The reason I involved you in the matter was I needed to eliminate suspicions and make sure the Sempere family hadn't had anything to do with—"

"You must think I'm an idiot." Daniel laughed bitterly, looking at Alicia with contempt. "And I must be, because until now I hadn't realized what you were, Alicia, or whatever in hell your name is."

"Daniel, please . . ."

"Don't touch me." Daniel stood and headed for the door.

Alicia sighed and dropped her face in her hands. She sought Fermín's eyes in search of support, but the little man was gazing at her as if she were a pickpocket caught in the act.

"As a first attempt it looks rather lame to me," he said. "I think you still owe us an explanation—even more so now, in view of the con you've tried to make us swallow. And that's without counting the explanation you owe me. If you really are Alicia Gris."

She smiled, dejected. "Don't you remember me, Fermín?"

The little man was staring at her as if she were an apparition. "I no longer know what I remember. Have you come back from the dead?"

"I suppose you could say that."

"And what for?"

"I'm only trying to protect you."

"I would never have guessed."

Alicia stood up and looked at Vargas.

"Go after him," said the policeman. "I'll take care of Lomana, and inform you as soon as I can."

Alicia nodded and set off in search of Daniel. Fermín and Vargas were left alone, looking mutely at each other.

"I think you're too hard on Alicia," Vargas said.

"How long have you known her?" asked Fermín.

"A few days."

"So you're in a position to certify that she's a living being, not a ghost?"

"I think she only looks like one."

"She does drink like a sponge, there's no denying that," remarked Fermín.

"You've no idea."

"A coffee with a dash of whisky before returning to the house of horrors?" Fermín offered.

Vargas accepted.

"Do you need company and logistical support to fish out the stiff?"

"Thanks, Fermín, but it's best that I do this on my own."

"Then tell me something, and please don't lie to me—you and I have been through enough battles to know bullshit when we see it. Is it me, or is this business worse than it smells?"

Vargas hesitated. "Much worse," the policeman agreed at last.

"Right. And that two-legged piece of excrement, Valls, is he still alive or is he pushing up poisoned daisies by now?"

Vargas, who seemed suddenly overcome with the exhaustion of the last few days, looked at Fermín with an expression of defeat.

"That, my friend, I think is the least of our worries now . . ."

15

DANIEL'S FIGURE WAS outlined in the distance, a shadow sheltering under the streetlamps of the Raval quarter. Alicia quickened her pace as much as she could. Soon the soreness in her hip returned. She struggled to shorten the distance separating her from Daniel, breathing with difficulty, a sharp pain searing through her bones.

When Daniel reached the Ramblas, he turned around and saw her. He threw her an angry look.

"Daniel, please, wait for me," called Alicia, holding on to a streetlamp.

Ignoring her, he set off again at a brisk pace. Alicia somehow managed to drag herself after him. Sweat covered her forehead, and the whole of her side was now an open wound aflame.

At the corner of Calle Santa Ana, Daniel looked over his shoulder.

Alicia was still there, limping in a way that disconcerted him. He paused to watch her for a moment and saw her lifting a hand, trying to catch his attention. Daniel shook his head and mumbled under his breath. He was about to give up and go home when he saw her fall, as if something had broken inside her. He waited a few seconds, but Alicia didn't get up. He hesitated, then walked toward her as she writhed on the ground. Her face under the streetlamp was drenched in sweat, and she was grimacing with pain. He felt the urge to leave her there to her fate, but drew a bit closer and knelt down beside her. Alicia was gazing at him, her face covered in tears.

"Are you playacting?" asked Daniel.

She stretched a hand out to him, and he helped her up. Her body shook with pain under his hands, and he felt a hint of remorse. "What's the matter?"

"It's an old wound," Alicia said, panting. "I need to sit down, please."

Holding her by the waist, Daniel led her to a café at the start of Calle Santa Ana that always closed late. The waiter knew him, and Daniel was sure that the following day the entire neighborhood would be served with an exhaustively detailed account of his arrival there on the verge of midnight with a young lady of shadowy charms in his arms. He guided Alicia to a table by the entrance and helped her sit down.

"Water," she whispered.

Daniel went up to the bar and spoke to the waiter. "Give me a bottle of water, Manuel."

"Just a bottle of water?" asked the man, winking knowingly.

Daniel didn't venture into detail. He returned to the table with a bottle of water and a glass. Alicia was holding a metal pillbox in her hand and trying to open it. He took it and opened it for her. She took two pills and swallowed them with a gulp of water, which dribbled down her chin and throat. Daniel was looking at her anxiously, not knowing what else to do.

She opened her eyes and looked at him, trying to smile. "I'll be all right in a minute."

"Maybe if you eat something it will kick in faster . . ."

Alicia shook her head.

"A glass of white wine, please . . ."

"Are you sure it's a good idea to mix alcohol with those?"

She nodded, and Daniel went off in search of the wine. "Manuel. Give me a glass of white wine and something to nibble."

"I have some mouthwatering ham croquettes."

"Whatever."

Back at the table, Daniel persisted until he'd gotten Alicia to eat one and a half croquettes with her wine and whatever those two white pills were.

Slowly she recovered her self-control, managing to smile as if nothing had happened. "I'm sorry you had to see me like this."

"Are you feeling better?"

She nodded, although her eyes had taken on a glassy, liquid tinge. Part of her, it seemed, was miles away.

"This doesn't change anything," Daniel warned her.

"I understand." Alicia spoke slowly, almost slurring her words.

"Why did you lie to us?"

"I didn't lie to you."

"Call it what you like. You've only told me one part of the truth, which comes to the same thing."

"Even I don't know the truth, Daniel. Not yet. However much I wanted to, I couldn't give it to you."

Despite himself, Daniel felt tempted to believe her. Perhaps he was even stupider than Fermín thought.

"But I'm going to find it," said Alicia. "I'm going to get to the bottom of this matter, and I can assure you I'm not going to keep anything from you."

"In that case, let me help you. It's in my own interest."

Alicia shook her head.

"I know that Mauricio Valls murdered my mother," said Daniel. "I have every right in the world to look into his face and ask him why. More than you and Vargas."

"That's true."

"Then let me help you."

Alicia smiled tenderly. Daniel looked away.

"You can help me by keeping yourself and your family safe," she said. "Vargas and I are not the only ones following this trail. There are others. Very dangerous people."

"I'm not frightened."

"That's what worries me, Daniel. Be frightened. Very frightened. And let me do what I know how to do." Alicia looked for his eyes and took his hand. "I swear on my life that I'm going to find Valls and make sure you and your family are safe."

"I don't want to be safe. I want to know the truth."

"What you want, Daniel, is revenge."

"That's my business. And if you don't tell me what's really happening, I'm going to find out for myself. I'm serious."

"I know. May I ask you a favor?"

Daniel shrugged.

"Give me twenty-four hours. If in twenty-four hours I haven't resolved this matter, I swear on whatever you want me to swear that I'll tell you everything I know."

He looked at her suspiciously. "Twenty-four hours," he conceded at last. "I also have a favor to ask you in exchange."

"Name it."

"Tell me why Fermín says you owe him an explanation. An explanation about what?"

Alicia lowered her eyes. "Many years ago, when I was a child, Fermín saved my life. It was during the war."

"Does he know?"

"If he doesn't, he suspects it. He'd given me up for dead."

"Is this wound you have from then?"

"Yes," she replied, in a way that made him think it was only one of many wounds Alicia was hiding.

"Fermín has also saved me," said Daniel. "Often."

She smiled, and made as if to get up. "Sometimes life sends us a guardian angel."

Daniel walked around the table to help her, but she stopped him. "I can manage on my own, thanks."

"Are you sure those pills haven't left you a bit . . . ?"

"Don't worry. I'm a big girl. Come on, I'll walk with you to your front door. It's on my way."

They walked together to the door of the old bookshop, where Daniel pulled out the key. They looked at one another silently.

"I have your word," said Daniel.

She nodded.

"Good night, Alicia."

She remained there, motionless, watching him with that glazed look. Daniel didn't know whether to attribute it to the drugs, or to the bottomless pit he could sense behind those green eyes. When he was about to go in, Alicia stood on her toes and brought her lips close to Daniel's. He moved his face away, and the kiss brushed his cheek. Without saying a word, Alicia turned and walked away, her silhouette evaporating in the shadows.

*

Bea had been watching them from the window. She'd seen them come out of the café on the street corner and approach their front door when the midnight bells rang out over the city's rooftops. The moment Alicia drew close to Daniel and he stood there, stock-still, lost in her eyes, Bea felt her stomach turn. She saw her get on her toes, ready to kiss his lips. Then she stopped looking.

She went slowly back to the bedroom and stopped for a moment outside Julián's bedroom. He was sound asleep. Bea closed his door and went on to her bedroom, then got back into bed and waited to hear the door. Daniel's footsteps moved stealthily along the corridor. Bea lay there in the semidarkness, staring at the ceiling. She listened to Daniel undressing at the foot of the bed and putting on the pajamas she'd left for him on the chair. She felt his body slip in between the sheets. When she turned her head, she saw that Daniel had his back to her.

"Where were you?" she asked.

"With Fermín."

16

HENDAYA OFFERED HIM a cigarette, but Fernandito refused it.

"I don't smoke, thanks."

"A wise man. That's why I can't understand why you don't call your father so he can come and fetch you and bring your papers. Then all this could be resolved. Or are you hiding something?"

The boy shook his head. Hendaya smiled amicably, and Fernandito remembered how he'd seen him blow the chauffeur's knees off with his gun a couple of hours earlier. The dark stain on the shirt collar was still there.

"I'm not hiding anything, sir."

"So . . . ?" Hendaya pushed the phone toward him. "One call, and you'll be free."

Fernandito swallowed hard. "I'd like to ask you not to force me to make this call. For a good reason."

"A good reason? And what is that, dear friend Alberto?"

"It's because of my father, who is ill."

"Ah, is he now?"

"It's his heart. He had a heart attack a couple of months ago, and he spent six weeks at the Clínico. Now he's home, recovering, but he's very weak."

"I'm very sorry."

"My father is a good man, sir. A war hero."

"War hero?"

"He entered Barcelona with the Nacionales. There's a photograph of him, parading along Avenida Diagonal, on the cover of *La Vanguardia*. We have it framed in our dining room. He's the third on the right. You should see it. They allowed him to march in the front row because of his bravery in the battle of the Ebro. He was a sergeant."

"You must all be very proud of him."

"We are, but the poor man hasn't really been himself after what happened to my mother."

"Your mother?"

"She died four years ago."

"My condolences."

"Thank you, sir. Do you know what the last thing my mother said to me before dying was?"

"No."

"Promise me you'll look after your father, and you won't upset him."

"And have you lived up to that promise?"

Fernandito lowered his eyes and looked contrite. He shook his head. "The truth is, I haven't been the son my mother raised, or the one my father deserves. Believe it or not, I'm a good-for-nothing."

"And there was I thinking you were a good kid."

"Not at all. A lost cause, that's me. All I do is give my poor father grief, as if he didn't have enough to cope with already. One day I'm chucked out of my job, the next I forget my ID card. See for yourself. A war-hero father and a useless idiot of a son."

Hendaya studied him cautiously. "Am I to understand from all this that if you call your father and tell him you've been held in the police station because you didn't have your ID on you, you'll upset him again?"

"That would finish him off, I'm sure. If a neighbor has to bring him here to fetch me in his wheelchair, I think he'd die of shame and grief to see what a disastrous son he's got."

Hendaya thought about the matter. "I understand, Alberto, but you must understand me too. You put me in a difficult position."

"Yes, sir, and you've already been very patient with me. I really don't deserve it. If it depended on me, I'd ask you to throw me in jail with all the worst scum, just to teach me a lesson. But I beg you to reconsider on account of my poor father. I'll write down my name, surnames, and address, and tomorrow you can come and ask any of our neighbors—if possible in the morning, as that's when my father is asleep, because of his medication."

Hendaya took the piece of paper Fernandito was handing him. "Alberto García Santamaría, Calle Comercio number thirty-six, fifth floor, door one," he read out. "What if some police officers come with you now?"

"If my father, who spends his nights awake looking out of the window and listening to the radio, sees me arriving with the police, he'll throw me out, which I would deserve, and then he'd have a massive coronary."

"And we don't want that to happen."

"No, sir."

"So how do I know that if I let you go, you won't go back to your old ways?"

Fernandito turned solemnly to face the official portrait of Franco hanging on the wall. "Because I'm going to swear to you before God and before the Generalissimo, cross my heart and hope to die."

For a few moments Hendaya looked at him with curiosity and a pinch of sympathy. "I see you're still standing, so you must be telling the truth."

"Yes, sir."

"Look here, Alberto. I like you, and the truth is that it's very late, and I'm tired. I'm going to give you an opportunity and cut you loose. I shouldn't, because rules are rules, but I've been a son too, and not always the best. You can go."

Fernandito looked toward the office door in disbelief.

"Go on, before I change my mind."

"A million thanks, sir."

"Thank your father. And don't do it again."

Quick as a flash, Fernandito stood up and left the office, mopping the sweat off his brow. He walked unhurriedly through the long hall of the political police, and when he passed the two officers who were observing him in silence, he greeted them: "Have a good evening."

As soon as he reached the corridor, he quickened his pace and hurried on toward the wide stairs leading to the ground floor. It wasn't until he'd walked through the main door and was on Vía Layetana that he allowed himself a deep breath and blessed the heavens, hell, and everything in between for his good fortune.

*

Hendaya watched Fernandito cross Vía Layetana and set off down the road. Behind him, he heard the approaching footsteps of the two officers who had guarded the boy.

"I want to know who he is, where he lives, and who his friends are," he said without turning around.

17

THE MIST FLOODING the streets of Vallvidrera left a trace of dew on Vargas's clothes. He watched the taxi pull away and walked toward the lights of the bar next to the funicular station. The place was deserted at that time of night, and a CLOSED notice hung on the door. Vargas looked through the glass front and scanned the interior. A waiter was drying glasses behind the counter, with only the radio and a mutt that a flea wouldn't have touched to save its life for company. Vargas rapped on the glass with his knuckles. The waiter looked up from his boredom. He glanced at Vargas, then shook his head slowly. Vargas pulled out his badge and knocked again, louder. The waiter sighed and walked around the bar and over to the door. The dog, woken from its stupor, limped along, acting as his bodyguard.

"Police," announced Vargas. "I need to use your telephone."

The waiter opened the door and let him in. He pointed to the phone by the entrance gate to the counter. "Shall I serve you anything, while we're at it?"

"A *cortado*, if it's not too much bother."

While the waiter was getting the coffee machine ready, Vargas picked up the phone and dialed the number for police headquarters. The dog planted itself next to him and observed him with dozing eyes and a feeble wag of the tail.

"Chusco, don't bother him," warned the waiter.

As Vargas waited for a reply, he and Chusco sized each other up, comparing their degrees of seniority and general wear and tear.

"How old is the dog?" asked the policeman.

The waiter shrugged. "When I bought the bar he was already here, and he couldn't even hold back his farts. And that was ten years ago."

"What breed is it?"

"Tutti-frutti."

Chusco flopped down onto one side and showed Vargas a bare pink belly. On the other end of the line someone cleared his throat.

"Get me Linares. Vargas here, from Central Police Headquarters."

Shortly afterward he heard a click on the line and the slightly mocking voice of Linares. "I thought you'd be back in Madrid by now, Vargas, collecting medals."

"I've stayed on a few days longer so I can catch one of those processions with papier-mâché giants and big-heads."

"Don't get too excited—all the seats are gone already. How can I help you at this time of night? Don't tell me you have bad news."

"That depends. I'm in Vallvidrera, in the bar next to the funicular station."

"The best views in all Barcelona."

"You can say that! A while ago I saw a corpse in a house on Carretera de las Aguas."

Vargas enjoyed Linares's reaction.

"Holy shit," Linares grunted. "Was that necessary?"

"Aren't you going to ask me who the deceased is?"

"You weren't going to tell me anyhow."

"I would if I knew."

"Maybe you could tell me what the hell you were doing at such a late hour up there. Walking in your sleep?"

"Tying up loose ends. You know how it is."

"Sure. And I suppose you expect me to get a judge out of bed now to sign it off."

"If it's not too much to ask."

Linares huffed again. Vargas heard him voicing instructions. "Give me an hour, or an hour and a half," he said to Vargas. "And do me a favor: don't find any more stiffs, if you don't mind."

"Will do."

Vargas put down the phone and lit a cigarette. A steaming *cortado* awaited him on the counter. The waiter looked at him, vaguely curious.

"You haven't heard anything," Vargas advised him.

"Don't worry, I'm as deaf as Chusco."

"Can I make another call?"

465

The waiter shrugged. Vargas dialed the number of the flat on Calle Aviñón. He had to wait a few minutes for an answer. At last he heard the receiver being picked up and the sound of soft breathing on the other end.

"It's me, Alicia. Vargas."

"Vargas?"

"Don't say you've forgotten me already."

A long pause. Alicia's voice sounded as if it was coming from inside a fish tank. "I thought it would be Leandro," she said at last, dragging her words.

"You sound odd. Have you been drinking?"

"When I drink I don't sound odd, Vargas."

"What did you take?"

"A little glass of warm milk before saying my prayers and going to bed."

"Where were you?" he asked.

"I was having a drink with Daniel Sempere."

Vargas was silent for a while.

"I know what I'm doing, Vargas."

"If you say so."

"Where are you?"

"In Vallvidrera, waiting for the police and the judge to come and remove the body."

"What did you tell them?"

"That I went to Mataix's house, trying to finish tying up loose ends, and I came across a surprise."

"And they bought that?"

"Of course not, but I still have good friends in the force."

"What are you going to tell them about the body?"

"That I don't recognize him because I'd never seen him before. Which is technically true."

"Does your friend know you've been taken off the case?"

"He probably found out before I did. He's always ahead of the game."

"As soon as the body is identified, the news will reach Madrid. And Leandro."

"Which gives us a few hours' leeway," Vargas said. "With luck, that is."

"Did Fermín tell you anything?"

"Pearls of wisdom. And that you two have a pending conversation."

"I know. Did he say what it was about?"

"We've become close, but not that close. I have a feeling Fermín thinks you're someone from his past."

"So what now?"

"Once the judge has signed the warrant for the body to be removed, I'll accompany the body to the morgue, arguing that it might be part of my investigation. I know the pathologist from my years in Leganés. He's a good man. I'll see what I can find out."

"You'll be there at least until sunrise."

"At least. I'll take a nap in the morgue. I'm sure they'll lend me a nice table," joked Vargas halfheartedly.

"Take care. And call me as soon as you know anything."

"Don't worry. You try to get some rest."

Vargas put down the phone and went over to the counter. He drank his coffee, which was lukewarm by now, swallowing it in one gulp.

"Shall I serve you another?"

"Perhaps I'd rather a large coffee with milk."

"A pastry to go with it? It's on the house. I'll have to chuck them tomorrow."

"All right, then."

Vargas pulled a horn off the dry croissant and examined it against the light, debating whether swallowing that thing was a good idea. Chusco, with the low-scruple threshold peculiar to the species, was watching him attentively and licking his lips in anticipation. Vargas let the piece of pastry fall, and Chusco captured it in mid-flight. The dog proceeded to devour the prize avidly and then panted at Vargas in eternal gratitude.

"Watch out, or you'll never get rid of him," warned the waiter.

Vargas exchanged another glance with his new best friend. He gave him the rest of the croissant, and Chusco swallowed it in one gulp. In this dog-eat-dog world, he thought, when you get old and even common sense hurts, a crumb of kindness or pity is a dish fit for the gods.

The ninety minutes promised by Linares turned into two long hours. When Vargas saw the headlights of the police car and the morgue van cutting through the mist as they came up the road, he paid for his coffees, adding a generous tip, and went out into the street to wait, cigarette in hand. Linares didn't get out. He rolled down the window and signaled to Vargas to get into the car and sit next to him in the back seat. One of his men was driving. A chubby individual wrapped in a coat and bearing a sullen expression sat in the passenger seat.

"Your Honor," Vargas greeted him.

The judge didn't bother to reply or acknowledge his presence. Linares threw him a sharp glance and smiled, shrugging. "Where are we going?" he asked.

"Close by. On Carretera de las Aguas."

While they drove down toward the entrance to the road, Vargas looked at his old colleague out of the corner of his eye. Twenty years in the force had taken their toll, and more. "You're looking well," he lied.

Linares chuckled. Vargas met the judge's look in the rearview mirror.

"Old friends?" asked the judge.

"Vargas doesn't have friends," said Linares.

"Wise man."

Vargas guided the driver through the dark track described by the road until the headlights outlined the iron gates of the Mataixes' house. The van from the morgue followed close behind. They got out of the car, and the judge took a few steps forward to look at the outline of the house through the trees.

"The body is in the basement," Vargas explained. "In a swimming pool. It's probably been there two or three weeks."

"No shit," said one of the assistants from the mortuary, who looked like a beginner.

The judge drew up to Vargas and looked him in the eye. "Linares says you discovered it during the course of an investigation?"

"That's right, Your Honor."

"And you haven't been able to identify it?"

"No, Your Honor."

The judge turned to look at Linares, who was rubbing his hands together to keep warm.

The second mortuary assistant, older and with an impenetrable expression, walked over to the group and tried to catch Vargas's eye. "One or several pieces?"

"Excuse me?"

"The deceased."

"One. I believe."

The man nodded. "Manolo, the large bag, the boat hook, and a couple of shovels," he said to his apprentice.

*

Half an hour later, while the morgue men were loading the corpse into the van and the judge was filling out forms on the police car's hood under the beam of a flashlight held by Linares's subordinate, Vargas noticed his old colleague standing next to him. Together, they silently watched the men struggle to lift the corpse, which was heavier than they'd expected, into the van. As they got on with the job, they bashed what must have been the corpse's head a couple of times, quarreling among themselves and swearing under their breath.

"Earth to earth," murmured Linares. "One of ours?"

Vargas checked that the judge was out of earshot. "Something like that. I'm going to need a bit of time."

Linares looked down. "Twelve hours, maximum. I can't give you any more."

"Hendaya . . . ," said Vargas.

Linares nodded.

"Is Manero in the morgue?"

"Waiting for you. I've already told him you were going there."

Vargas smiled in gratitude.

"Anything I need to know?" asked Linares.

Vargas shook his head. "How's Manuela?"

"Fat as a hog, just like her mother."

"That's how you like them."

Linares nodded solemnly.

"I don't suppose she remembers me," Vargas said.

"Not by name, but she still refers to you as 'that son of a bitch.' Fondly."

Vargas offered his friend a cigarette, but he declined. "What's happened to us, Linares?"

Linares shrugged. "Spain, I suppose."

"It could be worse. We could be in the bag."

"All in due time."

18

HE KNEW HE was being followed without needing to look behind him. As he turned the corner and headed up toward the cathedral, Fernandito glanced over his shoulder and saw them: two figures that had been trailing him since he left the police station. He quickened his pace, adjusting his course to keep close to the shadows of the front doors until he reached the end of the esplanade. There he paused for a moment, hiding under the canopy of a closed café, and saw that Hendaya's two henchmen hadn't lost him. He had no intention of leading them to his home, much less to Alicia's, so he decided to drag them along on a night tour of Barcelona, hoping he would eventually either tire them or shake them off by sheer good luck or an unlikely stroke of genius.

He set off toward Puertaferrisa, sticking to the middle of the road, as visible as a target in a firing range. The road was practically deserted at that time of night, and Fernandito wandered unhurriedly, passing the occasional drunk, a nightwatchman on duty, and the usual contingent of lost souls who prowled the streets of Barcelona into the early hours. Every time he looked back, Hendaya's hounds were there, keeping the same distance whether he walked faster or slower.

When he reached the Ramblas, he considered breaking into a run and trying to lose them in the narrow streets of the Raval, but that would give him away, and given his followers' patent skill, his chances would be slim. He decided to continue down the Ramblas until he reached the entrance to the Boquería market.

A cortege of vans had congregated outside the market doors, where, beneath a garland of lightbulbs, a large group of workers were unloading crates, supplying the stalls for the following day. Without thinking twice, Fernandito slipped between the columns of crates, his silhouette melting into those of the dozens of workers moving through the market's corridors. As soon as he felt he was out of sight of his pursuers, he scuttled off toward the rear of the enclosure. As he ran, the huge market with its vaulted ceiling opened up before him like a cathedral devoted to the art of fine foods, where the smells and colors of the universe conspired to form a great bazaar to meet the city's appetites.

He dodged heaps of fruit and vegetables, mounds of spices and canned food, boxes packed with ice and jelly like creatures that were still moving, avoiding bleeding carcasses hanging from hooks and receiving curses and shoves from butchers, young hands, and women in rubber boots at the greengrocer stalls. When he reached the back of the building, he found himself in a square full of empty wooden crates. He darted behind a pillar of boxes, his eyes riveted on the market's back exit. Thirty seconds ticked by without any sign of the two police officers. Fernandito took a deep breath and allowed himself a smile of relief.

His moment of calm was short-lived. The two policemen peered around the market door and paused to study the square. Fernandito sank into the shadows and slipped away.

As soon as he'd turned the corner onto a narrow street bordering the old Hospital de la Santa Cruz, toward Calle del Carmen, he bumped into her: peroxide blonde, skirt so tight it looked poised for an explosion, and the face of a decidedly unpious Madonna wearing flaming lipstick.

"Hello, darling," she said. "Shouldn't you be getting your hot cocoa ready before going to school?"

Fernandito eyed the tart and, above all, the promise of shelter offered by the doorway behind her. The building itself was most un-inviting. An individual with a sallow complexion acted as front desk man, occupying a cubicle the size of a confessional.

"How much?" Fernandito said, surveying the entrance to the nar-row street.

"That depends on the service. Today I have a special offer for altar boys and breast-feeding babes, 'cause when it comes to brea—"

"Fine," cut in Fernandito.

Having concluded the sales pitch, the hooker took his arm, pull-ing him toward the stairs. The customer had taken only three steps when he stopped to look behind him, perhaps alerted by the prud-ish radar all novices have inside them, or by the aromas emanating from the building. Fearing a financial loss in what was already a bear market of a night, she gave him a passionate squeeze and whispered in his ear, in the wettest of tones, "Come on, little birdie, come to Mama. I'm going to take you on an end-of-term trip that will sweep you off your feet."

As they walked past the cubicle, the attendant handed them the supply kit, which included soap, rubbers, and other assorted acces-sories. Fernandito followed the Venus-for-hire up the stairs without taking his eye off the entrance door. Once they'd turned the corner to the first-floor landing—which opened onto a cavernous corridor with rooms smelling of hydrochloric acid—the tart gave him an anxious look. "You seem to be in a bit of a hurry, love."

Fernandito sighed, and she searched his nervous eyes. The street bestows fast-track diplomas in psychology, and experience had taught her that if a customer didn't warm up at the mere promise of a good tumble and her lush, abundant good looks, he was likely to change his mind once he stepped into the filthy room that served as her of-fice. Or, worse still, that he might go back on his word before pulling down his trousers and beat a retreat without delivering on expecta-tions or fees. "Look, sweetheart," she said, "rushing is not a good idea when it comes to love, especially at your age. I've seen more ex-perienced sailors than you burst the cork with just one touch of this luscious bosom. You need to calm down and enjoy the whole thing like a cream cake. One little mouthful at a time."

Fernandito mumbled what the hooker took as capitulation before the irrefutable evidence of her firm flesh. The room was at the end of the corridor. On the way, the boy could hear the tunes of bump and grind filtering under the doors. Something in his face must have given away his scant familiarity with these matters.

"First time?" asked the tart, opening the door and ushering him in.

The boy nodded in anguish.

"Well, then, don't worry, novices are my specialty. Half the rich brats in Barcelona have passed through my consulting room to learn how to change their own diapers. Come in."

Fernando glanced at his temporary refuge. It was worse than he'd expected.

The room exhibited a full inventory of misery, exuding a stench that seemed to peel the green paint off the walls, leaving damp patches of a suspect nature. The minute bathroom, its door open onto the bedroom, featured a lidless toilet and an ocher-colored sink. Leaden light filtered through a tiny window, and the water pipes whispered a strange melody of gurgles and drips that inspired anything but the atmosphere of romance. A washbasin of considerable proportions at the foot of the bed suggested mysteries he'd rather not dwell on. The bed consisted of a metal frame, a mattress that may have been white about fifteen years ago, and pillows with a lot of miles on the clock.

"I think I'd better go home," he said.

"Relax, kid, now comes the best part. Once I've gotten you out of your trousers, this will look like the nuptial suite at the Ritz."

The hooker led Fernandito to the bed and helped him sit down, with a fair bit of pushing. Once her client had given in to her shoves, she knelt down in front of him and smiled with a tenderness that cut through the makeup and the sadness oozing from her eyes. A commercial patina in her expression ruined what little low-life poetry Fernandito had tried to imagine. The girl was looking at him expectantly.

"The gates of Paradise open only at the sight of coin, my darling."

Fernandito nodded. He rummaged in his pockets and pulled out his wallet. The tart's eyes lit up with expectation. He took the money he had on him and gave it to the woman without counting it. "It's all I've got. Is that all right?"

The hooker left the money on the bedside table and looked at him with studied sweetness. "I'm Matilde, but you can call me whatever you like."

"What do people call you?"

"Depends. Minx, whore, slut, or the name of their wife or mother. . . . Once, a repentant seminarist called me *mater*. I thought he meant 'water,' but it turns out that's 'mommy' in Latin."

"I'm Fernando, but everyone calls me Fernandito."

"Tell me, Fernando, have you ever been with a woman?"

He nodded with the slimmest of convictions. Not a good sign.

"Do you know what to do?"

"The truth is that I only want to be able to stay here for a while. We don't need to do anything."

Matilde frowned. The twisted ones were the worst. Determined to straighten out the situation, she proceeded to undo Fernandito's belt and pull down his trousers. He interrupted her.

"Don't be afraid, love."

"I'm not afraid of you, Matilde," said Fernandito.

She stopped and looked straight at him. "Is someone following you?"

Fernandito nodded.

"I see. Police?"

"I think so."

The woman stood up and sat next to him. "You're sure you don't want to do anything?"

"I just want to be here for a while. If you don't mind."

"Don't you like me?"

"That's not what I meant. You're very attractive."

Matilde chuckled. "Do you have a girl you like?"

Fernandito didn't answer.

"I'm sure you do. Go on, tell me, what's your girlfriend's name?"

"She's not my girlfriend."

The woman was looking at him inquisitively.

"Her name's Alicia," said Fernandito.

The woman's hand settled on his thigh. "I'm sure I know how to do things that your Alicia doesn't."

Fernandito realized that he didn't have a clue about what things Alicia knew or didn't know how to do, and it wasn't from lack of speculation.

Matilde observed him with curiosity. She lay down on the bed and took his hand. When he looked at her in the light of the anemic bulb, which gave her a yellowish hue, he realized that she was much younger than he'd imagined. She might have been only four or five years older than him.

"If you like, I could teach you how to caress a girl."

Fernandito choked on his saliva. "I know how to do that," he managed to articulate, rather dispiritedly.

"No man knows how to caress a girl, sweetheart. Take it from me. Even the most experienced men have fingers like ears of corn. Come, lie down next to me."

Fernandito hesitated.

"Undress me. Slowly. The slower you undress a girl, the faster you win her heart. Imagine I'm Alicia. I might even look a bit like her."

You're like chalk and cheese, thought Fernandito. Even so, the image of Alicia lying before him on the bed with her arms stretched over her shoulders clouded his eyes. He clenched his fist to stop the trembling.

"Alicia doesn't have to know. I'll keep the secret. Go on."

19

BURIED IN A dark corner of Calle Hospital's nether regions stood a somber building that looked as if it had never been touched by sunlight. An iron door forbade entrance, and there was no notice or sign to hint what was inside. The police car stopped in front of it. Vargas and Linares got out.

"Will that poor devil still be here?" asked Vargas.

"I don't suppose job offers are raining down on him," said Linares as he rang the bell.

After about a minute the door opened inward, and they were greeted by the reptilian glare of an unfortunately built little man, who admitted them with a somewhat unfriendly expression.

"I thought you were dead," he said to Vargas once he recognized him.

"I've missed you too, Braulio."

The old hands knew about Braulio, a humanoid creature with a skin weathered by formaldehyde and the unsure step of an old beetle. Braulio, man of yet untapped talents, acted primarily as errand boy and assistant to the pathologist. According to malicious gossip, he lived in the basement of the morgue, turning filth into an art form and drifting into old age in the safe haven provided by a decrepit, bug-ridden bed. He possessed a single change of clothes, which he was already wearing when, at the age of sixteen, he was admitted to the institution under unfortunate circumstances.

"The doctor is waiting for you," he said.

Vargas and Linares followed him through a litany of damp corridors tinged with a greenish half-light that led to the heart of the morgue. Legend had it that Braulio had arrived there thirty years earlier, after being run over by a tram opposite the San Antonio market while fleeing from the scene of a petty theft—a scrawny chicken or a handful of petticoats, depending on the version. The driver of the ambulance that picked him up, seeing the tangle of impossibly knotted limbs, pronounced him dead at the scene and, after loading him into the van as if he were a sack of rubble, stopped to have a few rounds of beer with a few pals of his in a bar on Calle Comercio before handing in the battered jumble of bloody bones at the police morgue in the Raval quarter, which was more on his way than the Hospital Clínico. Just as the trainee pathologist was about to dig his scalpel into him, the dying man opened his eyes, big as saucers, and jumped back to life. The event was declared a miracle of the national health system and enjoyed wide coverage in the local press, because this happened in the middle of the summer when newspapers liked to come out with curious news items and trivia to liven up the blistering heat. "Poor Wretch Revives Magically One Step Away from the Grave," the front page of *El Noticiero Universal* blared.

Braulio's fame and glory were short-lived, however, and in tune with the frivolity of the times. For it turned out that the person in question was exceedingly unsightly, and after his large intestine had become braided like a horse's mane, he suffered from chronic flatulence. The readers were put in the awkward position of having to forget all about him in great haste and concentrate again on the lives of music-hall singers and soccer stars. Poor Braulio, having drunk from the capricious fountain of celebrity, couldn't handle his return to the most ignominious of anonymities. He considered taking his own life by eating an enormous amount of rancid Lent fritters, but in a moment of mysticism that came upon him while sitting on the toilet—owing to the resulting severe colitis—he saw the light and understood that the Lord, in his manifold ways, had wanted him to exist in the shadows, at the service of rigor mortis and its accompanying mysteries.

As the years went by and boredom grew, the police force's fertile wit devised a most elaborate mythology around the figure, misadventures, and miracles of Braulio. According to this narrative, during his interrupted passage between this world and the next, Braulio had been adopted by a malevolent spirit who refused to go down to hell, feeling more comfortable in that Barcelona of the 1930s, which was—so experts maintained—its earthly equivalent.

*

"You still haven't got yourself a girlfriend, Braulio?" asked Linares. "With this perfume of stale black sausage you let out, they probably throw themselves at you, begging for your favors."

"I have plenty of girlfriends," Braulio replied, winking with a droopy, purplish eyelid that looked more like a patch. "And they're nice and quiet."

"Stop uttering such filth and bring the body, Braulio," ordered a voice from the dark. At the sound of his master's voice, Braulio hurried off.

Dr. Andrés Manero, pathologist and Vargas's old comrade in arms, stepped forward and held out his hand. "There are people you only see at funerals, but you and I don't even manage that: we only meet for autopsies."

"A sign that we're still kicking."

"You can say that, Vargas—you look as fit as a bull. How long since the last time?"

"At least five or six years."

Manero nodded with a smile. Even in the faint light floating around the room, Vargas noticed that his friend had aged more than normal. Soon they heard Braulio's uneven footsteps pushing the stretcher. The body was covered with a cloth that clung to it, becoming transparent where it touched the moisture.

Manero approached the stretcher and lifted the part of the shroud covering the face. His expression remained unchanged, but he turned to look at Vargas. "Leave us, Braulio."

The assistant raised his eyebrows in annoyance. "You don't need me, Doctor?"

"No."

"But I thought I was going to assist with—"

"You were wrong. Go out for a while and have a smoke."

Braulio threw Vargas a hostile look, being in no doubt that he was to blame for his not being allowed to take part in the forthcoming feast. Vargas winked back at him and pointed to the door.

"Clear off, Braulio," Linares ordered. "You heard the doctor. Go and have a really cold shower."

Visibly annoyed, Braulio set off, limping and cursing under his breath. Once they were rid of him, Manero removed the entire shroud and lit the strip of adjustable lamps hanging from the ceiling. A pale light of icy vapor carved out the outline of the body. Linares took a step forward, and after a quick glance at the corpse, let out a sigh. "God almighty . . ." Linares looked away and went over to Vargas. "Is it who it looks like?"

Vargas kept his eyes fixed on Linares's, but didn't reply.

"I'm not going to be able to cover this up," said Linares.

"I understand."

Linares looked down, shaking his head. "Is there anything else I can do for you?"

"You could get rid of the leech."

"I'm not following you."

"Someone is. One of yours."

Linares fixed his gaze on Vargas, his smile leaving him. "I have no one following you."

"It must have been someone from the top, then."

Linares shook his head. "If there was anyone doing that, I'd know. Mine or not mine."

"It's a young guy, quite bad. Smallish. A novice. His name's Rovira."

"The only Rovira in headquarters is in the archives. He's sixty and has enough shrapnel in his legs to open a hardware store. The poor man couldn't follow his own shadow if you paid him."

Vargas frowned.

Linares's face oozed disappointment. "I may be a lot of things, Vargas, but not someone who stabs his friends in the back."

Vargas was about to reply, but Linares raised a hand to silence him. The harm was done.

"You have until mid-morning," Linares said. "After that, I must file a report. This will have its consequences, as you know." He moved toward the exit. "Good night, Doctor."

*

Anchored in the shadows of the narrow street bordering the morgue, Braulio watched the figure of Linares disappear into the night. "I'll get you, you bastard," he said to himself. Sooner or later, every one of these cocky pricks who loved nothing more than disrespecting him would end up like all the rest, a piece of swollen meat laid out on a marble slab at the mercy of a well-sharpened blade and whoever knew how to handle it. And he was there to give them the farewell they deserved. It wasn't the first time, and it wouldn't be the last. Those who thought death was the final indignity life gave you were wrong. An extensive catalog of mockery and humiliations awaited backstage once the curtain had fallen, and good old Braulio was always there to collect a memento or two for his trophy case and make sure that they all stepped into eternity with their fair reward. He'd had his eye on Linares for some time. And he hadn't forgotten his buddy Vargas, either. Nothing keeps memory more alive than resentment.

"I'm going to bone you like a piece of ham and make myself a key ring with your nuts, you jerk," he murmured. "Before you know it."

Accustomed to listening to himself but never bored of it, Braulio smiled with satisfaction. He decided to celebrate the good fortune of his clever thoughts with a cigarette, to help fight off the cold permeating the streets at that late hour. He felt the outside pockets of his coat, which he'd inherited from a deceased with subversive leanings who had come to pay his dues a few weeks earlier, in conditions that proved there were still real experts with balls on the police payroll. The packet of Celtas was empty. Braulio buried his hands in his pockets and watched his breath forming spirals in the air. With what Hendaya would pay him when he told him what he'd just seen, he'd be able to buy a few cartons of Celtas and even a tub of fine Vaseline, the perfumed sort they sold at the rubber shop of Genaro the Chinaman. Some customers had to be treated with class.

*

The echo of footsteps in the dark roused him from his dreams. He looked carefully and noticed a silhouette forming among the folds of the mist. It was advancing toward him. Braulio took a step back and bumped into the entrance door. The visitor didn't seem much taller than he was, but he transmitted a strange calm and determination that made the few hairs remaining beneath Braulio's blondish hairpiece stand on end.

The individual stopped in front of Braulio and offered him an open packet of cigarettes. "You must be Señor Don Braulio."

Nobody had ever called Braulio Señor or Don in his entire life, and he discovered that he didn't like the sound of that address coming from the stranger's lips. "And who are you? Has Hendaya sent you?"

The visitor simply smiled and raised the packet of cigarettes up to Braulio, who accepted one. He then pulled out a gas lighter and held out the flame.

"Thanks," Braulio murmured.

"You're welcome. Tell me, Don Braulio, who's in there?"

"A pile of stiffs—what do you expect?"

"I'm referring to the living."

Braulio hesitated. "So Hendaya sent you, right?"

The stranger just fixed his eyes on him without losing his smile.

Braulio gulped. "The pathologist, and a policeman from Madrid."

"Vargas?"

Braulio nodded.

"How is it?"

"Excuse me?"

"The cigarette. How is it?"

"Very good. Imported?"

"Like all good things. You have keys, don't you, Don Braulio?"

"Keys?"

"To the morgue. I'm afraid I might need them."

"Hendaya didn't say anything about giving any keys to anyone."

The stranger shrugged. "Change of plans," he said, as he calmly slipped on a pair of gloves.

"Hey, what are you doing?"

The flash of the steel only lasted a second. Braulio noticed the blade of the knife, the sharpest cold he'd ever known in his miserable existence, sinking into his guts. At first he felt no pain, only that awareness of extreme clarity and weakness as the blade sliced his guts. Then, when the stranger sank the knife again into the lower abdomen, this time right up to the handle, and pulled it strongly upward, Braulio felt that cold turning to fire. A claw of red hot iron made its way toward his heart. His throat flooded with blood and drowned his screams, as the stranger dragged him into the alley and pulled out the bunch of keys fastened to his belt.

20

HE WALKED THROUGH the corridors in the half-light until he reached the passage leading to the autopsy room. A greenish halo filtered through the cracks in the door. He could hear the voices of the two men. They spoke like old friends, leaving silences that didn't require explaining and making jokes to ease the job at hand. Standing on his toes to look through the tinted glass circle crowning the door, he studied Vargas's profile as he sat on one of the marble slabs, and that of the pathologist, leaning over the corpse. He heard the doctor describe in all detail the fruit of his labors. He couldn't help smiling at the skill with which the pathologist unraveled the details of Lomana's last moments, without being disgusted by the smoothness of the cut or the precision with which he'd sliced the arteries and the windpipe of that lout, just to see him die on his knees and enjoy the panic in his eyes as the blood gushed through his hands. Among experts, it was only gentlemanly to recognize a job well done.

*

The pathologist also described the knife wounds that had been dealt Lomana on the torso when he grabbed the killer's legs, trying in vain to avoid being pushed to the edge of the swimming pool. There was no water in his lungs, he explained, only blood. Lomana had drowned in his own blood before sinking into the putrid water. The pathologist was an experienced man, a professional who knew his job and whose teachings inspired respect and admiration. There were not many like him. For that reason alone, the man decided to spare his life.

Vargas, the old fox, dropped questions here and there with remarkable insight—the watcher had to give him that. But it was obvious that he was groping around in the dark and that, apart from the particulars of Lomana's final agony, he would learn little from his visit to the morgue. While the man outside the door listened to the two inside, he debated whether he should withdraw for a few hours to take a rest or go in search of a prostitute to warm his feet until dawn. It seemed clear that Vargas's inquiries had reached a standstill, and there would be no need to take further steps in the matter. Those were his orders, after all. Not to make a move unless there was no other choice. Deep down, he was sorry. It would have been interesting to confront the old policeman and see whether he still had the guts to cling on to life. Those who resisted the inevitable were his favorites. And as for the luscious Alicia, he was reserving the final honor for her. With her he would certainly take his time and savor the reward for all his efforts. Alicia was not going to disappoint him.

It was another half hour before the pathologist concluded his examination and offered Vargas a glass of the liqueur he kept in the instrument cupboard. The conversation diverted toward topics that are de rigueur between old friends whose paths have parted—platitudes on the passing of time, on those fallen along the wayside, and other banalities on the tired subject of aging. Bored, the listener was about to leave and let Vargas and the pathologist drift away to the back of beyond when he noticed that the policeman was pulling a piece of paper out of his pocket, examining it under the lights hanging from the ceiling. The voices dropped to a murmur, and the man had to press his ear against the door to make out the words.

Dr. Manero noticed that the door to the room was moving slightly. "Braulio, is that you?"

When he didn't get a reply, the pathologist sighed and shook his head disapprovingly. "When I don't let him stay, he sometimes hides behind doors to eavesdrop."

"I don't know how you put up with him," said Vargas.

"I tell myself that it's almost better if he's here, pissing out, rather than wandering about in the big wide world, pissing in. At least this way we can keep an eye on him. Nice drink, eh?"

"What is it? Embalming liquid?"

"I keep it for when I have to take something along to weddings and first communions in my wife's family. Aren't you going to tell me about the case? What was this wretch Lomana doing in the swimming pool of an abandoned house in Vallvidrera?"

Vargas shrugged. "I don't know."

"Then I'll try with the living. What are you doing in Barcelona? If I'm not mistaken, you'd promised never to return."

"An unbroken promise doesn't deserve to be called a promise."

"And what's this you've got here?" asked Manero, pointing to the list of numbers Vargas was holding. "I always thought of you as a man of letters."

"Who knows? I've been carrying it around with me for days, and I don't know what it means."

"Can I have a look?"

Vargas handed it to the pathologist, who glanced at it while he sipped his liqueur.

"I was thinking that perhaps they were bank account numbers," said the policeman.

The pathologist shook his head. "I wouldn't be able to say what the ones in the right-hand column are, but the ones on the left are almost certainly certificates."

"Certificates?"

"Death certificates."

Vargas gave him a puzzled look.

Manero pointed to the column on the left. "Do you see the numbering? These numbers follow the old system. The numbering changed years ago, but in these you can still see the number of the document, book, and page. These bits are added later, but here we generate these numbers every day. Even your friend Lomana will have one for the rest of eternity."

Vargas downed his drink in one gulp and examined the list again as if he were looking at a jigsaw puzzle he'd been battling with for years, and it was suddenly starting to make sense. "What about the numbers in the right-hand column? They look as if they're correlated, but the sequence of the numbering is different. Could they also be certificates?"

Manero looked closer and shrugged. "Looks like it, but they're not from my department."

Vargas let out a sigh.

"Does this help you at all?" asked the pathologist.

The policeman nodded. "And where could I find the documents that correspond to these certificate numbers?"

"Where do you think? Where everything begins and ends in this life: in the Civil Registry."

21

THE GLIMMER OF light seeping through the bathroom window told Fernandito that dawn was at hand. He sat on the bed and glanced at Matilde, who had fallen asleep next to him. His gaze ran over her naked body, and he smiled.

She opened her eyes and looked at him serenely. "How's things, love? A bit more relaxed?"

"Do you think they'll have left by now?"

Matilde stretched and looked for her clothes, strewn by the foot of the bed. "Just in case, go out through the opening that leads to the alley. It will take you to one of the market entrances."

"Thanks."

"Thank *you*, sweetheart. Have you enjoyed it a little?"

Fernandito blushed, but he nodded as he got dressed in the morning gloom. Matilde stretched out an arm to grab the pack of cigarettes she'd left on the bedside table and lit one. She observed Fernandito as he slipped his clothes on in a hurry, his shyness and timidity almost intact despite the instruction he'd just received. Once he was ready, he looked at her. She pointed to the small window.

"This way?"

Matilde nodded. "But keep your eyes peeled, and don't break your neck. I want you to come back and see me in one piece. You will come back, won't you?"

"Of course," lied Fernandito. "As soon as I get my wages."

The boy stuck his head out of the window and studied the inner courtyard leading to the narrow lane Matilde had mentioned.

"Don't trust the stairs—they're a bit loose. You'd better jump, you're young."

"Thanks. And good-bye."

"Good-bye, darling. Good luck."

"Good luck," Fernandito replied.

He was about to slip through the small window when he heard Matilde's voice behind him. "Fernando?"

"Yes?"

"Treat her well. Your girlfriend, whatever her name is. Treat her well."

*

As soon as he'd abandoned the morgue, Vargas felt he was coming back to life after a prolonged interlude in purgatory. The liqueur poured out by Dr. Manero and, above all, the revelation about what half the numbers on that list signified had lifted his spirits. He could almost forget he hadn't slept a wink in far too many hours. His body betrayed his tiredness—if he'd stopped to think about it, he would have realized that his bones, and even his memory, were aching. But the hope that the small bit of information he had just uncovered might lead to something solid kept him resolutely on his feet.

For a moment he wondered whether he should go over to Alicia's apartment to share the news, but since he wasn't sure whether the list of death-certificate numbers Valls had carried with him in his secret journey from Madrid could provide any hard evidence, he decided to make sure first. He set off toward Plaza Medinaceli, an oasis of palm trees and gardens standing out amid the dilapidated palaces and the sea mist blowing in from the port, where soon the offices of the Barcelona Civil Registry would open their doors.

On his way, Vargas stopped at the Hostal Ambos Mundos in Plaza Real, where they were already serving breakfast and coffee to the children of the night who were dropping by for one last refreshment. He sat at the bar, signaled to a waiter—endowed with a prominent jaw and sideburns—and asked for a *serrano* ham sandwich, a beer, and a double black coffee with a shot of brandy.

"I've only got the expensive stuff left," warned the waiter.

"Then give me two shots," replied Vargas.

"If you're in the mood for celebrations, you might want a Montecristo cigar for dessert. They bring them to me straight from Cuba. Sheer class, the sort the mulatto girls roll between their thighs . . ."

"I won't say no."

Vargas had always heard it said that breakfast was the most important meal of the day, at least until lunchtime. To finish it off with a good Havana cigar could only bring good luck. Leaving a halo of

Caribbean smoke, he set off again, with a full stomach and mounting optimism. The sky was tinged with amber, and the misty light sliding down the facades made him think that this would be one of those rare days when he'd discover the truth, or something that looked sufficiently like it.

*

About fifty meters behind him, under a patch of shadow cast by the cornices of a decaying building, the eyes of the observer followed him relentlessly. With that cigar between his lips, full belly, and the air of someone steeped in false hopes, Vargas seemed to him closer to the end than ever. What little respect he'd managed to feel for the policeman was evaporating like the film of mist that still crept along the cobbled pavement beneath his feet.

He would never be like that, he told himself. He would never allow alcohol and complacency to cloud his judgment or let his body become a useless bundle of bones. He'd always found old people disgusting. If people didn't have the dignity to jump out of a window or under a train once decrepitude set in, somebody should shoot them, deal them a death blow, or remove them from circulation like mangy dogs as a matter of public health.

The observer smiled, never remiss in celebrating his own witty remarks. He was always going to be young, because he was smarter than the rest. He wasn't going to make the mistakes that allowed someone with Vargas's potential to become a sad reflection of his former self. Like that yokel Lomana, who had been kicked in the ass all his life and then died on his knees, holding on to his gullet with both hands while he, the observer, watched his eyes: the capillaries bursting, the pupils dilating into a black mirror. Another piece of shit who hadn't known how to get out of the way in time.

He wasn't afraid of Vargas. He wasn't afraid of what the cop could, or believed he could, discover. He bit his tongue so as not to laugh. Time was nearly up. And when there was no more need to follow Vargas, and all that business had concluded, he would be able to enjoy his reward: Alicia. The two of them alone, in no hurry. Just as the master had promised him. With enough time and skills to teach that velvet slut that there was nothing left to learn from her, and that, before dispatching her into the oblivion from which she should never have emerged, he was going to work her good and deep and show her what pain really was.

*

When Alicia opened her eyes, the light of dawn was blazing in the windows. She turned her head to one side and buried her face in the sofa cushion. She was still wearing yesterday's clothes, and the poisonous taste of bitter almonds lingered in her mouth, left by the pills soaked in alcohol. Something hammered in her ears. She half opened her eyes again and saw the bottle of pills on the table next to the remains of a glass of warm white wine, which she swallowed in one gulp. When she tried to fill it again, she discovered that the bottle was empty. Only when she groped her way to the kitchen to look for another one did she realize that the hammering she heard in her temples wasn't her pulse or the shadow of a migraine brought about by the pills, but the sound of someone knocking on her door. She held on to a chair in the dining room and rubbed her eyes. A voice on the other side of the door kept repeating her name insistently. She dragged herself to the entrance and opened the door. Fernandito, who looked as if he'd been to the end of the world and back, gazed at her more in alarm than relief.

"What time is it?" asked Alicia.

"Early. Are you all right?"

Alicia nodded with half-closed eyes and staggered back to the sofa. Fernandito closed the door and, before she fell on the way, held her upright and helped her land safely on the sofa.

"What is this stuff you take?" he wanted to know, examining the bottle of pills.

"Aspirin."

"They must be for horses."

"What are you doing here so early?"

"I was in El Pinar last night. I have plenty to tell you."

Alicia felt the table in search of cigarettes. Fernandito pushed them aside without her noticing.

"I'm all ears."

"It doesn't look like it. Why don't you take a shower while I make some coffee?"

"Do I smell bad?"

"No. But I think it will do you good. Come on, I'll help you."

Before Alicia could protest, Fernandito helped her up from the sofa and led her to the bathroom, where he sat her on the edge of the bath and let the water run, testing the temperature with one hand and making sure she wasn't going to keel over with the other.

"I'm not a baby," Alicia complained.

"Sometimes you act like one. Come on, into the water. Are you going to undress, or shall I do it?"

"In your dreams."

Alicia pushed him out of the bathroom and closed the door. She dropped her clothes on the floor, a garment at a time, as if she were shedding dead scales, and looked at herself in the mirror.

"Good God," she murmured.

A few seconds later the shock of cold water biting her skin returned her unceremoniously to the world of the living. Fernandito, who was preparing a pot of strong coffee in the kitchen, couldn't hold back a smile when he heard the shout from the bathroom.

*

A quarter of an hour later, buried in a bathrobe that was too large for her, her hair wrapped in a towel, Alicia heard the story of the night's events. While Fernandito talked, she sipped at the coffee in the large cup she held in both hands. When the boy had concluded his report, she downed the remaining coffee and looked him in the eyes.

"You shouldn't have put yourself in that dangerous situation, Fernandito."

"That's the least of it. That guy, Hendaya, hasn't the foggiest who I am. But I'm sure he knows who you are, Alicia. You're the one in danger."

"Where have you been since you managed to shake off the two policemen?"

"I found a sort of flophouse behind the Boquería market where I was able to wait."

"A sort of flophouse?"

"The lurid details for another day. What are we going to do now?"

Alicia sat up. "You're doing nothing. You've done enough already."

"What do you mean, nothing? After what happened?"

She drew closer to him. There was something different about him, in the way he looked at her and behaved. She decided not to pull at that thread. She'd wait for a more suitable moment.

"You're going to wait here for Vargas to return, and you're going to tell him exactly what you've told me. Word for word."

"What about you? Where are you going?"

Alicia pulled the revolver out of the handbag that lay on the table and checked that it was loaded.

Fernandito reverted to his usual shocked expression. "Hey . . ."

22

AT SOME POINT in his captivity, Mauricio Valls had begun to think of light as the harbinger of pain. In the dark he could imagine that those rusty bars were not confining him, that the walls of the cell did not ooze a film of filthy moisture that slid over the rock like black honey and formed a fetid puddle at his feet. Above all, in the dark he could not see himself.

The half-light in which he lived was only barely broken when, once a day, a strip of brightness opened up at the top of the stairs and a figure was outlined against it carrying the pot of foul water and a piece of bread that he devoured in a matter of seconds. The jailer had changed, but not his manners. His new custodian never stopped to look at him in the face or speak to him at all. He ignored Valls's questions, pleadings, insults, and curses. All he did was place the food and the drink next to the bars and leave.

The first time the new jailer came down, the stench issuing from the cell and the prisoner had made him throw up. From then on he almost always came down covering his mouth with a handkerchief and stayed as little as possible. Valls no longer noticed the smell, just as he barely felt the pain in his arm, or the dull throb of the purple lines that rose from his stump like a cobweb of black veins. They were letting him rot alive, and he no longer cared.

He had started to think that one day nobody would come down those steps anymore, that the door would never open again, and he'd spend the rest of what little life he had left in darkness, feeling his body decompose bit by bit and devour itself. He had often witnessed that ritual during his years as governor of the Montjuïc prison. With luck, it would take a matter of days. He had started to fantasize about the weakness and delirium that would take hold of him once the initial agonies of hunger had burned all the bridges. The cruelest part was the absence of water. Perhaps, when the grip of despair and torment became overpowering and he began to lick the sewage that seeped down the walls, his heart would stop beating. One of the doctors who had worked for him in the castle twenty years ago always said that God takes pity on motherfuckers first. Even in this respect, life was a bitch. Perhaps, at the last moment, God would also take pity on him, and the infection he could feel advancing through his veins would save him from the worst part of the end.

*

When the door opened again at the top of the stairs, he was dreaming that he had already died and was in one of those canvas sacks used to remove the corpses from the cells in Montjuïc Castle. He woke from his drowsiness to discover that his tongue was swollen and aching. He put his fingers in his mouth. His gums were bleeding, and his teeth moved when he touched them, as if they were attached to soft mud.

"I'm thirsty!" he groaned. "Water, please . . ."

The steps coming down the stairs were heavier than usual. A light went on with a roar of white noise. Sound was much more reliable than light in the cell. The world had been reduced to pain, the slow decomposition of his body, and the echoes of footsteps and pipes murmuring between those walls. Valls followed the path of the approaching footsteps with his ears. He became aware of a figure that had stopped at the bottom of the stairs.

"Water, please," he begged.

He crept up to the metal bars and strained his eyes. A beam of blinding light burned his retinas. A torch. Valls moved back and covered his eyes with the only hand he had left. Even like that, he could feel the light moving over his face and over his filthy body, covered in excrements, dried blood, and rags.

"Look at me," said the voice at last.

Valls removed his hand from his eyes and opened them very slowly. His pupils took a while to adapt to the light. The face on the other side of the bars was different, but it seemed strangely familiar.

"I said look at me."

Valls obeyed. Once dignity was lost, it was far easier than giving orders. The visitor went up to the bars and examined him carefully, passing the torch's beam over his limbs and his emaciated body. Only then did Valls realize why the face looking at him from the other side of the bars seemed familiar.

"Hendaya?" he gasped. "Hendaya, is that you?"

Hendaya nodded. Valls felt that his prayers were being answered. For the first time in days or weeks, he could breathe. It must be another dream. Sometimes, anchored among shadows, he held conversations with saviors who came to his rescue. He strained his eyes again and laughed. It was Hendaya. In the flesh.

"Thank God, thank God," he sobbed. "It's me, Mauricio Valls. Valls, the minister . . . It's me . . ."

He stretched out his arms toward the policeman, weeping with gratitude, ignoring the shame of being seen that way, half naked, mutilated, and covered in shit and urine. Hendaya took a step forward.

"How long have I been here?" asked Valls.

Hendaya didn't reply.

"Is my daughter Mercedes all right?"

Hendaya offered no answer. Valls stood up with difficulty, holding on to the bars until his eyes were level with Hendaya's. The policeman was looking at him with no expression. Was Valls perhaps dreaming again?

"Hendaya?"

The policeman pulled out a cigarette and lit it. Valls got a whiff of tobacco, the first time he'd smelled it in what seemed like years. It was the most exquisite perfume he'd ever sniffed. He thought the cigarette was for him until he saw Hendaya put it between his lips and take a long drag.

"Hendaya, get me out of here," he begged.

The policeman's eyes shone through swirls of smoke rising between his fingers.

"Hendaya. It's an order. Get me out of here."

The other man smiled and took a couple more drags.

"You have bad friends," he said at last.

"Where's my daughter? What have you done to her?"

"Nothing, yet."

Valls heard a voice rise into a desperate howl, not realizing it was his own. Hendaya threw the cigarette into the cell, at Valls's feet. The policeman didn't bat an eyelid when the prisoner, seeing him go back up the stairs, started to shout and bang the metal bars with his last remaining bit of strength.

Valls collapsed, exhausted, on his knees. The door at the top of the stairs sealed itself shut like a coffin. Darkness closed in on him again, colder than ever.

23

AMONG THE MANY adventures hidden in the heart of Barcelona, there are unassailable sites, and forbidding chasms. But for the truly fearless, there's the Civil Registry. Vargas faced the ancient structure, covered in soot, and sighed. Its veiled windows and its resemblance to a vast mausoleum seemed to warn the gullible not even to attempt the assault.

Once he'd negotiated the large oak door that kept mere mortals at bay, a heavy-looking counter loomed before him. Behind it, a little man with owlish eyes watched the world go by without even a hint of cordiality.

"Good morning," was Vargas's peace offering.

"It would be if these were opening hours. As the notice on the street clearly specifies, we open from eleven a.m. to one p.m. Tuesdays to Fridays. Today is Monday, and it's eight thirteen in the morning. Can't you read?"

Vargas, practiced in the art of dealing with this sort of petty tyrant—which many a public servant armed with an official stamp carries inside him—dropped his friendly expression and planted his badge two centimeters from the receptionist's nose. "But no doubt *you* can read."

The little man gulped, swallowing a month's worth of saliva and his bad temper. "At your service, Captain. Please forgive this misunderstanding. How can I help you?"

"I'd like to speak to whoever is in charge here, if possible, not a cretin like you."

The receptionist quickly picked up the phone and asked for someone called Señora Luisa. "I don't care," he murmured into the receiver. "Tell her to come out right now."

He put down the receiver and straightened his jacket. Once he'd rearranged himself, he looked at Vargas.

"The director's secretary will be with you right away."

Vargas sat down on a wooden bench without taking his eyes off the receptionist. Two minutes later a small woman with penetrating eyes appeared. Her hair was tied back and she wore rimless glasses. She raised an eyebrow, clearly realizing what had just happened. "Don't get angry with Carmona. He does his best. I'm Luisa Alcaine. How can I help you?"

"My name is Vargas, from police headquarters in Madrid. I need to check some certificate numbers. It's important."

"Don't say it's also urgent. That brings bad luck in this house. Let's have a look at those numbers."

The policeman handed her the list. Doña Luisa took a quick look and nodded. "The arrival or the departure numbers?"

"Excuse me?"

"These over here are death certificates, and these other numbers are birth certificates."

"Are you sure?"

"I'm always sure. My short height is just to mislead people." Luisa gave him a cunning catlike smile.

"Then I'd like to see both, please."

"Everything is possible in the miraculous world of Spanish bureaucracy. Follow me, if you'll be so kind, Colonel," Luisa said, holding a door open behind the counter.

"It's just Captain, I'm afraid."

"Shame. After the fright you gave Carmona, I thought you'd have a higher rank, to be honest. Don't they give you titles according to your height?"

"I've been shrinking for a while now. It's the mileage."

"I understand. I came here looking like a ballerina, and look at me now."

Vargas followed her down a seemingly endless corridor. "Is it me, or does this building seem bigger inside than out?"

"You're not the first person to notice. It grows a little every night. Rumor has it that it feeds on civil servants who are on leave and on legal clerks who come here to look up files and fall asleep in the consultation room. If I were you, I wouldn't drop your guard."

When they reached the end of the corridor, Luisa stopped in front of a huge door that looked like the entrance to a crypt. Someone had hung a piece of paper from the lintel with these words:

ABANDON ALL PATIENCE
ALL YE WHO VENTURE BEYOND THIS DOOR . . .

Luisa pushed open the door and winked at him. "Welcome to the magic world of official forms and two-peseta stamps."

A dizzying beehive of shelves, ladders, and filing cabinets spread out in a vast Florentine tableau under a vault of pointed arches. Something akin to a piece of stage machinery with lamps exuded a dusty light that hung like a ragged curtain.

"God almighty," murmured Vargas. "How can anyone find anything here?"

"The idea is not to be able to find it. But with a bit of ingenuity, a little persistence, and the expert hand of yours truly, one can find anything here, even the philosopher's stone. Show me the list."

Vargas followed Luisa to a wall stuffed with numbered files soaring up to the heavens. The director snapped her fingers, and two diligent-looking staff members appeared. "I'm going to need you to bring down the books from sections 1 to 8B from 1939 to 1943 and 6C to 14 from the same period."

The two minions set off in search of ladders, and Luisa invited Vargas to sit down at one of the consultation desks in the middle of the hall.

"Nineteen thirty-nine?" asked the policeman.

"All these documents still have the old numbering. The system changed in 1944, with the introduction of the national identity document. You're in luck, because a lot of the prewar files were lost, but the period between 1939 and 1944 is all here in a separate section that we finished putting in order a couple of years ago."

"Do you mean to say that all these certificates are from shortly after the war?"

Luisa nodded. "Stirring up the past, eh?" the civil servant hinted. "I applaud your bravery, though I'm not so sure about your prudence. There aren't many people who have the interest or the desire to rummage around there."

While they waited for the return of the two assistants with the requested books, Luisa studied Vargas with clinical curiosity. "How long since you last slept?"

He checked his watch.

"Just over twenty-four hours."

"Shall I ask for a coffee? This could take a while."

Two and a half hours later, Luisa and her two assistants had navigated through oceans of paper and finished the voyage by placing a small islet of volumes in front of Vargas, who could hardly keep awake.

He considered the task ahead and sighed. "Would you do the honors, Señora Luisa?"

"But of course."

While Vargas drank his third cup of coffee, Luisa sent her assistants away and proceeded to organize the registry books into two slowly increasing piles.

"Aren't you going to ask me what all this is about?" Vargas inquired.

"Should I?"

He smiled.

After a while, Luisa let out a sigh of relief. "Well, it should all be there. We'll go through the list again. Let's see."

Checking the numbers, she selected one volume after another. As she examined them, Vargas noticed that she was frowning.

"What?" he asked.

"Are you sure these numbers are correct?"

"They're the ones I have . . . Why?"

Luisa looked up from the pages and gazed at him in surprise. "No, nothing. They're all infants."

"Infants?"

"Children. Look."

Luisa placed the books in front of Vargas and compared the numbers, one at a time.

"Do you see the dates?"

Vargas tried to decipher that numerical mishmash. Luisa guided him with the tip of a pencil.

"They go in couples. For every death certificate there is one birth certificate. Issued on the same day, by the same civil servant, in the same division, and at the same time."

"How do you know?"

"Because of the control code. See?"

"And what does that mean?"

"I don't know."

"Is it normal for the same civil servant to issue two documents simultaneously?"

"No. And even less normal when they're from two different departments."

"What could have caused such a thing?"

"It's not standard procedure. At the time, certificates were noted down by districts. These were all processed in the central registry."

"And is that an irregularity?"

"Very much so. Moreover, these documents, if what is written down here is true, were all issued in a single day."

"And that's odd."

"Odder than two left feet. But that's just the start."

Vargas looked at her.

"All the deaths are certified in the Hospital Militar. How many children die in a military hospital?"

"And the births?"

"In the Hospital del Sagrado Corazón. All, with no exception."

"Could it be a coincidence?"

"If you're a man of faith. . . . And look at the ages of the children. They're also in pairs, as you can see."

Vargas took a closer look, but exhaustion was beginning to cloud his understanding.

"For every death certificate, there is one birth certificate," Luisa once again explained.

"I don't understand."

"The children. Every one of them was born on the same day as one of the deceased."

"Could I borrow all this?"

"The originals cannot leave the premises. You'd have to ask for copies and that would take at least a month, and only by pulling strings."

"Couldn't there be a faster way—"

"And more discreet?" Luisa completed.

"Also."

"Move to one side."

For the next half an hour, Luisa took paper and pen and wrote down an extract with the names, dates, certificate numbers, and codes of each document. Vargas followed her neat, elegant handwriting, trying to find the clue that would tell him what all of it meant. Only then, when his eyes were already drifting through the endless list of words and numbers, did he notice the names Luisa had just written down. "Just a minute," he interrupted.

Luisa moved to one side. Vargas looked back among the certificates and found what he was looking for.

"Mataix," he murmured.

Luisa leaned over the documents the policeman was examining. "Two girls. They died on the same day . . . Does that mean anything to you?"

Vargas's eyes slid down to the bottom of the certificates. "What's this?"

"The signature of the civil servant who issued the document."

The strokes were clean and elegant, the handwriting of someone who knew about appearances and protocol. Vargas formed the name silently with his lips and felt his blood turn to ice.

24

THE APARTMENT SMELLED of Alicia. It smelled of her perfume, her presence, and the aroma left by the touch of her skin. Fernandito had been sitting on the sofa for an eternity and a half, accompanied only by this fragrance and an anxiety that was starting to eat him alive. Alicia and her gun had left a quarter of an hour ago, but the wait was becoming interminable. Unable to stay still for another moment, he got up and went over to the large double windows that looked out on Calle Aviñón, to open them and get some fresh air. With a bit of luck, that disturbing aroma would escape in search of a new victim.

He let the icy breeze clear his conscience and went back inside, determined to wait, just as Alicia had asked him to do. His noble resolve lasted about five minutes. Soon he began to wander around the room, reading the titles of the books on the shelves, stroking the pieces of furniture as he walked by, studying objects he hadn't noticed on previous visits and imagining Alicia following that same path and touching the same things. *This isn't good, Fernandito. Sit down.*

The chairs avoided him. When he thought he couldn't find any new routes around the sitting room, he ventured down a corridor at the end of which were two doors. One led to the bathroom. The other one had to be the door to Alicia's bedroom. He suddenly felt himself blushing, a mixture of modesty, unease, and embarrassment. Before he reached the bathroom door, he turned and went back to the main room, where he sat on a chair and waited. A few heavy minutes dragged by, with no other comfort than the ticking of a grandfather clock. Time, Fernandito realized, always flows at the opposite speed to the needs of the person living through it.

He stood up again and went over to the window. No sign of Vargas. The world went by, distant and banal, five floors down. Without knowing how, he found himself again in the corridor. Outside the bathroom door. He stepped in and looked at his reflexion in the mirror. An open lipstick rested on a shelf. He picked it up and examined it. Blood red. He put it back again and walked out, feeling embarrassed. On the other side was the bedroom door. From the doorway, he could see that the bed was made. Alicia hadn't slept there. A thousand ideas assaulted him, and he killed them off before they could reach his mouth.

He took a few steps into the room and gazed at the bed. He imagined her lying there and looked away. He wondered how many men had been there, lying by her side, exploring her body with their hands and lips. He walked over to the wardrobe and opened it. Alicia's clothes were visible in the shadowy darkness. He brushed the hanging dresses with his fingertips, then closed the door. Opposite the bed stood a wooden chest of drawers. He opened the first drawer and found a whole stash of beautifully folded silk and lace garments. Black, red, and white. It took him a few seconds to realize what he was staring at. This was Alicia's underwear. He gulped. His fingers paused two centimeters from the material. He pulled back his hand as if the lace might burn him and closed the drawer.

You're an idiot, he told himself.

An idiot or not, he opened the second drawer. It contained silk stockings and some device with straps that had the look of something designed to hold them up and made him feel quite dizzy. He shook his head slowly and began to close the drawer. Just then the telephone started to ring with such fury that Fernandito thought his heart was coming unstuck, ready to shoot out of his mouth and crash against the wall. He slammed the drawer shut and ran panting back to the dining room. The telephone was hammering accusingly, like a fire alarm.

Fernandito approached it and watched it vibrate without knowing what to do. The bell rang incessantly for about a minute or more. When at last the boy placed his trembling hand on the receiver and lifted it, the bell stopped ringing. He let it drop back and took a deep breath, then sat down and closed his eyes. Something was pounding in his chest. It was his heart: it was throbbing, and seemed to have gotten trapped in his throat. He laughed at himself, finding comfort in his own foolishness. If Alicia could see him . . .

He was no good at this sort of thing. The sooner he bowed to the evidence, the better. The events of that night and his short experience at Alicia's service had proved to him that he was not made for a life of intrigue but rather for trade and public service. As soon as Alicia returned, he would give her his notice. And he'd better forget his visit to the sanctuary of his boss's undergarments. Worthier men had ruined themselves for much less, he told himself.

*

He was recovering his composure with these edifying thoughts when the telephone burst out ringing again. This time, in a reflex action, he picked it up and replied in a barely audible voice.

"Who's that?" roared the voice at the other end of the line.

It was Vargas.

"It's Fernandito," he replied.

"Tell Alicia to come to the phone."

"Señorita Alicia has gone out."

"Where has she gone?"

"I don't know."

Vargas swore under his breath.

"And you? What are you doing there?"

"Señorita Alicia ordered me to wait for you and tell you what happened last night."

"What happened?"

"I think it's better if I tell you in person. Where are you?"

"At the Civil Registry. Did Alicia say when she would be back?"

501

"She didn't say anything. She took a gun and left."

"A gun?"

"Well, technically speaking it was a revolver, one of those with a cylinder that—"

"I know what it is," Vargas cut in.

"Will you be coming?"

"In a while. I'll go by my room to take a shower and change my clothes—I look a real mess. Then I'll come by the apartment."

"I'll be waiting for you."

"You'd better. Oh, and Fernandito . . ."

"Yes?"

"Don't let me find out that you've been touching anything you shouldn't touch."

*

The blue tram slid along at the speed of tedium. Alicia had got to the stop just in time to jump on board when the driver was about to begin his ascent up Avenida del Tibidabo. The car was packed with a group of school kids, clearly just emerged from a boarding school. Two rather severe-looking priests guarded the boys on their journey, presumably an outing to the church at the top of Mount Tibidabo.

Alicia was the only woman in the tram. As soon as she sat down—in the seat a pupil had offered her at a signal from one of the priests—the raucous kids went so quiet one could hear their stomachs growl, or perhaps it was simply their hormones galloping through their veins. Alicia decided to look down and pretend she was traveling alone. The schoolboys, who seemed to be in their early teens, looked at her out of the corner of their eyes as if they'd never seen any creature like her. One of them, a red-haired brat riddled with freckles, who looked even more of a simpleton than most boys his age, was sitting right opposite Alicia and seemed to be hypnotized by her presence. His eyes had become fixed in a constant bouncing action between her knees and her face. Alicia looked up and held his gaze for a few seconds. The poor boy seemed to be choking, until one of the priests gave him a slap on the back of his neck. "Manolito, let's not get into trouble," warned the cleric.

The rest of the journey passed amid silence, furtive glances, and the occasional muffled giggle. The sight of bursting puberty is the best antidote to nostalgia, thought Alicia.

When they came to the end of the ride, she decided to stay seated while the two priests herded the boarders away as if they were cattle. She watched the mob file past and head for the funicular station, exchanging pushes and vulgar guffaws. The more excited ones turned to look at her and share comments with their mates. Alicia waited until the priests had led them all into the funicular station, as if they were herding them into a pen, and then stepped out of the tram. She crossed the small square, her eyes riveted on the imposing facade of El Pinar crowning the hill before her.

A couple of black cars were parked by the door of the restaurant called La Venta, just a few meters from the tram stop. Alicia knew it well; it was Leandro's favorite restaurant in the whole of Barcelona, and more than once he'd taken her there to teach her table manners and the etiquette of eating out at fancy places. *An elegant young lady doesn't just hold her knife and fork, she caresses them.* Alicia put her hand in her bag, felt her revolver, and unlocked the safety catch.

The vast property of El Pinar had two entrances. The main entrance, where cars drove in, was on Calle Manuel Arnús, just over a hundred meters from the square, following the road that wound its way around the hill toward the northern end of Carretera de las Aguas. The second entrance, an iron gate leading to a path with steps through the garden, was just a short distance from the tram stop. Alicia walked over to the gate and, as she had suspected, discovered that it was locked. She continued following the property wall toward the main entrance. There was a second house there, presumably the old living quarters of the property guards, which she imagined was being watched. As she proceeded around the hill, she noticed at least one figure standing at the top, guarding the outside of the house. Hendaya probably had more men dotted around, both outside and indoors.

She stopped halfway along, at an angle where she couldn't be seen from the main entrance, and examined the wall. It didn't take her long to work out where Fernandito had entered the property the night before. It didn't seem practicable in daylight. It was obvious that she would need help.

She returned to the square, where the tram was already beginning its descent, then made her way to La Venta and stepped into the restaurant. It was deserted at that time of day, and the kitchen wouldn't open for a few hours. She walked over to the bar and sat down on one of the stools. A waiter peered out from behind a curtain and approached her with a polite smile.

"A glass of white wine, please."

"Any preference?"

"Surprise me."

The waiter nodded and expertly took a wineglass, without making eye contact.

"May I use the phone?"

"Of course, miss. It's over there, at the end of the bar."

Alicia waited for the waiter to disappear again behind the curtain, took a sip of wine, and walked over to the telephone.

*

Fernandito was looking out of the window, trying to catch sight of Vargas among the pedestrians walking up Calle Aviñón, when the phone rang again behind him. This time he didn't hesitate before picking it up. "Where on earth are you? Weren't you coming?"

"Who was coming?" asked Alicia at the other end of the line.

"Sorry, I thought you were Captain Vargas."

"Have you seen him?"

"He called to say he was on his way here."

"How long ago?"

"About a quarter of an hour, more or less. He said he was at the Civil Registry."

Alicia let a moment of silence go by. Fernandito interpreted it as a moment of bewilderment.

"Did he say what he was doing there?"

"No. Are you all right?"

"I'm all right, Fernandito. When Vargas arrives, you must first tell him what you told me and then tell him that I'll be waiting for him in the bar next to the Tibidabo funicular station. La Venta."

"That's right next to El Pinar . . ."

"Tell him to hurry up."

"Do you need help? Do you want me to come over?"

"Don't even think of it. I need you to wait there until Vargas arrives, and do what I said. Have you understood?"

"Yes . . . Señorita Alicia?"

Alicia had hung up.

Fernandito was staring at the silent receiver when he noticed something out of the corner of his eye: a movement behind the windows of Vargas's rooms, on the other side of the street. The policeman must have gone up while he was on the phone to Alicia. The boy went over to the window to make sure that he was right. Vargas was on the street, walking up to the Gran Café.

"Captain Vargas!" Fernandito called out.

The policeman disappeared through a doorway. Fernandito looked again at the windows on the other side of the street, just in time to glimpse a figure drawing the curtains. Suddenly he was seized by a dark, cold certainty. He went to the door and started running down the stairs as fast as he could.

25

VARGAS NOTICED IT right away. His room key slid into the lock with difficulty, as if it had come across sharp edges in the mechanism, and when he turned it, the spring barely offered resistance. The lock had been forced.

Pulling out his gun, he gently pushed the door inward with his foot. The apartment—just two rooms separated by a curtain—lay in semidarkness. The curtains were drawn, and Vargas clearly remembered having left them open.

He cocked the hammer. A silhouette stood motionless in a corner. Vargas raised the weapon and aimed.

"Please, don't shoot! It's me!"

Vargas took a few steps forward, and the figure stepped out with his hands in the air.

"Rovira! What the hell are you doing here? I was about to blow your brains out."

The little spy, still wearing his shabby coat, was trembling as he looked at him.

"Put your hands down," said Vargas.

Rovira nodded repeatedly and obeyed. "I'm sorry, Captain. I didn't know what to do. I wanted to wait for you downstairs, but someone was following me, I'm sure, so I thought—"

"Hold your horses, Rovira. What are you talking about?"

Rovira took a deep breath and waved his hands about, as if he didn't know where to begin. Vargas closed the door and led him to an armchair.

"Sit down."

"Yes, sir."

Vargas grabbed a chair and sat facing Rovira.

"Start at the beginning."

Rovira swallowed hard. "I have a message for you from Superintendent Linares."

"Linares?"

Rovira nodded. "He was the one who ordered me to follow you and Señorita Alicia. Although I can assure you I've obeyed all the instructions you gave me and I've kept my distance so as not to bother you. And I've also reported the bare minimum."

"What message?" snapped Vargas.

"When he arrived at police headquarters, Superintendent Linares received a call. Someone from Madrid. From very high up. He's asked me to tell you that you're in danger, that you'd both better leave town. You and Señorita Alicia. He told me to go and look for you at the morgue and tell you. At the morgue, I was told that you'd already left for the registry."

"Go on."

"Have you discovered anything interesting there?" asked Rovira.

"Nothing that concerns you. What else?"

"Well, I went to the registry but was also told that you'd left, so then I hurried over here to wait for you. And it was then that I noticed you were being watched."

"Wasn't that your job?"

"Someone else other than me."

"Who?"

"I don't know."

"And how did you get in here?"

"The door was open. I think someone has forced the lock. I made sure there was no one hidden inside, and I drew the curtains so nobody could see I was waiting for you here."

Vargas looked at him for a long time, without saying a word.

"Have I done something wrong?" asked Rovira fearfully.

"Why didn't Linares phone me at the morgue?"

"The superintendent said the telephones at headquarters weren't safe."

"And why didn't he come in person?"

"He's in a meeting with that officer they sent from the ministry. Someone called Alaya or something like that."

"Hendaya."

Rovira nodded. "That's the one."

The guy was still trembling like a puppy. "Can you give me a glass of water, please?" he begged.

Vargas hesitated for a moment. He walked over to the chest of drawers and filled a glass from a half-full pitcher.

"What about Señorita Alicia?" asked Rovira behind him. "Isn't she with you?"

Rovira's voice was suddenly much closer. Vargas turned, glass in hand, to find Rovira standing right next to him. He no longer trembled, and his frightened expression had fused into an impenetrable mask.

Vargas never got to see the blade of the knife.

He felt a brutal stab in his side, as if someone had bashed his ribs with a hammer, and realized that the cutting edge had sunk so deep, it had perforated his lung. Vargas thought he saw Rovira smile, and when he tried to grab his revolver, he was struck by a second blow. The blade penetrated his neck right up to the handle. Vargas staggered. His vision clouded over, and he held on to the chest of drawers. A third knifing hit his stomach. He collapsed, falling flat on the floor. A shadow hovered over him. While his body surrendered amid convulsions, Rovira snatched his weapon from him, examined it with indifference, then chucked it on the floor.

"Piece of junk," he said.

Vargas searched those bottomless eyes. Rovira waited a few seconds and then dealt him two more stab wounds in the stomach, twisting the blade as he did so. The policeman spat out a surge of blood and tried to hit Rovira, or whoever that creature was who was tearing him apart. His fists barely touched the other man's face. Rovira pulled out the knife, soaked in his blood, and showed it to him.

"You son of a bitch," whispered Vargas.

"Look at me, you old shit. I want you to die knowing that with her, I'm not going to be so gentle. I'm going to make her last, and I swear she's going to curse you for having failed her while I show her all the things I can do."

Vargas felt a deep cold taking hold of him, paralyzing his limbs. His heart beat fast, and he could barely breathe. A tepid, slimy sheet was spreading under his body. His eyes filled with tears, and he was overcome by fear such as he'd never felt before. His murderer cleaned the knife on his lapels and put it away. He stayed there, squatting, looking into Vargas's eyes and relishing his agony.

"Can you feel it now?" he asked. "What is it like?"

Vargas closed his eyes and conjured up the image of Alicia. He died with a smile on his lips, and when the man he'd known as Rovira noticed it, such was his anger that even knowing Vargas was dead, he started hitting his face with his fists until his knuckles were raw.

*

Hiding in the doorway, Fernandito listened. He'd run up the stairs, and when he reached Vargas's door, he waited for a moment before calling. The sound of sharp blows on the other side stopped him. A rough voice was yelling furiously while those terrible punches landed on what sounded like flesh and bone. Fernandito wrestled with the door, but it was shut. After a while the blows stopped, and he heard footsteps approaching the door. Fear gripped him, and, swallowing his shame, he ran up the stairs to hide. Glued to the wall on the landing, Fernandito heard the door open. Footsteps began to descend. Fernandito stuck his head into the stairwell and saw a short man wearing a black coat. He hesitated a few moments, then went silently down to Vargas's door. It was ajar. He peeped into the doorway and saw the policeman's body, lying on a black sheet that looked like a liquid mirror. He didn't know what it was until he stepped on it, slipped, and fell headlong next to the body. Vargas, white as a marble statue, was dead.

For a moment Fernandito didn't know what to do. Then, seeing the policeman's weapon on the floor, he picked it up and hurtled down the stairs.

26

A SHROUD OF clouds was quickly spreading up from the sea, blanketing Barcelona. Sitting at the bar, Alicia turned when she heard the first clap of thunder. She gazed at the line of shadows crawling inexorably over the city. An electric spasm lit up the curtain of cloud, and shortly afterward the first drops of rain hit the windowpanes. In a couple of minutes the skies splintered, and the world plunged into dense gray darkness.

The roar of the storm accompanied her as she left the restaurant and made her way back to the stone wall surrounding the property of El Pinar. The curtain of water blurred all outlines a few meters away and provided cover for her movements. When she passed the garden entrance for a second time, she noticed that from there she could barely make out the front of the house. She walked around the property again and climbed up the wall at the point she had selected earlier. From there she jumped over to the other side, landing on a thick layer of dead leaves that softened her fall. Hiding among the trees, she made her way across the garden until she gained the main path, then followed it to the back of the large, sprawling house, where she found the kitchen windows Fernandito had mentioned in his account. Rain lashed furiously, running down the facade. Alicia drew close to one of the windows and peered inside. She recognized the wooden table, covered in dark stains, where Fernandito had seen Valentín Morgado die. There was nobody in view. Claps of thunder shook the building.

Alicia hit the windowpane with the butt of her revolver. The glass shattered. A second later she was inside.

*

Fernandito followed the stranger closely. He walked at a leisurely pace, as if he had only gone out for a stroll, not just killed a man in cold blood. The first flash of lightning lit up the streets, and people ran to take shelter from the rain beneath the arches of Plaza Real.

The murderer didn't quicken his step or give the slightest indication that he was looking for cover. He went on walking slowly toward the Ramblas. When he got there, he stopped on the pavement's edge. Coming closer, Fernandito could see that his clothes were sodden. For a moment he felt the urge to pull out Vargas's revolver, which he carried in his pocket, and fire a shot in his back. The murderer remained there, unmoving, as if he could feel Fernandito's presence and was waiting for him. Then, without any warning, he set off again, crossing the Ramblas into Calle Conde del Asalto, and headed toward the heart of the Raval quarter.

Fernandito hung back a bit until the stranger turned left at the corner of Calle Lancaster. Then he ran after the little man, rounding the corner just in time to see him disappear behind a door halfway along the block. He waited a few seconds and then slowly approached the door, keeping close to the wall. Dirty water poured down from the cornices, splashing his face and trickling under his coat collar. Opposite the spot where he'd seen the murderer enter, he stopped.

From afar the doorway had looked like the entrance to a residential property, but once closer Fernandito realized that it in fact led to the ground floor of some business. A rusty roll-up door sealed the front. A smaller door, cut into the metal, was slightly ajar. Over the lintel, a faded notice announced:

MANNEQUIN FACTORY
CORTÉS BROTHERS
TAILORING ACCESSORIES & WORKSHOP
ESTABLISHED 1909

The workshop looked abandoned, and had clearly been closed for years. Fernandito wavered. Everything seemed to be screaming at him to get away from that place and go in search of help. He'd retreated as far as the corner when the image of Vargas's crushed body and face stopped him. He turned around and went back to the workshop. Sticking his fingers over the edge of the small door, he opened it a fraction.

*

It was pitch-dark inside. He pulled the door right back and let the faint light filtering through the rain sketch a doorway into darkness. He stared at the outline of what appeared to be a shop like the ones he remembered from his childhood days—wooden counters, glass cabinets, and a few tumbled-down chairs. Everything was covered with what at first looked like sheets of transparent silk. Only after a few bewildered seconds did he realize they were cobwebs. A couple of naked dummies stood in a corner, wrapped in an embrace of webs, as if some giant spider had dragged them there to devour them.

A metallic echo was coming from somewhere deep within the premises. Fernandito narrowed his eyes and noticed that behind the dust-covered counter, a curtain led to a back room. It still swayed gently. He walked over and, almost unable to breathe, gently drew the curtain aside. A long corridor stretched before him. Suddenly the brightness behind him dimmed. He turned just in time to see that the wind, or perhaps someone's hand, had pushed the small entrance door, and it was slowly closing.

*

Alicia advanced through the kitchen, her eyes fixed on a door behind which voices echoed, muffled by the hammering of the rain. She heard footsteps on the other side, and the sudden bang of a heavy door closing. She stopped and, while she waited, examined the layout of the kitchen. The stoves, ovens, and grills looked as if they hadn't been used for a long time. Frying pans, pots, knives, and other utensils still hung from rails on the wall. The metal had turned a darker shade. A large marble sink was full of rubble. The center of the room was taken up by the wooden table, chains and straps tied to its legs and dry blood covering its top. She wondered what they had done with the body of Sanchís's chauffeur, and whether Victoria was still alive.

She walked over to the door and put her ear to it. The voices seemed to come from a nearby room. She was about to open the door a fraction to have a look when once more she heard what at first she'd thought was the sound of rain striking the windowpanes, a metallic drumming that seemed to come from deep down in the house. She held her breath and heard it again. Something or someone was banging a wall or a water pipe. She went over to listen by the well of a dumbwaiter. There she could hear it better, and tell that it came from below. There was something under the kitchen.

Alicia walked slowly around the room, rapping on the walls with her knuckles, but they seemed solid. A metal door was just visible in a corner. She unlocked the lever and opened it. On the other side she found a room, about six meters square, its walls covered in dusty shelving: perhaps an old pantry. The metal drumming could be heard more clearly here. She took a few more steps into the room and felt the vibration beneath her feet. Then she noticed it: a dark line that looked like a vertical crack in the wall at the far end. She drew closer and felt the wall. When she pushed it with both hands, the wall gave way. A strong animal stench of rot and excrement rose from inside. Nauseated, she covered her face with her hand.

A tunnel opened up before her, drilled through the stone, descending at an angle of forty-five degrees. A staircase of irregular steps ran down into the darkness.

Suddenly the drumming stopped. Alicia took one step down and listened. She thought she could hear a faint sound of someone breathing. Pointing her revolver forward, she descended another step.

On one side, hanging from a metal hook on the wall, was a long object. A torch. Alicia took it and, turning the handle, switched it on. A beam of white light penetrated the thick, damp darkness rising from the well.

"Hendaya? Is that you? Don't leave me here . . ." The voice came from the end of the tunnel, broken, barely human.

Alicia stepped down slowly until she glimpsed the metal bars. Raising the torch, she swept the inside of the cell with its beam. When she realized what she was seeing, her blood froze.

He looked like a wounded animal, covered in filth and rags. Wisps of grimy hair and a thick beard hid a yellow face with scratches all over it. The creature crawled up to the bars and stretched out a pleading hand. Alicia lowered her weapon and looked at the prisoner in astonishment. He placed his other arm between the metal bars, and she noticed that his hand was missing. It had been brutally amputated at the wrist, and the stump was covered with dry tar. The skin on that arm had a purplish tone.

Struggling to hold back her nausea, Alicia went over to the metal bars. "Valls?" she asked in astonishment. "Are you Mauricio Valls?"

The prisoner opened his mouth as if he were trying to form a word, but the only thing that came out of his lips was a harrowing groan. Alicia examined the cell's lock. A wrought-iron padlock sealed a chain looped around the bars.

She could hear the sound of footsteps through the walls. She didn't have much time. On the other side of the bars, Valls looked at her with eyes that were drowning in despair. She knew she couldn't get him out of there. Even supposing she could blow open the padlock with her gun, she assumed that Hendaya must have left at least two or three men in the house. She was going to have to leave Valls in his cell and go in search of Vargas.

The prisoner seemed to read her thoughts. He put his hand out and tried to grab her, but he barely had any strength left.

"Don't leave me here," he said, his tone somewhere between a plea and an order.

"I'll come back with help," whispered Alicia.

"No!"

She took his hand, ignoring the revulsion produced by the contact with that bag of bones someone had decided should rot to death in that hole. "I need you not to tell anyone I've been here."

"If you try to leave, I'll shout, you fucking whore, and they'll stick you in here with me."

Alicia looked him in the eye. For a moment she thought she could see the real Valls, or what little was left of him, in that living corpse. "If you do that, you'll never see your daughter again."

Valls's face fell apart, all the fury and despair dissolved in a second.

"I promised Mercedes I would find you," said Alicia.

"Is she alive?"

She nodded.

Valls leaned his forehead against the bars and wept. "Don't let them find her and hurt her," he begged.

"Who? Who would want to hurt Mercedes?"

"Please . . ."

Alicia heard footsteps again above that cavity. She stood up.

Valls gave her one last look, full of resignation and hope.

"Run," he moaned.

27

FERNANDITO STARED AT the door that was slowly closing, pushed by the wind. Darkness solidified around him. The silhouettes of the dummies and the glass cabinets disappeared into the shadows. When the gap in the doorway was just a chink of faint light, he took a deep breath. He'd followed that guy to his hideout with a purpose. Alicia was counting on him. Gripping the revolver firmly, he turned toward the corridor of shadows that plunged into the depths of the workshop.

"I'm not afraid," he whispered.

A light murmur reached his ears. He could have sworn it was a child's laughter. Very close. Just a few meters from where he stood. Footsteps dragged quickly toward him in the dark, and he was seized with panic. He raised his weapon and, without knowing quite what he was doing, pulled the trigger. A deafening roar hit his eardrums, and his arms flew up as if someone had hit his wrists with a hammer. A flash of sulfurous light lit up the passageway for a split second, and Fernandito saw him.

The man was advancing toward him, his knife held high and his eyes ablaze. His face was hidden beneath what looked like a leather mask.

Fernandito fired again and again, until the revolver slipped from his hand and he fell on his back. For a moment he thought the demonic silhouette he'd seen looming over him was by his side, and that the cold steel would touch his skin before he could recover his breath. He pushed himself backward and struggled to his feet. When he'd regained his balance, he hurled himself against the small door. It opened wide, and he fell headlong on the waterlogged street. He scrambled up again and, without looking behind him, ran off as if death were breathing down his neck.

*

They all called him Bernal. That wasn't his real name, but he hadn't bothered to correct them. He'd only been in that damned house that made your hair stand on end for a few days, at Hendaya's orders, but he'd seen enough. Enough to realize that the less that ripper and his team of butchers knew about him, the better. In just under two months he would fade away into retirement with a miserable pension as a reward for his burned-out life in the police force. At this point in the farce, his great dream was to die alone and forgotten in a dark, damp room in some boardinghouse on Calle Joaquín Costa. He'd rather die like an old hooker than as a bogus hero, honoring those pretty kids they were sending from the Ministry of the Interior: the new centurions, all of them cut from the same cloth, ready to clear the streets of Barcelona of poor wretches and third-rate reds who could barely stand up to pee, having spent half their lives hidden or walled up in prisons as crowded as beehives. There are times when it's more honorable to die forsaken than to live in glory.

The wrongly named Bernal was lost in these thoughts when he opened the door to the kitchen. Hendaya insisted on him making the rounds, and Bernal always followed orders to the letter. That was his specialty.

He only had to take three steps to notice that something was out of place. A gust of fresh air brushed his face, and he looked up toward the far end of the kitchen. A flash of lightning revealed the dented edges of the broken windowpane. He walked over to the corner and knelt down by the pieces of glass that had fallen from the window. A trail of footprints petered out over the dust—a light tread and tiny soles, with matching heel marks. A woman. The false Bernal weighed up the evidence. He stood up and walked over to the pantry room, then pushed the wall at the end and opened the entrance to the tunnel. He took a few steps down, until the reek that came from below advised him to stop. He turned back and was about to close the access when he noticed the torch hanging from the hook. It was swaying gently. The police officer closed the door and returned to the kitchen. He had a quick look around, and after mulling it over for a bit, he rubbed out the footprints with his foot and pushed the bits of glass into a dark corner. He wasn't going to be the one to tell Hendaya, when he returned, that someone had paid a surprise visit to the house. The last poor soul who gave Hendaya bad news had ended up with a broken jaw. And that was one of his right-hand men. They were not going to get his help. With a bit of luck, he'd be given a little medal in seven weeks' time, which he was planning to pawn to pay for the services of a classy tart with whom to bid farewell to this rotten world. If he managed to make it through this last assignment, he could still salvage a gray and ill-fated old age in which to forget what he'd witnessed during those last days in El Pinar, and convince himself that everything he'd done in the name of duty belonged to a man named Bernal, someone he'd never been, and never would be.

*

Hiding in the garden on the other side of the window, Alicia watched the policeman roam around the kitchen area, check the entrance to the tunnel, and then, inexplicably, rub out the footprints she'd left behind her. The policeman took one last look and then went back to the door. Making the most of the fact that the rain was still bucketing down, and not knowing for certain whether the officer would tell his superiors what he had discovered, Alicia decided to risk crossing the garden very quickly, going down the hillside and climbing over the wall. For the sixty seconds this took, she kept expecting a shot between her shoulder blades that never came.

After jumping down into the street, she ran back to the square, where the blue tram was starting its descent in the storm, and hopped onto the moving carriage. Ignoring the conductor's disapproving look, she collapsed onto a seat, soaking wet and trembling either from cold or relief—she wasn't sure which.

*

She found him sitting in the rain, huddled on the doorstep. Alicia walked through the puddles flooding Calle Aviñón and stopped in front of Fernandito. He raised his head and looked at her with tears in his eyes.

She knew even before he spoke. "Where's Vargas?" she asked.

Fernandito lowered his head. "Don't go up," he whispered.

Alicia went up, two steps at a time, ignoring the pain that drilled through her hip and fired up her side. When she reached the fourth-floor landing, she stopped in front of the half-open door to Vargas's rooms. A sickly-sweet smell floated in the air. She pushed the door inward and saw the body, lying over a shiny, dark sheet. A sudden chill took her breath away, and she held on to the doorframe. Her legs shook as she drew closer to the corpse.

Vargas's eyes were open. His face was a wax mask, so brutally beaten up she hardly recognized him. She knelt down beside him and stroked his cheek. He was cold. Angry tears clouded her eyes, and she stifled a moan.

Next to the body was a fallen chair. Alicia picked it up and sat down to gaze in silence at the corpse. The searing pain in her hip was raging through her bones. She struck her old wound hard, fist clenched. For a few seconds the pain blinded her, and she almost fell on the floor. She kept on hitting herself until Fernandito, who had been witnessing the scene from the doorway, held her arms and stopped her. He embraced her until he'd steadied her, then let her howl with pain until she could hardly breathe.

"It's not your fault," he said, over and over again.

When Alicia had stopped shaking, Fernandito covered the body with a blanket he found on an armchair.

"Look in his pockets," ordered Alicia.

The boy went through the policeman's coat and jacket. He found his wallet, a few coins, a piece of paper bearing a list of numbers, and a visiting card that read:

> **MARÍA LUISA ALCAINE**
> *Assistant Secretary*
> *to the Head Office*
> *of Archives and Documentation*
>
> CIVIL REGISTRY OF BARCELONA

He handed her what he'd found, and Alicia examined it. She kept the list and the card. The rest she returned to Fernandito, telling him to put it all back where he'd found it. Her eyes were riveted on Vargas's body, its shape visible under the blanket.

Fernandito waited a couple of minutes before walking back to her side. "We can't stay here," he said at last.

Alicia looked at him as if she couldn't understand him, or couldn't hear him.

"Give me your hand," he said.

She ignored him, trying to get up on her own. Seeing her wince in pain, Fernandito put his arms around her and helped her up.

Once she was on her feet, she took a few steps, trying to hide the fact that she was limping. "I'm OK on my own." Her voice was icy, her eyes impenetrable, no longer betraying any emotion, not even when she turned to Vargas for the last time.

She's closed and bolted all the doors, thought Fernandito.

"Let's go," she murmured, limping to the exit.

Fernandito held her arm and led her to the stairs.

*

They sat at a table in the far corner of the Gran Café. Fernandito asked for two large coffees with milk and a glass of brandy, poured the brandy into one of the cups, and handed it to Alicia. "Drink. It will warm you up."

Alicia accepted the cup and sipped at the coffee slowly. The rain scratched the windowpanes and trickled down, masking the gray blanket that had fallen over Barcelona. Once Alicia had recovered her color, Fernandito told her the whole story.

"You shouldn't have followed him to that place," she said.

"I wasn't going to let him get away."

"Are you sure he's dead?"

"I don't know. I fired two or three shots with Captain Vargas's gun. He couldn't have been more than two meters away. It was very dark . . ."

Alicia put her hand on Fernandito's and smiled weakly.

"I'm OK," he lied.

"Do you still have the weapon?"

Fernandito shook his head. "It fell when I was running away. What are we going to do now?"

Alicia was quiet for a few moments, her gaze lost in the windowpane. She could feel the pain in her hip throbbing in time to her pulse.

"Shouldn't you take one of those pills of yours?" asked Fernandito.

"Afterward."

"After what?"

Alicia looked him in the eye. "I need you to do something else for me."

Fernandito nodded. "Anything."

She looked in her pockets and handed him a key. "It's the key to my home. Take it."

"I don't understand."

"I want you to go up to the apartment. Make sure there's nobody there before you go in. If the door is open or the lock looks as if it's been forced, start running and don't stop until you get home."

"You're not coming with me?"

"Once you're in the dining room, look under the sofa. You'll find a box of documents and papers. Inside this box there's an envelope with a notebook inside it. The envelope is marked 'Isabella.' Have you understood?"

He nodded. "Isabella."

"I want you to take that box away with you. Hide it. Hide it where nobody can find it. Can you do that for me?"

"Yes. Don't worry. But—"

"No buts. If anything should happen to me—"

"Don't say that."

"If anything should happen to me," Alicia insisted, "you can't even go to the police. If I don't return to collect the documents, let a few days go by, then take them to the Sempere & Sons bookshop on Calle Santa Ana. The place where you picked those books up for me."

"Yes, I know."

"Before you go in, make sure nobody is watching the bookshop. If anything makes you the slightest bit suspicious, just walk past and wait for another moment. When you're there, ask for Fermín Romero de Torres. Repeat the name."

"Fermín Romero de Torres."

"Don't trust anyone else. You can't trust anyone else."

"You're scaring me, Señorita Alicia."

"If anything happens to me, give him the documents. Tell him I sent you. Tell him what happened. Explain that among these documents is the diary of Isabella Gispert, Daniel's mother."

"Who is Daniel?"

"Tell Fermín that he must read it and decide whether or not to give it to Daniel. He'll be the judge."

Fernandito nodded. Alicia smiled sadly. She held the boy's hand and pressed it hard. He took her hand to his lips and kissed it.

"I'm sorry I got you mixed up in this, Fernandito. And that I've left you with that responsibility. . . . I had no right."

"I'm glad you did. I won't fail you."

"I know. . . . One last thing. If I don't return . . ."

"You'll return."

"If I don't return, don't ask after me in hospitals, or in police stations, or anywhere else. Imagine that you've never known me. Forget me."

"I'm never going to forget you, Señorita Alicia. I'm that stupid . . ."

She stood up. It was obvious that the pain was devouring her, but she smiled at Fernandito as if it was just a passing discomfort.

"You're going to look for that man, aren't you?" he said.

Alicia didn't reply.

"Who is he?" asked Fernandito.

Alicia visualized the description Fernandito had given her of Vargas's murderer. "He calls himself Rovira," she said. "But I don't know who he is."

"Whoever he is, if he's still alive, he's very dangerous." Fernandito stood up, ready to accompany her.

Alicia stopped him, shaking her head. "What I need is for you to go to my house and do as I asked."

"But . . ."

"Don't argue. And swear you'll do exactly as I said."

Fernandito sighed. "I swear."

Alicia gave him one of her conquering smiles, the sort that had so often clouded what little sense God had given the boy, and limped away to the door. He watched her walk off in the rain, more fragile than ever, until he lost sight of her up the street. Then, after leaving a few coins on the table, he crossed the street to Alicia's building. In the hallway he bumped into the caretaker, his aunt Jesusa, who was trying to mop up the rain flooding the floor with a rag wrapped around the end of a broom. When she saw him walk past with a key in his hand, Jesusa frowned disapprovingly. Fernandito realized that the caretaker, who had a sharp eye for gossip and a hawk's eye for everything that didn't concern her, must have witnessed the scene in the Gran Café on the other side of the street, hand-kissing included.

"Haven't you learned your lesson yet, Fernandito?"

"It's not what it looks like, Auntie."

"I'd rather not say what it looks like, but as I'm your aunt, and the only member of the family who seems to have any common sense, I must tell you what I've told you a thousand times."

"That Señorita Alicia is not the right woman for me," Fernandito recited from memory.

"And that one day she'll break your heart, as they say on the radio," Jesusa completed.

That day had been left behind years ago, but Fernandito preferred not to stir things up. Jesusa went up to him and smiled tenderly, pinching his cheeks as if he were still ten years old. "I don't want you to suffer, that's all. Señorita Alicia—and you know how fond I am of her, as if she were family—she's a ticking bomb waiting to go off: when we least expect it, she'll explode and take everyone in her path with her, and may God forgive me for saying so."

"I know, Auntie. I know. Don't you worry, I know what I'm doing."

"That's what your uncle said the day he drowned."

Fernandito stooped down to kiss her on her forehead and charged up the stairs. He walked into Alicia's apartment, leaving the door ajar as he followed her instructions. The box she'd described was under the sitting-room sofa. He opened it, had a quick look at the pile of documents, and noticed, among them, the envelope marked "Isabella." He didn't dare open it.

He closed the box and wondered who this Fermín Romero de Torres was, who merited all Alicia's confidence, the person to whom she entrusted herself as her last salvation. He supposed that, in the great scheme of things, there were many other characters in Alicia's life about whom he knew nothing, and who played an infinitely more important role than his.

Perhaps you thought you were the only one . . .

He picked up the box and walked back to the door. Before stepping out and closing it, he took one last look at Alicia's apartment, convinced that he would never again set foot in it. When he reached the entrance hall, he saw his aunt Jesusa, armed with her large broom, still trying to hold back the rain filtering in through the main door. He stopped for a moment.

"You coward," he murmured to himself. "You shouldn't have let her go."

Jesusa interrupted her efforts and looked at him, intrigued. "What are you saying, sweetheart?"

Fernandito sighed. "Auntie, can I ask you a favor?"

"But of course."

"I need you to hide this box where nobody can find it. It's very important. Don't tell anyone you've got it. Not even the police, if they come around asking. No one."

Jesusa's face darkened. The caretaker took a quick look at the box and made the sign of the cross. "Oh dear, oh dear . . . What mess have you two got yourselves in?"

"Nothing that can't be fixed."

"That's what your uncle always said."

"I know. Will you do me this favor? It's very important."

Jesusa nodded solemnly.

"I'll be back soon."

"Do you swear?"

"Of course."

He went out into the rainy street, fleeing Jesusa's anxious look. There was so much fear in his body that he barely noticed the cold that chilled him to the marrow. On his way to what might well be the last day in his short life, he told himself that, thanks to Alicia, he had at least learned two things that would serve him forever—if he lived to tell the story, that is. The first was how to lie. The second, and this he was still smarting from, was that promises were a bit like hearts: once the first was broken, breaking the rest was a piece of cake.

28

ALICIA STOPPED ON the corner of Calle Lancaster and observed the entrance to the old mannequin factory for a couple of minutes. The small door Fernandito had gone through was still ajar. The building that housed the workshop was nothing more than a two-story gap of dark stone with a bulging roof. The windows on the first floor were boarded up with wooden planks and a few filthy cobblestones. Stuck to the facade was a cracked box of wires, and a knot of telephone cables peeped out through two holes drilled in the stone. Apart from these details, the place looked abandoned, like most of the old industrial workshops remaining in that part of the Raval quarter.

Edging along the facade to avoid being seen from the entrance, Alicia approached the workshop. The downpour had left the streets deserted, and she didn't hesitate to pull out her gun and point it straight into the doorway. Pushing the door wide open, she scanned the tunnel of light that shone into the hallway and then stepped in, holding her weapon in front of her with both hands. A slight draft came from inside, impregnated with the smell of old water pipes and what she guessed was kerosene or some other fuel.

The hallway opened into what must have once been the sales outlet for the workshop. A counter, a set of empty glass cabinets, and a couple of mannequins wrapped in something whitish and transparent presided over the room. Alicia walked around the counter toward the wooden beaded curtain that concealed the entrance to the back room. She was about to step through it when her foot knocked against a metal object. Without lowering her revolver, she glanced down briefly and saw Vargas's weapon. She picked it up, slipping it into her jacket's left-hand pocket, and drew aside the beaded curtain.

A corridor stretched out before her into the depths of the building. The smell of gunpowder still floated in the air. A chain of faint reflections swung from the ceiling. Alicia prodded the walls until she felt a round switch. She turned the peg, and a garland of low-voltage bulbs hanging from a cable lit up along the corridor. Their reddish half-light revealed a narrow passageway that sloped gently downward. A few meters from the entrance, the wall was spattered with dark stains, as if red paint had been sprayed over it. At least one of the bullets Fernandito had fired had struck its target. Perhaps more. The trail of blood continued along the floor and vanished down the passageway. A little farther on she found the knife with which Rovira had tried to attack Fernandito. The blade was bloodstained: Alicia realized it was Vargas's blood. She continued onward and didn't stop until she made out the halo of ghostly light shining through from the far end of the tunnel.

"Rovira?" she called.

A dance of shadows stirred at the bottom of the corridor, and she could hear the soft sound of something creeping slowly in the dark. Alicia tried to swallow, but her mouth was dry. Since she'd stepped into that corridor, she hadn't felt the pain in her hip or the chill of her drenched clothes. All she felt was fear.

She walked on to the end of the passage, ignoring the squeak of her soles as she stepped on the firm, damp, slimy floor.

"Rovira, I know you're wounded. Come out and let's talk."

Her own voice sounded fragile and fearful, but the direction in which the echo traveled served her as a guide. When she reached the end of the tunnel, she stopped. A large hall with tall ceilings spread out before her. She viewed the remains of the worktables, the tools and machinery on either side of the plant. A frosted glass skylight at the far end of the workshop illuminated a pale phantasmagoria.

They dangled from the ceiling, held up by ropes that made them look like hanged corpses, suspended half a meter from the ground. Men, women, and children, dummies dressed in the finery of older times, swayed in the half-light like souls trapped in a secret purgatory. There were dozens of them. Some displayed smiling faces and glassy eyes, others were half finished. Alicia's heart pounded in her throat. She took a deep breath and stepped into the pack of hanging figures. Arms and legs brushed gently against her hair and face, the figures swaying and stirring as she slowly advanced through them.

The echoing sound of the wooden bodies as they rubbed against each other spread through the plant. Beyond it she could hear a mechanical whir. The smell of kerosene intensified as she approached the far end of the workshop. Alicia left the forest of hanging bodies behind her and cast her eyes on a piece of industrial machinery that vibrated and gave off puffs of steam. A generator. A heap of discarded body parts lay on one side, dismembered heads, hands, and torsos tangled into a mass. It reminded her of the piles of bodies she'd seen in the streets during the war, after the air raids.

"Rovira?" she called again, more to hear her own voice than expecting a reply.

He was watching her from some dark corner, she was certain. She scanned the plant, trying to read the protruding shapes she could sense in the gloom. She didn't detect any movement. Behind the pile of mannequin remains, she noticed a door with cables running under it that connected to the generator. A meager electric light outlined the doorframe. Alicia prayed that Rovira's lifeless body was there, stretched out on the floor. She walked up to the door and kicked it open.

29

THE ROOM WAS rectangular, with black walls and no windows. It smelled damp and looked like a crypt. A row of naked bulbs ran across the ceiling, radiating a yellowish light and emitting a low, crackling buzz, as if a swarm of insects were creeping along the walls. Before she went in, Alicia scrutinized every centimeter of the room. There was no sign of Rovira.

A ramshackle bed, covered with a couple of old blankets, occupied one of the corners. A wooden box on one side acted as a bedside table. On the box was a black telephone, candles, and a glass jar full of coins. An old suitcase peeped out from under the mattress, together with a pair of shoes and a bucket. Next to the bed was a large wardrobe made of carved wood, the sort of antique piece one would expect to see in an elegant home, not in an industrial workshop. Its doors were almost shut tight, leaving a small opening. Alicia drew closer to the wardrobe, a step at a time, ready to empty her revolver. For a second she imagined Rovira inside, smiling and waiting for her to open the door.

She held the weapon firmly in both hands and gave one of the doors a kick. It opened slowly, bouncing off the frame. The wardrobe was empty. A bar held a dozen bare hangers. At the bottom of the wardrobe she found a cardboard box with just one word written on it:

SALGADO

She tugged at the box, and its contents scattered around her feet: jewels, watches, and other valuable objects. There were wads of notes that looked like they were no longer legal tender, tied up with strings. Gold ingots, melted down quickly and roughly. Alicia knelt down and stared at that loot, a small fortune. It must be the treasure that Sebastián Salgado, once a prisoner in Montjuïc, and the first suspect mentioned in the disappearance of Valls, had hidden in a locker of the Estación del Norte; the treasure he had dreamed of retrieving after the minister requested his pardon and set him free two decades later.

Salgado had never managed to recover the fruit of his crimes and pillage. When he opened that locker, all he found was an empty suitcase. He'd died knowing he was a thief beaten at his own game. Someone had gotten there ahead of him. Someone who knew about the loot and the plot involving the anonymous letters Valls had been receiving for years. Someone who had been pulling the strings of that whole business long before the minister disappeared.

The lights flickered for a moment, and Alicia turned around, startled. And then she saw it. It covered an entire wall, from floor to ceiling. She approached it slowly, and when she realized what she was looking at, she felt her knees weaken and let her arms drop.

The mosaic was made up of dozens, even hundreds, of photographs, newspaper clippings, and notes. It had been put together with extraordinary precision and the diligence of a silversmith. All the pictures, without exception, were of Alicia. She recognized snapshots from her first days in the unit, next to old photographs in which she was barely a child, dating from her years at the orphanage. The collection included dozens of snapshots taken from a distance, show-ing her walking along streets in Madrid or Barcelona, by the entrance to the Gran Hotel Palace, sitting in a café with a book, walking down the stairs of the National Library, shopping in the capital, even stroll-ing by the Crystal Palace in Retiro Park. One of the photographs showed the door to her room in the Hispania.

She found newspaper clippings giving details of cases in which she'd been involved but which, naturally, never mentioned Alicia or the unit, crediting only the police or the Civil Guard. At the foot of the mosaic was a table arranged like an altar on which she recognized all kinds of objects related to her: menus from restaurants she remem-bered having visited, paper napkins on which she'd jotted something down, notes signed by her, a wineglass with a lipstick mark on the rim, a cigarette stub, the remains of her train ticket from Madrid to Barcelona . . .

In a glass bowl at one end of the table, exhibited like relics, were a few bits of underwear she'd been missing since the night when someone, or something, had come into her apartment while she was under the effects of her medication. A pair of stockings was neatly spread out on the table and held down with pins. Next to the stock-ings lay the Víctor Mataix book from the *Labyrinth of the Spirits* series that had been stolen from her home. Alicia suddenly felt a strong urge to run away from that nightmarish place.

She never saw the figure that had risen slowly from among the pile of dismembered bodies behind her, on the other side of the door, and was advancing toward her.

30

WHEN SHE REALIZED what had happened, it was already too late. She heard labored breathing behind her and turned around, but had no time to aim her revolver. A brutal impact shook her to the core. The stabbing pain took her breath away, and she fell to her knees. Only then was she able to see him clearly and understand why she hadn't noticed him on her way in. A white mask covered his face. He was naked and carried an object that looked like some sort of industrial awl.

Alicia tried to shoot Rovira, but he skewered her hand with the metal spike. The revolver tumbled onto the floor. The man grabbed her by her neck and dragged her to the bed. He let her fall there and sat on her legs, holding them tight. He clutched her right hand, which he'd perforated with the awl, and leaned over to tie it to the metal bars of the bed with a piece of wire. As he did so, his mask slipped off and she saw his contorted face, almost touching hers. His eyes were glazed, and the skin on one side was peppered with the burns of a close-range gunshot. One of his ears was bleeding, and he smiled like a boy about to pull the wings off an insect, taking pleasure in its agony.

"Who are you?" asked Alicia.

Rovira observed her, enjoying the moment. "You think you're so clever, and you still haven't figured it out? I'm you. Everything you should have been. At first I admired you. But then I realized that you're weak, that I have nothing left to learn from you. I'm better than you. I'm better than you could have ever been . . ."

Rovira had left the awl on the bed. Alicia reckoned that if she could distract him for a second she might perhaps be able to grab it with her left hand, which was free, and thrust in into his neck or his eyes.

"Don't hurt me," she pleaded. "I'll do whatever you want . . ."

Rovira laughed. "My dear, what I want is precisely to hurt you. To hurt you a lot. I've earned it . . ."

Then he held her by her hair against the bed and licked her lips and her face. Alicia closed her eyes, groping around the blanket in search of the awl. Rovira's hands ran down her torso and stopped at the old wound on her side. She had touched the awl's handle when Rovira whispered in her ear: "Open your eyes, you whore. I want to see your face properly when you feel it."

She opened her eyes, knowing what was coming and praying that she might lose consciousness before the first blow. Rovira straightened up, raised his arm, and banged his fist down on her wound with all his might. Alicia let out a deafening howl. Rovira, the room, the light, the cold she felt in her body—everything was forgotten. All that existed was the pain flashing through her bones like an electric current, making her forget who she was and where she was.

Rovira laughed to see her body tighten like a cable and her eyes roll back. He lifted her skirt far enough to reveal the scar that covered her hip like a black spiderweb, exploring her skin with the tips of his fingers. He leaned over to kiss her wound and then struck her again and again until he'd damaged his fist against her hip bones. Finally, when no more sound came out of Alicia's throat, he stopped. Sinking into a well of agony and darkness, she'd gone into convulsions. Rovira recovered the awl and used its point to run over the web of dark capillaries visible under the pale skin of Alicia's hip.

"Look at me," he ordered. "I'm your substitute. I'll be much better than you. From now on, I'll be the favorite."

Alicia looked at him defiantly.

Rovira winked at her. "That's my Alicia," he said.

He died smiling.

He didn't get to see that Alicia was reaching for the revolver she'd kept in the left-hand pocket of her jacket. When he started to poke around in her wound with the awl, she had already placed the barrel under his chin.

"Clever girl," he whispered.

A moment later, Rovira's face was pulverized into a cloud of bone and blood. The second shot, at point-blank range, knocked him backward. The naked body fell onto its back at the foot of the old bed, a smoking hole in its chest, the hand still gripping the awl.

Alicia dropped the weapon and struggled until she freed her right hand from the bedstead. Adrenaline had spread a veil over the pain, but she knew it would be short-lived. Sooner or later, when it returned, she would pass out. She had to get out of that place as quickly as possible.

She managed to straighten up and sit on the bed. When she tried to stand up, she had to wait a couple of minutes; her legs wouldn't hold her, and she was seized by a weakness she couldn't quite comprehend. She felt cold. Very cold. At last she managed to get to her feet, almost shivering. She leaned against the wall. Her body and clothes were covered in Rovira's blood. She couldn't feel her right hand except for a dull throb. She examined the wound left by the awl. It didn't look good.

Just then, the telephone next to the bed rang. Alicia suppressed a scream.

She let it ring for about a minute, staring at it as if it were a bomb about to explode at any moment. Finally she lifted the receiver and put it to her ear. She listened, holding her breath. A long silence followed on the line. Above the light hum of the long-distance connection, she could hear slow breathing.

"Are you there?" said the voice.

Alicia felt the receiver shaking in her hands. It was Leandro.

The phone slipped from her hand, and she staggered toward the door. As she walked past the sanctuary Rovira had created, she stopped. Anger gave her enough strength to go into the workshop, find one of the kerosene cans standing next to the generator, and pour the contents on the floor. A thick liquid oozed through the room, surrounding Rovira's corpse, spreading a black mirror from which rose swirls of iridescent vapor. When she walked past the generator, she yanked off one of the cables, letting it fall on the floor.

As she made her way through the mannequins that hung from the ceiling toward the corridor that led to the exit, she could hear the crackling sound behind her. When the blaze caught, a sudden gust of air shook the figures surrounding her. An amber glow followed her through the passageway as she advanced, swaying and lurching from one wall to the other to keep herself on her feet. She had never felt so cold.

She prayed to heaven or hell not to let her die in that tunnel, to let her reach the frame of light just visible in the distance. Her flight seemed endless, as if she were scaling the guts of a beast that had swallowed her, climbing back up to its jaws so as not to be devoured. The heat penetrating through the tunnel from the flames behind her barely thawed the icy embrace wrapping itself around her. She didn't stop until she'd walked through the hallway and was out in the street. Feeling the rain caressing her skin, she breathed again. A figure was running toward her up the street.

She collapsed into Fernandito's arms. The boy hugged her and smiled, but he was staring at her, terrified. She put her hand on her belly, on the place where she had felt that first blow. Warm blood ran through her fingers and dissolved in the rain. She no longer felt pain, only cold, an icy cold telling her softly to let go, to close her eyelids and abandon herself to eternal sleep, which promised peace and truth.

She looked into Fernandito's eyes and smiled at him.

"Don't let me die here," she whispered.

31

THE STORM HAD swept the street of passersby and left the bookshop bereft of customers. Fermín decided to devote the day to assorted menial undertakings and a dash of low-level philosophizing. Taking no notice of the lightning flashes and the crashing rain, which seemed determined to knock down the shop window, he turned on the radio. Patiently, as if he were coaxing the lock of a safe, he turned the dial until he came across the sound of a big band that was launching into the first bars of "Siboney." At the first roll of the timbale drums, Fermín began to sway to the Caribbean rhythm and went back to the repair and restoration work of a six-volume edition of *The Mysteries of Paris* by Eugène Sue, with Daniel as his kitchen boy and helper.

"I used to kill this tune on the dance floor and sweep the chorus girls off their feet at the Tropicana when I was young and still had a good hip movement. What memories it brings. . . . If instead of good looks I'd had a talent for literature, I would have written *The Mysteries of Havana*," he proclaimed.

"Eros won, and Parnassus lost," Bea remarked.

Fermín walked over to her, keeping step with the music, his arms wide open, swinging his hips to the *clave* rhythm.

"Señora Bea, come, I'll show you the basic steps of the *son montuno*. Your husband dances as if he were wearing cement clogs, and you haven't been able to properly experience the frenzy of Afro-Cuban tempo. Let's go . . ."

Bea ran to hide in the back room, where she hoped to finish squaring the accounts and keep her distance from Fermín's bopping and crooning.

"Your wife can sometimes be as dull as the small print on a land-registry list," Fermín said.

"You're telling me," replied Daniel.

"Sound travels here," warned Bea's voice from the back room.

This pleasant atmosphere was broken when they heard a car braking suddenly on the wet street. When they looked up, they saw a taxi stop in the pouring rain outside the Sempere & Sons shop window. There was a sudden flash of lightning, and for a split second the car looked like a carriage made of molten lead smoldering in the rain.

"Leave it to a taxi driver . . . ," said Fermín.

The rest happened at the speed of disaster. A young boy soaked to the skin, face flattened by terror, came out of the taxi and when he saw the CLOSED notice on the door started banging the glass with his fists. Fermín and Daniel swapped glances.

"And they say nobody wants to buy books anymore," said Fermín.

Daniel walked over to the door and opened it. The boy, who looked as if he was on the verge of collapse, put his hand on his chest, took a deep breath, and asked, almost shouting, "Which of you is Fermín Romero de Torres?"

Fermín raised a hand. "That's me, the one with the muscles."

Fernandito rushed over to grab his arm, pulling at him. "I need you," he begged.

"Look, kid, don't take this the wrong way, but the most stunning of females have told me the same many a time, and I've known how to resist."

"It's Alicia," Fernandito panted. "I think she's dying . . ."

Fermín went pale. He looked at Daniel in alarm and, without saying a word, let Fernandito drag him to the street and get into the taxi, which sped away.

Bea, who had just poked her head around the back-room curtain and witnessed the scene, looked at Daniel in bewilderment.

"What was that?"

Her husband sighed despondently. "Bad news," he murmured.

As soon as he landed inside the car, Fermín came up against the taxi driver's eyes.

"Not you again," said the driver. "Where are we going now?"

Fermín tried to size up the situation. It took him a few moments to realize that the figure with skin as pale as wax and a faraway look lying on the back seat of the taxi was Alicia. Fernandito was cradling her head in his hands, struggling to hold back his tears of panic.

"Just keep going," Fermín ordered the taxi driver.

"Where to?"

"For now, just straight ahead. Step on it."

Fermín searched Fernandito's eyes.

"I didn't know what to do," stammered the boy. "She wouldn't let me take her to a hospital or a doctor and . . ."

In a brief moment of lucidity, Alicia gazed at Fermín and smiled sweetly at him. "Fermín, always trying to save me."

When he heard her shaky voice, Fermín's stomach and all its neighboring entrails shrank. Since he'd eaten a whole bagful of dry almond biscuits for breakfast, it was triply painful. Alicia dangled between consciousness and the abyss, so Fermín decided to shake the young boy for information, since he seemed the most scared of all three by far. "You, what's your name?"

"Fernandito."

"Can you tell me what's happened here?"

Fernandito began to sum up what had happened in the last twenty-four hours with so much rush and confusion of details that Fermín stopped him, deciding to establish practical priorities. He felt Alicia's belly and examined her bloodstained fingers.

"Helmsman," he ordered the taxi driver, "head for the Hospital del Mar. Fly!"

"You should have hailed a balloon. Look at the traffic."

"Either we get there in the next ten minutes, or I'll burn down this heap. You have my word."

The taxi driver grunted and pressed the accelerator. He and Fermín exchanged scowling glances through the rearview mirror.

"Don't quarrel, you two," Fernandito scolded them. "We're losing Señorita Alicia."

"Holy shit," swore the cabdriver, dodging the traffic on Vía Layetana on his way to the waterfront.

Fermín pulled a handkerchief out of his pocket and handed it to Fernandito. "Hold the handkerchief out of the window," he ordered him.

Fernandito nodded and did as he was told. Taking great care, Fermín lifted Alicia's blouse and found the hole left by the awl in her belly. Blood was gushing out of it.

"Jesus, Mary, and Joseph . . ." He pressed the wound with his hand and checked the traffic. Despite his grumbling, the taxi driver was performing juggling tricks with cars, buses, and pedestrians at breakneck speed.

Fermín felt his breakfast swiftly rising up his throat. "If at all possible, the idea would be to get to the hospital alive. One person at death's door is more than enough."

"Ask the Three Kings for miracles. And if not, you're welcome to take the wheel," replied the driver. "How's it going back there?"

"We could do better."

Fermín stroked Alicia's face and patted it gently, trying to revive her. She opened her eyes. Her corneas were bursting with blood from the blows. "You mustn't fall asleep now, Alicia. Make an effort to stay awake. Do it for me. If you like, I can crack dirty jokes or sing you some Frank Sinatra hits."

Alicia gave him a dying smile. At least she could still hear.

"Picture the Generalissimo in his hunting outfit, with his little beret and his boots. That always gives me nightmares and won't let me sleep."

"I'm cold," murmured Alicia weakly.

"We're almost there . . ."

Fernandito was watching her in dismay. "It's my fault. She kept asking me not to take her to any hospital, and she scared me," he said. "She kept assuring me that they'd look for her there—"

"It's to the hospital or to the graveyard," Fermín interrupted.

Fernandito looked as if he'd been hit in the face. He was only a kid,

Fermín remembered; he was probably more frightened than anyone else in the taxi. "Don't worry, Fernando. You did what you had to do. In moments like these, anyone can get his underwear in a knot."

Fernandito sighed, consumed by guilt. "If anything should happen to Señorita Alicia, I'll die . . ."

She took his hand and pressed it feebly.

"What if that man finds her . . . Hendaya?" Fernandito whispered.

"There's no fucking way anyone's going to find her," said Fermín. "I'll make sure of that."

With her eyes half-open, Alicia was trying to follow the conversation. "Where are we going?" she asked.

"To Can Solé. Their prawns with garlic resurrect the dead. Just the job, you'll see."

"Don't take me to a hospital, Fermín . . ."

"Who said anything about hospitals? That's where people die. Hospitals are statistically the most dangerous places in the world. Rest assured. I wouldn't take a bunch of lice to a hospital."

In an attempt to dodge the traffic that had solidified on the lower stretch of Vía Layetana, the taxi had moved into the oncoming traffic lane. Fermín saw a bus go past within a hairsbreadth of the window.

"Father, is that you?" called Alicia. "Father, don't leave me . . ."

Fernandito looked at Fermín, panic-stricken.

"Pay no attention, kid. The poor thing is delirious, she's hallucinating. It's quite common in the Spanish temperament. Boss, how's it going out there?"

"Either we all arrive alive, or we fall by the wayside," said the taxi driver.

"That's the spirit."

Fermín saw they were approaching Paseo de Colón at cruising speed. A wall of trams, cars, and humanity rose five seconds ahead. The driver clutched the wheel with all his might, muttering some verbal abuse.

Commending his soul to the goddess Fortune or whoever happened to be on call, Fermín smiled weakly at Fernandito. "Hold tight, son."

Never had a four-wheeled object sliced through the traffic on Paseo de Colón so recklessly, provoking a roar of hoots, insults, and curses. Having crossed the avenue, the taxi plunged into the area leading to La Barceloneta, where it pulled into a street as narrow as a sewage tunnel, taking with it a team of motorbikes parked on the edges.

"Bravo, maestro!" Fermín chanted.

At last they sighted the beach and a purple-tinged Mediterranean. The taxi swung into the hospital's front entrance and stopped opposite two ambulances, letting out a deep mechanical groan of surrender and scrap metal. A veil of steam emerged from the sides of the bonnet.

"You're a star," Fermín declared, patting the driver's shoulder. "Fernandito, take this champion's name and his number plate, we'll send him a Christmas hamper, with ham and *turrones* included."

"I'll be quite happy as long as you never hail my taxi again."

Twenty seconds later a squadron of nurses took Alicia out of the car, placed her on a stretcher, and rushed off with her to the operating room, while Fermín ran alongside her, his hands pressing the wound.

"You're going to need a few hectoliters of blood," he warned. "You can take as much as you like from me. I may have a lean frame, but I have more liquid reserves than the national park of Aigüestortes."

"Are you related to the patient?" asked a porter who came up to him at the entrance to the surgery department.

"I'm the alternate father figure and designated parental backup," replied Fermín.

"And what does that mean?"

"It means get out of my way or I'll find myself in the painful need to catapult your scrotum up your neck by kneeing you in the balls. Are we clear?"

The porter stood to one side, and Fermín accompanied Alicia until she was snatched from his hands and he saw her land, pale as a ghost, on an operating table. The nurses were cutting off her clothes with scissors, exposing her battered body, covered in bruises, scratches, and cuts, and revealing the wound from which blood flowed unremittingly. Fermín caught a glimpse of the dark scar clamped onto one of her hips, spreading across her anatomy like a web about to devour her. He clenched his fists to stop his hands from shaking.

Alicia searched him with eyes that were veiled with tears, a feeble smile on her lips. Fermín prayed to the Limping Devil, the perennial favorite patron of doomed scenarios, not to take her away yet.

"What's your blood group?" asked a voice next to him.

Holding Alicia's gaze, Fermín stretched out one of his arms.

"O negative, universal and top quality."

32

IN THOSE DAYS, science had yet to unravel the enigma of why time slows to a fraction of its cruising speed inside hospitals. Once Fermín had emptied himself of what he deemed, at a glance, a barrel of blood, he and Fernandito settled down in a waiting room with a view of the beach. From the window they could see the citadel of shacks of the Somorrostro, a vast shantytown beached between a sea and a sky sealed together by leaden clouds. Farther on lay the mosaic of crosses, angels, and pantheons of the Pueblo Nuevo Cemetery. The sight offered an ominous reminder to the poor souls enduring endless hours in the hospital waiting room. Fernandito gazed at the scene like a condemned man, while the more prosaic Fermín devoured a gigantic spicy sausage sandwich he'd managed to secure at the coffee shop, washing it down with a Moritz beer.

"I don't know how you can eat now, Fermín."

"Having donated eighty percent of my bloodstream and probably the sum total of my liver, I need to restock. Like Prometheus, but without those big ugly birds."

"Prometheus?"

"One must read, Fernandito. Not everything in adolescence is jerking off like a monkey. Besides, being a man of action, I have a very swift metabolism that requires me to consume over three times my body weight in prime steak every week in order to maintain this stupendous physique in combat form."

"Señorita Alicia barely eats," ventured Fernandito. "Drinking, well, that's another matter . . ."

"We each have to wrestle with our appetites. In my case, for example, since the war, I'm constantly ravenous. You're young and can't understand that."

Fernandito watched in resignation as Fermín proceeded to devour his feast. After a while, an individual who looked like a district lawyer poked his head around the waiting-room door, carrying a file, and cleared his throat to announce his presence. "Are you relatives of the patient?"

Fernandito sought Fermín's gaze, who put a hand on the boy's shoulder to imply that from then on he would take care of the talking. "The word 'relative' doesn't quite do justice to the bond that unites us to her," he said, shaking the crumbs off his jacket.

"And what word would you use to define such a bond, if it's not too much to ask?"

Fernandito had naively assumed that he had begun to master the art of fibbing until he witnessed the performance given by the master at work, Fermín Romero de Torres, while Alicia was plunging into the darkness of surgery. As soon as the individual had introduced himself as assistant to the hospital management and made clear his intention of inquiring what had happened and asking for documentation, Fermín fired off a rhapsody of such fine embroidery that he reduced the bureaucrat to a state of babbling stupefaction.

The first thing he did was to identify himself as the right-hand man to the civil governor of Barcelona, the regime's blue-eyed boy in the province. "We cannot be discreet enough concerning what I have to tell Your Excellency," he pronounced.

"The wounds suffered by the young lady are extremely serious, and of a clearly violent nature. I'm obliged by law to inform the police . . ."

"I wouldn't recommend it unless you want to make your debut by tomorrow noon at the latest as assistant receptionist at the roadside dispensary behind the slaughterhouse of Castellfollit."

"I don't follow you."

"That much is obvious. Kindly sit down and take note."

Fermín then began to unfold the epic account of how Alicia, now fictionally rechristened Violeta LeBlanc, a fashionable courtesan, had been procured by the governor and a few friends of his from the Department of Labor to provide them with a fine sample of her famed services out on the town, all expenses paid by contributions from the Trade Union Organization. "You know how these things are. A few glasses of brandy here, a lace petticoat there, and they all turn into boisterous children. The Spanish male is very macho, and here, by the Mediterranean coast, the salty vapors of the sea wantonly embolden the spirit . . ."

Fermín elaborated on the story, explaining that given the governor's penchant for exotic role-play and other tussles of a notoriously risqué nature, the sweet Violeta had ended up seriously wounded in the line of duty. "Alas, the heyday of the sturdy tart is well behind us," he concluded.

"But—"

"Between you and me, it goes without saying what a scandal would result were such an incident to become known. Remember that the governor has a saintly wife and eight children, enjoys five vice presidencies in savings banks, and is the main shareholder in three construction companies where equity interests are held by sons-in-law, cousins, and other relatives of men in top positions of our esteemed government, as is traditional in our beloved motherland."

"I understand, but the law is the law, and I have an obligation—"

"You have an obligation to Spain and to the good name of its best, just like me and like my squire here, Miguelito, this fine young man sitting over yonder, looking as if he's just crapped himself in his pants, and who is, believe it or not, the second godson of none other than the marquis of Villaverde. Miguelito, tell him."

Fernandito nodded repeatedly.

"And what do you want me to do?" protested the manager.

"Look, in cases of such a delicate nature—and believe me, I have a lot of experience in the field—what behooves a man of vision and patriotic flair is to fill in the forms with names borrowed from any of the great Spanish classics, for it has been proven that the finest pens in the business have little weight on the reading list recommended by police headquarters, and that way nobody notices the substitutions."

"But how I am to do anything so ridiculous?"

"Leave the paperwork to me. You just concentrate on the generous emoluments you will receive for having performed your civic duty courageously. This is the way to save Spain, a little bit every day. This isn't like Rome. Here traitors do get paid."

The management assistant, who had acquired a purplish shade and seemed to be defying salubrious blood-pressure levels, shook his head and adopted a royal expression of indignation. "And you? Aren't you going to tell me your name at least?"

"Last name LaMancha, first name Quixote, at your service and the service of the Generalissimo."

"This is disgraceful."

Fermín looked him firmly in the eye and nodded. "Precisely. And what do we do in this country with such disgraces but sweep them under the carpet and cash in on them?"

*

An hour later, Fermín and Fernandito were still waiting for news from the operating room. At Fermín's request, the boy had drunk a hot cup of cocoa and was beginning to revive and regain some calm.

"Fermín, do you think they've swallowed all that stuff you told them? Haven't you gone a bit too far with those lurid details?"

"Fernandito, we've planted the seed of doubt, and that's what matters. When it comes to lying, what one must consider is not the plausibility of the fib but the greed, fear, and stupidity of the receiver. One never lies to people; they lie to themselves. A good liar gives fools what they want to hear and allows them to free themselves from the facts at hand and choose the level of self-delusion that fits their foolishness and moral turpitude. That's the secret. Oldest trick in the world."

"What you've suggested is terrible," Fernandito objected.

Fermín shrugged. "Depends how you look at it. In this farcical world of ours, where leopards try to hide their spots and lambs think themselves lions, falsehood is the glue that keeps all the bits together. People get so used to lying and repeating other people's lies, either because they're afraid or out of self-interest, resentment, or sheer stupidity, that they end up lying even when they think they're telling the truth. It's the failing of our times. The honest, decent person is a species in danger of extinction, much like the plesiosaur or the well-read burlesque dancer."

"I can't accept what you're saying. Most people are decent and good-hearted. The trouble is that a few bad apples give a bad name to the rest. I have no doubt about that."

Fermín patted the boy's knee affectionately. "That's because you're still very green and a bit of a simpleton. When you're young, you see the world as it should be, and when you're old you start to see it as it really is. You'll be cured of it eventually."

Fernandito hung his head. While the boy battled with the blows of misfortune, Fermín scanned the horizon and noticed a couple of nurses in tight uniforms advancing up the corridor. Their pleasing architecture and the way they wiggled as they walked produced a tickling sensation in the nether regions of his soul. For want of anything better to occupy his mind while waiting, his eyes bored into them expertly. One of the nurses, who looked like a junior and couldn't have clocked more than nineteen years on her meter, threw him a look as she went by to indicate that the likes of him were never, ever going to taste such delicious fruit, and then laughed. The other one, who seemed more feisty when it came to dealing with idle visitors hanging around the corridors, looked at him severely.

"You pig," murmured the young woman.

"The worms are going to have a feast one day . . . ," said Fermín.

"I don't know how you can think about such things when Señorita Alicia is hovering between life and death," said Fernandito.

"Do you always speak in clichés or did you learn to express yourself by watching the newsreels?" replied the bibliographic adviser to the Sempere & Sons bookshop.

A long silence followed. Finally Fermín, who was starting to peer beneath the piece of cotton wool that had been taped to his arm after he gave blood, noticed that Fernandito was looking at him out of the corner of his eye, fearful of opening his mouth again.

"What's the matter now?" Fermín asked. "Do you need to pee?"

"I was wondering how long you've known Señorita Alicia."

"You could say we're old friends."

"But she'd never mentioned you before."

"That's because we haven't seen each other for over twenty years, and we each thought the other was dead."

The boy stared at him in bewilderment.

"What about you? Are you a naive, aspiring lover boy caught in the spiderweb of the queen of the night, or an eager goody-goody?"

Fernandito thought it over. "More like the first, I suppose."

"Don't be embarrassed, life's like that. Learning how to differentiate between why one does things and why one says one does them is the first step toward getting to know oneself. And from there to no longer being a cretin, there's still quite a way to go."

"You speak like a book, Fermín."

"If books spoke, there wouldn't be so many deaf people around the place. What you need to do, Fernandito, is start preventing others from writing your dialogue. Use the head God planted on your neck and write your own script. Life is full of black marketeers eager to stuff their audience's brains with nonsense because that allows them to stay on their high horses and keep the carrot dangling. Do you understand?"

"I don't think so."

"That explains a lot. But still, making the most of the fact that you're a bit calmer now, I'm going to ask you to tell me, once again, everything that happened. This time, from the beginning, in proper order and with no stylistic flourishes. Do you think it feasible?"

"I can try."

"Go on, then."

This time Fernandito didn't leave a drop in the inkwell. Fermín listened intently, assembling the pieces from the puzzle that was beginning to form in his mind with hypotheses and speculations.

"Those documents and the diary of Isabella you mentioned," he said, "where are they now?"

"I left them with my aunt Jesusa. She's the caretaker in the building where Señorita Alicia lives. She can be trusted."

"I don't doubt it, but we're going to have to find a safer location. In the world of criminal investigation, it is well known that caretaker's lodgings provide many good uses, but confidentiality isn't one of them."

"Whatever you say."

"And I'm going to ask you to keep all the things you've told me between us two. Not a word to Daniel Sempere."

"Understood."

"That's good. Listen, have you any money on you?"

"A few coins, I think . . ."

Fermín put out an open palm. "I have to make a call."

*

Daniel answered at the first ring.

"For God's sake, Fermín, where the hell are you?"

"Hospital del Mar."

"Hospital? What happened?"

"Someone tried to murder Alicia."

"What? Who? Why?"

"Please calm down, Daniel."

"How am I going to calm down?"

"Is Bea around?"

"Of course, but—"

"Put her on the phone."

A pause, voices arguing, and finally the calm tones of Bea on the phone. "Tell me, Fermín."

"I don't have time to go into detail, but Alicia very nearly died. Right now she's in the operating room, and we're waiting for news."

"We?"

"Me and a kid called Fernandito who seems to have worked as an assistant and lackey for Alicia. I know how this is sounding, but try to be patient."

"What do you need, Fermín?"

"I've tried to contain the matter with a bit of fine wording, but I have a feeling we won't be able to stay here much longer. If Alicia survives this, I don't think the hospital will be a very safe place. Someone might try to finish the job."

"What do you propose?"

"I suggest we take her somewhere where nobody can find her, as soon as possible."

Bea let a long silence go by. "Are we thinking the same thing?"

"Great minds think alike."

"And how do you plan to get her out of the hospital and take her there?"

"I'm formulating a strategy as we speak."

"Heaven help us."

"O ye of little faith . . ."

"What must I do?"

"Get hold of Dr. Soldevila," said Fermín.

"Dr. Soldevila retired and hasn't worked for at least two years. Wouldn't it be better . . . ?"

"We need someone we can trust," replied Fermín. "Besides, Soldevila is an eminent doctor and knows all the tricks. I'm sure he'll be delighted if you tell him I've asked you."

"The last thing I heard him say was that you were a scoundrel, that he was fed up to his back teeth with you pinching his nurses' bottoms, and that he didn't want to see you ever again."

"Water under the bridge. He's very fond of me."

"If you say so. . . . What else do you need?"

"Provisions for at least one week for a patient who has just survived a stabbing in the abdomen, another in the hand, and a beating that would have left a Basque weight lifter out of action."

"My God . . ."

"Concentrate, Bea. Provisions. The doctor will know what will be needed."

"He's not going to like any of this at all."

"That's where your charm and powers of persuasion come in."

"Delightful. I suppose she'll need clean clothes and that sort of thing."

"That sort of thing. I leave it all to your sound judgment. Is Daniel still there?"

"With his ear glued. Do you want me to send him over to you?"

"No. Tell him to stay put and keep calm. I'll call you both back when I have some news."

"We'll be here."

"It's what I always say: if you want things to turn out well, you must put a woman in charge."

"Stop the flattery, Fermín. I can see you coming a mile off. Anything else?"

"Keep your eyes peeled. It wouldn't surprise me if the bookshop was being watched."

"That's all we needed. Understood. Fermín?"

"Yes?"

"Are you sure we can trust this woman?"

"Alicia?"

"If that's her real name . . ."

"It is."

"And the rest? Is that also true?"

Fermín sighed. "We're going to give her a chance. Will you do this for me, Bea?"

"Of course, Fermín. Whatever you say."

Fermín hung up the phone and went back to the waiting room. Fernandito watched him anxiously. "Who were you talking to?"

"To common sense."

Fermín sat down and gazed at the boy. He reminded him so much of Daniel when he was younger that he was even starting to like him. "You're a good guy, Fernandito. Alicia will be proud of you."

"If she lives, that is."

"She'll live. I've already seen her return from among the dead once before, and those who learn the trick never forget it. I speak from experience. To return from the dead is a bit like riding a bike, or unfastening a girl's bra with a single hand. It's all a question of getting the knack."

Fernandito smiled weakly. "And how does one do that?"

"Don't tell me you don't know how to ride a bike."

"I mean undoing a bra with a single hand."

Fermín patted his knee and winked conspiratorially. "You and I have a lot to talk about . . ."

As luck would have it, before Fermín was able to start Fernandito off on a crash course on the verities of life, the surgeon appeared in the waiting-room doorway and, letting out a long sigh, collapsed, exhausted, on one of the chairs.

33

THE SURGEON WAS one of those youngish men who start to lose their hair before their thirties from too much thinking. He was tall and thin, with a profile like a pencil and intelligent eyes that surveyed the scene behind a pair of glasses known in those days as Truman glasses in honor of the trigger-happy American president who dropped atomic bombs the size of school buses on the Empire of the Sun.

"We've managed to stabilize her, close the wound, and control the hemorrhage. For the moment there is no infection, but I've got her on antibiotics, just as a precaution. The wound was deeper than it seemed. It's a miracle that it didn't slice her femoral artery, but the stitches were very complicated, and at first they didn't hold. They will keep on holding if the inflammation subsides, if there is no infection, and if we're lucky. Only God knows."

"But will she pull through, Doctor?"

The surgeon shrugged. "That will depend on what progress she makes in the next forty-eight hours. The patient is young, and her heart is strong. Someone weaker would not have survived the operation, but that doesn't mean that she's out of the woods, not by a long stretch. And if there's an infection . . ."

Fermín nodded, taking in the medical report. The doctor's eyes were studying him with surgical curiosity. "May I ask how the patient got the wound on her right hip?"

"A childhood accident. During the war."

"I see. It must cause her terrible pain."

"She's very long-suffering, although I must admit that sometimes it affects her character."

"If she survives this, I could help her. There are new reconstruction procedures that weren't even known twenty years ago, and they might reduce her pain. Nobody should have to live like that."

"It will be the first thing I'll tell Violeta when she wakes up."

"Violeta?" asked the doctor.

"The patient," Fermín specified.

The surgeon, who was nobody's fool, looked sidelong at him. "Look, this is none of my business, and I don't know what story you've foisted on poor old Coll, but someone has beaten this woman brutally and almost killed her. Whoever has—"

"I know," Fermín cut in. "Believe me, I'm well aware of it. When do you think we can move her out of here?"

The surgeon raised his eyebrows in astonishment. "Move her out of here? At best, the patient has a month of complete rest ahead. Violeta, or whatever her name is, isn't going anywhere unless you want to arrange a fast-track funeral for her. I'm serious."

Fermín studied the surgeon's face. "What about transferring her to another place?"

"It would have to be another hospital. But I wouldn't recommend it."

Fermín nodded his head gravely. "Thank you, Doctor."

"Not at all. In a couple of hours, if all goes well, we'll take her up to a room on the main floor. Until then you won't be able to see her. I'm saying this because you might like to go out and get some fresh air. Or you may have some arrangements to make, if you know what I mean. For the moment, as I say, the patient is stable and the prognosis is moderately optimistic."

"Moderately?"

The surgeon gave him an ambiguous smile. "If you want my personal opinion, and not that of the surgeon, this young lady doesn't want to die yet. Some people survive out of pure anger."

Fermín assented with a quick nod. "Women are like that. They get something into their heads and . . ."

Fermín waited until the surgeon had left them alone before poking his head out into the corridor and survey the situation. Fernandito joined him. Two figures dressed in very unmedical-looking uniforms were advancing slowly from the end of the passage.

"Hey, aren't those the fuzz?"

"Excuse me?" asked Fernandito.

"Policemen. Don't you read comic books?"

"Now that you mention it, they do look like—"

Fermín grunted and pushed Fernandito back into the waiting room.

"Do you think the manager has alerted the police?" asked the boy.

"This is going to be more complicated than I thought. There's no time to lose. Fernandito, you're going to have to lend me a hand."

"I'll lend you two, if need be. Order away."

"I want you to go back to the Sempere & Sons bookshop and speak to Bea."

"Bea?"

"Daniel's wife."

"And how will I know——"

"You can't go wrong. She's the cleverest of the bunch, and besides, she's a stunner, but a modest one, so don't get the wrong idea."

"And what do I say to her?"

"That we're going to have to play the queen's gambit sooner than we'd anticipated."

"The queen's gambit?"

"She'll understand. And tell her to send Daniel over to warn Isaac."

"Isaac? What Isaac?"

Fermín huffed, exasperated by Fernandito's slow reflexes.

"Perhaps Isaac Monturiol, inventor of the submarine. Plain Isaac. Do I need to write it down for you?"

"No, it's all engraved on my mind."

"Well then, beat it, we're already late."

"What about you? Where are you going?"

Fermín winked at him. "A war can't be won without the infantry."

34

BY THE TIME Fermín left the hospital and went down to the beach, the storm had passed. The wind blew onshore, dragging in waves that broke on the sand barely a few meters from the rim of the shantytown—a vast citadel of huts spreading as far as the eye could see, right up to the walls of the Pueblo Nuevo Cemetery. Even the dead had a better home than that lot of lost souls who scraped together an existence at the edge of the sea, Fermín told himself.

A chorus of suspicious looks greeted him as he walked up an alleyway flanked by hovels. Ragged children, haggard women, and men who looked twice their age watched as he walked by. Soon a quartet of wild-looking youngsters appeared, surrounding him and barring his way.

"Are you lost, *payo*?"

"I'm looking for Armando," said Fermín, without a hint of nervousness or fear.

One of them had a scar across his face, running from forehead to cheek. He stepped forward with a menacing grin and looked defiantly into Fermín's eyes.

Fermín held his gaze. "Armando," he repeated. "I'm a friend of his."

The youth sized up his opponent, whom he could have eliminated with a mere slap, and finally he smiled. "Weren't you the dead one?" he asked.

"I changed my mind at the last minute," said Fermín.

"On the beach," said the young man, pointing with his head.

Fermín signaled his gratitude, and the youths stood to one side. Then he continued along the alleyway for about a hundred meters, his presence now ignored by the locals. The path turned toward the sea, and Fermín heard children's voices and laughter coming from the beach. He walked on and soon became aware of what had drawn the children to the water's edge.

The storm had pushed in an old cargo ship, which had run aground just a few meters from the shore. Its hull had listed to port, and the keel and propellers peeped over the foam. The waves had knocked most of the cargo overboard. A flock of seagulls fluttered among the floating remains of the wreckage while the crew tried to salvage what it could and the children celebrated the disaster in party spirit. In the distance rose an endless forest of chimneys and factories. Above them clouds slid along the sky, carrying the echo of thunderclaps and the glow of the storm.

"Fermín," said a deep, calm voice next to him.

He turned to find Armando, prince of gypsies and emperor of the forgotten world of El Somorrostro. He wore an impeccable black suit and carried his patent leather shoes in his hand. He'd rolled up his trouser legs to walk along the damp sand and watch the children play in the surf.

Armando pointed at the scene of the shipwreck. "The misfortune of some is the bonanza of others," he declared. "What brings you to these parts, dear friend, misfortune or bonanza?"

"Despair."

"Never a good counselor."

"But very convincing."

Armando smiled and nodded. He lit a cigarette and offered the packet to Fermín, who declined the invitation.

"They tell me you were seen leaving the Hospital del Mar," said Armando.

"You have eyes everywhere."

"I suspect that what you need are hands, not eyes. How can I help you?"

"By saving a life."

"Yours?"

"I already owe you mine, Armando. What brings me here is a life I should have saved many years ago. Destiny placed it in my hands, and I failed."

"Destiny knows us better than we know ourselves, Fermín. I don't think you failed anyone. But I sense that haste is required. Give me the details."

"It can be complicated. And dangerous."

"If it were easy and safe, I know you wouldn't insult me by coming to ask for my help. What's the name?"

"Alicia."

"A love?"

"A debt."

*

Hendaya knelt down by the body and removed the blanket. "Is that him?" he asked.

When he didn't get a reply, he turned around. Linares, behind him, was staring at Vargas's corpse as if he'd just been slapped in the face.

"Is it, or isn't it?" Hendaya insisted.

Linares nodded, closing his eyes briefly.

Hendaya covered the face of the dead policeman again and stood up. He walked calmly around the room, casually examining the clothes and objects scattered about. Apart from Linares, two of his men were waiting in patient silence.

"I'm told that before he came back here, Vargas was in the morgue with you," he said to Linares. "Can you fill me in?"

"Captain Vargas had found a dead body the night before, and he called to inform me about it."

"Did he say under what circumstances he found the body?"

"During the course of an investigation he was working on. He didn't discuss the details of the case with me."

"And you didn't ask him?"

"I presumed that Vargas would give me the details when the time was right."

"You had that much trust in him?"

"As much as in myself," replied Linares.

"Interesting analogy. Nothing like having good friends in head-quarters. And tell me, were you able to identify the body?"

Linares hesitated for a moment. "Vargas suspected it was some-one called Ricardo Lomana. The name must ring a bell. He was a colleague of yours, I think."

"Not of mine. But yes, the name sounds familiar. Did you file a report on these events to the relevant department?"

"No."

"Why was that?"

"I was awaiting confirmation from the pathologist."

"But you were going to do it."

"Of course."

"Of course. Meanwhile, did you tell anyone in the police station about Vargas's suspicions regarding Lomana's identity?"

"No."

"No?" Hendaya insisted. "No assistant?"

"No."

"Does anyone else, apart from the pathologist and his staff, the judge, and the police officers who came with you, have any knowledge of the removal of the corpse?"

"No. What are you insinuating?"

Hendaya winked at him. "Nothing. I believe you. . . . And do you know where Vargas was going when he left the morgue?"

Linares shook his head.

"To the Civil Registry," said Hendaya.

Linares frowned.

"You didn't know?"

"No," Linares answered. "Why should I know?"

"Didn't Vargas mention it to you?"

"No."

"Are you sure? Didn't Vargas call you from the registry to ask you something?"

Hendaya was smiling, enjoying the game. Linares held his gaze.

"No."

"Does the name Rovira ring a bell?"

"It's quite a common surname."

"Is it in the police station?"

"I think there's someone there with that name. He works in the archives and is about to retire."

"Has anyone asked you about him recently?"

Linares shook his head again. "Can you please tell me what we're talking about?"

"About a crime, my friend. A crime that was committed against one of ours, one of the best. Who could have done something like this?"

"A professional, obviously."

"Are you sure? To me it looks more like the work of a petty thief."

"A petty thief?"

Hendaya nodded confidently. "This neighborhood isn't trustworthy, and God knows these Catalans are capable of stealing their mothers' drawers on their deathbed while they're still warm. It's in their blood."

"No third-rate petty thief would have had a chance against Vargas,"

Linares argued. "You know that as well as I do. This wasn't done by an amateur."

Hendaya gave him a long, calm look. "Come on, Linares. There are professional petty thieves. Hard men, with no scruples. You know that. And your friend Vargas, let's face it, wasn't in very good shape. The years don't lie."

"The investigation will have to determine that."

"Unfortunately there won't be one."

"Just because you say so," snapped Linares.

Hendaya smiled with satisfaction. "No, not because *I* say so. I'm nobody. But if you know what's good for you, you won't expect anyone else to tell you."

Linares bit his tongue, then said, "I'm not going to accept that. Not from you, nor from anyone else."

"You've had a good run, Linares. Let's not fool ourselves. You haven't gotten where you have by playing the hero. Heroes don't make it to the end. Don't do anything silly now, two minutes away from a golden retirement. Times are changing. And you know I'm saying this for your own good."

Linares shot him a look of contempt. "What I know is that you're a son of a bitch, and I couldn't give a shit who you're working for. This isn't going to stop here. Call whoever you need to call."

Hendaya shrugged, and Linares turned around and headed for the exit.

Hendaya caught the eye of one of his men and nodded. The policeman set off behind Linares. The other one came over, and Hendaya gave him a questioning look. "Any signs of that whore?"

"There was only one body in the workshop. Not a sign of her. We've been through the apartment on the other side of this street. Nothing. None of the neighbors have seen her, and the caretaker assures me that the last time she saw her was yesterday, when she was going out."

"Is she telling the truth?"

"I think so, but if you like, we can soften her up a bit."

"That won't be necessary. Comb the hospitals and first-aid clinics. If she's in one of them, she will have given a false name. She can't be very far."

"What if they call from Madrid?"

"Not a word until we find her. Let's make as little noise as possible."

"Yes, sir."

35

IT WAS THE best dream she'd ever had.

Alicia woke up in a room with white walls that smelled of camphor. A distant murmur of voices rose and fell in a tide of whispers. The first thing she noticed was the absence of pain. For the first time in twenty years, she wasn't suffering. The pain had vanished completely, taking with it that world she'd inhabited almost all her life. In its place she found a space where light traveled through the air like a dense liquid, colliding with specks of dust that floated in the atmosphere, forming iridescent sparks.

Alicia laughed. She could breathe and feel her body resting. There was no more agony in her bones, and her spirit was rid of that biting metal clamp that had always imprisoned her. The face of an angel leaned over her and looked into her eyes. The angel was very tall; he wore a white coat, and had no wings. He barely had any hair either, but he carried a hypodermic syringe, and when she asked him whether she was dead, and whether this was hell, the angel smiled and said it depended how one looked at it, but she shouldn't worry. She felt a small prick, and a torrent of liquid happiness spread through her veins, leaving a warm trail of peace.

A small devil appeared behind the angel. He was lean and had a huge nose, a nose that could have inspired Molière to write a comedy or Cervantes to invent an epic tale.

"Alicia, we're going home," the little devil announced in a voice that seemed strangely familiar.

A spirit with jet-black hair stood next to him. His features were so perfect that Alicia felt like kissing his lips, running her fingers through that fairy-tale hair, and falling in love with him, even if

555

only for a while, enough for her to think she was awake and had bumped into the happiness that some careless person had dropped along the way.

"May I caress you?" she asked him.

The dark prince, for surely he was at least a prince, looked at the little devil uncertainly.

The devil made a gesture to indicate he need pay no attention to her. "That's my blood running through her veins: it's made her forget her decorum momentarily and left her on the wrong side of immodesty. It'll pass."

At a sign from the prince, a whole gang of dwarfs materialized, except that they weren't dwarfs and were all dressed in white. Between the four of them, they lifted her off the bed by tugging at the sheets, and placed her on a stretcher. The prince took her hand and squeezed it. He would make a wonderful father, thought Alicia. The way he squeezed her hand and his velvety touch very much confirmed it.

"Would you like to have a child?" she asked.

"I've got seventeen, my dear," said the prince.

"Go to sleep, Alicia, you're embarrassing me," said the little devil.

But she didn't sleep. Holding her beau's hand and riding aboard the magic stretcher, she went on dreaming as she rode through endless corridors decorated with a crest of white lights. They sailed through elevators and rooms haunted with laments, until Alicia felt that the air was getting colder and the pale ceilings changed into a celestial vault of clouds, stained red by the touch of a cotton-wool sun. The little devil placed a blanket over Alicia, and, following instructions from the prince, the dwarfs lifted her into an incongruous-looking carriage—incongruous, considering this was a fairy tale, because it had no steeds to pull it, nor was it decorated with copper spirals but only a cryptic message on the side:

LA PONDEROSA

COLD MEATS

WHOLESALE

AND HOME DELIVERY

The prince was closing the carriage doors when Alicia heard voices, someone ordering them to stop and shouting threats at them. For a few minutes she was left alone while her champions confronted a posse of peasants, for the air was filled with the unmistakable echo of blows with fists and clubs. When the little devil returned to her side, his hair stood on end, his lip was split, and he wore a victorious smile. The vehicle set off with a rattling movement, and Alicia had the strange impression that she could smell cheap spicy sausage.

*

The ride seemed endless. They plowed through avenues and lanes, following the twisted map of the labyrinth, and when the doors opened and the dwarfs, who had grown and now looked like ordinary men, pulled her out on the stretcher, Alicia noticed that the carriage had miraculously turned into a van and they were in a narrow, dark street that cut a swath through the shadows. The little devil, who suddenly bore Fermín's unmistakable features, told her she was very nearly safe and sound. They carried her up to a large carved oak door, behind which a man with sparse hair and vulturine eyes peeked out. The man looked at both sides of the street and whispered, "Come in."

"This is where I say good-bye," announced the prince.

"Give me a kiss, at least," Alicia murmured.

Fermín rolled his eyes. "For God's sake, kiss her, or we'll never be done."

And with all his dark grace, Prince Armando kissed her. His lips tasted of cinnamon, and by any reckoning he knew how to kiss a woman: with art, composure, and the long experience of an artist who takes pride and pleasure in his work. Alicia allowed a chill to run through her and stir forgotten corners of her body, and then she closed her eyes, sealing off the tears.

"Thank you," she whispered.

"Unbelievable," said Fermín. "Anyone would say she was fifteen. Thank goodness her father isn't here to see it."

What sounded like the mechanism for a cathedral clock sealed the door behind them. They went down a long, palatial corridor peopled with frescoes of fabulous creatures that appeared and disappeared in the light of the oil lamp carried by the keeper of the place. The air smelled of paper and magic, and when the passageway opened up into a large hall with a vaulted ceiling, Alicia saw it.

A labyrinth of shimmering forms ascended toward an immense glass dome. Moonlight, split into a thousand blades, poured down from up high and threw into relief the seemingly impossible geometry of a spell made up of all the books, all the stories, and all the dreams in the world. Recognizing the place she had dreamed of so often, Alicia stretched out her arms to touch it, fearing it would vanish in the air. Next to her appeared the faces of Daniel and Bea.

"Where am I? What is this place?"

Isaac Montfort, the keeper who had opened the doors for them and whom Alicia recognized after so many years, knelt down beside her and stroked her face.

"Alicia, welcome back to the Cemetery of Forgotten Books."

36

VALLS WAS BEGINNING to suspect that he had imagined it. The visions faded, and he was no longer sure whether he'd dreamed about the woman who had come down the stairs to the door of his cell and asked him whether he was Minister Valls. At times he doubted that it had actually happened. Perhaps he'd dreamed it. Perhaps he was just another wreck of humanity rotting in the cells of Montjuïc Castle who, overcome by delirium, had come to believe that he was his jailer and not who he really was. He seemed to remember a case like that—Mitjans, his name was. Mitjans had been a famous playwright during the years of the Republic, and Valls had felt enormous contempt for him because life had given him everything that he, Valls, had longed for and had been unable to achieve. Mitjans, who like so many others had been the object of his envy, had ended his days in the castle, no longer knowing who he was, in cell 19.

But Valls knew who he was, because he remembered. And as that bedeviled David Martín had once told him, one is what one remembers. That is why he knew that that woman, whoever she was, had been there, and that one day she, or someone like her, would return to free him. He wasn't like Mitjans, or all those other wretches who had died under his command. He, Mauricio Valls, would not die in that place. He owed it to his daughter Mercedes, the person who had kept him alive all that time. Perhaps that was why, every time he heard the door to the basement open and footsteps coming down the darkened stairs, he would look up, his eyes full of hope. Because this could be the day.

It must have been early morning—he'd learned to tell the time of day in relation to the cold. He knew there was something different, because they never came down so early. He heard the door and heavy footsteps. Slow footsteps. A figure materialized in the dark. He carried a tray that gave off the most delicious aroma he had ever smelled.

Hendaya left the tray on the floor and lit a candle that he placed in a candlestick. "Good morning, Minister," he announced. "I've brought you your breakfast."

Hendaya pushed the tray until it was close to the metal bars, then lifted the lid covering a plate. A vision appeared: a juicy fillet steak in a creamy pepper sauce, with roast potatoes and sautéed vegetables. Valls could feel his mouth salivating and his stomach turning.

"Medium rare," said Hendaya. "Just as you like it."

On the tray there was a basket with small bread rolls, silver cutlery, and linen napkins. The drink, an exquisite Rioja, nestled in a Murano wineglass.

"Today is a great day, Minister. You deserve it." Hendaya slipped the tray under the bars.

Valls ignored the cutlery and the napkin and grabbed the piece of meat with his hand. He shoved it into his toothless mouth and began to devour it with a ferocity he didn't recognize in himself. He wolfed down the meat, the potatoes, and the bread. He licked the plate until it shone and drank that delicious wine until there wasn't a drop left in the glass.

Hendaya observed him nonchalantly, with a pleasant smile, taking a long drag on his cigarette. "You must excuse me: I ordered a dessert, but they haven't delivered it."

Valls pushed the tray to one side and grabbed the metal bars, his eyes fixed on Hendaya.

"You seem very surprised, Minister. I don't know whether it's because of the festive menu or because you were expecting someone else."

The pleasures of the feast were beating a retreat. Valls slumped down again in the far end of the cell. Hendaya stayed where he was for a few minutes, leafing through a newspaper while he finished his cigarette. When he was done, he threw the butt away and folded the paper. Noticing that Valls was looking intently at the newspaper, he remarked, "Perhaps you would like some reading material? A man of letters like you must miss his daily reading."

"Please," Valls implored.

"But of course!" said Hendaya, walking over to the bars.

Valls stretched out his remaining hand, a plea on his face.

"In fact it brings good news today. To tell you the truth, it was when I read it this morning that I thought you deserved a proper celebration." Hendaya flung the newspaper inside the cell and headed up the stairs. "All yours. You can keep the candle."

Valls fell upon the paper and grabbed it. The pages had gotten all tangled when Hendaya threw it, and it took him a while to put it back in order with a single hand. When he'd managed to do so, he drew the candle closer and skimmed over the front page.

At first he couldn't make out the letters. His eyes had been confined to that place far too long. What he did recognize was the full-page photograph. It was a snapshot taken in El Pardo Palace. He was posing in front of a large mural, wearing the navy pinstripe suit he'd had tailored in London three years before. It was the last official photograph Mauricio Valls's ministry had distributed. The words emerged slowly, like a shimmering image underwater.

A GREAT SPANIARD DIES

DEATH OF MINISTER MAURICIO VALLS IN TRAFFIC ACCIDENT

THE GENERALISSIMO DECLARES THREE DAYS OF OFFICIAL MOURNING

Mauricio Valls was a shining light in the firmament of a new, large and free Spain, reborn from the glory of the war's ashes. He embodied the highest values of the Regime and took Spanish letters and culture to unforeseen heights.

—Press Agency/Editorial Office, Madrid, January 9, 1960

Spain has awoken in shock at the news of the immeasurable loss of one of its favorite sons, Don Mauricio Valls y Echevarría, minister for national education. The tragedy happened late last night, when the car in which he was traveling with his driver and bodyguard crashed on kilometer 4 of Carretera de Somosaguas, on his way back to his private residence after a late meeting in El Pardo with other members of the cabinet. The first reports suggest that the accident happened when a tanker truck, traveling in the opposite direction, punctured one of its wheels. The driver lost control and swerved onto the wrong side of the road, crashing against the minister's car, which was traveling at high speed. The tanker was carrying a load of fuel, and the crash caused a huge explosion that was heard by residents in the area, who immediately informed the authorities. Minister Valls and his driver died on the spot.

The driver of the tanker, Rosendo M. S., from Alcobendas, passed away before emergency services could resuscitate him. A huge blaze resulted from the collision, and the bodies of both the minister and his bodyguard were badly burned.

The government has called an emergency meeting of the cabinet this morning, and the head of state has announced that he will issue an official communiqué later in the day, in person, from El Pardo Palace.

Mauricio Valls was fifty-nine years old, and had devoted over two decades to serving the regime. His loss leaves a big void in Spanish letters, on account of both his work at the head of his ministry and his distinguished career as publisher, author, and academic. Senior officials of all the public institutions and the most renowned figures in our letters and culture have visited the ministry to express their condolences and mark the admiration and respect Don Mauricio inspired in all those who knew him.

Don Mauricio Valls leaves a wife and daughter. Government sources have informed us that the funeral chapel will be open to all members of the public who wish to pay their last respects to this universal Spaniard, from five o'clock this afternoon in Oriente Palace. The editorial board and the entire staff of this newspaper also wish to express the same profound shock and grief felt by all at the loss of Don Mauricio Valls, a shining example of the highest levels to which a citizen of our country can aspire.

¡Viva Franco! ¡Arriba España! Don Mauricio Valls: ¡presente!

AGNUS DEI

❧

JANUARY

1960

I

VICTORIA SANCHÍS AWOKE between linen sheets, ironed and perfumed with lavender. She was wearing beautifully tailored silk pajamas. She touched her face and noticed that her skin smelled of bath salts, and her hair was clean, although she didn't remember having washed it. She couldn't remember anything.

She sat up, far back enough to be leaning on the velvet headboard, and tried to work out where she was. The bed, large, with pillows that invited surrender, presided over an ample bedroom decorated in a plush, elegant style. A soft light filtered through a large window with white curtains, revealing a chest of drawers adorned with a vase full of fresh flowers. Next to the chest of drawers stood a dressing table, placed under a mirror. There was also a desk. The walls were covered with embossed paper, and there were a number of watercolors of pastoral scenes, ostentatiously framed.

She drew the sheet to one side and sat on the edge of the bed. The pastel colors in the carpet at her feet matched the rest of the room's decor to perfection. The setting had been put together with professional taste by an expert hand. It was both warm and impersonal. Victoria wondered whether this was hell.

She closed her eyes and tried to understand how she had gotten here. The last thing she remembered was the house in El Pinar. The images came back to her little by little. The kitchen area. She was tied hand and foot to a chair with bits of wire. Hendaya had knelt down next to her and was interrogating her. She spat in his face. A brutal blow knocked her onto the floor. One of Hendaya's men lifted the chair. Two other men were bringing in Morgado and tying him to a table. Hendaya was questioning her again. She kept silent. Then the policeman took a gun and blew off Morgado's knee, shooting at point-blank range. The chauffeur's screams were breaking her heart. She had never heard a man howl with pain like that. Hendaya questioned her again, calmly. Struck dumb, she shook with terror. Hendaya shrugged and walked around the table, placing the barrel of the gun on the chauffeur's other knee. One of the captain's thugs held her head so that she couldn't look away. "Look what happens to people who try to fuck with me, you whore." Hendaya pulled the trigger. A cloud of blood and pulverized bone splashed his face. Morgado's body was going into spasms as if some high-voltage current was running through it, but no more sound came out of his mouth. Victoria closed her eyes. Moments later came the third shot.

Nausea suddenly hit her, and she jumped out of bed. A half-open door led to the bathroom. She collapsed on her knees by the toilet and vomited bile. She went on retching until she could no longer bring out a drop of saliva, then leaned against the wall, sitting on the floor, panting. She looked around her. The bathroom, a creation made of pink marble, was pleasantly warm. On the wall, a built-in loudspeaker exuded the murmur of a string orchestra performing a sugary version of a Bach adagio.

Victoria recovered her breath and stood up, leaning on the walls. Her head was spinning. She walked over to the sink and let the water run. After washing her face and getting rid of the bitter aftertaste in her mouth, she dried herself with a thick, soft towel, which she dropped by her feet. She staggered back to the room and slumped back onto the bed. Although she tried to erase the images from her mind, Hendaya's blood-spattered face seemed branded with a hot iron on her retinas.

Victoria looked around at this strange place in which she had awoken. She didn't know how long she had been here. If this was hell, and it deserved to be, it looked more like a luxury hotel. Soon she fell asleep again, praying she would never wake up.

2

THE NEXT TIME Victoria opened her eyes, she was blinded by the sunlight behind the curtains. She could smell coffee. She stood up and found a silk dressing gown that matched her pajamas. There was also a pair of slippers at the foot of the bed. She heard a voice behind the door that seemed to lead to another room in the suite. Moving closer, she stopped to listen. The soft tinkling of a teaspoon in a china cup. Victoria opened the door.

A short corridor led to an oval room. On a table in the middle of the room, breakfast was set for two: a pitcher of orange juice, a basketful of bread rolls and pastries, a selection of jams, cream, butter, scrambled eggs, crispy bacon, sautéed mushrooms, tea, coffee, milk, and brown and white sugar lumps. The smell it all gave out was wonderful, and despite herself, Victoria's mouth began to water.

A middle-aged man, of middling height, middling baldness, and middling middlingness, was sitting at the table. When he saw her come in, he stood up courteously, smiled affably, and offered her the chair opposite him. He wore a black three-piece suit and had the pallid complexion of those who live behind closed doors. If she'd passed him in the street, she would barely have noticed him, or would have taken him for a midrange civil servant, or perhaps a provincial notary visiting the capital to go to the Prado Museum and the theater.

Only when one stopped to observe him closely did one notice his pale eyes, limpid and piercing, enlarged behind glasses whose oversize tortoiseshell frames lent him a vaguely effeminate air. His gaze seemed shrouded in perpetual calculation as he watched her, almost without blinking.

"Good morning, Ariadna," he said. "Please sit down."

Victoria looked around her. She seized a candlestick she found on a shelf and brandished it menacingly.

Completely unperturbed, the man lifted the lid off one of the trays and sniffed. "It smells marvelous. You must be hungry."

He made no move to approach Victoria, but she kept the candlestick raised.

"I don't think you're going to need that, Ariadna," he said calmly.

"My name isn't Ariadna. My name is Victoria. Victoria Sanchís."

"Please sit down. You're safe here and you have nothing to fear."

Victoria's eyes were lost in that hypnotic gaze. A whiff from the breakfast reached her again. She realized that the fierce pain she felt in her guts was simply hunger. She lowered the candlestick and left it on the shelf, then slowly made her way to the table. Without taking her eyes off the man, she sat down.

He waited for her to be seated before pouring a cup of coffee for her. "Let me know how much sugar you want. I like it very sweet, although the doctor tells me it's not good for me."

She watched him prepare the coffee. "Why did you call me Ariadna?"

"Because that's your real name. Ariadna Mataix. Isn't that right? Still, I can call you Victoria if you prefer. I'm Leandro."

Leandro stood up briefly and held out his hand. Victoria didn't shake it. He sat down again graciously. "Scrambled eggs? I've had some, and they're not poisoned—I hope."

Victoria wished the man would stop smiling that way, making her feel guilty for not repaying his perfect kindness.

"It's a joke. Of course there's nothing poisoned. Eggs with bacon?"

Victoria surprised herself by accepting. Leandro smiled with satisfaction and served her, sprinkling a little salt and pepper over the small pile of steaming eggs. Her host had the easygoing manner of an expert chef.

"If you'd rather have anything else, we can ask for it. The room service here is excellent."

"This is fine, thanks."

She almost bit her tongue for saying "thanks." Thanks for what? To whom?

"The croissants are delicious. Try them. The best in town."

"Where am I?"

"We're in the Gran Hotel Palace."

Victoria frowned. "In Madrid?"

Leandro nodded and offered her the basket with the pastries. She hesitated.

"They're freshly made. Take some, or I'll end up eating them all, and I'm on a diet."

Victoria stretched her hand out to take a croissant, and as she did so, noticed the needle marks on her forearm.

"We had to sedate you. I'm sorry. After what happened in El Pinar ..."

Victoria jerked back her arm. "How did I get here? Who are you?"

"I'm your friend, Ariadna. Don't be afraid. You're safe here. That man, Hendaya, won't be able to hurt you ever again. Nobody will be able to hurt you again. You have my word."

"Where's Ignacio, my husband? What have they done to him?"

Leandro looked at her tenderly and smiled weakly. "Go on, first eat a bit and recover your strength. Later I'll let you know what happened. I'll answer all your questions. I promise. Trust me and be calm."

Leandro had a gentle voice, and he constructed sentences with poise. He chose words the way a perfume maker chooses fragrances for his formulas. Despite herself, Victoria discovered that she was beginning to relax; the fear that had seized her was slowly disappearing. The food, hot and delicious, the warm air issuing from the radiators, and the serene and fatherly presence of Leandro were making her want to let go. "How I wish all this were true."

"Was I right, or wasn't I? About the croissants, I mean."

Victoria nodded timidly.

Leandro wiped his lips with his napkin, folded it slowly, and pressed a service-bell ringer on the table. A door opened instantly, and a waiter appeared. He removed the breakfast service without saying a word or looking at Victoria once. Alone with Victoria again, Leandro adopted a sorrowful expression, crossed his hands on his lap, and lowered his eyes. "I'm afraid I have bad news, Ariadna. Your husband, Ignacio, has passed away. I'm terribly sorry. We arrived too late."

Ariadna felt her eyes filling with tears. They were tears of anger, because she had known that Ignacio was dead without having to be told by anyone. She pressed her lips together and looked at Leandro, who seemed to be considering her state of mind.

"Tell me the truth," she managed to utter.

Leandro nodded repeatedly. "This isn't going to be easy, but please listen to me. Afterward you can ask me whatever you like. But first I want you to see something."

Leandro got up and walked over to pick up a folded newspaper lying on a small tea table in a corner of the room. He returned to the table and handed it to Victoria. "Open it."

She took the paper without understanding. She opened it and looked at the front page.

DEATH OF MINISTER MAURICIO VALLS
IN TRAFFIC ACCIDENT

Victoria let out a stifled scream. The newspaper fell from her hands, and she began to sob and moan uncontrollably. With utmost tact, Leandro approached her and gently put his arms around her. Victoria allowed herself to be hugged and took refuge in that stranger, trembling like a child. Leandro let her lean her head on his shoulder, stroking her hair while she shed the tears and the pain she had accumulated all her life.

3

"WE'D BEEN INVESTIGATING Valls for a long time. We opened the case after a report from the compliance commission of the Banco de España detected some financial irregularities in the transactions of the National Consortium for Financial Restructuring—a consortium that had been presided over by Miguel Ángel Ubach, your father . . . or, I should say, the man who passed himself off as your father. For some time we'd been suspecting that the consortium was just a smokescreen, rubber-stamping everything that had been expropriated, or simply stolen, during and after the war, to be shared among a chosen few. Like all wars, ours ruined the country and further enriched a few who were already too rich before it started. That's why wars are fought. In this case, the consortium was also used to repay favors, pay for betrayals and services, and buy silence and complicity. It was a means to attain promotion for many—among them, Mauricio Valls. We know what Valls did, Ariadna. What he did to you and your family. But that is not enough. We need your help to get to the bottom of this."

"What for? Valls is dead."

"To see that justice is done. Valls is dead, yes, but many hundreds of people whose lives he destroyed are still alive and deserve justice."

Victoria glanced at him suspiciously. "Is that what you're looking for? Justice?"

"We're looking for the truth."

"And who are you, exactly?"

"We're a group of citizens who have sworn to serve the country because we want to make Spain a fairer place, more honest and more open."

Victoria laughed.

Leandro looked at her, his expression serious. "I don't expect you to believe me. Not yet. But I'm going to prove to you that we're the ones who are trying to change things from inside the regime, because there's no other way of changing them. To regenerate this country and give it back to the people. We're the ones risking our lives so that what happened to you and your sister, what happened to your parents, never happens again; to make sure that those who committed such crimes pay for them and the truth becomes known. Because without truth there is no justice, and without justice there is no peace. We're for change and progress. We're the ones here to end a state that serves only those few individuals who have hidden behind institutions to shield their privileges, at the expense of workers and disadvantaged people. And not because we're heroes, but because someone has to do it. There's no one else. That is why we need your help. If we join forces, it will be possible."

They gazed at one another throughout a long silence.

"What if I don't want to help you?"

Leandro shrugged. "Nobody can force you to do this. If you decide that you don't want to join us, that you don't care whether others who have suffered the same fate don't get justice, I'm not going to force you. It's in your hands. Valls is dead. The easiest thing for a person in your situation would be to leave all this behind and begin a new life. Who knows, perhaps I would do the same in your place. But I think you're not that kind of person. I think that deep down you don't care about revenge, but about justice and truth. As much as we do, or more so. I think you want those who are to blame to pay for their crimes. And I'm sure you want their victims to get their lives back and to be assured that those who lost theirs for their sake didn't do so in vain. But it's in your hands. I'm not going to stop you. There's the door. You can leave this place whenever you wish. The only reason we've brought you here is that here you're safe. Here we can protect you while we try to get to the bottom of this matter. It depends on you."

Victoria turned her head to look at the door.

Leandro poured himself another cup of coffee, dissolved five lumps in it, and sipped it calmly. "When you ask, a car will pick you up and take you wherever you want to go. You'll never see me again or get news from us. You only have to ask."

Victoria felt a knot in her stomach.

"You don't have to decide now. I know what you've been through, and I know you're confused. I know you don't trust me, or anyone. It's perfectly understandable. Nor would I, in your place. But you've got nothing to lose by giving us an opportunity. One more day. Or a few hours. At any moment, without having to give your reasons to anyone, you can leave. But I hope you don't—I beg you not to. Give us this opportunity to help others."

Victoria looked down and saw that her hands were shaking.

Leandro smiled with infinite gentleness. "Please . . ."

At some point, through her tears, she consented.

4

FOR AN HOUR and a half Leandro reconstructed what they had been able to uncover.

"I've been trying to piece together the facts for some time. What

I'm going to do is summarize what we know, or think we know. You'll see that there are some gaps, and that we're probably wrong on some points. Or on many. That's where you come in. If you like, I'll tell you what I think happened, and you correct me whenever I'm wrong. All right?"

Leandro had a soothing voice that invited one to surrender. Victoria wanted to close her eyes, be cocooned for a time in the warm embrace of that voice, framed by the velvety outline of words that acquired sense, no matter what their meaning was.

"All right," she agreed. "I'll try."

The man smiled with such gratitude and warmth that he made her feel safe and protected against whatever lay in wait beyond the walls of that place. Little by little, unhurriedly, he told her the story she knew only too well. The account began when she was just a small girl and her father, Víctor Mataix, met a man called Miguel Ángel Ubach, a powerful banker whose wife—a regular reader of Mataix's books—had persuaded him to hire Mataix to ghostwrite his autobiography in exchange for a substantial sum of money.

Victoria's father, who was going through financial difficulties, accepted the assignment. After the war, the banker and his wife paid the Mataix family an unexpected visit in their home next to Carretera de las Aguas in Vallvidrera. Señora Ubach was a beauty queen straight out of a magazine, and quite a bit younger than her husband. She didn't want to ruin her perfect figure by bringing a child into the world, but she liked children, or the idea of having them and letting her servants bring them up, almost as much as she liked pet cats and a well-mixed vodka martini. The Ubachs spent the day with the Mataix family. By then her parents had given her a sister, Sonia, who was still a baby. When they left, Señora Ubach kissed the girls goodbye and declared that they were adorable. A few days later a group of armed men returned to the Mataixes' house in Vallvidrera. They arrested her father and took him to the prison in Montjuïc Castle, and they took Victoria away with her sister, leaving their mother behind, so badly wounded they presumed she was dead.

"Am I correct up to now?" asked Leandro.

Victoria nodded, drying her angry tears.

That very night those men separated them, and she never saw Sonia again. They told her that if she didn't want her little sister to be killed, she must forget her parents, because they were a pair of criminals. And from then on, they said, her name would no longer be Ariadna Mataix but Victoria Ubach. They explained to her that her new parents were Miguel Ángel Ubach and his wife Federica, and that she was very lucky. She would live with them in the most beautiful house in all of Barcelona, a mansion called El Pinar. She would have servants at her disposal, and whatever she wished for would be hers. Ariadna was ten.

"From then on the story becomes confused," warned Leandro.

They discovered, he explained, that Víctor Mataix had been shot in Montjuïc Castle, like so many others, on the orders of Mauricio Valls, the prison governor, although the official report said he had committed suicide. Leandro believed that Valls had sold Ariadna to the Ubachs in exchange for favors that would help him rise in the regime, together with a bundle of shares in a bank that had been recently set up. These shares had been expropriated from estates of hundreds of people who were imprisoned and in many cases executed shortly after the end of the war.

"Do you know what happened to your mother?"

Victoria nodded, pressing her lips together.

Leandro told her how, as far as they knew, the day after her husband and daughters had been kidnapped, her mother, Susana, managed to gather her strength and made the mistake of going to the police to report what had happened. She was immediately arrested and interned in a psychiatric hospital in Horta, where she was kept in solitary confinement and underwent electric shock treatments for five years, until they decided to abandon her in some deserted area on the outskirts of Barcelona, once they realized she couldn't even remember her name.

"Or at least that's what they believed."

Leandro explained that Susana had survived on the streets of Barcelona by begging, sleeping rough, and eating food she stole from rubbish bins, hoping that one day she would be able to recover her daughters. That hope is what kept her alive. Years later, Susana found a newspaper among the rubble in an alleyway of the Raval quarter, with a photograph of Mauricio Valls and his family. By then he was a very important man who had left his days as prison governor behind him. In the photograph Valls posed with a little girl, Mercedes.

"Mercedes was none other than your little sister, Sonia. Your mother recognized her because Sonia had been born with a mark she could never forget."

"A mark in the shape of a star on the base of her neck," Victoria heard herself saying.

Leandro smiled as he nodded. "Valls's wife suffered from a chronic illness that prevented her from having children. Valls decided to keep your sister and bring her up as his own child. He called her Mercedes, after his late mother. Stealing what she could, Susana managed to put together enough money to take a train to Madrid. Once she was there, she spent months spying on the playgrounds of all the schools in Madrid, hoping to locate your sister. By then she had built herself a new identity. She lived in a squalid room in the Chueca area and at night worked as a seamstress in a workshop. During the day she searched the Madrid schools. And when she had almost given up hope, she found her. She saw her from a distance, and knew it was her daughter. She began to go there every morning. She would approach the playground railings and try to catch the girl's attention. She managed to talk to her a couple of times. She didn't want to frighten her. When she realized that Mercedes . . . that Sonia no longer remembered her, your mother was on the point of taking her own life. But she didn't give up. She kept going there every morning, hoping to see her, even if it was just for a few seconds, or to speak to her if the child came over to the railings. One day she decided that she should tell her the truth. She was caught by Valls's bodyguards as she stood by the railings, talking to your sister. They blew her brains out with a single shot in front of the girl. Would you like me to stop for a bit?"

Victoria shook her head.

Leandro continued to narrate what he knew about how Victoria had grown up in the golden prison of El Pinar. In time, Miguel Ángel Ubach was summoned by the Generalissimo to head a group of bankers and dignitaries who had financed his army, and put in charge of designing a new economic structure for the State. Ubach left Barcelona and moved with his family to a large house in Madrid, which Victoria always hated and from which she escaped, disappearing for a few months, until she was found in strange circumstances on a beach in San Feliu de Guíxols, a small town about a hundred kilometers from Barcelona.

"This is one of the big gaps in the story we have put together," said Leandro. "Nobody knows where you were during those months, or who with. All we know is that one night in 1948, shortly after you returned to Madrid, the Ubach residence went up in flames. It was reduced to ashes, and both the banker and his wife Federica died in the blaze."

Leandro searched her eyes, but Victoria kept silent.

"I do realize that it's very difficult and painful to talk about this, but it's important that we know what happened during those months when you disappeared."

She pressed her lips together, and Leandro nodded patiently. "It doesn't have to be today," he said, and continued with his story.

Orphaned and heiress to a huge fortune, Victoria was left under the guardianship of a young lawyer named Ignacio Sanchís who had been named the executor of the Ubachs' estate. Sanchís was a brilliant man whom Ubach had taken under his protection from a young age. An orphan, he had studied with a scholarship awarded by the Ubach Foundation. It was rumored that in fact he was the illegitimate son of the banker, the fruit of an illicit relationship he'd had with a well-known actress of the time.

Little Victoria always had a special bond with Sanchís. They were both surrounded by all the luxuries and privileges the Ubach empire could buy, and yet they were alone in the world. Ignacio Sanchís often came to the family house, where he would conduct business matters with the banker in the garden. Victoria would spy on him from the attic windows. One day, after Sanchís came across her unexpectedly when she was swimming in the pool, he told her he'd never known his parents and had grown up in La Navata orphanage. From then on, whenever Sanchís came to the mansion, Victoria no longer hid and would come down to greet him.

Señora Ubach didn't like Ignacio, and did not allow her daughter to speak to him. He was a nobody, she said. The matriarch staved off her boredom by meeting her young lovers in luxury hotels in Madrid, or sleeping it off in her bedroom on the third floor. She never became aware that her daughter and the young lawyer had become good friends, that they shared books and a complicity that nobody in the world, not even Señor Ubach, could have imagined.

"One day I told him we were the same," Victoria confessed.

After the tragic death of the Ubachs in the fire that destroyed their house, Ignacio Sanchís became her legal guardian until she came of age, when he married her. There was a lot of gossip, of course. Some called it the greatest marriage for money of the century.

Victoria smiled bitterly when she heard those words.

"Ignacio Sanchís was never a husband to you, at least not in the way everyone thought he was," said Leandro. "He was a good man who had discovered the truth and married you to protect you."

"I loved him."

"And he loved you. He gave his life for you."

Victoria sank into a long silence.

"For many years you tried to take justice into your own hands with the help of Ignacio and of Valentín Morgado, who had been in prison with your father and whom your husband hired as a chauffeur for you. Together you forged a plan to lay a trap for Valls, and you managed to capture him. What you didn't know is that someone was watching you. Someone who couldn't allow the truth to be disclosed."

"Is that why they killed Valls?"

Leandro nodded.

"Hendaya?" asked Victoria.

He shook his head. "Hendaya is just a foot soldier. We're looking for the person pulling the strings behind him."

"And who is that?"

"I think you know."

Victoria shook her head slowly, confused.

"Maybe you're not aware of it right now."

"If I'd known, I would have ended up in the same cell as Valls."

"Then perhaps we can find out together, with your help and our resources. You have already suffered enough and put yourself in enough danger. It's our turn now. You and your sister were not the only ones. You know that. There are many, many more. Many don't even suspect that their life is a lie, that everything was stolen from them . . ."

She nodded.

"How did you find out? How did you come to the conclusion that you and your sister hadn't been the only ones?"

"We managed to get a list with document numbers. Numbers of birth and death certificates that had been forged by Valls."

"Who did they belong to?" asked Leandro.

"To children of the prisoners who'd been locked up in Montjuïc Castle after the war, when he was the prison governor. All disappeared. Valls would first jail and murder the parents. Then he kept the children. He made out a death certificate at the same time as he forged a birth certificate with a new identity for the children, and then sold them to well-positioned families in the regime in exchange for favors, money, and power. It was a perfect plan, because once the new parents had accepted the stolen children, they became accomplices, and had to keep their mouths shut forever."

"Do you know how many of these cases there were?"

"No. Ignacio suspected there may have been hundreds."

"We're talking about a very complex operation. Valls couldn't have done all that on his own."

"Ignacio thought he must have had an accomplice, or various."

"I agree. In fact, I daresay that Valls was possibly only a cog in the machine. He had the access, the opportunity, and the greed. But I find it hard to believe that he could devise such a complex plot."

"That's what Ignacio said."

"Somebody else, someone we still haven't uncovered, is the brain of this whole operation."

"The black hand," said Victoria.

"Excuse me?"

She smiled weakly. "It's from a story my father used to tell me when I was a child. The black hand. The evil that always stays in the shadows and pulls the strings . . ."

"You must help us find him, Ariadna."

"So do you think that Hendaya is receiving orders from Valls's partner?"

"That's the most likely thing, yes."

"That means it must be someone inside the government. Someone powerful."

Leandro nodded. "That's why it's so important not to rush into anything and act very cautiously. If we want to capture him, we must first know the whole truth, with names, dates, and details, and discover who knew about this matter and who is implicated. Only if we find out who was in the know will we be able to get to the bottom of all this."

"What can I do?"

"As I said, help me reconstruct your story. I'm sure that if we join up all the pieces of the jigsaw, we'll find the mastermind behind the plot. Until then, you won't be safe. That's why you must stay here and let us protect you. Will you?"

Victoria looked uncertain at first, but then she nodded.

Leandro leaned forward and took her hands in his. "I need you to know that I'm grateful for your bravery, for your courage. Without you, without your fight and your suffering, none of what we are trying to do would be possible."

"I just want justice to be done. Nothing else. Never in my whole life have I thought that what I wanted was revenge. Revenge doesn't exist. All that matters is the truth."

Leandro kissed her on the forehead: a paternal kiss, protective and noble, which made her feel less alone, even if only for an instant.

"I think we've done enough for one day," he said. "You need to rest. We have a difficult task ahead."

"Are you leaving?" asked Victoria.

"Don't worry. I'll be close by. And I want you to know that you're guarded and protected. I'm going to ask your permission to let us shut this door. It's not to keep you locked in, but to stop anyone who is not allowed to enter from trying to get in. Do you think you can do that?"

"Yes."

"If you need anything, all you have to do is press this bell, and some-one will be with you in a matter of seconds. Whatever you may need."

"I'd like to have something to read. Would it be possible to get hold of some of my father's books?"

"Of course. I'll have them sent up to you. Now you must try to rest."

"I don't know if I'll be able to sleep."

"If you like, we can help you . . ."

"Sedate me again?"

"It's just a help. It will make you feel better. But only if you want."

"All right."

"I'll be back tomorrow morning. We'll start to piece together ev-erything that has happened, bit by bit."

"How long will I have to stay here?"

"Not long. A few days. A week at most. Until we know who is be-hind all this. Until the culprit has been arrested, you won't be safe anywhere else. Hendaya and his men are looking for you. We man-aged to rescue you from El Pinar, but that man isn't going to give up. He never gives up."

"How did it happen? I don't remember."

"You were dazed. Two of our men lost their lives to get you out of there."

"And Valls?"

"It was too late. Don't think about that now. Rest, Ariadna."

"Ariadna," she repeated. "Thank you."

"Thank *you*," said Leandro on his way to the door.

As soon as she was left alone, she was gripped by a sense of un-ease and an emptiness she couldn't quite understand. There wasn't a single clock in the entire room. When she drew back the curtains, she saw that the windows were locked and covered on the outside with a translucent paper that let in the light but completely blocked the view.

She began to wander aimlessly around the room, struggling to stop herself from pressing that bell Leandro had left on the table in the lounge. At last, after exploring every corner of the suite, she re-turned to her bedroom, worn out. She smiled at herself.

"The truth," she heard herself whisper.

5

LEANDRO STUDIED THE pale, sorrowful face on the other side of the mirror. Ariadna exuded the perfume of broken souls who have become lost along the way, though they think they're moving forward. He had always been fascinated by the idea that if one knew how to read the language of looks and of time, one could guess, just by gazing at a face, what that face had looked like as a child, and relish the moment when the world had stuck its poisoned dart in it, and its spirit had begun to grow old. People were like puppets or clockwork toys. They all had a hidden mechanism that allowed one to pull their strings and make them run in whatever direction one wished them to run. The satisfaction he felt, or perhaps it was only a sustenance, came from that surrender, that confused desire to which sooner or later they succumbed to give themselves over to his wishes, to receive his blessing and offer him their soul in exchange for a smile of approval and a look that would make them believe.

Sitting next to him, Hendaya watched her suspiciously. "I think we're wasting our time, sir," he said. "If you give me an hour, I'll get everything she knows out of her."

"You've had more than enough hours already. Not everything is meat for slicing. You do your work, and I'll do mine."

"Yes, sir."

Shortly afterward the doctor appeared on the scene. Leandro had selected him with great care. He had the good-natured look of a family doctor, a kindly, bespectacled sixty-year-old with the mustache of a judicious man, someone who could well have been a lovable uncle or grandfather; someone before whom not even the most sanctimonious woman would feel embarrassed to undress, but rather would let his tepid hands palpate her private parts while she looked up to heaven and murmured, "What hands you have, Doctor."

He wasn't a qualified doctor, but nobody would have said so when they saw him in his gray suit, with his doctor's bag and his experienced older man's limp. He was a chemist, in fact, and one of the best. Leandro watched him help Ariadna lie down on her bed, uncover her arm, and search her pulse. The syringe was small and the needle so fine that she didn't seem to notice it. Leandro smiled to himself when he saw how Ariadna's eyes glazed over and her body lost its rigidity. In a matter of seconds she had fallen into that chemically induced drowsiness that would keep her there for at least sixteen hours, possibly more, considering her fragile constitution. She would float in a dreamless calm, in a state of utter suspension and pleasure that would slowly dig its claws into her guts, veins, and brain. Day by day.

"Isn't that going to kill her?" asked Hendaya.

"Not with the right dosage," said Leandro. "At least for now."

The doctor put his instruments back in his bag, covered Ariadna, and left the bedroom. As he walked past the mirror, he gave a respectful nod.

"Anything else?" asked Leandro, hearing Hendaya's impatient breathing behind him.

"No, sir."

"Then I'm grateful to you for having brought her to me safe and sound, but there's nothing more for you to do here. Go back to Barcelona and find Alicia Gris."

"She's most probably dead, sir . . ."

Leandro turned around. "Alicia is alive."

"With all due respect, how can you know?"

Leandro stared at Hendaya as if he were a beast of limited intelligence in a stable.

"Because I know."

6

ALICIA OPENED HER eyes in the dim candlelight. The first thing she noticed was that she was too thirsty to be dead. The second thing was the face of a man with white hair and beard, sitting next to her. He was gazing at her from behind tiny round lenses, and his features reminded her vaguely of the God figure in one of the catechism books of her years in the orphanage.

"Are you from heaven?" asked Alicia.

"Don't get carried away. I'm from the neighborhood."

Dr. Soldevila took her wrist and felt her pulse, checking his watch. "How are you feeling?"

"I'm very thirsty."

"I know," said Dr. Soldevila, without making any move to offer her something to drink.

"Where am I?"

"Good question." The doctor pulled back the sheets, and Alicia felt his hand over her pelvis. "Do you feel the pressure?"

She nodded.

"Pain?"

"Thirst."

"I know. But you must wait."

Before covering her, Dr. Soldevila's eyes paused on the black scar wrapping around her hip. Alicia could read the horror that his eyes were trying to hide. "I'll give you something for that. But be careful. You're still very weak."

"I'm used to the pain, Doctor."

Dr. Soldevila sighed and covered her up again.

"Am I going to die?"

"Not today. I know this sounds silly, but try to relax and rest."

"As if I were on holiday."

"Something like that. Try to, at least."

Dr. Soldevila stood up, and Alicia heard him murmur a few words. Footsteps approached, and a circle of figures appeared around her makeshift bed. She recognized Fermín, and Daniel and Bea. There was a man with them. He had sparse hair and eagle eyes, and she had the feeling she'd known him all her life but couldn't quite place him. Fermín was whispering to Dr. Soldevila. Daniel smiled with relief. Bea, next to him, was looking suspiciously into Alicia's eyes.

Fermín knelt down beside her and placed his hand on her forehead. "This is the second time you've almost died on my watch, and I'm starting to get fed up to my back teeth. You have the mien of a corpse, granted, but other than that, you look like a million pesetas, so how are you feeling?"

"Thirsty."

"That doesn't make sense to me. You've swallowed at least eighty percent of my bloodstream."

"Until all the anesthetic has been eliminated, she mustn't drink," Dr. Soldevila explained.

"Piece of cake, you'll see," Fermín remarked. "Cleansing the body of anesthetics is like shedding a few years of Catholic school: free your nether regions a bit, and the rest will follow."

Dr. Soldevila threw him a poisonous look. "Try not to tire the patient with such filth, if that's not too much to ask."

"The silence of the grave will be observed," Fermín declared, crossing himself to make the point.

Dr. Soldevila grunted. "I'll be back tomorrow morning. Until then, you'd better take turns. At the slightest sign of a fever, inflammation, or infection, come and fetch me. Day or night. Who's going to take the first turn? Not you, Fermín—I can see you coming."

Bea spoke first. "I'll stay," she said in a tone that made it very clear that this was not open to debate. "Fermín, I left Julián with Sofía, but I'm not too happy about it because he always gets his way with her. I've called Bernarda and asked her to come around and keep an eye on him. You can use our bedroom. I've left clean sheets on the chest of drawers, and Bernarda knows where everything is. Daniel will sleep on the sofa."

Daniel glanced at his wife, but kept his mouth shut.

"Don't worry. I'll make sure the little one sleeps like a log. A dash of brandy and honey in his milk will work wonders."

"Don't even dream of giving my son any alcohol. And for goodness sake don't talk to him about politics, because then he goes around repeating everything."

"Yes, ma'am. Information power cut decreed sine die."

"Bea, remember the antibiotic injections. Every four hours," said the doctor.

Fermín grinned innocently at Alicia. "Don't worry," he said. "Doña Bea, who may seem a bit of a dragon today, gives injections like an angel. Her father is diabetic, you see, and although there is nothing sweet about him, she became so skillful at pricking, she'd be the envy of those panther mosquitoes on the Nile, or whatever those bugs are called in that part of the world. She learned to give injections as a child, since there was no one else in the family who dared, and now she pricks us all, me included, considering I'm a difficult patient because I have steel buttocks and I bend all the needles due to my muscular tension."

"Fermín!" Bea shouted.

Fermín performed a military salute and winked at Alicia. "Well, my dear vamp, I leave you in good hands. Try not to bite anyone. I'll be back in the morning. Pay attention to everything Señora Bea tells you, and if possible try not to die."

"I'll do my best. Thanks for everything, Fermín. Once again."

"Don't remind me. Come on, Daniel. Looking dumbfounded won't speed up the healing process."

Fermín left, dragging Daniel behind him.

"All clear, then," said the doctor. "Now, how does one get out of here?"

"I'll see you out," said the keeper.

*

They were left alone. Bea pulled up a chair and sat down next to Alicia. They regarded one another without uttering a word. Alicia ventured a smile of gratitude. Bea gazed at her, inscrutable.

After a while the keeper poked his head in and sized up the situation. "Doña Beatriz, should you need anything, you know where to find me. I've left you a few blankets and the medicines with the doctor's instructions on the shelf."

"Thanks, Isaac. Good night."

"Good night, then. Good night, Alicia," said the keeper. His footsteps faded away down the corridor.

"Everyone seems to know me here," said Alicia.

"Yes, everyone seems to know you. A pity nobody knows for certain who you really are."

Alicia nodded, giving Bea another meek smile, which Bea again didn't return. A long, heavy silence fell between them. Alicia's eyes roamed over the walls, which were covered with books from floor to ceiling. She knew Bea's gaze was still fixed on her.

"Can you tell me what you're simpering about?" asked Bea.

"Oh, just something silly. A while ago I dreamed that I was kissing a very handsome man, and I don't know who he was."

"Do you have a habit of kissing strangers, or is that only when you're under anesthetic?"

Bea's tone of voice cut like a knife blade, and as soon as the words had left her mouth she regretted them. "I'm sorry," she murmured.

"Don't be. I deserve it," said Alicia.

"In just over three hours, it will be time for the antibiotic. Why don't you try to sleep a bit, as the doctor ordered?"

"I don't think I could. I'm frightened."

"I thought nothing frightened you."

"I'm good at pretending."

Bea was about to say something, but she bit her tongue.

"Bea?"

"What?"

"I know I have no right to ask you to forgive me, but—"

"Forget about that for the moment. I don't have to forgive you for anything."

"But would you, if I asked you to?"

"Your friend Fermín says that if someone wants to be forgiven, he should go to the confessional, or buy himself a dog. For once, and because he can't hear me, I'll admit he's right."

"Fermín is a wise man."

"He has his moments. But don't tell him, or he'll become unbearable. Now try to get some sleep."

"May I hold your hand?" asked Alicia.

Bea hesitated, but in the end accepted Alicia's hand. They were silent for a long time. Alicia closed her eyes and began to breathe slowly. Bea looked at that strange creature who made her feel fear and compassion at the same time. Soon after she arrived, when Alicia was still delirious, the doctor had examined her, and Bea had helped him undress her. She still had that image engraved on her mind: the horrifying wound that mauled her side.

"Daniel is a lucky man," murmured Alicia.

"Are you trying to flatter me?"

"A married woman and a mother? I would never dare."

"I thought you were supposed to be asleep," said Bea.

"So did I."

"Does it hurt?"

"Do you mean the wound?"

Bea didn't reply.

Alicia still had her eyes closed. "Just a bit," she said. "The anesthetic has numbed it."

"How did you get it?"

"It was during the war. In the bombings."

"I'm sorry."

Alicia shrugged.

"It helps me keep suitors away."

"I bet you have loads."

"None worth the candle. The best men fall in love with women like you. They only want me to fantasize about."

"If you're trying to make me feel sorry for you, forget it."

Alicia smiled.

"Don't think they don't fantasize about me," ventured Bea with a chuckle.

"I haven't the slightest doubt."

"Why are they so stupid sometimes?" asked Bea.

"Men? Who knows. Perhaps it's because nature is a mother, though a cruel one, and she leaves them silly at birth. But some of them aren't that bad."

"That's what Bernarda says."

"And your Daniel?"

Bea sharpened her eyes. "What about my Daniel?"

"Nothing. He seems to be a nice guy. A good soul."

"He has his dark side, believe me."

"Because of what happened to his mother? To Isabella?"

"What do you know about Isabella?"

"Very little."

"You were a much better liar without the anesthetic."

"Can I trust you?"

"I can't see you have much choice. The question is whether I can trust you."

"Do you doubt it?"

"Absolutely."

"There are things about Isabella, about her past . . . ," Alicia began. "I think Daniel has a right to know them, but I'm not sure whether in fact it would be better if he never did."

"Alicia?"

Alicia opened her eyes and found Bea's face almost touching hers. She felt her pressing her hand tightly.

"Yes."

"I'm going to ask one thing of you. I'll only tell you once."

"Whatever you say."

"Don't ever think of harming Daniel or my family."

Alicia held that gaze, which became so commanding she hardly dared to breathe.

"Swear you won't."

Alicia gulped. "I swear."

Bea nodded and sat back in her chair again. Alicia saw her half close her eyes.

"Bea?"

"What is it now?"

"There's something . . . The other night, when I walked with Daniel to your front door . . ."

"Shut up and go to sleep."

7

THE PASSING STORM had given Barcelona that electric-blue tinge that can only be enjoyed on certain winter mornings. The sun had kicked away the clouds, and a clean light floated in the air, so liquid it could have been bottled. Señor Sempere, who had woken up with unalloyed optimism and, ignoring the doctor's advice, downed a large cup of black coffee that tasted wonderfully rebellious, decided that it was going to be a memorable day.

"We're going to have more takings than a Molino variety show during Lent," he announced. "You'll see."

While he was removing the CLOSED notice from the bookshop door, he noticed that Fermín and Daniel were whispering in a corner.

"What are you two scheming?"

They turned around with that stupid expression on their faces that indicated a budding conspiracy. They looked as if they hadn't slept for a week, and if the bookseller's memory served him correctly, they were wearing exactly the same clothes as the day before.

"We were remarking on the fact that every day you look younger and more dashing," said Fermín. "Young women of a marriageable age must be throwing themselves at your feet."

Before the bookseller was able to reply, the doorbell tinkled. A gentleman with crystal-clear eyes and impeccable business attire walked up to the counter and smiled placidly.

"Good morning, sir, how may we help you?"

The visitor began to remove his gloves unhurriedly. "I was hoping you'd be able to answer a few questions," said Hendaya. "Police."

The bookseller frowned and shot a quick look at Daniel, who had gone so pale he'd acquired the color of Bible paper, the sort used to print the complete works of universal classics.

"Go ahead."

Hendaya smiled politely and pulled out a photograph that he left on the counter. "If you'd be so kind as to come over and have a look."

The three congregated behind the counter and proceeded to examine the photograph. It was a picture of Alicia Gris, looking about five years younger, smiling at the camera and putting on an air of innocence even a babe in arms wouldn't have swallowed.

"Do you recognize this young lady?"

Señor Sempere picked up the photograph and looked at it carefully. He shrugged and passed it on to Daniel, who repeated the ritual. The last person to inspect it was Fermín, who, after lifting it up against the light, as if it were a counterfeit note, shook his head and handed it back to Hendaya.

"I'm afraid we don't know this person," said the bookseller.

"I must say, she does look a bit roguish, but her face doesn't ring a bell," Fermín corroborated.

"No? Are you sure?"

All three denied in unison.

"You're not sure, or you haven't seen her?"

"Yes we are, and no we haven't," Daniel replied.

"I see."

"May I ask who that is?" asked the bookseller.

Hendaya put the photograph back. "Her name is Alicia Gris, and she's a fugitive from justice. She has committed three murders, that we know of, in the last few days. The most recent was yesterday, when she killed a police captain named Vargas. She's very dangerous and may be armed. She's been seen in this part of town during the last few days, and some of your neighbors say she came into the bookshop. One of the shop assistants in the bakery on the corner is quite sure she saw her with one of the employees from this bookshop."

"She must have made a mistake," replied Señor Sempere.

"That's possible. Does anyone else work here, apart from you three?"

"My daughter-in-law."

"Maybe she'll remember her?"

"I'll ask her."

"If you remember anything, or if your daughter-in-law does, please call this telephone number. It doesn't matter what time it is. The name is Hendaya."

"We'll do that."

The policeman gave a friendly nod and headed for the door. "Thank you for your help. Have a nice day."

They stayed behind the counter without saying a word, watching Hendaya cross the street slowly and stop by the café on the other side. There an individual in a black coat came up to him, and the two talked for about a minute. The individual nodded, and Hendaya set off down the street. The man in the black coat glanced briefly at the bookshop and stepped into the café. He sat at the table by the window and remained there, vigilant.

"Can someone tell me what's going on?" asked Señor Sempere.

"It's complicated," ventured Fermín.

Just then the bookseller caught sight of his niece, Sofía, who was returning from taking Julián to the park. She was grinning from ear to ear.

"Who was that handsome hunk who just left?" she asked from the door. "What's the matter? Has someone died?"

*

The conclave took place in the back room. Fermín broached the subject without further delay.

"Sofía, I know you adolescents keep your brains on the back burner while you wait for the hormonal tsunami to abate, but if the handsome snake you've just seen leaving the bookshop, or any other individual using any old pretext, appears and asks you whether you've seen, know, have heard of, or have the faintest idea of the existence of Señorita Alicia Gris, you're going to lie with that Neapolitan grace God has given you and say no, you've never seen her in your life, and you'll say so looking as dumb as your neighbor Merceditas, or I swear that, even though I'm not your father, or your legal guardian, I'll stick you in a cloistered convent from which you'll not be allowed out until you find Sir Winston Churchill devilishly handsome. Are you with me?"

Sofía nodded remorsefully.

"Now go to the counter and pretend you're doing something useful."

Once they'd gotten Sofía out of the way, Señor Sempere confronted his son and Fermín.

"I'm still waiting for you to explain what the hell is going on."

"Have you taken your blood pressure medication?"

"With my coffee."

"What a grand idea. All you need to do now is to dunk a dynamite cartridge in it, as if it were a sponge finger, and then we can all pat you on the back."

"Don't change the subject, Fermín."

Fermín pointed at Daniel. "I'll take charge of this. You go out there and behave as if you were me."

"And what does that mean?"

"Keep your eyes peeled. Those dickheads are staking out the shop and will be waiting for us to make a wrong move."

"I was going to take over from Bea . . ."

"Take over from Bea?" asked Señor Sempere. "Take over from what?"

"A number of issues," Fermín cut in. "Daniel, don't leave the premises. I'll go. I have experience in matters of military intelligence, and I can slip out like an eel. Go on, beat it. It mustn't look as if we're scheming."

Daniel walked through the back-room curtain reluctantly, leaving them alone.

"Well?" asked Señor Sempere. "Are you going to tell me once and for all what's going on here?"

Fermín smiled meekly. "Do you fancy a Sugus?"

8

THE DAY PROVED endless for Daniel. The hours dragged by as he waited for Bea and let his father tend to the customers. Fermín had left, shortly after palming off one of his byzantine tales on Señor Sempere, consisting of monumental fibs whispered in confidential tones, which he hoped would silence the man's questions, for a few hours at least, and appease his alarm.

"We must appear more normal than usual, Daniel," he'd said shortly before sneaking out through the back-room window into the square of the church of Santa Ana, to avoid detection by the officer Hendaya had left watching the bookshop.

"And when have we ever been normal?"

"Don't get all existential now. As soon as I see that the coast is clear, I'll slip out and take over from Bea."

Bea appeared at last around noon, when Daniel's hair was beginning to gray and he'd bitten his nails up to his elbows.

"Fermín has told me everything," she said.

"Did he get there all right?"

"Apparently he stopped on the way to buy some sweet biscuits he couldn't resist because he says they're called 'nun's farts,' and some white wine."

"White wine?"

"For Alicia. Which Dr. Soldevila has confiscated."

"How is she?"

"Stable. The doctor says she's still weak, but there's no infection and she doesn't have a fever."

"Did she say anything else?"

"What about?"

"Why do I have the feeling that everyone is trying to hide something from me?"

Bea stroked his cheek. "Nobody is hiding anything from you, Daniel. Where's Julián?"

"At the nursery school. Sofía took him."

"I'll go and collect him this afternoon. We have to keep up an appearance of normality. Where's your father?"

"Back there, fuming."

Bea lowered her voice. "What did you tell him?"

"Fermín foisted one of his epic poems on him."

"I see. I'm off to the Boquería market to get a few things. Do you want anything?"

"A normal life."

*

Halfway through the afternoon, Daniel's father left him alone in the shop. Bea hadn't returned yet, and Daniel, worried and in a filthy mood because he felt duped, had decided to go up to the apartment with the excuse that he was going to take a nap. For days now he'd harbored the suspicion that Alicia and Fermín were keeping something from him. And now, it seemed, Bea had joined them.

He spent a couple of hours mulling over the matter, winding himself up and gnawing away at his soul. Experience had taught him that in such cases it was better to act dumb and pretend not to have noticed. After all, that was the role he was always given in the show. Nobody expected good old Daniel, the poor motherless boy, the perpetual adolescent with nothing on his conscience, to find things out. That's what the others were there for, to bring him the answers written down and even the questions to boot. Nobody seemed to have noticed that he hadn't been wearing short trousers for years. Sometimes even little Julián looked at him out of the corner of his eye and laughed, as if his father had come to the world to play the fool and look like a simpleton while the others revealed life's mysteries to him.

I'd laugh at myself too if I could, thought Daniel. Not that long ago he'd been able to make fun of his own shadow, to humor Fermín and his jibes, to embody the eternal naive boy adopted by his quixotic guardian angel. It had been a good part to play, and he'd felt comfortable with it. He would have loved to continue being the Daniel that all the others around him saw, and not the Daniel who, in the early hours, when Bea and Julián were fast asleep, would grope his way down to the bookshop, take shelter in the back room, and push the plaster panel hidden behind a broken old radiator.

There, at the very bottom of a box, covered by a thick pile of dusty old books, was the scrapbook filled with the press clippings about Mauricio Valls he'd been stealing from the newspaper library in the Ateneo. The public life of the minister was recorded in those pages, year after year. He knew every one of those news items and press releases by heart. The last one, the one about his death in a traffic accident, was the most painful.

Valls, the man who had stolen his mother from him, had got away.

*

Daniel had learned to hate that face, so eager to be photographed in vainglorious poses. He'd come to the conclusion that you never really know who you are until you learn to hate. And when you really hate, when you abandon yourself to that anger that burns you inside, that slowly consumes what little good you thought you had in your baggage, you do it secretly. Daniel smiled bitterly. Nobody thought him capable of keeping a secret. He'd never been able to, even as a child, when keeping secrets is an art and a way of staving off the world and its emptiness. Not even Fermín or Bea suspected that he kept that folder hidden there, containing the scrapbook in which he so often took refuge, feeding the darkness that had grown inside him since discovering that Mauricio Valls, the great white hope of the regime, had poisoned his mother. It was all conjecture, they told him. Nobody could know the truth of what had happened. Daniel had left the suspicions behind him and lived in a world of certainties.

And the worst of them all, the most difficult to contemplate, was that justice would never be served.

The day he'd dreamed of, poisoning his soul, the day he would find Mauricio Valls, make him look into his eyes and see in them the hatred he had fed—that day would never come. Nor would he pick up the gun he'd bought from a black marketeer who sometimes did business in Can Tunis, which he kept wrapped in rags at the bottom of the box. It was an old gun, dating from the war, but the ammunition was new and the guy had taught him how to use it.

"First you get him in the legs, below the knees. And you wait. You watch him try to pull himself along. Then shoot him in his guts. And you wait. You let him writhe. Then you shoot on the right side of his chest. And you wait. You wait for his lungs to fill with blood, until he chokes in his own shit. Only then, when you think he's already dead, do you empty the last three bullets into his head. One in the back of the neck, one in his temple, and one under his chin. Then you throw the gun into the Besós River, near the beach, and let the current take it away."

Perhaps the current would also take with it, forever, the anger and the pain now rotting inside him.

"Daniel?"

He looked up and saw Bea. He hadn't heard her come in.

"Daniel, are you feeling all right?"

He nodded.

"You look pale. Are you sure you're all right?"

"I'm fine. A bit tired, from not having slept. That's all." Daniel gave her his sweet smile, the one he'd been dragging around since he was a schoolboy, the smile he was known for in the neighborhood.

Good old Daniel Sempere, the son-in-law all good mothers would want for their daughters. The man who hid no shadows in his heart.

"I've bought you some oranges. Don't let Fermín see them, or he'll eat them all in one go, like last time."

"Thanks."

"Daniel, what's the matter? Aren't you going to tell me? Is it because of what's happened with Alicia? Because of that policeman?"

"Nothing's the matter. I'm a bit worried. It's normal. But we've gotten out of worse fixes. We'll get out of this one."

Daniel had never known how to lie to Bea. She looked into his eyes. For months now, what she saw in them had scared her. She drew closer to him and hugged him. Daniel let her put her arms around him, but he didn't say anything, as if he wasn't there.

Bea walked away slowly. She put the shopping bag on the table and lowered her eyes. "I'm going to pick up Julián."

"See you soon."

9

FOUR DAYS WENT by before Alicia could get out of bed without help. Time seemed to have stopped in midair since she'd arrived in that place. She spent most of the day swaying between wakefulness and sleep, without leaving the room where she'd been installed. The room had a brazier, which Isaac fed every few hours, and the gloom was barely broken by the light of a candle or an oil lamp. The medication Dr. Soldevila had left to ease the pain plunged her into a heavy drowsiness from which she occasionally emerged to find Fermín or Daniel watching over her. Money might not buy you happiness, but chemicals can sometimes perform miracles.

When she did recover a vague sense of who and where she was, she would try to utter a few words. Most of her questions were answered before she asked them. No, nobody was going to find her there. No, the dreaded infection had not happened, and Dr. Soldevila thought Alicia was making good progress, although she was still weak. Yes, Fernandito was safe and sound. Señor Sempere had offered him a part-time job making deliveries and picking up sets of books bought from private owners. He was always asking after her, but, according to Fermín, not quite as much since he'd bumped into Sofía in the bookshop. He had managed to beat what seemed impossible: his own infatuation track record.

Alicia was happy for him. If he was going to suffer, let it be for someone worthwhile.

"He does fall in love easily, poor thing," said Fermín. "He'll have a dreadful time during his stay on this planet."

"Those who aren't able to fall in love suffer all the more," Alicia let drop.

"I think the medication is affecting your cerebellum, Alicia. If you start picking up a guitar and singing Sunday-school songs, I'll have to ask the medicine man to reduce your dosage to that of baby aspirin."

"Don't take away the only good thing I've got."

"What a fiend you can be, Mother of God."

The virtues of vice were underestimated. Alicia missed her glasses of white wine, her imported cigarettes, and her space for solitude. The medication kept her sufficiently dazed to allow the days to go by in the warm company of those good people who had conspired to save her life and seemed more anxious about her survival than she herself was. Sometimes, when she was submerged in that chemical balm, she told herself that the best thing would be to touch bottom and remain there in a never-ending stupor. But sooner or later she would wake up again and remember that only people who have settled all their debts deserve to die.

More than once she had woken up in the dim room to find Fermín sitting in a chair opposite her, looking thoughtful.

"What time is it, Fermín?"

"Your time: the witching hour."

"Don't you ever sleep?"

"I've never been one for naps. What I go for is insomnia elevated to an art form. I'll catch up on sleep when I die." Fermín gazed at her with a mixture of tenderness and suspicion that exasperated her.

"Haven't you forgiven me yet, Fermín?"

"Remind me what it is I must forgive you for. I'm vaguely confused." ·

Alicia sighed. "That I let you believe I'd died that night during the war. That I let you live with the guilt of thinking that you'd failed me and my parents. That when I returned to Barcelona, and you recognized me in the train station, I pretended not to know you and allowed you to think you were going mad or seeing ghosts."

"Ah, that." Fermín gave her a caustic smile, but his eyes shone with tears in the candlelight.

"Are you going to forgive me, then?"

"I'll take it into consideration."

"I need you to forgive me. I don't want to die carrying this burden."

They gazed mutely at one another.

"You're a lousy actress."

"I'm a great actress. The trouble is that with all the junk the doctor is prescribing, I keep forgetting my lines."

"I don't feel at all sorry for you, you know."

"I don't want you to feel sorry for me, Fermín. Not you, nor anyone else."

"You'd rather they were afraid of you."

Alicia smiled, baring her teeth.

"Well, I'm not scared of you either," he declared.

"That's because you don't know me well enough."

"I liked you better before, when you played the part of a poor dying damsel."

"So, do you forgive me?"

"What does it matter to you?"

"I don't like to think that it's because of me that you go around being the guardian angel of people—of Daniel and his family."

"I'm the bibliographic adviser to the Sempere & Sons bookshop. The angelic attributes are your invention."

"Are you sure you don't think that if you save someone decent, you'll save the world, or at least the possibility that something good might be left in it?"

"Who said you're someone decent?"

"I was talking about the Semperes."

"Don't you do the same thing, deep down, my dear Alicia?"

"I don't think there is anything decent to save in the world, Fermín."

"Even you don't believe that. The trouble is that you're afraid of finding out that there is."

"Or the opposite, in your case."

Fermín let out a grunt and dug his hand in his raincoat pocket in search of sweets. "Let's not get all corny. You stick to your nihilism, and I'll stick to my Sugus sweets."

"Two unmistakable values."

"And no two ways about it."

"Go on, give me a good-night kiss, Fermín."

"You and your kisses!"

"On the cheek."

Fermín hesitated, but in the end he leaned over and brushed her forehead with his lips. "Go to sleep, for Christ's sake, you demon woman."

Alicia closed her eyes and smiled. "I love you very much, Fermín."

When she heard him crying quietly, she stretched out her hand until she found his. And so, holding each other, they fell asleep in the warmth of a dying candle.

10

THE KEEPER OF that place, Isaac Montfort, brought Alicia a tray twice or three times a day with a glass of milk, a few slices of toast with butter and jam, and some fruit or a pastry from the Escribá Patisserie, the sort he bought every Sunday—for he too had his weaknesses beyond literature and a hermit's life, especially if they involved significant amounts of pine nuts and custard cream. After much pleading, Isaac began to bring her old newspapers, even though Dr. Soldevila wasn't too happy about it. That is how she was able to read everything the press had published about the death of Mauricio Valls and feel her blood boil again.

This is what has saved you, Alicia, she thought.

Good old Isaac was a small, fierce-looking man, but he had a tender nature and had developed a soft spot for Alicia he was barely able to hide. He said she reminded him of his late daughter. Nuria was her name. He always carried two pictures of her in his pocket. One was of a rather mysterious-looking woman, who smiled sadly; the other showed a happy little girl hugging a man Alicia recognized as Isaac, a few decades younger.

"She left me before knowing how much I loved her," he said.

Sometimes, when he brought in the tray with her food and Alicia struggled to swallow two or three mouthfuls, Isaac would be overcome by a wave of memories and start telling her about his daughter Nuria, and about his regrets. Alicia listened to him. She suspected that the old man hadn't shared that sorrow with anyone, but fate had chosen to send him a stranger who resembled the person he had most loved, so that now, when it was too late, when he was no longer of any use to anyone, he could find some comfort by trying to save Alicia and give her an affection that didn't belong to her. Sometimes, when he talked about his daughter, the old man would start to cry, haunted by that memory. Then he would leave Alicia and not return for hours. The most sincere pain is experienced alone. Alicia felt secretly relieved when Isaac took his infinite sadness to a corner to drown in it. The only pain she hadn't learned to tolerate was to see old people cry.

*

They all took turns watching over Alicia and keeping her company. Daniel liked reading to her from books he borrowed from the labyrinth, especially books by someone called Julián Carax, for whom he felt a special fondness. Carax's pen made Alicia think of music and chocolate cakes. The times she spent with Daniel every day, listening to him read from Carax's pages, allowed her to lose herself in a forest of words and images that she was always sad to leave. Her favorite was a short novel called *Nobody*, whose last paragraph she ended up learning by heart, and would whisper to herself when she was trying to get to sleep:

In war he made a fortune, and in love he lost everything. He was destined not to be happy, never to taste the fruit which that late spring had brought to his heart. He knew then that he would live the rest of his days in solitude's perpetual autumn, with no other company or memory than longing and remorse, and that when someone asked who had built that house and who had lived in it before it became a haunted ruin, people who had known it and were familiar with its accursed history would look down and say, in a very faint voice and hoping the wind would blow away their words: nobody.

She soon discovered that she couldn't talk about Julián Carax to anybody, least of all to Isaac. The Semperes had shared some sort of history with Carax, and Alicia thought it best not to rummage around in the family's shadows. Isaac, in particular, couldn't bear to hear Carax's name without turning purple with anger. As Daniel explained to her, Isaac's daughter Nuria had been in love with Carax. The old man believed that all his poor daughter's misfortunes, which had led to her tragic death, were due to Carax, a strange character who, she learned, had once tried to burn all the existing copies of his own books. Had the keeper not been sworn in to his post, Carax would have been able to count on his enthusiastic help.

"It's best not to mention Carax to Isaac," said Daniel. "Come to think of it, better not mention him to anyone."

The only person among them all who saw Alicia as she was, and who didn't have any imaginary ideas or qualms, was Daniel's wife. Bea bathed her, dressed her, combed her hair, and gave her the medication, her eyes conveying that constraint presiding over their relationship, which they had both implicitly established. Bea would take care of Alicia; she would help her to heal and recover so that, as soon as possible, she could get out of their lives and disappear forever, before she could hurt them.

Bea, the woman Alicia would have liked to be and who, with every day spent in her company, she realized she never would. Bea, who spoke little and asked even less, but who understood her better than anyone. Alicia had never been one for hugs and gestures, but more than once had felt the urge to embrace her. Luckily she always restrained herself at the last second. A quick glance at Bea was enough for Alicia to know that this was not a parish church performance of *Little Women*, and that they both had a task to accomplish.

"I think you'll soon be rid of me," Alicia would say.

Bea never took the bait. She never complained. She never reproached her. She changed her bandages with the utmost care. She applied an ointment, something Dr. Soldevila had gotten his trusted chemist to prepare for him, on the old wound. It eased the pain without poisoning her blood. When she did so, she showed neither pity nor compassion. She was the only person, excepting Leandro, in whose eyes Alicia hadn't glimpsed horror or apprehension when they saw her naked and realized the extent of the wounds that had destroyed part of her body during the war.

The only point where they could come together in peace and without shadows on the horizon was little Julián. Their longest and most peaceful chats usually took place when Bea bathed Alicia with a bar of soap and jugs of warm water heated up by Isaac on a camping stove he had in the room he used as office, kitchen, and bedroom. Bea adored the child with a devotion Alicia knew she could never even begin to understand.

"The other day he assured us that when he grows up," Bea said, "he wants to marry you."

"I suppose that as a good mother you've warned him that there are wicked girls in the world who are not at all suitable for him."

"Of which you must be the queen."

"That's what all my potential mothers-in-law have always said. And rightly so."

"On such matters being right is the least of it. I live surrounded by men, and for a long time I've known that most of them are immune to logic. The only thing they learn about, and not all of them do, is the law of gravity. Until they fall flat on their faces, they don't wake up."

"That maxim sounds like one of Fermín's."

"Everything is catching, and I've spent years listening to his pearls of wisdom."

"What else does Julián say?"

"His latest idea is that he wants to be a novelist."

"Precocious."

"You've no idea."

"Are you going to have any more?"

"Children? I don't know. I'd like Julián not to grow up alone. It would be nice if he had a little sister . . ."

"Another woman in the family."

"Fermín says that would dilute the excess of testosterone that dulls the mind of the clan. Except for his, which he alleges can't even be dissolved with turpentine."

"And what does Daniel say?"

There was a long silence.

Bea shrugged. "Daniel says less every day."

*

As the weeks went by, Alicia could feel her strength coming back. Dr. Soldevila examined her twice a day. Soldevila was not a man of many words, and the few he used, he dedicated to the concerns of others. Sometimes Alicia caught him looking at her out of the corner of his eye, as if he were wondering who this creature was and wasn't sure he wanted to know the answer.

"You have scars from a lot of old wounds. Some are serious. You should start thinking about changing your habits."

"Don't worry about me, Doctor. I have more lives than a cat."

"I'm not a vet, but the theory is that cats only have nine lives, and I can see you're almost running on empty."

"One more will suffice."

"Something tells me you're not going to devote it to charity work."

"It depends on how you look at it."

"I'm not sure what I'm most worried about, your health or your soul."

"A priest as well as a doctor. You're quite the catch."

"At my age, the difference between the practice and the confessional becomes blurred. Still, I think I'm too young for you. How's the pain going? The pain in your hip, I mean."

"The ointment helps."

"But not as much as what you were taking before."

"No," Alicia admitted.

"How much were you taking?"

"Four hundred milligrams. Sometimes more."

"God almighty. You can't go on taking that. You know, don't you?"

"Give me a good reason."

"Ask your liver, if you two are still on speaking terms."

"If you hadn't confiscated my white wine I could invite you to a little drink, and you and my liver could have a chat."

"You're a hopeless case."

"That's something we all three agree on."

*

Most of them were beginning to make plans for her funeral, but Alicia knew she had gotten out of purgatory, even if perhaps it was just on a weekend leave. She knew because she was recovering her dismal view of the world and losing her appreciation for the moving, tender scenes of the last few days. Once again the dark breath of years gone by colored everything, and the pain drilling like iron through her hip bones reminded her that her tenure as the delicate flower–like invalid was about to expire.

The days had regained their customary rhythm, and the hours that slipped by during her healing process began to taste of wasted time. The person who showed the most anxiety about her was Fermín, whose role alternated between a prematurely hired mourner and an amateur mind reader.

"May I remind you of what the poet said," Fermín would intone, reading her evil spirits: "revenge is a dish best served cold."

"He must have mistaken that for gazpacho. Poets usually starve to death, and they don't have a clue about cuisine."

"Tell me you're not thinking of doing anything stupid."

"I'm not thinking of doing anything stupid."

"What I want is for you to reassure me."

"Bring a notary public along, and we'll make it official."

"I have quite enough with Daniel and his newly acquired criminal tendencies. I've discovered that he's got a hidden gun! Can you believe it? Holy Mother of God. Only a couple of days ago he was still picking his nose, and now he's hiding pistols as if he were a puppet of the Anarchists."

"What have you done with the gun?" asked Alicia, with a smile that made Fermín's hair stand on end.

"What could I do? I hid it again. Where nobody will find it, of course."

"Bring it to me," whispered Alicia, seductive.

"No way. I'm getting to know you. I wouldn't bring you a water pistol. You'd be capable of filling it with sulfuric acid."

"You've no idea what I'm capable of," she snapped.

Fermín looked concerned. "I'm beginning to imagine it, crocodile woman."

Alicia wielded her innocent smile again.

"Neither you nor Daniel know how to use a weapon. Give it to me before you get hurt."

"So you can be the one to hurt someone?"

"Let's say I promise I won't hurt anyone who doesn't deserve it."

"Oh, fine. Why didn't you mention that before? In that case I'll bring you a machine gun and a few grenades. Fancy any caliber in particular?"

"I'm serious, Fermín."

"Exactly. What you have to do is get better."

"The only thing that will get me better is doing what I have to do. It's the only thing that will guarantee that you're all safe. And you know it."

"Alicia, I'm sorry to say that the more I hear you, the less I like the tone and drift of your conversation."

"Bring me the weapon. Or I'll get hold of one."

"So you can die in a taxi again, but this time for real? Or chucked into an alleyway? Or in a cell at the hands of butchers who will cut you up into little pieces for fun?"

"Is that what's worrying you? That I might be tortured or killed?"

"It has crossed my mind, yes. Look, between you and me, and

don't take this personally, I'm up to my eyeballs with you dying on me all over the place. How am I going to bring children into the world and be a decent father if I'm unable to keep alive the first child I became responsible for?"

"I'm not a child anymore, nor are you responsible for me, Fermín. Besides, you're brilliant when it comes to keeping me alive, and you've already saved me twice."

"Third time's the charm."

"There won't be a third time."

"And there won't be a weapon. I'll destroy it today. I'll crush it and scatter the bits over the docks of the port: I'll feed them to those rubbish-eating fish, the ones with a fat belly you see on the surface, stuffing themselves with pigswill."

"Not even you can prevent the inevitable from happening, Fermín."

"It's one of my specialties. The other is dancing cheek to cheek. End of discussion. You can look at me with those tiger eyes as much as you like, you're not going to scare me. I'm not Fernandito or any of those bumpkins you manage so skillfully by flashing your black stockings."

"You're the only person who can help me, Fermín. All the more so now that we have the same blood in our veins."

"Which at this rate is going to last you as long as a turkey at Christmastime."

"Don't be like that. Help me get out of Barcelona and find me a weapon. The rest is my business. You know that deep down it will be good for you. Bea would agree with me."

"Ask her for the pistol and see what she says."

"Bea doesn't trust me."

"And why might that be?"

"We're wasting precious time, Fermín. What do you say?"

"Just piss off, and I won't say go to hell because that's where you're going, headfirst."

"That's no way to speak to a young lady."

"You're as much a lady as I'm a sumo wrestler. Take a swig of that stuff of yours, and go back to your coffin to sleep it off before you do something evil."

When Fermín got tired of arguing, he would leave her alone. Alicia would have a bit of dinner with Isaac, listen to the stories about Nuria, and when the old keeper retired, would pour herself a glass of white wine (a couple of days earlier, she'd discovered where Isaac hid the bottles confiscated by the doctor) and leave the room. She would walk down the corridor until she reached the hall with the high vaulted ceiling, and there, under the breath of the midnight light cascading down from the top of the cupola, she would stare at the vision of the great labyrinth of books.

Guided by a lamp, she entered the corridors and tunnels. She limped up the cathedral-like structure, negotiating rooms, junctions, and bridges that led to hidden halls crossed by spiral staircases or by hanging footbridges forming arches and buttresses. On the way she stroked the hundreds and thousands of books that awaited their readers. Sometimes she'd fall asleep on a chair in one of the rooms she found on her itinerary. Every night the route was different.

The Cemetery of Forgotten Books had its own geometry, and it was practically impossible to walk past the same place twice. More than once she'd gotten lost and had taken a while to find the way back down to the exit. One night, when dawn was beginning to glimmer above, Alicia emerged at the very top of the labyrinth and found herself standing on the same spot where she'd landed after falling through the broken dome, that night of the air bombings in 1938. When she looked down into the abyss, she glimpsed the minute figure of Isaac Montfort at the foot of the labyrinth. The keeper was still there when she reached the bottom.

"I thought I was the only one with insomnia," he said.

"Sleep is for dreamers."

"I've made some chamomile tea—it helps me sleep. Would you like a cup?"

"If we add a dash of something to it."

"The only thing I have left is some old brandy I wouldn't even use to unclog the water pipes."

"I'm not fussy."

"And what will Dr. Soldevila say?"

"What all doctors say: what doesn't kill you makes you fat."

"You could do with getting a bit fatter."

"It's on my to-do list."

She followed the keeper to his room and sat at the table while Isaac prepared two cups of herbal tea and, after sniffing at the brandy bottle, poured a few drops into each one.

"It's not bad," said Alicia, tasting the cocktail.

They sipped their spiked chamomile in peace and quiet, like old friends who don't need words to enjoy each other's company.

"You're looking well," said Isaac finally. "I suppose that means that you'll leave us soon."

"I'm not doing anyone any good by staying here, Isaac."

"The place isn't bad," he assured her.

"If I didn't have matters to resolve, no other place in the world would seem better than this."

"You're welcome to return whenever you like, although something tells me that once you leave, you won't be coming back."

For an answer, Alicia smiled.

"You'll need clothes and things," the old man pointed out. "Fermín says that your home is being watched, so I don't think it would be a good idea to collect anything from there. Somewhere I have a few of Nuria's clothes that might suit you."

"I wouldn't want to—"

"I would consider it an honor if you accepted my daughter's things. And I think my Nuria would like you to have them. Besides, I think you must be the same size."

Isaac went over to a wardrobe and pulled out a suitcase that he dragged up to the table. He opened it, and Alicia had a look. There were dresses, shoes, books, and other objects whose sight made her feel an immense sadness. Although she'd never met Nuria Montfort, she'd started to get used to her haunting presence, listening to her father talk about her as if she were still by his side. When she saw the remains of a life contained in an old suitcase, which a poor old man had kept to save the memory of his dead daughter, she couldn't find the right words. All she could do was nod.

"They're good quality," she said, for she had a keen eye for labels and the feel of fabrics.

"My Nuria spent all she had on books and clothes, poor thing. Her mother always said she looked like a film star. If you'd only seen her. It was a joy to look at her . . ."

Alicia moved some of the dresses in the suitcase to one side and noticed something peeping through the folds. It looked like a white figure, about ten centimeters high. She picked it up and examined it under the light of the lamp. It was an angel made of painted plaster, with its wings open wide.

"I haven't seen that for years. I didn't know Nuria had kept it. It was one of her favorite toys, from when she was a little girl," Isaac explained. "I remember the day we bought it, at the fair of Santa Lucía, next to the cathedral."

The figurine's torso felt as if it had an empty hole in it. When she placed her finger over it, a tiny door opened, and Alicia saw it had a hidden compartment.

"Nuria liked to leave me secret messages inside the angel. She used to hide it somewhere in the house, and I had to find it. It was a game we shared."

"It's beautiful," said Alicia.

"Keep it."

"No, I wouldn't dream of it . . ."

"Please. This angel hasn't given any messages for a long time. You'll know how to put it to good use."

That was how, for the first time in her life, Alicia began to sleep with a little guardian angel to whom she prayed she would soon be able to get away, leave those good souls behind, and set off on the path she knew awaited her on her return to the heart of darkness.

"You won't be able to come there with me," she whispered to the angel.

LEANDRO ARRIVED EVERY morning at exactly half past eight. He waited for her in the room where breakfast had just been brought in, together with a vase of fresh-cut flowers. By then Ariadna Mataix had been awake for an hour. The person in charge of waking her up was the doctor, who now had set aside all formalities and entered the bedroom without knocking first. A nurse always came with him, but Ariadna had never heard her speak.

The first thing was the morning injection, the one that allowed her to open her eyes and remember who she was. Then the nurse would get her up, undress her, take her to the bathroom, and put her under the shower for ten minutes. She dressed her with clothes Ariadna remembered and thought she'd bought sometime or other, every day a new outfit. While the doctor took her pulse and checked her blood pressure, the nurse combed her hair and put on her makeup, because Leandro liked to see her looking smart and presentable. By the time she sat at the table with him, the world had resumed its place.

"Did you have a good night?"

"What is it they're giving me?"

"A gentle sedative, as I said. If you'd rather, I'll ask the doctor to stop administering it."

"No. No, please."

"As you wish. Would you like something to eat?"

"I'm not hungry."

"A little orange juice, at least."

Sometimes Ariadna threw up her food or experienced such intense nausea that she would lose consciousness and fall off her chair. When that happened, Leandro pressed the bell, and seconds later somebody appeared who would lift her and wash her again. In such cases the doctor would give Ariadna another injection, bringing on a state of icy calm that she craved so badly she was often tempted to pretend she was fainting so she could get another fix. She no longer knew how many days she'd been there. She measured time by the space between the injections, between the balm of an unconscious sleep and the awakening. She'd lost weight, and her clothes were falling off her. When she saw herself in the bathroom mirror, she wondered who that woman was. She longed constantly for the moment when Leandro would end the daily session so that the doctor would return with his magic bag and his knockout potions. Those moments when she felt her blood was on fire until she lost consciousness were the closest to happiness she could remember ever having experienced.

"How are you feeling this morning, Ariadna?"

"All right."

"I thought that today we could talk about those months in which you disappeared, if you don't mind."

"We already spoke about that the other day. And the day before that."

"Yes, but I think that bit by bit new details are emerging. Memory is like that. It likes to play tricks on us."

"What do you want to know?"

"I'd like to return to the day you ran away from home. Do you remember it?"

"I'm tired."

"Hold out a bit longer. The doctor will be here very soon, and he'll give you a tonic to make you feel better."

"Can it be now?"

"First we'll talk, and then you can take your medicine."

Ariadna nodded. Every day the same game was repeated. She no longer remembered what she'd told him and what she hadn't. What did it matter? It no longer made sense to keep anything from him. They'd all died. And she was never going to get out of there.

"It was the day before my birthday," she began. "The Ubachs had organized a party for me. All my girlfriends from school had been invited."

"Your girlfriends?"

"They were not my real friends. It was bought friendship, like everything else in that house."

"Was that the night you decided to run away?"

"Yes."

"But someone helped you, right?"

"Yes."

"Tell me about that man. David Martín, wasn't it?"

"David."

"How did you meet him?"

"David was a friend of my father's. They'd worked together."

"Had they written books together?"

"Radio serials. They'd written one called *The Ice Orchid*. It was a mystery story set in nineteenth-century Barcelona. My father didn't allow me to listen to it because he said it wasn't suitable for little girls, but I used to sneak away and listen to it on the radio in our house in Vallvidrera. Very low."

"According to my reports, David Martín was sent to prison in 1939, when he was trying to cross the frontier and return to Barcelona at the end of the war. He spent some time imprisoned in Montjuïc Castle, at the same time that your father was there, and was pronounced dead toward the end of 1941. You're talking about 1948, seven years after this. Are you sure the man who helped you escape was Martín?"

"It was him."

"Couldn't it have been someone who pretended to be him? After all you hadn't seen him for a number of years."

"It was him."

"OK. How did you meet up again?"

"Doña Manuela, my tutor, used to take me on Saturdays to Retiro Park. To the Crystal Palace, my favorite place."

"Mine too. Is that where you met Martín?"

"Yes. I'd seen him a few times. From a distance."

"Do you think it was just a coincidence?"

"No."

"When did you first speak to him?"

"Doña Manuela always carried a bottle of anise liqueur in her bag, and sometimes she would fall asleep."

"And then David Martín would come over?"

"Yes."

"What did he say to you?"

"I can't remember."

"I know it's difficult, Ariadna. Make an effort."

"I want the medicine."

"First tell me what Martín said to you."

"He would talk about my father. About the time they'd spent together in prison. My father had spoken to him about us. About what had happened. I think they'd made some sort of pact. The first one who managed to get out of there would help the family of the other."

"But David Martín didn't have a family."

"He had people he loved."

"Did he tell you how he managed to escape from the castle?"

"Valls had ordered two of his men to take him to an old house next to Güell Park and murder him. They used to kill a lot of people there, and they buried them in the garden."

"And what happened?"

"David said there was someone else there, in the house, who helped him escape."

"An accomplice?"

"He called him the boss."

"The boss?"

"He had a foreign name. Italian. I remember because it was the same as that of a famous composer my parents liked a lot."

"Can you remember the name?"

"Corelli. He was called Andreas Corelli."

"That name doesn't appear in any of my reports."

"Because he didn't exist."

"I don't understand."

"David wasn't well. He imagined things. People."

"Do you mean to say that David Martín had imagined that Andreas Corelli person?"

"Yes."

"How do you know?"

"Because I know. David had lost his mind, or what little mind he had left, in prison. He was very ill, and he didn't realize."

"You always call him David."

"We were friends."

"Lovers?"

"Friends."

"What did he say to you on that day?"

"That he'd spent three years trying to get access to Mauricio Valls."

"To take revenge on him?"

"Valls had murdered someone he loved very much."

"Isabella."

"Yes. Isabella."

"Did he tell you how he thought Valls had murdered her?"

"He'd poisoned her."

"And why did he come to look for you?"

"To keep the promise he'd made to my father."

"Is that all?"

"And because he thought that if I could provide him with access to my parents' house, sooner or later Mauricio Valls would turn up there, and he'd be able to kill him. Valls often visited Ubach. They had some businesses together. Financial interests. Otherwise it was impossible to get to Valls, because he always had his bodyguards with him or was protected somehow."

"But that never happened."

"No."

"Why?"

"Because I told him that if he tried to do it, they'd kill him."

"He must have imagined that already. There must have been something else."

"Something else?"

"Something else you said to him to make him change his plans."

"I need my medicine. Please."

"Tell me what you told David Martín that made him change his mind, so that he abandoned the plan that had brought him to Madrid to take his revenge on Valls and instead decided to help you escape."

"Please . . ."

"Just a tiny bit more, Ariadna. Afterward we'll give you your medication, and you'll be able to rest."

"I told him the truth. That I was pregnant."

"I don't understand. Pregnant? Who by?"

"By Ubach."

"Your father?"

"He wasn't my father."

"Miguel Ángel Ubach, the banker. The man who had adopted you."

"The man who had bought me."

"What happened?"

"At night he would often come to my bedroom, drunk. He told me his wife didn't love him, he said she had lovers, that they no longer shared anything. He would start crying. Then he'd rape me. When he got tired of it, he said it was my fault, he said I tempted him, he said I was a whore, like my mother. He beat me and assured me that if I said anything about this to anyone, he'd have my sister killed. He knew where she was, he said, and a call from him would be enough to have her buried alive."

"And what did David Martín say when he heard that?"

"He stole a car and got me out of there. I need the medicine, please . . ."

"Of course. Right now. Thank you, Ariadna. Thanks for your frankness."

I 2

"WHAT DAY IS it today?"

"Tuesday."

"It was also Tuesday yesterday."

"That was a different Tuesday. Tell me about your escape with David Martín."

"David had a car. He'd stolen it, and he kept it hidden in a garage in the Carabanchel district. That day he told me that the following Saturday he'd drive it around to one of the gates of the park at noon. When Doña Manuela fell asleep, I had to start running and meet him in the entrance opposite Puerta de Alcalá."

"And did you?"

"We got into the car and hid in the garage until it was dark."

"The police accused your tutor of having been an accomplice in your kidnapping. They interrogated her for forty-eight hours, and then she was found in a ditch on the road to Burgos. They'd broken her legs and arms, and then shot her in the back of the neck."

"Don't expect me to feel sorry for her."

"Did she know that Ubach abused you?"

"She was the only person I ever told."

"And what did she say?"

"To keep quiet. She said important men had their needs, and that in time I'd realize that Ubach loved me very much."

"What happened that night?"

"David and I left the garage with the car and spent the whole night on the road."

"Where were you going?"

"We traveled for about two days. We would wait until it was dark, and then we'd take byroads or country lanes. David made me lie down in the back seat, covered with blankets so no one could see me when we stopped at gas stations. Sometimes I'd fall asleep, and the moment I woke up I could hear him talking, as if there was someone with him, sitting in the passenger seat."

"That Corelli individual?"

"Yes."

"And didn't that scare you?"

"It made me feel sorry."

"Where did he take you?"

"To a place in the Pyrenees where he'd hidden for a few days after returning to Spain at the end of the war. Bolvir, that was the name. It was very close to a small town called Puigcerdá, almost on the border with France. There was a large abandoned house there that had been a hospital during the war. I think it was called La Torre del Remei. We spent a few weeks in that place."

"Did he tell you why he was taking you there?"

"He said it was a safe place. There was an old friend of David's there, someone he'd met when he crossed the frontier, a local writer named Alfons Brosel. He brought us food and clothes. Without him we would have starved or died of cold."

"Martín must have chosen that place for some other reason."

"The village brought back memories. David never told me what had happened there, but I know it had a special meaning for him. David lived in the past. When the worst of the winter came, Alfons advised us to leave and gave us a bit of money with which to continue the journey. The people in the town had started to gossip. David knew of an enclave on the coast where another old friend of his—a rich man called Pedro Vidal—had a house he thought would make a good hiding place, at least until the summer. David knew the house well. I think he'd stayed there before."

"Was that the village where you were found a few months later? San Feliu de Guíxols?"

"The house was about two kilometers outside the village, in a place called S'Agaró, next to the bay of San Pol."

"I know it."

"The house was among the rocks, in a place called Camino de Ronda. Nobody lived there in the winter. It was a sort of housing development, with big summer mansions belonging to wealthy families from Barcelona and Gerona."

"Is that where you spent the winter?"

"Yes. Until spring."

"When they found you, you were alone. Martín wasn't with you. What happened to him?"

"I don't want to talk about that."

"If you like, we can have a break. I can ask the doctor to give you something."

"I want to leave this place."

"We've talked about this before, Ariadna. You're safe here. Protected."

"Who are you?"

"I'm Leandro. You know that. Your friend."

"I don't have friends."

"You're nervous. I think we'd better leave it for today. Have a rest. I'll tell the doctor to come."

It was always Tuesday in the suite of the Gran Hotel Palace.

"You're looking very well this morning, Ariadna."

"I have a bad headache."

"It's the weather. The pressure's very low today. It happens to me too. Take this, and it will pass."

"What is it?"

"Just aspirin. Nothing else. By the way, we've been checking what you told me about the house in S'Agaró. You were right, it was owned by Don Pedro Vidal, a member of one of the wealthiest families in Barcelona. From what we've been able to find out, he was a sort of mentor to David Martín. The police report specifies that David Martín murdered him in his Pedralbes residence in 1930, because Vidal had married the woman he loved, someone called Cristina."

"That's a lie. Vidal committed suicide."

"Is that what David Martín told you? It seems that deep down he was a very vindictive man. Valls, Vidal . . . People do crazy things because of jealousy."

"The person David loved was Isabella."

"You've already told me that. But it doesn't quite fit in with the information we have. What linked him to Isabella?"

"She'd been his apprentice."

"I didn't know novelists had apprentices."

"Isabella was very stubborn."

"Is that what Martín told you?"

"David talked about her a lot. It's what kept him alive."

"But Isabella had been dead for almost ten years."

"Sometimes he forgot. That's why he'd gone back there."

"To the house in S'Agaró?"

"David had been there before. With her."

"Do you know when that was?"

"Just before the start of the war. Before he had to flee to France."

"Is that why he came back to Spain, even though he knew they were looking for him? Because of Isabella?"

"I think so."

"Tell me about your time there. What did you do?"

"David was already very ill. By the time we got to the house, he could barely tell the difference between reality and what he thought he saw and heard. The house brought back a whole lot of memories. I believe that deep down he went back there to die."

"So David Martín is dead?"

"What do you think?"

"Tell me the truth. What did you do during those months?"

"Look after him."

"I thought he was the one who was meant to look after you."

"David could no longer take care of anyone, much less himself."

"Ariadna, did you kill David Martín?"

<h1 style="text-align:center">13</h1>

"WE HADN'T BEEN there a month when David got worse. I'd gone out to get some food. A few peasants came along every morning with a cartful of groceries and set themselves up by the old bathhouse and the restaurant they called La Taberna del Mar. At first it was David who went there, or to the village, to find provisions, but there came a point when he couldn't leave the house. He suffered from terrible headaches, fever, nausea . . . Almost every night he paced around the house, delirious and talking to himself. He believed Corelli would come and get him."

"Did you ever see this Corelli?"

"Corelli didn't exist. I told you. He was someone who lived only in David's imagination."

"How can you be sure?"

"The Vidals had built a small wooden jetty that stretched out into the sea from the little cove below the house. David would often go there and sit at the far end, gazing at the sea. That's where he held his imaginary conversations with Corelli. Sometimes I would walk over to the pier and sit down next to him. David wouldn't notice that I was there. I heard him talk to Corelli, just as he had done in the car when we fled from Madrid. Then he would wake up from his trance and smile at me. One day it began to rain, and when I took his hand to take him back home, he hugged me, crying, and called me Isabella. From then on he no longer recognized me, and he spent the last two months of his existence convinced that he was living with Isabella."

"It must have been very hard for you."

"No. The months I spent taking care of him were the happiest, and the saddest, of my life."

"How did David Martín die, Ariadna?"

"One night I asked him who Corelli was and why he was so afraid of him. He told me Corelli was a black soul—those were his words. David had agreed to write a book commissioned by Corelli, but he had betrayed him by destroying the book before Corelli could get his hands on it."

"What sort of a book?"

"I'm not quite sure. Some sort of religious text or something like that. David called it *Lux Aeterna*."

"So David thought Corelli wanted to take his revenge on him."

"Yes."

"How, Ariadna?"

"What does it matter? It has nothing to do with Valls or with anything."

"Everything is connected, Ariadna. Please, help me."

"David was convinced that the baby I carried in my womb was someone he had known and lost."

"Did he say who?"

"He called her Cristina. He hardly ever spoke of her. But when he mentioned her, his voice seemed to shrink with remorse and guilt."

"Cristina was the wife of Pedro Vidal. The police also accused Martín of her death. They assured us that he'd drowned her in a lake in Puigcerdá, very near the old house in the Pyrenees where he took you to."

"Lies."

"Perhaps. But you're telling me that when he spoke about her, he showed signs of guilt . . ."

"David was a good man."

"But you yourself said that he'd completely lost his mind, that he imagined things and people who were not there, that he thought you were his old apprentice, Isabella, who had died ten years earlier. . . . Weren't you afraid for yourself? For your baby?"

"No."

"Don't tell me it didn't cross your mind to leave that house and run away."

"No."

"All right. What happened next?"

14

"IT WAS AT the end of March, I think. David's health had improved over the last few days. He'd found an old wooden boat in a shed at the bottom of the cliff, and almost every morning, early, he would row out to sea in it. I was already seven months pregnant and spent my time reading. The house had a library, and there were copies of almost all the works by David Martín's favorite author, someone I'd never heard of, called Julián Carax. In the afternoon we'd light the fire in the sitting room, and I would read aloud to him. We read them all. We spent those two last weeks reading the latest novel by Julián Carax, *The Shadow of the Wind*."

"I don't know it."

"Almost nobody knows it. They think they do, but they don't really. One night we finished reading the book in the early hours. I went to bed, and two hours later I felt the first contractions."

"You had two months to go . . ."

"I started to feel a terrible pain, as if I'd been stabbed in the womb. I panicked. I shouted David's name. When he pulled back the sheet to pick me up in his arms and take me to the doctor, they were soaked in blood . . ."

"I'm sorry."

"Everyone is sorry."

"Did you get to the doctor?"

"No."

"And the baby?"

"It was a girl. She was stillborn."

"I'm very sorry, Ariadna. Perhaps we'd better stop for a while and call the doctor to give you something."

"No. I don't want to stop now."

"All right. What happened next?"

"David . . ."

"Relax, take your time."

"David took the corpse in his arms and started to whine like a wounded animal. The little girl's skin was bluish. She looked like a broken doll. I wanted to get up and hug them both, but I was very weak. At dawn, when it was beginning to get light, David took the baby, looked at me for the last time, and asked to be forgiven. Then he left the house. I dragged myself over to the window. I saw him go down the steps in the rocks to the jetty. The wooden boat was moored at the very end. He got into it with the girl's body wrapped in a few rags and started to row out to sea, looking toward me the whole time. I raised a hand, hoping he'd see me, hoping he'd come back. He went on rowing until he stopped about a hundred meters from the coast. The sun was peering over the sea by now, making it look like a lake of fire. I saw David's figure stand up and take something from the bottom of the boat. He proceeded to hit the keel, again and again. It only took a couple of minutes to sink. David stayed there, motionless, with the baby in his arms, staring at me until the sea swallowed them both forever."

"What did you do then?"

"I'd lost a lot of blood and was very weak. I spent a couple of days with a fever, thinking that everything had been a nightmare and that any moment now David would come back in through the door. After that, when I was able to get up and walk, I started going down to the beach every day. To wait."

"To wait?"

"For them to return. You must think I was as mad as David."

"No. I don't think that at all."

"The peasants who came every day with their cart had seen me there. They came over to ask me whether I was all right and gave me something to eat. They said I didn't look well and offered to take me to the hospital in San Feliu. It must have been them who alerted the Civil Guard. One of their patrols found me asleep on the beach and took me to the hospital. I was suffering from hypothermia, pneumonia, and an internal hemorrhage that would have killed me within twelve hours if I hadn't been taken to the hospital. I didn't tell them who I was, but it didn't take them long to find out. There were search warrants with my picture in all the police stations and Civil Guard barracks. I was admitted to a hospital and spent two weeks there."

"Didn't your parents come to see you?"

"They weren't my parents."

"I mean the Ubachs."

"No. When at last I was discharged, two policemen and an ambulance picked me up and took me back to the Ubachs' mansion in Madrid."

"What did the Ubachs say when they saw you?"

"The señora, for that's how she liked me to call her, spat in my face and called me a bitch and an ungrateful whore. Ubach summoned me to his office. The whole time I was there, he didn't even bother to look up from his desk. He explained that they were going to send me to a boarding school near El Escorial, and that I'd be able to come home for a few days at Christmas, so long as I behaved myself. The next day they took me there."

"How long were you at the boarding school?"

"Three weeks."

"Why for such a short time?"

"The head of the school discovered that I'd told my roommate, Ana Maria, what had happened."

"What did you tell her?"

"Everything."

"Including the stealing of children?"

"Everything."

"And she believed you?"

"Yes. Something like that had also happened to her. Almost all the girls in the boarding school had a similar story."

"What happened?"

"A few days later they found her hanging in the boarding-school attic. She was sixteen."

"Suicide?"

"What do you think?"

"And you? What did they do to you?"

"They took me back to the Ubachs' house."

"And . . . ?"

"Ubach gave me a beating and locked me in my room. He told me that if I ever told lies about him again, they'd stick me in a mental hospital for the rest of my life."

"And what did you say?"

"Nothing. That very night, while they slept, I sneaked out of my room through the window and locked the door of the Ubachs' bedroom, on the third floor. Then I went down to the kitchen and opened the gas taps. They kept drums of kerosene for the generator in the basement. I walked all around the first floor, sprinkling kerosene on the floor and the walls. Then I set fire to the curtains and went out into the garden."

"You didn't run away?"

"No."

"Why not?"

"Because I wanted to see them burn."

"I understand."

"I don't think you can understand. But I've told you the whole truth. Now you tell me something."

"Of course."

"Where's my sister?"

15

"YOUR SISTER IS now called Mercedes, and she's in a safe place."

"Like this one?"

"No."

"I want to see her."

"Soon. First tell me about your husband, Ignacio Sanchís. I can't quite understand how Miguel Ángel Ubach, who had all the top law firms in the country at his service, decided to make a promising but inexperienced young man his executor. Have you any idea why?"

"Isn't it obvious?"

"No."

"Ignacio was Ubach's son. He fathered him with a chorus girl he used to see when he was young. Her name was Dolores Ribas, and she was a regular in the music halls of the Paralelo district. Because Ubach's wife—the señora—didn't want to ruin her figure by having children, Ubach supported Ignacio secretly. He paid for his schooling, and when Ignacio came of age, he made sure he enjoyed plenty of opportunities, enabling him to join a law practice, which Ubach then took on."

"Did Sanchís know? Did he know Ubach was his real father?"

"Of course."

"Is that why he married you?"

"He married me to protect me. He was my only friend. He was an honest and decent man."

"So it was a sham marriage?"

"It was the most real marriage I've ever seen, but if you're referring to that, no, he never laid a finger on me."

"When did you start planning your revenge?"

"Because he had access to all the Ubach documentation, Ignacio put two and two together regarding Valls. It was his idea. By going through the story of my real father, Víctor Mataix, we found out about some of his prison companions, from David Martín to Sebastián Salgado, and Morgado, whom he hired as a chauffeur and bodyguard. But we've already talked about that . . . no?"

"It doesn't matter. Was it also your idea to use David Martín's ghost to frighten Valls?"

"It was my idea."

"Who wrote the letters that you sent Valls?"

"I did."

"What happened in November 1956 in the Círculo de Bellas Artes, here in Madrid?"

"The letters were not achieving what we had hoped for. The idea had been to instill an increasing fear in Valls and make him believe there was a plot, orchestrated by David Martín, to take revenge on him and reveal the truth about his past."

"To what end?"

"To get him to make a false move and return to Barcelona to confront Martín."

"Which you achieved."

"Yes, but we were forced to apply more pressure."

"And that was the murder attempt in 1956?"

"Among other things."

"Who perpetrated it?"

"Morgado. He wasn't supposed to kill Valls, just scare him and convince him he wasn't safe even in his own bunker, and never would be until he came in person to Barcelona to silence David Martín once and for all."

"But he would never be able to find him, because he was dead."

"Exactly."

"What other things, as you were saying, did you do to apply pressure?"

"Ignacio paid a member of his house staff to leave one of my father's books, *Ariadna and the Scarlet Prince*, in Valls's office in Villa Mercedes. It was the night of the masked ball. There was a note in the book, and the list with the numbers of the forged documents we'd discovered until then. It was the last note he received. After that he couldn't take it any longer."

"Why did you never go to the police or the press?"

"Don't make me laugh."

"I'd like to go back to the matter of the list."

"I've already told you everything I know. Why is that list so important to you?"

"It's a question of getting to the bottom of this business. So we can see justice is done. To find the real architect of this nightmare that you and so many others have lived through."

"Valls's partner?"

"Yes. That's why I have to insist."

"What do you want to know?"

"I'd like you to make an effort and try to remember. The list, you say it only included numbers? Not the names of the children?"

"No. Just the numbers."

"Do you remember how many? More or less."

"There must have been about forty."

"How did you get hold of those numbers? What made you think there were more cases of children stolen from parents murdered on Valls's orders?"

"Morgado. When Valentín began working for the family, he told us he'd heard of entire families that had disappeared. Many of his old prison mates had died in the castle, and then their wives and children had vanished without a trace. Ignacio told Valentín to give him a list of names, and he hired Brians, the lawyer, to make discreet inquiries in the Civil Registry and try to find out what had happened to those people. The easiest to find were the death certificates. When he saw that they were mostly issued on the same day, he suspected, and looked up the birth certificates with the same date."

"How ingenious of Brians. Not everyone would have thought of doing that."

"When he made that discovery, we began to think that if Valls had done what it looked like he'd done in those cases, there could be many more. In other prisons. In families we didn't know, all over the country. Hundreds. Perhaps thousands."

"Did you tell anyone about your suspicions?"

"No."

"And you didn't investigate anyone beyond those cases?"

"Ignacio was planning to do that. But he was arrested."

"What happened to the original list?"

"That man kept it. Hendaya."

"Are there copies?"

Victoria shook her head.

"Didn't you or your husband make at least one? For security?"

"The ones that existed were at home. Hendaya found them and

destroyed them there and then. He was very clear that it was the best thing to do. All he wanted to know was where we'd hidden Valls."

"Are you sure?"

"Completely. I've already told you a few times."

"I know, I know. And yet, even so, somehow I can't quite believe you. Have you lied to me, Ariadna? Tell me the truth."

"I've told you the whole truth. What I don't know is whether you have too."

Leandro's eyes, devoid of all expression, rested on her as if they'd just noticed her presence. He smiled weakly and leaned forward. "I don't know what you're referring to, Ariadna."

She could feel her eyes fill with tears. The words slid out of her lips before she realized she was uttering them. "I think you do know. You were in the car, weren't you? The day they came to arrest my father and take my sister and me away. You were Valls's partner . . . the black hand."

Leandro gazed sadly at her. "I think you're mistaking me for someone else, Ariadna."

"Why?" She was barely able to speak.

Leandro stood up and walked over to her. "You've been very brave, Ariadna. Thanks for your help. I don't want you to worry about anything. It has been a privilege to know you."

Ariadna looked up and confronted Leandro's smile, a balm of peace and compassion. She wanted to lose herself in that smile and never wake up again. Leandro leaned forward and kissed her on the forehead.

His lips were cold.

*

That night, while the doctor's magic potion made its way through her veins one last time, Ariadna dreamed about the Scarlet Prince of the stories her father had written for her, and she remembered.

Many years had passed, and she could barely recall her parents' faces, or her sister's. She could only do so in dreams. Dreams that always took her back to the day those men arrived to take her father away and kidnap her and her sister, leaving their mother for dead in the house in Vallvidrera.

That night she dreamed that she could once again hear the rumble of the car approaching through the trees. She remembered the echo of her father's voice in the garden. She looked out the bedroom window and saw the black carriage of the Scarlet Prince stopping by the fountain. The door of the carriage opened, and light turned to shadow.

Ariadna felt the touch of ice-cold lips on her skin, and the silent voice bled like poison through the walls. She wanted to run and hide with her sister inside a wardrobe, but the Scarlet Prince's eyes saw everything and knew everything. Huddled in the dark, she listened to his footsteps, as the architect of all nightmares slowly approached.

16

A PUNGENT AROMA of eau de cologne and American tobacco preceded him. Valls heard his footsteps coming down the stairs, but refused to give him the satisfaction. In lost battles, the last defense is indifference.

"I know you're awake," said Hendaya at last. "Don't make me throw a bucket of cold water over you."

Valls opened his eyes in the half-light. The cigarette smoke emerged from the shadows and drew jellylike shapes in the air. The glow of the embers lit up Hendaya's eyes.

"What do you want?"

"I thought we could talk."

"I've got nothing to tell you."

"Do you feel like smoking? They say it shortens one's life."

Valls shrugged. Hendaya smiled, lit a cigarette, and handed it to him through the bars.

Valls accepted it with trembling fingers and took a drag. "What do you want to talk about?"

"About the list," said Hendaya.

"I don't know what list you mean."

"The one you found in a book in your office at home. The one you had on you the day they captured you. The one that contained about forty numbers of birth and death certificates. You know what list."

"I don't have it anymore. Is that what Leandro is looking for? Because he's the person you're working for, isn't he?"

Hendaya settled down again on the stairs and looked at him with indifference. "Did you make a copy?"

Valls shook his head.

"Are you sure? Think about it."

"Perhaps I made a copy."

"Where is it?"

"Vicente had it. My bodyguard. Before we got to Barcelona, we stopped at a gas station. I asked Vicente to buy a notebook, and I copied the numbers there so that he too had a copy, in case something happened and we had to separate. He knew someone he could trust in the city, and he was going to ask that person to locate the certificates and destroy them, after we'd got rid of Martín and found out who else he'd given that information to. That was the plan."

"And where's that copy now?"

"I don't know. Vicente had it on him. I don't know what they've done with his body."

"Is there any other copy apart from the one Vicente had?"

"No."

"Are you sure now?"

"Yes."

"You know that if you lie to me, or you hide something from me, I'll keep you here indefinitely."

"I'm not lying."

Hendaya nodded and fell into a long silence. Valls was afraid he would go and leave him alone again for another twelve hours. He'd reached the point at which Hendaya's brief visits were the only event he could look forward to.

"Why haven't you killed me yet?"

Hendaya smiled as if he'd been waiting for the question, for which he had a perfectly rehearsed answer. "Because you don't deserve it."

"Does Leandro hate me that much?"

"Señor Montalvo doesn't hate anyone."

"What must I do to deserve it?"

Hendaya was looking at him with interest. "From my experience, those who boast the loudest about their wish to die fall apart at the last moment when they see the wolf's teeth, and plead like little girls."

"It's ears."

"What?"

"The Spanish saying is 'To see the wolf's ears.' Not teeth."

"I always forget we have a distinguished man of letters as our guest."

"Is that what I am? One of Leandro's guests?"

"You're no longer anything. And when the wolf jumps upon you, and it will, the first thing you'll notice will be its teeth."

"I'm ready."

"I don't blame you. Don't think I'm not aware of your situation and what you must be going through."

"A compassionate butcher."

"A thief thinks everyone steals. You see, I know about sayings too. I propose a deal. Between you and me. If you behave well and help me, I'll kill you myself. It will be clean. A shot in the back of the neck. You won't even notice. What do you say?"

"What must I do?"

"Come over. I want to show you something."

Valls moved over to the bars of the cell. Hendaya was looking for something inside his jacket, and for a second Valls prayed it was a revolver and he'd blow off his head right there. What he pulled out was a photograph.

"I know someone was here. Don't bother to deny it. I want you to have a good look at this photo and tell me whether this is the person you saw."

Hendaya showed him the picture. Valls nodded.

"Who is it?"

"Her name was Alicia Gris."

"Was? Is she dead?"

"Yes, although she doesn't know it yet," Hendaya replied, putting away the snapshot.

"May I keep it?"

Hendaya raised his eyebrows in surprise. "I didn't think you were sentimental."

"Please."

"You miss female company, eh?" Hendaya smiled magnanimously, then, with a sneer, threw the photograph inside the cell. "All yours. I must say, she's a real stunner in her own way. Now you'll be able to look at her every night and jerk off with both hands. Sorry, with one."

Valls looked at him blankly.

"Keep behaving yourself and piling up those points. I'll keep a hollow-point bullet for you as a farewell gift, a reward for all the services you've offered the fatherland."

Valls waited until Hendaya had disappeared up the stairs before kneeling down to pick up the photograph.

17

ARIADNA KNEW THIS was the day she was going to die. She knew the moment she woke up in the suite of the Gran Hotel Palace and opened her eyes to discover that one of Leandro's minions had left a parcel on the desk while she was asleep. It was tied with a ribbon. She pulled aside the sheets and staggered to the table. It was a large white box with the word PERTEGAZ inscribed on it in gold letters. Beneath the ribbon was an envelope with her name handwritten on it. When she opened it, she found a large card:

Dear Ariadna,
Today is the day when you can finally be reunited with your sister.
I thought you'd like to look your best and celebrate that at last
justice will be done, and you'll never again have to fear anything
or anyone. I hope you like it, I chose it personally for you.

Yours,
Leandro

Ariadna caressed the edges of the box before opening it. For a second she imagined a poisonous snake creeping up its side, ready to leap onto her neck the moment she lifted the lid. The inside was covered with soft tissue paper. She removed the first layer and found a complete set of underwear in white silk, stockings included. Beneath the underwear was an ivory-colored wool dress, with shoes and a bag to match. And a scarf. Leandro was sending her to her death dressed as a virgin.

She washed herself on her own, with no help from the nurses. Then she slowly put on the garments Leandro had chosen for the last day of her life and looked at herself in the mirror. All she needed was the white coffin and the crucifix in her hands. She sat down to wait, wondering how many white virgins had been purified in that luxurious cell before her, how many luxury Pertegaz boxes Leandro had ordered to say good-bye to his damsels with a kiss on their forehead.

She didn't have to wait long. Barely half an hour later she heard the sound of the key slipping into the lock. The mechanism gave way softly, and the kind doctor, with his friendly face of the trusted family surgeon, poked his head around the door with that docile, compassionate smile that always accompanied him, like his bagful of wonders.

"Good morning, Ariadna. How are you feeling this morning?"

"Very well. Thank you, Doctor."

He slowly drew closer, leaving the bag on the table. "You're looking very pretty and elegant. I hear this is a big day for you."

"Yes. Today I'm going to be reunited with my family."

"That's wonderful. Family is what really matters in life. Señor Leandro has asked me to offer you his deepest apologies for not being able to greet you personally. An urgent matter has cropped up, and he'll be away temporarily. I'll let him know you looked splendid."

"Thanks."

"Shall we administer a tonic to give you a bit more strength?"

Ariadna stretched out her naked arm submissively. The doctor smiled, opened his bag, and pulled out a leather pouch that he unrolled over the table. Ariadna recognized the twelve numbered bottles attached with elastic bands, and the metallic box for the hypodermic syringe.

The doctor leaned over her and took her arm delicately. "If I may."

He began to feel her skin, which was covered in the marks and bruises of countless injections. While he explored the front of her forearm, her wrist, the space between her knuckles, and tapped the skin gently, he smiled at her. Ariadna looked into his eyes and lifted the skirt of her dress to reveal her thighs. There were also needle marks there, but farther apart.

"If you like you can prick me here."

The doctor affected a show of utmost modesty and nodded discreetly. "Thank you. I think it will be better."

She observed him as he prepared the injection. He'd chosen the bottle marked number nine. She'd never seen him choose that bottle before. Once the syringe was ready, the doctor searched for a spot on the inside of her left thigh, right above the top of the new silk stocking she'd just pulled on.

"It might hurt a bit at first, and you might feel the cold. It will only be for a few seconds."

Ariadna watched the doctor as with concentration he drew the needle to her skin. When the point was one centimeter from her thigh, she spoke.

"You didn't use the cotton wool with alcohol today, Doctor."

The man looked up briefly in surprise, and smiled hesitantly.

"Do you have daughters, Doctor?"

"Two, God bless them. Señor Leandro is their godfather."

It happened in barely a second. Before the doctor had finished uttering those words and could return to his task, Ariadna grabbed his hand powerfully and thrust the needle into his throat. A bewildered look flooded the eyes of the good doctor. His arms fell to his sides, and he began to shake, the syringe stuck in his neck. The solution became tinted with blood. Ariadna held his gaze, gripped the syringe, and emptied its contents into his jugular vein. The doctor opened his mouth without uttering a sound and fell on his knees. She sat down again on the chair and watched him die. He took two to three minutes.

Then she leaned over him, pulled out the syringe, and wiped the blood off on his jacket lapel. She put the syringe back in its metal box, returned the bottle marked with a 9 to its place, and folded the leather pouch. Kneeling beside the body, she found a wallet from which she took a dozen or so hundred-peseta notes. She donned the beautiful jacket that came with the dress and the matching hat. Finally, she picked up the keys the doctor had left on the table, the pouch with the bottles, and the syringe, and put them inside the white handbag. She tied the scarf around her neck and, carrying the bag under her arm, opened the bedroom door.

The suite's sitting room was empty. A vase full of white roses rested on the table where she had shared so many breakfasts with Leandro. She walked over to the door. It was locked. One by one she tried the doctor's keys until she found the one that opened it. The corridor, a wide carpeted gallery flanked by paintings and statues, reminded her of a large luxury cruiser. It was deserted. The echo of background music and the hum of a vacuum cleaner in a nearby suite floated in the air. Ariadna walked slowly. She passed an open door with a cleaning cart and saw a maid picking up towels inside. When she reached the hallway with the elevators, she met a smartly dressed middle-aged couple, who stopped speaking the moment they noticed her.

"Good morning," said Ariadna.

The couple replied with a small nod, keeping their eyes glued to the floor. They waited in silence. When the doors of the elevator opened at last, the gentleman allowed Ariadna in and received a steely look from his companion. They began the descent. The lady examined her out of the corner of her eye, sizing her up and circling around her clothes like a bird of prey. Ariadna smiled at her politely, and the lady replied with a cold, cutting smile. "You look like Evita," she said.

The caustic tone made it clear that the appreciation had not been a compliment. Ariadna simply looked down modestly. When the doors opened onto the ground floor, the couple didn't move until she'd walked out.

"Probably an expensive tart," she heard the gentleman behind her murmur.

The hotel foyer was packed. Ariadna noticed a boutique with luxury items a few yards away and took refuge there. Seeing her come in, an obliging sales assistant looked her up and down, and once she'd estimated the cost of what she was wearing, smiled at her as if she were an old friend. Five minutes later Ariadna left the shop sporting a pair of Dior sunglasses that covered half her face, her lips lit up with the most garish pink lipstick she had been able to find. Only a few accessories separate the virgin from the luxury courtesan.

This is how she walked down the wide stairs leading to the exit, pulling on her gloves as she felt the eyes of guests, concierges, and other hotel staff taking an X-ray of every detail of her body. Slowly, she told herself. When she reached the main door, she stopped, and the doorman who held it open for her looked at her with a mixture of greed and complicity.

"A taxi, gorgeous?"

18

AN ENTIRE LIFE devoted to medicine had taught Dr. Soldevila that the hardest illness to cure is habit. That afternoon, just like every afternoon since he'd taken that damned decision to close his office and succumb to the second deadliest plague known to man—retirement—the good doctor opened the balcony of his flat on Calle Puertaferrisa and stuck his nose out. The day, he thought, like almost everything in the world, was already going downhill.

Lamps adorned the streets, and the sky had acquired the pink hue of those wonderful cocktails served at the Boadas Bar with which the doctor rewarded his liver from time to time for a life of practicing what he preached. That was the signal. Armed with coat, scarf, and his doctor's bag, and under cover of his Barcelona-gentleman's hat, Soldevila stepped out into the street to his daily meeting with that strange spirit called Alicia Gris, placed in his path thanks to the intrigues of Fermín and the Semperes. A spirit for whom he felt infinite curiosity and a weakness that made him forget, in his long, sleepless nights, that he'd spent thirty years without touching a woman in good health.

Sauntering down the Ramblas, ignoring the city's bustle, he was mulling over the certainty that, luckily for her and unluckily for him, Señorita Gris had recovered from her wounds with a speed he attributed not to his medical abilities but to the concentrated malice running through the veins of that shadowy creature. Soon, he lamented, he would have to discharge her.

He could always try to convince her that she should come by his office every now and then for what professionals call a follow-up, but he knew that such an attempt would be as futile as asking a Bengal tiger that had just been let out of its cage to return every Sunday morning before church to drink its little saucer of milk. Probably the best thing for everyone, except for Alicia herself, was that she should disappear from their lives, the sooner the better. All he had to do was look into her eyes to make that diagnosis and know that it was the most accurate one he'd made in his long career.

Such was the melancholy that overcame the old doctor at the thought of having to say good-bye to someone who would surely be his last patient that he was unaware, as he walked into the dark tunnel of Calle Arco del Teatro, that among the shadows hovering around him there was one that let off a peculiar perfume of strong eau de cologne and imported Virginia tobacco.

During the past week he'd learned to locate the large door of that place whose existence he'd had to swear he would not reveal even to the Holy Ghost, unless he wanted Fermín to come around to his house for an afternoon snack every day and tell him dirty jokes. "It's best if you come alone," they'd told him. Security reasons, alleged the Semperes, whom he would never have suspected capable of getting mixed up in such complex machinations. One spent one's life rummaging around people's internal organs only to discover that one hardly knew them. Life, like appendicitis, was a mystery.

And so, lost in his thoughts and his determination to submerge himself once again in that enigmatic house they all called the Cemetery of Forgotten Books, Dr. Soldevila put his foot on the doorstep of the old palace and grabbed the demon-shaped knocker, ready to rap on the door. He was about to give the first knock when the shadow that had been following him since he'd left his front door materialized next to him and placed the barrel of a revolver on his temple.

"Good evening, Doctor," said Hendaya.

Isaac watched Alicia with a touch of suspicion. Not given to trivialities, he'd noticed with some alarm that in the past few weeks he'd allowed something very close to affection for the young woman to grow inside him. He blamed the passing years: they softened everything. Alicia's presence during those weeks had forced him to reconsider the chosen solitude of his retirement among books. As he watched her recover and return to life, Isaac had felt the memory of his daughter Nuria rekindle. Far from fading, it had sharpened over time until Alicia's arrival had once again opened the wounds he didn't even know he carried inside him.

"Why are you looking at me like that, Isaac?"

"Because I'm a silly old man."

Alicia smiled. Isaac had noticed that when she did that, she bared her teeth, exuding a malicious air. "A silly man who becomes old or an old man who becomes silly?"

"Don't make fun of me, Alicia, even if I deserve it."

She gazed at him tenderly, and the old keeper had to look away. When Alicia removed that dark veil, even if it was just for a few moments, she reminded him so much of Nuria that he felt a lump in his throat and could barely breathe.

"What's that you've got there?"

Isaac showed her a wooden case.

"Is it for me?"

"My farewell gift."

"Do you want to get rid of me already?"

"Not me."

"So what makes you think I'm leaving?"

"Am I wrong?"

Alicia didn't reply, but accepted the case.

"Open it."

Inside she discovered a golden nib attached to a mahogany pen holder, and a bottle of blue ink that glowed in the candlelight. "Was it Nuria's?"

Isaac nodded.

"It's the present I gave her on her eighteenth birthday."

Alicia examined the nib, a piece of true craftsmanship.

"Nobody has written anything with it for years," said the keeper.

"Why don't you?"

"I have nothing to write."

Alicia was about to dispute his statement when two dry knocks spread their echo through the palace. After a pause of five seconds, there were two more knocks.

"The doctor," said Alicia. "He's finally learned the code."

Isaac nodded and stood up. "Who says you can't teach an old dog new tricks?"

The keeper picked up one of the oil lamps and set off toward the corridor that led to the entrance.

"Start trying it out," he said. "There's some blank paper there."

Isaac walked down the long, curved passage, carrying the lamp in his hand. He only used it when he was going to receive someone. When he was alone, he didn't need it. He knew that place like the back of his hand and preferred to walk through its heights and depths in the pallid half-light that always floated inside the building. When he reached the big front door, he stopped and set the lamp down on the floor. Using both hands, he clasped the crank that activated the bolt's mechanism. He'd noticed that he was beginning to find it more of an effort than usual, and every time he pushed, he felt a pressure on his chest that he hadn't felt before. Perhaps his days as the keeper of the place were numbered.

The bolt's machinery, which was as ancient as that place, was made up of an elaborate system of springs, levers, and cogs, and it took between ten and fifteen seconds to unlock all its points of attachment. Once the door was released, Isaac pulled the bar that activated the counterweight system and allowed him to move the heavy oak structure while barely touching it. Dr. Soldevila stood there, silhouetted against the doorframe.

"As punctual as ever, Doctor," Isaac began.

A second later, the doctor's body fell inside, flat on its face, and a tall angular figure blocked the access.

"Who . . . ?"

Hendaya pointed his revolver between Isaac's eyes and kicked the doctor's body out of the way. "Shut the door."

Alicia dipped the nib in the inkwell and slid it across the paper, drawing a brilliant blue line. She wrote her name and watched the ink slowly dry. The pleasure of the blank page, which at first always smells of mystery and promise, vanished as if by magic. As soon as one begins to place the first words on it, it becomes clear how in writing, as in life, the distance between intentions and results is much the same as that between the innocence with which one undertook the first and accepted the second. She was about to write a sentence she remembered from one of her favorite books when she paused and looked toward the door. Leaving the pen on the paper, she scanned the silence.

She knew immediately that something was wrong. The absence of the murmurings that usually could be heard between the two old veterans, the uncertain echo of irregular footsteps, and a poisoned silence she could feel in the air made the hairs on the back of her neck stand on end. She looked around and cursed her luck. She'd always thought she would die some other way.

19

IN ANY OTHER circumstance Hendaya would have shot dead the two old men as soon as he'd gained access to the building, but he didn't want to alert Alicia. Dr. Soldevila lay practically unconscious after the blow on the back of his head that had knocked him over. Experience told Hendaya that he needn't worry about him for at least half an hour.

"Where is she?" he asked the keeper in a whisper.

"Where's who?"

Hendaya hit Isaac's face with the revolver and heard the crunch of a bone. The keeper fell on his knees and then collapsed on one side, groaning. Hendaya crouched down, grabbed him by his neck, and yanked at him. "Where is she?" he repeated.

The old man's nose was bleeding profusely. Hendaya placed the barrel of his weapon under his chin and looked him in the eye. Isaac spat in his face.

A brave one, thought Hendaya. "Come on, Granddad, let's not make a scene now, you're a bit over the hill to act the hero. Where's Alicia Gris?"

"I don't know what you're talking about."

Hendaya smiled. "Do you want me to break your legs, Grandpa? At your age a broken thigh bone doesn't mend . . ."

Isaac kept his lips sealed. Hendaya held him by the nape and dragged him inside. They walked through a wide, curved gallery behind which he sensed a fleeting brightness. The walls were covered with frescoes depicting fantastic scenes. Hendaya wondered what sort of a place this was. When they reached the end of the corridor, he found himself facing a gigantic vaulted hall that seemed to rise to the heavens. The sight made him lower his revolver and let Isaac fall like a dead weight.

It looked like an apparition, a dreamlike vision floating on a cloud of spectral light. A vast labyrinth swirling around itself grew into an uprising of tunnels, walkways, arches, and bridges. The structure seemed to sprout from the very ground, scaling an inconceivable geometry, until it scratched the large opaque-glass dome crowning the vault.

Hendaya smiled to himself. Hidden in the shadows of an old Barcelona palace was a forbidden city of books and words that he would set fire to after chopping beautiful Alicia Gris up into little bits. This was his lucky day.

*

Isaac was dragging himself along the floor, leaving a trail of blood. He wanted to call out, but all he could produce was a moan, and he could barely keep himself conscious. He heard the man's footsteps approaching again and felt his foot between his shoulders, pressing him down on the floor.

"Steady there, Grandpa."

Hendaya grabbed Isaac's wrist and lugged him to one of the columns supporting the vaulted ceiling. A trio of narrow pipes ran down the column, fastened to the stone with metal hooks. Hendaya pulled out a pair of handcuffs, attached one handcuff to one of the

643

pipes, and closed the other around Isaac's wrist until he felt it biting into the skin.

Isaac let out a muffled scream. "Alicia's gone," he panted. "You're wasting your time . . ."

Hendaya ignored the old man and scanned the shadows. Candle-light glowed behind a doorframe in a corner. The policeman held his gun with both hands and edged his way toward the door, keeping close to the wall. The anxiety in the old man's eyes confirmed that he was on the right track.

He stepped into the room, his weapon raised. In the middle stood a makeshift bed with its sheets pulled to one side. A chest of draw-ers was set against a wall, covered with medicines and other sup-plies. Hendaya examined every corner and dark area before going any farther into the room. The air smelled of alcohol, of wax, and of something sweet and floury that made him salivate. He walked over to a small table standing next to the bed, with a candle resting on it. There he found an open ink bottle and a wad of sheets of paper. On the first of these, in sloping, free-flowing handwriting, he read:

Alicia

Hendaya smiled and went back to the doorway. He looked at the keeper, who was still struggling with the handcuffs that tied him to the pipe. Farther away, by the entrance to the labyrinth of books, he noticed a slight wavering of shadows, as if a raindrop had fallen on the surface of a pond, leaving a trail of ripples spreading across the water. As he walked past Isaac, he picked up the oil lamp without bothering to look at the keeper. There'd be time enough to settle the score with him.

When he reached the foot of the huge structure, Hendaya stopped to gaze at the basilica of books soaring before him. He spat to one side. Then, after checking that the revolver's magazine was full and there was a bullet in the chamber, he stepped into the labyrinth, fol-lowing the scent of Alicia and the echo of her footsteps.

20

THE TUNNEL TRACED a slight upward curve that drove into the center of the structure and narrowed as Hendaya left the entrance behind him. The walls were lined with book spines from top to bottom. A coffered ceiling sealed the passage, made out of old leather book covers on which one could still read titles in dozens of different languages. After a while he reached an octagonal hallway with a table in its center. The table was packed with open books, lecterns, and a lamp shedding a soft golden light. A web of corridors spread in multiple directions, some descending, others climbing upward.

Hendaya stopped to listen to the sound of the labyrinth, a sort of murmur, as if of old wood and paper in constant movement, barely perceptible. He'd decided to take one of the descending corridors, assuming that Alicia would try to find another way out, hoping that he would get lost inside and give her time to escape. That's what he would have done in her place. A second before entering the passage, however, he noticed it. A book hung from one of the shelves, as if someone had started to pull it out but left it dangling, about to fall. Hendaya drew closer and read the title:

ALICE THROUGH
THE LOOKING GLASS
LEWIS CARROLL

"So we're in the mood for games?" he asked out loud, his voice echoing through the tangle of tunnels and halls. There was no answer. Hendaya pushed the book back against the wall and continued along the passage, which soon started to go uphill, becoming ever steeper, eventually forming steps under his feet at short distances. The farther he penetrated into the labyrinth, the more he felt that he was moving through the bowels of a legendary creature, a leviathan of words that was perfectly aware of his presence and of every step he took. He raised the lamp as far as the corridor's vaulted ceiling allowed him and kept walking. Some ten meters farther on, he stopped dead in his tracks. In front of him loomed the figure of an angel with wolfish eyes. A fraction of a second before firing, he realized that the figure was made of wax. Its hands, which were large and looked like tongs, held a book he'd never heard of before:

PARADISE LOST

JOHN MILTON

The angel guarded another oval hall, twice the size of the previous one. The room was flanked by glass cabinets, curved shelves, and niches laid out like a burial chamber for books.

Hendaya sighed. "Alicia? Stop fooling around and show your face. I only want to talk to you. As one professional to another."

Walking across the room to the point from which new corridors set out, he listened carefully. Here again, next to the curve where the gloom darkened, a book peeped out from a shelf in one of the passageways. Hendaya clenched his teeth. If Leandro's whore wanted to go on playing cat and mouse, she was going to get the surprise of her life.

He didn't bother to see what new book Alicia had chosen in her trajectory toward the heart of the labyrinth. "Up to you," he said, taking that corridor, which rose very steeply.

For almost twenty minutes Hendaya climbed what appeared to be a colossal piece of stage machinery. On his way he crossed large halls and walked over balustrades suspended between arches and walkways from which he was able to see that he'd climbed far more than he'd estimated. The figure of Isaac, handcuffed to the water pipe below, now seemed minute. He looked up toward the dome, sprawling and swirling into increasingly elaborate configurations above him. Every time he thought he'd lost the trail, he found the spine of a book peeping out at the entrance to a new tunnel, leading to yet another hall from which the path forked into endless twists and spirals.

The labyrinth went on mutating as he ascended toward its zenith, its intricate design using arches and ventilation shafts to allow the entrance of vaporous beams. Mirrors set at different angles spread the eerie, floating light. Every new room he found was increasingly populated by paintings and contraptions that he could barely make out. Some figures looked like unfinished automatons; paper or plaster sculptures hung from the ceiling or were encased in the walls, like creatures hidden in coffins made of books. An indefinable sense of vertigo and unease took hold of him, and soon he found his gun slipping between his sweaty fingers.

"Alicia, if you don't come out, I'm going to set fire to this pile of shit and watch you burn alive. Is that what you want?"

At a noise behind him, he turned. A round object the size of a fist, which at first he thought was a ball or a globe, was rolling down a set of stairs from one of the tunnels. He knelt down to pick it up. It was the head of a doll with a disquieting smile and glass eyes. A second later the air was filled with the tinkle of a metallic melody. It sounded like a lullaby.

"You bitch," he muttered.

He raced up the stairs, his temples throbbing. The strains of music led him to a circular room that opened onto a balustrade flooded by a dense, almost liquid shaft of light. Seeing the glass dome on the other side, he realized that he'd reached the summit. The music came from the back of the room. On either side of the doorway stood pale figures encased between books, like mummified bodies abandoned to their fate. The floor was covered with open volumes, which Hendaya trampled on as he made his way across the room to a small built-in cupboard that looked like a reliquary. He could hear the music playing inside it.

Hendaya opened the small door carefully.

A music box made with mirrors tinkled on the cupboard floor. Inside the box, an angel with open wings turned slowly in a hypnotic trance. The sound gradually petered out as the mechanism unwound and the angel was left suspended in mid-flight. It was then he noticed a reflection on one of the mirrors in the music box. One of the figures he had taken for plaster corpses when he came in had shifted.

Hendaya felt the hairs on the back of his neck stand on end. He spun around and fired his gun three times at the figure silhouetted against the bright light. The layers of paper and plaster that made up the effigy were ripped apart, leaving a cloud of dust floating in the air. The policeman lowered the weapon slightly and strained his eyes. Only then did he notice a gentle movement in the air next to him.

He turned, and when he tightened the revolver's hammer again, he recognized the dark glow of two penetrating eyes emerging from the shadows.

The nib of the pen perforated Hendaya's cornea and cut through into his brain, so deep it scratched the bone at the back of his skull. He collapsed instantly, like a puppet whose strings had been severed, his trembling body stretched out over the books.

Alicia knelt, snatched the weapon he still held in his hand, and, using her feet, pushed the body toward the balustrade. Then she kicked it over the edge and watched it fall into the abyss, still alive, and smash against the stone floor with a dead, humid echo.

21

ISAAC SAW HER come out of the labyrinth. She limped slightly and held a gun in her hand in such a natural way, it made his blood run cold. He watched her approach the place where Hendaya's body had crashed against the marble floor. She was barefoot, but didn't hesitate before stepping through the pool of blood that spread around the corpse. Leaning over Hendaya's body, she looked through his pockets and pulled out a wallet. She examined it, keeping a wad of notes and discarding the rest. Then she felt his jacket pockets and drew out a set of keys, which she also kept. After glancing dispassionately at the dead body for a few moments, Alicia grabbed something sticking out of Hendaya's face and pulled hard. Isaac recognized the pen he'd given her barely an hour earlier.

Slowly, Alicia walked over to Isaac. She knelt down beside him and unlocked his handcuffs. Isaac, trembling, not realizing that his own eyes were brimming with tears, searched hers. Alicia gazed back at him impassively, as if she were trying to make clear to that poor old man that she was not a reincarnation of his lost daughter.

She wiped the pen on her nightdress skirt and handed it to him. "I could never be like her, Isaac."

The keeper dried his tears but said nothing. Alicia offered him her hand and helped him get up. Then she walked over to the little bathroom next to the keeper's room. Isaac heard the water run.

After a while Dr. Soldevila staggered in. Isaac waved at him, and he came over.

"What happened? Who was that man?"

Isaac pointed his head toward the knot of limbs embedded on the floor, some twenty meters away.

"Good God . . . ," murmured the doctor. "And the young lady?"

*

Alicia emerged from the bathroom, wrapped in a towel, and went into Isaac's room. The doctor looked inquisitively at Isaac, who shrugged. Soldevila walked over to Isaac's door and peered around. Alicia was putting on some of Nuria Montfort's clothes.

"Are you all right?" asked the doctor.

"I'm fine," replied Alicia, not taking her eyes off the mirror.

Dr. Soldevila shelved his amazement, sat down on a chair, and gazed at her in silence while she explored a toilet bag that had belonged to Isaac's daughter and chose a few cosmetics. She put on her makeup conscientiously, outlining her lips and eyes with precision as, once again, she built a character that fit in much better with the scene of her actions than did the weakened body the doctor had become accustomed to caring for during the past few weeks. When his eyes met hers in the mirror, Alicia winked at him.

"As soon as I've left," she said, "you're going to have to get in touch with Fermín. Tell him the body needs to disappear. Tell him to go see the taxidermist in Plaza Real, and say I sent him. He has the necessary chemical products."

Alicia stood up, swirled around once to check herself in the mirror, and, after putting the gun and the money she had taken from Hendaya's body into a black bag, headed for the door.

"Who are you?" asked Dr. Soldevila as she walked past.

"The devil," Alicia replied.

22

AS SOON AS Fermín saw the good old doctor walk in through the bookshop door, he knew it was open season for shocks. Soldevila showed unmistakable signs of having been very professionally punched in the face. Daniel and Bea, who were behind the counter trying to balance the month's accounts, opened their mouths wide and rushed over to help.

"What happened, Doctor?"

Dr. Soldevila let out a snort that sounded like a bursting balloon and hung his head dejectedly.

"Daniel, bring out the bottle of strong brandy your father hides behind the *Exemplary Lives of the Saints* collection," Fermín ordered.

Bea took the doctor to a chair and helped him sit down. "Are you all right? Who did this to you?"

"Yes, and I'm not entirely sure," he replied. "In that order."

"And Alicia?" asked Bea.

"I wouldn't worry about her, honestly . . ."

Fermín sighed. "She's flown off?"

"Wrapped in a cloud of sulfur."

Daniel handed the doctor a glass of brandy to which he offered no resistance. He downed it in one gulp and let the concoction do the trick. "Another, please."

"What about Isaac?" asked Fermín.

"He stayed behind, meditating."

Fermín crouched down next to the doctor and looked into his eyes. "Come on, Your Eminence, out with it—and, if possible, holding back on the editorializing."

*

When he'd finished his account, the doctor asked for a third glass, as a nightcap. Bea, Daniel, and Fermín joined him cautiously.

After a tactful silence, Daniel opened the discussion. "Where could she have gone?"

"To right a wrong, I imagine," said Fermín.

"Please speak plainly, Your Graces," said the doctor. "When I studied medicine, the Sempere family mysteries were not on the curriculum."

"Believe me when I say I'm doing you a favor by suggesting you go home," Fermín advised. "Place a veal steak like a beret on your head and leave us to untangle this mess."

The doctor nodded. "Must I expect more gunmen? I'm just asking in case I need to be prepared."

"Not for the time being, I think," said Fermín. "But perhaps it wouldn't be a bad idea to leave town and go off to a spa in Montgat for a couple of weeks. Take a merry widow with you and work on the elimination of a kidney stone, or any other corpuscle that may have got stuck in your urinary tract."

"For once, I wouldn't say no," said the doctor.

"Daniel, why don't you do us the favor of taking the doctor home and making sure he gets there in one piece?" suggested Fermín.

"Why me?" Daniel protested. "Are you trying to get me out of the way again?"

"If you'd rather, I'll send your son Julián along. But I think the mission requires someone who has at least taken his first communion."

Daniel agreed reluctantly. Fermín felt Bea's eyes fixed on the back of his neck, but he preferred to ignore it for the time being. Before saying good-bye to Dr. Soldevila, he poured him one last glass of brandy and, seeing there was still a shot of liquor left in the bottle, downed the remains in one swig.

Free at last of Daniel and the doctor, Fermín collapsed on the chair and covered his face with his hands.

"What was all that the doctor said about the taxidermist and making a body disappear?" asked Bea.

"Some unpleasant matter that unfortunately will have to be resolved," said Fermín. "One of the two most annoying things about Alicia is that she's always right."

"What's the other?"

"That she doesn't forgive. Did she say anything to you these last few days that might allow us to guess what was going through her mind? Think carefully."

Bea hesitated, but then shook her head.

Fermín nodded resignedly and got to his feet. He took his coat from the stand and prepared to hit the road on a winter's afternoon that did not look promising. "Then I'd better go off to meet the taxidermist. Let's see if I come up with any ideas on the way."

"Fermín?" Bea called, before he'd reached the door.

He stopped, but didn't turn around.

"There's something Alicia didn't tell us, isn't there?"

"I suspect there are a lot of things, Doña Bea. And I think she did that for our own good."

"But there's something that has to do with Daniel. Something that can hurt him a lot."

At this point Fermín turned around and smiled sadly. "But that's what you and I are here for, isn't it? To stop something like that from happening."

Bea looked straight at him. "Be very careful, Fermín."

*

Bea watched Fermín leave in a blue twilight that threatened sleet. She stood there, looking out as people filed along Calle Santa Ana, hidden under scarves and coats. Something told her that winter, the real winter, had just collapsed on them without warning. And this time it would not go unnoticed.

23

FERNANDITO LAY ON the bed in his room, his gaze lost in the small window that gave onto the inner courtyard. The room, or cupboard, as everyone called it, shared a wall with the laundry room and had always reminded him of scenes set in submarines he sometimes saw in the matinee shows of the Capitol Cinema—only far gloomier and less cozy. Even so, that afternoon, thanks to the wondrous alchemy of hormones, which he tended to mistake for a spiritual or mystical experience, Fernandito floated in seventh heaven. Love, with a capital L and a tight skirt, had knocked on his door. Technically it hadn't knocked; it had just walked past his door, to be precise. Yet he believed that, like a stubborn toothache, fate didn't let go of you until you faced it with courage. All the more so where love was concerned.

The epiphany that had managed to banish, once and for all, the ghost of the treacherous Alicia and the entire spectral femme-fatale number that had ensnared him since early adolescence, had taken place a few days ago. Love, even when it implodes, leads to another. That's what the *boleros* certified. Their lyrics might be as sickly sweet as a cream cake, but they were almost always well grounded when it came to the science of loving. His unholy infatuation with Señorita Alicia had led him to meet the Sempere family and be offered a job by the kind bookseller. And from there to paradise, only chance had played a part.

It happened the morning he arrived at the bookshop to report for duty as delivery-boy-at-large. As fate would have it, at that precise moment a creature of disturbing charms and a slippery accent was running about the shop. From the conversation the Semperes were having, Fernandito gathered that her name was Sofía, and after a few inquiries he discovered that the girl in question was none other than the niece of Sempere the bookseller and a cousin of Daniel. It appeared that Daniel's mother, Isabella, was of Italian descent, and Sofía, who hailed from the city of Naples, was spending some time with the Semperes while she studied at Barcelona University and perfected her Spanish. All these minutiae, of course, were but a mere technicality.

Eighty-five percent of Fernandito's cerebral matter, not to mention other lesser parts, became devoted to the contemplation and adoration of Sofía. The girl must have been about nineteen, give or take a year. Nature, with her infinite cruelty toward timid young men of a marriageable age, had opted to endow her with such fulsome and suggestive shapeliness, and such a pert little walk, that the mere sight of it all drove Fernandito into a paroxysm of near cardiac arrest. Her eyes, the shape of those lips, and the white teeth and pink tongue he glimpsed when she smiled dazzled the poor boy. He could spend hours imagining his fingers caressing that Renaissance mouth and moving down that pale throat on their way to the valley of paradise, emphasized by those tight woolen sweaters the signorina wore, which proved beyond a doubt that Italians had always been the true masters of architecture.

Fernandito half closed his eyes and ignored the noise of the radio in the dining room of his family home and the shouts of neighbors, conjuring up instead the image of Sofía languidly reposing on a bed of roses, or any other vegetable equipped with petals, offering herself to him in the full blossom of youth so that he, with firm hands expert in all kinds of fasteners, zips, and other mysteries of the eternal feminine, could strip her bit by bit by means of kisses, or maybe bites, and end up burying his face in that incomparable oasis of perfection that heaven had so kindly placed right below the belly button of all women. Fernandito remained in his daydream, convinced that if the Lord above struck him dead at that very moment with a destructive bolt for such lewd thoughts, it would have been worth it.

But instead of a purifying shaft of lightning, the phone rang. Footsteps, heavy as a digging machine, traipsed up the corridor, and the door of the cabin opened suddenly to reveal the large silhouette of Fernandito's father, sporting a vest and loose trousers and holding a chorizo sandwich in one hand. "Get up, you useless twit," he announced. "It's for you."

Torn away from the clutches of paradise, Fernandito dragged himself to the end of the corridor. There, in a hidden corner, stood the telephone beneath a plastic figure of Christ his mother had bought in the monastery of Montserrat. The figure's eyes lit up when you pressed the switch, lending it a supernatural glow that had given Fernandito years of nightmares. As soon as he picked up the receiver, his brother Fulgencio poked his head around to spy on him and make faces, his one great talent.

"Fernandito?" asked a voice on the line.

"Speaking."

"It's Alicia."

His heart missed a beat.

"Can you speak?" she asked.

Fernandito threw a rope-soled shoe at Fulgencio, who ran off to hide in his room. "Yes. Are you all right? Where are you?"

"Listen carefully, Fernandito. I need to be away for a while."

"That doesn't sound at all good."

"I need you to do me a favor. It's important."

"Anything you ask."

"Do you still have the papers that were in the box I asked you to take from my apartment?"

"Yes. They're in a safe place."

"I want you to look for a handwritten notebook that has 'Isabella' written on the cover."

"I know the one. I haven't opened it, eh? I don't want you to think ..."

"I know you haven't. What I want you to do is give it to Daniel Sempere. Only to him. Have you understood?"

"Yes ..."

"Tell him that I told you to give it to him. That it belongs to him and nobody else."

"Yes, Señorita Alicia. Where are you?"

"It doesn't matter."

"Are you in danger?"

"Don't worry about me, Fernandito."

"Of course I worry ..."

"Thanks for everything."

"This sounds like a good-bye."

"You and I know that only corny people say good-bye."

"And you could never be corny. Even if you tried."

"You're a good friend, Fernandito. And a good man. Sofía is a very lucky woman."

Fernandito turned to steaming crimson. "How do you know?"

"I'm happy to see that at last you've found someone who deserves you."

"Nobody will ever be like you, Señorita Alicia."

"Will you do what I asked?"

"Of course."

"I love you, Fernandito. Keep the keys to the flat. You'll need a place to take your girl to. It's your home now. Be happy. And forget me."

Before he could say another word, Alicia had hung up. Fernandito swallowed hard and, drying his tears, put down the receiver.

24

ALICIA WALKED OUT of the telephone booth. The taxi was waiting for her a few meters farther on. The driver had pulled down the window and was enjoying a cigarette, his thoughts miles away. When he saw her approach, he prepared to throw the cigarette butt away. "Shall we go?"

"Just one minute. Finish your cigarette."

"The gates close in ten minutes . . ."

"In ten minutes we'll be out of here," said Alicia.

She headed up the hill toward the forest of mausoleums, crosses, angels, and gargoyles covering the mountainside. The sunset had dragged a shroud of red clouds over Montjuïc Cemetery. A curtain of sleet swayed in the breeze, spreading a veil of crystal specks before her. Alicia walked up a path and climbed a few stone steps leading to a balcony populated by tombs and sculptures of ghostly figures. There, standing out against the light of the Mediterranean, stood a gravestone that was slightly tilted.

ISABELLA SEMPERE

1917–1939

Alicia knelt by the grave and placed her hand on the headstone. She remembered the face in the photographs she had seen in Señor Sempere's apartment, and in the picture Brians had kept of his old client—in all likelihood, also his unmentionable love. She recalled the words she'd read in the notebook and knew that, even though she hadn't met her, she had never felt as close to anyone as she did to that woman whose remains lay beneath her feet.

"Perhaps it would be best if Daniel never knew the truth and never found Valls or the revenge he longs for," she said. "But I can't decide for him. Forgive me."

Alicia unbuttoned the coat she'd borrowed from the keeper, put her hand in the inside pocket, and pulled out the carved figure he'd given her. She examined the little angel with open wings he'd bought for his daughter in a Christmas market stand so many years ago, inside which she'd hidden messages and secrets for her father. She opened the hollow space and looked at the note she'd written on a scrap of paper on her way to the cemetery.

Mauricio Valls
El Pinar
Calle Manuel Arnús
Barcelona

She rolled up the note and slipped it into the hollow, then put the lid back on and placed the angel figure at the foot of the headstone, between the vases of dry flowers.

"Let fate decide," she murmured.

When she got back to the taxi, the driver was waiting for her, leaning against the car. He opened the door for Alicia and returned to the wheel. Through the rearview mirror he saw her open her bag and pull out a bottle of white pills. She put a handful of them in her mouth and chewed, lost in thought. The driver handed her a water bottle lying on the passenger seat. Alicia drank. At last she looked up.

"Where to?" asked the taxi driver.

She showed him a wad of notes.

"There's at least four hundred duros there," he ventured.

"Six hundred," she specified. "They're yours if we reach Madrid before dawn."

25

FERNANDITO STOPPED ON the other side of the street and looked at Daniel through the bookshop window. It had started to snow when he left the house, and by now the streets were almost deserted. He observed Daniel for a few minutes, waiting to make sure he was alone in the bookshop. When Daniel walked over to the door to hang the CLOSED sign, Fernandito emerged from the shadows and stood in front of him, a frozen smile on his face.

Daniel looked at him in surprise and opened the door. "Fernandito, if you're looking for Sofía, she's spending the night at her friend Sita's in Sarriá, to study for some exam or—"

"No. I was looking for you."

"Me?"

The boy nodded.

"Come in."

"Are you alone?"

Daniel gave him a puzzled look. Fernandito stepped into the bookshop and waited for Daniel to close the door.

"Yes, what is it?"

"I have something for you on behalf of Señorita Alicia."

"Do you know where she is?"

"No."

"What is it?"

Fernandito dithered for a moment, and then pulled out what looked like a school notebook from inside his jacket. He handed it to Daniel, who accepted it with a smile at the apparent innocence accompanying that air of mystery. As soon as he read the word on the cover of the notebook, his smile vanished.

"Well . . . ," said Fernandito. "I'll leave you. Good night, Don Daniel."

Daniel nodded without taking his eyes off the notebook. Once Fernandito had left the bookshop, he turned off the lights and sought refuge in the back room. He sat down at the old desk that had already belonged to his grandfather, turned on the reading lamp, and closed his eyes for a few seconds. He felt his pulse accelerating, and his hands shook.

The cathedral bells rang out in the distance as he opened the notebook and began to read.

ISABELLA'S
NOTEBOOK

1939

My name is Isabella Gispert, and I was born in Barcelona in 1917. I'm twenty-two years old and I know I will never reach my twenty-third birthday. I write these words knowing for certain that I only have a few days left to live, and that I will soon have to leave behind those to whom I am most indebted in this world: my son Daniel and my husband Juan Sempere, the kindest man I have ever known. I will die without having merited all the trust, love, and devotion he has given me. I'm writing for myself, taking with me secrets that don't belong to me and knowing that nobody will ever read these pages. I'm writing to reminisce and to cling to life. My only wish is to be able to remember and understand who I was and why I did what I did while I am still able to do so, and before the consciousness that I already feel weakening abandons me forever. I'm writing even if it hurts, because loss and pain are the only things that keep me alive, and I'm afraid of dying. I'm writing to tell these pages what I can't tell those I love, for fear of hurting them and putting their lives in danger. I'm writing because as long as I'm able to remember, I will be with them one more minute . . .

I

The image of my body wasting away in the mirror of this bedroom makes it hard for me to believe it, but once, a long time ago, I was a child. My family had a grocery behind the church of Santa María del Mar. We lived in a house at the back of the shop. There we had a patio from which we could see the top of the basilica. I liked to imagine it was an enchanted castle that went out for a stroll every night through the streets of Barcelona and returned at dawn to sleep in the sunlight. My father's family, the Gisperts, came from a long line of Barcelona traders, and my mother's, the Ferratinis, from a family of Neapolitan sailors and fishermen. I inherited the character of my maternal grandmother, a woman with a rather volcanic temperament who was nicknamed La Vesubia. We were three sisters, but my father used to say he had two daughters and one mule. I loved my father very much, despite the fact that I made him very unhappy. He was a good man who managed groceries better than he managed his daughters. Our father confessor used to say that we all come into this world with a purpose, and mine was to contradict.

My two older sisters were more docile. It was clear to them that their objective was to make a good marriage and better themselves in the world according to the rules of social etiquette. Much to my poor parents' disappointment, I declared myself a rebel when I was eight and announced that I would never get married, that I would never wear an apron, not even in front of a firing squad, and that I would be a writer or a submariner (Jules Verne had me confused on that point for a while). My father blamed the Brontë sisters, whom I always talked about devotedly. He thought they were a bunch of libertarian nuns entrenched in the old city walls who had lost their minds during the riots of 1909 and now smoked opiates and danced cheek-to-cheek among themselves after midnight. "This would never have happened if we'd sent her to the Teresian mothers," he complained. I must admit that I never knew how to be the daughter my parents would have wished me to be, or the young girl the world I was born into expected. Or perhaps I should say I didn't want to. I always went against everyone's wishes: against my parents' wishes, my teachers' wishes, and, when they all grew tired of battling with me, my own.

I didn't like playing with the other girls: my specialty was decapitating dolls with a catapult. I preferred to play with boys, who were easily bossed around, although sooner or later they discovered that I always beat them, so I had to start managing on my own. I think that's when I began to have that feeling of always being distant and separate from the rest. In that respect I was like my mother, who used to say that deep down we were always alone, especially those of us born female. My mother was a melancholy woman with whom I never got along, perhaps because she was the only one in the family who understood me a little. She died when I was still a child. My father got married again, to a widow from Valladolid who never liked me and who, when we were alone, called me "little tart."

After my mother died, I realized how much I missed her. Perhaps that's why I started going to the university library, for which she'd managed to get me a reader's card before she died, without telling my father, who thought all I needed to study was the catechism, and all I needed to read were the lives of saints. My stepmother hated books. Their very presence offended her; she hid them inside cupboards so they wouldn't ruin the decor of the house.

The library is where my life changed. I didn't even open the catechism by chance, and the only saint I enjoyed reading about was Saint Teresa, for I was utterly intrigued by those mysterious ecstasies, which I associated with shameful practices that I don't even dare tell these pages. In the library I read everything I was allowed to read, and especially what some people told me I shouldn't read. Doña Lorena, a wise librarian who used to be around in the afternoons, always prepared a pile of books she described as "books all young ladies should read and nobody wants them to read." Doña Lorena said that the level of barbarism in a society is measured by the distance it tries to create between women and books. "Nothing frightens a loutish person more than a woman who knows how to read, write, and think, and moreover shows her knees." During the war she was sent to the women's prison, and they say she hanged herself in her cell.

I knew from the start that I wanted to live among books, and I began to dream that one day my own stories would end up in one of those tomes I so worshiped. Books taught me to think, to feel, and to live a thousand lives. I'm not ashamed to admit that, just as Doña Lorena predicted, the day came when I also started liking boys. Too much. I can tell these pages and laugh about how my legs trembled when I saw some of the young men who unloaded boxes in the Borne market and looked at me with hungry smiles, their torsos covered in sweat, their skin tanned and, I was sure, tasting of salt. "Oh, what I'd give you, gorgeous," one of them told me, before my father locked me up in the house for a week, a week I devoted to fantasizing about what that daring young man wanted to give me, while feeling a bit like Saint Teresa.

To tell you the truth, the boys of my age didn't interest me much. Besides, they were somewhat afraid of me. I'd beaten them at everything except in competitions to see who could pee farthest in the wind. Like all girls of my age, whether they admit it or not, I preferred older boys, especially the ones who fit into the category defined by all mothers as "the unsuitable ones." I didn't know how to doll myself up or look my best, at least at first, but soon I learned to tell when boys liked me. Most of them turned out to be the complete opposite of books: they were simple and could be read instantly. I suppose I never was what is known as a good girl. I'm not going to lie to myself. Who wants to be a good girl voluntarily? Not me. I would corner the boys I liked in a doorway and instruct them to kiss me. Since a lot of them were paralyzed with fear or didn't even know how to begin, I would kiss them. My exploits reached the parish priest's ears, and he deemed it necessary to perform an immediate act of exorcism, for these were clear signs of demonic possession. My stepmother had a nervous breakdown caused by the shame I'd put her through. It lasted a month. After that episode she declared that I would end up at least as a cabaret artist, or go straight to the "gutter," her favorite expression. "And then nobody will want you, you little tart." My father, who was at his wit's end as to what to do with me, began making arrangements to send me to a strict religious boarding school, but my reputation preceded me, and as soon as they realized who I was, they refused to admit me for fear I might contaminate the other boarders. I write all this without embarrassment because I think that if I committed a sin at all during my teenage years, it was simply that of being too innocent. I broke a heart or two, but never with malice, and then I still believed that nobody would ever break mine.

My stepmother, who had declared a special devotion for Our Lady of Lourdes, never lost hope. She prayed to her constantly, begging that one day I would settle down, or that a tram would run me over and I'd be out of the way once and for all. My salvation, suggested the parish priest, had to come about by channeling my troubled instincts in the Roman Catholic way. An urgent plan was put together for me to become engaged, whether I liked it or not, to Vicentet, whose parents owned the patisserie at the entrance to Calle Flassaders, and who, according to my parents, was a good match. Vicentet had a soul as soft as powdered sugar; he was as tender and supple as the sponge cakes his mother made. I could have eaten him up in half a morning, and the poor guy knew it, but our respective families thought that our union would be a way of killing two birds with one stone—setting up the "boy," and putting that little tart Isabella back on the straight and narrow.

Vicentet, blessed art thou among confectioners, adored me. For him, poor soul, nothing in the whole wide world could be more beautiful or purer than Isabella. When I walked past, he would gaze at me like a sacrificial lamb, dreaming of our wedding banquet at the Siete Puertas and our honeymoon trip on a pleasure boat to the breakwater point in the port. I, of course, made him as unhappy as I could. Unfortunately for all the Vicentets of the world, and they're not few in number, the heart of a girl is like a fireworks stand under the summer sun. Poor Vicentet, how he suffered because of me. I was told that in the end he married a second cousin from Ripoll who was about to become a novice and would have married the statue of the unknown soldier if that would have saved her from the convent. Together they still bring babies and sponge cakes into the world. He had a lucky escape.

✳

As foreseeable, I stuck to my guns and ended up doing what my father had always feared—even more than the possibility that Grandmother La Vesubia might come and live with them. Now that books had poisoned my feverish brain, his most dreaded nightmare was that I should fall in love with the worst sort of creature in the universe, the most treacherous, cruel, and malevolent to have ever set foot on earth, whose main purpose in life, aside from satisfying his infinite vanity, was to cast unhappiness on those poor souls who commit the serious mistake of loving him: a writer. And for that matter, not even a poet, a variety my father thought of as more or less a harmless daydreamer, who could be persuaded to find an honest job in a grocery store and leave his verses for Sunday afternoons after church. No, it would be the worst variety of that species: a novelist. Those were beyond repair, not welcome even in hell.

The only living writer in my world was a somewhat eccentric individual, to put it kindly, who had settled in the neighborhood. After some inquiries I discovered that he lived in a large old house on Calle Flassaders, near the pastry shop belonging to Vicentet's family. According to rumors from old gossipmongers, land registrars, and a very bigmouthed night watchman called Soponcio who knew all the tittle-tattle in our streets, the house was haunted and its occupant was a bit soft in the head. His name was David Martín.

I'd never seen him because, supposedly, he only came out at night and hung out in places not suitable for young ladies and respectable people. I didn't consider myself either one or the other, so I forged a plan to make our destinies collide, like two trains hurtling out of control. David Martín, the only living novelist in a radius of five streets from my home, didn't know yet, but very soon his life was going to change. For the better. Heaven or hell would send him just what he needed to straighten out his dissolute existence: an apprentice, the great Isabella.

2

The story of how I became David Martín's official apprentice is long and detailed. Knowing him, it wouldn't surprise me if David himself had left his own account of it somewhere, an account in which my character won't be exactly that of the heroine. The fact is that, despite his iron resistance, I managed to sneak into his house, his strange life, and his consciousness, which in itself was a haunted house. Perhaps it was destiny, perhaps it was the fact that, deep down, David Martín was a tormented spirit who, without knowing it, needed me much more than I needed him. "Lost souls who find one another at midnight," I wrote at the time as part of my training, in an attempt at a melodramatic poem that my new mentor declared highly dangerous for diabetics. He was like that.

I've often thought that David Martín was my first real friend in this life, after Doña Lorena, that is. He was almost twice my age, and sometimes it seemed to me that he'd lived a hundred lives before meeting me, but even when he avoided my company or we quarreled about something trivial, I felt so close to him that despite myself I understood that, as he sometimes joked, we were "two devils in a pod." Like many good-natured people, David liked to hide in a shell of gruff cynicism, but despite the numerous jibes he threw at me (no more than the ones I threw at him, to be fair) and however hard he pretended not to, he always showed me great patience and generosity.

David Martín taught me many things: how to create a sentence, how to think about language and all its devices as an orchestra in search of a musical score, how to analyze a text and understand how it is constructed and why . . . He taught me to read and write again, but this time I knew what I was doing, why, and what for. And above all how. He never tired of telling me that in literature there is only one real theme: not what is narrated, but how it is narrated. The rest, he said, was decoration. He also told me that writing was a profession one had to learn, but was impossible to teach: "Whoever doesn't understand that principle may as well devote their life to something else, for there are lots of things to be done in this world." He was of the opinion that I had less of a future as a writer than Spain had of being a reasonable country, but he was a born pessimist, or what he called an "informed realist," so, true to myself, I contradicted him.

*

With David I learned to accept myself just as I was, to think for myself, and even to love myself a little. During the time I spent living in his ghost-ridden house we became friends, good friends. David Martín was a solitary man, who burned his bridges with the world without realizing it, or perhaps he did it deliberately because he thought that nothing good would ever come across them. His was a broken soul, an item that had been damaged since childhood and which he was never able to mend. I began by pretending to hate him, then tried to hide the fact that I admired him, and finally I made an effort not to show that I felt sorry for him, because it infuriated him. The more David tried to push me away, and he never stopped trying, the closer I felt to him. Then I stopped contradicting him in everything and only wanted to protect him. The irony of our friendship is that I came into his life as an apprentice and a nuisance, but deep down it was as if he'd always been waiting for me. To save him, perhaps, from himself or from all that stuff he had trapped inside him, which was eating him alive.

You only truly fall in love when you don't realize it's happening. I fell in love with that broken, profoundly unhappy man long before I began to suspect that I even liked him. He, who always read me like an open book, feared for me. It was his idea that I should work in the Sempere & Sons bookshop, where he'd been a customer all his life. It was his idea to convince Juan, who would end up being my husband and who at the time was "the young Sempere," to court me. In those days Juan was as shy as David could be brazen. In a way they were like day and night; in David's heart it was always night.

By then I'd begun to realize that I would never be a writer, or even a submariner, and that the Brontë sisters would have to wait for another, more like-minded candidate to succeed them. I had also started to realize that David Martín was ill. A chasm opened up inside him, and after an entire existence spent fighting to maintain his sanity, when I came into his life David had already lost the battle with himself and was losing his mind, like sand slipping through his fingers. If I'd heeded common sense, I would have run away, but by then I'd already started to enjoy contradicting myself.

*

In time, a lot of things were said about David Martín, and terrible crimes were attributed to him. I am convinced—and I think I knew him better than anyone else—that the only crimes he committed were against himself. That is why I helped him escape from Barcelona, after the police had accused him of murdering his protector, Pedro Vidal, and Vidal's wife Cristina—with whom he thought he was in love, in that stupid and fatal way some men imagine they love a woman they can't tell apart from an apparition. And that's why I prayed he would never return to this city, that he would find peace in some faraway place, that I would be able to forget him, or eventually persuade myself that I had. God only listens when one prays for what one doesn't need.

I spent the next four years trying to forget David Martín, and thinking I had almost managed to do so. Having abandoned my dreams of writing, I'd made my other dream, that of living among books and words, a reality. I worked in the Sempere & Sons bookshop, where, after the death of Grandfather Sempere, Juan had become Señor Sempere. Our engagement was one of those prewar affairs—a modest courtship, cheeks caressed, strolls on Sunday afternoons, and stolen kisses under marquees during the street fiestas in Gracia, when no family members were spying on us. There were no trembling legs, but that wasn't necessary either. One can't live one's whole life as if one were always fourteen.

Juan didn't take long to propose to me. My father accepted his proposal in three minutes flat, full of gratitude to Saint Rita, patron saint of impossible causes, as he glimpsed the improbable sight of his daughter dressed in white bowing before a priest and doing as she was told. Barcelona, city of miracles. When I said yes to Juan, I did it with the conviction that he was the best man I would ever meet, that I didn't deserve him, and that I'd learned to love him not only with my heart but also with my mind. My "yes" wasn't that of a young girl. How wise I felt. My mother would have been proud of me. All those books had served some purpose. I accepted his hand knowing that what I most desired in the world was to make him happy and raise a family with him. And for a while I actually believed that that was how it would be. I was still so innocent.

3

People live inside their hopes, but the landlord of fate is the devil. The wedding was going to take place in the church of Santa Ana, in the little square just behind the bookshop. The invitations had been sent, the wedding banquet organized, the flowers bought, and the car that was supposed to drive the bride to the church door booked. Every day I told myself I was thrilled, that at last I was going to be happy. I remember one Friday in March, exactly one month before the ceremony, when I was left alone in the bookshop because Juan had had to go to Tiana to deliver an order to an important customer. I heard the tinkle of the doorbell, and when I looked up, I saw him. He'd barely changed.

David Martín was one of those men who don't grow old, or who only do so inside themselves. Anyone would have joked that he must have made a pact with the devil. Anyone but me, who knew that in the hallucinations of his soul he was convinced that it was so, although his private devil was an imaginary character who lived in the back room of his mind under the name of Andreas Corelli, a Parisian publisher and such a sinister individual he seemed to have emerged from David's own pen. In his mind, David was convinced that Corelli had hired him to write an accursed book, the founding text of a new faith of fanaticism, anger, and destruction that would set fire to the world forevermore. David carried the burden of that raving fantasy and many others, and believed unquestioningly that his literary demon was hunting him down because he, true to character, hadn't thought of anything better to do than betray him, break their agreement, and destroy the present-day Malleus Maleficarum at the very last moment, perhaps because the shining kindness of his unbearable apprentice had made him see the light as well as the error of his ways. And that's where I came in, the great Isabella, an unbeliever who didn't even believe in lottery tickets, who thought that the perfume of my youthful charms and a time spent without breathing the stuffy air of Barcelona (where, moreover, the police were looking for him) would be enough to cure his madness. As soon as I looked into his eyes, I knew that four years wandering around God knows where hadn't cured him one iota. The moment he smiled at me and told me he'd missed me, my soul was shattered. I began to cry, and cursed my luck. When he touched my cheek, I knew I was still in love with my very own Dorian Gray, my preferred lunatic, and the only man I had always yearned to have his way with me.

*

I can't remember what words we exchanged. That moment is still a blur in my memory. I think that everything I'd built up in my imagination during the years of his absence collapsed on me in five seconds, and when I managed to crawl out from under the rubble, all I could do was write a hasty note to Juan that I left by the cash register:

> I must leave. Forgive me, my love,
>   Isabella

I knew the police were still looking for David; a month didn't go by without some member of the force coming by the bookshop to ask whether we'd had any news of the fugitive. I left the bookshop holding on to David's arm and dragged him to the Estación del Norte. He seemed delighted to have returned to Barcelona and looked at everything with the nostalgia of a dying man and the innocence of a child. I was terrified, and all I could think of was where to hide him. I asked him whether he knew of any place where nobody could find him, and nobody would think of looking.

"The Great Assembly Room in the city hall building," he said.

"I'm serious, David."

I was always a woman of bright ideas, and that day I had one of my craziest. David had once told me that his old mentor and friend, Don Pedro Vidal, had a house in a remote corner of the Costa Brava called S'Agaró. At the time the house had served him as a gentleman's pad, that familiar institution of the Catalan bourgeoisie, a place where well-do-to male members of good society took young ladies, prostitutes, and other candidates for hidden love encounters through which to vent their energetic temperaments without soiling the immaculate marriage bond.

Vidal, who kept various addresses for that purpose in the comfort of Barcelona, had always offered David his hideout by the sea whenever he wished, because he and his cousins only used it during the summer, and even then only for a couple of weeks. The key was always hidden behind a stone on a ledge next to the entrance. With the money I'd taken from the cash register in the bookshop, I bought two tickets to Gerona and from there another two to San Feliu de Guíxols. S'Agaró was just two kilometers farther on, in the bay of San Pol. David didn't put up any resistance. In the train, he leaned on my shoulder and fell asleep.

"I haven't slept for years," he said.

We arrived in San Feliu in the evening, with nothing but the clothes we were wearing. I decided not to take one of the horse carts waiting outside the station, instead making the journey to the villa on foot under cover of darkness. The key was still there. The house had been closed for years. I opened all the windows wide and left them like that until dawn appeared over the sea at the foot of the cliff. David had slept like a baby all night, and when the sun touched his face, he opened his eyes, sat up, and drew close to me. He held me tight, and when I asked him why he'd come back, he said he'd realized that he loved me.

"You have no right to love me," I said.

After three years of idleness, La Vesubia, who had always been inside me, reappeared. I started to shout at him, venting all the anger, all the sadness, all the longing he had left in me. I assured him that knowing him was the worst thing that had ever happened in my life, that I hated him, that I didn't want to see him ever again, that I wanted him to stay in that house and rot there forever. David nodded and looked down. I suppose that's when I kissed him, because I was always the one who had to kiss first, and in a split second I shattered the rest of my life. The priest of my childhood days had been wrong. I hadn't come to this world to contradict everyone, but to make mistakes. And that morning, in his arms, I made the greatest mistake I could ever have made.

4

One doesn't become aware of the emptiness in which one has allowed time to go by until one truly lives. Sometimes life—not the days that have burned away—is just an instant, a day, a week, or a month. One knows one is alive because it hurts, because suddenly everything matters, and because when that brief moment is over, the rest of one's existence becomes a memory to which one tries in vain to return while there is some breath left in one's body. For me that moment was contained in the weeks I lived in that large house overlooking the sea with David. I should say with David and the shadows that he carried inside him and that lived with us, but then I didn't care. I would have gone with him to hell if he'd asked me to. And I suppose that, in my own way, that's what I ended up doing.

At the foot of the cliff there was a shed with a couple of rowing boats, and a wooden jetty that stretched out into the sea. Almost every morning, at dawn, David would sit at the end of the jetty to watch the sunrise. Sometimes I would join him, and we'd swim in the cove shaped by the cliff. It was March, and the water was still cold, but after a while we'd run home and sit by the fireplace. Then we would take long walks along the path bordering the cliffs, which led to a deserted beach the locals called Sa Conca. In the small wood behind the beach there was a gypsy camp where David bought provisions. Back home, he would cook and we'd have dinner in the evening while we listened to some of the old records Vidal had left in the house. Many evenings, right after sunset, a strong north wind would start up, blowing among the trees and banging the shutters.

We had to close the windows and light candles all over the house. Then I would spread a couple of blankets in front of the fireplace and take David's hand, because although he was twice my age and had lived more than I could even begin to imagine, he was always shy with me, and I was the one who had to guide his hands so he could undress me slowly, the way I liked him to do. I suppose I should be ashamed to write these words and conjure up these memories, but I have no modesty or shame left to offer the world. The memory of those nights, of his hands and lips exploring my skin, of the happiness and pleasure I lived between those four walls, all that, together with the birth of Daniel and the years I've had him by my side and seen him grow, are the most beautiful things I will take with me.

Now I know that the real purpose of my life, the one not even I could have foreseen, was to conceive my son Daniel during the weeks I spent with David. And I know the world would judge me and condemn me to its heart's content for having loved that man, for having conceived a son in sin and in hiding, and for lying. The punishment, be it fair or unfair, did not wait. In this life nobody is happy for free, not even for an instant.

*

One morning, while David was walking down to the jetty, I got dressed and went down to the bathhouse and the restaurant called La Taberna del Mar, at the foot of the bay of San Pol. From there I called Juan. It was now two and a half weeks since I'd disappeared.

"Where are you? Are you all right? Are you safe?" he asked me.

"Yes."

"Are you going to come back?"

"I don't know. I don't know anything, Juan."

"I love you very much, Isabella. I'll always love you. Whether or not you come back."

"Aren't you going to ask me whether I love you?"

"You don't have to explain anything to me if you don't feel like it. I'll wait for you. Always."

Those words sank into me like a dagger, and when I got back home, I was still crying. David, who was waiting for me by the door of the house, hugged me.

"I can't go on being here with you, David."

"I know."

Two days later, one of the gypsies from the beach came over to warn us that the Civil Guard was asking about a man and a young girl who had been seen in the area. The guards had a photograph of David, and said he was wanted for murder. That was the last night we spent together. The following morning, when I woke up under the fireplace blankets, David had gone. He'd left a note in which he told me to go back to Barcelona, marry Juan Sempere, and be happy for the two of us. The night before, I'd confessed that Juan had asked me to marry him and that I'd accepted. Even now, I don't know why I told him that—whether I wanted to push him away from me or wanted him to beg me to elope with him in his descent to hell. He decided for me. When I'd told him he had no right to love me, he'd believed me.

I knew there was no sense in waiting for him. That he wasn't going to return that afternoon or the next day. I cleaned the house, covered the furniture with sheets again, and closed all the windows. I left the key behind the stone in the wall and made my way to the train station.

I knew I was carrying his child in my womb as soon as I stepped into the train in San Feliu. Juan, whom I'd called from the station before leaving, came to meet me. He hugged me and didn't ask me where I'd been. I didn't even dare look him in the eye.

"I don't deserve your love," I confessed.

"Don't talk nonsense."

I was cowardly and afraid. For me. For the child I knew I carried inside me. A week later, I married Juan Sempere in the church of Santa Ana, as had been arranged. We spent the wedding night in the Fonda España. The following morning, when I woke up, I heard Juan crying in the bathroom. How beautiful life would be if we were able to love those who deserve it.

Daniel Sempere Gispert, my son, was born nine months later.

5

I never quite understood why David Martín decided to return to Barcelona during the last days of the war, in January of this year, 1939. The morning he left the house in S'Agaró and disappeared, I thought I would never see him again. When Daniel was born, I left behind the young girl I'd once been and the memory of the time we'd spent together. I've lived these years looking no further than caring for Daniel, being the mother I should be for him, and protecting him from a world I have learned to see through David's eyes. A world of darkness, of resentment and envy, of meanness and hatred. A world in which everything is false and everyone lies. A world that shouldn't deserve to survive, but a world into which my son has come and from which I need to protect him. I never wanted David to know of Daniel's existence. The day my son was born, I swore to myself that he would never know who his father had been, because Daniel's true father, the man who devoted his life to him and brought him up by my side, Juan Sempere, was the best father he could ever have had. I did this because I was convinced that if one day Daniel discovered, or suspected, the truth, he would never forgive me. And even so, I would do it again.

David Martín should never have returned to Barcelona. Deep down I believe that if he did, it was because he somehow suspected the truth. Perhaps that was the real punishment reserved for him by the devil he carried in his soul. The moment he crossed the frontier, we were both doomed.

He was arrested a few months ago after crossing the Pyrenees, then taken to Barcelona, where the cases pending against him were reopened. They also charged him with subversion, treason against the state, and God knows what other absurdities. He was locked up in La Modelo, together with thousands of other prisoners. These days people are murdered and imprisoned in vast numbers in all big cities in Spain, and even more so in Barcelona. It's open season for revenge, for annihilating the opponent, our great national calling. As was to be expected, the brand-new crusaders of the regime crept out from under the stones and ran to take up positions in the new order of things, ready to climb up the ranks of the new society. Many of them have crossed the lines and changed sides once or even a number of times for convenience and self-interest. No person who has lived through a war with their eyes open can ever again believe we're better than any wild animal.

One might think that things could get no worse, but there's no bar low enough for meanness when it holds the reins. An individual appeared on the horizon, someone who seemed to have come to the world to embody the spirit of the times and the place. I imagine there are plenty like him among the scum that always rises to the surface when everything else founders. His name is Mauricio Valls, and, like all great men in small times, he is a nobody.

6

I suppose one day all the newspapers in the country will publish great eulogies of Don Mauricio Valls and sing his praises to the four winds. Our land abounds with characters of his ilk, men who never lack a retinue of flatterers crawling around to pick up the crumbs that fall from their table, once they've reached the top. For the time being, before that moment comes, and it will, Mauricio Valls is still just one of many, an outstanding candidate. During these last few months I've learned a great deal about him. I know he began as one more bookworm in café gatherings—a mediocre man with no talent or trade who, as usually happens, made up for his failings with an enormous vanity and insatiable hunger for recognition. Estimating that his merits would never earn him a penny or the position he coveted and felt entitled to, he decided to carve out a career for himself, cultivating a clique of like-minded chums with whom to exchange privileges, excluding those he envied.

*

Yes, I'm writing in anger and resentment, and I'm ashamed of it, because I no longer know, nor do I care, whether my words are fair or not, whether I'm judging the innocent or whether the fury and the pain that burn me to the core are also blinding me. During these past months I've learned to hate, and it terrifies me to think that I'll die with this bitterness in my heart.

The first time I heard his name was shortly after I found out that David had been captured and imprisoned. At the time Mauricio Valls was a young pup of the new regime, a loyal follower who had made himself a name by marrying the daughter of a tycoon in the business and financial setup that had supported the Fascist Nacionales. Valls had started his days as an aspiring man of letters, but his greatest triumph was to seduce a poor soul and lead her down the aisle: a young woman born with a cruel illness that since adolescence had wasted away her bones and confined her to a wheelchair. A rich and unmarriageable heiress, a golden opportunity.

Valls must have imagined that his move was going to catapult him to the top of the national Parnassus, to some important position in the Academy or some prestigious post in the court of Spanish arts and culture. He hadn't factored in that there were plenty of others who, like him, had begun to appear like late-blossoming flowers out of nowhere when it was clear which side would win the war, all queuing up for the great day.

When the time came for sharing the rewards and booty, Valls received his with a lesson on the rules of the game. The regime didn't need poets but jailers and inquisitors. And so, without expecting it, he received an appointment that he considered degrading and well below his intellectual gifts: governor of the prison of Montjuïc Castle. Of course, someone like Valls never wastes an opportunity. He knew how to profit from this reversal of fortune by getting into the regime's good books, preparing for his future promotion, and while he was at it, incarcerating or exterminating all adversaries, real or imaginary, on his long list, or disposing of them as he pleased. How David Martín ended up on that list is something I will never be able to understand, although he wasn't the only one. For some reason Valls's fixation with Martín has been twisted and obsessive.

As soon as Valls found out that David Martín had been sent to La Modelo, he requested his transfer to Montjuïc Castle and didn't rest until he saw him behind the bars of one of his cells. My husband Juan knew a young lawyer, a customer at the bookshop, called Fernando Brians. I went to see him to find out what I could do to help David. Our savings were practically nonexistent, and Brians, a good man who has become a great friend in these difficult months, agreed to work for free. Brians had contacts in Montjuïc, especially one of the jailers, Bebo, and was able to discover that Valls had some sort of a plan regarding David. Valls knew David's work, and although he never tired of describing him as "the world's worst writer," he was trying to persuade David to write, or rewrite, a sheaf of pages bearing Valls's name, with which Valls believed he could establish his own reputation as an author, backed up by his new position in the regime. I can just imagine David's reply.

Brians tried everything, but the charges brought against David were too serious. The only thing left to do was to beg for Valls's clemency, that the treatment David received in the castle not be what we all imagined. Ignoring Brians's advice, I went to see Valls. Now I know that I made a mistake, a very serious mistake. By going there, if only because Valls saw me as one more possession belonging to the object of his hatred, David Martín, I made myself the focal point of his greed.

Like so many of his sort, Valls was quickly learning how to take advantage of the anxieties of his prisoners' relatives. Brians kept warning me. Juan, who suspected that my relationship with David and my devotion for him went beyond a noble friendship, was concerned about my visits to Valls in the castle. "Think of your son," he would say. And he was right, but I was selfish. I couldn't just abandon David in that place if there was something I could do. It was no longer a question of dignity. Nobody survives a civil war with even a scrap of dignity to boast about. My error was not realizing that Valls didn't want merely to possess or humiliate me but to destroy me. He'd finally understood that this was the only real way he had to hurt David and bend him to his will.

All my determination, all the naïveté with which I tried to persuade Valls, was turned against us. It made no difference how much I praised him, how much I pretended to respect and fear him, how much I humiliated myself by begging for his compassion toward his prisoner. Everything I did was just fuel for the fire inside Valls. I now know that in my attempt to help David, I ended up condemning him.

When I realized all this, it was already too late. Bored with his work, with himself, and with the slow arrival of his days of glory, Valls filled his time with fantasies. One of them was that he'd fallen in love with me. I thought that if I could convince him that his fantasy had a future, perhaps Valls would show some magnanimity. But he also got tired of me. In despair, I threatened to unmask him, to make public who he really was and how far his cruelty went. Valls laughed at me and at my ingenuousness, but he wanted to punish me. To wound David and deal him his fatal blow.

Barely a week and a half ago, Valls asked me to meet him at the Café de la Ópera, in the Ramblas. I went to the meeting without saying a word to anyone, not even my husband. I was sure that this was my last chance. I was mistaken. That very night I knew something had gone wrong. In the early hours I woke up feeling nauseous. In the mirror I saw that my eyes looked yellow, and some stains had appeared around my neck and on my chest. At daybreak I began to throw up blood. Then the pain began. A cold pain, like a knife carving you up inside, making its way through your body. I grew feverish, unable to keep down liquids or solids. My hair fell out in clumps. The muscles of my entire body tensed up like cables, making me scream with pain. Blood came out of my skin, my eyes, my mouth.

The doctors and hospitals haven't been able to help me. Juan thinks I've caught an illness, and there is still hope. He can't bear the thought that I'm going to abandon him and my son Daniel, whom I have failed as a mother by allowing my desire, my yearning to save the man I thought was the love of my life, to supplant my duty.

I know Mauricio Valls poisoned me that night in the Café de la Ópera. I know he did it to hurt David. I know I only have a few days left to live. Everything has happened very fast. My only comfort is laudanum, which numbs the pain inside me, and this notebook in which to confess my sins and my faults. Brians, who visits me every day, knows that I'm writing to stay alive, to contain this fire that is devouring me. I've asked him to destroy these pages when I die, and not to read them. Nobody must know what I have explained here. Nobody must know the truth, because I've learned that in this world truth only hurts, and God loves and helps those who lie.

I have nobody left to pray to. Everything I once believed in has deserted me. Sometimes I don't remember who I am, and rereading this notebook is the only thing that lets me understand what is happening. I will write until the end. To remember. To try to survive. I'd like to hug my son Daniel and make him understand that whatever happens, I will never abandon him. That I'll be with him. That I love him. Dear God, forgive me. I didn't know what I was doing. I don't want to die. Dear God, let me live one more day so I can hold Daniel in my arms and tell him how much I love him . . .

THAT NIGHT, LIKE so many others, Fermín had gone out in the small hours to stroll through the deserted streets of Barcelona, which were sown with frost. Remigio, the neighborhood nightwatchman, knew him, and when he saw him walk by always inquired about his insomnia. He'd learned that word from a phone-in radio program for lonely women that he listened to avidly because he identified with almost all the sorrows expressed in it, including one referred to as menopause, which intrigued him no end and which he thought could be cured by vigorously scraping one's privates with a pumice stone.

"Why call it insomnia, when what they mean is conscience?"

"You're a philosopher, Fermín. If I had a woman like yours waiting for me, all nice and warm between the sheets, there's no chance I'd be the only sleepless guy in town. And wrap yourself up. The winter might have come late, but it's come with a vengeance."

An hour of wrestling with the biting breeze that was sweeping the streets with sleet convinced Fermín that he should make his way to the bookshop. He had some work to catch up on, and he'd learned to enjoy those moments alone in the shop before the sun came out or Daniel came down to open up. He headed along the corridor of blue light stretching along Calle Santa Ana and glimpsed a distant pale glow tinting the glass of the shop window. Fermín slowed down as he drew closer, listening to the echo of his footsteps, and stopped a few meters away, sheltering from the wind in a doorway. Too early even for Daniel, he thought. Maybe what he'd said about conscience was going to turn out to be contagious.

He was debating between going back home to wake Bernarda up with a strenuous demonstration of Iberian virility, or going into the bookshop to interrupt Daniel doing whatever he was doing (above all to make sure this didn't include firearms or any sharp objects), when he caught sight of his friend walking through the shop entrance and stepping into the street. Fermín sank back into the doorway until he felt the door knocker sticking into his lower back and discovered that Daniel was locking the door and setting off toward Puerta del Ángel. He was in his shirtsleeves and was carrying something under his arm, a book or a notebook. Fermín sighed. That didn't look good. Bernarda would have to wait to find out a thing or two.

For almost half an hour Fermín followed Daniel through the knot of streets leading down to the port. He didn't need to move too skillfully or surreptitiously; Daniel seemed so lost in thought, he wouldn't have noticed a group of tap-dancing ballerinas if they'd been following him. Trembling with cold and cursing himself for having lined his coat with pages from a sports paper—porous and unreliable for such occasions—instead of using the extra-thick pages from the Sunday edition of *La Vanguardia*, Fermín was tempted to call out to his friend. But he thought better of it. Daniel was advancing as if in a trance, unaware of the sleety mist clinging to his body.

Finally Paseo de Colon opened up before them and, beyond it, the tableau of sheds, masts, and sea mist guarding the docks of the port. Daniel crossed the avenue and walked around a couple of stationary trams that waited for dawn to break. He entered the narrow alleyways between the cavernous sheds, colossal warehouses storing mountains of cargo. At the breakwater of the port, a group of fishermen getting their nets and tackle ready to go out to sea had lit a fire in an empty diesel drum to keep warm. As Daniel approached, they moved to one side, seeing something in his expression that did not encourage conversation. Fermín hurried on. As he drew closer, he could see Daniel throwing the notebook he'd been carrying under his arm into the flames.

Fermín went up to his friend and smiled at him weakly from the other side of the diesel drum. Daniel's eyes shone in the light of the fire.

"If what you're trying to do is catch pneumonia," ventured Fermín, "may I remind you that the North Pole is exactly in the opposite direction."

Daniel ignored his words and stood there, staring at the blaze as it devoured the pages, which shriveled among the flames as if an invisible hand were turning them one by one.

"Bea must be worried, Daniel. Why don't we go back?"

Daniel looked up and gazed blankly at Fermín, as if he'd never seen him before.

"Daniel?"

"Where is it?" asked Daniel, in a cold voice that lacked all inflection.

"Excuse me?"

"The gun. What have you done with it, Fermín?"

"I gave it to the Sisters of Charity."

A frozen smile surfaced on Daniel's lips. Fermín, who had never felt so close to losing Daniel forever, stepped closer and put his arm around him. "Let's go home, Daniel. Please."

At last Daniel nodded, and little by little, in complete silence, they made their way back.

*

Dawn was breaking when Bea heard the door of the apartment open and Daniel's footsteps in the hall. She'd been sitting for hours in the dining-room armchair, a blanket over her shoulders. Daniel's figure appeared in the corridor. If he saw her, he did nothing to show it. He walked past her and made his way to Julián's bedroom, which was in the back, overlooking the small square by the church of Santa Ana. Bea stood up and followed him. She found Daniel in the bedroom doorway, gazing at the sleeping child.

Bea put her hand on his shoulder. "Where were you?" she whispered.

Daniel turned around and looked into her eyes.

"When is all this going to end, Daniel?" she murmured.

"Soon," he said. "Soon."

LIBERA ME

MADRID

JANUARY

1960

I

IN THE GRAY, metallic dawn Ariadna faced the long avenue bordered by cypress trees. She held a bunch of red roses in her hand, which she'd bought on the way, by the entrance to a graveyard. There was complete silence. Not a single birdsong could be heard, no breeze dared caress the blanket of dead leaves covering the cobblestones. With no other company than the sound of her own footsteps, Ariadna covered the distance to the large spiked gates guarding the entrance to the estate, crowned with the words

VILLA MENOEDEO

Mauricio Valls's palace loomed behind an Arcadia of gardens and groves. Towers and dormers punctuated an ashen sky. Ariadna, a speck of white in the shade, studied the shape of the house that could be glimpsed between statues, hedges, and fountains. She thought it looked like a monstrous creature that had crept up, fatally wounded, to that corner of the forest. The gate was half open. Ariadna stepped in.

As she walked, she noticed the railway tracks running through the gardens, circling the perimeter of the estate. A miniature train, with a steam engine and two cars, seemed to be stranded among the bushes. She kept walking along the paved path leading up to the main house. The fountains were dry, their stone angels and marble Madonnas blackened. The trees' branches were covered in countless white chrysalises, now empty, like miniature tombs made of candy floss. A swarm of spiders hung from threads in the air. Ariadna crossed the bridge over the large oval swimming pool. Its water, greenish and covered in a fine layer of shiny algae, was strewn with the corpses of small birds, as if some curse had made them drop from the sky. Farther away were empty garages and staff buildings, buried in the shadows.

Ariadna climbed the stairs leading to the front door. She knocked three times before realizing that it too was open. Looking back, she took in the atmosphere of ruin that permeated the estate: with the fall of the emperor and his privileges, the servants had fled the palace. Ariadna pushed open the door and stepped into the house. It already smelled of a graveyard, of oblivion. A velvety half-light tightly gripped the network of corridors and staircases opening up before her. She stood there, motionless, a white specter at the doors of purgatory, staring at the dead splendor with which Mauricio Valls had dressed up his days of glory.

A faraway lament reached her ears. It came from the first floor and sounded like the feeble whine of a dying animal. She walked up the wide staircase unhurriedly. The walls hinted at the outlines of stolen paintings. On either side of the stairs were empty pedestals on which she could still make out the marks left by looted figures and busts. When Ariadna reached the first floor, she stopped and listened for the moaning again. It came from a room at the end of the corridor, which she headed slowly toward. The door was ajar, and a powerful stench wafted from it, brushing her face.

Ariadna walked across the darkened room and approached a four-poster bed. In that light it looked like a funeral hearse. An arsenal of machines and instruments sat idly on one side of the bed, disconnected and pushed back against the wall. The carpet was strewn with rubble and abandoned oxygen tanks. Ariadna stepped over those objects and pulled back the veil surrounding the bed. Behind it she discovered a human figure twisted upon itself, as if its bones had turned to jelly and its whole anatomy had been recast by pain. The figure's bloodshot eyes, enlarged on a skeletal face, observed her suspiciously. That guttural groan, halfway between weeping and suffocation, came out of her throat once more. Señora Valls had lost her hair, her nails, and most of her teeth.

Ariadna gazed at her without compassion. She sat down on one side of the bed and leaned over her. "Where's my sister?" she asked.

Valls's wife tried to form words. Ariadna ignored the stink she gave off and drew her face close to her lips.

"Kill me," she heard her plead.

2

HIDDEN IN THE dolls' house, Mercedes saw the woman go through the villa's gates. Dressed in ghostly white, she advanced very slowly in a straight line, carrying a bunch of red roses. Mercedes smiled. She'd been waiting for her for days. Death, dressed in Pertegaz couture, at last visited Villa Mercedes before hell swallowed it up, leaving in its place a barren land where grass would never grow again, where wind would never blow.

She had climbed onto one of the windowsills in the dolls' pavilion, where she'd been living since the staff abandoned the house, soon after the news of her father's death. At first Doña Mariana, her father's secretary, had tried to stop them, but that same evening some men dressed in black had come and dragged Doña Mariana away. Mercedes had heard gunshots behind the garages, but she didn't want to go there and look. Over the next few nights they took away the paintings, the statues, the furniture, the clothes, the cutlery, and whatever else they fancied. They would arrive at sunset like a starving pack. They also took all the cars and destroyed the walls of the sitting rooms, looking for hidden treasures that they didn't find. When there was nothing left, they went away and never returned.

One day she saw two police cars come in. With them came some of the bodyguards she remembered from her father's security staff. For a moment she hesitated, wondering whether to go out and meet them, tell them everything that had happened, but when she saw them go up to her father's workroom in the tower and loot everything inside it, she hid again among the dolls. There, among hundreds of figures that looked into the void with glass eyes, nobody found her. They abandoned the lady of the house to her fate after disconnecting the machines that preserved her in her state of eternal torment. She'd been howling for days, but still hadn't died. Until that day.

That day Death was visiting Villa Mercedes, and soon Mercedes would have the ruins of the house all to herself. She knew that everyone had lied to her. She thought her father was alive and safe somewhere, and that as soon as he could, he'd return to her side. She knew, because Alicia had promised her. She had promised she would find her father.

*

When she saw Death walk up the stairs to the entrance of the house and step inside, Mercedes became doubtful. Perhaps she was mistaken. Perhaps that white figure she had taken for the Grim Reaper was only Alicia, who had come back to fetch her and take her to her father. It was the only thing that made sense. She knew Alicia would never abandon her.

She stepped out of the dolls' pavilion and walked over to the main house. Inside, she heard footsteps on the first floor and ran up the stairs just in time to see the white figure go into the lady's room. The stench filling the corridor was terrible. She covered her mouth and nose with her hand and walked up to the doorway. The figure in white was leaning like an angel over the lady's bed. Mercedes held her breath. Then the figure took one of the pillows and, covering the lady's face, pressed hard while her body shook with convulsions, until it lay still.

The figure turned around slowly, and Mercedes was seized by the iciest cold she had ever felt. She was wrong. It wasn't Alicia.

Death, all dressed in white, approached her slowly and smiled. She offered Mercedes a red rose, which she accepted with trembling hands. "Do you know who I am?" she asked.

Mercedes nodded. Death embraced her with immense affection and gentleness. The young girl let herself be caressed, containing her tears.

"Shhh," whispered Death. "Nobody is going to separate us ever again. Nobody will hurt us anymore. We'll always be together. With Mommy and Daddy. Always together. You and I . . ."

3

ALICIA WOKE UP on the back seat of the taxi. She sat up and realized she was alone. The windows were steamed up. She wiped the pane with her sleeve and saw that they'd stopped at a gas station. A streetlamp projected a yellowish beam that vibrated every time a truck thundered past on the road. In the distance, a leaden dawn was spreading across the sky, sealing it without leaving a single crack. She rubbed her eyes and rolled down the window. A sudden gust of icy air pulled her out of her drowsiness. A stabbing pain ran through her hip. She let out a moan and held her side. Soon the pain subsided to a dull throb, a warning of what was to come. The wisest thing would have been to take a pill or two before the pain sharpened, but she wanted to stay alert. She had no other choice. After a few minutes, she saw the profile of the taxi driver emerging from the gas station bar, carrying two paper cups and a bag with greasy stains. He raised a hand to greet her and walked briskly around the car.

"Good morning," he said as he sat down at the wheel again. "It's cold as hell out there. I've brought you some breakfast. More roadside delicacy than continental, but at least it's hot. Coffee with milk and some deep-fried pastry sticks that looked good. I asked them to pour a bit of brandy into the coffee, to lift the spirits."

"Thanks. Let me know what I owe you."

"It's all included in the fare, full board. Go on, eat a bit. It will do you good."

They had their breakfast in silence, inside the car. Alicia wasn't hungry, but she knew she needed to eat. Every time another one of those heavy-duty trucks went by, the rearview mirror vibrated and the whole car shook.

"Where are we?"

"Ten kilometers outside Madrid. A couple of delivery-van drivers told me there are Civil Guard controls at most of the entrances of the main roads coming from the east, so I thought we could make a detour and go in through the Casa de Campo road or through Moncloa."

"And why would we do that?"

"I don't know. It just occurred to me that a Barcelona taxi entering Madrid at seven o'clock in the morning might attract attention. Because it's yellow, that's all. And we two make a bit of an odd couple, no offense. But you're the boss."

Alicia finished her coffee in one gulp. The brandy burned like gasoline, but warmed her bones a little. The taxi driver was looking at her out of the corner of his eye. Alicia hadn't paid much attention to him until then. He was younger than he seemed, with reddish hair and pale skin. His glasses were held together over the nose bridge with insulating tape, and he still looked like a teenager.

"What's your name?" asked Alicia.

"Mine?"

"No. The taxi's."

"Ernesto. My name is Ernesto."

"Do you trust me, Ernesto?"

"Are you trustworthy?"

"Up to a point."

"I see. Do you mind if I ask you a rather personal question?" said the taxi driver. "You don't have to answer if you don't want to."

"Fire ahead. What's on your mind?"

"That's what's on my mind, actually. Firing. Earlier, when we left Guadalajara, we took a sharp bend, and all the stuff in your bag ended up on the back seat. As you were asleep, I didn't want to bother you, and I put it all back . . ."

Alicia sighed, nodding. "And you saw that I'm carrying a gun."

"Well, yes. And it didn't look much like a water pistol, although, quite frankly, I'm no expert on the subject."

"If that makes you feel more at ease, you can drop me off here. I'll pay you what we agreed, and then I'll ask one of your truck-driver friends in there to drive me up to Madrid. I'm sure one of them will agree."

"I haven't the slightest doubt about that, but I wouldn't feel too happy about it."

"Don't worry about me. I can handle myself."

"No, I'm not worried about you. I'm worried about the truck drivers, to be honest. I'll take you, which is what we'd agreed, and no more discussions." Ernesto started the car and pressed both hands on the wheel. "Where are we going?"

*

They found a city shrouded in fog. A wave of mist crept over the towers and domes crowning the rooftops on Gran Vía. Veils of metallic steam wafted through the streets, wrapping themselves around cars and buses that were trying to advance with their headlights barely scratching the fog. The traffic moved forward slowly, blindly, and the figures of pedestrians on the pavements looked like frozen ghosts.

When they drove past the Hotel Hispania, her official residence during those past years, Alicia looked up to gaze at what had been her window. They continued advancing through central Madrid under that shroud of darkness, until the silhouette of Neptune's fountain rose before them.

"Where now?" asked Ernesto.

"Keep going until Lope de Vega, turn right, and then go up along Duque de Medinaceli, which is the first street."

"Weren't you going to the Hotel Palace?"

"We're going to the back of the hotel. The kitchen entrance."

The taxi driver nodded and followed her instructions. The streets were almost deserted. The Gran Hotel Palace took up an entire block shaped like a trapezoid, a city in itself. He drove around the perimeter until they came to a corner where Alicia asked him to park behind a van from which men were unloading boxes with bread loaves, fruit, and other food supplies.

Ernesto lowered his head to look up at the monumental facade.

"Here you are. As promised," she said.

The driver turned around to find a wad of notes in Alicia's hand. "Wouldn't you rather I waited for you?"

Alicia didn't reply.

"Because you are coming back, aren't you?"

"Take the money."

The driver hesitated.

"You're making me waste my time. Take the money."

Ernesto accepted his pay.

"Count it."

"I trust you."

"It's up to you."

Ernesto watched her as she pulled something out of her bag and then slipped it under her jacket. He was sure it wasn't a lipstick.

"Listen, I don't like this. Why don't we leave?"

"You're the one who's leaving, Ernesto. As soon as I get out, return to Barcelona and forget you ever saw me."

The taxi driver felt his stomach shrink. Alicia put her hand on his shoulder, pressed it affectionately, and stepped out of the car. A few seconds later Ernesto saw her vanish into the Gran Hotel Palace.

4

THE HEART OF the grand hotel was already working full tilt as it coped with the first breakfast sitting. An army of cooks, kitchen boys, and waiters came in and out of the kitchen areas and tunnels, pushing trolleys or carrying trays. Alicia edged around the commotion with its aroma of coffee and a thousand delights, receiving a few surprised looks, although everyone was too busy to focus on what was obviously a lost guest or, more likely, a luxury courtesan slipping out discreetly at the end of her work shift. Because of this code of invisibility that prevails in all luxury hotels, Alicia was able to play that card unabashed until she reached the service elevators. She stepped into the first one, which she shared with a maid carrying towels and bars of soap who looked her up and down with a mixture of curiosity and envy. Alicia gave her a friendly smile, as if to imply that they both walked on the same side of the street.

"So early?" asked the maid.

"Early bird catches the worm."

The maid nodded shyly. She got out on the fourth floor. When the doors closed and the elevator continued up to the last floor, Alicia pulled out the bunch of keys from her handbag and looked for the golden one Leandro had given her two years earlier. "It's a master key.

It opens all the rooms of the hotel. Including mine. Make good use of it. Never enter a place if you don't know what awaits you."

*

The service elevator opened onto a small hidden passage next to the cleaners' cupboards and laundry rooms. Alicia hurried down the passage to the door that led into the main corridor, which went around the entire floor. She opened it cautiously. Leandro's suite was on one of the corners hanging over Plaza de Neptuno. She stepped into the corridor and walked toward the suite. On the way she passed a guest who was returning to his room, probably after having had his breakfast. He smiled politely. Alicia smiled back. When she rounded the bend in the corridor, she saw the door to Leandro's suite. There were no bodyguards posted outside the entrance. Leandro hated that type of display; he'd always advocated discretion and an absence of melodrama. But Alicia knew that at least two of his men must be nearby, either in a neighboring room or going through the hotel, at that very moment. She reckoned she had, at best, five to ten minutes.

Pausing in front of the door to the suite, she looked right and left, then quietly put the key in the lock and turned it gently. The door opened, and Alicia slipped inside. She locked the door behind her and stood there for a few seconds, leaning her back against it. A small entrance hall led to a corridor at the end of which was the oval room, set beneath the dome of one of the towers. Leandro had been living there as far back as she could remember. She crept toward the room, her hand resting on the weapon in her belt. The room was in semidarkness. The door to the suite's bedroom was ajar, projecting a shaft of light. Alicia heard water running and a whistling she knew well. She walked across the oval room to the door and opened it wide. At the far end was the bed, empty and unmade. To the left was the bathroom door, which was open, letting out a delicate vapor scented with soap. Alicia stopped in the doorway.

His back to her, Leandro was shaving meticulously in front of the mirror. He wore a scarlet bathrobe and matching slippers. The bath, full of steaming water, waited on one side. A radio murmured a tune that Leandro was whistling. Alicia met his eyes in the mirror, and he smiled warmly, without a hint of surprise.

"I've been expecting you for days. You will have noticed that I told the boys to get out of the way."

"Thanks."

Leandro turned and wiped the foam off his face with a towel. "I was thinking of them. I know you've never liked teamwork. Have you had breakfast? Shall I order something for you?"

Alicia shook her head. She pulled out the pistol and pointed it at his belly. Leandro poured a bit of aftershave on his hands and massaged his face.

"I take it that's poor Hendaya's weapon. Good thinking. I suppose it's pointless to ask you where we can find him. I'm only saying this because he had a wife and children."

"Have a look in a tin of cat food."

"That's my girl. Shall we sit down?"

"We're fine here."

Leandro leaned against the dressing table. "As you wish. What's up?"

Alicia hesitated for a moment. The easiest thing would be to shoot now. Empty the gun and try to get out of there alive. With luck she would reach the service stairs. Who knows, perhaps she would make it to the lobby before being shot down.

Leandro, as usual, read her thoughts. He gave her a look of compassion and paternal affection as he slowly shook his head. "You should never have left me. You don't know how much your betrayal has hurt me."

"I have never betrayed you."

"Please, Alicia. You know perfectly well that you've always been my favorite. My masterpiece. You and I are made for one another. We're the perfect team."

"Is that why you sent that vermin to kill me?"

"Rovira?"

"Was that his name?"

"Sometimes. He was meant to be your substitute. I only sent him so he could learn from you and watch you. He admired you a lot. He'd been studying you for two years. Every dossier. Every case. He said you were the best. My mistake was to think that perhaps he could take your place. Now I've come to accept that nobody can replace you."

"Not even Lomana?"

"Ricardo never really understood his role. He would volunteer uncalled-for judgments and poke his nose where he shouldn't, when all that was required of him was brute force. He confused his loyalties. Nobody can survive in this business without being clear about where those lie."

"And where do yours lie?"

Leandro shook his head.

"Why don't you come back to me, Alicia? Who will take care of you like me? I know you as if you were my flesh and blood. I just have to look at you to know that right now pain is eating you raw, but you haven't taken anything because you want to stay alert. I look into your eyes, and I see you're afraid. Afraid of me. And that hurts. It hurts so much . . ."

"If you want a pill, or even the entire bottle, it's all yours."

Leandro smiled sadly, muttering under his breath. "I admit that I was wrong. And I apologize. Is that what you want? Because if you like, I'll go down on my knees. I'm not embarrassed. Your betrayal hurt me a great deal—it blinded me. Me, the one who's always taught you that one should never make decisions in anger, pain, or fear. You see, I'm human too, Alicia."

"You're going to make me cry."

Leandro's smile now betrayed malice. "Do you see how, deep down, we're the same? Where will you be better off than by my side? I have grand plans for us. I've been thinking a lot these past few weeks, and I've understood why you want to leave this. Moreover, I've realized that I want to leave it too. I'm sick and tired of cleaning up after incompetent idiots. You and I are made for other things."

"Oh, are we?"

"Well, of course. Or did you imagine we would always be dealing with other people's messes? That's over. I've set my sights on something far more important. I'm also leaving all this behind. And I need you to be by my side, I need you to come with me. Without you, I can't do it. You know what I'm talking about, don't you?"

"I haven't a clue."

"I'm talking about politics. This country is going to change. Sooner or later. The General won't last forever. New blood is needed. People with ideas. People who know how to manage the world out there."

"Like you."

"Like you and like me. You and I, together, can do great things for this country."

"Such as murdering innocent people and stealing their children to sell them?"

Leandro sighed, a look of annoyance spreading over his face. "Don't be naive, Alicia. Those were other times."

"Was it your idea, or Valls's?"

"Does it matter?"

"It matters to me."

"It was nobody's idea. It's simply the way things happened. Ubach and his wife took a fancy to Mataix's daughters. Valls saw an opportunity. And then came others. It was a time for opportunities. And there's no supply without demand. I just concentrated on doing what I had to do and making sure the matter didn't escape Valls's control."

"It looks like he didn't quite pull it off."

"Valls is a greedy man. Unfortunately greedy people never know when it's time to stop abusing their position, so they force things until they blow up. That's why, sooner or later, they fall."

"Is he still alive, then?"

"Alicia . . . What do you want from me?"

"The truth."

Leandro laughed to himself. "The truth? You and I know such a thing doesn't exist. The truth is an agreement that allows innocent people not to have to cope with reality."

"I haven't come here to listen to your book of quotations."

Leandro's look hardened. "No, you've come here to poke around where you know you mustn't. As you always do. To complicate everything. Because that's how you do everything. That's why you left me. That's why you betrayed me. That's why you come here now to talk to me about truth. Because you want me to tell you that yes, you're better than me, better than all this."

"I'm not better than anyone else."

"Of course you are. That's why you've always been my favorite. That's why I want you back by my side. Because this country needs to have people like you and like me. People who know how to control it. How to keep it in line, and calm, so it doesn't all turn into a sack full of rats again, living to feed their hatred, their envy, and their spiteful anger, rats who eat one another alive. You know I'm right. You know that even though we're always being blamed for everything, without us this country would go to hell. What do you say?"

Leandro gazed at her at length and, when he didn't get a reply, walked over to the bathtub. He turned his back to her and removed his robe. Alicia looked at his naked body, pale like the belly of a fish. He grabbed the golden bar on the marble wall and slowly immersed himself in the bath. Once he was lying in the tub, the steam caressing his face, he opened his eyes with a hint of sadness.

"Everything should have been different, Alicia, but we're children of our time. Deep down, it's almost better this way. I always knew it would be you."

Alicia let the gun drop.

"What are you waiting for?"

"I'm not going to kill you."

"Then why have you come?"

"I don't know."

"Of course you know."

"What are you doing?"

Leandro stretched out a hand to the telephone extension hanging from the bathtub wall. Alicia aimed at him again.

"You know what this is like, Alicia. . . . Operator. Yes. Put me through to the Ministry of the Interior. Gil de Partera. Yes. Leandro Montalvo. I'll wait. Thank you."

"Put the phone down. Please."

"I can't do that. The order never was to save Valls. The order was to find him and silence him, so that none of this sad business would come out in the open. And we were on the point, once again, of crowning the mission with success. But you didn't listen to me. That's why now, much against my will, I'm going to have to order the death of all those people you have involved in your adventure. Daniel Sempere, his wife, and all his family, including that fool who works for them, and all those to whom, in your crusade for redemption, you've had the ill-fated idea of blurting out what they should never have known. You've wanted it this way. Fortunately you've led us to them. As usual, even when you don't try, you're the best. Operator? Yes, Minister. Same here. That's right. I have news—"

One shot was enough. The receiver slipped from Leandro's hand and fell on the floor by the bathtub. His head tilted to one side as he bestowed upon her a look poisoned with affection and longing. A scarlet cloud spread under the water, masking the reflection of his body. Alicia stood there, motionless, watching as he bled with every throb, until his pupils dilated and his smile froze into a mocking grin.

"I'll wait for you," he whispered. "Don't be long."

A second later the body slid slowly, and Leandro Montalvo's face sank into the blood-filled water, its eyes still open wide.

5

ALICIA PICKED THE receiver up and put it to her ear. The line wasn't connected. Leandro had not called anyone. She pulled out the bottle of pills and swallowed a couple, chewing them and mixing them with a gulp of expensive brandy Leandro kept in a small cabinet in the sitting room. Before leaving the suite, she cleaned Hendaya's gun thoroughly and dropped it on the carpet.

The walk down to the staff passage seemed interminable. Two of the elevators were coming up, so she used the stairs, walking down as fast as possible. Once again she made her way through the tangle of corridors around the kitchen area. Finally she was on the last stretch to the exit, convinced that at any moment she would feel the bullet hit her back and fall headlong, to die like a rat in the tunnels of the Gran Hotel Palace basement, the court of the Scarlet Prince.

Out on the street, a gust of sleet brushed her face. She stopped for a moment to recover her breath. The taxi driver was still standing by the cab, in the same place he'd dropped her, waiting anxiously. As soon as Ernesto saw her, he ran toward her and, without saying a word, grabbed her arm and led her to the cab. He sat her in the passenger seat and hurried across to take the wheel.

Sirens could already be heard in the distance when the engine started and the taxi glided off toward Carrera de San Jerónimo. As they drove past the main entrance to the Palace, at least three black cars were parked outside the hotel doors. A number of men were running inside, pushing aside anyone they met on their way. The taxi driver continued calmly, pressed the indicator, and melted into the traffic driving downhill toward Recoletos. Once they were there, hidden in a swarm of cars, buses, and trams creeping along in the fog, he let out a sigh of relief and for the first time dared to look at Alicia. Tears ran down her face, and her lips were trembling.

"Thanks for waiting for me," she said.

"Are you feeling all right?"

Alicia didn't reply.

"Shall we go home?"

She shook her head. "Not yet. I must make one last stop . . ."

6

THE TAXI CAME to a halt in front of the spiked gates. Ernesto turned off the engine and gazed at the profile of Villa Mercedes peeping through the trees. Alicia was also examining the house, not saying a word. They stayed there for about a minute, allowing the silence that enveloped that place to seep in slowly.

"It looks like there's nobody here," said the taxi driver finally.

Alicia opened the car door.

"Shall I accompany you?" asked Ernesto.

"Wait for me here."

"I'm not going anywhere."

Alicia stepped out of the taxi and walked up to the gates. Before going in, she turned to look at Ernesto, who smiled weakly and raised a hand. He looked petrified with fear.

She slipped through the bars and set off toward the house through the gardens, passing statues, and at one point catching sight of the steam engine through the trees. Only her own footsteps over fallen leaves broke the silence, and there were no signs of life other than a tide of black spiders, scuttling around her feet and dangling from chrysalises stuck to branches on the trees.

At the top of the main staircase, the door to the house stood open. She paused and looked around. The garages were empty. Villa Mercedes gave off a menacing air of devastation and abandonment, as if all its inhabitants had left in the middle of the night, fleeing from a curse. She walked slowly up the steps to the doorway and stepped into the hall.

"Mercedes?"

The echo of her voice vanished into a litany of empty rooms and corridors. Somber passages fanned out on either side. Alicia walked over to the entrance of a grand ballroom into which dead leaves had been blown by the wind. The curtains fluttered in the draft. The blanket of spiders had crept up from the garden and now spread over the white marble tiles.

"Mercedes?" she called again.

Once more her voice became lost in the bowels of the house. A sickly sweet smell was coming from the top of the stairs. She began to walk up, following the trail of scent, which led her to the room at the end of the corridor. She stepped into the room but stopped midway. A cloak of black spiders covered the corpse of Señora Valls. They had begun to devour her.

Alicia ran back into the corridor, opening one of the windows facing the inside patio to let in the fresh air. As she did so, she noticed that all the windows overlooking the atrium were closed, except for one in a corner of the third floor. She walked back to the main staircase and climbed the stairs to the third floor. A long corridor ran off into the gloom. A double white door was visible at the end of the passage. It was ajar.

"Mercedes, it's Alicia. Are you there?"

She approached slowly, scanning for shapes behind curtains, or among the shadows outlined between doorways on either side of the corridor. When she came to the end of the passage, she placed her hands on the door and waited.

"Mercedes?"

She pushed the door inward.

The walls were pale blue, and displayed a constellation of pictures inspired by stories and legends. A castle, a carriage, a princess, and all kinds of fantastic creatures flew across a sky studded with silver stars over the vaulted ceiling. Alicia realized that this was a nursery, a paradise for privileged children, with as many toys as a child could dream of. The two sisters were waiting at the far end of the room.

The bed was white. It was crowned by a wooden headboard carved into the shape of an angel with its wings outstretched, gazing at the room with infinite devotion. Ariadna and Mercedes were dressed in white. They lay on the bed, holding hands, each clasping a red rose against her chest with the other hand. A box holding a syringe and glass phials rested on the bedside table, next to Ariadna.

Alicia could feel her legs trembling, and she had to cling to a chair. She never knew how long she remained there, whether it was barely a minute or an hour. All she remembered was that when she went down the stairs and reached the ground floor, her feet took her to the ballroom. There she went to the fireplace. A box of long matches sat on the mantelpiece. She lit one and began to circle the entire perimeter of the mansion, setting fire to curtains and other fabrics. When she felt the flames raging behind her, she left that house of death. She crossed the garden again without looking back, while Villa Mercedes burned, a black pyre rising to the heavens.

IN PARADISUM

⌁

BARCELONA

FEBRUARY

1960

I

AS HE'D DONE every Sunday since he became a widower, over twenty years before, Juan Sempere rose early, made himself a strong cup of coffee, and put on his Barcelona gentleman's suit and hat to go down to the church of Santa Ana. The bookseller had never been a religious man, unless Alexandre Dumas could be considered an ex cathedra addition to the list of saints. He liked to park himself in the last pew and witness the ceremony in silence. He stood up and sat down out of respect at the priest's indications, but he didn't take part in the chanting, the prayers, or the communion. Since Isabella's death, he and the heavens, not the greatest communicators at the best of times, had little to say to one another.

The parish priest, who was aware of Juan's convictions, or his lack of them, always welcomed him, reminding him that this was his home, whatever he believed. "We each live our faith in our own way," he would say. "But don't quote me, or they'll send me off to the missions, hoping I get eaten by an anaconda." The bookseller always replied that he wasn't a man of faith, but that in that chapel he felt closer to Isabella, if only because it had been the scene of their marriage and her funeral, separated by just five years, the only happy years he remembered having lived.

That Sunday morning, as usual, Juan Sempere sat in the last pew to hear mass and watch how the early birds of the neighborhood—a mishmash of devout women and sinners, lonely people, insomniacs, optimists, and those retired from the business of hope—came together to beseech the Lord, in his infinite silence, to remember them and their fleeting existences. He could see the priest's breath sketching prayers of vapor as he spoke. The congregation listed toward the only gas heater the parish church's budget allowed, but even that appliance, despite the assistance of Madonnas and saints who interceded from their niches, could not work miracles.

The priest was about to consecrate the Holy Host and drink the wine that, in that bitter cold, the bookseller wouldn't have said no to, when he glimpsed out of the corner of his eye a figure sliding down the pew and sitting down next to him. Sempere turned to find his son Daniel, whom he hadn't seen in church since his wedding day. All he needed now was to see Fermín come in holding a missal to decide that in fact his alarm clock had gone on strike, and what he was seeing was just part of a pleasant winter Sunday's dream.

"Everything all right?" asked Juan.

Daniel nodded with a meek smile and turned to look at the priest, who was starting to distribute communion among the parishioners while the organist, a music teacher who made Sunday appearances at various churches in the area and was a customer at the bookshop, played as best he could.

"Judging by the crimes committed against Johann Sebastian Bach, Maestro Clemente's fingers must be frozen stiff this morning," he added.

Daniel nodded again. Sempere gazed at his son, who for some days now had seemed lost in thought. Daniel carried inside him a world of absences and silence that Sempere had never been able to enter. He often recalled that dawn, fifteen years ago, when his son had woken up screaming because he could no longer remember his mother's face. That morning the bookseller had taken him for the first time to the Cemetery of Forgotten Books, perhaps hoping that the place and what it signified might fill the emptiness that losing Isabella had left in their lives. He had watched him grow and become a man, get married, and bring a child into the world, and yet he still woke up every morning fearing for him and wishing Isabella were by his side, to tell him the things he would never be able to say. A parent never sees his children grow old. To a father's eyes, they always seem like those kids who once looked up at him with veneration, convinced that he had the answers to all the mysteries of the universe.

That morning, however, in the half-light of a chapel far from God and from the world, the bookseller looked at his son and for the first time thought that time had begun to pass for him too, that he would never again see the boy who lived only to remember the face of a mother who would never return. Sempere tried to find words with which to tell Daniel that he understood, that he was not alone, but the darkness hanging over his son like a poisoned shadow scared him. Daniel turned toward his father, and Sempere read anger and hatred in his eyes such as he'd never seen, not even in the eyes of old men whose lives had already been condemned to misery.

"Daniel . . . ," he whispered.

His son put his arms around him, hushing him and holding him tight, as if he feared something might snatch him away. The bookseller couldn't see his face, but he knew his son was weeping silently. And for the first time since Isabella had left them, he prayed for him.

2

THE BUS LEFT them at the gates of Montjuïc Cemetery shortly before noon. Daniel took Julián in his arms and waited for Bea to get down first. Never before had they taken the boy there. A cold sun had burned away the clouds, and the sky projected an expanse of metallic blue that seemed out of place with the scenery. They walked through the portal of the city of the dead and began their ascent. The path running along the hillside bordered the old part of the graveyard built at the end of the nineteenth century and was flanked by mausoleums and tombs of theatrical architecture that invoked angels and phantoms wrought in intricate chaos to the greater glory of the vast fortunes and families of Barcelona.

Bea had always detested visiting the city of the dead, where all she saw was a morbid staging of death and a poor attempt at convincing terrified visitors that ancestry and good names persevere even in the hereafter. She deplored the idea that an army of architects, sculptors, and artisans had sold their talents to construct such a sumptuous necropolis and populate it with statues in which the spirits of death leaned over to kiss the foreheads of children born before the days of penicillin, where ghostly damsels were trapped in spells of eternal melancholy, and where inconsolable angels, stretching out over marble tombstones, wept the loss of some rich colonial butcher who had earned both fortune and glory through the slave trade and the bloodstained sugar of the Caribbean islands. In Barcelona, even death dressed up on Sundays. Bea detested that place, but she could never say that to Daniel.

*

Little Julián gazed at all that grotesque carnival of earthly vanities with haunted eyes. He pointed at the figures and labyrinthine structures of the mausoleums with a mixture of fear and amazement.

"They're just statues, Julián," his mother told him. "They can't do anything to you, because there isn't anything here."

As soon as she'd uttered those words, she was sorry. Daniel didn't look as if he'd heard them. He'd barely parted his lips since he'd returned home in the early hours without explaining where he'd been. He'd lain down next to her in the bed, without speaking, but hadn't slept at all.

At daybreak, when Bea asked him what was wrong, Daniel stared at her but said nothing. Then he undressed her angrily. He took her forcibly without looking her in the face, holding down her arms over her head with one hand and brusquely opening her legs with the other.

"Daniel, you're hurting me. Stop, please. Stop."

He ignored her protests and charged at her with a fury Bea couldn't remember, until she freed her hands and stuck her nails into his back. Daniel cried out in pain, and she pushed him to one side with all her strength. As soon as she'd gotten rid of him, Bea jumped out of the bed and covered herself with a dressing gown. She wanted to shout at him, but she withheld her tears. Daniel had curled up into a ball on the bed and was avoiding her eyes.

Bea took a deep breath. "Don't ever do that again, Daniel. Ever. Have you understood? Look at me and answer."

He looked up and nodded. Bea locked herself in the bathroom until she heard the door of the apartment close behind Daniel. An hour later, he came back. He'd bought some flowers.

"I don't want flowers."

"I thought I'd go and visit my mother," said Daniel.

Sitting at the table and holding a cup of milk, little Julián observed his parents and noticed that something wasn't right. You could fool the whole world most of the time, but never Julián, not for a minute, thought Bea.

"Then we'll come with you," she replied.

"You don't have to."

"I said we'll come with you."

*

When they reached the foot of the small hill crowned by a terrace overlooking the sea, Bea stopped. She knew Daniel wanted to visit his mother alone. He tried to hand the child to her, but Julián refused to leave his father's arms.

"Take him with you. I'll wait for you down here."

3

DANIEL KNELT DOWN in front of the headstone and left the flowers next to it. He stroked the letters engraved on the stone:

ISABELLA SEMPERE
1917–1939

He remained there with his eyes closed until Julián started to babble in that incomprehensible tone he adopted when he had something on his mind.

"What's the matter, Julián?"

His son was pointing at something at the foot of the headstone. A small figure peeped through the petals of some dried flowers in the shadow of a glass vase. It looked like a plaster statuette. Daniel was quite sure it hadn't been there the last time he'd visited his mother's grave. He picked it up and examined it. An angel.

Julián, who was staring at the figurine with fascination, leaned over and tried to snatch it. When he did so, the angel slipped, fell on the marble, and broke. It was then that Daniel noticed something sticking out from one of the two halves: a piece of rolled-up paper. He set Julián down and picked up the angel figure. When he unrolled the paper, he recognized Alicia Gris's handwriting:

Mauricio Valls
El Pinar
Calle Manuel Arnús
Barcelona

Julián was looking at Daniel attentively. Daniel kept the piece of paper in his pocket and gave the boy a smile that didn't seem to convince him. He was observing his father the way he did when he had a fever and lay on the sofa. Daniel left a white rose on the gravestone and picked his son up again.

Bea was waiting for them at the foot of the little hill. When he was by her side, Daniel hugged her without saying a word. He wanted to beg her forgiveness for what had happened that morning and for everything else, but couldn't find the words.

Bea's eyes found his. "Are you all right, Daniel?"

He hid behind that smile that hadn't convinced Julián, and convinced Bea even less. "I love you," he said.

That night, after putting Julián to bed, they made love slowly in the half-light. Daniel passed his lips over her body as if he feared it was the last time he'd be able to do so. Then, as they lay in each other's arms, under the blankets, Bea whispered in his ear: "I'd like to have another child. A girl. Would you like that?"

Daniel nodded and kissed her forehead. He went on caressing her until Bea fell asleep. Then he waited for her breathing to turn slow and heavy. He got up quietly, gathered his clothes, and put them on in the dining room. Before leaving, he stopped in front of Julián's bedroom and opened the door a fraction. His son was sleeping peacefully, hugging a cuddly crocodile Fermín had given him, which was twice his size. Julián had christened it "Carlitos," and there was no way he would go to sleep without it, despite all Bea's attempts to substitute for it something more manageable.

Daniel resisted the temptation to go into the bedroom and kiss his son. Julián was a light sleeper and had a particularly sensitive radar for his parents' movements around the house. When he closed the door of the apartment, he wondered whether he would ever see him again.

4

DANIEL JUMPED ONTO the night tram from Plaza de Cataluña just as it was starting the slide along the rails. There were only about half a dozen passengers inside, all hunched up with cold, swaying to the rattling of the tram with their eyes half closed, oblivious to the world. Nobody would remember having seen him there.

For about half an hour the tram climbed up the city streets, meeting hardly any traffic. They went past deserted stops, leaving a trail of blue sparks on the cables and a smell of electricity and burned wood. Every now and then one of the passengers came back to life, staggered to the back exit, and got off without waiting for the tram to stop. During the last stretch of the ascent, from the corner of Vía Augusta and Calle Balmes to Avenida del Tibidabo, Daniel traveled alone with only a lethargic conductor who snoozed on his stool at the back and the driver, a little man joined to the world by a cigar that shed plumes of yellowish smoke smelling of gasoline.

When he reached the final stop, the driver let out a celebratory puff and rang the bell. Daniel stepped out, leaving behind him the amber bubble of light surrounding the tram. In front of him, unfolding toward a vanishing point, was Avenida del Tibidabo, with its parade of mansions and palaces scaling the mountainside. High above, a silent sentinel keeping watch over the city, stood the silhouette of El Pinar. Daniel felt his heart racing. He pulled his coat tight and started walking.

As he went past number 32 in the avenue he looked up to gaze at the old house of the Aldayas from the gate, and was overcome by memories. In that large old house he'd found and almost lost his life an eternity ago—that is to say, a few years back. Had Fermín been with him, he would surely have found a way of improvising some irony about how that avenue seemed to describe his destiny and how only a fool would think of carrying out what he had in mind while his wife and child slept their last night of peace on earth. Perhaps he should have brought Fermín along with him. He would have done everything in his power to stop him, and not allowed him to do anything crazy. Fermín would have come between him and his duty, or simply his dark desire for vengeance. That is why he knew that, that night, he had to face his destiny alone.

When he reached the small square that crowned the avenue, Daniel kept in the shadows. He walked toward the road surrounding the hill above which loomed the dark, angular silhouette of El Pinar. From a distance the house looked as if it was perched in the night sky. Only when one drew closer did one become aware of the size of the estate surrounding it and the huge scale of the building. The grounds—a landscaped mountain—were surrounded by a stone wall that bordered the road. An adjoining villa crowned with a tower guarded the main entrance, whose ornate wrought-iron gate dated from the days when metal work was still an art form. Farther down was another entrance, a stone porch built into the wall with a lintel announcing the name of the mansion. Behind that second entrance, a long maze of steps wound its way up through the gardens. It looked like a long climb. The gate seemed as solid as the one at the main entrance, and Daniel concluded that he'd have to climb the wall, vault over, and reach the house by walking through the trees, hoping he wouldn't be seen. He wondered whether there were any dogs, or hidden guards. From the outside he couldn't see any lights. El Pinar emitted a funereal air of loneliness and neglect.

After a couple of minutes' observation, he chose a point in the wall that seemed more sheltered by the trees. The stone there was damp and slippery, and it took him a few tries before he could reach the top and jump over to the other side. As soon as he'd landed on the blanket of pine needles and fallen branches, he felt the temperature drop around him, as if he'd entered an underground tunnel.

Daniel began to climb stealthily up the hill, stopping every few meters to listen to the murmur of the breeze through the leaves. After a while he reached a stone path that led from the main entrance to the esplanade surrounding the house. He followed it until the facade rose before him. He scanned the area around him, which was enveloped in silence and a dense gloom. If there was anyone else in that place, they had no intention of making their presence known.

The building rested in shadow, the windows dark. The only sounds were those of his own footsteps and the wind whistling through the trees. Even by the faint light of the moon, Daniel could tell that El Pinar had been virtually abandoned for years. He gazed around, puzzled. He'd expected guards, dogs, or some sort of armed surveillance. Perhaps he had secretly been hoping for it—for someone who might try to stop him. There was nobody.

He walked over to one of the large windows and pushed his face against the cracked pane, seeing only darkness inside. He walked around the structure and came to a small patio adjoining a glazed gallery. He peered inside but didn't see any light or movement. Grabbing a stone, he broke a glass pane in the door, then put his hand through the gap and opened it from the inside. The smell of the house embraced him like an old, wicked spirit that had been waiting anxiously for him. He took a few steps forward, and noticed that he was shaking, and still holding the stone in his hand. He didn't let go of it.

The gallery led to a rectangular space that must once have been a formal dining room. Daniel walked through it and into a sitting room with large, intricately shaped windows, from which one could gaze down on the whole of Barcelona, more distant than ever. He went on exploring the house, feeling as if he was walking through the hull of a sunken ship. The furniture was shrouded by a pale murkiness, the walls darkened, the curtains frayed or fallen. At the heart of the house was an inner courtyard, its walls rising to a cracked roof through which beams of moonlight fell like swords of steam. He heard a low sound and a flapping of wings up high. On one side stood a sumptuous marble staircase, more suited to an opera house than a private home. Next to the stairs was an old chapel. The face of a Christ nailed to the cross could be made out in the half-light, tears of blood rolling down his cheeks and an accusatory look in his eyes. Farther on, beyond the doors to various closed rooms, a larger open door seemed to sink into the very bowels of the mansion. Daniel walked over to it and stopped. A light draft brushed his face, and with it came a smell. Wax.

He took a few more steps forward through a corridor and saw a more ordinary-looking staircase, once used, he assumed, by the staff. A few meters farther on, the corridor opened up into an ample room with a table in the middle, and near it, some fallen chairs. It was the old kitchen area, Daniel realized. The smell of wax came from there. A soft flickering light illuminated the surrounding walls and a large dark stain on the table, left by something that had spilled over the edge and splashed on the floor like a liquid shadow. Blood.

"Who goes there?"

The voice sounded almost more scared than Daniel himself. He stopped and searched for cover among the shadows as footsteps slowly approached.

"Who goes there?" came the voice again.

Clutching the stone firmly, Daniel held his breath. A figure loomed, holding a candle in one hand and a shining object in the other. All of a sudden it stopped, as if sensing Daniel's presence. Daniel studied its shadow. A gun trembled in its hand. The figure took a few steps forward, and in a flash Daniel saw the hand holding the weapon cross in front of the doorway where he was hiding.

His fear turned to anger, and before he realized what he was doing, he threw himself on the figure, hitting the hand with the stone as hard as he could. He heard bones cracking, and a howl of pain. The weapon fell to the floor. Daniel hurled himself on the bearer of the gun, unleashing all the fury he'd been holding inside as he beat the figure's face and torso with his bare fists. The figure tried to cover its face and shouted like a terrified animal.

The fallen candle, still burning, had created a pool of wax that now ignited. In its amber light, Daniel saw the panic-stricken face of a fragile-looking man. He stopped, disconcerted. The man, breathing with difficulty, his face covered in blood, looked at him without understanding. Daniel grabbed his gun and pressed the barrel against one of the eyes of the man, who let out a groan.

"Don't kill me, please . . ."

"Where's Valls?"

The man still didn't seem to understand.

"Where's Valls?" Daniel repeated. He could hear the steely tone in his voice, and a hatred he didn't recognize.

"Who is Valls?" stammered the man.

Daniel made as if to hit his face with the gun. The man closed his eyes, trembling, and Daniel suddenly realized he was beating up an elderly person. He retreated and sat down with his back to the wall. Taking a deep breath, he tried to recover his self-control. The old man had curled into a ball and was whimpering.

"Who are you?" Daniel sighed at last. "I'm not going to kill you. I only want to know who you are, and where Valls is."

"The guard," the old man groaned. "I'm the guard."

"What are you doing here?"

"They said they'd come back. They told me to feed him and wait for them."

"Feed who?"

The old man shrugged.

"Valls?"

"I don't know his name. They left this gun with me and ordered me to kill him and throw him into the well if they didn't come back in three days' time. But I'm not a murderer . . ."

"How long ago was this?"

"I don't know. Days ago."

"Who told you he would come back?"

"A police captain. He didn't give me his name. He gave me money. It's yours if you want it."

Daniel shook his head. "Where's that man? Valls."

"Downstairs . . ." The old man pointed to the metal door at the far end of the kitchen.

"Give me the keys."

"Have you come to kill him, then?"

"The keys."

The old man looked in his pockets and handed him a bunch of keys.

"Are you with them? With the police? I've done everything I was told to do, but I couldn't kill him . . ."

"What's your name?"

"Manuel. Manuel Requejo."

"Go home, Manuel."

"I have no home. . . . I live in a shed, back there, in the woods."

"Leave this place."

The old man nodded. He got on his feet with some difficulty, holding on to the table to steady himself.

"I didn't mean to hurt you," Daniel said. "I thought you were someone else."

Avoiding his eyes, the man dragged himself toward the exit.

"You're going to do him a favor," he said.

5

BEHIND THE METAL door was a room in which a few shelves held cans of food. There was an opening on the wall at the far end, and beyond it Daniel thought he could make out a tunnel hollowed out in the stone, descending steeply. As soon as he stuck his head into the opening he was hit by an intense odor rising from underground, an animal stink of excrement, blood, and fear. Covering his face with his hand, he listened through the shadows. A flashlight was hanging on the wall. He switched it on, sending the beam of light into the tunnel. Steps carved out of the rock disappeared into a well of darkness.

He went down slowly. The walls oozed damp, and the ground was slippery. He reckoned he must have descended some ten meters by the time he saw the end of the stairs. There the tunnel widened and spread into a recess the size of a room. The stench was so powerful that it clouded the senses. As he swept through the darkness with the flashlight, he saw the bars separating the two halves of the chamber hollowed in the rock. Daniel shone the beam around the cell without understanding. It was empty. Until he heard the murmur of laborious breathing and noticed a corner with shadows that unfolded into a skeletal silhouette, he didn't realize he'd been mistaken. There was something trapped in there, creeping toward the light, something he had trouble identifying as a man.

Eyes that were burned by the dark, eyes that seemed not to see, veiled by a layer of white. Those eyes were searching him. The silhouette, a tangle of rags covering a bag of bones that was swathed with dried blood, filth, and urine, grabbed one of the bars and tried to stand up. He only had one hand. Where the other one should have been, there was only a festering, burned stump. The creature remained close to the bars, as if he wanted to smell Daniel. Suddenly the creature smiled, and Daniel realized he'd seen the gun he was holding.

Daniel tested various keys in the bunch until he found one that fit into the lock. He opened the cell. The creature inside looked at him expectantly. Daniel recognized in him a pale reflection of the man he'd learned to hate. Nothing remained of his regal face, of his arrogant demeanor and his haughty presence. Someone, or something, had ripped out everything that could be taken from a human being until all that remained was a longing for darkness and oblivion. Daniel raised the gun and aimed it at his face. Valls laughed joyfully.

"You killed my mother."

Valls nodded repeatedly and hugged Daniel's knees. He then groped for the gun with his only hand and pulled it up to his forehead. "Please, please," he beseeched through his tears.

Daniel cocked the hammer. Valls closed his eyes and pressed his face hard against the barrel.

"Look at me, you son of a bitch."

Valls opened his eyes.

"Tell me why."

Valls smiled without understanding. He'd lost a few teeth, and his gums bled. Daniel turned his face away and felt nausea rising to his throat. He closed his eyes and evoked the face of his son Julián, asleep in his bedroom. Then he pulled the gun away, opened the cylinder, letting the bullets fall to the waterlogged floor, and shoved Valls aside.

Valls stared at him, first in confusion, then in a panic, and started picking up the bullets, one at a time, holding them out to Daniel with a trembling hand. Daniel threw the gun to the far end of the cell and grabbed Valls by the neck. A ray of hope lit up Valls's eyes. Daniel held him tight and hauled him out of the cell and up the stairs. When he reached the kitchen area, he kicked open the door and went outside, without ever letting go of Valls, who staggered behind him. He didn't look at him or speak to him. He just pulled him down the garden path until they reached the metal gate. There he looked for the key in the bunch the guard had given him and opened it.

Valls had begun to moan, terrified. Daniel shoved him out into the road. The man fell on the ground, and Daniel grabbed his arm again, pulling him back to his feet. Valls took a few steps and stopped. Daniel kicked him, forcing him to continue. He pushed him until they reached the small square where the first blue tram awaited. Dawn was breaking, the sky unfurling into a reddish cobweb that spread over Barcelona and set the distant sea ablaze. Valls went down on his knees and looked up at Daniel imploringly.

"You're free," said Daniel. "Go!"

Don Mauricio Valls, a shining light of his day, limped away down the avenue.

Daniel stayed there until his silhouette merged into the grayness of that early hour. He sought refuge in the waiting tram, which was empty. Sitting down on one of the benches at the back, he pressed his face against the window and closed his eyes. After a while he dozed off.

When the conductor woke him, a clear sun was already sweeping away the clouds, and Barcelona had a clean smell.

"Where are you going, boss?" asked the conductor.

"Home," said Daniel. "I'm going home."

After a while the tram began its descent. Daniel set his gaze on the horizon extending at the foot of the wide avenue, feeling that there was no resentment left in his soul, and that for the first time in many years he had woken up with the memory that would stay with him for the rest of his days: the face of his mother, a woman who would always be younger than he was now.

"Isabella," he whispered. "I wish I'd been able to know you."

6

THEY SAY THEY saw him arrive at the entrance of the metro station, and that he went down the stairs in search of the tunnels, as if he wanted to crawl back to hell. They say that when passersby saw his rags and noticed the stench he gave off, they moved to one side and pretended not to see him. They say he got into one of the trains and looked for shelter in a corner of the car. Nobody approached him, nobody looked at him, and nobody wanted to admit, later, that they'd seen him.

They say the invisible man wept and moaned in the car, begging for someone to have pity and kill him, but no one would even exchange a glance with such a wreck. They say he wandered all day through the underworld, changing trains, waiting on the platform for another train to take him through the mesh of tunnels hidden beneath the labyrinth of Barcelona, and from that train to the next train, and the next, leading nowhere.

They say that at the end of that afternoon, one of those accursed trains came to a halt at the line's terminus station, and when the beggar refused to get out and showed no signs of hearing the orders being shouted at him by the conductor and the stationmaster, they called the police. As soon as the police officers arrived, they stepped into the carriage and approached the tramp, who didn't respond to their orders either. Only then did one of the policemen get close to him, covering his nose and mouth with his hand. He poked him gently with the barrel of his gun. They say that the body then collapsed, lifeless, on the floor, and the rags covering him opened up to reveal a corpse that seemed to have already begun to decompose.

His only piece of identification was a photograph he held in his hand, showing an unknown young woman. One of the officers took the photograph of Alicia Gris, and for a few years he kept it inside his locker at the police station, convinced that it was none other than Death, who had left her visiting card in the hands of that poor devil before sending him to his eternal damnation.

The funeral services collected the body and transported it to the morgue, where all destitute people ended up, together with unidentified bodies and the abandoned souls the city left behind every night. At dawn, two workers put him into a canvas bag bearing the stench of hundreds of other bodies that had made their last journey inside it, and lifted it into the back of a truck. They drove up the old road bordering Montjuïc Castle, which was outlined against a sea of fire and a thousand silhouettes of angels and spirits in the city of the dead, figures that seemed to have gathered there to spit their last insult at him as he made his way to the common grave where in another life he, the beggar, the invisible man, had sent so many whose names he barely remembered.

When they reached the grave, an endless well of bodies covered with lime, the two men opened the bag and let Don Mauricio Valls slide down the hillside of cadavers until he reached the bottom. They say he fell faceup, his eyes open, and that the last thing the men saw before leaving that forsaken place was a black bird perching on his body and gouging them out with its beak, while all the bells of Barcelona tolled in the distance.

BARCELONA

APRIL 23, 1960

I

CAME THE DAY.

Shortly before dawn, Fermín woke up with his hormones raging. Heeding the call, he descended on an unsuspecting Bernarda and showered her with one of his morning love specials that would leave her exhausted for a week and the bedroom furniture askew, while rousing vigorous protests from the neighbors on the other side of the wall.

"Blame it on the full moon," Fermín apologized to the lady next door, greeting her through the laundry room window overlooking the inner courtyard. "I don't know what comes over me. I seem to be transformed."

"Yes, but instead of transforming into a wolf, you turn into a pig. See if you can't control yourself—there are children living here who haven't yet taken their first communion."

As was usually the case with Fermín in the aftermath of one of his arduous early performances, he felt the appetite of a tiger. He made himself a four-egg omelette with bits of chopped ham and cheese, which he polished off with a half-kilo French loaf and a small bottle of champagne to boot. Satisfied, he crowned it all with a small glass of *orujo* and proceeded to put on the prescribed attire for confronting a day that showed all the signs of possible complications.

"Will you tell me why you've dressed yourself like a diver?" asked Bernarda from the kitchen doorway.

"Out of precaution. In fact it's an old raincoat lined with copies of one of the regime's newspapers. Not even holy water gets through this material. Something to do with the ink they use. They say a big one's coming."

"Today, Sant Jordi's day?"

"The ways of the Lord may be unknowable, but they're often a pain in the butt," Fermín chipped in.

"Fermín, no blaspheming in this house."

"I'm sorry, my love. I'll take the pill for my agnosticism right away, and it will pass."

Fermín wasn't lying. For some time now, a day of countless biblical disasters had been forecast to fall upon Barcelona, city of books and roses, on the day of its most beautiful celebration. The panel of experts had agreed in full: the National Meteorology Service, Radio Barcelona, *La Vanguardia*, and the Civil Guard. The last drop before the proverbial deluge had been added by the well-known fortune teller Madame Carmanyola. The fortune teller was famous for two things. One was her condition as a morbidly obese nymph, which hid the fact that she was really a full-bodied man from Cornellá called Cucufate Brotolí, reborn into a hirsute womanliness—after a long career as a notary—to discover that what she really liked, deep down, was to dress as a tart and shake her rear end to the sensual hand-clapping of flamenco. The other was her infallible gift for weather forecasts. Quality and technical issues aside, the fact of the matter was that they were all in agreement. This Sant Jordi's day was set to rain cats and dogs.

"Well, in that case perhaps you'd better not bring the stall out onto the street," Bernarda advised.

"No way. Don Miguel de Cervantes and his colleague Don Guillermo de Shakespeare didn't die in vain on the same date—strictly speaking—the twenty-third of April. Surely on this day of all days, we booksellers should be up for the challenge. Today we'll be putting books and readers together, even if the ghost of General Espartero bombs us from Montjuïc Castle."

"Will you at least bring me a rose?"

"I'll bring you a cartload of the fullest and most scented ones, my little sugar."

"And remember to give one to Señora Bea. Danielito is a bit of a disaster, and I'm sure he'll forget at the last minute."

"I've been changing the boy's proverbial diapers for too many years now to forget strategic details of such importance."

"Promise me you won't get wet."

"The wetter I get, the more fecund and fertile I'll become."

"Oh, dear God, we'll be going straight to hell."

"All the more reason to make the most of it while we can, my love."

After assaulting his adored Bernarda with an array of kisses, pinches, and cuddles, Fermín stepped out into the street, convinced that at the eleventh hour a miracle would occur, and the sun would appear, as bright as in a Sorolla painting.

On his way he stole the caretaker's newspaper—it served her right for being a gossip and a Fascist sympathizer—and confirmed the latest predictions. They were forecasting thunder, lightning, hailstones the size of crystalized chestnuts, and gale-force winds likely to sweep millions of books and roses into the sea, forming an isle like Sancho Panza's Barataria, stretching as far as the eye could see.

"I wouldn't bet on it," said Fermín, donating the paper to a poor soul who was sleeping it off, wedged in a chair next to the Canaletas kiosk.

Fermín wasn't the only one to have that feeling. Barcelonians are peculiar creatures, never wasting an opportunity to contradict acknowledged truths such as weather maps or Aristotelian logic. That morning, which dawned with a sky the color of the trumpets of death, all the booksellers had gotten up early, ready to bring their bookstands out into the street and if necessary face tornadoes and typhoons.

When he saw the display of camaraderie along the Ramblas, Fermín felt that the optimists would surely triumph that day. "That's what I like to see. Show them what we're made of. Let it pour down, but they won't make us budge."

The florists, armed with an ocean of red roses, had shown no less courage. At 9:00 on the dot, the streets in central Barcelona were all decked out for the great day of books, hoping that the troubling prophecies would not scare away sweethearts, readers, and all the absentminded folk who'd congregated punctually every April 23 since 1930 to celebrate what was, in Fermín's view, the most glorious holiday in the known universe.

At 9:24, as was not to be expected, the miracle occurred.

A SAHARAN SUN drilled through Daniel's bedroom curtains and shutters and slapped him in the face. He opened his eyes and witnessed the marvel in disbelief. Next to him lay Bea's naked back, which he proceeded to lick from her neck all the way down, until she woke up giggling and turned around with a start. Daniel embraced her and kissed her lips slowly, as if he wanted to drink her. Then he moved the sheet aside and took pleasure in gazing at her, caressing her belly with his fingertips until she caught his hand between her thighs and licked his lips with enjoyment.

"It's Sant Jordi. We'll be late."

"I'm sure Fermín has already opened the shop."

"Fifteen minutes," conceded Bea.

"Thirty," replied Daniel.

They ended up with forty-five, give or take a minute.

*

Halfway through the morning, the streets began to liven up. A velvety sun and an electric blue sky draped the city, while thousands of citizens came out into the sunshine to stroll through hundreds of bookstalls set up along pavements and promenades. Señor Sempere had decided to place his stall opposite the bookshop, in the middle of Calle Santa Ana. A number of tables crammed with books displayed their wares in the sunshine. Behind the tables, helping readers, wrapping up books, or simply watching the crowds walk by, was the entire Sempere team. Fermín, who had rid himself of his raincoat, fronted the lineup in his shirtsleeves. Next to him stood Daniel and Bea, minding the accounts and the cash register.

"Where's the promised deluge?" asked Daniel when he joined the ranks.

"On its way to Sicily, where they need it more. Hey, Daniel, you're looking pretty roguish this morning. I guess spring is in the air . . ."

Señor Sempere, together with Don Anacleto—who always joined them as a support troop and was a deft hand at wrapping books—sat on chairs and recommended titles to the undecided. Sofía fired up young men who went over to the stall to check her out and ended up buying something. Next to her, Fernandito smoldered with jealousy and a little pride. Even the neighborhood watchmaker, Don Federico, and his occasional paramour, Merceditas, had come along to help.

The person who most enjoyed it all, however, was little Julián, who delighted in watching the parade of people carrying books and roses. Standing on a box next to his mother, he helped her count the coins while he polished off the Sugus reserves he'd found in the pockets of Fermín's raincoat. At some point in the middle of the day, Daniel stood there, looking at him and smiling. Julián hadn't seen his father in such a good mood for ages. Perhaps now that shadow of sadness that had followed him for so long would go away, just like those storm clouds that everyone was talking about and nobody had seen. Sometimes, when the gods aren't looking and destiny loses its way, even good people get a taste of good luck in their lives.

3

DRESSED IN BLACK from head to toe, her eyes hidden behind sunglasses that reflected a crowded Calle de Santa Ana disappearing into the distance, Alicia took a few steps forward. She sheltered under the arches of a front door and furtively observed the Sempere family as they sold books, chatted with passersby, and enjoyed that special day in a way she knew she never would.

She smiled when she saw Fermín snatch books from gullible readers and change them for others; when she saw Daniel and Bea brush against one another and exchange glances in a language that filled her with envy but that she knew she didn't deserve; or Fernandito entranced with his Sofía, and Grandfather Sempere gazing at his family and friends with satisfaction. She would have liked to walk up to them and say hello. Tell them they no longer had anything to fear, and thank them for having let her enter their lives, even if just for a short time. She wanted, more than anything in the world, to be one of them, but taking that memory with her would be reward enough. She was about to leave when she encountered a look that made time stop.

Little Julián was staring at her, a sad smile on his face, as if he could read her thoughts. The boy raised a hand, waving good-bye. Alicia returned the gesture. A moment later, she had disappeared.

"Who are you waving to, sweetheart?" asked Bea when she saw her son looking hypnotized, his eyes riveted on the crowd.

Julián turned to look at his mother, and reached for her hand. Fermín had come over to stock up on the Sugus reserve, which he naively thought was still in his raincoat, and found his pockets empty. He'd turned to look at Julián, ready to raise hell, when he too noticed the boy's expression and followed his enraptured glance.

*

Alicia.

Fermín felt her in her absence, with no need to see her, and blessed the heavens, or whoever had taken those clouds to other pastures, for having returned her to him one more time. Perhaps Bernarda was right after all, and in this lousy world, sometimes, some things did end the way they should.

He grabbed his raincoat and leaned toward Bea, who was just accepting payment for a whole set of Sir Arthur Conan Doyle books from a young boy with very thick glasses.

"Listen, boss, Junior here has cleared out my ammo, and my blood sugar has plunged to Russian Revolution levels. In view of the fact that everyone here, except for that halfwit Merceditas, is overqualified for the job at hand, I'm going off to see if I find some quality confectioner's to top up my provisions. And while I'm out and about, I'll buy a rose for Bernarda."

"I have some roses reserved at the florists by the entrance to the church," said Bea.

"What you don't think of . . ."

Bea watched him hurry off and frowned.

"Where's Fermín going?" asked Daniel.

"God knows . . ."

4

HE FOUND HER at the far end of the docks, sitting on a suitcase. She was smoking in the sun, watching a crew loading trunks and boxes onto a liner that cast its whiteness over the waters of the port. He settled down next to her. They sat in silence for a while, enjoying each other's company without having to say anything.

"Big suitcase," he said at last. "And there was I thinking that of all women, you must be the only one who knows how to travel light."

"It's easier to leave bad memories behind than good shoes."

"Well, as I've only got one pair . . ."

"You're an ascetic."

"Who collected them for you? Fernandito? The rascal, he's certainly learning to keep things to himself."

"I made him swear he wouldn't say anything."

"How did you bribe him? With a French kiss?"

"Fernandito only has kisses for Sofía, and so it should be. I've handed him the keys of the flat, so he can live there and sin at will."

"We'll leave that piece of information away from Señor Sempere's ears. He's the girl's legal guardian."

"Good idea."

Alicia looked at him. Fermín became lost in those feline eyes, deep and unfathomable. A well of darkness. She took his hand and kissed it.

"Where on earth were you?" asked Fermín.

"Here and there. Tying up loose ends."

"Around someone's neck?"

Alicia proffered an icy smile. "There were things that had to be resolved. Stories to piece together. I've been doing my job."

"I thought you'd retired."

"I only wanted to leave my slate clean," she said. "I don't like leaving things unfinished."

"And weren't you going to come and say good-bye?"

"You know that I'm not one for farewells, Fermín."

"It would have been good to know that you were still alive and in one piece."

"Did you doubt it?"

"I had my moments of weakness. It's age. One starts feeling uneasy, seeing the sharks circling. They call it composure."

"I was going to send you a postcard."

"Where from?"

"I haven't decided yet."

"I have a feeling this liner isn't off to the Costa Brava."

Alicia shook her head. "No. It's going a bit further."

"That's what I thought. Seems like a very long ship to me. May I ask you a question?"

"So long as it has nothing to do with the journey's end . . ."

"Is the Sempere family safe? Daniel, Bea, the granddad, Julián?"

"It is now."

"And to what hell did you have to descend to make sure innocent people are able to live in peace, or at least in placid ignorance?"

"To none that wasn't already on my path, Fermín."

"Those cigarettes smell good. They look expensive. Of course. You've always had a taste for fine, beautiful things. My tastes lie more on the ordinary side, and I like to watch my pennies."

"Would you like one?"

"Why not? In the absence of Sugus, one must find a way to feed the monkey. The fact is, I haven't smoked a cigarette since the war, when they were made out of butts and peed-on grass. I'm sure the product has improved."

Alicia lit a cigarette and handed it to Fermín. He admired the lipstick mark on the filter before taking a drag.

"Are you going to tell me what really happened?"

"Do you really want to know, Fermín?"

"I have a condition that prompts me to want to know the truth at all times. You can't imagine the amount of distress this ailment brings to those of us who could otherwise live so content in a state of blissful ignorance."

"It's a very long story, and I have a boat to catch."

"You must have a bit of time left to enlighten a poor ignorant fool before weighing anchor."

"Are you sure you want me to tell you?"

"I'm like that."

For almost an hour, Alicia told him everything she could remember, from her days in the orphanage and on the streets to when she began to work at the orders of Leandro Montalvo. She told him about her years under Leandro, about how she'd ended up believing she'd lost her soul along the way, never suspecting it was hidden inside her, and about her refusal to continue working for him. "Valls's case was supposed to be my passport to freedom, my last assignment."

"But there never is such a thing, is there?"

"No, of course not. You're only free up to the point where you ignore the truth."

Alicia told him about the meeting at the Gran Hotel Palace with Gil de Partera, and the assignment she and Captain Vargas, her imposed work partner, had been given: to help uncover the pieces of an investigation that was going nowhere.

"My mistake was not to realize that the assignment was a deception. From the start. In fact, nobody wanted to save Valls. He'd made too many enemies. And too many blunders. He'd broken the rules of the game by abusing his privileges and endangering the safety of his accomplices. When the trail of his crimes turned back on him, they abandoned him. Valls thought there was a conspiracy to murder him, and he wasn't altogether wrong. But he'd left so much blood on his path, he no longer knew where the bullet would come from. For years he thought the ghosts of his past had returned to get revenge on him—Salgado or his Prisoner of Heaven, David Martín, so many others . . . What he didn't suspect was that those who really wanted to finish him off were the ones he thought were his friends and protectors. When you're in power, nobody stabs you face-to-face, always in the back and with an embrace. Nobody at the top wanted to save him or find him. They just wanted to ensure that he would disappear, and that the trail of all the things he'd done would be permanently erased. There were too many hands implicated. Vargas and I were simply tools. That is why, in the end, we too had to disappear."

"But my Alicia has more lives than a cat and was able to dodge the Grim Reaper once more . . ."

"By the skin of my teeth. I think I've already spent all the lives I had left, Fermín. It's time I also left the stage."

"May I tell you that I'll miss you?"

"If you're going to get sentimental on me, I'll chuck you into the water."

The ship sounded its horn, spreading its echo throughout the entire port. Alicia stood up.

"Can I help you with the suitcase? I promise to stay on dry land. Pleasure boating brings me bad memories."

He went with her as far as the gangway, where the last passengers were already filing through. Alicia showed her ticket to the boatswain who, thanks to a generous tip, told a porter to carry the lady's suitcase to her cabin.

"Will you come back to Barcelona one day? This city is bewitched, you know. It gets under your skin and never lets go . . ."

"You'll have to look after her for me, Fermín. And Bea, and Daniel and Señor Sempere and Bernarda, and Fernandito and Sofía, and above all yourself and little Julián, who one day will make us all immortal."

"I like that. The bit about being immortal, especially now that my bones are beginning to creak."

Alicia put her arms tightly around Fermín and kissed him on the cheek. He knew she was crying, and didn't want to look her in the face. Neither of them were going to lose their dignity just when they were about to get away with it.

"Don't even think of standing here bidding me farewell from the dock," warned Alicia.

"Don't worry."

Fermín lowered his eyes as Alicia's footsteps disappeared up the gangway. He turned around without looking up and set off walking, his hands in his pockets.

He found Daniel at the end of the dock, sitting with his legs dangling over the edge. They exchanged glances, and Fermín sighed.

He sat down beside Daniel. "I thought I'd managed to give you the slip."

"It's that new cologne you drench yourself in. I could even trail you in the fish market. What did she tell you?"

"Alicia? Stories to keep one awake at night."

"You might like to share them."

"Some other day. I'm an expert when it comes to insomnia and I don't recommend it."

Daniel shrugged. "I think the advice comes a bit too late."

The echo of a ship's horn flooded the port. Daniel tipped his chin toward the liner as it cast off and began to pull away from the quayside. "Those are the ones that go to America."

Fermín nodded.

"Fermín, do you remember, years ago, when we used to come and sit down here, and we'd solve the world's problems?"

"That was when we thought they could still be solved."

"I still think they can be."

"Because deep down you're still a kid, even if you shave now."

They stayed there, watching the liner cutting through the reflection of the whole of Barcelona across the waters of the port, its wake of white foam breaking up the greatest mirage in the world. Fermín didn't look away until the stern of the ship was lost in the sea mist that swept through the mouth of the port, escorted by a flock of seagulls.

Daniel gazed at him pensively. "Are you all right, Fermín?"

"As fierce as a bull."

"Well, I don't think I've ever seen you look so sad."

"That's because you need to have your eyes checked."

Daniel didn't insist. "What do you say? Shall we get going? What if I treat you to a few glasses of bubbly at the Xampanyet, just like old times?"

"Thanks, Daniel, but I think I'll say no today."

"Don't you remember? Life is waiting for us . . ."

Fermín smiled, and for the first time, Daniel realized that his old friend didn't have a single hair on his head that wasn't gray.

"It's waiting for you, Daniel. Memories are all I have waiting for me."

Daniel pressed his arm affectionately and left him alone with his memories and his conscience.

"Don't be long," he said.

1964

EVERY TIME HIS son Nicolás asked him how one became a good journalist, Sergio Vilajuana replied with the same maxim: "A good journalist is like an elephant: he has a good nose, good ears, and above all, he never forgets."

"What about the tusks?"

"He's got to take care of those, because there's always some well-armed individual who wants to take them from him."

That morning, like every other morning, Vilajuana had taken his youngest son to school before heading for the editing room of *La Vanguardia*. The stroll helped him to sort out his ideas before delving into the maelstrom of the newsroom to battle with the topics of the day. On arriving at the newspaper's headquarters on Calle Pelayo, he came across Jenaro, an office boy who for the last fifteen years had been trying to persuade the editor to admit him into the sports section as an unpaid trainee, a maneuver by which he hoped to be allowed into the president's box at the Barcelona Soccer Club, the great ambition of his life.

"That will be the day you learn to read and write, Jenaro," the editor in chief, Mariano Carolo, would always say. "Miracles don't happen even in Lourdes, and at this rate, unless you go there to mop the floor, they won't even let you into the box to watch a children's qualifying round."

As soon as he saw him come through the door, Jenaro went up to Vilajuana with a serious expression.

"Señor Vilajuana, the censor from the ministry is waiting for you," he murmured.

"Again? Have these people nothing better to do?"

Vilajuana peered into the newsroom from the doorway and located the unmistakeable silhouette of his favorite censor, a slick-haired individual with a pear-shaped body who was standing guard by his desk.

"Ah, by the way, a parcel came for you," said Jenaro. "I don't think it's a bomb, because it fell on the floor and we're still in one piece."

Vilajuana picked up the parcel and decided to do a U-turn and avoid the censor's visit. The man was a bore. He'd been trying for weeks to corral Vilajuana and tell him off about an article he'd written on the Marx brothers that, the censor argued, constituted an apologia for an international Communist conspiracy.

*

He walked over to a bar in the darkest corner of Calle Tallers, nicknamed the Filthy Arms by the journalists, cabaret artistes, and assorted fauna native to the northern tip of the Raval quarter who frequented it. After ordering a coffee, he took cover at a table in the far back, where not a single ray of sunlight had ever penetrated. He sat down and examined the parcel. It was a padded envelope, reinforced with wrapping tape and addressed to him at *La Vanguardia*. The stamp, half erased by the vagaries of the post, was from the United States of America. The sender's address simply read:

A.G. 🐚

Next to the initials was a design identical to the spiral staircase that appeared on the covers of all Víctor Mataix's novels in the *Labyrinth of the Spirits* series.

Vilajuana opened the envelope and pulled out a wad of documents tied together with string. Under the knot he saw a card with the letterhead of the Algonquin Hotel in New York, which read as follows:

A good journalist will know how to find the story that needs to be told . . .

Vilajuana frowned and untied the knot. After unfolding the bundle of papers on the table, he tried to decipher the resulting confusion of lists, cuttings, photographs, and handwritten notes. It took him a couple of minutes to understand what he was staring at.

"Good God," he whispered.

That afternoon, Vilajuana sent a message saying he'd caught a highly infectious virus that turned the entire digestive system into a minefield and would not be able to come in all week for fear of condemning the entire team to a constant pilgrimage to the toilet. By Thursday, Mariano Carolo, who could smell a rat, turned up at Vilajuana's home carrying a roll of toilet paper.

"Forewarned is forearmed," he said.

Vilajuana sighed and let Carolo in. The editor made his way to the sitting room. When he saw the entire wall covered in papers, he got closer and ran his eyes over it. "Is this what I think it is?" he asked after a while.

"I'd say it's only the beginning."

"And what is your source?"

"I wouldn't know where to begin."

"I see. Is it reliable, at least?"

"I believe so."

"I suppose you're aware that if we publish something like this, they'll close down the newspaper, you and I will end up teaching grammar in some forsaken backwater village, and our dear owner and publisher will have to exile himself to some hard-to-get-to mountainous country in central Europe."

"I'm well aware."

Carolo looked anxiously at Vilajuana and rubbed his stomach. Since he'd become the paper's editor, he developed ulcers even in his dreams. "And there was I, so content with being the Catalan Noël Coward," he murmured.

"The truth is, I don't know what to do," said Vilajuana.

"Do you have a lead?"

"Yes, there's a trail I can follow."

"OK. This is what we're going to do. I'll say you're preparing a series of features on a relatively unexplored aspect of the Generalissimo: his secret but sublime work as screenwriter."

"Hollywood's greatest loss."

"What a magnificent headline. Keep me informed. I give you two weeks."

Vilajuana spent the rest of the week analyzing the documents and organizing them in a tree diagram. When he stared at it, he felt as if the tree was just one among many, and that beyond the four walls of that room a whole forest awaited him. Once he'd digested the documentation and its implications, the question was whether to follow the trail or not.

Alicia had provided him with almost all the pieces of the puzzle. The rest depended on him. After a couple of sleepless nights, he made up his mind. His first stop was the Civil Registry, a cavernous building beached in front of the port, home to a purgatory of archives and bureaucrats that seemed to have blended together in perfect symbiosis. He spent a few days there, delving into a chasm of files without finding anything. He was beginning to think that Alicia's trail was a false one when, on the fifth day, he bumped into an old doorman on the point of retirement who spent his time stuck to a transistor radio, listening avidly to league matches and phone-in programs in a broom cupboard full of mops and provisions. The new crop of civil servants referred to him as Methuselah because he was the only one to have survived the last administrative purge. The new centurions, more polished and better trained than their predecessors, were doubly hermetic, and none would explain to him why, however hard he tried, he couldn't find the registry books for death and birth certificates in the city of Barcelona before 1944.

"That's from before the system change," was the only answer he ever got.

Methuselah, who always managed to push his broom under Vilajuana's feet while the journalist was trying to navigate through folders and boxes of documents, finally took pity on him. "What in heaven's name are you looking for, my good man?"

"I'm beginning to think it's the Holy Shroud."

Thanks to a few coins and the companionship generated by ostracism, Methuselah ended up telling him that, in fact, what he was looking for was not papers but a person.

"Doña María Luisa. Things were different when she ran things around here. Don't get me started."

The attempts at finding this Doña María Luisa ran smack into the same wall.

"That person has retired," the new director told him, in a tone that implied that if he knew what was good for him, he'd leave the matter well alone and take a walk along La Barceloneta to enjoy the views.

It took a couple of weeks to locate her. María Luisa Alcaine lived near Plaza Real in a tiny apartment at the top of a block of flats with no elevator and no hope of having one, surrounded by dovecotes and unfinished terraced roofs, with boxes of papers piled up from floor to ceiling. The years of retirement had not been kind to her. The woman who opened the door looked vanquished.

"Doña María Luisa Alcaine?"

"Who are you?"

Vilajuana had anticipated the question and prepared an answer, which he hoped would keep that door open, even if only for a few seconds.

"My name is Sergio Vilajuana, and I'm a journalist working for *La Vanguardia*. I've been sent to see you by a friend of an old acquaintance of yours, Captain Vargas. Do you remember him?"

Doña María Luisa gave a deep sigh and turned around, leaving the door open behind her. She clearly lived alone in that hole and was dying of cancer, or of neglect. She chain-smoked as if the cigarettes were jelly beans, and when she coughed, she sounded as if she was bringing up her soul in bits.

"It won't make any difference now," she said. "Sit down. If you can find a spot."

That afternoon María Luisa told him how, years before, when she was still secretary to the director, a captain from the police force called Vargas had come to the Civil Registry. "A handsome man, the sort you rarely see nowadays."

Vargas had shown her a list with numbers of death and birth certificates that seemed to correlate—the same list Vilajuana had received years later, neatly typed out.

"So you remember?"

"Of course I remember."

"Do you know where I could find the registry books containing those records prior to 1944?"

Maria Luisa lit another cigarette and took a drag that Vilajuana thought would finish her off. When she emerged from a cloud of smoke that looked as if something inside her had exploded, she signaled to him to follow her.

"Help me," she said, pointing at a mountain of boxes piled up in one of the kitchen cupboards. "It's the two at the back. I brought them home to prevent them from being destroyed. I thought Vargas would come back for them one day and that, with luck, he'd come back for me too. After all these years, I imagine that good old Captain Vargas must have beaten me in the race to paradise."

María Luisa told Vilajuana that as soon as Vargas had left the registry that day, she had started to put two and two together. Rummaging through the documents, she kept finding more and more numbers that had been switched and cases in which it was obvious that the procedures had been manipulated.

"Hundreds of children. Stolen from their parents, who were probably murdered or imprisoned until they rotted alive. And that's only as far as I was able to go in a few days. I took home what I could, because as soon as they started asking about Captain Vargas and his visit, I saw it coming. This is all I was able to save. A week after Vargas came to search the records of the registry, there was a fire in the archives. Everything prior to 1944 was lost. I was blamed for the disaster and dismissed two days later. If they'd known that I'd taken all these documents home, God knows what they would have done to me. But they thought the entire archive had been destroyed in the blaze. The past doesn't disappear, however hard idiots try to forget it and con men try to fake it and resell it as new."

"What have you done all these years?"

"Die. Decent people are killed slowly in this country. Quick deaths are reserved for scoundrels. They kill people like me by ignoring us, shutting all the doors in our faces and pretending we don't exist. For a couple of years I sold lottery tickets on the sly in the metro tunnels, until they found out and took that away from me too. I wasn't able to find anything else. Since then I've lived off the charity of my neighbors."

"Have you no family?"

"I had a son, but he was told his mother was a stinking red, and I haven't seen him in years." María Luisa looked at Vilajuana with a smile that was hard to make out.

"Can I do anything for you, María Luisa?"

"You can tell the truth."

Vilajuana sighed. "To be honest, I don't know whether I'll be able to do that."

"Do you have children?"

"Four."

Vilajuana was trapped in the eyes of that dying woman. He didn't know where to hide.

"Do it for them. Tell the truth for them. When you're able to, and in whatever way you're able to. But don't let us die. There are so many of us by now. Someone must lend us their voice."

Vilajuana nodded. María Luisa held out her hand, and he shook it.

"I'll do what I can," he said.

*

That night, while he was tucking in Nicolás, his son fixed him with his gaze.

"Dad?"

"Yes?"

"An elephant question."

"Let's have it."

"Why did you become a journalist? Mommy says that Granddad wanted you to be something else."

"Your grandfather wanted me to be a lawyer."

"And you paid no attention to him?"

"On certain occasions—none of which should apply to you or to the immediate future—a father must be disobeyed."

"Why?"

"Because some fathers, unlike yours, make mistakes when they judge what is best for their children."

"I meant, why did you want to be a journalist?"

Vilajuana shrugged. "Because of the amazing pay and the regular hours."

Nicolás laughed. "No, seriously. Why?"

"I don't know, Nico. That was a long time ago. Sometimes, when you grow older, what at first seemed very clear isn't as clear anymore."

"But the elephant doesn't forget. Even if they try to cut its tusks off."

"I suppose it doesn't."

"So . . . ?"

Vilajuana nodded and gave in. "To tell the truth. That's why I became a journalist."

Nicolás weighed his reply pensively. "And what is the truth?"

Vilajuana turned off the light and kissed his son's forehead. "That is something you're going to have to ask your mother."

Stories have no beginning and no end, only doors through which one may enter them.

A story is an endless labyrinth of words, images, and spirits, conjured up to show us the invisible truth about ourselves. A story is, after all, a conversation between the narrator and the reader, and just as narrators can only relate as far as their ability will permit, so too readers can only read as far as what is already written in their souls.

This is the golden rule that sustains every artifice of paper and ink. Because when the lights go out, when the music ends and the stalls are empty again, the only thing that matters is the mirage that has been engraved in the theater of the imagination all readers hold in their mind. This, and the hope every maker of tales carries within: that readers will open their hearts to these little creatures made of ink and paper, and give them a part of themselves so they can be immortal, even if only for a few minutes.

And having said these words a little more solemnly than the occasion probably merits, we had now better land at the end of the page and ask our friend the reader to accompany us at the closing moment of this story, to help us find the most difficult thing for a poor storyteller who is trapped in his own labyrinth: the exit door.

Prelude to
The Labyrinth of the Spirits
(*The Cemetery of Forgotten Books*, volume IV),
by Julián Carax.
Edited by Émile de Rosiers Castellaine.
Paris: Éditions de la Lumière, 1992.

JULIÁN'S
BOOK

I

I ALWAYS KNEW that one day I would end up writing this story. The story of my family and of that Barcelona haunted by books, memories, and secrets in which I grew up and which has followed me all my life, even when I knew that it was probably no more than a paper dream.

My father, Daniel Sempere, had tried before me, and almost lost his youth in the attempt. For years the good bookseller would sneak away in the early hours, when he thought my mother had fallen asleep, and tiptoe down to the bookshop to lock himself up in the back room. There, by the light of a candle, he would wield his flea-market fountain pen and fight an endless duel with hundreds of pages until dawn.

My mother never reproached him for it. She feigned—the way so many things are feigned in a marriage to keep it on an even keel—that she hadn't noticed. His obsession worried her almost as much as it worried me: I was beginning to fear my father was going off his rocker like Don Quixote, only the other way around: not from too much reading but from too much writing. She knew my father needed to make that voyage alone, not because he harbored any literary ambitions but because confronting the words was his way of discovering who he really was and trying to recover the memory and the spirit of the mother he had lost when he was four years old.

I remember one day when I woke up with a start shortly before dawn. My heart was beating furiously, and I could hardly breathe. I had dreamed that my father was dissolving into the mist, and I was losing him forever. It wasn't the first time. I jumped out of bed and ran down to the bookshop. I found him in the back room, still in a solid state, a battlefield of crumpled pages strewn around his feet. His fingers were ink-stained and his eyes were bloodshot. He'd placed an old photograph of Isabella on the desk, taken when she was nineteen, the one we all knew he always carried with him because he was terrified of forgetting her face.

"I can't," he whispered. "I can't give her life back to her."

I held back my tears and looked into his eyes. "I'll do it for you," I said. "I promise."

My father, who always smiled at my occasional outbursts of seriousness, embraced me. When he let go of me and saw that I was still there and I had been speaking in earnest, he offered me his fountain pen. "You'll need this. I don't even know what side it's supposed to write with . . ."

I studied that dreadful-looking gadget and slowly shook my head. "I'll use a typewriter," I declared. "An Underwood, the professional's choice."

I'd seen that phrase, "the professional's choice," in a newspaper ad, and it had impressed me. It was quite something to think that just owning one of those contraptions of the size and tonnage of a steam engine might transform you from an amateur journalist to a professional writer.

My declaration of intentions must have caught my father by surprise. "So now you want to be a professional writer? With an Underwood and all that?"

While we're at it, I thought dreamily, one with an office on the top floor of a Gothic skyscraper, imported cigarettes galore, a dry martini in one hand and a muse sitting on my lap, wearing blood-red lipstick and expensive black underwear. That, anyway, is how I imagined the professionals at the time, at least the ones who created those detective novels that soaked up my sleep, my soul, and some other things too. Great expectations aside, I didn't miss the slight hue of irony beneath my father's affectionate tone. If he was going to question my vocation, we were bound to argue.

"Yes," I replied dryly. "Like Julián Carax."

Take that, I thought.

My father raised his eyebrows. The blow had confused him. "And how do you know what Carax writes with, or even who he is?"

I adopted the mysterious expression I had patented to imply that I knew more than everyone imagined. "I know loads."

At home, the name Julián Carax was always mentioned in a whisper behind closed doors, protected by veiled looks and kept out of children's reach, like one of those medicines tagged with a skull and crossbones. Little did my parents know that by the time I was eight, I'd discovered, in the top drawer of the dining-room cupboard (which I reached with the help of a chair and a wooden box), a collection of Julián Carax novels republished by a family friend called Don Gustavo Barceló. They were hidden behind two tins of Camprodón biscuits, which I polished off entirely, and a large bottle of muscatel wine that almost threw me into a coma at the tender age of nine.

By the time I was ten, I'd read them all twice over and, although I probably hadn't understood them fully, been captivated by a prose that ignited my imagination with images, worlds, and characters I would never, ever forget. Having reached that point of sensory intoxication, I was quite sure that my ambition was to learn to do what this Carax did, and become his most outstanding successor in the art of telling tales. But I had the feeling that to achieve this, I first had to find out who he was, and why my parents had always preferred me not to know anything about him.

By good luck, my honorary uncle, Fermín Romero de Torres, didn't share my parents' information policy. By then Fermín no longer worked in the bookshop. He visited us often, but there was always an aura of mystery concerning what his new occupation was, and neither Fermín nor any member of my family volunteered to clarify it. Still, whatever his new job, it seemed to provide him with ample time for reading. He had recently taken in a number of anthropology treatises that had led him to come up with some formidable speculative theories, an occupation that, he said, helped him avoid kidney colic and expel stones the size of loquat seeds [sic] through the urinary system.

According to one of those peculiar theories, forensic evidence accumulated over the centuries proved that, after millennia of supposed evolution, humans had managed to eliminate a bit of body hair, perfect their loincloths, and refine their tools, but little else. From this premise, a second part of the theorem was inexplicably arrived at, and it went something like this: what the said threadbare evolution had not achieved even remotely was to understand that the more one tries to hide something from a child, the more he is set on finding it, be it a sweet or a postcard with outrageous chorus girls flaunting their charms to the wind.

"And thank goodness that's the way things are, because the day we lose the spark that makes us want to know things, and young people are content with the nonsense dressed in tinsel sold to them by the current popes of bullshittery—be it a miniature electrical appliance or a battery-run chamber pot—and become incapable of understanding anything that lies beyond their backsides, we'll return to the age of the slug."

I would laugh and say, "This is apocalyptic," making use of a word I'd learned from Fermín that always earned me a Sugus sweet.

"That's what I like to hear," he would reply. "So long as we have youngsters who know how to manage five-syllable words, there will be hope."

Perhaps it was due to Fermín's bad influence, or maybe to all those tricks I'd learned in the thrillers I devoured as if they were sugared almonds, but soon, by virtue of my enthusiasm for tying up loose ends, eavesdropping on furtive conversations, rummaging in forbidden drawers and, above all, reading all the pages my father thought had ended up in the wastepaper basket, the enigma of who Julián Carax had been and why my parents had decided to christen me with his name began to clear up. And wherever my skills of deduction and detection didn't reach, Fermín and his magisterial impromptu lectures filled in, supplying me on the sly with clues for solving the mystery, and connecting the different strands of the story.

That morning, as if he didn't have enough worries already, my father was served a double shot: that his son wanted to be a *professional* author, and that, moreover, I knew the entire cache of secrets he'd always tried to hide from me, probably more out of modesty than anything else. To his credit, I must say that he took it quite well. Instead of yelling and threatening to lock me up in a boarding school, the poor man just stood there staring at me, not knowing what to say.

"I thought you would want to be a bookseller, like me, like your grandfather, and like my grandfather before him, and like almost all the Semperes since time immemorial . . ."

Realizing that I'd caught him off guard, I decided to shore up my position.

"I'm going to be a writer," I said. "A novelist. To crown it all, I think one says."

That last phrase I let slip as a bit of humorous padding, but clearly my father didn't find it funny. He crossed his arms, leaned back in his chair, and studied me cautiously. The puppy was showing a rebellious streak that didn't please him. Welcome to fatherhood, I thought. You bring children into the world, and this is what you get.

"That's what your mother has always said, but I thought she just said it to tease me."

More in my favor. The day my mother makes a mistake will be when Judgment Day happens to fall on April Fool's. But, being allergic to resignation from birth, my father was still stuck in his warning attitude, and I feared a speech to dissuade me was on its way.

"At your age I also thought I had what it takes to be a writer," he began.

You could see him coming like a meteorite wrapped in flames. If I didn't disarm him now, this could become a sermon on the dangers of devoting one's life to literature. And I knew, because I'd often heard it from those starving authors who visited the bookshop—the ones to whom we had to sell on credit, and even treat to a snack—that literature showed as much devotion to its loyal followers as a praying mantis to its consort. Before my father got too worked up, I cast a melodramatic look over the battlefield of scattered pages on the floor and rested my eyes on him again without saying a word.

"As Fermín says," he admitted, "wise men make mistakes."

I realized that my counterargument could work as a bridge to his main premise, i.e., that the Semperes didn't have scribblers' blood, and booksellers also served literature without exposing themselves to absolute ruin and misery. Since, deep down, I suspected that the good man was as right as a saint, I went on the offensive. In a rhetorical duel one must never lose the initiative, even less when the opponent looks like he's winning.

"What Fermín says is that wise men own up when they some-times make mistakes, but idiots always make mistakes, even though they never admit it and always think they're right. He calls it his Ar-chimedean Principle of Communicable Imbecilities."

"Oh, does he?"

"Yes. According to him, an idiot is an animal who doesn't know how to, or is unable to, change his mind," I machine-gunned back.

"You seem extremely well versed in Fermín's philosophy and sci-ence."

"Are you saying he's wrong?"

"What he is, is disproportionately interested in speaking ex cathe-dra."

"And what does that mean?"

"To piss outside the pot."

"Well, in one of these pissy ex cathedra moments, he also told me there's something you should have shown me ages ago."

My father looked confused for a moment. Any hint of a sermon had evaporated, and now he was staggering around without knowing where the next punch would come from.

"He said what?"

"Something about books. And about the dead."

"The dead?"

"Something or other about a cemetery. The bit about the dead is my idea."

In fact, what had been going through my mind was that this busi-ness might have something to do with Carax, who in my personal canon combined the notion of books and the dead to perfection.

My father considered the matter. A flash crossed his eyes, as it always did when he had an idea. "I suppose on that point he was probably right."

I sniffed the sweet scent of victory surfacing somewhere.

"Go on, go upstairs and get dressed," said my father. "But don't wake your mother."

"Are we going somewhere?"

"It's a secret. I'm going to show you something that changed my life, and might change yours too."

I realized I'd lost the initiative, and the ball was in his court. "At this hour?"

My father smiled again and winked at me.

"Some things can only be seen in the dark."

2

THAT DAWN MY father took me to visit the Cemetery of Forgotten Books for the first time. It was the autumn of 1966, and a drizzle had decorated the Ramblas with little puddles that shone like copper tears as we walked. The mist I had so often dreamed about accompanied us, but it lifted when we turned into Calle Arco del Teatro. A dark breach lay before us, and soon a grand palace of blackened stone emerged from its shadows. My father knocked on the large front door with a knocker in the shape of a devil's face. To my surprise, the person who opened the door to us was none other than Fermín Romero de Torres, who smiled mischievously when he saw me.

"About time," he said. "All that cloak-and-dagger business was giving me stomach cramps."

"Is this where you work now, Fermín?" I asked, intrigued. "Is this a bookshop?"

"Something like that, although there isn't much in the comic book section. . . . Come on in."

Fermín accompanied us through a curved gallery whose walls were painted with frescoes of angels and legendary creatures. Needless to say, by then I was in a trance. Little did I know that the wonders had only just begun.

The gallery led us to a hall with a vaulted ceiling that rose into infinity under a cascade of prodigious light. I looked up, and a labyrinthine structure materialized before my eyes. The tower formed in a never-ending spiral, like a reef on which all the libraries of the world had been shipwrecked. I advanced slowly, openmouthed, toward that castle woven together of all the books ever written. I felt as if I'd entered the pages of one of Julián Carax's stories, afraid that if I dared to take one more step, that instant would turn to dust and I'd wake up in my room.

My father appeared by my side. I looked at him and took his hand, if only to convince myself that I was awake and that place was real.

He smiled. "Julián, welcome to the Cemetery of Forgotten Books."

It took me quite a while to recover my pulse and reconnect to the laws of gravity. Once I had calmed down, my father murmured these words to me through the gloom:

"This is a place of mystery, Julián, a sanctuary. Every book, every volume you see here, has a soul. The soul of the person who wrote it and of those who read it and lived and dreamed with it. Every time a book changes hands, every time someone runs his eyes down its pages, its spirit grows and strengthens. This place was already ancient when my father brought me here for the first time, many years ago. Perhaps as old as the city itself. Nobody knows for certain how long it has existed, or who created it. I will tell you what my father told me, though. When a library disappears, or a bookshop closes down, when a book is consigned to oblivion, those of us who know this place, its guardians, make sure that it gets here. In this place, books no longer remembered by anyone, books that are lost in time, live forever, waiting for the day when they will reach a new reader's hands. In the shop we buy and sell them, but in truth books have no owner. Every book you see here has been somebody's best friend. Now they only have us, Julián. Do you think you'll be able to keep such a secret?"

My gaze was lost in the immensity of the place and its sorcery of light. I nodded, and my father smiled.

Fermín offered me a glass of water and stood there, looking at me. "Does the kid know the rules?"

"That's what I was about to tell him," said my father.

My father then gave me a detailed list of the rules and responsibilities that had to be accepted by all new entrants to the secret brotherhood of the Cemetery of Forgotten Books, including the privilege of being able to adopt a book in perpetuity and become its protector for life.

While I listened to him, I began to wonder whether he hadn't had some ulterior motive to have chosen that exact day to bombard my eyes and my brain with that vision. Perhaps, as a last resort, the good bookseller hoped that the sight of that city populated by hundreds of thousands of abandoned tomes, by so many forgotten lives, ideas, and universes, might serve as a metaphor of the future that awaited me if I persisted in my obstinate belief in being able, one day, to earn a living from literature. If that was his intention, the vision had quite the opposite effect. My vocation, which until then had been a mere child's daydream, became etched on my heart that day. And nothing my father or anyone might say could make me change my mind.

Destiny, I suppose, had made the choice for me.

In my long wanderings through the tunnels of the labyrinth, I chose a book titled *The Crimson Tunic*, a novel belonging to a cycle called *The City of the Damned*, whose author was someone called David Martín, of whom I'd never heard until then. Or perhaps I should say that the book chose me; when at last I rested my eyes on the cover, I had the strange feeling that the copy had been waiting there for me for some time, as if it knew that on that dawn I would bump into it.

When at last I reemerged from the edifice, and my father saw the book I held in my hands, he turned pale. For a moment he looked as if he would collapse.

"Where did you find that book?" he murmured.

"On a table in one of the rooms. . . . It was standing up, as if someone had left it there for me to find."

My father and Fermín exchanged mysterious glances.

"Is something the matter?" I asked. "Should I choose another one?"

My father shook his head.

"It's destiny," murmured Fermín.

I smiled with excitement. That was exactly what I had thought, even if I didn't quite know why.

*

I spent the rest of the week in a trance, reading the adventures narrated by David Martín, savoring every scene as if I were observing a large canvas where the more I explored, the more details and landscapes I discovered. My father also retreated into his daydreaming, although his worries seemed to be anything but literary.

Like many men, by then my father was beginning to suspect that he'd stopped being a young man, and he often revisited the scenes of his early youth, looking for answers to questions he still didn't fully understand.

"What's the matter with Dad?" I asked my mother.

"Nothing. He's just growing."

"Isn't he past the growing age?"

My mother gave a patient sigh. "You men are like that."

"I'll grow fast, and you won't have to worry."

My mother smiled. "We're in no hurry, Julián. Let life take care of that."

In one of his mysterious journeys to the center of his navel, my father came back from the post office carrying a parcel that came from Paris. Inside it was a book called *The Angel of Mist*. Anything with angels and mist in it sounded totally up my alley, so I decided to investigate, even if only because of the expression on my father's face when he'd opened the parcel and seen the cover of the book. After some research I concluded that it was a novel written by a certain Boris Laurent, a pen name, I later discovered, for none other than Julián Carax. The book came with a dedication that made my mother cry—and she never was one to run for the handkerchief at the first chance—and finally convinced my father that destiny had us all caught by a place he wouldn't be explicit about, but that, I surmised, required delicate handling.

To be honest, I was the one who was most surprised. For some reason, I had always supposed that Carax had been dead since time immemorial (a historical period comprising everything that had taken place before my birth). I always thought that Carax was another of the many phantoms from the past lurking in the haunted palace of the official family memory. When I realized that I had been mistaken and that Carax was alive, kicking, and writing in Paris, I had an epiphany.

As I caressed the pages of *The Angel of Mist*, I suddenly understood what I had to do. That is how the plan was hatched that would allow me to fulfill that destiny, a destiny that for once had decided to pay a house call, and many years later would give birth to this book.

3

LIFE WENT ON at a steady pace, between revelations and fantasies, as it usually does, without paying too much attention to all of us who travel hanging on it by our fingertips. I enjoyed two childhoods: the first was quite conventional, if such a thing can ever be, and was the one others saw; the second was an imaginary childhood, and the one I truly lived. I made some good friends, most of them books. In school I was bored stiff and acquired the habit of spending my time in the classroom with my head in the clouds, a habit I still retain. I was lucky enough to come across a few good teachers, who treated me with patience and agreed that the fact that I was always different wasn't necessarily something bad. It takes all sorts to make a world, including a few Julián Semperes. Still, I probably learned more about the world reading between the four walls of the bookshop, visiting libraries on my own, or listening to Fermín, who always had some theory, advice, or practical warning to offer, than in all my years of schooling.

"At school they say I'm a bit odd," I once admitted to Fermín.

"Well, that's good news. We'll start worrying the day they tell you you're normal."

For better or for worse, nobody ever accused me of that.

*

I suppose my adolescence offers a little more biographical interest because at least I lived a greater part of it outside my head. My paper-filled dreams and my ambitions of becoming a soldier of the pen without perishing in the attempt were gaining strength, even though they were somewhat restrained, I must admit, by a certain dose of realism acquired as time went by and I observed the workings of the world. Halfway through my journey, I had already realized that my dreams were forged with impossibilities, but that if I abandoned them before charging into battle, I would never win the war.

I was still confident that one day the gods on Mount Parnassus would take pity on me and allow me to learn how to tell stories. Meanwhile, I stocked up on raw material, hoping the day would come when I'd be able to premiere my own factory of dreams and nightmares. Slowly, I compiled everything related to the history of my family, its many secrets, and the thousand and one narratives that made up the little universe of the Semperes, an imagined world I had decided to name The Cemetery of Forgotten Books.

Aside from discovering everything discoverable and whatever resisted discovery about my family, I had two great passions at the time: one magical and ethereal, which was reading, and the other mundane and entirely predictable, which was pursuing silly love affairs.

Concerning my literary ambitions, my successes went from slender to nonexistent. During those years I started a hundred woefully bad novels that died along the way, hundreds of short stories, plays, radio serials, and even poems that I wouldn't let anyone read, for their own good. I only needed to read them myself to see how much I still had to learn and what little progress I was making, despite the desire and enthusiasm I put into it. I was forever rereading Carax's novels and those of countless authors I borrowed from my parents' bookshop. I tried to pull them apart as if they were transistor radios, or the engine of a Rolls-Royce, hoping I would be able to figure out how they were built and how and why they worked.

I'd read a report in a newspaper about some Japanese engineers who practiced something called reverse engineering. Apparently these industrious gentlemen disassembled an engine to its last piece, analyzing the function of each bit, the dynamics of the whole, and the interior design of the device in question to work out the mathematics that supported its operation. My mother had a brother who worked as an engineer in Germany, so I told myself that there must be something in my genes that would allow me to do the same thing with a book or with a story.

Every day I became more convinced that good literature has little or nothing to do with trivial fancies such as "inspiration" or "having something to tell" and more with the engineering of language, with the architecture of narrative, with the painting of textures, with the timbres and colors of the staging, with the cinematography of words, and the music that can be produced by an orchestra of ideas.

My second great occupation, or I should say my first, was far more suited to comedy, and at times touched on farce. There was a time in which I fell in love on a weekly basis, something that, in hindsight, I don't recommend. I fell in love with a look, a voice, and above all with what was tightly concealed under those fine-wool dresses worn by the young girls of my time.

"That isn't love, it's a fever," Fermín would specify. "At your age it is chemically impossible to tell the difference. Mother Nature brings on these tricks to repopulate the planet by injecting hormones and a raft of idiocies into young people's veins so there's enough cannon fodder available for them to reproduce like rabbits and at the same time sacrifice themselves in the name of whatever is parroted by bankers, clerics, and revolutionary visionaries in dire need of idealists, imbeciles, and other plagues that will prevent the world from evolving and make sure it always stays the same."

"But Fermín, what has all this to do with anxieties of the heart?"

"Spare me the sugary lyrics, I know you only too well. The heart is an organ that pumps blood, not sonnets. With a bit of luck some of that circulation reaches the brain, but on the whole it ends up in the gut and, in your case, in the loins—which, if you're not careful, will take over your brain until you reach your twenty-fifth birthday. Keep the testicular mass well away from the rudder, and you'll come into port. Fool around, and your life will go by without your doing anything useful."

"Amen."

My free time was divided between romances in dark alleyways, exploring under blouses and skirts in the back row of some decrepit neighborhood cinema with more or less success, parties at La Paloma Ballroom, and strolls along the breakwater, holding hands with my girlfriend of the moment. I won't go into further detail because there was no significant event worth reporting until I reached my seventeenth birthday and collided head-on with a creature named

Valentina. Any self-respecting sailor has an iceberg waiting for him; mine was called Valentina. She was three years older than me (which for practical purposes seemed more like ten), and she left me in a catatonic state for a few months.

I met her one autumn afternoon when I'd gone into the old French Bookshop on Paseo de Gracia to shelter from the rain. She had her back to me, and something about her made me draw closer and look at her out of the corner of my eye. She was leafing through a novel by Julián Carax, *The Shadow of the Wind*, and if I dared to go up to her and open my mouth, that's because in those days I felt indestructible.

"I've read this book too," I said, parading a level of wit that proved Fermín's circulation theories beyond all doubt.

She looked at me with emerald eyes that were sharp as blades, and blinked so slowly I thought time had stopped. "Lucky you," she replied.

She returned the book to the shelf, turned around, and made her way to the exit. I just stood there, glued to the floor for a few seconds, fuming. When I recovered my wits, I grabbed the book from the shelf, took it to the cashier, paid for it, and ran into the street, hoping my iceberg hadn't sunk under the sea forever.

The sky was the color of steel, and pearls of rain were pelting down. I caught up with her while she waited at the traffic light to cross Calle Rosellón, ignoring the rain.

"Should I call the police?" she asked, without turning her head.

"I hope not. I'm Julián."

Valentina huffed. She turned her head and fixed those sharp eyes on me again. I smiled like an idiot and handed her the book.

She raised an eyebrow and, after a moment's hesitation, accepted it. "Another Julián? Do you form a brotherhood or something like that?"

"My parents named me after the author of this book. He was a friend of theirs. It's the best book I've ever read."

My luck was decided by the scenery, as usually happens on such occasions. A flash of lightning streaked the facades on Paseo de Gracia with a silver hue, and the rumble of the storm crept angrily over the city. The traffic lights turned green. Before Valentina could send me packing or call a policeman, I played my last card.

"Ten minutes. A coffee. If in ten minutes I haven't earned it, I'll vanish and you'll never set eyes on me again. I promise."

Valentina looked at me, hesitating and repressing a smile. The rain was to blame for everything.

"OK," she said.

And there I was, believing my life had changed the day I decided to be a novelist.

*

Valentina lived on her own in a top-floor flat on Calle Provenza. From there one could contemplate the whole of Barcelona, something I rarely did because I preferred to contemplate her in the different stages of undress to which I inevitably tried to reduce her. Her mother was Dutch, and her father had been a well-known Barcelona lawyer whose name even I knew. When he died, her mother decided to return to her country, but Valentina, by now an adult, decided to remain in Barcelona. She spoke five languages and worked for a lawyer's practice founded by her father, translating lawsuit reports and multimillion-dollar cases for big companies and families with a box in the opera house going back four generations. When I asked her what she wanted to do with her life, she glanced back at me with that look that always entranced me. "Travel," she said.

Valentina was the first person I allowed to read my modest attempts at writing. She had a tendency to keep her tenderness and her demonstrations of affection for the more prosaic part of our relationship. When it came to giving me her opinion on my literary dabblings, she would say that all I had of Carax was his first name. Deep down I agreed with her, so I didn't take it badly. Perhaps for that reason, and because I thought nobody in the world could better understand the plan I'd been nursing for years, one day when I felt particularly well prepared to receive a slap in the face, I told her what I was planning to do as soon as I reached my eighteenth birthday.

"I hope you're not going to ask me to marry you," said Valentina.

I suppose I should have known how to interpret the clue fate was hinting at; all my big scenes with Valentina began with rain hot on my heels or scratching the windowpanes. That one was no different.

"What is the plan?" she said at last.

"To write the story of my family."

· We'd been together for almost a year, if that procession of afternoons between sheets in her studio up in the clouds could be called being together, and although I knew by heart every pore of her skin, I still hadn't learned to read her silences.

"And . . . ?" she asked.

"Isn't that enough for you?"

"Everyone has a family. And all families have a story."

With Valentina you always had to earn everything. Whatever it was, it had to be won. She turned away from me, and that is how, addressing that beautiful naked back, I set out, for the first time in a loud voice, the idea that had been running through my mind for years. It was not a brilliant presentation, but I needed to hear it from my own lips to believe in it.

I had a beginning: a title. *The Cemetery of Forgotten Books.* For years I'd been carrying a blank notebook around with me, on whose cover I'd written, in bold, ostentatiously elegant handwriting:

The Cemetery of Forgotten Books

A novel in four volumes

by

Julián Sempere

One day Fermín had caught me, pen in hand, staring spellbound at the first blank page of the notebook. He inspected the cover and, after letting out a sound that could be described as a cross between grunting and breaking wind, intoned:

"Accursed be those whose dreams are made of paper and ink, for theirs will be the purgatory of vanity and disappointment."

"By your leave, would Your Excellency be so kind as to translate that solemn aphorism into plain speech?"

"I suppose silliness makes me go all biblical," he said. "You're the one who pretends to be a poet. Work out the semantics."

I'd worked out that the magnum opus, a product of my feverish juvenile imagination, would reach a devilish size and a body weight close to fifteen kilos. The way I dreamed of it, the narrative would be divided into four interconnected volumes that would work like entrance doors into a labyrinth of stories. As the reader advanced into its pages, he would feel that the story was piecing itself together like a game of Russian dolls in which each plot and each character led to the next, and that, in turn, to yet another, and so on and so forth.

"It sounds like the instructions for piecing together an Erector set or an electric train."

My sweet Valentina, always so eloquent.

"It does have a whiff of an Erector set," I admitted.

I had tried to sell her my highfalutin letter of intent without feeling embarrassed, because it was, word for word, the one I'd written when I was sixteen, convinced that half my work had been already accomplished with it. The fact that I'd had the nerve to copy that idea straight out of *The Shadow of the Wind*, the novel I'd given Valentina the day I met her, was the least of it.

"Hasn't Carax done that already?" asked Valentina.

"Everything in life has been done by someone before, at least anything worth doing," I said. "The trick is to try to do it a bit better."

"And there you go, with all the modesty of youth."

Accustomed as I was to having jugs of ice-cold water poured on me by my beloved iceberg, I continued with my presentation, as determined as a soldier jumping out of his trench and advancing with a shout against the hail of machine guns.

According to my infallible plan, the first volume would focus on the story of a reader, in this case my father: on how, when he was young, he'd discovered the world of books—and, by extension, life—through an enigmatic novel by an unknown author concealing a huge mystery, the sort that leaves you drooling at the mouth. All that would provide the foundation for building, in one stroke of the pen, a novel that would combine all known and unknown forms.

"While you're at it, it could also cure the flu and the common cold," remarked Valentina.

The second volume, replete with a morbid, sinister aftertaste, seeking to goad the mainstream reader, would narrate the macabre wanderings of an ill-fated novelist, courtesy of David Martín, who would chart, in the first person, how he loses his mind, and drag us along in his descent into the hell of his own madness, thus becoming an even less reliable narrator than the Prince of Hell, who would also stroll around the novel's pages. Or perhaps he wouldn't, because it would all be a game in which the reader is the one who must finish the jigsaw puzzle and decide what kind of book it is.

"What if you're left in the lurch, and nobody feels like taking part in this game?"

"It will have been worthwhile all the same," I said. "There will always be someone who will take up the challenge."

"Writing is for optimists," Valentina declared.

The third volume, assuming some charitable reader had managed to survive the first two and not decided to board a different tram heading for a happy ending, would save us momentarily from the underworld and offer us the story of a character, the character par excellence and the voice of the official conscience of the story, that is to say, my adoptive uncle, Fermín Romero de Torres. His story would show us, with picaresque spirit, how he became the person he was, and his many misadventures in the most turbulent years of the century would reveal the lines connecting all the parts of the labyrinth.

"At least here we'll have a good laugh."

"Fermín to the rescue," I agreed.

"And how does this monstrosity end?"

"With fireworks, a grand orchestra, and stage machinery, special effects in full force."

The fourth installment, fierce and enormous, spiced with perfumes from all the earlier ones, would lead us at last to the center of the mystery, uncovering all the puzzles with the help of my favorite fallen angel of mist, Alicia Gris. The saga would contain villains and heroes, and a thousand tunnels through which the reader would be able to explore a kaleidoscopic plot resembling that mirage of perspectives I'd discovered with my father in the heart of the Cemetery of Forgotten Books.

"And you don't appear?" asked Valentina.

"Only at the end, and it's a very small part."

"How modest."

From her tone, I already guessed what was about to hit me.

"What I don't understand is why, instead of talking so much about this story, you don't just get on and write it."

I had asked myself that question about three thousand times during the last few years.

"Because talking about it helps me to imagine it better. And above all, because I don't know how to do it. That's where my plan comes in."

Valentina turned around and looked at me, confused. "I thought that was the plan."

"That is the ambition. The plan is another thing."

"What?"

"That Julián Carax write it for me," I revealed.

Valentina stood there staring at me with that look that opened corridors into one's soul. "And why would he do that?"

"Because, deep down, it's also his story, and the story of his family."

"I thought Carax was in Paris."

I nodded.

Valentina half closed her eyes. Icy, intelligent, my adored Valentina. "In other words, your plan is to go to Paris to find Julián Carax, supposing he's still alive, and convince him to write a three-thousand-page novel in your name with that story that supposedly is so important to you."

"More or less," I admitted.

I smiled, prepared to take the hit. Now she'd tell me I was thoughtless, naive, or a dreamer. I was ready to suffer any blow except the one she gave me, which, of course, was the one I deserved.

"You're a coward." She stood up, collected her clothes, and dressed, facing the window. Then, without looking at me, she lit a cigarette and let her eyes wander over the horizon of the Ensanche rooftops under the rain.

"I'd like to be alone," she said.

Five days later I walked up those steps again to Valentina's attic, only to find the door open, the room empty, and a bare chair facing the window. On the chair was an envelope with my name on it. I opened it. Inside were twenty thousand French francs and a note:

> *Bon voyage et bonne chance.*
>
> V.

When I stepped into the street, it had started to rain.

*

Three weeks later, on an afternoon when we had gathered a group of readers and regular customers in the bookshop to celebrate the publication of a first novel by a good friend of Sempere & Sons, Professor Alburquerque, something happened that had been widely expected for some time—something that would alter the history of our country, or at least bring it back to the present.

It was almost closing time when Don Federico, the neighborhood watchmaker, came in to the bookshop looking very flustered, hauling a contraption that turned out to be a portable television set he'd bought in Andorra. He put it down on the counter and gave us all a solemn look.

"Quick," he said. "I need a socket."

"A plug is what you need," joked Fermín, "like everyone else in this country, otherwise you won't get anywhere."

Something in Don Federico's expression suggested that the watchmaker was in no mood for lighthearted banter. Professor Alburquerque, who already suspected what it was all about, helped him connect the machine. A noisy gray screen materialized, projecting a halo of flickering light throughout the bookshop.

Alerted by the commotion, my grandfather peered around the back-room curtain and looked inquisitively at us all. Fermín shrugged.

"Let everyone know," ordered Don Federico.

While they were sorting out the position of the aerials, we congregated in front of the television set as if we were acting out some sort of ritual. Fermín and Professor Alburquerque began placing chairs. Soon all of us—myself, my parents, my grandfather, Fermín, Don Anacleto (he'd seen the glaring light on his way back from his afternoon stroll and thought we were watching a pop show, so he'd come in to nose around), Fernandito and Sofía, Merceditas, and the customers who were there for the launch of Professor Alburquerque's book—found ourselves filling those improvised stalls, unsure of what we were waiting for.

"Do I have time to go for a wee and get popcorn?" asked Fermín.

"If I were you, I'd try to hold out," warned Professor Alburquerque. "I have a feeling this is going to be momentous."

Finally Don Federico twisted the aerials around, and the static window dissolved into the gloomy black-and-white frame that was broadcast by Televisión Española in those days. Against the grand, velvety background the face of an individual came into view. He looked like a cross between a provincial notary and Mighty Mouse and wore a tearful and contrite expression.

"Franco has died," announced the then prime minister, Arias Navarro, amid sobs.

From the sky, or from somewhere else, a silence of unfathomable weight fell upon us. If the clock hanging on the wall had still been working, the pendulum would have stopped in mid-flight. What follows happened more or less simultaneously.

Merceditas burst into tears. My grandfather turned as pale as a meringue, probably fearing he would hear the rumble of tanks heading up Avenida Diagonal, and the declaration of another war. Don Anacleto, so prone to rhapsody and verse, went mute and began to visualize the burning of convents and other festivities. My parents looked at one another in bewilderment. Professor Alburquerque, who didn't smoke, borrowed a cigarette from the watchmaker and lit it. Fernandito and Sofía, ignoring the commotion, smiled at one another as if they were returning to their enchanted world, and went on holding hands. Some of the readers who had gathered there made the sign of the cross and left in shock.

I looked around for some adult in full possession of his mental faculties and met with Fermín, who was following the speech with cold interest and utter calm. I sat down next to him.

"Look at him," he remarked, "like a sniveling child, as if he'd never done anything bad in his life, and yet he's signed more death sentences than Uncle Joe Stalin."

"What's going to happen now?" I asked anxiously.

Fermín smiled at me serenely and patted me on the back. He offered me a Sugus, peeled one for himself—lemon flavored—and sucked it with satisfaction. "Don't worry, nothing's going to happen here. Skirmishes, pantomimes, and hypocrisy en masse for a while, that's for certain, but nothing serious. If we're unlucky, some idiot might go too far, but whoever holds the reins won't let anything get out of hand. It wouldn't be worth it. There'll be a fair amount of hullabaloo, but most of it will come to nothing. Records will be broken in the Olympic sport of coat turning, and we'll see heroes emerging from under the sofa. The usual stuff in these cases. It's going to be like a long constipation. It won't be easy, but slowly the turd will come out, or at least the bit that hasn't yet metabolized. And in the end, it won't get too nasty, you'll see. For the simple reason that it wouldn't benefit anyone. After all, this is a market stall of different interests, dressed up more or less successfully for popular consumption. Setting aside the puppet shows, the only thing that matters is who will be ruling, who will have the keys to the cash register, and how they're going to split up other people's money among themselves. On their way to the booty they'll spruce everything up, which is badly needed. New scoundrels will appear, new leaders, and a whole choir of innocents with no memory will come out into the streets, ready to believe whatever they want or need to believe. They'll follow whichever Pied Piper flatters them most and promises them some shoddy paradise. This is what it is, Julianito, with its highs and lows, and it's only as good as it gets, which is better than nothing. There are those who see it coming and go far away, like our Alicia, and there are those of us who stay with our feet stuck in the mud, because anyhow we don't have anywhere better to go. But don't worry about the circus. We've now come to the clown acts, and the trapeze artists will take a while to arrive. It's probably the best thing that could have happened to us all. As far as I'm concerned, and I am not that much concerned, I'm happy with it."

"And how do you know Alicia has gone so far away?"

Fermín smiled mischievously. "Touché."

"What have you not told me?"

Fermín grabbed my arm and led me to a corner. "Another day. Today is a day of national mourning."

"But—"

He left me before I could respond and went back to the congregation, which was still reeling at the death of the man who had been head of state for the last four decades.

"Are you going to propose a toast?" asked Don Anacleto.

Fermín shook his head. "I don't toast anyone's death," he said. "I don't know about you, but I'm going home to see Bernarda, and, God willing, try to get her as knocked up as science will allow. I suggest that, logistics permitting, you all do the same. And if not, then read a good book, like the one by our dear friend here, Professor Alburquerque. Tomorrow will be another day."

*

And another day came, and then another, and a few months went by during which Fermín artfully slipped away and left me in the dark about his insinuations regarding Alicia Gris. Guessing that he would tell me what he had to tell me when the moment was right, or just whenever he felt like it, I made use of Valentina's francs and bought myself a ticket to Paris. It was 1976, and I was nineteen.

My parents were unaware of the real reason for my trip, which I attributed to a desire to see the world, although my mother always suspected my true intentions. I was never able to hide the truth from her—as I had once told my father, I kept no secrets from her. My mother knew about my goings-on with Valentina and my ambitions, which she always supported, even when I periodically touched rock bottom and swore I was abandoning them because of my lack of talent and courage.

"Nobody succeeds without failing first," she assured me.

775

I knew my father was annoyed, although he wouldn't tell me. He didn't approve of my trip to Paris. According to him, what I should be doing was making my mind up and devoting myself once and for all to whatever it was I was going to do. If I wanted to be a writer, I'd do better to start taking it seriously. And if I wanted to be a bookseller, or parakeet trainer, or anything else, then ditto.

I didn't know how to tell him that what I needed was to go to Paris and find Carax, because it made no sense at all. I had no arguments with which to support the idea; I simply knew it in my heart. He didn't come to the station, saying he had to go to Vic for a meeting with his distinguished colleague, Señor Costa, a doyen of the profession and possibly the wisest dealer in the secondhand book business. When I got to the Estación de Francia, I bumped into my mother, sitting on one of the platform benches.

"I bought you a pair of gloves," she said. "I hear it's freezing in Paris."

I hugged her. "Do you also think I'm mistaken?"

My mother shook her head.

"One has to make one's own mistakes, not other people's. Do what you have to do and come back soon. Or whenever you can."

*

In Paris I found the world. My scant budget allowed me to rent an attic the size of an ashtray crowning a building on the corner of Rue Soufflot, which was the architectural equivalent of a Paganini solo. My watchtower hung over Place du Panthéon. From there I could gaze over the whole of the Latin Quarter, the terraced roofs of the Sorbonne, and the entire Left Bank.

I suppose I rented it because it reminded me of Valentina. When I looked out for the first time and saw the crest of dormers and chimneys surrounding the attic, I felt I was the most fortunate man on the planet. I spent the first few days making my way through an extraordinary world of cafés, bookshops, and streets strewn with palaces, museums, and people breathing a freedom that dazzled a poor novice like me, who came from the Stone Age with a heap of fluttering dreams in his head.

The City of Light granted me a gentle landing. In my comings and goings I struck up conversation, in appalling French and gesticulating speech, with young and old people, with creatures from another world. There was also the occasional beauty in a miniskirt who laughed tenderly at me and told me that, although I was as green as a lettuce, she thought me *très adorable*. Soon I began to think that the universe, which was only a small part of Paris, was full of Valentinas. In my second week as an adopted Parisian I persuaded one of them, without much effort, to come up and enjoy the views from my bohemian attic. It didn't take me long to discover that Paris was not Barcelona, and that here the rules of the game were very different.

"The things you've missed from not speaking French, Fermín . . ."

"Qui est Fermín?"

It took me a while to wake up from the enchantment of Paris and its mirages. Thanks to one of my Valentinas, Pascale, a redhead with a haircut and an air reminiscent of Jean Seberg, I managed to find a half-day job as a waiter. I worked in the mornings and during lunch in a café opposite the university called Le Comptoir du Panthéon, where I got a free meal after ending my shift. The owner, a kind gentleman who couldn't quite understand why, being Spanish, I wasn't a bullfighter or a flamenco dancer, asked me whether I'd come to Paris to study, in search of fortune and glory, or to perfect my French, which, more than perfecting, needed open-heart surgery and a brain transplant.

"I've come in search of a man," I admitted.

"And there was I thinking that you rather fancied young ladies. You can tell Franco has died. . . . A couple of days without a dictator, and you Spaniards have already become bisexual. Good for you. One must live, life's too short. *Vive la différence!*"

That reminded me that I'd come to Paris for a reason, and not to escape from myself. So the following day I began my search for Julián Carax. I started by visiting all the bookshops that lit up the pavements of Boulevard Saint-Germain, asking after the writer. Pascale, with whom I'd ended up becoming good friends, even if she'd made it quite clear that our thing under the sheets had no future (apparently I was *trop doux* for her taste), worked as a copy editor in a publishing house and knew a lot of people in the Parisian literary world. Every Friday she went along to a bookish gathering in a café of the literary quarter frequented by writers, translators, publishers, booksellers, and all the fauna and flora that inhabits the jungle of books and its surroundings. The crowd would change, depending on the week, but the rules were unvaried: to smoke and drink in huge quantities, maintain heated discussions about books and ideas, and go for one's opponent's throat as if one's life depended on it. Most of the time I listened and sank into a hallucinogenic cloud of tobacco while I tried to slide my hand under Pascale's skirt, an affectation she considered very gauche, bourgeois, and uncouth.

It was there that I was lucky enough to meet some of Carax's translators, who had traveled to the city for a symposium on translation at the Sorbonne. An English novelist called Lucia Hargreaves, who had grown up in Mallorca and returned to London for love, told me she hadn't heard about Carax for ages. His German translator, Herr Peter Schwarzenbeld, a gentleman from Zurich who preferred warmer regions and moved around Paris on a folding bicycle, explained that he had a feeling that Carax now devoted his time exclusively to composing piano sonatas and had adopted a new name. His Italian translator, Signor Bruno Arpaiani, confessed that for years he'd been picking up rumors that a new novel by Carax was about to appear, but he didn't believe them. All in all, nobody knew anything tangible concerning Julián Carax's whereabouts, or what had become of him.

At one of those café gatherings I happened to meet a remarkably clever gentleman called François Maspero, who had been a bookseller and a publisher and was now translating novels to great acclaim. Maspero had been Pascale's mentor when she first arrived in Paris, and he agreed to invite me to a coffee at Les Deux Magots, where I was able to give him a rough idea of my plan.

"A very ambitious plan, young man, and very complicated too, but . . ."

A few days later, I bumped into Monsieur Maspero in the neighborhood. He told me he wanted to introduce me to a young German lady with steely composure and a quick brain who divided her time between Paris and Berlin and spoke more languages than I could name. She devoted herself to discovering literary marvels and secrets, which she then placed with different European publishers. Her name was Michi Strausmann.

"She might know something about Carax . . ."

Pascale, who admitted that she wanted to be like Fräulein Strausmann when she was older, warned me that she was not a tender little flower and didn't suffer fools gladly. Monsieur Maspero very kindly set up a meeting with the four of us around a café table in the Marais area, not far from what had once been Victor Hugo's home.

"Fräulein Strausmann is an expert on Carax's work," he said by way of introduction. "Tell her what you told me."

So I did. She replied with a look that would have made the best soufflé collapse. "Are you an idiot?" she asked, in perfect Spanish.

"I'm in training," I admitted.

After a while the Valkyrie softened her heart and admitted she'd been too severe with me. She confirmed that, like everyone else, she'd had no news of Carax for quite a while, much as she would have wanted to.

"Julián hasn't written anything for a long time," she told me. "Nor does he answer letters. I wish you luck with your proposal, but . . ."

"Have you any address where I could write to him?"

Fräulein Strausmann shook her head. "Try Currygan and Coliccio. That's where I used to send my letters to him, and where I lost track of him years ago."

Pascale explained that Madame Currygan and Tomaso Coliccio had been Julián Carax's literary agents for over twenty-five years, and promised she'd arrange for them to see me.

*

Madame Currygan's agency was on Rue de Rennes. Legend had it in the trade that over the years she had turned her office into an exquisite orchid garden, and Pascale advised me to take a new plant for her collection as an offering. Pascale was a friend of the members of the so-called Currygan Brigade, an imposing quartet of women of different nationalities who worked for Madame Currygan and through whose good auspices I managed to secure an audience with Carax's agent.

Flowerpot in hand, I turned up at the agency. The members of the Currygan Brigade (Hilde, Claudia, Norma, and Tonya) mistook me for the errand boy from the corner florist. As soon as I opened my mouth, however, my identity was revealed. Once the mistake had been clarified, they led me to the office where Madame Currygan awaited. When I stepped in I noticed a glass cabinet with the complete works of Julián Carax and a splendid botanical garden. Madame Currygan listened patiently while she enjoyed a cigarette with which she filled the room with floating cobwebs.

"Yes, Julián did talk about Daniel and Bea sometimes," she said. "But that was a long time ago. I haven't heard from Julián in ages. He used to visit me often, but . . ."

"Did he get ill?"

"I suppose one could say he did, yes."

"What with?"

"Melancholy."

"Perhaps Signor Coliccio will know something about him."

"I doubt it. I speak to Tomaso every week on work matters, and from what I gather he hasn't heard from Julián either for at least three years. But you can try. Let me know if you find anything out."

Her colleague Don Tomaso lived in a barge on the banks of the Seine, together with his wife, an editor called Elaine. The barge was packed with books and anchored half a kilometer west of the Île de la Cité. Elaine received me on the quayside with a warm smile. "You must be the boy from Barcelona," she said.

"That's me."

"Come on board. Tomaso is reading an unbearable manuscript and will be glad for the interruption."

Signor Coliccio had the air of a sea dog and wore a captain's cap. He had silvery hair, but still preserved the smile of a mischievous child. After listening to my story, he remained silent for a while before speaking his mind.

"Look, young man. There are two things that are practically impossible to find in Paris. One of them is a decent pizza. The other is the whereabouts of Julián Carax."

"Let's say I give up on the pizza, and make do with Julián Carax," I ventured.

"Never give up on a good pizza," he advised. "What makes you think that Julián, supposing he's still alive, will want to speak to you?"

"Why should he be dead?"

Don Tomaso gave me a look that was bathed in sorrow. "People die, especially those who would do better to stay alive. Perhaps it's because God needs to make room for the huge amount of jerks with which he enjoys peppering the world."

"I need to believe that Carax is alive," I said.

Tomaso Coliccio smiled. "Speak to Rosiers."

Émile de Rosiers had been Julián Carax's editor for many years. A poet and author in his free time, Rosiers had developed a long career as a successful editor in various Parisian publishing houses. Throughout his working life, he had also published, both in Spanish and French translations, the works of some Spanish authors either banned by the regime or living in exile, as well as books by prominent Latin American authors. Don Tomaso explained that not long ago, Rosiers had been named editor in chief of a small but prestigious firm, Éditions de la Lumière. Their office was close by, so I made my way there.

Émile de Rosiers did not have much free time, but he was kind enough to invite me to lunch in a café just around the corner from his office, on Rue du Dragon, and listen to me.

"I like the idea of your book," he said, perhaps out of politeness, or because of genuine interest. "*The Cemetery of Forgotten Books* is a great title."

"It's all I have," I admitted. "For the rest I need Monsieur Carax."

"As far as I know, Julián has retired. A while ago he published a novel under a pseudonym, although not with me, and nothing after that. Utter silence."

"Do you think he's still in Paris?"

"It would surprise me. I would have heard something, or had news from him. Last month I saw his old Dutch publisher, my friend

Nelleke, who told me that someone in Amsterdam had told her that Carax had sailed to the Americas two years ago and died halfway through the voyage. A few days later another person told her that Carax had actually reached dry land and now spent his time writing television serials under a pseudonym. Choose the version you like best."

Rosiers must have read the despair on my face, after following so many false trails day after day. "Do you want a piece of advice?" he asked.

"Please."

"It's practical advice I give all budding authors when they ask me what they should do. If you want to be a writer, write. If you have a story to tell, tell it. Or try."

"If to become a writer all one needed was a story to tell, everyone would be a novelist."

"Imagine how awful, a world full of novelists," joked Rosiers. "The end of all times."

"Probably the last thing the world needs is one more."

"Let the world decide that," Rosiers advised once again. "And if it doesn't work out, don't worry. All the better for you, according to statistics. But if one day you manage to capture on paper with some skill something like the idea you have just described to me, come and see me. I might be interested."

"And until then?"

"Until then, forget about Carax."

"The Semperes never forget. It's a congenital illness."

"In that case I feel sorry for you."

"Then perform an act of charity."

Rosiers hesitated. "Julián had a good friend. I believe he was his best friend. His name was Jean-Raymond Planaux. He had nothing to do with this absurd business of ours. An intelligent, levelheaded guy, with no nonsense about him. If anyone knows anything about Julián, he'll be the one."

"Where can I find him?"

"In the catacombs."

I should have started there. Since this was Carax we were dealing with, it seemed inevitable that if there was any hope left of finding his trail on the face of this earth, it would be in a setting straight out of one of his books: the catacombs of Paris.

*

Jean-Raymond de Planaux Flavieu was a solid-looking bear of a man, a trifle intimidating at first sight, but who soon revealed his friendly disposition and a tendency to joke. He worked in the marketing office of the firm managing the Paris catacombs and was in charge of their advertising, tourist promotion, and everything related to that particular context of the hereafter.

"Welcome to the world of death, kid," he said, giving me a handshake that crunched my bones. "What can I do for you?"

"I wondered whether you could help me find a friend of yours."

"Is he alive?" He laughed. "I don't spend much time among the living."

"Julián Carax."

As soon as I'd uttered that name, Monsieur Planaux frowned, canceled his happy expression, and leaned forward with a threatening and protective air, cornering me against the wall.

"Who the hell are you?"

"Julián Sempere. My parents named me after Monsieur Carax."

"I don't care whether they named you after the inventor of the public urinal."

Fearing for my safety, I tried to take a step backward. The thick wall, probably connected to the catacombs, stopped me. I could see myself wedged in there in perpetuity between a hundred thousand skulls.

"My parents knew Monsieur Carax," I said in a conciliatory tone. "Daniel and Bea."

Planaux's eyes drilled into mine for a few seconds. I reckoned there was a fifty percent chance that he would smash my face in. The other fifty percent looked uncertain.

"Are you the son of Daniel and Beatriz?"

I nodded.

"From the Sempere bookshop?"

I nodded again.

"Prove it."

For almost an hour I recited the same speech I'd delivered to Carax's old agents and to his publisher. Planaux listened to me attentively, and I thought I glimpsed an air of sadness that intensified as I reeled off my story.

When I'd finished, he pulled a cigar out of his jacket and lit it, producing a cloud of smoke that threatened to bury the whole of Paris. "Do you know how Julián and I met?"

I shook my head.

"When I was young, we worked together in a third-rate publishing house. That was before realizing that this death business has much more future than literature. I was one of the sales reps, and would go out to sell the junk we mostly published. Carax worked for a salary, writing horror stories for us. The amount of cigars like this one we smoked late at night, in the café below the publishing company, watching all the girls go by . . . Those were the days. Don't be stupid: don't grow old, it doesn't bring you any nobility, knowledge, or shit skewered on a stick that's worth it. I think that's an expression from your country I once heard Julián use, and I found it very apt."

"Do you know where I could find him?"

Planaux shrugged. "Julián left Paris long ago."

"Do you know where he went?"

"He didn't say."

"But you can guess."

"You're sharp."

"Where?" I insisted.

"Where do people hide when they're old?"

"I don't know."

"Then you'll never find Julián."

"In memories?" I ventured.

Planaux gave me a smile wounded with sadness.

"Do you mean he went back to Barcelona?" I asked.

"Not to Barcelona—to what he loved."

"I don't understand."

"Nor did he. At least not for many years. It took him his whole life to realize what it was he had loved most."

All those years listening to stories about Carax, and I felt as lost as the day I arrived in Paris.

"If you are who you say you are, you should know," Planaux stated. "And if your answer is 'literature,' I'll give you a beating you'll never forget. But I don't think you're that stupid."

I swallowed hard. "I think I know what you're referring to. Or who."

"Then you know what you must do."

*

That evening I bade farewell to Paris, to Pascale, to my dazzling career in the catering industry, and to my nest in the clouds, and headed for the Gare d'Austerlitz. I spent all the cash I had left on a third-class ticket and took the night train back to Barcelona. I arrived at dawn, having survived the journey thanks to a couple of charitable pensioners from Lyon who were returning from visiting their daughter and shared the delicious food they'd bought that afternoon in the market on Rue Mouffetard, while I told them my story in the small hours of the night.

"Bonne chance," they said when they got off the train. "Cherchez la femme . . ."

When I got back, and for the first few days, everything looked small to me, and closed and gray. The light of Paris had stayed trapped in my memory, and the world had suddenly become large and distant.

"So, did you see *Emmanuelle*?" asked Fermín.

"An impeccable screenplay," I said.

"Just as I imagined. The envy of Billy Wilder and company. And tell me, did you find the Phantom of the Opera?" Fermín gave the smile of a devil. I should have imagined he knew perfectly well why I'd traveled to Paris.

"Not exactly," I admitted.

"So you're not going to tell me anything juicy."

"I thought you were the one who was going to tell me something juicy. Remember?"

"First solve your mystery, and then we'll see."

"That seems unfair to me."

"Welcome to Planet Earth," said Fermín. "Go on, impress me. Say something in French. 'Bonjour' and 'Oh là là' don't count."

"Cherchez la femme," I said.

Fermín frowned. "The classic maxim of any self-respecting thriller . . ."

"Voilà."

*

Nuria Montfort's grave lies on a promontory among trees, in the old part of Montjuïc Cemetery. It has a view of the sea and is not far from Isabella's tomb. It was there, one summer's evening in 1977, after unsuccessfully searching every corner of a Barcelona already receding into the past, that I found Julián Carax. He'd left fresh flowers on the headstone and was sitting on a stone bench facing the grave. He remained there for almost an hour, talking to himself. I didn't dare interrupt him.

I found him again in the same place the following day, and the next. Julián Carax had realized only too late that the person he loved most in the world, the woman who had given her life for him, would never be able to hear his voice again. He went there every day and sat opposite her grave to talk to her and spend what was left of his life in her company.

It was he who came up to me one day and stood there, looking at me in silence. The skin he'd lost in the fire had grown again and lent him an ageless face with no expression, which he hid beneath a bushy beard and an old-fashioned homburg hat.

"Who are you?" he asked. There was no hostility in his voice.

"My name is Julián Sempere. I'm the son of Daniel and Bea."

He nodded slowly. "Are they well?"

"Yes."

"Do they know you're here?"

"Nobody knows."

"And may I ask you why you're here?"

I didn't know where to begin. "May I buy you a cup of coffee?"

"I don't drink coffee," he said. "But you can buy me an ice cream."

My face must have betrayed my surprise.

"When I was young, there were hardly any ice creams. I've discovered them late, like so many other things . . ."

*

That is how, that slow summer evening, after having dreamed of that moment since I was a child, and having ransacked Paris and Barcelona trying to find him, I ended up in a milk bar in Plaza Real sharing a table with Julián Carax, whom I bought two scoops of strawberry ice cream and a rolled wafer. I ordered an iced lemonade, because the damp heat that pervades Barcelona summers was already looming.

"What can I do for you, Señor Sempere?"

"If I tell you, you'll take me for a fool."

"I have a feeling you've been looking for me for some time. And since in the end you've found me, I would only take you for a fool if you didn't tell me."

I drank half the lemonade in one gulp, to gather strength. Then I set out my idea. He listened attentively, showing no sign of disapproval or reservation.

"Very ingenious," he concluded at the end of my speech.

"Don't laugh at me."

"It wouldn't occur to me. I'm telling you what I think."

"What else are you thinking?"

"That you're the one who should write this story. It belongs to you."

I shook my head slowly. "I don't know how to. I'm not a writer."

"Get yourself an Underwood. The professional's choice."

"I didn't know that ad had also appeared in France."

"It ran everywhere. Don't trust ads. An Olivetti would also do the job."

I smiled. At least I shared a sense of humor with Carax.

"Let me show you something," Carax offered.

"How to write?"

"That's something you'll have to learn on your own," he replied. "Writing is a profession that can be learned, but nobody can teach it. The day you understand what that means will be the day you start learning to be a writer."

He opened up the black linen jacket he was wearing and pulled out a shiny object. He placed it on the table and pushed it toward me. "Take it," he invited.

It was the most fabulous pen I had ever seen, the queen of all Montblancs. Its nib was made of gold and platinum, and had I still been a child I would have thought that only masterpieces could flow from it.

"They say it originally belonged to Victor Hugo, although I'd only take this in a metaphorical sense."

"Did fountain pens exist in Victor Hugo's day?" I asked.

"The first piston fountain pen was patented in 1827 by a Romanian called Petrache Poenaru, but it wasn't until the eighteen eighties that it was perfected and began to be commercialized on a large scale."

"So technically it could have been Victor Hugo's."

"If you insist. . . . Let's say that from the dubious hands of Monsieur Hugo it passed on to the no less illustrious and more likely hands of one Daniel Sempere, a good friend of mine. Eventually it crossed my path, and I've been keeping it all these years, waiting for the day when someone, someone like you, came to collect it. About time."

I shook my head energetically, pushing the pen back toward his hands. "I won't hear of it. I can't accept it. It's yours."

"A pen doesn't belong to anybody. It's a free spirit that stays with one while that person needs it."

"That's what a character in one of your novels said."

"They always accuse me of repeating myself. It's a disease that affects all novelists."

"I've never caught it. A sign that I'm not one."

"Just give it time. Take it."

"No."

Carax shrugged and put the pen back. "That's because you're not ready yet. A pen is like a cat—it only follows the person who will feed it. And just as it comes, it goes."

"What do you think of my proposal?"

Carax took the last spoonful of his ice cream. "This is what we'll do. We'll write it together. You give it all the force of youth, and I'll put in the old dog's tricks."

I was stunned. "Are you serious?"

He stood up and tapped my shoulder. "Thanks for the ice cream. Next time it's on me."

*

There was a next time, and many more. Carax always asked for two scoops of strawberry ice cream, whether it was summer or winter, but he never ate the rolled wafer. I would take what I'd written and he would go through it, cross things out, and rearrange the words on the page as if they were notes on a music score.

"I'm not sure this beginning is the right one," I would say.

"A story has no beginning and no end, only points of entry."

Every time we met, Carax went carefully through the new pages I handed him. He pulled his pen open and made notes that he would then use to point out, with endless patience, what I'd done wrong, which was almost everything. Point by point he would show me what didn't work, giving me the reason why and explaining in detail how it could be fixed. His analysis was extraordinarily meticulous. For every error I thought I'd made, he'd show me fifteen whose existence I hadn't even suspected. He pulled apart every word, every sentence, and every paragraph, and put them together again like a goldsmith working with a magnifying glass. He did all this without condescension, as if he were an engineer telling an apprentice how combustion or steam engines work. Sometimes he would question turns of phrase and ideas that I thought were the only things likely to be saved that day, most of which I'd copied from him.

"Don't try to imitate me. Imitating another writer is a prop. It helps you learn and find your own voice, but it's a beginner's thing."

"And what am I?"

I never knew where he spent his nights or the time he didn't share with me. He never said, and I never dared ask him. We always arranged to meet in cafés and bars in the old town. The only condition was that they must serve strawberry ice cream. I was aware that every afternoon he went to his appointment with Nuria Montfort. The first time he read the section in which she appears as a character, he smiled with a sadness that still overwhelms me. Julián Carax had lost his tear ducts in the fire that disfigured him and couldn't cry, but never in my life have I known anyone breathe the shadow of loss the way he did.

I like to think that we became good friends. As far as I'm concerned, at least, I've never had a better one, nor do I think I ever will. Perhaps because of the affection he felt toward my parents, perhaps because that strange ritual of reconstructing the past helped him come to terms with the pain that had consumed his life, or perhaps simply because he saw in me something of himself, he stayed by my side, guiding my steps and my pen, through all the years it took me to write those four novels, correcting, crossing out, and rearranging to the end.

"To write is to rewrite," he kept reminding me. "One writes for oneself, and one rewrites for others."

*

Of course, there was life beyond the fiction. A great deal happened during the years I devoted to rewriting once and a thousand times every page of the saga. True to my promise not to follow in my father's footsteps and head up the bookshop (after all, he and my mother were more than capable of running it), I'd managed to find a job in an advertising agency that, in another twist of fate, was located on Avenida del Tibidabo number 32, the old mansion of the Aldayas where my parents had conceived me one distant stormy night in 1955.

My work in the peculiar genre of advertising never seemed particularly memorable to me, but to my surprise my salary grew every month, and my value as a word and image mercenary was on the rise. The years went by, and I left a considerable trail of television, radio, and press advertisements behind me, for the greater renown of luxury cars that made rising executives drool, banks that were ever determined to make the small saver's dreams come true, electrical appliances that promised happiness, perfumes that led to a frenzied love life, and the endless gifts that thrived in those days in Spain. In the absence of the old regime, or at least of its more visible censors, the country was growing, modernizing itself at the increasing speed of too much money in circulation, while displaying stock-market indexes that left the Swiss Alps in the shade. When my father learned how much I was earning, he asked me whether what I did was legal.

"It's legal, yes. But ethical? That's another matter."

Fermín was delighted, showing no scruples about my prosperity. "As long as you don't get too full of yourself and lose your way, make money now that you're young, which is when it serves some purpose. And a loaded bachelor like you, well, what can I say? With the number of willing knockouts there must be in this publicity business, where everything is pretty and shiny . . . I wish I'd been able to have a taste of that in the postwar crap we were landed with, where even virgins had mustaches. Go for it. Enjoy all this, now's the moment. Have adventures, you know what I mean, go over the limits that can be gone over, but remember to jump off the train in time. Some professions are only for the young, and unless you're a main shareholder of this little shack—something I can't see you becoming, because we both know you have matters to be dealt with in the less well paid writing business—it would be folly to remain in such a powder keg beyond thirty."

Secretly I was ashamed of what I did, and of the obscene amount of money I was being paid to do it. Or perhaps that's what I liked to believe. The fact is that I accepted my astronomical salary happily and squandered it as soon as it hit my bank account.

"There's nothing shameful in that," Carax remarked. "On the contrary, it's a profession that thrives on wit and opportunity. If you know how to play your cards, it will allow you to buy your freedom and a bit of time so that, once you abandon it, you can become who you really are."

"And who am I really? The inventor of advertisements for soft drinks, credit cards, and luxury cars?"

"You'll become who you believe you are."

Deep down, I was less interested in who I was than in who Carax thought I was, or could be. I kept on working on our book, as I liked to call it. That project had become my second life, a world at whose doors I hung the disguise with which I walked around everywhere, and took hold of the pen or the Underwood or whatever, submerging myself into a story that for me was infinitely more real than my prosperous earthly existence.

*

Those years had changed all our lives to some extent. Not long after Alicia Gris was his guest, Isaac Montfort had announced that the moment had come for him to retire from active duty. He proposed that Fermín, who by then had become a father for the first time, take over from him as keeper of the Cemetery of Forgotten Books.

"It's time we put a scoundrel in charge," Isaac said.

Fermín had asked for Bernarda's permission, and she ended up agreeing to move to a ground-floor flat next to the Cemetery of Forgotten Books. There Fermín built a secret connecting door leading to the tunnels of the palace, and converted Isaac's rooms into his new office.

Taking advantage of the fact that at the time I was working on the ad account of a well-known Japanese electronic brand, I got Fermín a colossal color television set, the kind that were starting to be called "top of the line." Fermín, who once considered television as the Antichrist, modified his opinion when he discovered that it broadcast Orson Welles films—"he *really* knows, the rogue," he'd say—and, above all, films starring Kim Novak, whose pointed brassieres still fueled his faith in the future of humanity.

After a few bumpy years during which I even thought their marriage was on the rocks, my parents managed to overcome a few hurdles about which neither would give me an explanation and, to everyone's astonishment, presented me with a late sister whom they christened Isabella. Grandfather Sempere was just able to cradle her in his arms before dying a few days later from a massive heart attack that surprised him while he was lifting a box holding the complete works of Alexandre Dumas. We buried him next to his beloved wife Isabella with a copy of *The Count of Monte Cristo*. Losing his father made mine suddenly grow old for us all, and he was never the same again. "I thought Granddad would live forever," he said the day I found him crying, hiding in the bookshop's back room.

Fernandito and Sofía got married, as everyone had foreseen, and moved into Alicia Gris's old apartment on Calle Aviñón, in whose bed the groom had previously, and secretly, earned flying colors in his nonofficial inauguration with Sofía, thus finally turning all the theory acquired with Matilde into practice. In time, Sofía decided to open a small bookshop specializing in children's books, which she christened the Little Sempere. Fernandito got a job in a department store where, in years to come, he would become head of the book section.

In 1981, shortly after the failed coup that almost took Spain back to the Stone Age or something worse, Sergio Vilajuana published a series of reports in *La Vanguardia* in which he uncovered the case of hundreds of children stolen from their parents, mostly political prisoners who had disappeared during the first postwar years in the prisons of Barcelona and then been murdered to eliminate their trail. The resulting scandal reopened a wound that many didn't know about and others had wanted to cover up. Vilajuana's articles, which prompted a series of investigations that are still ongoing today and have generated oceans of documentation, charges, and civil and criminal cases, encouraged many to come forward and start recovering official accounts of the darkest years in the country's history, accounts that had been left buried all that time.

The reader will be wondering whether, while all this was going on, the ineffable Julián Sempere was alone, devoting himself by day to the mercenary industry of advertising and by night to Our Holy Lady of Literature. Not exactly. The task of writing the four books I had planned with Carax had begun as an escape to paradise, but became a monster that started to devour what was closest to me, which was myself. The monster, which had arrived in my life as a guest and then refused to leave, had to learn to live with the rest of my ghosts. In honor of my other grandfather, David Martín, I too took a peek over the chasm that all writers carry inside them, and ended up holding on to the edge by my fingertips.

In 1981 Valentina reemerged from the mists of time to appear in my life once again, in a scene that Carax would have proudly called his own. It happened one afternoon when my brain was turning to jelly and dripping down my ears. I had taken shelter once again in the French Bookshop, the setting of the original crime, and was loitering by the tables displaying recent publications when I saw her again. I stood stock-still, like a salt statue, until she looked around and saw me. She smiled, and I broke into a run.

*

She caught up with me at the traffic lights on Calle Rosellón. She'd bought me a book, and when I took it, without even looking to see what it was, she put her hand on my arm.

"Ten minutes?" she asked.

And yes, it soon began to rain. Although that was the least of it. Three months later, after furtive meetings in another one of her attics with views of half the northern hemisphere, we moved in together, or I should say that Valentina moved in with me, because by then I had a grand apartment in Sarriá with more space and more emptiness than I needed. This time Valentina stayed two years, three months, and one day. However, though she broke my heart, she also left me with the best gift anyone could have given me: a daughter.

We christened Alicia Sempere in August 1982. The following year, after a few comings and goings that I never quite understood, Valentina went away again, this time for good. Alicia and I were left on our own, but never alone. The little one saved my life, and taught me that none of the things I did would have had any meaning were it not for her. During the years I worked finishing those accursed books, even if only to be finally rid of them, Alicia was by my side, giving me back what I'd learned to disbelieve in: inspiration.

There were some fleeting relationships, potential adoptive mothers for Alicia—generous spirits I always ended up driving away. My daughter would tell me she didn't like me to be alone, and I would tell her that I wasn't.

"I've got you," I assured her.

I had her and all my gallery of ghosts trapped between reality and fiction. In 1991, thinking that if I didn't do it now, jump off the train once and for all, I'd lose what little truth remained in my soul, which wasn't much, I abandoned my lucrative career in the advertising business and spent the rest of the year finishing the books.

By then I could no longer ignore that Julián Carax was unwell. I'd gotten into the habit of thinking he was ageless, and that nothing could happen to him. I'd started to think of him the way one thinks of a father, someone who will never abandon you. *I thought he was going to live forever.*

*

Julián Carax no longer ordered strawberry ice cream when we met up. When I asked him for advice, he barely crossed things out or made amendments. He said that I'd already learned to fly alone, that I'd earned my Underwood and I no longer needed him. It took me a long time to understand, but in the end I couldn't go on fooling myself. I realized that that monstrous sadness he had always carried inside had returned to finish him off.

One night I dreamed I was losing him in the mist. I went out to search for him in the early hours. I looked relentlessly in all the places where we'd met during those years. I found him at daybreak, on September 25, 1991, lying over the grave of Nuria Montfort. In his hand was a case containing the pen that had belonged to my father, and a note:

Julián:
I'm proud to have been your friend and I'm proud of everything I've learned from you.
I'm sorry not to be by your side to see you succeed and achieve what I never could or knew how to achieve myself, but I am reassured by the certainty that, although you may find it hard to believe at first, you no longer need me, just as you never needed me. I'm going to join the woman I should never have left. Take care of your parents and of all the characters in our narrative. Tell our stories to the world, and never forget that we exist so long as someone remembers us.

Your friend,
Julián Carax

That afternoon I found out that the space next to Nuria Montfort's grave belonged, so I was told, to the city of Barcelona. Spanish institutions have a relentless voracity for other people's money, and so, pulling at the thread, we settled on an astronomical figure that I paid on the spot, making good use for once of the copious amounts I'd received for the saga of the sports cars and the Christmas commercials for champagne with more ballerinas in tow than Busby Berkeley's subconscious.

*

We buried my master, Julián Carax, one Saturday at the end of September. My daughter Alicia came with me, and when she saw the two graves lying side by side, she pressed my hand and told me not to worry, as now my friend would never be alone.

I find it hard to speak about Carax. Sometimes I wonder whether there isn't something in me from my other granddad, the unfortunate David Martín, and I invented Carax, just as David Martín invented his Monsieur Corelli so he could remember what never happened. A couple of weeks after the burial I wrote to Madame Currygan and Signor Coliccio in Paris, to let them know Carax had passed away. In my letter I asked them to tell his friend Jean-Raymond Planaux, if they thought it appropriate, and whoever else they considered should know. Madame Currygan replied, thanking me for my letter and telling me that, shortly before his death, Carax had written to tell her about the manuscript we'd been working on together all those years. She asked me to send it to her as soon as I'd finished it. Carax taught me that a book is never finished and that, with luck, it's the book that leaves us so we don't spend the rest of eternity rewriting it.

At the end of 1991 I made a copy of the manuscript, almost two thousand pages long, this time, yes, typewritten with an Underwood, and sent it to Carax's old agents. I didn't think I'd ever hear back from them. I began to work on a new novel, following, once again, my master's advice.

Sometimes it's best to put your mind to work and exhaust it, rather than let it rest, in case it gets bored and starts eating you up alive.

A few months went by between the writing of that novel that

had no title and long walks through Barcelona with Alicia, who had started to want to know everything.

"Is the new book about Valentina?"

Alicia never referred to Valentina as her mother, but called her by her name.

"No. It's about you."

"Liar."

During those long walks I learned to rediscover the city through my daughter's eyes, and I realized that the gloomy Barcelona my parents had lived in had slowly cleared, without us even noticing. The world I once imagined I could remember now lay dismantled. It had become a stage set, perfumed and carpeted for tourists, those lovers of sun and beaches who refused to notice the end of an epoch, however hard they looked—an epoch that hadn't so much collapsed as dissolved into a fine film of dust that can still be breathed in the air.

Carax's shadow continued to follow me everywhere. My mother often came to visit me, bringing little Isabella along so that my daughter could show her all her toys and books, which were many but didn't include a single doll. The fact is that Alicia hated dolls and would knock their heads off with a catapult in the school playground. She always asked me whether it was all right to do that, knowing that the answer was no, and whether I'd had any news of Valentina, knowing also that the answer was invariably the same.

I never wanted to talk to my mother about Carax, about the mysteries and silences of all those years. I knew, somehow, that she imagined it, because I never had any secrets from her beyond the ones she pretended to accept.

"Your father misses you," she would say. "You should come by the bookshop more often. Even Fermín asked me the other day whether you'd become a Carthusian monk."

"I've been busy trying to finish a book."

"For fifteen years?"

"It turned out to be harder than I expected."

"Will I be able to read it?"

"I'm not sure you're going to like it. In fact, I don't know whether it's a good idea to try to publish it."

797

"May I know what it's about?"

"About us. About us all. It's the story of the family."

My mother looked at me without saying a word.

"Perhaps I should destroy it," I suggested.

"It's your story," she said. "You can do what you think best with it. And now that Granddad is no longer here and things have changed, I don't think anyone will care about our secrets."

"What about Dad?"

"He'll probably be the person who would most appreciate reading it. Don't imagine we weren't all aware of what you were doing. We're not that stupid."

"Do I have your permission, then?"

"You don't need mine. And if you want your father's, you'll have to ask him for it."

I visited my father early one morning, when I knew he'd be alone in the bookshop. He pretended not to be surprised when he saw me, and when I asked him how the business was doing, he didn't want to tell me that the Sempere & Sons accounts were in the red, and he'd already received two offers to buy the bookshop and replace it with a souvenir shop selling figurines of the Sagrada Familia and Barça T-shirts.

"Fermín has warned me that if I accept, he'll set fire to himself outside the shop."

"What a dilemma," I remarked.

"He misses you," he said, in that way he had of attributing to others the feelings he was unable to recognize in himself. "How about you? How are things going? Your mother says you've left that job making commercials, and now all you do is write. When will there be something I can sell here?"

"Did she tell you what sort of a book it was?"

"I've presumed you've changed the names and some of the more lurid details, even if only to make sure you don't scandalize the neighbors."

"Of course. The only one who appears showing it all is Fermín—he deserves it. He's going to get more fans than Elvis Presley."

"So shall I start clearing a space in the shop window?"

I shrugged. "I got a letter this morning from two literary agents to whom I sent the manuscript. It's a series of four novels. A Paris editor, Émile de Rosiers, is interested in bringing them out, and a German editor, Michi Strausmann, has also made an offer for the rights. The agents tell me there might be further offers, but first I must polish up a million details. I've set two conditions: the first, that I needed my parents' permission and that of all my family to tell this story. The second, that the novel should be published under the authorship of Julián Carax."

My father looked down. "How is Carax?"

"In peace."

He nodded.

"Do I have your permission?"

"Do you remember, when you were little, that day when you promised to tell the story for me?"

"Yes."

"All these years I haven't doubted for a single day that you would. I'm proud of you, son."

My father hugged me as he hadn't done since I was a child.

*

I visited Fermín in his rooms at the Cemetery of Forgotten Books, in July 1992, the day the Olympic Games' opening ceremony was due to take place. Barcelona was clothed in light, and an aura of optimism and hope floated in the air, something I'd never felt before and would probably never experience again in the streets of my city. As soon as I got there, Fermín gave me a military salute. He looked very old to me, although I didn't want to tell him.

"I thought you were dead," he declared.

"I'm doing my best. You look as fit as a bull."

"It's the Sugus sweets, they caramelize me."

"It must be that."

"A birdie told me you're going to make us famous," Fermín let drop.

"Especially you. When you get offers to model for an advertising campaign, don't think twice about consulting me. I still know a lot about all that."

"I'm only planning to accept the racy ones for male underwear," replied Fermín.

"Do I have your permission, then?"

"You have my blessing, given out to the four corners of the world. But I don't think that's the only reason why you came."

"Why do you always suppose I have hidden motives, Fermín?"

"Because your mind is as twisted as a spring. I mean it as a compliment."

"So why do you think I've come?"

"Probably to marvel at my still fertile wit, and perhaps for an account we have that is still pending."

"Which of them?"

Fermín took me to a room he always kept under lock and key to protect it from the onslaught of his many offspring. He asked me to sit down in a large armchair he'd bought at the Encantes flea market. He sat down on a chair next to me, took a cardboard box, and placed it on his knees.

"Do you remember Alicia?" he asked. "It's a rhetorical question."

I could feel my heart missing a beat.

"Is she alive? Have you heard from her?"

Fermín opened the box and pulled out a handful of letters.

"I never told you, because I felt that it was best for us all, but Alicia returned to Barcelona in 1960 before leaving forever. It was Sant Jordi Day, the twenty-third of April. She came back to say good-bye, in her own way."

"I remember it perfectly. I was very young."

"And you still are."

We looked at one another in silence.

"Where did she go?"

"I said good-bye to her on the docks and saw her board a ship that was sailing to the Americas. Since then, every Christmas, I've received a letter with no sender's address."

Fermín handed me the wad with over thirty letters, one for every year. "You can open them."

All the envelopes had a photograph inside. The stamp showed that each one had been sent from a different place: New York, Washington, DC, Seattle, Denver, Santa Fe, Portland, Philadelphia, Key West, New Orleans, Santa Monica, Chicago, San Francisco . . .

I looked at Fermín in astonishment. He began to hum the national anthem of the United States of America, which on his lips sounded like a *sardana*. Each photograph had been taken with the sun behind her and showed a shadow, the silhouette of a woman, outlined against a panoramic view of parks, skyscrapers, beaches, deserts, or forests.

"Was there nothing else?" I asked. "A note? Something?"

Fermín shook his head. "Not until the last one. It arrived last Christmas."

I frowned. "How do you know it was the last one?"

He handed me the envelope.

The postmark showed it had been sent from Monterey, California. I pulled out the photograph and stared at it in disbelief. For once the image didn't show just a shadow. There was Alicia Gris, thirty years on, looking at the camera and smiling from what seemed to me the most beautiful place in the world, a sort of peninsula with cliffs and mysterious forests that stretched out into the sea through the mist of the Pacific Ocean. On one side, a sign read POINT LOBOS.

I turned the photograph over and met with Alicia's handwriting;

The end of the road. It was worth it. Thanks again for saving me,
Fermín, once and so many times. Save yourself too and tell Julián
to make us all immortal: we always trust he will.

I love you
Alicia

My eyes filled with tears. I wanted to believe that in that dreamlike place, so far from our Barcelona, Alicia had found her peace and her destiny.

"May I keep it?" I asked in a broken voice.

"It's yours."

I knew then that at last I'd found the final piece of my story, and that, from that moment on, what awaited me was life and, with luck, fiction.

EPILOGUE

~&~

BARCELONA

AUGUST 9, 1992

A YOUNG MAN, already showing a few gray hairs, walks through the streets of a shadowy Barcelona under a moon that spills in a silver ribbon over Rambla de Santa Mónica, guiding his steps. A girl of about ten holds his hand, her eyes full of mystery at the promise her father made her in the evening, the promise of the Cemetery of Forgotten Books.

"Alicia, you mustn't tell anyone what you're about to see today. No one."

"Then it will be our secret," she says in a whisper.

Her father sighs, hiding behind that sad smile that has followed him through life. "Of course. It will be our secret, always."

It is then that the sky explodes into a tree of light, and for a moment the fireworks of the closing ceremony capture the night of a Barcelona that will never return.

Shortly afterward father and daughter, like figures of vapor, merge with the crowds that flood the Ramblas, their footsteps forever lost in the labyrinth of the spirits.

AUTHOR'S NOTE

Illustration inspired by an image
of the interior of the Sagrada Familia,
photographed by Francesc Català-Roca.

ABOUT THE AUTHOR

CARLOS RUIZ ZAFÓN is the author of eight novels, including the international bestselling and critically acclaimed Cemetery of Forgotten Books series: *The Shadow of the Wind*, *The Angel's Game*, *The Prisoner of Heaven*, and *The Labyrinth of the Spirits*. His work, which also includes prizewinning young adult novels, has been translated into more than fifty different languages and published around the world, garnering numerous international awards and reaching millions of readers. IIe lives in Los Angeles.

ALSO BY
CARLOS RUIZ ZAFÓN

THE PRISONER OF HEAVEN
A Novel
"Invoking the atmosphere of Dumas, Dickens, Poe and Garcia Marquez, Carlos Ruiz Zafón retains his originality and will hold his rightful place among the storytelling masters of literature."
—*Book Reporter*

Internationally acclaimed, *New York Times* bestselling author Carlos Ruiz Zafón creates a rich, labyrinthine tale of love, literature, passion, and revenge, set in a dark, gothic Barcelona, in which the heroes of *The Shadow of the Wind* and *The Angel's Game* must contend with a nemesis that threatens to destroy them.

▰HarperCollins*Publishers*
DISCOVER GREAT AUTHORS, EXCLUSIVE OFFERS, AND MORE AT HC.COM.